SEASON
WARRIORS
&
WOLVES

THE AURAN CHRONICLES

WENDY HEISS

This is for you. If you have made it this far into the series, this book is my love letter to you. Thank you for loving this story despite its flaws.

PS: Mother, I beg, put the book down. I know you still wish this was a self help book, and it is a self help book, just...not the kind of self help you're thinking of.

Author's note

Conent Warnings

This is a dark fantasy series, so please do not skip the content warnings below.
Gore, death, mutilation, murder, war, torture, mention of child torture, decapitation, blood, vulgar language, self harm, violence, child abuse, emotional and physical abuse, loss of loved one. Depiction of panic attacks, anxiety, depression and PTSD. Scars, alcohol abuse, hallucinations, derealisation and dissociation, mention of infertility, mention of genocide.

And lastly, explicit content. This series is intended to be read by mature readers (18 +) as there are several explicit scenes. (Please don't tickle me about the amount of it. These are two very horny individuals who think they're about to die, okay.)

PS: Yes, you are indeed correct, Snow does go on with her villainous activities.

The Aura

Thousands of years ago, the eight prime Gods of Ithicea descended on the realm of Numen. After taking a liking to the human lands, they bestowed the realm with gifts and blessings of their own powers. Amongst their blessed were the Aura—humans veiled in god-like magic, true believers and humans of true hearts, deemed pure by the Gods.

The Elementals

Order of the Sun
Aura blessed by Goddess Cyra of sun and healing

Glare
Medi healer
Magi healer

Order of Sky and Air
Aura blessed by God Nubil of sky, thunder and clouds

Elding
Nimbus
Zephyr

Bruma Caste
Aura blessed by god Krig of winter, war and wisdom.

Verglaser

Order of Life and Soil

Aura blessed by Goddess Plantae of
earth and rebirth

Senchi
Shinze

The Spirituals

Order of the Dark

Aura blessed by Goddess Henah of moon,
darkness, shadows and empathy

Umbra
Empath
Obscur

Order of Fire

Aura blessed by God Adan of fire and truth

Scarlet

Crafter Order

Magic wielders, different from Aura, blessed by God Celesteel of
magic, otherworld and spirits

Dark Crafter

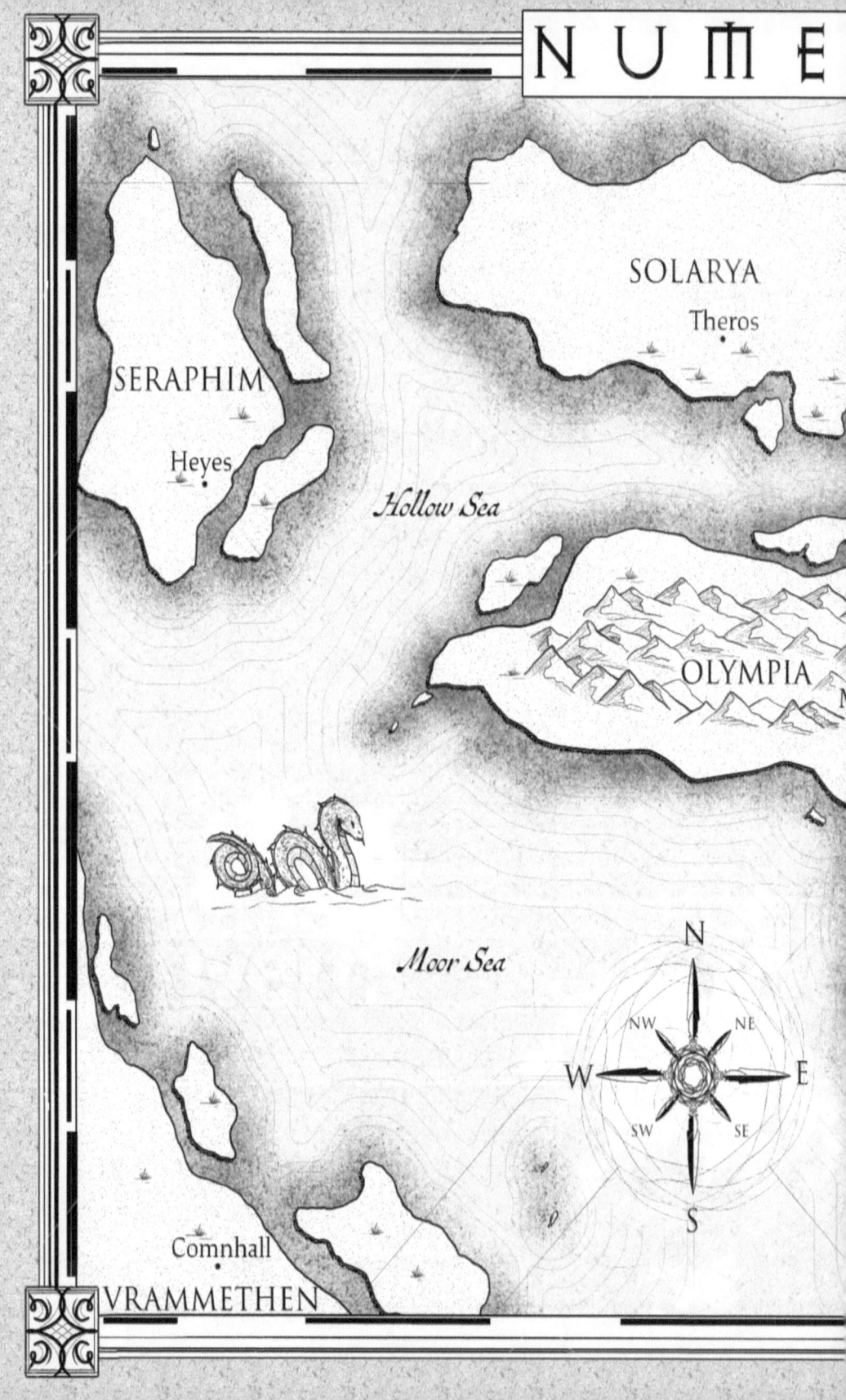

SOLARYA

Theros

SERAPHIM

Heyes

Hollow Sea

OLYMPIA

Moor Sea

N

NW   NE

W   E

SW   SE

S

Comnhall

VRAMMETHEN

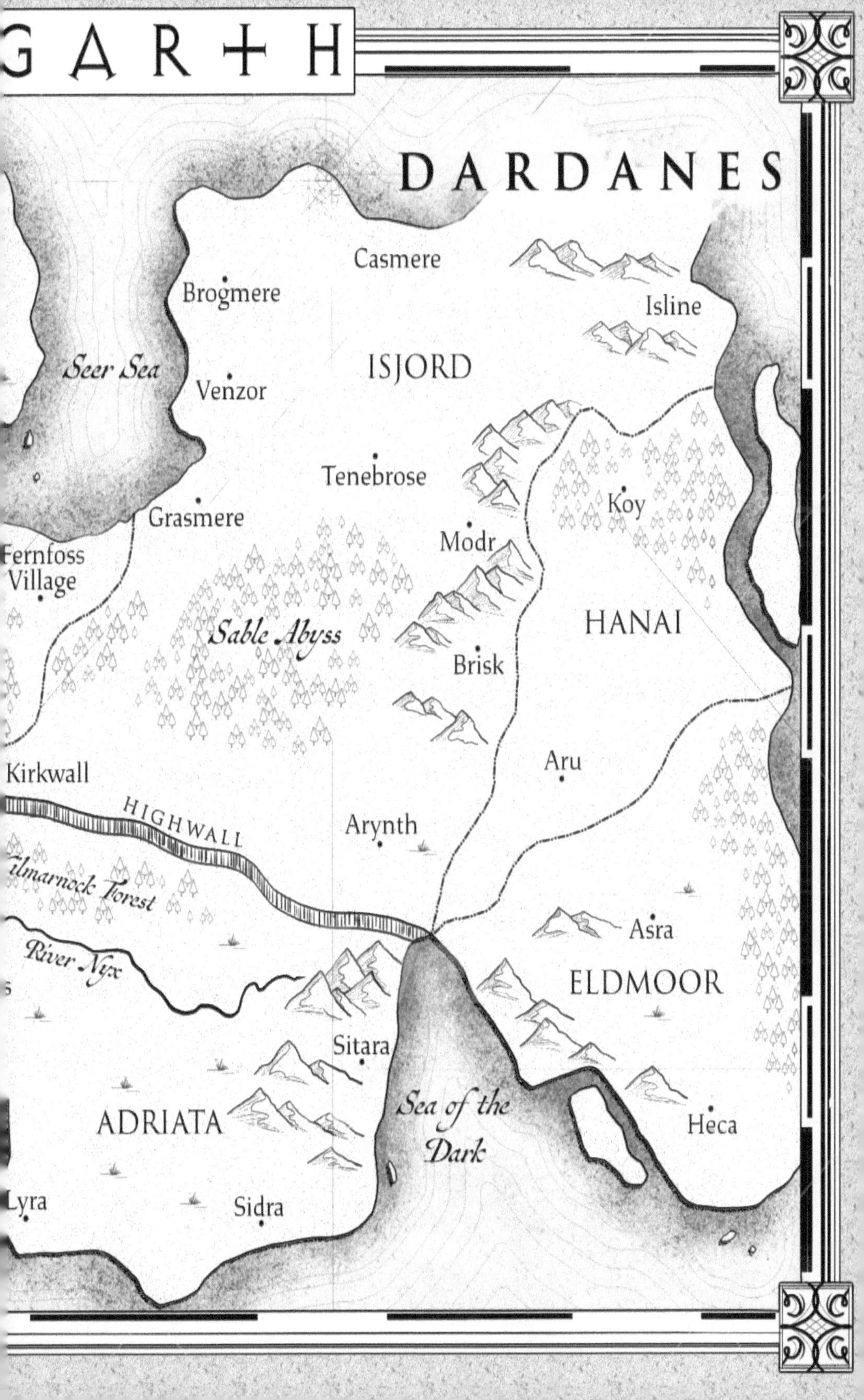

GAR✝H

DARDANES

Seer Sea

Brogmere

Casmere

Isline

Venzor

ISJORD

Tenebrose

Koy

Grasmere

Modr

Fernfoss
Village

Sable Abyss

Brisk

HANAI

Aru

Kirkwall

HIGHWALL

Arynth

Ilmarnock Forest

River Nyx

Asra

ELDMOOR

Sitara

ADRIATA

Sea of the
Dark

Heca

Lyra

Sidra

Black or White?

Snowlin

I'D BEEN HOLDING MY breath past the point I could see straight. But if I breathed, I'd feel the cold bodies slithering over my skin and wrapping around my limbs. Feel their scales scratching my unhealed wounds. Or their weight straining my tied wrists even harder against the chains holding me upright.

The hisses had eventually turned into a distant echo, and my consciousness was slowly faltering, my body surrendering to the hold of the shackles binding me. Though each time I did slip away into the darkness inside my mind, the sting of fangs etched into my flesh and muscle jolted me awake, to keep me aware of what they were inflicting on me and of their cold presence.

The shiver crawling up my skin reminded me of a memory I had locked away with more than force and magic. Father used to lock me in these pits filled with serpents to train fear out of me when I was younger. I had taught myself not to blink and barely breathe loud enough to make sure I wouldn't pass out while cold and scaly long bodies had brushed me, wrapped around me, and bit me to the point I had not woken for days. The memory was now a silent dog whistle that father used to remind me of fear though he'd utilised the very same method to strip me of it. He had wanted me to fear only one. To only fear him.

But there was no fear I felt.

Only hatred. Burning hatred. Red and raw. It boiled quietly inside of me. Inside the hearth they had failed to extinguish. A hearth of ebbing embers that had suddenly caught flame again. It was overpowering. And it felt so...good. So disgustingly good.

Even deep within the walls hiding me, I could feel the vibrations of the rumbling thunder outside obeying my call to waken them, to make them come alive. Though it was short lived because the chains binding me heated up and tightened, branding my skin with unbearable pain. But it was enough for the serpents climbing my body to drop to the floor and skitter away from me, coiling and wrapping around themselves, tucking their heads in.

That...that was fear. They stank of it. Their cold blood turning warm, filling with a kind of venom they so rarely tasted themselves...fear and more fear.

It was so silent. Until the trickle of blood seeping from my wounds slowly dripped to the damp floor that barely grazed my feet, creating a muffled echo. The sound bothered me more than the ache of my stretched limbs, or the burns and the cuts, the hunger or the fog.

Father was revelling in my insanity.

And so were the Gods.

Do *you* take pleasure in my insanity, too?

A hand patted my cheek. "Who are you talking to?"

My eyes hurt to open. To stare at the woman who had robbed me. "The only one listening," I rasped, my voice barely a whisper.

She fluttered her pale lashes, leaning close to my face. "I'm glad you are up for a conversation. I've come to have a little chat with you."

"We spoke. Not even that long ago."

Her bony hand wrapped around my jaw, her black painted nails digging into my cheeks. "Are you losing your mind so soon?" She chuckled, giving my head a shake. "What did I say in your little head?"

"Don't know. I don't speak snake, you pathetic bitch."

She slapped me, hard. And I laughed harder. So hard it hurt. And it hurt so good.

"You don't get to speak to me like that," she bellowed, the sound reverberating down the empty corridors outside of the open dungeon door.

"Mel, it's too late to play mommy with me." My eyes dropped to her stomach hidden between layers of Isjordian tulle and lace, and it made me laugh until I couldn't breathe. "What a strong heartbeat from such a small thing. You might not have a red heart for me to pluck out, so thank you for growing another one."

Her mouth pulled into a cruel sneer and she raised a brow at me. "I've got the Night Prince locked just a few corridors from you. Perhaps he will be eager to answer me."

"Pass him my greetings," I said, slightly bowing my head to her. Was she so gullible? That man was made of death while she bowed to it. While she was a servant to what he could command by simply drawing a breath. The only answers she was getting out of him were cocktail recipes.

She cocked her head back. "You will eventually tell me where your Olympian friends hide. Whether I take an eye or a kidney out of your—" She trailed a finger down my tattooed band of blessing curving around my ring finger. "Brother-in-law."

"Is that what you wish to know? Where Olympians hide? That much I'll tell you."

Her brows hiked up. "Isn't that just sweet. Do tell."

I leaned forward as much as the chains would allow me, and whispered, "My father's nightmares."

Her jaw ticked and she stepped back, shouting to the guards as she exited, "Throw the snakes back in with her and don't take them out until the floor is covered in her blood."

My chest rattled with the shaky breath I drew to laugh one last time. "Oh, Melanthe," I crooned over the echo of her steps retreating down the corridors. "I'm going to gut you like a little squealing piglet."

I chuckled as the guards lowered down to their shivering knees and threw the snakes back in. "Boo," I whispered, and they all scuttered away like frightened mice.

Part I
Queen's Gambit

1

White Pawn to E4

Snowlin

MY CHEEK RESTED AGAINST a damp floor, and all I could see between my burning eyelids was a pair of black leather boots that had stomped on my limbs restlessly for what I'd counted to be hours. They were coated with specks of crimson, soaked with blood—my blood.

He kicked my stomach hard and turned me on my back, resting a hard sole right over my neck to cut whatever little flow of air was entering my lungs. "Not fighting anymore?" Renick snarled, pressing harder.

He'd folded his sleeves back to keep the blood from staining his shirt, revealing skin that was no longer marked by our bargain. Where the band of magic had once been, now remained only a strip of mangled and burnt scar tissue. Which part of his soul had he sold to have it removed? Did he have anything even worth selling? Who had he sold it to so that the Death God had allowed him to cheat our bargain?

Though lightheaded, I managed to conjure one of my charming smiles. "Neither did your daughter."

He hit me again and again, till more blood bubbled in my mouth and the sharp taste of metal grew intense enough that I vomited. "Where is she?" he growled in my face, pinching my jaw hard enough to break it. "I know you haven't killed her."

I kicked my head forward with whatever energy I had left, knocking him back. "You're right. I haven't." Then I lunged towards him, and hit him over and over until all my knuckles had broken, my skin chafed and stained red with his blood. Till I felt no need to scream. Till I'd silenced my anger again. I leaned into his ear. "My friend did though. He sucked all the air out of her little lungs. I didn't kill her, but I did watch life leave her body little by little after she told me everything I needed to know about you, Nick dearest. You should have not broken our bargain." I trailed the back of my hand against his forehead. "How will I see you suffer now? It was going to be so good. You were going to suffer so, so...good."

There was nothing.

No satisfaction at his pain or how his blood felt against my skin.

Given up, I laid there on the ground beside him, feeling life seep out of me from all bleeding corners. I should be thinking of nothing. My mind should be empty.

But it was not.

Hot tears rolled down my temples, my vision blurring.

It was not.

All I could see with my eyes open was her. All I could see with my eyes closed was still her.

Bleeding.

Lifeless.

Slain.

"Show them hell," she had told me. But which hell would give me her back? Who would give her back? Who would let me have her again?

Demir clicked his tongue as he entered the room, his mouth curling in distaste at Renick's twisted remains. "Remember what I told you at the start?" he asked, crouching before me. "Everyone you kill will rot in here with you. And we've got to get rid of rotten flesh one way or another. The snakes will have to return." He cocked his head to the side, studying the fresh bite marks all over me. "We don't want that, do we?"

"He is not dead," I croaked out just a second before Renick groaned and rolled to his side. He shook like a slighted beast, baring his teeth at me. "Why would I kill him when someone else can do it for me?"

The Bruma Commander crawled to me, but not fast enough.

"If he dies, who will keep feeding Verglasers mirkroot to kill them for me?" I said a moment before he could strike or silence me.

Demir shot to his feet and pried him off of me, gripping his jacket and holding him back. "What is she talking about?"

Renick's eyes had gone wide enough to pop out of their sockets. "Nothing! How can you trust a word she says? I told you about all of her lies and plans. She lies again! She fucking schemes again!" he nearly screamed.

I hummed, shaking my head. "He started doing it before I even returned to Isjord," I revealed, pushing myself to my corner. "To make them more powerful and please father. But they die. They die very quickly. And no one knows because he sends them off to die in missions as a disguise." I turned to him. "Have I missed something, Nick?" Did he really think I needed to weaken my father's army this much as to let him hurt me more than I needed him to hurt me?

"Lying bitch!" he spat, trying to get to me again. "Olympian scum. She is lying! Always lying."

Chuckling, I rested my head back on the wall. "Yeah, yeah."

Demir narrowed his eyes on me over his shoulder, still not letting go of Renick. "If you want me to kill him, you've got to give me more than that."

And so it started. I'd delayed them enough. I'd bought Kilian enough time.

Leaning forward, I said, "Taste their blood, sailor boy."

Renick clung to Demir's, shaking his head. "It is not true. It is not true, Demir, you have to believe me."

"Farewell," I murmured, watching him get dragged away like a dog.

What was one pawn? Nothing. I'd sacrificed worse.

Forty-one days. No sun. No moon. I'd seen nothing for forty-one days. It was almost the end of it. The end of was supposed to be my taming. Father had not changed his ways even after so many years. This was the fault and weakness of every Isjordian—their mechanical and conformist ideas and old ideologies that they obliged to and enforced. What a strange fault to have. Predictability was so avoidable.

First, they tried to beat the fight out of me. Though I did not fight back at all. There was no fight to fight back. They kept throwing guards and soldiers at me like live feed to a snake. Whoever beat me was too weak to satiate my thirst for blood, so I did not bother. And whoever ordered them to beat me just wanted me to submit. Otherwise I would not be breathing at this very moment. Father kept no prisoners. He saw no joy in torture.

So, I gave them my submission. I gave them what they wanted of me.

Though my skin had cracked and bruised, and my bones ached and groaned, I felt reborn, the most alive I had felt in a long, long while. The more I hurt, the more I rose above caring about it. I felt nothing. Nothing at all. Not even a little bit. That pounding ache inside my rib cage had numbed it all out.

It pleased them to see me so weak and surrendered, and their satisfaction had clouded every other sense and thought because they'd accepted that human looking submission I wore, the bloodied mask and gown I donned over this skin they'd thought monstrous not long ago, the quiet tunes I played, the shaky tears I shed. I played right into their deepest and most twisted desires.

Then they starved me. A trick humans use to teach their pets obedience and dependence. And I obeyed even though they'd barely starved me out of the very thing that fed me most—violence, pain, and anger. Food fed the human, and the human in me was weak. Soldiers did not go to war for you because you filled their stomach with food, they fought for you because you fed them rage. A full stomach sent you to the toilet, anger sent you to battle.

Once my father had taught me submission, obedience, dependence, and starvation, he would come for the next thing.

Power. He'd come for my power. The one thing I'd always denied him.

And power I would give him.

The air was thick with dust and smoke enough to make me cough every minute of my eternally long days, and like every time I coughed, the taste of blood weighted on my tongue and the groans of pain crawling up my throat slowly became uncontainable. I couldn't feel a lick of my magic, not only because of the craft chains sucking in every bit that flowed out of me, but because the whole room I was locked in was painted corner to corner in craft runes that glowed red the more I struggled, the more I fought to draw power.

So tired...I was so tired.

The three figures who had granted me a visit every day for the past month or so stood silently still before me. One had their features pulled in disgust, the other pursed with impatience, while the last one was simply and merely...silent.

Nothing. There was nothing in Demir's face which had always been so brightly painted with his emotions. "I still don't understand what game you are playing at."

"Come closer," I hoarsely murmured, peeling my body from the damp floor. "I'll explain it to you."

He crouched down until we were face to face. "So?"

And in the midst of having my heart ripped open, I decided that if they were to take my heart entirely, I would rip theirs too by doing what only I know how to do best—dish out retribution. If she had been alive, she would have tried to convince me otherwise. Would have tried to make me reason. She...she would have reminded me that I have all I want. But she was not here.

"It is no game I am playing." *This was war.*

He huffed. "You did not give up until the bitter end. That little trick you played with the lords and the walls cost us months of work. You did that to give time to the Night King, and you are doing this to give him more time."

"You're not as smart as you think you are, sailor boy. Time?" That made me cackle. "I'm simply petty. Imagining my father's face when those walls came down has been my greatest gift these days. I dream about it. Fantasise about it. It is the only thing keeping me alive. How many died crushed under rock and cement? Fifty thousand? A hundred thousand? More? How many guards has he stationed over the ruins from fear that everyone will want a piece of his frosted cake? I could bet that all the chaos could be seen from the height of Islines."

Slowly, I crawled closer to him so I could see the colour change on his green irises—so I could finally see his emotions betray him. "Wouldn't it be such a shame if the old Krigborns knew that the Isjordian throne has no heir? Wouldn't it be just so unfortunate if they knew that father has no one lined up and eligible to take his crown? No son, no brother, no daughter—not one who he can crown at least. An unborn child is no heir. And Fren is the pure consequence of unfortunate reproduction, she is no queen. She would be dethroned within the hour by Isjordians themselves." I clicked my tongue. "And if I might make a wild guess, father has not found Reuben where he sent him to be."

His brows pulled together and he stood up so quickly that the poor man got a little whiplash. There. Pure realisation settled on those dull eyes of his, turning my grin vile. "No, you *are* playing."

"No. Not me," I said, leaning back on the cold wall of my cell. "But someone is. I just happen to have a piece of cheese on a string and the rats gather just like that."

"You have no connection to the outer world."

"How certain are you about making that bet?" I chuckled. "As certain as you were about the walls?"

"*Very* certain."

I rolled my head back to look at the stained ceiling. "Give me a day."

"What are you proposing?"

I'd even surprised myself at how good I'd become at bluffing. "With him. I will propose it to him, not his squire." I tilted my head to the side. "Vas, son of Zoltan, waste of what could have been just a wank."

I was certain that the sting of his fist had truly left me deaf in one ear, but it was absolutely worth it.

Two days. That is all it took for my father to resist temptation, to think and strategize a way out of the mess I'd made on his behalf and to finally come to a conclusion that I was...well...right.

"You wanted to speak with me," father finally said, stepping inside my dark room, looking around the empty space only so he wouldn't have to look at me. As always. He'd always avoided looking at me—at what he did to me.

So he came. As predicted. Fear was a funny little man. "No, *you* wanted to speak with me." I raised my chained hands. "I am in no place to make demands. *You* came here. That can't possibly mean anything else besides that you're in an absolute shithole of a...situation." Resting my chin on top of my knees, I sighed and fluttered my lashes at him. "You take it from here since I'm not feeling particularly talkative."

He cocked his yellow head back and glared at me. "You were right in what you told Demir."

After all, it took two to dance a waltz of manipulation. "Was I?"

He bent down, and though we were at quite a distance, I could see his slimy gaze glinting in the midst of foreign darkness as he snarled. "Well played."

"My, thank you."

He reached to grab my hand, lifting it up and inspecting the black tattoo curling around my ring finger and down my hand. I knew why he laughed next. "First thing I taught you was to never attach yourself to another. You went and did just that. Have I been such a horrid teacher? I'd be disappointed if it wasn't profiting from your foolishness. In fact, I am quite grateful for your stupidity."

I curled my fingers around his, holding onto him while I leaned closer to whisper, "You're scared of him, aren't you?" There was a long stretch of silence as he measured my reaction. "It's okay, papa," I cooed, tilting my head to the side to study that new, strange, and foreign thing in his gaze. The way unfamiliar fear marred the pale yellow of his irises. "It is normal to be afraid of my husband. The most normal thing you have probably ever done. In fact, it is the most human thing you have ever done, the most human you have ever looked." *So weak.*

"I've rarely been afraid, my rose."

"You've also rarely told the truth."

He raked his slimy gaze over me, over the scars and the wounds he always had refused to see. So much disgust in the eyes of the man who had given me life. "Look what you've done to yourself."

My grip tightened around his hand, and he hissed when I forced ice to grow like claws over my fingertips. My whole body violently shook, and blood began dripping from the corners of my mouth and down my eyes and nose from the strain of magic.

"Not just of my husband, you're afraid of me, too. Aren't you?" I chuckled. "How many feet underground are you holding me while you clutch your witch tightly at night for safety? Do I haunt your dreams, papa? You look like a painting in mine. Torn to shreds. Bleeding dry. Air drained out of your pitiful lungs."

His gaze shivered as he focused on the stream of blood gushing from my wrists, and almost snapped a muscle when he forced his eyes to meet mine. "Madness. There is nothing else to explain you, daughter. Simply madness."

"Well, well, doesn't your blood run well through me."

He stood and stomped away. And just before he shut the doors, I said, "It was nice doing business with you."

2

Black Pawn to E5

Snowlin

SNOW, THERE WAS SO much of it. Everywhere. On everything. Cold and frost had swallowed all sorts of life around Isjord which now remained only a thick coat of blistering white. It was the middle of July, yet it felt as if it was the start of January. My eyes had yet to accustom even though it had been a whole week since I'd left the Tenebrose dungeons. My body, too, wasn't dealing well with withdrawal, it craved violence and pain. It had taken a dozen healers and too many days to heal my limbs that still slightly ached when I made a sudden move.

The phantom chains on my neck, wrists, and ankles rattled with the slightest movement I made away from the window and towards my bed. And the pain of the magic-forged metal binding me, not only tied but powerless, had long turned dull and offered me no consolation at all. My insides were just as hollow. My flesh and organs had thinned and starved to make space for the grief I swallowed with each breath I took since seeing Nia bleed out before me.

You are insane, her words and laughter echoed around the room, over and over.

"So you keep saying," I whispered back, laying down on the bed.

I forced myself to breathe out the memory—to concentrate on what had kept just sane enough. After all, I didn't need to be entirely sane, not with what I was about to do. It wasn't exactly revenge as it was a pure need for the destruction of all and everything.

The old woman who was tasked to serve me was rather quiet. Even her steps were light, almost on purpose. She'd stolen a glance or two but had not looked at me otherwise. She set down a rose-coloured dress on the foot of my bed before waddling to me and reaching for my hand. She almost startled me when she pulled me to sit up. "Get up, girl," she finally rasped, glancing at the doors as if she had revealed a royal secret and was about to be punished. "Or they will get you to your feet. It's been days, and they can see well that you are able to walk now."

"They can try," I said, standing and pulling my arm from her grip, almost sending her stumbling back from the force.

She followed right after me despite her age. "Comply," she said quietly, pulling on my clothes and helping me into the bath. "It is easier." Her eyes darted to the still fresh wounds all over me and she sighed, her wrinkled face dropping with such despicable pity. "Much easier."

I dipped into the warm water and leaned back on the bath. "I'm in no need of sympathy. If you have a dagger I could borrow, on the other hand—"

"No sympathy from me, girl," she said almost cruelly, pouring water on my hair and face. "I've got no sympathy left to give. Only my thanks."

I opened my eyes and took a small piece of crumpled paper from her shaking hands. *For saving Nissa, I will forever be in your debt. A mother's debt.*

She put a finger to her lips and continued washing my hair while I tried to process the words written.

Why would I need an old woman's debt? I'd done for Nissa as much as she'd done for me. It had been a bargain. I was owed nothing, but I was too tired to argue and was sure that my room was veiled and surveyed by Melanthe. Causing this woman's death would serve me nothing. No death should go unprofitable, it would be such a waste.

She got me dressed, combed my hair, and neatly plaited it. Once she'd gotten me settled on the settee facing the arched glass window facing the winter garden, she let in a few young servants in with trays of food. They all stopped and bowed their heads politely one after the other after laying down the food and leaving. It got my attention for a moment, but Nissa's mother shook her head in warning to not ask.

The girls knew of what I'd done for Nissa. And it somewhat mattered.

"Eat," she said, backing towards the door and leaving.

My stomach gurgled at the soft smell of herbs, but the thought of eating made me rush to the sink and heave out what little bit of water I had drank before. "Mother-fucker."

A little laughter trickled at the back of my mind, and I looked up at the mirror, watching the twirling black shadows starting to bleed red, leaking out of the reflection and down the walls, painting everything red—blood red, thick and stained with sin.

"Something funny?" I asked, my words slurring, the world spinning.

Yes, they whispered back, a mocking laughter following.

My fingers shook as I tried to grasp the sides of the white porcelain to steady myself, but no limb of mine obeyed at all, they were locked in place like my eyes were—staring at the abyss of my own mind. And soon, the exhaustion, the sleeplessness, and hunger made me give up to the slumbering spell that monster in the mirror chanted. My body hitting the floor with a thud.

That evening, I was called to dinner for the first time since I'd surfaced from the dungeons. Father had ordered the servants to dress me in some of the finest silks, laces, and skirts some of the noble women of Isjord wore. The only thing they had not touched was my hair.

And from the look on his face when I arrived at the dining chambers, it had been a mistake, and a servant would lose a hand for it.

It was only him and I, no one else.

I sat across from him, and that was enough to trigger his ego. "Stand and come here. Sit in your place."

"No."

"Stand!" he shouted.

And I calmly repeated, "Again, no."

He sneered, huffing and puffing. "You have no power here."

"It is a seat, father, calm down. The air is not so stale over here with the stench of delusion and treachery." It wasn't about a seat. It was about control. Slowly, without him realising, I'd take it all. One rank and file at a time, like he did. If the king wanted me to slow my steps, I'd slow them.

He leaned back in his chair, glaring at me under his nose. From the way satisfaction weighted easily on his features, I could tell he was plenty satisfied by my state. "I've called a crowd for tomorrow," he announced confidently, cutting through his lamb.

I nodded. "You are an excellent jester, they will for sure enjoy your play."

His jaw ticked at my nonchalance. "For your crowning."

I plucked a few grapes from the fruit platter and munched while I waited for him to continue, but it seemed it was my turn to speak because he said nothing at all after that. "What, would you like me to prepare a speech or something?"

He leaned back on his seat. "I'm surprised by your easy cooperation given your rabid history."

"A transaction," I said, poking my fork in some slices of cheese. "For Malik Castemont's life, my help. I give nothing for free. You must know because you took him with the purpose to use him against me, didn't you? You are clearly struggling to retrieve the Octa Virga pieces since you resorted to tricking me into doing it for you. And since you've yet to kill me, yet to kill the Night Prince, tortured me just enough to teach me a lesson not to hurt me, I think you need us both—more so me I suspect considering I'm up here and asked to prepare a speech. Skygard blood and all, correct?"

Silence rang around the empty room. Both our gazes clashed, and neither of us relented to looking away first. His eyes were hardened with control and mine were glazed with violence inside the hottest kilns of fury there were.

My lips curled up into a smirk. "Finally got to tie that second shackle on me," I said, lifting my cup to a toast. "To your victory."

He followed suit, lifting the cup, but stopped from drinking when I added, "And your inevitable loss."

His smile was gruntled when he lowered his wine cup on the table. "You will learn to give up, my rose. Sooner than later. I will be here to watch you crumble to your own foolishness. To your own unfound sense of eminence."

"Perhaps we can learn together. Our first father-daughter activity." I clapped my hands together once, and the guards behind him flinched and quickly reached for their weapon. Steel hissed against their scabbards, only stopping when they caught the way my eyes gleamed with satisfaction. So afraid. So malleable. No Isjordian would have reacted this way. They thought of their king as a God, and trusted his power to override all. The men around him were no Isjordians. No Isjordian would have disrespected their king this way, to think him weak and afraid as how they'd made him look now. "Look at us bonding. At last."

He hunched over his food again, his knife screeching sharply against the porcelain. "You've lost, child. Don't be delusional."

"Can't help it. It is hereditary."

His expression turned cruel, but he didn't say anything for a long while, chewing leisurely on his meat. "After your crowning you will be sent to retrieve the Seraphim piece first," he revealed as if only to sour the taste of the sweet grapes I was chewing on, the only thing I'd eaten in days.

Of course he would lose no time. "I need to train."

He sneered. "Train?"

"You don't expect me to get your sceptre with my charming banter and gorgeous face, do you now?" Though I probably could, I would rather not—I had other plans on how to spend my charming banter and good looks. "I've spent a month without moving, let alone using magic."

"You will train," he said after a while, still measuring my intentions—still measuring the fact that I had magic.

"With someone of my calibre, preferably." *Demir, give me Demir so I can learn how to gut him properly. So I can learn to slay him and send him right back to his creator in tiny, little pieces of lizard.*

"Demir will see to it."

My. Was I mind bending now?

The dining room doors behind me drew open, and a very pregnant Melanthe stepped inside, head high and glowing. She slowed her step when she took notice of me and carefully walked around the table to her seat, her leery eyes gleaming for the first time with what looked like pure, unadulterated satisfaction. Indeed, father and she were not only made of the same cloth, but they were also cut from it, too. Like that, an odd realisation struck me. It had all come in a full circle and much to her plan, hadn't it? All of it. Every little bit of it. My father wasn't the only one scheming. She'd been doing the same, too. Gods, for how long?

"Melanthe," I crooned, slicing an apple and offering her a saccharine smile. "If you are here, who is scaring away the crows from our grains?" I would rip her apart. Bit by bit, until I would see her soul flaying from the rotting bones that held it.

For a moment, her eyes faltered, and she glanced shortly at my father. She kissed his cheek and sat across from me, folding a napkin over her swollen stomach and cutting through her meal. Quietly.

Fascinatingly disgusting. Guts, bile, and vomit had never made me gag, but this somewhat did. "Ignoring me now?" I asked, leaning back on my seat, trying to calm the heartburn that was threatening to spill sickness all over my dinner. "How boring of you."

"Trying to keep your spirits high and maybe we can get over this farce as quickly as possible," she said, her mouth curling with a smirk.

I sipped my drink to wash a death threat from my tongue. She would not have the satisfaction of seeing my anger, only its repercussions. "Is that what you told yourself when you made up a false lover to chase my father's attention all while deceiving your own sister to get back her support after she almost left you covenless?" Had taken me a little moment to piece it all together, but all of it had been right there. All laid before me.

Father glanced at Melanthe who had just narrowed her eyes on me. "I see my niece has gone around spreading lies."

"Visha had someone to learn from. She speaks so dearly of you. But how very you, Mel dearest. You couldn't stand not being the centre of his world, could you? But how pathetic to think that any woman of his has ever been the centre of his world enough that jealousy would stir him into caring about you. Tell me," I said. "Did you expect my father to kill you for your little schemes back then? To hang you right in front of everyone. To parade your body like a piglet before his people. It seems rather extreme." I glanced at my dear, quiet papa. "But the things we do for love, right?"

If I could no longer stir the galley, I'd bring harsh waters to it.

"I wouldn't worry about me, Snowlin," she said softly despite all the visible anger on her stiffened body. "You've got plenty else to worry about."

"It would surprise you that for now, I worry most about you." My eyes dropped to her stomach, and she immediately dropped a hand over it. "Being in your condition is not easy. We would want nothing bad happening to my little sister." I took another sip to drown the words I wanted to vomit at her. "Would we now?"

"Would be a shame if I sowed your mouth shut," she said, leaning forward on the table, her fingers glowing red with magic that gave the air a rotten stench variegated with mint. "Won't need that to get the sceptre, would you now?"

Such a fragile ego she had. It was not fun at all crushing something so pallid. I picked an apple from the table and took a little bite before throwing it directly at her head. Her and father's eyes went huge when the fruit hit the witch right where her brains should be.

"How brave," I said, stretching back on my chair, "to sit there threatening me and not three tons of cement apart from me." Without losing her gaze, I reached and got the butter knife, twirling the dull thing around my fingers. "Sow my mouth shut. My eyes, too. Cut my limbs. Carve my skin. But at the end of it all, you will be dead. Real dead. I will watch life fade from those eyes. And I'm not as merciful as your God. It hurt, Mel. It will hurt a lot." Taking a deep breath, I lowered the knife down, fighting temptation and putting on a smile for my father. "Pass me the salt, please." I took the container from the servant and sprinkled it all over us and the table. "I know it won't ward off witches, but I'm hoping it will work on bitches," I said, flicking some at a snarling Melanthe.

She dusted the sprinkles off her clothes and turned to my father. "You will let her talk to me like that?"

He sighed and leaned back, throwing his napkin on the table all mad at his interrupted meal. "What does it cost to lower your head and just eat like a normal fucking person, child?"

"Hearts and a couple livers. Why, you got them?" I leaned forward, fluttering my lashes at him. "We could bargain."

"Silas!" Melanthe bellowed.

I nailed the butter knife on the table, the rose wood cracking under the force, making her flinch. "Hush. He is doing it for you. Come on, papa," I pouted. "A little one."

My fingers were blood red and numb, enough to not feel the sharpness of thorns dig into them while I stood in front of my mother's grave, holding her favourite white rose. Wolves howled restlessly further inside the city and the forest around the crumbled castle walls, their call was stranger than usual. Desperate. The wind, too. It no longer blew north like it had done since the time of Gods. Only haphazardly all around. Uncontrollably. Furiously. Madly.

"I'm glad you're not here," I said, hoping that she would reply to me again. "It must have been so lonely here all alone." The two graves around her were empty. She'd always been alone. This is why she had stuck to me for so long. "Is she with you, ma? Tell me that she is. Is my Nia with you?"

Silence howled worse than the wind and the wolves.

She didn't reply.

"Can you hear me?"

She couldn't, could she?

No one did.

Except *you*. Only *you* can.

Demir was waiting at the exit of the winter gardens, just as angry as Melanthe had been when I struck a deal with my father for silence. "Why only one rose?" he asked. "You only took one rose when you went in there."

Maybe he had felt the air in Adriata. Maybe he had always doubted something. Whatever it was, I didn't need him lurking close to them. "Have you ever lost someone you cared about, Vas?" I asked, breaking a rose stem, feeling the trickle of blood stream down my sleeve when more thorns dug on my skin.

He didn't answer for a while. "Yes."

The white petals stained red when I cupped the flower and brought it to my face to smell the nothingness it offered. "Family?"

He suddenly looked so human. "Yes, family."

"Good." I threw the rose at him and laughed. And my eyes gleamed when he dropped it almost as if it had burned. Maybe it had. Maybe. "Very good. Was it painful? Did they die in agony? Tell me. Did they beg? Did they suffer?"

He was still looking at the bloodied rose on the ground. "A human death. Old age."

"Mmm, much, much better. The cruellest death of all. Aren't you glad to have escaped it?"

His eyes lifted to mine, flashing in that unnatural green they turned sometimes. "Very."

"You and her," I said, trailing a finger over the rose bushes. "You were locked together in Nephthys. Seems so unlike any other punishment issued for your tomfoolery. So unlike Fader."

"You call love tomfoolery as if you did not bargain to have your soul attached to another's."

"How much you know," I hummed. "How little you are actually allowed to partake in. Did it sadden you? To never know what it feels to tie your soul to another?"

"Aurora and I were one in more ways than your Gods dictate."

Men always thought their cocks were some sort of magical wands, so I was not surprised he believed that. "Aurora," I said, plucking another rose. "What did she promise you?"

His eyes dropped to the petals I was picking one by one. "Nothing."

"Oh, it must have been something. You know how I know that?" I asked, tying my hands behind me, the thorny stem digging on my palm. "Because she was not the first divine thing you have come across, Vas. Interestingly, you've come across much in your little human life. Bargained favours with them, too—so many favours. Even sailed the Sea of the Dark in hopes of meeting Golgotha—attempted—because it was there you met Esmeray who could not reach Golgotha either. Sweet Esmeray, the traveller who knew everything and the woman who Aurora had a close bond with here in Numen. So much so that she dedicated a whole diary to her."

He glared at me, his jaw ticking, his unnatural breaths returning to his furious chest all of a sudden. "A diary?"

"Of course. You helped her write it, didn't you? Isn't that why you approached something you loathed by nature?" Aurora had been a little test pet for those two. This idiot and Esmeray had been two conspiring and conniving idiots. Just not idiotic as Aurora.

He cocked his head back. "Intentions change. Feelings change. And I never made such a deal with Esmeray."

"Esmeray was special, wasn't she? Special to you."

His teeth were set tightly. "A friend."

"Hm. Is that what they call back stabbers these days? Friends?"

He studied me intently. "You think you know something I don't?"

"Yes, though I've promised not to tell a soul," I whispered to him. "But since you have no soul, you might as well know that the woman you trusted enough to run that little experiment with had another experiment of her own. *Sa keeler miia horra.* Loosely translating to *'The wrath of Gods'* in your old tongue. The one thing she was struggling to leave a trace of in her diaries where she'd taken upon herself to document everything godly. Gods had been everything to the land. Loving, giving, caring, shunning, encouraging. The one thing they had not done, was punish. Esmeray sought to see that—to know of Gods as much as she could. And she had the perfect set up already." I flashed him a grin. "Every night that I went to sleep with sore eyes decoding those books was worth it. *Orro m'ah sa bolaam'as.*"

Son of the seas, as Esmeray had called him.

After Macaria had come to us, there had been no doubt that reading the diaries would not cost the world more than Silas would. Kil, Thora, Mal, and I had spent every waking moment going through them. We'd learnt so much. Of his intentions in luring Aurora to speak of her gifts for Esmeray to document. The White Flame Guardian had been as curious about him as he'd been about her, so she had not doubted his intentions.

I knew him well. Very well.

Yet, there was one little thing I had yet to figure out.

His fear.

The one thing Esmeray had not written down. I suspected that had been their deal. He would give her what she needed, and she would write him in exaltation, make him appear like a human God as he'd always desired. And as all Gods, he also could not have flaws. Luckily for me, in arrogance you could always find mistakes, so many in between lines to read. What made him invincible also made him fragile.

My chains rattled when I lifted a hand to pat his heartless chest. "How can I use more than one rose when there will be so many graves that will need them? At your expense, nonetheless."

3

White Knight to F3

Snowlin

THE BRITCHES FIT ME too loosely, so the tailor had made sure to cut all of my jackets long to hit right below my knee and as snug to my body as possible to protect me from this bizarre cold that had struck the winter kingdom right in the middle of summer.

Nissa's mother clicked her tongue and sighed as she put my clothes on, lifting a piece of cake to my mouth from time to time and pinching my chin, reminding me to chew.

I closed my eyes in an attempt not to throw up all that I'd eaten, and she slapped my cheek. "Don't you dare, girl."

"Did you just hit me?" I sneered, swallowing a bite of the dry cake.

"Pain seems to be the only thing to bring you back among us. Where do you go in there?" she asked, tapping a finger on my brow.

"Nowhere nice."

"That I figured," she said, swiping her thumbs under my eyes. She wiped the tear beads on her apron and sighed once again, holding her skirts up to kneel before me and put my boots on. "Is it because of your husband?"

This time the warm tears slid down my cheeks before she could wipe them away. "My sister."

"I don't know your sister," she murmured low enough for only me to hear. "But no sister wants to see the other the way you are now. Eat, breathe, fight. For her sake if not for yours."

"What would it matter? She can no longer nag me for it."

"Then why are you alive at all?"

"Because she told me to show them hells. Until I do so, I will breathe. And then I will hunt them beyond until their pain is stained across the whole eight heavens and seven hells."

There was some type of horror in her face, but not one from fear. And though she didn't speak the words, nor whisper them, I saw each letter slip silently from her lips.

"Gods help us."

There was one God who could hear her. And she stood right before her. Intending to help none.

The knock was short before he opened the door, making Nissa's mother jump to her feet and hurry away. Demir stood at the threshold, eyes taking me from top to bottom before he nodded, almost pleased at what he saw. "It's time."

"What a grace. To be fetched by the hand of the king himself."

He reached me and pulled hard on my arm. His other hand sank in my hair and tugged hard. "Because I know you are very capable of taking down a trained beast even chained."

"You flatter me. Severely."

His luminescent eyes dropped to my hand on his chest, shaking as it curled right over his heart. He scoffed. "Don't you think it is time to mourn your losses and move on?"

"What losses?" I asked, reaching even closer to him. "I've lost nothing. You took from me." The choking heat around us suddenly turned dull and sharp like the cold radiating from the winter outside. I shook from the unusual strength I conjured to hold back from tearing him apart.

He sucked in a short breath and choked on a stream of blood when enough ice grew on my fingertips to pluck his heart out of his chest. Taste of blood filled my mouth from the resistance of my magic against Melanthe's bonds wrapped around me, but I would do it again. And again. Until I was satisfied.

I wiped the blood gushing down my nose and mouth with the back of my glove and spat the rest to the ground. "Pitiful. Such pity I feel for you, sailor boy," I said, dropping the warm organ to the floor and cleaning my hand on his jacket. "Shall we? I'd hate to be late to my own celebrations."

The crowd was unusually small for what my father considered a celebration. Especially what I would think the naming of his heir would look like. But none mattered when father intended this news to reach beyond mountains and possibly seas.

I was sure the looks directed at me were not because of how fabulous the navy attire fit my body and how it made my eyes stand out. Or the old and heavy jewellery that only queens had worn before me. Or the chains tied to my limbs that rattled with every step I took—though I was sure Melanthe had cast some sort of veil or glamour to conceal them. My father wouldn't want the brand new Crown Princess paraded around in chains. Certainly, they were not staring at me because I had lost half of my weight, or because for the first time I was unable to conceal my hatred from my features, or because my muscles had strung so tight from anger and grief that I looked like I'd gone half mad. Certainly, those were not it. Because there was caution in their perusal. There was hesitation in their gestures and the way they breathed. They were holding back their inhales as if I were to suddenly deny them of air.

They now knew what I was.

They knew of my power.

They knew I'd resided amongst them, that I'd hidden amongst them.

They knew they had brushed danger, stared at danger, laughed at danger, played with danger, and had never even realised.

Father had not wasted a moment to brag about his creation. Probably stirred much more into that pot of lies only to sharpen the taste of his power.

"Come, child," father's voice boomed around the quiet hall, and he extended a hand towards me from the height of his dais.

Noise slowly began returning inside the room when I climbed the gilded stairs to my father and sat beside him, where Eren had once sat.

Silence fell again when father raised a hand, and announced, "I thank you for joining us today." He rested a hand on my arm, and I fought a flinch. "As you know, since the passing of my son, the crown suffered a great loss. I lost a child and Isjord lost their heir."

A little giggle escaped me, and father shot me a deadly look before continuing, "It has been a long mourning time. The same long time that the position as my heir has remained empty. And empty it will no longer be. Snowlin will take my crown one day, as my blood and as my chosen heir. I name her heir. My heir. The next Isjordian Queen." He squeezed my arm as if he knew I was a breath away from cackling.

The room gasped, their attention turning to me. Few were appalled amongst the fearful. Appalled as in upset. Which consequently made me irked. Isjordians and their audacity truly were a case to be studied.

"What about her marriage to the Night King?" one asked.

It was like I'd been thrown into a fire at the mention of his name, and the world around me melted entirely. If I dared think of him...the world would burn with everyone in it, and I would have not cared at all. But the world couldn't burn anymore, not when he was in it, too, so I didn't think of him at all.

"A sham," father lied, making my attention snap to him. "We have been planning to study the nightlands for a while after what happened thirteen years ago. My daughter agreed to help in those endeavours as she was the most affected by them. She was willing to risk herself for what they did."

I shot my father an amused look. Really? Is that what we are going with now?

"And she did well," he continued while holding my stare. There were cruel intentions behind the eyes that I'd inherited. "We learned plenty. Of their plans of war amongst many things." He glanced at my gloved hand, at where beneath laid the mark of our love—the mark that my father intended to use against Kilian—and he smiled.

Another round of gasps echoed about the room.

His new court stood silent, observing the reactions of the rich that held Isjord together while they were being lied to.

Father needed their support, needed their riches to fund his armies, needed their reach through the realm. He was not only using me as bait for rumours and to squash the challenge to his crown, he was also using me as a bargaining pawn for their unconditional help.

However, I needed them, too.

"It is true," I said loudly, sitting up straight in my seat, and father's grip on his chair turned deadly. "All that father said is true. We've been working on it for years. In fact, for a decade."

Someone stepped forward, breaking from the crowd. "Though I believe that to be the truth, Your Highness, there are other matters," the man said, refusing to look at me. "Your father is a man of tradition, and to crown you heir is...for lack of a better word—strange. The future of our kind is bright and so is his reign. He has sired many children and he will sire many more." He turned to my father. "With all due respect, Your Majesty, when were you to make us aware of these plans? We have been feeding gold and young children to your armies for months now, don't we deserve a better explanation? Why now? Why her?"

"What is there to understand?" I asked, cutting father off just as he was about to speak. "Would you rather I demonstrate why you can never find someone like me to crown as the next one to rule your kingdom?"

He lifted a brow and glanced at my father. "Demonstrate?"

I shot Melanthe a look, hoping the bitch would understand what I'd meant. Standing and extending my hands forward, I let electricity skitter around my fingers. "Pretty, isn't it?" Then heavy lightning hit the ground outside, and everyone shot up to their feet, staring out of the large, stained windows as packed thunder rained down on the shield over Tenebrose. The hiss of magic touching magic vibrated in the air until my very bones began rattling. When Melanthe finally snapped to the realisation that her veil was faltering, I felt my magic drain, only flakes of it remaining now, caged and chained behind her binding spells. The chains around my wrists burned and sizzled with smoke and heat, threatening to crack from the force of power assaulting them. I dusted my hands to cool down my skin and sighed. "Not so pretty when it touches you though. Your flesh will melt right over your bone like gravy."

The room was stunned into absolute silence and resolute fear, their wide eyes landing on to the fractured veil above the city, the hiss of smoke fluttering towards the skies, and the relentless crackling thunder that drummed heavily despite the locks on my power. Father and Melanthe included. If they only knew that was like taking a breath for me. If they only knew how much worse I was capable of doing.

The man cleared his throat and turned to me again. "You are powerful—"

"The most powerful," I clarified, giving him a saccharine smile. Yet my biggest strength had never been breaking bones, but minds.

He cleared the obvious distress from his throat, and said, "The Night King is powerful, too. We've made enemies with Solarya, Hanai, and even the unblessed are refusing our trade because of him."

How could I argue with that? I glanced over my shoulder at my father and pouted. "Ouch."

Father pulled on my arm and sat me back down in my seat. "This war is ours. The Night King will do nothing as long as I hold his brother down in our dungeons."

If only he knew how wrong he was.

The man bowed his head at the both of us. "Let us hope that is true, my king."

"Leverage," I said, crossing a leg over the other. "Magic. Gold. A powerful heir. What more can a kingdom need?" Giving each and every one of them a sweet smile, I said, "I will do right by my given title. With all of you by my side, this kingdom will reign power over the realm. Power that no other Krigborn King has ever offered this land. Perhaps time did indeed call for a queen." Then I will watch you drown in all of it—choke on greed.

"We will hold onto that promise, Your Highness."

"And hold onto it tightly," I replied.

He and the others shared a look, and it took everything in me not to smile with victory when I saw the hopeful looks they exchanged.

News of my crowning would travel fast. Father would make sure of that. And I was going to use every reward that came with it.

When the hall began emptying, father stood and offered me a hand. "Join me for lunch."

"Busy, I'm afraid," I said, standing.

He raised a brow, almost amused, and grabbed my arm. "With what?"

"Training."

"After training then."

"I will see my brother-in-law afterward."

His grip on me turned painful. "Are you now?"

"Father, I will slit my throat here, right in front of you, with my own nails before I even lift one single finger to help you if Malik Castemont is not well and safe. The only way for me to know so is to see it with my own beautiful eyes. It is the least you can do since I am cutting your time to find the sceptre pieces before my husband finds a way to rip your guilty little soul out of your lungs."

He still held tightly onto me, his fingers bruising my skin. "You played that game a little too well, my rose. Don't do it again."

"Why, what will you do? Hurt me? Beat me? Starve me?" I asked, pouting. Pulling my arm from his grip, I descended the stairs. "If you are so sure of your victory, why are you so afraid, *papa?*"

"I will not let you stir my court and my people again."

Mine, too, father. For a while, they are my people, too. "Whatever you say, *my king.*"

4

Black Knight to C6

Snowlin

MOREGAN STOOD RIGHT IN the middle of the training court, rather annoyed at having to train me. Though disappointed I wasn't getting to play around with Demir, I was finally getting the chance to learn what my father's business was with the usurped old Krigborn Queen. How had he come across such a precious possession?

"You are my match?" I asked, crossing my arms and raking an unimpressed look over her.

"I've lived hundreds of years more than you, little girl."

"Perhaps try and live a few hundred more and you might just survive me." I craned my neck back at Demir. "Is this a joke?"

"Most sceptre locations are veiled, either suppressing magic or concealing it all together." He leaned on the court fence and pointed his chin to a high balcony where Melanthe stood watching us. "She will free parts of your magic. Consider this a suppressed environment."

I scoffed. Suppressed?

They all shot up, some screaming, shouting, cursing, and staggering backwards when sharp ice shards shot up from the ground for a mile around us, even making Demir bleed a little.

At the click of my fingers, the ice cracked and exploded into even smaller ice shards, floating slowly in the air before gathering into a swirling mist around Demir.

The man began turning green—literally. "Melanthe, stop it—"

He did not have the time to finish the order because each and every one of the thousand floating ice shards pierced his flesh faster than what lighting would have struck land.

The chains on my wrists burned and I hissed from the pain piercing my body. The shock made me sway on my feet and I dropped to the ground, clutching my stomach. It made me laugh. Too hard perhaps because there was not a pipsqueak of a sound in the air besides mine. "Melanthe," I cooed loudly, still curled up on the ground. "How

I am going to skin you."

Demir was still vomiting out blood while a bunch of healers picked out the shards of ice from his body.

One limb at a time, I got myself up again and faced the witch. "Am I training or what?"

Moregan's brows had dropped low enough to cover her eye lids, but she still took a stance, lifting both of her hands in front of her how I had seen only one man do before. Knees bent, arms extended forward, one palm facing me and the other facing her.

Eren.

How was this possible?

"Did they make your train my brother in Ulv Islet?" I asked, imitating her position. I was a fast learner. Copying and adapting was what I was most gifted at.

She glanced at Melanthe. "Stop talking."

"Funny," I said, swiftly blocking her attack by swerving to the side. "Father made you his prisoner and his heir's tutor."

"I wasn't his tutor."

"So, you do know my brother."

She pushed the palming facing me forward, and the snow below our feet rose from the ground, hardening as it shot in my direction. Only for it to meet mine. The crash made splinters of ice fly around and about. "Knew. Briefly," she said, switching the side of her other palm to face me before snow rose from behind me, hardening again and aiming for my back.

Except that it crashed against a wall of my own ice that rose quicker than her magic did. "Why was my brother being taught by you?"

"Ask your father."

"Maybe I will just ask my brother."

She attacked me again. Shards of ice flying half an inch or so away from grazing my cheek. "Speaking to the dead now?"

"Why? Anyone you want me to greet in your stead? They let you make any friends in Ulv Islet?"

"Stop talking!" she hissed, running in my direction, and snow twirled around my body to engulf me under it.

Everything melted right off before it even touched me when lightning skittered over my skin, enshrouding us inside a steamy, thick white fog.

Sharp edged ice grew in my palm, and I ran to meet her in the middle. I wrapped a hand around her throat and squeezed tightly, pointing the honed tip to her gut. "Fearful then. Fearful now," I murmured in her ear, keeping an eye on our surroundings still concealed by the mist, feeling each heartbeat still pulse in the distance and giving me enough alone time with Moregan. "Fear is a complex currency, don't you think? He has your loyalty. What are *you* winning from it?"

She pushed me off, unsheathing a curved anlace from her baldric. "I told you to shut up," she snarled, swinging her blade, twirling around after each time I blocked her and each time I blocked her. She was quick on her feet and tactical, more than gifted, saving her energy for careful and precise strikes. But like most, she fought with anger—and anger was blinding.

"Did he force the potion down your throat?" I continued, ice flying in the air again, scratching and burning skin. "Or did you just love feeling like an animal, so you decided to become one as well?"

Row, row this fucking boat gently down the angry seas.

Her body crashed against mine, knocking me to the ground. Her fist met my jaw before I could push her off. "He was locked there, too," she said between clenched teeth, hitting me again. "With me and others. Sometimes for days and sometimes for weeks. Did you ever see his own scars, little sister?"

I knocked her jaw back with the heel of my palm, and she rolled off of me, dizzy and bleeding from her mouth. "You taught him?" I asked, stabbing a sharp shard of ice through her palm, and pinning her to the floor. "Such a kind heart, *Ice Queen*."

Her eyes fluttered open. "He was put there to learn." She pulled her hand through the ice, freeing and punching me. The skin and bone began mending as if there had not been an injury to begin with. "Shame he never did. It would have spared me all this bullshit."

I laughed. "Oh, he did learn. But praise the Gods that he never had to prove himself." No one but me, him, and the skies had seen what he'd done to protect me and Thora. How many souls he'd drained out of air. Anyone who doubted our magic, anyone who had seen, felt, or smelled something to indicate what we were. No one could count the bodies that he'd left behind without no one knowing. Alaric had taught him precision, resistance, and agility, how to triple and quadruple the impact of a bean size amount of his magic into the magnitude of an avalanche with the fatality of a hurricane.

At some point, even I'd been thankful that he'd sworn to never draw magic again.

The question that poked my relentless thoughts was why had he never told me he'd been taught by this one, too?

Or perhaps he had.

And I just...didn't remember. Like I didn't remember much from back then. It was like my mind had simply erased anything it had deemed too severe.

I caught her fist again and pushed my elbow back hard on her face. "What did my father lose in there?" I asked, pointing to the scar in the middle of her head, and she flinched—hard. "It hasn't even healed properly. That is some dark, dark business."

She attacked me again, viciously, not sparing me a single moment to attack back. "Is this how you fight?"

"No. Is this how you answer?"

Magic rose in the air one more time, but I held back and let her have her fun, let her unleash all that pent up adorable frustration. "No."

I twisted around, missing all of her attacks, and using the heel of my foot, I stomped on her knee, making her stumble to the ground. "Other soldiers have little scars, faded scars, burnt marks, some even look like moles from a distance," I said, pointing to the side of my neck where most of the soldiers who stank of dark magic had a small unhealed scar. "You're the only little beast with one this big and no scar on your neck."

When her attention slipped to Melanthe, I laughed. "There. Got you. You were the first one they turned. Interesting. Actually, no, it is not. I lied. You're a prime Verglaser. The best test subject. No surprise there at all."

"How...how did you know?" she panted.

"That's enough," Demir said, finally on his feet and huffing with rage as he tore through the mist around us. "Get out of there, Moregan."

Even after all that, I was feeling oddly refreshed. Refreshed enough that I was cruising down to the dungeons where father kept Mal.

The guards behind me followed swiftly along with a hooded Crafter who had not even let out a breath since she'd stepped before me. She was the only one who had looked remotely afraid. But she wasn't only afraid of me. From the way she nervously glanced down the corridor, how her heart started beating louder the closer to the dungeon gates we got, told me that she was afraid of what was down there, too. Or who.

The heavy gates groaned when four guards pulled them open. The stink of craft almost made me gag. It had not been this heavy even around me. Did they really need all of this to contain Mal?

From the pale faces down the narrow alley leading to a fortified cell, I realised that it probably wasn't even enough. He was a spiritual Aura. He could find crumbs to feed his magic from someone's yawn alone. Emotion was a weapon. And in Mal's hands, it was beyond deadly, too.

He stood in the middle of an iron cage with nothing but a bed in it, sat on the ground, his hands resting on top of his bent knees while his head hung low between them. "Sister-in-law," he croaked, lifting his head up. Though half hidden from the shadows, I could see his grin. "What a treat for the sore eye."

The guards shivered and shifted on their feet, their knuckles turning white because of how hard they'd gripped their spears.

"Mal—" His name was all I was able to murmur, my chest suddenly heavy with the weight of all that had happened. And memories—so many memories. Haunting and taunting memories.

He stood and reached me, fitting his arms between the metallic bars and pulling me into an embrace. "Don't let them," he said in my ear, his whole body shaking. "Don't fucking let them win."

I drew in a stuttering breath, clutching his shirt to draw him closer. He'd kept me alive this far. He'd kept me from turning this place inside out. From pulling the flaming hells inside the heart of winter. "Tell me they have not hurt you."

His fingers dug where he held me. "No. They have not hurt me. Have you heard from Kil?"

I shook my head. "Nothing."

"That is not good."

Finally, I looked up at him. Though I knew Melanthe must be listening to our conversation, I couldn't resist asking, "You think something has happened to him?"

He snorted, pinching my cheek. "Has he been this soft around you? That fucker is terrifying. Silas better have a few pairs of drawers in his closet. But considering he likes to start shit, he might like sitting in it, too."

For the first time, I felt my mouth rise into a genuine smile which fell quickly when I saw the matted blood under his jacket. "Mal, you...you said he hasn't hurt you."

"It would be foolish to think he could take the closest person to the night throne and not try to poke a few answers out of him. It's nothing," he added, resting a hand on my shoulder. "It is nothing."

I shook my head. "He cannot hurt you. He knows it."

"Won't stop him from trying, Snow. Let it go now." He cupped the back of my head and sighed. "You won't let it go, will you?"

"We will see."

"He let you come down here."

I raised a brow at him. "You know why he spared you."

He shook his head. "He could've...he could've taken her, too, if he had wanted to threaten you with obedience. Silas must have thought the chances that Kil will fall for his traps are double if he has you and me both. But he doesn't know my brother like me and you do. if anything, he's fucked up twice as bad."

That offered some relief, and I nodded. "He won't come. I really hope that is the truth."

"He would have come for her, too. He would come for anyone he loves," he said, lightly squeezing the back of my neck. "And Kil is night. He has always moved under shadows. If you don't see him, it is then you know that he is coming."

Mal's words echoed around me long after my visit. *If you don't see him, it is then you know that he is coming.*

"Stop staring at the walls, girl," Nissa's mother said, pushing me back on the bed and throwing the blanket over me. "And go to sleep. You look like you belong serving soup down in the kitchens."

I grabbed her arm when she was about to leave. "Can you turn off all the candles? And draw the curtains. I don't want to see any light at all."

She nodded despite my odd request. "I know, girl. I know. You ought to ask me every night the same thing." Murmuring under her breath and shaking her head, she did as told. "No wonder you look like you do."

"Insult my attitude, but stay clear of insulting my beauty, old hag."

"Beauty my old arse."

When I closed my eyes, there was always some harrowing memory flashing behind them. But for a little while, I only wanted to think of him. Without thinking of anything else. Just him. Of him and the words he'd said to me in the dark.

The quiet entirety of it, the absolute darkness...I found comfort in it now like he did. The quiet was not frightening either. The shadows were so still that I wanted them to move, to stir awake the Snow they had created, so she could battle the monsters now hiding in the light.

If I just let go…if I just let my eyelids rest for a brief moment, I could hear him, too. *My love.*

The trip to Seraphim had been cancelled. That was all I had been told, and then I'd been ordered to not step anywhere between my room and the training grounds which my father had now moved indoors, inside some old closed quarters. A week. Then two. Almost another third one had passed, and I'd done just that. Darsan whispers had brushed past my ears, alleging that Melanthe was having health issues and could not portal the ships past Solaryan waters. Nissa's mother, on the other hand, told me that Verglasers had not even been able to break the Seer Sea ice to even move the ships an inch, which I doubted to be a lie told for everyone to spread in order to cover the truth—the one I could not still get close enough to no matter how hard I tried. Moregan had only grunted and sneered at me during training, seeming to have grown accustomed to my taunting words. While I'd not seen Demir or the witch. And that was only until the start of this week, when my father had fetched me from my room himself, looking quite jolly. And then he'd proceeded to drag me all over Isjord.

He had paraded me through every city and before every Isjordian he could find. It seemed he wanted even the dead to know that his kingdom had a long path ahead with a newer, stronger heir of Krigborn blood.

Did he realise what beast he was creating? Had he stopped to see the footprints his fear was leaving behind? How his people were starting to look at me. At *me* alone. Not their king.

Father was still prattling about with some Casmere merchant about the shortage of coal that was causing his trade to go bankrupt.

Coal. How could coal be in shortage in Isjord? Everyone in this kingdom even had their milk with a side of coal.

People were still staring at me from the distance as I moved from one market stall to the other, perusing mindlessly and trying not to concentrate on how badly I needed to pee. All the smiles I'd been given, the flowery wishes, and adoring bows I'd received were really making my bladder anxious.

A flash of red silk caught my attention—bright ruby, just how Kilian liked it. Then like a dam, all of our memories poured out. As if to taunt me.

What was he doing now? Was he alone like I was?

"You like it?"

I turned at the sound of my father's voice and let go of the soft fabric, not wanting to taint my like for it. "Yes, I think I've found the perfect material to wear at your funeral."

His jaw clenched and ticked briefly, and he grinned all teeth, still cautious of the attention on us. "You are funny, my daughter."

"I'm going to rip you apart," I said, laughing, playing along for our audience. "It will be glorious."

"Sometimes, I cannot tell if you are plainly insane or—"

"There is no *or*. I am plainly insane. Play blood games and win bloody prizes, papa." Turning to the merchant standing behind the stand, I pointed to the fabric. "Twelve yards, please."

The merchant hurried to fulfil my request. "That is quite a bit of material. Are you making a gown with it, princess?"

"Indeed," I said, giving father a sweet smile. "A ball gown. For a very special occasion. Oh, and I must see some sparkly fabric of sorts. The sparkliest one you've got."

The merchant nodded and went to the back while I turned to my dear father. "Nothing screams funeral more than diamonds and glitter. And since no sun or moon will be shining on your death, I might as well take upon the honour."

All of a sudden, a wave of dizziness washed over me, and my sight coated black before flashing with visions that were not mine.

City. People. Snow. Howling wind. Deafening sounds that were making my ears bleed.

I put a hand to my chest, trying to calm the erratic heartbeat drumming against the bone. Except that my heart was beating at a steady pace. And the one I was feeling was not mine.

They were not visions. It was not my heartbeat.

Memphis. It was my bonded.

I hadn't realised father was gripping my arm to hold me upright. "What's wrong with you now?"

"Let me be," I said, pulling my arm out of his grip. To my luck, he just sneered and turned on his merry way.

Carefully, I looked overhead, narrowing my eyes at the dark clouds that had not stopped pouring thick pellets of snow for hours now. And in the midst of white and grey, I saw a flash of black disappearing inside clouds before reappearing on the other side again.

No.

No.

"Memphis," I growled under my breath, hoping Melanthe's craft had not blocked it entirely. "Go!" My bonded was more careless than me, but she knew not to do this. "Go, I said!"

A group of soldiers rushed to my father's side, animatedly explaining something to him while pointing to the city entrance.

Shit.

I turned to my guard. "What is happening?"

"A snowstorm."

"A what?"

"They have been quite perennial these past few weeks. The wind is too harsh these days, it is raising the settled snow and the one falling. It has brought many casualties."

"Storm. It's because of a storm." I looked up at the skies again, Memphis finally disappearing without reappearing again.

The Skye. Memphis always flew with them.

"When did it start?"

"A few weeks ago, Your Highness. But your father's Crafter has travelled South to Eldmoor to seek help from her coven and a few white witches have arrived this morning from Whitebridge to warm up our skies. We should be rid of it in no time."

Hells.

I giggled. "A snowstorm."

He knew. My damn father knew there were no snowstorms. Is that why he had brought me out in public? He'd intended to use me as a trap for my people. He'd wanted to lure them out of hiding by using me.

"Father," I shouted, and everyone turned to me. "I'm feeling so unwell. Can I retreat inside?"

He sneered at me, looking around at all the people that had heard. "Of course, child. Of course you might."

I nodded, gathering my skirts and following a guard leading me inside a tavern. "Be careful," I shouted at him again. "It looks like the snowstorm is turning around, *papa*."

5

White Bishop to B5

Kilian

THE LOOK BEYOND THE Highwall was grave. All was pale behind the thicket of snow that had drowned the two villages close to us almost to the point that Isjordians were no longer leaving their homes.

Help came rarely, meaning that Silas's priorities were no longer his people. If he didn't have my wife and brother, I would have been tempted to go down there and give my aid to those who were struggling to even purchase flour for their bread or make a hearth big enough to boil water for their tea.

Memphis returned and shifted into a large cat, nudging my knee so I could offer her a pat for being the best girl around. "Did you see her again today?" I asked, rubbing her back. She'd been the most alive these past few days than she'd been in a long while all because of seeing her bonded again.

The animal let out a little happy yowl, and my chest hurt.

"She is well, isn't she? Tell me she is well."

Instead of answering me, she reached and rested her head on my shoulder. And it was all it took for my insides to knot and twist again.

My eyes drew shut as I pressed my brow to hers. "You've got to tell me, Memphis. Please, tell me."

"Your Majesty," Tristin called, and I looked up at the commander. "This could be the last time we will be able to fly on Isjordian skies. Silas has brought Glares and Magi-Healers on his patrols. I have four soldiers with burn wounds laying at the healers. He is either attempting to keep the cold under control by increasing the sunlight over his lands or knows what we are doing."

I shook my head, still patting Memphis. "Besides me, you, Larg, and Triad no one knows where we are sending you. Silas might be aware that there are Olympians around, but is definitely undermining your numbers considering. If he knew the truth, he'd be sending far worse than Glares and white witches your way. Snow has always been right. His biggest fear remains you."

She looked around uncomfortably. "I do not wish to allude, my king, but someone from your court could have let Silas know about more than just our existence."

"No one in my court but those closest to me know about what lies beyond the mist—they know of your existence, sure, but nothing beyond what everyone had already been speculating. And Cai has not observed any movement in Myrdur since Snow got the sceptre."

"What will we do next? It looks like they are still trying to sail west to Seraphim."

"We will have to let them. We have his metal, coal, horses, fruit, oils, and spices. If we take too much, he will tie it all back to us. We have to move slower now." He'd made so many enemies and I'd made all of his enemies my allies. Everything that was meant to go in or out of Isjord first went by me now.

"You are playing Snow's game a little too well."

I smiled down at Memphis. "She is a good teacher, and her model was almost flawless."

"Almost?" she asked, her brows hiking up in amusement.

"Good sabotage usually comes from within. She never planted a mole or a spy in my court, probably because she trusted no Adriatian. But Silas already welcomed my wife inside his court. The heir announcement was never his plan, it was hers. The foundations are crumbling from right under his feet and he doesn't even know it."

"You put too much faith in her reasoning," Eren said, climbing up the stairs to the wall tower.

"She is my faith. It would be absurd if I didn't. And my faith is smart—the smartest. She has survived Silas too many times to count, and she will survive him again." I stood and took the letter he handed to me, the envelope still sealed with my crest. "I gather Magnus refused contact again."

"Fifth letter, Kilian. It has to mean something."

"It means nothing. Magnus will never join Silas, and Silas never had a plan to make allies, only to demilitarise kingdoms with his deals and bargains. If Solarya is cutting contact with us, Magnus must be thinking Snow has betrayed me."

He leaned against the terrace wall, looking at the slim horizon made of nothing but pure white snow. "Or maybe he is disappointed to hear that you've hidden the truth about her powers to him."

"No, he would understand. Magnus would understand why we would have wanted to hide that side of hers."

Heavy, quick steps sounded from the stairwell, and we all turned to watch the little Skygard sister heavily pant, limping and exhausted as she reached us. "I hate...hate stairs." She stretched back, wiping sweat from her brow. "It's my training time. You were supposed to be there already to train me."

"Are you telling me that you finished reading the books Atlas assigned you to read?" Her lashes fluttered for a moment. "Yes."

"Thoroughly."

She was unphased. "Define thoroughly."

Nesrin led a stomping group of soldiers up the wall tower and turned to bow at me, a wide smile and few shadows I didn't like colouring her exterior. Her eyes went to Thora who stood by my side, glaring back at her.

As far as Nesrin knew, Thora was just someone I had taken under my wing to train and make part of my court eventually. It was the best way to keep her safe. But of course, she suspected something else.

The little sister tilted her head to the side and raised a brow at her. "I've already told you that I am not an Empath, Nesrin. If you have something to say, you have to say it. Whatever language you like, even."

The councillor raised her chin. "No priestess needs to hover around the king. You've got plenty to learn to be wasting your time before the entrance exam you're supposedly taking soon."

The little Skygard stepped forward. "And no councillor needs to hover around the king's castle quarters when they've been told a million times that they are not welcome there. Especially at night when they're sneaking in like a thief, but wearing lace and with their tits out rather than a mask and dagger in their hand. If you passed your own exams with so little knowledge and skill, then I shan't worry about mine."

Nesrin staggered a little, blinking between her and I, a deep flush of embarrassment climbing up her neck. I hadn't known that she'd been trying to enter my quarters again. She cleared her throat. "Could I have a moment with you later, Kilian?"

"There is a meeting later this evening at court. Whatever there is to discuss, let me know then."

She nodded, her attention drifting to Thora briefly before she joined the rest of her soldiers.

Thora sighed, looking bored. "One day I'm going to turn her lungs into wet, bloody prunes. I hate prunes."

"You seem to hate *her*."

"You should see her little group of arse lickers that follow her around all day, praising and fawning over her like she is some...*queen*."

That was something I didn't like either. "Her father was influential."

"Heard he was almost pretty flammable as well. He is probably loving hell."

That made me chuckle. "You're sweating."

She wiped the wet beads from her temple and looked down at her feet, focusing there for a moment. "It is pretty high up—there were a lot of stairs, I mean."

"You don't need to come up here, Thora."

"What if she shows up down there or up here? If father comes again or threatens us with someone else. What if she escapes? What if she needs help? I want to be here if that happens. I keep missing her again and again. I've been useless so many times and I'll never be useless again." She turned to me. "This is why you need to keep training me, not make me fall asleep in uncomfortable places such as the library."

"You can read in your room next time. Atlas will let you borrow the books."

Her face scrunched up all disappointment and she glanced back at her brother who was quietly chuckling by the edge of the tower. "Obscur Asteri," she mumbled between her teeth, retreating towards the stairs. "More like...obscuring my will to live."

Eren sighed, leaning over the terrace ledge.

"You don't like this, do you?" I asked. "That she is choosing to take control instead of hiding from what she is. Like you are."

He shot me a glare. "You used to be so much kinder."

"No, you've just become an old, grumpy man. Now get off my Highwall, I need the guards to actually do some guarding, not flutter their lashes at you."

I woke to something jerking uncontrollably under my arm. Memphis's large feline body laid beside me like every night for the past few months. But this time it was different from the others. Her heartbeat drummed loud enough to fill all corners of the room and her whole body shook. Her bond with Snow was still strong despite the distance and magic keeping them apart. I knew she still felt Snow. I knew what her nightmares, anxiousness, discomfort, and pain meant.

"What do you see?" I asked, stroking her face.

She let out a broken yowl and tucked her head under the duvet again.

"Please," I murmured, swallowing down a lump in my throat. "Let me see, too."

She jumped up, shaking her head and morphing into a thin, black snake, twirling around the balcony pillars and disappearing into the gardens below.

There would be no sleep for me tonight either.

I lit every candle in the room, even the ones she didn't like the smell of. The more the space brightened, the more I could see remnants of her shadows still dancing around the room. Twirling, swaying, and even angrily stomping in places. Her shadows slipped away from my touch every time I reached near them, so I only sat at the edge of my bed, watching. This time they hovered around the library, her phantom fingers circling over the books there. Over the Esmeray Diaries and Eamon's Book of Dreams. She'd spent most of her last days there before being taken by Silas, reading and studying. It was why remnants of her presence and shadows lingered so heavily over them.

Like every night before, I reached and piled them all up on my table.

No matter how many times I skimmed them, there was nothing left from Snow's notes on the diaries that I'd not gone through.

I pulled Eamon's Book of Dreams out one last time for tonight, stopping at the title page for a moment. The only page I'd not actually looked at in the whole book. There were scribbles all over. Writing I knew well.

The most delicate writing, so soft and sophisticated. I knew the pretty hands that had inked the pages. I prided myself that I knew her extremely well. But her intelligence, that was one thing I kept continuously failing to praise enough. Snow had a fascinating mind. The most fascinating mind I knew.

She'd written '*Book of Dreams?*' all over. The word *dreams* was underlined and with several question marks following after.

"What were you up to, my heart?"

I flipped through the book, tracing a finger over the pages to note where the word *dream* had been highlighted again with a light pencil. Too many times to count, Snow had underlined the word on every page she had found it, no matter the meaning. The thick book ended with him passing the duty as keeper of Nephthys to his son, and it was the only page where there was no mention of the word *dream*. And right on the inner back cover, there was a little mirror glued on top of the old leather. Thin. Rectangular. Framing barely my eyes. And there was a little note below it with her handwriting again.

There are no reflections in dreams.

I remained frozen for a moment.

Hells.

"Smart girl," I murmured to myself, picking up my jacket and heading down to Visha's quarters.

The tired Crafter poked her head out on the first knock. "It is the hour of the dead. Unless you've been slain and this is your spirit, good night."

I slid my hand between the doors, stopping her from shutting me out. "Vas and Aurora were entrapped inside a dream veil in Nephthys Island."

She blinked once. "A dream veil?"

"When Eamon was going in and out of Nephthys, he documented everything meticulously. The smallest of things such as the locks he used, the exact direction his boat took, how many times he turned the key on the lock, his breaks, the foods he ate, when he ate. Think, Visha, why would he be doing that? Eamon travelled back and forth to that island for centuries. The effect that the dream craft must have had on him along with the presence of the Sea of the Dark, it all would have caused him daily issues. Hallucinations. Memory loss. Derealisation. The whole book is a log. A detailed log of everything, so he would not forget, so he would be sure everything was done correctly, so others would read and know that he made no mistakes in his guard in case something was to happen. Tell me why he is the only one to leave a book behind?"

Her eyes widened just the slightest. "The other keepers did not live long enough."

"Exactly. His son died thirty years later. His grandson was almost the same age, too. Every guard after him died young, and then Aurora was freed. Eamon began documenting only when he could no longer remember. He kept a mirror at the end, as a reminder that he was awake when he wrote in it. Snow always wondered why the two had been locked together considering that Fader cursed them with separation."

"Why not a nightmare veil? Or fear? Terror? Anguish?" She rubbed her eyes. "It would make more sense. Vas also couldn't cross any of the ones protecting the sceptre."

"Correct, but also very wrong. Vas fought the veil of fears in Isjord, and even managed to get through the Hanaian one with some effort, so why is it that he could not get out of Nephthys? What is the difference between the two veils, Visha?"

"One seeps inside you to sicken the mind. The other alters what is around you without getting inside your mind. Both taunt. One with what fear you have and the other with what you fear you can never have."

"Over and over. For centuries. It would make a God sick, let alone a man."

"You think that is what he fears? Losing sense of reality or being lured into something they desperately desire until their heart is broken to the point of death? Is this what Snow was looking for?"

"No. Just as Snow said, Vas did not love Aurora. If he did love her, that veil would have been nightmares. It would have fed on what he felt for her and hurt him through it. Fader knew what he was doing. He was showing them both each other's dreams.

None which overlapped the other's. That is torture. Reminding them they fought and broke rules for nothing. Reminding them they deceived each other for nothing."

The witch chewed on her bracelet bead. "Macaria would know about this. We always assumed that they had been bound with godly magic, but it would make sense." She sighed. "I doubt we can use this against Aurora though, not without access to the sceptre."

My hands gathered into fists at my side. "I was not thinking of using it on Aurora."

6

Black Pawn to A6

Snowlin

THE TRIP TO SERAPHIM through the rough waters of the Seer Sea had probably shifted my organs all over and tangled them with each other considering how sick even walking made me. Not to mention that the place stank of fish and salt, and that the next thing I could possibly retch out was only my poor, innocent lungs.

Demir manoeuvred us around the massive camp that my father had raised in Heyes. He'd been in some sour mood lately, and for some reason, he kept holding a palm against his chest almost as if it hurt.

The heat was not as bad as it had been years ago when I'd visited with my father. Though it was still muggy, the air wasn't as stifling. Seraphim skies were a dark grey, not because of any storm or thunder, but from the lingering soot that never cleared since the burn of the Fire Kingdom five hundred years ago. Aurora had been the one to burn it. She'd been the one to turn what once had been the richest kingdom in the realm into a hot rock filled with only scorched ruins. Even five hundred years later, Seraphim had not managed to rebuild itself from that destruction.

There was not even one Seraphim folk around in what Seraphim land we'd stepped on since our arrival. It was strange to say the least and not strange at all when you thought about it better. Why conquer when you could quietly spread like fungus and overtake it all. That was Silas Krigborn's strategy. But it seemed strange that no winter and snow had settled on the land even though he'd almost claimed it as his and Isjord's. And that probably meant that Aurora's damage was more severe than I'd thought.

Hammer scales flew all around me as swordsmiths beat the hot iron into weapon casts. They flung the barely finished blades into piles of weapons behind them, not even caring to check for quality or even wait for them to cool off. Perhaps they didn't need to. Father would not care if a sword would be used well and fair in the hands of a soldier. If it could pierce flesh, it was good enough. There were too many hands to equip with weapons, little time, and not enough forgers. If my father was looking to arm his soldiers in Heyes, it meant he planned to send them either south to

Vrammethen, or west to The Sayuri and then Hanai. Considering they had changed
to thinner sails that eased tacking manoeuvres, they were planning to sail against the
wind—so most likely Hanai.

Faint whispers brushed my ears while we made our way closer to the heart of the
camp. The sound of hammers suddenly flailed. And almost everyone raised their eyes
and bowed their heads as if I was some sort of a saviour.

There was so much hope in their eyes that I wanted to crush. But that was until I
saw the soldiers following us along.

Children.

Barely in their teens.

I saw my brother in them.

I saw myself.

Then I saw countless graves filled with soft bones and barely any adult teeth.

There was no sense of nobility or responsibility in me, doubtful that it was something I could feel towards these people, but rage against my father did assault my senses
for a strong minute. At how far he was willing to go and how much worse he intended
to do.

Kilian would hate this. To have to fight them. To not be able to spare them. To have
to plan against them and not nurture and plead them away from this.

"I didn't tell you to stop," Demir hissed in my ear, discreetly tugging on my chains
for me to follow.

There were several bodies inside the main tent which had been turned into a
war room. Some I'd seen before and others that I wouldn't have thought I'd see on
my father's side. Adriatians, Solaryans, and Eldmoorians stood alongside Isjordian
Captains.

They all avoided my gaze when I reached their side while Demir exchanged news
with those who he had left in charge here.

"You've made your families really proud, I hope," I said to no one in particular,
settling on a chair.

"Says the one who has betrayed our king one too many times to count," an Adriatian muttered under his breath, sneering at me.

I peeled off my left glove and raised my hand up to show him why I could never and
would never betray my husband. "I never betrayed anyone. Just because you cannot
see the shackles, does not make me a traitor. And just because you hated me enough
to betray your kind, does not make you righteous." I put my glove back on and turned
slightly over my shoulder to them. "When this is over, I will find your mothers, fathers,
wives and husbands, daughters and sons, and I will slaughter them as food for my
bonded. It will not satiate my own stomach, but I am sure as hells it will please my
soul."

Demir's face turned from bored to surprised to concerned and to angry in a matter
of seconds while he listened to the soldier animatedly trying to explain something to
him. He shot me a quick glance before completely turning his back to me, trying to
disguise his hushed words though I was no master in lip reading.

"Heard that a single ship hasn't made it past Mahara's channel," someone murmured in Darsan to another.

"They say a witch is blocking them," another said.

"Stronger than Melanthe?"

"So they say."

"I heard," another whispered, "the winds have been mad, too."

"It's like a curse," another snarled. "No salt, no spices, no coal, or oil. Nothing. The winter lands are falling under the same curse as ours. Except there are no lilies this time."

"Galanthus," another murmured, and realisation struck me. "Instead of lilies, there are snow flowers growing in the middle of summer when the cold is the harshest it has ever been. It makes no sense."

"Gods make no sense," another huffed.

"Neither do men," I said in Darsan, and they all went quiet. "You believe in curses and prophecies, make vile claims and take vile actions based on them, but make no sound or blink no eye when men do worse than Gods or prophecies or curses. Do you know what that is called?" I glanced at them again. "Hypocrisy. Amongst many other names that I've yet to learn in your tongue."

Had Kilian been messing with my father all this time without him even possibly knowing? If they couldn't cross the Mahara channel, it meant that Kilian was playing my game with my father. Keeping them away from necessities. Starving Isjord.

Then it all made sense.

The change in people's reaction to me. The sudden support. The hope. The doubt. Humans remained oddly human after all. Pointing at a non-existent curse rather than back at their own faults. And making up a saviour when there was no need for saving in the first place.

I'd not even realised Demir was a foot from me when he spoke, "If you don't wipe that grin off your face, they might think you're mad, little heiress."

Instead, I flashed him an even brighter one. "What can I do when the joke walks right up to me?"

"Hope you can find humour in the fact that we will leave for the sceptre piece as early as tomorrow morning."

"Absolutely. Let's see what you've been struggling to do for...what? Years?" I leaned forward, resting an elbow on my knee. "How did poor you even find them without me?"

He leaned in, resting his hands on my chair and caging me in. "I was there when it was said that the blood of a Skygard would be the one to raise Aurora from the sceptre. I was there when your ancestor took it apart five hundred years ago. So, I did just that. Used the blood of a Skygard to look for her." He put a hand on my shoulder and grinned. "Almost got your uncles. Had they not vanished into thin air like they did. The noble act cost me two more decades. I had to spend years recovering from the damage they caused to my body. A body that by Gods should have not been harmed the way it did." He pushed my hair back. "But I am prepared for this Skygard."

Gods...Gods, how many roots did this rotten plant even have? "You were there that night?" Is this why they had been able to take down the Elding during the night of the *Draugr*?

"How do you think your grandfather died, the mighty King of Skies—The Unbreakable Dragon? I have to give it to him though, he did kill me about four dozen times before he got tired and overwhelmed fighting me and your father all whilst trying to protect his people."

The land. The restless souls. The lifeless air. The Fogling. Was it because of him?

"That's right," he taunted.

Cold tears slipped down my face, my breath misting from the cold air spreading. "You used my kin?"

"For a little while. You had a cousin, the last thought to be Eldingchild left after both your uncles died. But he, too, died shortly after we took him down to Ulv Islet. Grief, apparently. Once blood went rotten, it was no worth to me. And though your father never really intended to use your mother as a breeding mare, he was forced to. When that prophecy was written, there was no doubt. He was convinced enough to have you three. We thought your brother was the Elding. He certainly had all the other Skygard traits. Noble, kind, persevering. I could swear that the wind beat at his pace and bowed at his order. There was something about that brother of yours, something I'd never seen anywhere else. Silas kept him in Ulv Islet for some time while I was healing there. Silas was convinced that he was what we needed, but I could not smell the Elding in him like I did when we faced one another in Hanai. Imagine my surprise. Imagine your father's." He wiped my tears with his knuckles and then licked the wet skin. "That day when I saw you, I saw my salvation. With a little Delcour craft and what little blood we had from the young Elding before, we managed to locate some sceptre pieces. The tricky part was retrieving them. Those trials were made only for you to solve." His jaw tightened and red rage flashed in his face. "The Elder Crafters had tried to make sure I wouldn't be able to enter them. I had to turn into this, and yet...everything kept me from her. Everything!" he thundered, and I flinched back in my chair.

He'd struggled to enter the temple because of the veil of fears. Like the soldier had said. My lips trembled when I asked, "What are you most afraid of, Vas?"

He pulled back a little, frowning. "What?"

I gripped his shirt to hold him still while my eyes dug into his, searching and searching into that dead and listless abyss. Trying to find the gate to a soul. "Spiders. Snakes. Death. The God of Death. Fire. Heights." His eyes glistened from the reflection of mine when I whispered, "Lightning. Denial. Hell. Separation." I chuckled. "Me. The Night King."

Except...the gate was open, and nobody was fucking home.

He tried to push me off, but I held him tightly, the air chilling entirely at my vile satisfaction. My smile slipped on easily despite the loose tears falling down my face when I leaned forward, our faces not an inch apart. "I thank you for your candour."

Men were fools. They always jumped into the pool of someone's tears only for them to drown from within, forgetting they were inside hellish waters to begin with. Grief was always grief. It could not be twisted.

He gripped my chains, making the metal dig into my skin and rub hard enough to make me bleed. "Prisoners only have dreams, princess."

The tears would not stop, and it somehow made me laugh even harder. "Sweet, sweet dreams knowing you lay in your cold bed afraid." And happy thoughts knowing that my father, this fool, and his witch had no idea who they were holding prisoner and what they were creating after everything they revealed to me. The joke really told itself. The shadows in the mirror were laughing along. Hysterically. Hungry. So hungry.

We know, they whispered from every reflective surface inside the tent, swords and shields and puddles of water. Their excitement even made the air tremble.

I put a finger to my lips. "Shhhh. He doesn't know that."

Demir sat up straight, his face entirely unreadable. Cautiously, he retreated away, his eyes never leaving mine.

Ruin. Ruin had settled everywhere. Not like in Olympia. It was a different type of ruin. The earth below my feet was scorched and covered with black ash and burnt gravel while hot steam leaked from pockets of air between the plates of land that had survived the wrath of divine anger.

Shrubs, ferns, moss, and whatever had grown over the old city remains were lit in a slow white flame that burned without consuming the plant. The land was cursed to burn forever. A long, long eternity.

We reached a large statue climbing nearly to the clouds. It was one I could recognise without a second look. I'd seen paintings, embroidery, miniatures, and many other designs of the Fire God. The giant statue of Adan holding the ever-burning flame that had once cast a huge shadow over the city of Heyes was now but pieces and so was the everfire—the first ever flame to have been lit in Numengarth. Seraphim folk had divided the burning blessing, safely preserving the pieces of the everfire and hiding them in secret hearths and temples and caves after their fall five hundred years ago.

A group of men waved at our party and led us further inside what seemed to be a maze of rock surrounded by thick-stemmed, fire red lianas blanketing their surface—the only life I'd seen not lit by fire.

"Don't touch anything," Demir warned when we turned into a narrower corridor.

Something was not right.

It felt like a thousand eyes were upon me, watching and tracing each of my steps.

The boot soles felt softer, melting from the heat radiating from underneath us. Rivulets of sweat were dripping down my temples, and I had never wanted to crawl out of my own skin more than at that moment. I hated the heat as much as I hated the cold.

Demir's back muscles contorted, his spine arching and his limbs twisting as he shifted into his green form. "This is as far as we have gone before," he growled, pulling me forward. "You go in."

Courage as soft as their brains.

I scoffed, walking past him and into a crack between two collapsed stones leading to a dark cavity that stank of sulphur and smoke. My feet constantly tripped on much smaller rocks littering the ground which I could not see. Then...something slithered around my leg, and I halted, steadying my breaths and pulse. There was something I'd missed in the midst of the deafening silence, something that my senses had failed to catch. Not exactly life. Neither death.

But nothing happened for long minutes.

When I took another step, the thing slithered around both my legs. The further inside I went, the further up my body it crawled. And soon, it began burning an icy sting. Immediately, I stepped back, and they slithered away from me.

"The hells," I breathed out fast, stumbling back when my entire body felt as if I was in flames.

Isjordian soldiers ran to my side, helping me to the ground before a fainting spell almost knocked me unconscious.

"We've lost about a dozen Crafters and a thousand men and Aura trying to just take a few steps in," Demir's gravelly revealed.

I began patting down where I'd been burned. Except...my legs looked fine and the britches did not even have a single burn mark on them and neither did my boots. I pulled one side of my trousers up to reveal black charred marks on my skin that hurt more than I remembered burns to hurt.

"Adan's fire," an Isjordian Captain said, handing me some sort of an ashy powder. "Put it on the wound, princess. It's just winter moss."

My body was about to go into shock from the stinging pain, so I immediately reached to rub the powder on my skin, heaving with relief when the sting somewhat dissipated.

I looked around, my breaths turning a frosty white and the ground beneath my feet began coating in ice at my command, stretching and covering every inch around us for miles.

"It will not work," the captain said. "The fire melts right through our blessing. We have tried freezing the lianas, pulling them, and cutting them, but they always grow back in a matter of minutes."

Could they not sniff the heavy stink of dark craft variegated in the air with the traces of smoke? "Because they are created by the magic of a prime Crafter," I said, ice spreading further over the red leafy crawlers. "Caramel and honey might taste the same, but they are not the same. My magic stems directly from Gods while yours is simply a matter of luck." I stepped inside the cave again. "How dumb can one be." Months. It had taken these idiots months to realise something so plain.

Carefully, I took one step after the other towards where the darkness dove into a depth of black I'd never witnessed before. I reached a hand forward, electricity dancing between my fingers to illuminate my surroundings.

The further in I went, the more that shiver down my spine tingled while the heavy whispers outside grew even more faint. I was inside the veil, I could feel the suffocating feel of it and its harrowing call it emitted, yet nothing was happening.

The corridor was endless. I had walked for long minutes when I stopped and listened to the slight disturbance in the air. The humidity vibrated, and I bent down to rest my palm against the stony floor below my feet. A steady beat resembling steps tickled my palm, growing louder and presumably closer to me. What could be heavy enough to cause that?

A wave of unnatural heat hit me when I stood, and then a pair of large, piercing titian eyes glowed in front of me, followed by a loud growl that made the ruins over us rattle, sending dust and gravel flying around. The creature spat fire around me, giving the cave light.

What in the seven hells?

The auburn dragon shifted on its massive claws, attempting to bat its wings that were chained all over to the walls around us.

My eyes widened with fascination, and I pushed my dagger back to its sheath. Four centuries since they were thought gone. The one Dyurin blessed creature that had struggled to survive within our small human world stood right before my eyes. Tales and old words said that dragons did not belong to any godly realms, that they derived from another human pane. Some even said that they had crawled behind their masters and riders and snuck into Numengarth. And as punishment, they were not allowed back into their homes.

My mouth had parted a little as I stared at it. Awe filled my voice as I murmured, "Look at you. Aren't you beautiful."

The dragon's skin flashed a pearlescent coral when it leaned its face closer to me. The creature sniffed the air, lowering its nostrils near my face, flashing claws and teeth that were the size of my body. When it didn't give any more of a reaction than growl at me, I carefully stepped forward, reaching a hand to its face.

"Nice dragon," I cooed, getting closer and closer. "Pretty dragon. Polite dragon. Vegetarian dragon. You look like you like your vegetables." I stumbled back, dropping to the ground when it growled again, sniffing me and breathing hard. I stood and dusted my clothes when it didn't turn me into some measly appetiser. "Yeah, I don't like to be touched either."

The dragon huffed in response, curling into itself and closing its eyes.

I blinked. "Wait a damn minute. Where is the bloody sceptre?"

Its eyes drew open for a moment and its head pointed to the floor under us.

"Very good dragon. Under?" I asked, kneeling down.

A huff.

"I take that as a yes."

I brushed the thick layer of dust over the ground with my gloved hand to reveal aquamarine mosaic tiles. Fuck. Considering the massive space, this would take me all day.

"Hey," I whispered to the dragon. Why was I whispering? "Hey!"

The dragon opened its eyes again, looking all mad at me and not very vegetarian.

I pointed at the floor. "A bit of help? Nice dragon helps the very nice Guardian, ey?"

The thing didn't budge. Then it suddenly breathed out a cloud of fire that almost turned me into a skewered Guardian. The dust caught fire almost like lint, flying about and fizzling out in the air, disappearing into nothing.

My mouth went slack at what laid below the layer of time. Carefully, I stepped back to the furthest corner of the room, inspecting the picture that the mosaic tiles had created.

It looked like a map of sorts. And in its middle stood a circle that faintly resembled a craft halo. But instead of runes, it had star constellations. Eight of them. All the ones I knew by heart. Except that there were not just simple constellations. They lined perfectly to match the ultimate perfect tale.

Impossible.

It had to be.

"My snowflake," my mother whispered, crawling under my blanket where I had been hiding for the past hour. "One should always be able to see the stars. How can you see the

stars under here?"

"I don't like them. I hate the stars, ma."

"They would be so upset to hear that. Do you know they all have names? My best friend taught me all of them. She used to say that if you happen to see them all at the same time, the gates to all worlds out there would open for you," she said, luring me out of my hiding. Her eyes fell to the bruises on my face and her gaze glistened like the night sky, but so much prettier. She wiped her tears away. "Do you...do you want to go see if we can find them, too? Perhaps we will be lucky and they will welcome us."

"Would they allow me, too?"

"Why would they not?"

"Because I am useless. To papa, to you, to Eren and Thora. To everyone."

"You are so precious, my snowflake. To much more than just this one cruel world."

Ales. Sidus. Letum. Lumen. Tellus. Levis. Nix. Eurus. All eight constellations that framed the eight prime heavens.

A gate to not just any heaven or world.

A gate to all of them—all that was in between, around, and in the middle of the space we lived in.

Beyond them, too. Realms upon realms that resided amongst, along, parallel, and beyond our own. Wherever you wished—the gates would take you there. It was what my mother had said. What the old folk tales said.

It had to be a lie. A tale. My mother had told me tales.

But then my mother had also lied to me too many times to count.

I looked up at the dragon. "Do I have to...portal somewhere?" Would I even be allowed to enter or even leave this realm? We couldn't enter the heavens, but other realms...that I didn't know.

The creature huffed, pointing to the centre of the halo where one single star was drawn. Paleagus. Or as they called it in Numen—Ithicea.

My hand hovered over the drawing, hesitant. There was something odd about the chalky design, it almost looked worn out in places compared to the rest of the tiles. I traced the greying patch over and over until I could make out the shape of what had caused the colour to rub off.

"Feet." The shape was of two feet. Immediately, I got up and stood right on top of the star.

Nothing. I spun round, made a pose too, yet nothing. The moment I shifted to step away, a tile plaque sank into the ground. And another. Eventually, all of them did, sinking an inch into the ground one after the other. Then, as if I was thrown into a sinkhole, the reality around me began spinning, turning with such force that the gravity holding me upright suddenly began crushing me under it, and I collapsed to my knees. The cave disappeared, and so did the dragon. The vortex dimmed and then completely darkened.

The spinning darkness swallowing me in its belly marred with flashes of violet, specks of silver and gold. And then it suddenly stopped and settled. My mouth parted open at the star constellations around me that were not even feet away from my touch. So many stars. So many worlds. They all brushed past my fingertips as they floated into the space around me.

Heaviness settled on my chest at the realisation of what hovered before my eyes.

Reaching forward, I grazed my fingers over a dazzling formation that glistened like the blink of a firefly. The second my skin met warmth, a vortex violently spun from the glittering specks to form a circle portal that framed a dark forest. One I couldn't recognise. Crimson skies. Tall, dark, and lifeless redwood trees growing from black earth and soil. Stale air. Grainy and grey wind.

Cries of an infant drew my attention, and I searched the distance beyond the portal, my eyes landing on a small child abandoned at the foot of a large rotten bole. She was small, her hair was white and pale, and she had the darkest eyes I had ever seen. For a moment, as our gaze met in the distance, the child stopped crying, her wondrous onyx eyes widening.

Death, a voice echoed in my ear. *Death. Death. Death. Death.* It chanted with such desperation and warning that a cry vibrated from my chest.

And then I saw it. The vision flashing before my eyes. Bodies among bodies laid around me, melting below the scorched earth that had lit in white fire. Pearlescent feathers burned as they slowly fell to the ground, gathering around the bloodied body of a white-haired woman with golden wings. Another body laid dead at my feet—Vas was in his human form, one scorched hand reaching out to his dead lover. And at the centre of all the chaos stood...me. Kneeling on the ground, my own blade piercing my chest. Distant calls rang with my name, voices I knew well. Pleas and cries were muddled with hoorahs of victory. Soldiers jumped around in the far distance, celebrating, throwing my father's head around while calls of my name grew fainter and fainter until they disappeared.

The white-haired child cooed, and then all of it vanished. Only the flutters of it remained in my mind. Until it resembled the call of a distant memory. Leaving my body trembling, my breaths shuddering, tears streaming down my eyes, and a heavy weight pressing against my ribcage. A hand went to my chest, reaching to touch the wound that had felt so real.

"Cerina!" a harsh voice called almost desperately from somewhere beyond the forest. "Cerina!"

I flinched at the sound and pulled my hand back to my side, causing the portal to disappear and return to the previous arrangement of stars that kept floating away and disappearing between the rest.

I took a breath. Letting what I'd seen melt at the back of my already sick mind.

Then I laughed.

And laughed.

I braced both hands on the ground while more stuttering laughter overtook me. The choked sounds travelled down the space around me, growing and bouncing even louder. "She can die," I whispered, nearly coughing from the sickening laughter spilling out of me. One...two stray tears burned a trail down my cheeks, dripping on the black space below my fingers, glistening against it. My stomach twisted and sickness grew into a big ball inside the pit of my insides. "She can die."

"And so will you," a voice whispered at the back of my mind.

"The sceptre," I said, wiping away my face and ignoring the snickering shadows. "Take me to the sceptre."

The entire thing disappeared, returning me to the cave.

What?

"The sceptre. Where is the fucking sceptre?" I asked, hitting the stone beneath me.

I stood, looking around for another chamber, but nothing...there was nothing else. Had I even gone through the first veil? Or any veil at all?

"You already passed the veil of fears," a sweet voice called from somewhere behind me, and I spun around, electricity frying the air at my call, but she was not afraid.

The girl was beyond beautiful. A luring beauty that seemed too untrue to be anything but a trap. The light cast by dragon flames revealed golden brown skin and dark coppery hair that fell below her waist. Her feet looked like they almost floated under her emerald skirts when she stepped towards me. "But the biggest fear lies beneath your feet. That is the last trick that the Elder Crafter put in this room for when the next Skygard would need to raise the White Flamed Guardian again. Knowledge can be a curse. A cast and a spell worse than any craft. But then, not knowing the danger of the power you hold makes you selfish. Like it made my father."

I blinked at her. "You're King Kegan's daughter, aren't you?"

Her smile was polite and gentle, and it almost hid the sadness painted on the rest of her face. "They called me Nilsa."

"You're alive."

She nodded. "For what I did, I offered to serve as the sceptre's guard and prevent anyone who wants to cause the same destruction that my father did. I might not be an *Ybris*, but once I was just as strong."

"You must know—"

"We both have selfish fathers, Guardian," she said, parting her skirts to the side and pulling a silver rod out of a leather sheath hidden between them. She held the sceptre piece in her palms, extending them to me. "The difference is that I did it for glory and you are doing it to keep your loved ones safe."

"It might bring destruction."

She lifted a brow. "Do you not want it?"

I stepped forward and took it from her, the rod gleaming white at my touch. "What about you?"

"I will remain here until you return it back to the safety of my hands."

"Your world might need you. Your people might need you. If they only knew you are alive, that a prime Scarlet is still alive, one bearing the surname and blood of a Veranesi, they would not surrender to the guilt of their old king's fault. Not to my father's oppression either."

"I have faith that someone good will lead them back to glory—blood of a prime Scarlett or not, blood of the Veranesi line or not. Fire rages, it cannot be oppressed."

I frowned. "Are you chained here?"

"Willingly."

"And if you chose to leave?"

"I gave up that right."

"By word of mouth and not in a curse or craft."

"To me, it holds the same weight."

She might be the Scarlet in this room, but my nerves were simmering hotter than the Drayrior Volcano up north of this burnt island. "You will get out."

She blinked fast. "Excuse me?"

"Are you hearing what I am saying at all? There is war. After my father takes my kingdom, he will come for this one next. Perhaps he already has. We cannot afford to be gracious and repent for our faults. We cannot afford to be sad. I cannot afford to weep for my friend who was killed! Yet you sit here, doe eyed and unafraid while your people, mine, and everyone else is suffering when you could be beside them fighting. Your people surrendered their blessings. They gave up on power that could serve to hold this realm safe. They chose to keep doing so despite what was thrust upon them—famine, war, control, slavery. They had no one to guide them, to tell them that they bear no fault. The fault was not theirs. I made mistakes, too! I let my father live when I had the chance to kill him! And I am going to make sure that I fix my mistakes. Not repent for them. Not surrender my magic just because it can do harm. Fire and lightning are a blessing. A coin Gods tossed. We chose which side it lands on."

Her chest rose fast. "I did what it felt right to do."

"Well, does it still *feel* right?" *King Kegan's daughter had a pure soul*, Visha had said. This, what stood in front of me, was deemed pure? Since when did selfishness become a trait of the pure?

The look she had on told me that there was no convincing her otherwise. But then...it was in her blood. Fire was stubborn.

I turned, giving her my back and heading towards the dragon. The creature got in its legs and stumbled back when a honed ice blade grew in my hold.

I took the chains binding the creature and froze them, striking my blade on the now fragile links to break them.

It took me an hour to get all of them down, and by the end, I dropped to the ground, panting. The dragon lowered its nostrils to sniff me before curling its massive body around mine.

Tentatively, I reached my hand to its face again and stood. "Go. Leave! And while you do so, burn every tent, building, ship, and soldier holding the wolf crest that you see on your path. Burn every winter born. Burn them all. Then head southeast, follow the moon and the star of the south, under where the Henah blessed rest," I ordered. "Find the castle by the Moor Sea, with grand gardens and ivory walls. Don't hurt them. They will not hurt you back." I pulled my glove off and showed the dragon my left hand marked with our union—two souls made one had the same scent to Dyurin's creatures. The dragon's eyes drew shut for a moment before it huffed almost in agreement. "Others might want to chain you again, but he will keep you safe. I promise."

"Jayre cannot leave the cave," the Fire Princess said. "He hasn't seen any humans besides me in five hundred years."

"What luck Jayre has found today. Isjordians give the warmest welcome," I said, waving the creature off. Chuckling, I turned to her. "They burn impeccably well, I'll tell you that."

Nilsa still stood in the corner, her brown eyes wide, watching the dragon shuffle in its claws, stretching its sore wings and crawling towards the exit. "This is not how it is supposed to go."

I stretched my neck and limbs, preparing for what I was to find outside. "Well, how was it supposed to go?"

"Goodness always prevails."

Dropping my head back, I cackled. What in the unicorn and siren filled world did she live on? "No, evil prevails." And on que, faint sounds of struggle and anguish began seeping inside the cave.

She frowned. "Out of all, you should be the last one to think so."

"I've seen cruelty of both human and divine. Out of all, I ought to be the first one to think so."

Jayre's growls made the cave walls shake, pebbles and dust raining over us, and Nilsa took a gentle step towards me. "Why must we cause more destruction when we know the consequences?"

"Why must I endure when I can end it? Ruin what wants to ruin me first."

Her eyes widened, dropping to the sceptre, and her mouth parted in a breathless gasp. "You want to try to kill the Guardian? But she is blameless."

Few had left me speechless in this lifetime. "On second thought, stay here actually. I'll sort your kingdom out myself."

She stepped forward. "You will anger the Gods!"

I spread dirt all over the portal before leaving. "I guess you've never seen *me* angry."

I held my breath in the dark silence of the tunnel leading me outside.

Then I heard it.

Screams of agony ringing so loudly that they echoed like a pure symphony under the hollow cave walls.

There, there.

Clutching the sceptre piece, I turned to Nilsa one last time. "Hide here, ashamed, or fight out there with your people who have had to bow even lower beyond the shame of their last king only so they could kiss my father's feet."

My eyes burned from the heat when I emerged from the cave. Chaos like no other surrounded me. Blistering fire crawled up to the skies, stretching for miles ahead, emerging over the Isjordian camps that had turned into a hot hearth. Demir stood between the piles of burned bodies, heaving, his eyes red and wide and half mad as they followed the dragon disappearing in the distance.

His nostrils flared and he spun to me, stomping in my direction and growling with fury until I lifted the sceptre between us, making him halt his unnecessarily dramatic attack.

"Got it."

He lifted clawed hand to my face, trailing a sharp finger down my cheek. "You are unscathed. How is that so?"

"The dragon was protecting it. I couldn't get to the sceptre unless it left the cave. Took me a bit to trick it."

"Trick it? That creature had your scent all over," he snarled.

I stepped forward. "Do you think I did it with the power of my thoughts?" I snarled right back, throwing him the sceptre piece with all the strength I could muster. "Got you the fucking thing. What more do you want?"

He gripped the rod tightly, then glowered and growled at me one last time before dragging me after him. "This will have consequences," he spat out.

The soot stained with blood and gore and the echoing screams was...cathartic. If he wasn't going to kill me, my heart would stop from excitement. I skipped along after him. "I'm so, so very scared."

Nissa's mother had done exactly what I had told her to do after my return from Seraphim. And so efficiently, she had spread the word far and wide, within the walls of the castle and outside. From the other maids to the kitchen servants, cooks, traders, markets, and the rest of the folk of Tenebrose. It had taken barely days for all of them to think I'd fought off a dragon and survived while trying to protect Isjordian camps all while getting my father's weapon to his holy war.

Soldiers and servants alike murmured to each other when I made my way to the training courts, feigning a small limp. I'd not even let the Medi-Healer touch the bruise from my father's slap. My consequences were looking a lot like trophies.

Along with sympathy, they offered something else. Something looking a lot like respect.

Melanthe, as usual, had narrowed her eyes on me from the balcony where she always overlooked my training. But this time, her attention slipped to my surroundings. To everyone who was looking at me. The way her face began to fall, the alarming confusion dropping along with her brows, it was all so satisfying.

"Shall we?" I asked a sneering Moregan, shedding my jacket.

7

White Bishop takes C6

Snowlin

It was the middle of August and they had just finally managed to arrange a safe trip through Eldmoor. Whatever Kilian was doing to delay them, it was working.

We'd travelled not even longer than an hour through portal after portal, effectively avoiding any witch from Red Coven before Melanthe began directing us towards a dead forest. The air reeked with a scent of old death and was filled with haunting voices that spoke through the wind. And the start of the autumn chill did not do much to help my twisted imagination either.

The ground crunched beneath my feet when I'd stepped on a pile of bones—human bones. Lovely. What a way to ruin good leather boots.

A scream brought me out of my sorrow for the poor animal that had been turned into shoes. One of the Isjordian soldier's accompanying us scrambled backwards until her back hit a dead tree. Her eyes were filled with horror, fixed ahead onto...nothing.

Melanthe sighed, and loudly called out loud, "Guinevere, enough with your petty tricks."

A young witch appeared from behind a massive pile of animal bones, snickering as she surveyed the terrified Isjordian soldiers. "Sorry, sister. But it is always so funny how afraid they are of us."

And it was, actually.

But unfortunately, I was playing on their team now. "It will be funny, too, when they skin your kind and make hogs wear your flesh coat as a party outfit for their hog gatherings," I said, giving her a saccharine smile, and my father's soldiers chuckled.

Her smile wilted and she stood frozen for a moment before shooting Melanthe a glance. "The *Ybris* is with you? You didn't mention anything about bringing her. The others, they—"

"Of course she is with me, Guin. She will go down the tomb to get the sceptre piece for us," Melanthe explained, ushering all of us forward and lifting up a veil placed to conceal a two-story house that looked older than Krig's balls.

Guinevere, the young witch, walked right beside me, staring at me while we entered the mansion. The staring did not end at all. Only grew more intense.

"You're making your kind really proud," I chuckled, turning to stare back at her.

She lifted her chin and looked away. "Urinthia deceived us. She no longer deserves our respect or loyalty."

"I'm no Eldmoorian, but even I know you swear no loyalty to anyone who is not the one to bless you. You vow your word and your soul to the God of Death, and he appointed your Grand Maiden. Are you that unafraid? Of your own God? How very brave of you, young Guin."

She cleared her throat, blinking a little fast and struggling to say something for a long while. "Our...our God stands behind Melanthe. He let her exit Caligo unscathed."

That made me chuckle. "Your God stands behind no one. And unscathed is an understatement for what she bargained for her return," I whispered, and she frowned, looking between me and her new leader who had turned to scowl at us like the fires of hells.

"Get away from her, Guinevere," my new and improved step-mother ordered.

"Why, Mel dearest?" I asked, lifting up my chained wrists and making the links jiggle. "What can poor me possibly do in these conditions? Unless you come a little closer. Then I can strangle you like my father did years ago." Blowing her a kiss, I whispered, "I'm into it if you're into it."

When a few witches chuckled under their breath, the cuffs on my wrists tightened and burned, making me groan in pain.

An Isjordian soldier stepped forward, grabbing onto my hand. "My princess, your skin is bleeding," he said with alarm, reaching for a handkerchief to wrap around my wrist and turning to Melanthe. "What have you done to her, witch?"

I pressed my lips together and fluttered my lashes at a seething Melanthe. "You're hurting me."

Uneasiness filled the room when all Isjordian soldiers turned their heavy stares at the once dead and soon to be dead witch. The temperature had dropped low, and a shiver of satisfaction licked my spine when the black chains glowed red and suddenly loosened up a little, giving me some relief.

I squeezed the soldier's hand and offered a small thanks to him before following behind Melanthe. Several red heads in all kinds of hues turned when I entered what looked like a dining room that had been turned into a war room. On top of the oval wood table was laid a map of Eldmoor. Several twisted, short twigs formed a star over the edge of Heca. Presumably over where the sceptre was hidden.

I'd barely caught a glimpse of it when the door was shut right in my face, making me hiss a curse under my breath.

"Why are you letting the witch treat you as such, princess?" a soldier asked, offering me a clean napkin to change the blood soaked one.

"Family," I shrugged. "We ought to be forgiving of raging bitch behaviour." Spinning to her, I asked, "Tell me, where are we exactly?"

"About three miles inside of Lissis Forest."

I blinked. "Inside the Deadlands?" Shit.

"We are safe," she assured. "The witch has promised us safety."

My brows hiked up. No one stepped in the Deadlands and was promised safety. This part of Eldmoor was nothing but a giant graveyard.

It was the hour of the dead when we left the makeshift coven that Melanthe and her merry band of traitor witches had created. The moon was crimson red, draping a bloody hue over the cloudy skies and over the barren forest that hissed with murmurs of the dead and creatures who restlessly prowled from one snag to another as they followed our entourage along.

The air cried in warning the deeper we got into the forest, it begged for us to turn back. The wind whispered and then howled for us to rethink, to return.

The witches had lifted a glowing red palm in the air to form a veil of protection around us. To keep away any predator of the night that fed on souls—the creatures that had inhabited these forests even before Celesteel had stepped here. It had been why he'd chosen this land to bless as his. He'd felt death here almost as if he had felt it in Caligo. And the merciful God had offered these tortured creatures relief. He'd turned parts of Eldmoor into lands of the dead to protect them from desiring and grieving for a life they could no longer live. Us stepping in here was a temptation to them. Walking this part of the land was challenging Celesteel. The witches were breaking more than divine laws, they were disrespecting their God. And I could practically taste their fear on my tongue. Or was it whatever perfume Melanthe had sprayed on that was tickling my gag reflexes?

I knew we'd arrived at our destination when silence rang loud around us. Not a touch of wind, no clouds or moon above us, no animal, no trees, or soil beneath my feet. The ground was stone, the air was solid, the skies were a vortex of swirling ruby.

A monolith stood tall before us. Solid black steel with three glistening red words engraved in it. Daughter. Sister. Mother.

Celesteel was the son of the most powerful deity to coexist alongside Fader, or as they had once called him—the God of Some. The Goddess of Nothing, Nihilia, his mother, birthed *Death, Nightmares, Silence, Darkness, Chaos, Temptation, Greed, Desire,* and *Emptiness.* The nine Gods of Nothingness. Both of her children, *Death* and *Darkness,* Henah and Celesteel, had decided to serve Fader and make Ithicea the centre of their realms, looking to part ways with *taking,* and *giving* instead—even death and darkness could nurture. Despite his powers and what he was, Celesteel had given somewhat of a life to all the lands he'd blessed. Through women. By giving women power. Ultimate power and reign over death. Because he'd found out that women...they were life itself. They'd nourished the land, air, animals, and humans, too. They became mothers, daughters, sisters, and leaders. They were compassionate and nurturing. It is said throughout his scriptures that Goddess Plantae, his lover and perhaps the most powerful woman, was the one who had convinced him to side with Fader—the same woman who had then given his own land life. And women had brought Eldmoor back to life, too.

Right beneath that monolith stood the grave of the first Grand Maiden, buried on the land where only a daughter, sister, and mother could step on without being claimed by the God of Death as a willing servant of the Otherworld. No man dared. No man could dare. There was no man who was that unafraid of death to step in here.

And considering that Demir, the only man who could not be claimed by Celesteel, had not come with us, it meant that Melanthe doubted Fader's gift of life. Perhaps, our Vas was not so eternal after all.

I could bet that Celesteel had fumed at Fader's decision—a decision that had broken the very rules he had created, the boundaries between life and death.

Melanthe gathered her skirts and pulled on my chains, forcing me to follow after her and her sisters into the land that belonged to Celesteel.

The further into the forest behind the monolith we dove, the thicker the knotty branches grew, making it barely possible to move through them. The witches helped one another fit through the tight space between the dense branches that locked into another to keep us back. Few grunts and cuts later, we faced an open plain field covered in dark ash that still poured from the crimson-stained clouds overhead. There was nothing beyond it though I was sure we were facing the Sea of the Dark from this point. It looked like the grey desert stretched for miles and miles and perhaps endlessly. No sea of any sort in sight.

However, the electric feel of the air beyond betrayed the meticulous work of whoever had crafted this ruse. I reached a hand forward and felt the thick gelatinous veil of an illusion that was playing games with my mind—the desert was only a trick veil protecting whatever laid beyond it.

And before I could pull my hand back, something grabbed onto me and dragged me to the other side.

Blistering heat assaulted my senses and I cringed when hot air entered my lungs, almost making me breathe out steam.

"Flames, flames, flames," a strident voice screamed right into my ear.

My lids peeled open and I jerked away from the flaking body standing next to me. Seven sweet hells.

Pieces of rotten flesh barely clung to the skeleton of a woman. Her chestnut brown hair was the only thing that remained untouched, long and curled almost to the back.

She cackled, bits of flesh dropping, melting right off the bone. "We burn. All burns. You will burn, too."

I looked behind me, where the witches along with Melanthe should have been but no longer were.

The bloody remnants of the tittering woman reached me again, and she extended a careful hand for me to take. "I take you to the flames. You will burn beautifully."

"Hellfire," I murmured to myself at the sight of the black rose tattoo on her wrist. The brand of Ghenna, the Guardian of Hellfire. "The elder Crafter hid the sceptre inside hellfire?" To burn inside flames that will forever burn you but not kill you.

She jumped and giggled. "Oh, oh, aren't you a bright one!"

I huffed a bored sigh and threw a glare at the illusion veil behind me.

Cowards.

"They cannot come," the...thing said. "Children born out of Celesteel's blessing can catch hellfire in the scorched lands because the seventh part of our soul is made of hellfire, too. Unlike yours. Your soul, every part of it, is made of frost and lightning. Come, come," she ushered me, taking us down a stairwell leading inside a cave under the barren stone where we were standing.

"Why did you enter...uhm—" Where were we exactly?

"The scorched lands," she finished for me, guiding me down the tunnel. "I never entered. I just never left."

"What?"

"Do you know," she started, already panting and breathless from the walk, "what happens when a Summoner brings something from beyond the walls of this realm?"

"You can't summon something beyond this realm."

"Oh, but you can," she giggled. "Or could. At least in my time. I summoned fire from the beyond. I wanted a taste of it. And fire I got. A whole piece of land from Ustrina. The Seventh Hell of Fire. The Heaven of Hellfire."

My feet stopped and I turned to look at her. "You did this?" She'd summoned a hell on Numengarth?

"With a little bit of prime blood, some knowledge on godly runes, and the hair of a vengeful spirit." She laughed again, more bits of flesh dangling around and flaking, and I held back a gag. "Come, come, we are here."

I cocked a brow at her and at where she was pointing. A fire pit burned to the roof of the narrow corridor, blocking the small path entirely. "You cannot mean we need to go through the fire."

She put a hand on my back and pushed me towards it. "You cannot burn, child of Nubil and Krig."

Before I could ask, she turned around and headed back up where we had come from, murmuring more words to herself, "We burn. All burns. You will burn, too."

Tentatively, I reached my hand to the flame, and pulled back almost immediately, cradling my burned fingers to my stomach. "Fuck!" Only when I felt my dormant magic slowly coat my skin with ice did I realise what she had meant.

Coating all of my skin in hoar frost, I reached for the fire again and jumped through it. Ice hissed at the touch of flames and mist coated my vision for a short second, but I did not burn. Though I had stepped right into hells from the look of it.

I was standing on top of a floating piece of rock, surrounded by three tall cliffs that cradled a crater sputtering and spilling a ruby red lava down the edges and onto the never-ending ocean of fire below it.

"What a pleasant surprise," someone behind me said, and I spun to face a man clad in the purest and deepest colour of black I'd ever seen. His eyes were a shade of red that turned a deep burgundy when they focused on me. Those strange pupils hollowed and spun, almost seeming to swallow all that they saw. He ran a gloved hand through his short, dark locks covering his brow and gave me a calculated grin. "You are another type of Skygard. An interesting type."

"Who are you?"

"No pleasantries? I thought you humans enjoyed that." He laughed and pointed a finger at me. "But you're far from being a human, aren't you?"

"You're one to talk."

He pushed from where he was leaning against rock and walked towards me, only stopping when I unsheathed a dagger and then another, holding them to my side.

"You can't hurt me," he said, severely entertained by the challenge.

I almost burst a vein attempting to call upon a fraction of lightning, but it was worth the headache because he raised both hands and retreated a step.

He chuckled, the sound so dark that the fire around us turned a deeper shade of red. "Caught me in a lie." He flicked a hand in the air, and the sceptre piece floated right between us, tempting me. "Have it. I presume that is what you came down here for."

I extended a palm to him. "Throw it."

He smiled and waved his hand forward, making the sceptre piece float and land right in my palm.

I raised a brow at him. "What's the catch? Want me to fight a fire sprite, play a game of chess, make you a sandwich, hem your trousers?"

He leaned against the rock again, looking beyond amused. "By right and order of Fader, I can hand the descendant of Zephyr the sceptre piece. If it had been anyone else, I would have been less pragmatic, Snowlin."

"You know who I am?"

"You've been donating magic to my realm for years, we ought to get familiar with one another at some point."

"Your realm?"

"One of them. One of the hells I reign over."

Impossible. "You're a Prince of Hells?"

he flashed me a grin. "You can call me Ezekiel."

I froze. He was Visha's betrothed? "The Prince of Ustrina?"

"In the flesh," he said, bowing his head to me. "Yet not entirely. A projection if you might call it so since it is not possible for me to step in Numen anymore."

"And this is a hobby of yours?" I asked, looking around.

"Word spread fast that you bested the God of Waters. I had to see for myself what all the fuss was about."

"My husband did, not I."

"Ah, the godling," he said, crossing his arms over his chest. "What a fascinating pair."

The question left my lips before I could stop it, "Why did your father let him return from the Otherworld?"

"He owed Nubil a favour and was rather pleased to cash it in and be done with your petty God."

"Nubil asked for his return?"

"I was as surprised as you are. The God of Skies is rather fond of his debts."

Nubil had asked Celesteel to let Kilian back. The one I owed my undying gratitude was Nubil?

"Any more questions for me, Guardian?" he asked when I remained quiet. "I'm rather entertained."

"Visha will not marry you," I said.

"Visha is not who I am meant to marry. Your kin is."

What was he on about? "She is not my kin."

"Lilith will become your kin. In time."

I frowned. "Lilith—" My words froze. He knew Melanthe's unborn child's name. "Her you might have," I spat, heading back towards the fire pit.

"Ah," he called as I was about to leave. "I'd catch a burn mark or two, or your father will begin doubting your ancestry. Keep my future wife safe. I am owed a debt. Which if improperly collected will cause an issue to the realm you are *burning* to protect."

I halted. More words left my lips before I could think the whole thing through, "Make a bargain with me."

He blinked for a moment and then smirked. "Such wrong words have little been spoken but are always welcomed. And what can you offer me that I cannot take and don't already have?"

"A life you were meant to have but never can."

I handed the sceptre piece to Melanthe who had the most stunned expression painted across her rather unexciting face.

"What is it, Mel dearest? Did you want me to get you a souvenir or something?"

"You got the sceptre?"

"My, I wonder what else could possibly impel me to go sightseeing right inside a hell pit."

A cloud of red lifted the sceptre piece from my hand, and Melanthe opened a chest, guiding it safely inside.

The moment we exited the Deadlands, the main guard removed his coat and threw it over my shoulders. He signalling his head to the healer standing behind everyone to begin patching up my burns. "They are not severe, princess," he said, letting his magic cool the charred flesh.

"I'm not new to burns."

The man's face turned stolid, and his eyes darted briefly to the scar on my face. "Hold in there, Your Highness. The realm will one day be yours to freeze when you sit on the throne. And you will not need a witch or a beast to do so," he said, glancing at Melanthe.

"Not many want to see me take the throne," I said carefully.

He shook his head. "More than you think are on your side," he assured. "Many more than you think. New times are coming. And you are just what new times need. The old Gods are gone and so are their kings."

I hid a victorious smile beneath a cringe when a healer began mending my burnt flesh.

My ears suddenly began itching and I threw a look behind my shoulder at the witches crowding around Melanthe who had turned and was watching me as if she'd seen a spirit.

Did they know who resided behind the Elder Crafter's veil? Did they know who I had met? Could they smell the bargain I'd just made?

8

Black Pawn takes C6

Snowlin

THE AIR WAS COLDER today, silent, and almost careful. As if it expected something to happen. As if it was silently waiting. Just as it had been silently waiting for the past, most uneventful week of my life.

I had trained with only Moregan who was like a cracked crock pot, leaking a few truths here and there each time her anger steamed.

Demir was nowhere to be seen.

Father had only joined dinner twice.

And I had not seen Melanthe since Eldmoor.

It meant only one thing. Melanthe was about to give birth.

The two Adriatian oafs who were on morning guard duty had taken a seat on my right and left, caging me between them. They stared ahead at the grey walls while I ate my breakfast in the servant halls where I'd been coming these past couple of days, seeing that I'd become part of the landscape and no longer a portrait.

The only sounds in the halls came from the steam leaking out of the pots that boiled my father's dinner, the slow and almost careful steps of servants that stirred and salted the food, and the sound of my knife cutting through whatever vegetable quiche the cook had managed to cook separately from the meaty main dishes.

To my unfortunate luck, it was too quiet. So I had to be fast.

After a quick glance at all the entrances, I flipped the cutlery in my hold and plunged them as hard as I could into the two men guarding me, piercing their throats through and through. But not enough to kill them immediately as the steel was as dull as my patience.

"Shhhh," I shushed, glancing over my shoulder at the servants who still had not noticed me twisting the silverware deeper into their flesh and the blood slowly dripping down the tiled floor.

The men choked and twisted for a little while before their bodies turned limp and threatened to topple over. Grabbing onto their clothes, I pulled them upright. Once their limp corpses were staying somewhat still, I gently pushed my chair back and stood, wiping some small specks of blood away and dusting my long jacket.

A girl gasped from somewhere behind me and dropped a basket stuffed with corn onto the floor, causing the indigestible vegetable to roll out everywhere.

I put a finger to my lips, and she completely stilled, not even breathing.

Everyone in the kitchen had stopped moving and caused the silence to grow even louder. I met all of their stares, and when no one made a single move, my smile turned uncontainable. "I beg a favour," I said quietly, putting my gloves back on.

Not even a fruit fly moved.

An elderly cook stepped forward and gulped before asking, "Of what sort?"

There we go. "Take the bodies out to the waste piles."

Her mouth dropped open. "If...what if the guards see?"

"Why would they see what you throw out?" I had worked in the kitchens for years and that had never happened. The order of things was drilled into my brain, hence why I had chosen to act at his time of day.

She shot everyone in the room a look before nodding. "We will see to it, princess."

I nodded back, and before leaving, I bent down and grabbed a corn, handing it to the shaking servant who couldn't look away from the two dead men. "We take what we want by fire or by blood. But remember," I said, taking her clammy hand and wrapping it around the corn. "Fire makes smoke and smells."

She nodded shakily. "Will you really be queen as they say?"

"We will see. If the blood will stain or not."

I poked my head out of the kitchen exit leading to the corridors overlooking the back winter garden that no one used besides servants. No guards were in sight. I suppose that today I was not my father's biggest worry. If that child died, he was doomed. If Melanthe died, he was twice as doomed.

And I wished the witch nothing but a healthy, long, painful, and overdrawn birth.

Clutching the stolen daggers tightly, I moved down the corridor, heading the opposite way from where everyone was.

The further away I moved, the more I could feel the tingle of magic itch my fingertips. The witch was in labour. My binds were loosening. Her magic was weakening.

Guards were stationed in front of the castle temple, all armed up to their necks just as Nissa's mother had warned me. Turning round, I made my way back towards the winter gardens and right inside the apple tree maze resting beside the old quarters of Edric, the first King of Isjord.

Empty of life. Empty of death. The quarters were void, and the brisk wind made the dark wooden doors creak as it crashed against them.

I tugged on a red apple hanging from the oldest tree in Isjord and bit into the sweet fruit before pushing inside the forgotten space.

The heavy scent of magic still lingering inside made me dizzy for a moment. Pure magic. Unadulterated and unspoiled. Prime magic. The touch of the first king was everywhere, still eerily present.

"Bet you feel a bit ashamed," I murmured, hoping the fucker could hear me. "For reproducing."

Nissa's mother had taken weeks to figure out for me where Melanthe's lair hid. I'd had my doubts that the temple would be where it was since the day I'd caught her kneeling before Krig. A loyal servant of Celesteel such as her would never fall to her knees for another God—not unless forced to.

Edric's quarters were the one place Alaric had wanted me to stay far away from. And I had obeyed since the last thing I wanted was a long conversation with a spirit. But I'd also read that the first king had a direct entrance to the temple from his quarters.

It took me more than ten minutes to figure my way around, pulling and tugging on everything that could lead to a hidden door. Until the candle holder I grabbed from a table twisted, making the tiles groan and shift, opening enough for a body to go through. A long corridor led me right into an open plane cave filled with tables and cabinets carrying potions, herbs, books, dust, spider webs, and most importantly, a rotten stench that was coming from one particular direction.

My, my.

What a treat.

Every shade of every herb, potion, powder, and Crafter book was spread out before me.

Carefully, I drew open a wooden cabinet to find stacks and stacks of blood vials lining it. The scent...good Gods, the scent. My stomach recoiled.

"What do we have here," I whispered to myself as I not so carefully picked up a pretty blue glass vial filled with a cinnamon smelling liquid.

"First rule," Nia had once told me years ago after a Crafter had tricked me into drinking some dizzying portion, *"If it smells sweet, it means danger. A sour taste is just water and consumable herbs. What is foul smelling is a trick, water enchanted to deceive you into thinking it's dangerous. Remember, death in a bottle tastes the sweetest."*

I had not realised that I'd been standing still and lost for a long while recalling that memory. Not until I heard voices coming from outside the temple. Quickly, I poured small drops of the cinnamon smelling liquid into the blood vials, hoping to spoil whatever Melanthe had been cooking.

Then I leaned over the herbs, sniffing them one after the other until I found what I needed. Blue gyre for a little dark magic problem, and grey lock powder. Once I pocketed what Nia had told me was a paralysing herb, I went searching for what could cover my magical scent that I most probably had left all over the cave. The same thing that Lysander had me eat, breathe, wash in, and spray every day since I was born.

I ground a bit of ember salt and rubbed it all over me, making sure to sprinkle some around the room before leaving.

Moregan moved slowly along the corridors after leaving the training courts, her attention set forward towards wherever she was heading. I had learned two things after following her around almost all afternoon. She often lost sense of her surroundings. And that her memory often failed her. Twice she had gotten lost along the corridors. Whatever father had done to her in Ulv Islet clearly still affected her.

And grudges were such a profitable thing to capitalise on.

I followed swiftly behind her, my steps light and airy on the hard stone floors. The closer I got to her, the more her steps slowed. And then stopped entirely when I wrapped a hand around her neck and pressed the dagger to her jugular, hard enough to poke a small wound that gushed with thick, almost black blood.

"Shhh," I hissed in her ear. "The more you move the more the poison will spread." She bared all her teeth at me. "You think that can kill me?"

"Kill you? Why would I ever want to kill you?" She made to move but I tightened my grip around her and forced her to stay put. "You will want to hear what I have to say."

She growled and tried to move again...but she couldn't.

"Grey lock," I said. "In about ten more seconds, all of your body will lock in place, paralysed. Everything except your tongue. Now hurry those nice feet of yours." I pushed her forward and into her chambers where she stumbled and almost crashed against a chair, her body convulsing and trembling until it began locking in place like a rusty lock.

"Hm." I moved around her bedroom and studied the nothingness of it all. "What a simple life for a fallen queen. Very humble," I said, sitting at the edge of her bed and leaning back on my elbows. "Or maybe pitiful is a better word." I nodded. "Yeah, I'm leaning more towards *pitiful*. Wouldn't you think so, Skadi?"

Her eyes shot wide. "How...how do you know?"

"What did my father promise you?" I leaned forward on my knees and studied her. "To take over the Islines and return your crown? Perhaps revenge on your sister? Or a position in his one and only kingdom of butterflies and hopeful peace?"

Her nostrils flared. "And you'd like to know...why?"

"Because I can also offer you something. Something better. Something that isn't a lie."

After laughing cruelly, her mouth pulled into a snarl. "Your head is in Nubil's clouds, little queen of nothing."

"I'd say my feet, not my head." I stood and walked around the room, observing her unlocked prison again. "Have you heard of Zephyr, the Guardian of Lightning, Nubil's second in command?"

"I've heard of many dead Gods."

"How about one that is alive?"

She narrowed her eyes on me but said nothing.

"Has my father told you the true reason why he bred children of Skygard blood? Why he made sure to erase any trace of my bloodline afterward? Surely not, right? Why would he want you to know that I am able to control Aurora, that I am not only chosen by Gods to control Aurora, but also one of their kind."

Her eyes widened just the slightest. "What?"

"Zephyr was my...well, he was something of mine. I am of his blood."

She scoffed, shaking her head. "Impossible."

"Quite the contrary. I presume he has also lied about why he wants the unblessed metal, too."

"Where are you trying to go with this?"

"I am stating your options, Skadi. When me and my husband open war on my father, what side will you be on? Mine. Or dead."

"There will be no war. Your father will make sure of that."

"There will always be war where me, him, and greed spin on the same wheel. How can he take this realm when I've got my hands in it? When my husband can turn his life dark before he could breathe out the cold air he lives on? Silas's promises are false as he is. A false God who needs a godly armour to control the sceptre that only I, blood of Zephyr and born a Skygard, can. Think," I said, tapping a finger on her temple. "Why do you think he had me, why did he make sure to kill anyone who was of my blood, why does he need to create an *anima accissor* armour?"

"You're saying Silas cannot control the sceptre."

"I'm saying, no one can control the sceptre, not just him—no one who is not me, my brother, or my sister. And that is why he sired the three of us. Father will fail. Like all those before him did, including Tenebrose, who I am sure you know has tried to raise the Guardian before as well."

"And why do you need me to believe all this?"

"Because you were Queen of the Islines. You were the queen of what my father fears most."

Her pupils moved fast. "Silas fears nothing."

I snorted. "He made me heir because of your sister. Because of you. Because of every heir of Krigborn blood—everyone who can claim his throne. Everyone has a fear beyond what one calls a fear. Father's fear is that—the claim on his throne. Isjordians are loyal to my father because he is a Krigborn and that alone. They do not care for him, nor do they respect him beyond that. They fear him, but they fear spiders and woodlice just as much. He knows what hides in the Islines, the power of the Isea people. Raw power. He wants to use you as he uses me, to control his peoples' loyalty and the Islines when time comes. Your people call my father and every king before him a false king, so what makes you think they will not do the same? What makes you think they will accept him? He needs you more than you think. You're his way to them. To their trust."

She shook her head. "He gave me back power. The strength that my own people took."

"To break you. Not to harden you. And he has broken you. I've seen it."

Her eyes lowered and she took a moment and a few loud inhales before rolling her green gaze to me. "There is nothing that I or you can do about it. Leave before Demir returns. At least for the sake of the man you are giving up your fight to protect."

"I never gave up my fight. Otherwise, I would not be here." I bent down to her till we were face to face. "Me and you will fall into an agreement."

"Leave," she growled. "You say another word, and this will end up in your father's ears."

My mouth curved into a smirk. "If you tell him a single word of what I told you, he will end you. You know too much, and he trusts you too little—presuming he trusts you to begin with. Which I highly doubt."

Her eyes widened in realisation and her mouth gaped, opening and closing, struggling to find words.

"That's right," I said, crouching down before her and tapping my finger on top of my head. Her body recoiled a little despite the poison in her system. "I killed him, you know. I gave Aryan Krigborn the most dishonourable death there is. You owe me a little bit for that. His head cracked open like a watermelon. Just...less juicy? The man did not have much to work with. His brains barely fed a crow or two."

Noise from behind the doors dragged my attention, and I put a finger to my lips.

She sucked in a sharp breath when someone rasped a fist over the wood so urgently that the door shook on its hinges.

She turned to me. "If they find you here, they will think I am your ally, and this would have been all for nothing. Go!" she whispered harshly.

"Play for my father, but win for me," I offered. "Help me scare him, and I will help you get your revenge. I am particularly good at that. Unlike my father, I cannot offer you your crown back, but what I can offer is the head of who took it from you. If that is what you want and wish."

Another loud knock shook the doors.

She swallowed. "Scare him?"

"He will not be stopped, not with all that he has gathered, but he can be delayed."

"I cannot bargain with you, Melanthe would know. She has marked everyone after what you did with the old lords."

"No bargain. From one Krigborn to another, Skadi, an agreement between two of the same blood." I pulled a vial from my pocket and tipped it to her lips. After several seconds, I extended a hand to her. "*Kha ramal arê khâz.*" *My word for yours*, I recited in old Ysolt.

She hesitated, her hands gathered in tight fists at her side. When another knock rang again violently, she thrust a hand forward, bracing mine. "*Khâz ramal arê khân.*" *Your word for mine.*

When the fist pounded on her door relentlessly, she pulled away, and shouted, "What?"

"General, you are being called by Demir," someone shouted back from behind the door. "To check on the princess."

"The bitch can wait," she responded, and threw me a side glance.

I raised my brows at her and mimed an offended reaction, putting a hand over my heart. "*Ouch.*"

The soldier continued, "General, this is urgent. Demir thinks she might be up to something."

That made me smile. "Oh, dear," I whispered. "Better hurry."

"Let me get dressed," she shouted back, rolling her eyes. "And I will be right out."

"We will wait," the guards answered.

Panicked, she turned to face me. "Windows. Use the windows to get out."

I frowned, looking down at my attire. "That's very unladylike. I will leave after you."

"Princess," she hissed. "Hell will break loose if I do not find you in your room."

"There are shortcuts everywhere, Moregan. Relax," I said, taking a seat on her settee. "No one will know I've even said a word today."

I'd just laid down after my bath and opened my book when Demir burst through my bedroom doors, heaving and panting while he directed his scathing glare on me.

"Down boy," I crooned, flipping my pages to where I'd been reading the other night. "No danger here."

"Where are your guards?"

My brows flew up and I glanced at the doors before blinking up at him. "What guards?"

"Don't play with me," he growled.

Pushing up, I stood and looked out at the two guards stationed by my door. "There."

"The ones from this morning. They have not reported back, nor have they returned to their quarters."

"How would I know?"

He neared me almost chest to chest as he harshly whispered the words out between gritted teeth, "Do not fucking play with me."

My frown was slow and natural. "Something has happened," I stated more than asked while drawing more confusion to my expression. The mask slipped on so quickly and effortlessly that it surprised me, too. "You know how loyal Adriatians are to their faith." I clicked my tongue. "To trust them so profoundly only for them to run away with your secrets. Off to another king or queen who will lead them to destroy what they fear and what their faith does not forgive. First it was me. And now my father. One monster for the other. I'd say pray that they've just run away from fear and not because they are looking for another king to spy for." I chuckled. "But who would you pray to? Bones and rot?"

He took a long moment to study all of me. The more he stared, the more it dawned on him that I was clueless. Because I truly was. I did not know where they were. Presuming that the servants had already sent away the castle waste to be disposed of in some hole or fire far from here.

He retreated a couple steps back, still clenching his jaw and fists from the rage he did not know where to direct it at. "You will stay in your room."

"I was staying in my room, dear."

"The child is born."

That took me by surprise. Not the birth. Him telling me. When I glanced back at him, the emotion on my face was as natural and real as it could get. "Born?"

"Early this afternoon."

"And why are you telling me?"

His vile grin was back. "We are only a couple steps away now. Thought I'd remind you."

"How thoughtful of you."

"Do you think I do not understand your game?"

"Game?"

His jaw was set tight. I knew how to tickle some nerves. It was my speciality. "Your father is not fooled. No one is. But keep playing nice."

"Dear, if I don't play nice," I started, approaching him and running a hand over his silent chest. "How do I get to rip your lover apart, feather by feather, hm? I need for her to rise from whatever grave she is buried in."

"Whatever keeps you happy."

"A blanket with Guardian feathers would make me very pleased," I said, giving him a saccharine smile. "With you I'm going to make a pair of lovely, green leather boots."

My laughter filled every corner of the room and seeped all the way down the corridor before the doors were shut with a thud.

As usual, Moregan waited for me on the training grounds, her focus set forward. Nothing in her reactions to me had changed. She was an intelligent woman who knew to play the crowd well.

Demir studied me intently when I climbed the court fence and approached the old queen. It was almost as if the bastard could smell something wrong.

So, I did what I do best—I played. Putting on my sweetest smile, I said, "What has soured your candy, dearest? You're particularly ugly today."

Moregan's face twisted with a snarl, and she took a fighting stance opposite me. "All mouth and no action, as usual."

I blocked her fist and twisted under her elbow, releasing her and pushing back. "I've heard otherwise actually."

She spat on the ground and lunged for me again. This time, a shard of ice extended from her elbow when she threw it back, aiming it at my stomach. And she made me bleed. Perfect.

"Moregan!" Demir bellowed, climbing the court and reaching my side to cup the wound. "Have you gone insane?"

"She...she—" Moregan mumbled, blinking at the large wound gushing out blood.

"I've told you to not let her get to you," he said, blocking my wound with a hand whilst signalling his soldiers.

"I'm sorry," the bald general offered quietly, throwing me a quick look before fleeing the courts.

Demir hissed, crawling back and away from me, staring at his sizzling palms coated with my blood.

Hm. Strange. Nia had told me that the herb only neutralised dark magic, not that it would literally scald it. It was worth all the upset belly I'd gotten from ingesting blue gyre. Seeing him trying to comprehend what had just happened nearly made me cry from amusement.

"Help me up, sailor boy. I might need to see a healer," I said, dropping to the floor from the dizziness caused by the blood loss.

His attention snapped to me, and he stood, backing away, looking almost afraid. "The guards will take you back to your room." His shaking hands curled into fists and he quickly fled the scene.

Poor Demir. If it did that to his hand, what would it do to his stomach now that Nissa's mother and the rest of the servants had sprinkled it all over his food? And where he slept. And the clothes that he wore.

9

White Pawn to D4

Kilian

FIVE MONTHS. FIVE LONG months had passed since Snow and Mal had been taken by Silas.

A season had changed, and another was about to. But thankfully, Silas had yet to complete the sceptre, let alone weld it together. At least that is what Elias had managed to slip by the last time we'd had contact.

"Are you certain?" Visha asked, still holding tightly onto the vial containing a partial solution to one of my issues.

I reached my hand forward. "Quite certain."

She still held onto it, pulling it back from me. "Dreams are sent by your Goddess, and you know it well, if you chose to suppress them—"

I took the vial from her hand and downed it. "If she is not in my dreams, why should I dream at all. I don't care for the nonsense of Gods. Or their warnings. If Silas marching around with a divine weapon, three armies, and holding hostage two of the people I love most in this lifetime are not enough of a warning, then I don't know what is."

She frowned. "Snowlin really *is* bad company."

"Any news from Eldmoor?" I asked, tossing the small flask into the crackling fire pit.

"It seems the shortage of herbs is affecting Silas's Crafters. Red Coven had seen Melanthe's sisters lurking around the illegal markets. No ingredients means no more beasts."

"Good," I said, standing. "Have Macaria order merchants to sell them cheap substitutes."

"Why?"

"Because I'm not done fucking with Silas just yet. If they look hard enough, they will find what they need elsewhere. If we give them something that could ease their needs, for cheaper, quicker, and with low effort, then not only will they be casting faulty craft, but they will be under our surveillance. We can put two and two together just by knowing what they buy most. What veils they have around the walls, how they treat their sick, what they feed their beasts, how they create those beasts."

She nodded. "I will make Macaria aware immediately."

"Good."

Penelope raised her head from the feet-long book before her and offered me a small smile.

I tousled her hair as I went by to leave. "Don't work her too hard, Visha."

Thora had chosen to train in Olympia again despite the obvious cautionary looks she threw around the cliff where the upper training grounds stood. And even though she had chosen it on purpose to train her fear along with her muscles and magic, she was regressing rather than progressing. Because forcing yourself to like something you despise and fear never works.

For the tenth time in the last hour, she threw her attention to the height below us and struggled to evade my rather gentle attacks.

"Thora," I called, knocking her weapon out of her hands, but she unsheathed her daggers, coming for me again.

A flick of a wrist was all that it took me to pry them off of her.

She dropped down to the ground and sprawled on the gravelly floor. "I'm useless with weapons. Why can't we train with magic?"

"Because magic can become unreliable, and your father has recruited some of the best Crafters in the realm who can disarm your magic with a look if you're caught in their traps."

She glanced at the cliff again and seemed as if she was holding her breath.

I sighed and sat next to her. "Holding your breath? Does that even help?"

Her attention snapped to me and she sunk inside herself again. "A little, but then I start getting dizzy. And I hate feeling dizzy. It reminds me of that time when Snow and I caught the red shivers after we went to play with some winter squirrels."

"Have you thought about trying to jump?"

Her eyes shot wide, and she shook her head fast as if I was about to push her off the cliff. Except that she would eventually make that jump herself. No pushing included. Unless she wanted to be pushed.

"I'm not jumping."

"I can jump with you."

She thought about it for a moment, pacing back and forth. "You think this will help?"

"Might. Might not. Unless you try, you will never know. Do you even want to try?"

"I do."

She didn't. "You don't have to rush this. Healing is a slow process."

She raised her eyes to me. "There is nothing ripped, torn, or bleeding, no wounds either. I bear no scars like Eren or Snow. So what am I even healing, Kilian?"

"What hurts you without scars is often worse." I tapped a finger on her brow. "Snow uses pain to unlock herself out of there and you use it to lock yourself back inside. If you're relying on it even just slightly, still reminding yourself of it, those scars are not scars, they are still wounds. Why poke at them, Thora, why do you retreat back in there, inside that wound?"

She gathered her knees to her chest, resting her chin on them. "The reality is easier inside my head. Eren is happy there and Snow is happy there." She turned to me. "But she was happy here as well. With you. With us. And I don't want to miss it anymore. I want to see her happy in this reality, too. So I will try and stay in it for as long as I can. Mal was helping me, and it was working. Thank you for taking over. Though you do suck at it a little."

I chuckled. "I will always be here, Thora, for anything you need." I extended my hand to her and faded the two of us to Adriata. "You like water," I said as we made our way to lunch. "Perhaps you can first try a low height. A pool or a nearby diving cliff children play on."

She didn't respond.

"It is alright, Thora, if you do not—" I halted and spun to her, except that she was no longer beside me. She'd stopped in the middle of the stairs, looking over the training court where my brother's soldiers were being led by their second in command. Her eyes had fixed on Neo who had leaned back on the fence, looking at the younger soldiers trying to execute his commands.

"See anything you like?" I asked, trying not to smile.

She nodded and pointed a finger directly at my brother's second in command. "I want him."

That made me laugh—hard.

The younger Skygard frowned at me. "What? Can't I have him?"

"Doesn't work like that."

Her brow shot up and she walked up the rest of the stairs to me. "Says who?"

"Mal won't like it. Are you alright with that?"

"Malik is not my brother or my father."

Same song sung by two sisters. "Neo is his soldier—a brother, almost."

"Unless Malik wants him for himself, he can learn to mind his own business. And yes, I want to try jumping here first. When you're done longingly staring at a single black hair you find in your room, please take me there. I don't feel comfortable doing that with anyone else."

"I do not stare at her hair longingly," I said.

She waved a hand over her head. "Yes, you do."

"I miss her." *So much. So much it was ripping me apart.*

She cupped both hands over her mouth, and shouted back, "I miss her, too."

A portal opened behind me, a breathless Caiden coming out of it. "We've spotted Vas again."

"Perfect."

Driada had sat on the veranda overlooking the lavender gardens when I returned to Amaris. Her gaze remained fixed and lost in the distance despite the massive needle she held between her trembling fingers.

I kneeled before her, and her chestnut eyes dropped to me, a smile gracing her delicate features that had thinned far too much lately. Carefully, I pried the sewing material from her hands and set it beside her, bringing her hands to my face to warm them up. "It is getting cold, Driada."

"I'm waiting for Mal, he returns from school around now."

I shed my jacket and threw it around her shoulders. "Shall we wait together?"

She nodded, taking my hand in her cold one. I had never been big on physical contact, but I had always held her hand every evening while we'd waited for Mal to come back home when he was young.

We waited a while. Past sunset. Past dusk. Past twilight.

Thought she would eventually remember that he was not here without me breaking her heart again like every other night.

"He is not coming, is he?" she asked, two stray tears falling down her hollow cheeks. "Neither is Henrik."

"They have not gone to the same place, Driada. I will get my brother back."

She patted my hand and laid her head on my shoulder. "Of course, my boy. You always take care of your brother. I worry for nothing, don't I?"

Night fell overhead and a strange quiet settled inside my chest. A warning quiet. And a type of quiet I had often searched as a cure to what my magic needed to feed on.

Death.

I raised a hand to her forehead. "Ada?"

The rosy walls of her room had never appeared grimmer despite the colourful life Mal had given them with his skills and paint brushes. Every time our father had shouted and ignored her, my brother had added another flower to her walls to make her happy. I'd never realised the true extent of the hate I carried in my heart for my father until I noticed that there was not an inch of white left to peek through anywhere in the walls.

Driada's small frame laid sunken in the middle of her large bed. Even though she shivered, she'd insisted on holding my hand. Her eyes peeled open and her mouth quivered into a small smile. "Please, son," she whispered, reaching a hand to cup my face. "Don't keep holding onto me. Let it take me. Do not upset the God of Death. Do not make him your enemy."

"He made me his enemy when he set his sights on you out of everyone." I shook my head. "I will not surrender before him. I will not surrender you to him." For years I had tricked death, and I would do it until I no longer could. To keep her alive, I'd do much worse.

"It has been the greatest honour to have been your...to have been there for you growing up."

"My mother," I said, kissing her hand. "You can say it. You are my mother."

"Thank you," she whispered, tears streaming down her temples. "Thank you, son. My perfect sons. Mal will understand. He will understand if I leave."

"What about me? What if I don't understand? What about me, Driada?"

Her breathing grew into a sharp rattle. "You will forgive me. I know it. In time you will forgive me, too."

Thora burst through the doors, crying and struggling to breathe as she climbed on top of the bed and curled herself next to Driada. "Please," she murmured, laying her head on her shoulder. "Please, you've still not shown me how to cross stitch. You can't leave me. Don't leave me. Not you, too."

Driada's smile was faint but warm. "I won't."

"You are. I can feel it." Thora looked up at me. "Please. Do something!"

I couldn't. I could do nothing. I was death and darkness and shadows yet I couldn't do anything. Not even keep those I loved safe.

Larg, Triad, and Alaric showed up next, kneeling beside her bed as she took her slow last breaths. The room slowly filled with more and more people who adored her. Atlas rushed to my side, clinging to the back of my jacket, sobbing with his head buried under his robes. Everyone eventually came as Driada took her last breath. Except the two people she loved most. Except for my brother and wife.

Would I have to mourn them, too? Should I have already mourned them?

10

Black Pawn takes D4

Snowlin

FATHER HAD THROWN WARNING looks my way all throughout the meeting even though I had not said one word. And Demir had pushed his chair so close to mine that I could almost feel his scales bristling against my precious and expensive wool britches.

His court also kept glancing my way as if they expected me to interrupt. But that wasn't my intention. Nor a part I needed to play anymore. Before, I had to be loud to deter attention from my real intentions, intended to be challenging to bring out the worst from those I needed answers from, and disrespectful in order to know who wasn't aware how to bow regardless of whether they respected me or not. Now, they feared my silence more, and that made me quite pleased. Enough not to huff a single sigh or snort at some of their stupid plans.

Melanthe was still recovering from birth, and I had yet to see my brand-new sibling. Though I was sure they had probably taken her somewhere else and far from here.

I was chained. Without magic. Weaponless. Guarded. Yet they still thought me to be capable of causing her harm. I was so flattered that my eyes could almost water had this dry winter air not shrivelled my eyeballs to the size of peas.

Moregan had not stopped trying to get my attention and that was bothering me quite a bit considering that Demir could basically sniff intentions before they were even thoughts in my brain. And Gara—sweet Gara sat before me, so proud. When my eyes landed on the thick, marred scar around her wrist where our bargain had been, she flinched, pulling on her long sleeve to hide it from me.

"Princess," someone called, and I returned to attention. "What are your thoughts on it?"

The looks that father and Demir gave the general who'd asked me told me they were not pleased to know of my opinion on accepting a trade with southern Eldmoorian merchants.

"Why southern?" I asked, curious actually.

The general cleared his throat, not even a bit bothered by his king's glare. "They seem to be the only ones with enough stock, Your Highness. Hanai has cut trade with most of the continent and the market doesn't seem able to satisfy demand and hiked up most prices which caused Crafters to not produce a majority of the potions, herbs, and medicine we need. We've been lucky and have been offered all the products we needed by these merchants. At a high price, however."

I fought a grin. "Gold is an inexpensive cost in this economy, isn't it?"

"These days everything is an expensive cost, Your Highness," someone mumbled, and father's jaw ticked.

"Well, gold comes to us, right? Is gold still doing that, or has it gotten cold feet these days?" I asked, trying to rein in a joyous smile when all of them ducked their heads like ostriches.

"Your warm jests do lighten up the air, Your Highness," the new Casmere Lord said. "I appreciate you trying to soften the grave situation."

Oh my. Grave?

Father cleared his throat, and everyone sat back upright at ninety degrees. "Let's call this a day. My daughter in law has a small child to look after all alone, I mustn't delay her."

"Yes," I said. "You must bring my niece to see me sometime, Gara. I'd love to meet the adorable little thing."

The new Lady of Grasmere looked uncomfortable but nodded, quickly standing and rushing to leave after curtsying to my father.

"Where are you going?" he asked before I could make a run for it with all the rest of his court.

"I visit mother's grave sometimes in the afternoons when the weather is not as bad."

"I've been told." He stood and reached me. "I will join you."

"Why, do you need to piss or something?"

He bared his teeth at me. "Child—"

"You've done nothing but fuck with her life. Stay clear of fucking with her death. You owe it to her to forget her, to not even think about her, mention her, or even dare ponder on her memory. Not even a bit. Even if it is thrust upon you to remember her, force yourself to forget it. If not for the sake of her, for the sake of you. Because I swear, father, I will make it my mission to rip her existence out of your mind."

He slapped me, then grabbed my jaw and backed me to the wall, hard. "I loved her," he growled in my face. "You wretched thing. I loved that woman."

He flinched when my cackles echoed about the room. "You loved nothing more than watching her slowly die off. The way your eyes lit up seeing her wither into herself—that...that I will never forget. The night she gave her life for me, she was happy to do it. And you know what I think? She was not happy to save me." My voice shook. "No, she was thrilled to leave *you*. So spare me the bullshit, it is getting exhausting. If you really loved her, then why...why did you want this more than you wanted her? Why do you want this so much?"

His mouth pursed and he retreated, taking a seat on his bejewelled and gilded chair. "I've never told you stories when you were little, my rose." He pointed for me to take a seat. "How about I tell you one now?"

"If you must torture me some way."

After I took a seat, he gave me an eerie smile, too soft to belong to a man like him—too gentle to be given to me. "Do you know of the date I was born?"

"Yes, I light a candle on that day and wish you death each year. Right at the stroke of midnight. Maybe I will light a dozen next year or maybe I'll just light an entire fire. If we are lucky, the northern wind will pick it up and spread it over the forest, down the city, and around the walls. Maybe it will burn everything. If I am lucky, maybe it will burn you, too." I drew a long, deep breath, pretty satisfied with my daydream. "Where were we? Something about the unfortunate day you were born."

Anger nearly burst that vein in his brow, but to my unfortunate luck, he calmed down, sighing. "The day I was born, child, was one of the holiest days in our kingdom. A comet crossed the Isjordian skies when I took my first breath, grazing our kingdom so close that it almost kissed land. Songs were sung, praises were raised, expectations exploded with words that I would grow to become the greatest king Isjord had ever crowned. And I did—I did become great. However, there was always someone I bowed to. First it was a teacher or a priest, then my father, his advisor, a battalion commander or two—I bowed to respect, hierarchy, and fear sometimes, too. I thought it would change once I became king, once my useless and witless father died, but it actually worsened. I needed to bow to many more when I sat on my throne." He leaned forward. "And the worst was that I had to bow to a God, too. One who had left this land for me to make it better without doing anything and receiving everything. Praise, adoration, loyalty. No matter what I did, it was at his grace. So, I burned temples first. Reprinted Eirlys liber to say exactly what I wanted and needed it to say. I burned all the original scriptures, vandalised statues, redrew Guardians and Hodr as a dark presence looming over us. And then," he said, grinning, "I slowly killed their God and the prayers sent to him. Soon, I will become their new one. After all, there were beings who once were merely mortals and made of bleeding flesh and breakable bones who became through praise and prayer...divine. But first, all must praise and pray to me, the ultimate faith. If not by choice, it will have to be by force. When Aurora wipes out the rest of the realm, there will only be me. I will give hell and heaven out of my palm. They will have to beg. They will have to pay. They will have to bow."

Just when I thought I'd seen all the roots of this rotten garbage, the plant turns out to be a fucking potato. Shock is what I should be feeling. Problem is, I was beyond tired of his antics to even feel anything. Leaning forward, I said, "You need a hobby. That's it. Collecting stamps or something." I clicked my fingers. "Making mugs. Definitely some ceramics need to be involved. Mm, how about pottery? Or perhaps I can add a knitting class to my prisoner list of duties. Do you have a steady hand?"

"I had hope that you would understand," he said, sighing and pinning a disappointed look on me. "Me and you are made of the same stuff, child. You remind me too much of my younger self to not appreciate the effort and skill I've put into this. If you weren't my greatest disappointment, you would have been my biggest achievement."

I rolled my eyes. "If your murder wasn't my greatest regret, it would have been my biggest pleasure." I stood and gestured to him in the holy sign, two fingers on my brow and two on my heart. "To Hodr, might it welcome us all. People pray for heaven, praise a God for the fruit they will receive, not for what power they have or how it will serve them. The fruit you are offering is rotten. Spoiled. Something they have already tasted, grown sick off." Bowing a little too dramatically, I retreated towards the door. "How about collecting coins? No?"

I'd just laid a rose on my mother's grave when another presence filled the empty space. Moregan hid under the maze wall shadows, her face concealed under a cloak.

I glanced at her over my shoulder. "What was so important that it couldn't wait?"

"Adriata's queen mother has died. I thought you might want to know."

The world spun around me for a moment and my knees gave away. Dread, so much dread crossed my sight until it blurred and darkened.

Driada was dead?

It had to be a lie. Kilian would have not let her die. My Kilian would have fought the God of Death himself to keep her here. At least until she could see Mal again. Not now. He wouldn't...she...she couldn't have died. "Lies," I whispered.

"I'm afraid not."

My eyes drew shut and air entered my lungs too sparingly to let me speak. "How did the news come about?"

"Silas's spies. The information comes from a close source."

"Close?"

"From his court."

His spy. Someone close to Kilian. It had to be. "And do you know who it is?"

"No. Just that it is the same person who gave away your friend's and the prince's location in Eldmoor. The information is collected at Highwall through sparse code words. Adriatian patrol is too tight to let much slip out, but enough to know the most important bits."

No matter how much I tried to distract the pain knotting on my chest, it was too severe to ignore. I didn't know there were so many tears left in me to spare for another. Silencing my grief didn't help either because sobs escaped as worse sounds—pained whimpers that made my throat scratch and bleed.

"Are you...are you alright?" Moregan asked after a while.

No. Maybe I was not.

Adriatian guards followed me closely up until I took that turn towards the dungeons. The two blocked my path, weapons drawn. "The king has denied permission for visits."

"Since when is my wretched father your king, you miserable cunts?" I reached until his blade was pressed to my ribs and tearing through my clothes.

He drew back, stunned, but I pushed again till he was forced to sheath his sword into its holster. "The king—"

"Will do what? Kill me? Kill you?"

"Yes."

"Do I look like I care? If he kills me or you? Out of my way." I pushed past them, rushing until more guards began to block my way. When someone reached to grab me, I spun around and grabbed onto a dagger strapped to their baldric, piercing their chest before turning to face the others. More blood spilled over the tiles when another tried to grab me.

"Let her," Demir's voice boomed down the corridor, and everyone stepped back immediately. He coughed, a hand coming to rest on his chest. "Remember, princess, it was your choice to do so."

There was no air in my lungs when I stood before his dark cell. His large body had hunched over where he'd sat on the ground, his face shielded away from me by shadows and hair.

I just stood there for too long a while. Wordless. How could one tell another they had lost their mother?

He didn't move, not even acknowledge me though he'd seen me. Not for a while. "She is dead, isn't she?"

"She is," I whispered, forcing myself forward only to come to another halt when a string of light hit part of his face, and I saw dried blood paint his skin. All I could hear was the sound of my heart. And a loud thud urging and drumming for blood. "Stand," I ordered, my spine straightening.

He stretched a little. "I've just sat."

"Malik, stand!" my voice echoed around the empty room, and thunder rained down because of my splintering calm. I felt the chains on my limbs heat and tighten, my magic resisting and battling Melanthe's craft.

He obeyed, slowly standing and walking up to me. Half of his face was soaked in blood and there were deep scars across his left eye—across his missing left eye. "Snow—"

Thunder blasted outside, and blood leaked out of my mouth, nose, and eyes from the way my magic drummed against the seal on my back, freeing itself, only to be blocked by Melanthe.

Before he could finish his sentence, I rushed out and headed for my father's chambers despite Mal's echoing pleas to not retaliate. I stopped right before I'd reached his doors, when I heard two soft voices accompany his boisterous laughter and the squeal of a new-born.

"Father, she is adorable," Fren squealed.

Each inhale was harder to take than the other. My fingers shook from the urge to either close my fist and make my palms bleed, or sink them into their flesh and make another bleed for me. Voices drummed around my head, helplessly and unable to escape me through actions I often took to lessen their call—through murder and torture. Incessant, they called, chanted, even begged. To kill.

"She is," Melanthe said, laughing. *"We might need to crown her soon. Right, Silas?"*

"In time, yes," my father said, his laughter following.

I counted like Cai had taught me. Concentrated like Kil would have wanted me to.

I remembered my Nia and then Mal, the one I was staying alive for. Every possible move flashed before my eyes as I measured my next step. It was a gambit, and I was too far into the game to lose just pawns.

He'd touched my knight.

After taking a few deep breaths that disagreed with my tightening chest, I carefully stepped back and headed to my room where Nissa's mother was changing my bedding.

The woman stopped when she saw whatever expression was painted on my face and swallowed hard.

Get Moregan, I mouthed, and she nodded, listening to the instructions I gave her.

11

White Queen takes D4

Snowlin

SILENCE HAD BECOME SO present these days in the dining hours that I could practically see the anxiousness in each of my father's forehead wrinkles.

I'd just lifted the fork holding a golden mushroom to my mouth when bells rattled like thunder around us. The sort of bells that had only rang once before in Isjord. The day when prince Tenebrose was crowned King of Isjord—the same sound that would only ring again when his throne would be contested or threatened.

Melanthe's eyes went as big as saucers, and she turned to my father. "Cannot be."

Father stood, wiping his mouth and heading out. "I'm sure it is false. There are many new soldiers around, it takes nothing to ring the wrong bell."

Fren was clueless. "What is false, papa?"

"You all stay here," he said, buttoning his jacket.

Melanthe stood and followed shortly behind. "I'm not sitting having breakfast while you are out there."

How romantic. I stopped chewing the bite of orange, gaging a little, and sipping water to wash down the taste of citrusy bile.

It was only Fren and I left when another round of bells rang, and the sound of stomping soldiers grew faint towards the distance of the now crumbled castle walls.

"What is with you?" the sea urchin squeaked out, looking me up and down in disgust.

I offered her a smile and bit on some lovely, sweet grapes. Father had a gift for choosing the best fruit merchants, they were delicious. "What is with you, dearest sister?" Lifting a brow, I leaned in. "Is the bedchamber dry? You look like you're in heat. Poor thing."

"You're not in a position to worry about me."

"I meant Elias. Poor Elias."

Her eyes narrowed and she opened her mouth to speak when a blast rang near us.

Guards and a Crafter rushed into the dining room and ushered us outside and towards the throne room. Smoke coiled towards the skies and all too close to the castle, signalling that the attack was not far from us.

Fren screamed when something crashed against the castle walls, shaking its whole foundations and causing all paintings to fall, crash, and splinter to pieces.

"Your father's halls are protected," the Crafter shouted, pushing us inside the open throne room space. "Do not come out until we deal with this."

"Deal with what?" Fren screamed, shaking like a baby rattle.

Today I would learn two things.

One: how afraid could father truly be?

The Crafter gave us one last shove inside. "An old creature from the Islines. The old Krigborns are attacking."

"Cannot be," the bastard girl said. "Father said they would never have the guts to attack us. They don't have armies. They are barbarians!"

And two: how small was an unblessed brain. Theoretically and practically.

The doors slammed shut an inch or so away from my face and a bolt was rammed in place along with several other locks, locking us away from danger.

Now, you all might be thinking: why is Snow running away from a big bad monster? Snow can take the big bad monster. Snow is not afraid of big bad monsters. Snow is stronger than big bad monsters. Snow is a bigger and far worse monster.

And I will tell you that you are quite correct.

"Where did that come from?" Fren huffed in frustration behind me. After a minute of silence, she asked, "Shouldn't you be out there with the guards?"

I turned round to her, my smile wide. "Yes, I should be."

Her eyes dropped to the knife I pulled from under my jacket. "What...what are you doing?" She moved behind one of her massive guards. "Don't be stupid. You're chained like a dog and without your precious magic."

"Magic is overrated. And I kind of prefer it the good old bloody way."

I had underestimated Moregan. Father had underestimated Moregan. The woman was capable of much, and in my hands, she was capable of too much. Only Gods knew how she had managed to sneak an Isline creature inside these walls. I was terribly curious to know. *You* must be, too. And so was the shadowy reflection on the bloodied blade I was holding before me.

It had been almost an hour since they had locked everyone in here alone with me, and they had yet to figure out their mistake. Or so I thought.

My excitement picked up when I heard footsteps grow louder and louder near the doors. Doors which flew open in no time by someone who knew that he had been fooled.

Awestruck, my father stood there with his entourage, staring at the distance of the throne room with me perched on his bloody dais which was quite literally...bloody. His eyes dropped to the ground for a short sweeping second before they met mine again. And when our gazes clashed, I flashed him a wicked smile.

"What have you done?" he harshly and breathlessly whispered. He did not shout or threaten. My poor father was in shock.

"Done? Me? Nothing." I pointed the end of my blood-stained knife at him. "What have *you* done?"

"Snowlin!" he roared, the whole room blistering with blue ice, crawling and draining all the heat in the room.

It only stopped when I rested my foot on top of the decapitated head on the ground. "Me and you entered an agreement," I said, lifting my wrists up in the air and shaking the chains. "This is not the first time you have chained me."

"You will regret this, child," he threatened, baring his teeth, "I'm glad you've not realised what I'm capable of, I'd love to catch you by surprise again."

Flicking my foot back, I kicked the head and watched it roll down the throne steps and travel all the way down in front of him. The man tore his eyes away from the upper quarter of his daughter, breathing like a beast and looking like he was about to be sick.

His threats were ageing and boring me at this point. "Do you know what is worse than an angry woman?" I asked, standing. "One with nothing to lose. Take away the one thing I don't want to lose and see if you would ever be able to control me. Father, I would have let you beat and skin me ten thousand ways to hells and never even lifted a finger to help." I pointed my knife at him again, and all of his entourage jumped before him, lifting their swords in my direction. All which severely entertained me. "*You* went and touched him. *You* broke our agreement, you hurt the one thing that you are using to control me. Didn't you? But was it at least worth it? Did you manage to torture a groan out of him? A sigh? A plea of help? Surely one thing, right? Something worth invoking my anger for." They had thought Mal could be broken. But they didn't know that Mal had been broken long ago and there was very little left to break. He would never betray his brother, his kingdom, his oath, and his blessing no matter how much he loathed it. Did they even know who Mal was and what he was capable of? If there was a God I feared, it would be him. And luckily, he too was on my side.

Slowly, I descended the small set of stairs and approached him. "You will take a healer down to him. A nice one. A polite one. Next time I go down there, I'd like to see both of his eyes when I talk to him."

"You don't know what you have done."

We were not even a foot away from one another. One pair of soulless eyes gazing into another pair of soulless eyes. "You might be a villain, father, but I am *the* villain." I gestured the knife between us. "Let's coexist. Despite the thrill it gives me to prove you a point," I said, throwing the blade to the floor and wiping my hands on my dress, "I really don't have the energy for it. And I don't like half arsing things like today. You taught me to be more meticulous than this. Disappointing you is something I want to correct as your new heir. And I only aim to please from now on."

He was the first to break our locked gaze when he looked over at Fren's dismantled body. And then something beautiful happened. Something stunning. He shook from rage and pain and grief and whatnot.

He raised a hand to wrap around my throat and squeezed hard enough to cut all air from my lungs. "Next time I throw you in with my snakes, I'll make sure to have starved them for months."

"I am already in it," I rasped breathlessly. "Now, are you quite done? If you're not going to bite, let me go. This is enough family time for me today."

Even though he had let go, I could still feel the mark of his fingers on my skin. It hurt to swallow, and it hurt to breathe, but then again, he'd done worse to me.

Satisfied, I strutted out of the throne room, humming to myself. "*Hush, little baby, don't say a word, Papa's going to buy you a mockingbird.*" I gave Melanthe a smile when I brushed past her. "*And if that mockingbird don't sing, Papa's going to buy you a diamond ring.*"

Demir's eyes trailed me all the way down the corridor, not once leaving mine.

Well, I was quite satisfied with my consequences. Especially when I saw the sly smiles that the Isjordian guards wore when I walked past them to my room. Their heads lowered, bowing before me.

Yet...I felt so dull. Grey. Hollow.

So tired.

I was so tired.

It wasn't until I found Nissa's mother sitting at the edge of my bed with a tray of tea in her hands that I collapsed to my knees, attempting to drown the silent sobs threatening to rip my throat that burned worse than hellfire. I dug my fingers on the rug beneath me, trying to keep a promise I'd broken so often after I'd given it to the man I loved—to the man who would wear my pain and hurt with me, and for me. The man who had lost his mother, too. The man I couldn't hold in my arms as he had held me when the world had taken from me. The man I was starving to touch, to breathe in, to comfort.

When Nissa's mother wrapped her arms around me, it broke something I'd tried to hold from breaking. I cried against her chest until I'd shattered every inch of strength I had tried to preserve to avenge my sister. How many more did I have to avenge? How much longer did I have to grieve loss for? How much longer did I have to keep losing?

The old woman sighed, rubbing a soft palm to my back. She brushed her fingertips on my neck and her jaw trembled as she spilled silent tears for me. "This world is so cruel to you, child."

"It wants my anger."

"We either die angry or live long enough to know it was really grief to start with. Grief heals. You can heal it, child. Let the word take from you, but don't let it take *you* because of your anger."

"*Why not,*" that voice purred at the back of my mind. "*What is there left to lose?*"

So much.

So, so much.

"Shut up," I murmured back. "Shut up."

Time. I had bought Kilian the time he would have lost. While he would bury Driada, father was burying Fren. I had not just killed his child, I'd possibly killed an alliance between Elias and him. Father could not afford to lose Elias. People trusted him. People loved him, respected, and looked up at him, more so now that he'd taken his father's spot.

The new heir of Venzor had not spared me a single glance, and it was enough to tell me that father was looking to blame someone for what had happened that day—him probably being the first suspect. A calculation I had not made.

Kilian would figure out how to take father down before he could raise the Guardian. Father was waiting for him to make the first move. Waiting to catch him knowing he had just the right bait. He'd even waited to retrieve the Vrammethen piece last. I was glad Kilian knew better and that he mostly reasoned with his brain and not his heart.

Though priests in Isjord were known to keep it simple during funerals, this one did indeed not keep it simple. For at least an hour, he had praised and raised all sorts of prayers for a woman who was not even blessed, let alone Krig blessed. Had Fren been alive, she would have loved to know, so there is that.

By the time the last lines of Eirlys liber were recited, a thick blanket of snow had covered all the attendants. Except for my father. The man was steaming from anger, hot enough to not let a pellet of snow set on him.

He had not spoken a word to anyone. But he chose to speak to me, however and very unfortunately, "I tried to raise a soldier, make you the pinnacle of power, but you became a monster who slays its own kin mercilessly."

Touching, really. "Became?" I asked, throwing the white rose on Fren's casket and turning in my seat to face him. "I am all your doing. From the way I walk, talk, and even the way I breathe. I am what you made. You emptied me of feel. You marked me with pain. You fed me hate. You taught me rage. I. Am. All. You."

Beat her until she cannot feel a kick anymore. Break her right hand so she can learn to use her left. Break both her legs so she can learn to stand on pain. Make her bleed until her blood turns black. Make her bleed until she forgets to rely on it to live.

Break. Take. Ruin.

It was all he had done to me.

Every scar on my body reminded me of it, what I was beneath them remained the wound he'd made me to be. "You have never humanised me, father. Why should I humanise you?"

"It would have been so simple," he whispered harshly, resting a hand on my cheek and brushing his thumb over my skin, his eyes boring into mine. "To obey me. You would have had the life you wanted. I can still give you it. You want to burn, then burn. Every life you would have wanted I would have given you permission to take. And the power to rule, I was going to hand it to you." His hold on me grew harsher. "I can still hand it to you. The throne was made for you. This could be yours. The new world I create can all be yours. No more Adriatians. No more of those who can hurt you."

I pushed his hand off and wiped my cheek. "I don't want your throne. I want to watch it burn. Preferably with you still sitting on it."

"My king," Elias called, and I stilled. "Could I have a word?"

I turned to face my friend and ally. "My condolences for your loss."

His face hardened, jaw ticking with what looked like anger. Ignoring me, he turned to my father again who was intently watching our exchange. To my luck, he had thought Ivar was the one to make the deal with me, not his son. "I do not want this to delay us, Silas. The first chance we get, I'd like for us to leave for Breshall."

Us? Breshall? The sceptre was in the isles?

"We will, son. It looks like the weather is also clearing up for us," my father said, throwing a look west, towards the distance of the Venzor shores that were unnaturally bright and clear compared to the skies above us.

"True, and the Mahara channel has been easier to cross. Do I join the troops east or wait to join you west? The seas are home to me like all the Venzors before, you might need me in Breshall."

East? What troops? Wait. Had my people stopped guarding the channel?

Father glanced briefly at me from the corner of his eye. "No, I predict we could leave as early as the end of this week. You don't need to abandon your squadrons, they need your lead. Your guide through our forests is the best among our men. Demir will sail with us along with Melanthe."

"Good to hear, Your Majesty. I will let my squadron know that we will not be joining and remain guarding the east."

Sailing? We were going to sail there? There were camps east now?

"Don't be hard on yourself, Elias," father offered, patting his shoulder and throwing me a look. "It was an unfortunate loss." The second Elias was out of earshot, he turned to me. "You've ruined more than her life."

I rolled my eyes. Did he really think I cared? "They would have made very ugly babies. I did him a favour."

To resist temptation and strike me in front of everyone, he turned and headed where his court members had gathered.

Mission accomplished. Peace at last.

I craned my head around, observing the grieving bunch that had gathered, and found a surprising observation—almost all of them were staring at me. So I raised a hand, wiggling my fingers and offering them a gentle smile.

"*Ybris*. Exiled princess. Mistress of bloodshed," an old, nerve pinching voice said from behind me, and I turned to face Cerelia Krigborn. "Now kin slayer. What will they call you next?"

"I'd say queen slayer," I said, raking my eyes over her frail looking corpse, "but it looks like someone else has been doing all the slaying for me."

"I come in peace."

"All white flags flung around me usually and eventually turn red. Yours is already drenched too far in the blood of my kin." A stuttering laughter shook my entire body when she didn't flinch at the accusation and became ready to deny her partake in it as usual. "You knew all along."

She searched around for a moment, blinking. "Knew what?"

"What your youngest son was doing. He was always your favourite, wasn't he? You used to spoil that dry brain cunt rotten. You knew he kept Thora and Eren alive. If Eleonor was aiding Aryan, that means you knew, too. My, my. What will father think of this treachery? Most importantly, how will he react?"

"Nonsense. You're telling nonsense," she whispered harshly, stealing a look at him.

"It is all nonsense."

I clicked my tongue. "Poor auntie Eleonor. To die at the hands of the brother who adores her to pieces. Quite a tale, will it not be?"

She began shaking a little uncontrollably. "Nonsense."

I wrapped her pearls around my finger until they were choking her. "Every day that I think this soiled blood cannot be more spineless, I keep being proven wrong."

She clutched my hands, and pleaded, "Do not do this."

I leaned forward, giving her a smile. "Why should I not?"

"You want something."

"I want everything," I said, picking some lint from her jacket that was soaked in perfume. "But you cannot give me everything, can you?"

"Snowlin, grandchild," she begged on the verge of tears, "please."

"On your knees. Beg on your knees and perhaps I'll consider sparing your precious daughter from my father's wrath."

She looked around, at the graveyard still filled with Isjordians of the highest ranks. "Please, do not do this."

I pulled away and made to leave when she dropped to her knees. "Please."

Silence suddenly fell over the snowy expanse filled with mourners and relentless spirits, all their attention focused on my prideful grandmother standing on her knees before me, clutching my dress.

"How does it feel?" I asked, staring down at her. "How does humiliation feel?" After a good, solid minute, I looked around, concern pulling on my face. "Someone help me. My grandmother is not feeling well."

Elias rushed to her, wrapping an arm around her middle, and helping her up. "Are you feeling unwell, Your Majesty?"

She looked up at me, at my grin. "Y-yes."

"Nonsense," I said, turning to him and pointing my head at Cerelia's pocket where I'd slipped the letter I'd written last night, knowing I was finally going to get to see him. "She's feeling spectacular. But are you, dear old friend?"

"Absolutely," he answered, bowing his head just slightly to me before helping Cerelia to a seat, his hand sneaking inside her pocket to grab the letter.

12

Black Queen takes D4

Kilian

THE SKIES OF ADRIATA that usually burned by the summer sun had been murky and filled with soot all through august as forgers had beaten and carved metal into weapons for days to no end. Yet it was still not enough. The last note Elias had sent a month ago counted a growing number of beasts. People from all over, not only Isjordians, were joining Silas's side of the war, volunteering their own bodies and betraying their faith. The world the way I knew it was gone in a blink. The new Gods were now human. The old were still silent. And fear was inciting resistance not prayers.

Each city in Isjord was housing beasts and soldiers by the millions. And even though numbers had never scared us, these numbers did.

Larg picked up a sword from the stands and lifted it up, inspecting the weapon that was missing only one element to make it as dangerous as I was—a small piece from the heart of a sphinx. The last one Cai had managed to buy from the illegal markets in Seraphim had been already used. And the rest of the scraps left were now being embedded in smaller weapons, utilised in any way possible—even if it was only a pin, it would do.

My godfather grunted, throwing the sword into the rest of the pile. "Have you spoken to the Autumn Queen about the latest shipments you stole from Silas?"

The shipment had been men and women. Olympians. "I am about to head to her now. But I have to speak to Alaric first about it."

He grabbed my arm. "If he knows—if Silas finds out that it was you who intercepted his ships and stole perhaps his most prized possessions, he will hurt them. You heard what the soldiers said. Silas had paid three years worth of gold to those tradesmen. Searched far and wide for those ten Zephyrs."

"Slavers, not tradesmen, and Silas will never find out."

"Son," he said, stopping me again, and I sighed, knowing what was to come. "Get some sleep, alright?"

"It is too bright." *Too dark. Too quiet. Too loud. Too empty.* I needed her. It was not about want. My soul needed its other half.

He pinched the bridge of his nose and threw a look over the stables. "What are you going to do about the...dragon? Our people are starting to make up tales again, and it's pressing on my bloody nerves."

I felt myself smile. "I'm going to do nothing. It's her dragon."

"You still think she sent it?"

"Olympian spies sent word from Mahara's channel that new Isjordian ships had docked Seraphim waters around the time it came to us. She sent that dragon," I said, dusting my hands. "And I could also make a bet that it might have done some damage on the way here on her behalf. Tristin's Nimbus had seen burnt wreckage of Isjordian ships floating around the Moor and Seer waters."

"I don't know how she is surviving Silas, let alone doing all this."

"He needs her."

"And your brother?"

"Silas needs him to control her and pressure me into keeping still."

"He will kill them once they get that last sceptre."

"Not on my watch."

He grabbed my arm again. "You will not catch his beast. You need to let it go. We lost a dozen good men on that last stunt we pulled with him."

"Negative," I said, walking away from him. "Not when I saw the fucker choke on his own blood long enough to know that he, too, fears death."

We'd hunt him down again. He could not keep still forever, not with Visha's traps lurking on every corner outside of the city he was hiding inside. Visha's dream veil had been almost successful, she'd managed to trap him long enough to let my darkness wrap around his heart. Had Melanthe not portalled him out of it, I would have perhaps made him my prisoner. But next time, I wasn't going to play as nice.

Alaric sat at the edge of an empty bed positioned in the middle of the almost empty room, holding a folded blanket on his lap. I've often found him here these days. He could no longer bear looking at the gravestone—so much so that he had almost ordered for it to be removed. He'd almost ordered every gravestone removed had Cai not stepped in. The two had fought, argued, and then not spoken since.

Grief had its way into hollowing, weakening, and thickening one's feelings all at once.

"*He doesn't know,*" Alaric had told me a few months back. "*He doesn't know how it feels to bury a child and prepare the grave to bury another.*"

"His mother made this for him when she was pregnant with him," he said, putting the blanket back on the bed. "Amara didn't know how to stay still, she always had to be moving and fighting and training, so her husband made her knit. Then she would sit down for hours. She made this first. Sebastian was her biggest joy and she tasked me with his protection." He laughed bitterly. "For some reason, everyone thought I could raise their children. Except one. Samuel was right in a way to fear children—to fear having a family." He stood and gave me a tight smile despite the grave fog of pure grief weighing on his shoulders. "I've failed every single child I was given. Cai is right, the Gods are cruel, and they make fun of us in the cruellest of ways. They handed me what I wanted most just to show me how incapable I was to want what they would never give me in the first place."

"That is not true."

He shook his head. "If I have to bury her, son, bury me, too." It took him a moment to unravel from his own tangled emotion. "You said there was something I needed to know this morning at the court gathering. What is it?"

"We've managed to stop another shipment from Silas. Aura."

His frown deepened. "People?"

"Olympians."

The old man's eyes squeezed tightly shut. "Where from?"

"Slave traders. These are soldiers. Trained to obey their master's orders. They haven't eaten or drank anything at all, no matter what. Oryn has been trying all day to figure out if they are under craft, but none of us think so. They were conditioned. Tortured. They all have no voice either, tongues were cut out. Silas was probably going to use them against us."

"I'll go there at once."

I grabbed him before he left, and asked, "Where is she?"

"Went to visit the old man," he said, patting my shoulder and sliding past me.

Every afternoon, I'd faded to the heights of Drava, right by the cliff overlooking the Dravan Isle and Mahara's channel. Twelve grave stones lined the edge of it, all bearing one surname—Drava. And right before the very last one, the grave that was yet to turn a shade of a dark grey and stain with moss, stood the heir of Drava, mourning the man who had given up his life for hers. Silently, she let the western wind beat against her body as she stood before Alastair's grave and lowered down a crown of anemones, and then another beside it, over Sebastian's.

"Macaria sends word that they have found another heart," Nia croaked, reaching a hand to her throat, her voice still faint despite the work of the best Crafters and Medi-Healers who had helped her recover after Alaric had fed the rest of his life force to her.

I nodded. "Send Cai. The witches seem to have taken a liking to him."

She managed to wear a rare smile. "They think him fearsome. I've learned that they tend to be kinder to those they fear."

"Is he still—" *Being a dick.*

"Still. But aren't we all?" she asked, raising her gaze up to mine and offering me pity in the form of a sigh and a head shake. "You look terrible. At least shave. She is obsessed with that chin of yours. You will disappoint her if she doesn't see it first thing." When

I didn't say anything, she asked, "Any news?"

"None."

"It has been weeks since Silas got the Eldmoorian sceptre piece. It won't be long now till he goes for Vrammethen. She will resurface."

"Or something has happened to her," I said, needing to share the worry that had been clawing at my chest since I'd last heard of her. "And he can't advance with getting the last piece."

"My little sister has been born," Thora said, stepping out of a portal. "That is why they've waited."

Right behind her stood Elias. "Before you all strangle me with questions, yes, she is well and so is your brother. Well—"

"Well?" I asked a bit louder than I should.

He cleared his throat. "I'm a widower." We were all stunned a little before he continued, "As you can guess—"

Thora jumped up and down, quickly finishing the sentence for him, "Snow killed Fren. Very badly."

He nodded. "Silas had been...messing with your brother and Snow found out. The rest of it I believe you can figure out. Both are safe and well though."

Messing? Messing how?

"Should you be here considering that you will now be Silas's main point of concern?" Nia asked Elias who seemed rather content despite the events.

"They are quite busy at present," he said, dropping to sit on a stone. "Silas has prepared ships for sail to Vrammethen even though we have no idea how they plan on crossing the Solaryans, the channel guarded by the unblessed, or even your ships. He knows that he has you to get through, Kilian, and that is why he left the unblessed piece for last. He knows you will strike now."

"Portals, that is how they will cross," Visha said, slowly climbing up the stone steps that led to the small terrace cliff. "Sequences of portals considering the size of the military he will take with him knowing that he expects Kilian to be waiting for him there. That kind of craft would consume a considerable amount of magic. And that is without considering the fact that Vrammethen is the furthest from Eldmoor, making it twice as hard to draw that much power all the way there. I'm more than certain that all of his Crafters will be focusing on this journey. Which means that their city veils will be weak. And their hold on Snow and Malik even weaker."

Elias shot to his feet and then sat back down just as quickly.

Visha threw him an unimpressed look. "Elias. Glad to see that Silas has not made you food for his beasts."

The Venzor heir smirked. "Come on, V, I know you have been worried sick about me."

"Oh, yes," she boredly drawled, walking to my side. Not a single muscle in her face moved to indicate any form of emotion, but her shadows were sneaking out a little behind whatever veil she wore to mask them.

Nia stepped forward, fearing that we wouldn't be able to hear her. "Wouldn't that give us an open door to Tenebrose? It would be least protected."

"It could," Elias said. "Moregan is apparently on our side. She could help us inside while I keep the outside safe."

She gaped. "Moregan? As in general Moregan? Silas's Moregan?"

Elias shrugged at Nia's astonishment. "Snow is convincing in her ways." The man raised a brow at me. "Yes, Kilian? You've resisted long enough, ask away."

Ignoring Nia's and Thora's chuckles, I asked, "Have you seen her?"

"Only at the funeral, but I've heard plenty from servants and soldiers. They seem...taken with this heir thing."

"Taken?"

"Really pleased with Snow as a choice for the throne. And Snow seems to make them feel...confident, stronger."

"She is playing again," Cai's voice filled the pocket of air formed by the clouds around us. He came and dropped down beside Elias. "How is Silas reacting to the support?"

Elias shrugged again. "Too busy to pay attention to what lowly soldiers and maids say. I would think he doesn't care or hasn't noticed."

Her friend turned to me. "We could use that."

"How, Cai?" Nia asked. "Isjordians won't open the doors to Tenebrose just because they have started to like Snow."

He crossed his arms over his chest. "Divide and conquer has always been Her Majesty's grand scheme of things."

"You think she did this on purpose, don't you?" I asked, not bearing to look at the accusatory shadows gathering around him. "You think she wanted to waltz right inside Silas's torture once again."

He rolled his eyes to me. "And what makes you think so?"

"Your teenage hormonal attitude. Do you need to be held or something?"

Nia stepped between us despite us not making any move, threatening or not. But she knew none of us needed to even take a breath to hurt the other. "How about we go down for dinner before Alaric dispatches his hounds?"

"How about he stops growling at the mention of my wife?"

The general sneered at me. "Don't worry, there might not be a wife to growl about soon."

I faded right before him and grabbed the front of his jacket before fading again further away and crashing him against rock. "I might cut you some slack, Caiden. But only for the sake of her. Knowing that she loves this hollow corpse of a thing you are. But I am not her. And as you said, she is not here. So be very mindful of how you speak about the other half of me."

A hand pulled on my shoulder. "Let him go, Kilian," Eren said, trying to pull me from Caiden.

Pushing him off, I stepped back. "Aren't you a lucky fucker. Another soul cares for you."

Caiden threw his anger at someone else not even a second after being angry at me. He glared at Eren, and there was so much disdain where there should not be any. "There was no need for the interference, *my prince*. I can take good care of myself."

Hurt flushed across Eren's face, but he didn't say anything to him. He actually ignored his lover altogether. "What now? Only one sceptre piece left. What happens to my sister now?"

"I happen," I said.

"You have a plan?"
"I do. It's only a matter of time now."

13

White Knight takes D4

Snowlin

"We head to Vrammethen in two days," father announced, leaning back on his chair.

I stopped chewing. "We?" The *us* that he'd mentioned to Elias at the funeral made sense now. So, he was coming with us. Interesting.

He nodded. "I will join you on this last trip. As you know, their sceptre piece will complete the Octa Virga."

That felt like a lie somehow. Considering that Melanthe would be half as strong there and that they were probably already struggling to safely cross the Seer Sea, let alone Mahara's channel, his presence signalled something else. Either a trap for Kilian or for the unblessed rulers.

"There is something I need to do first—something you owe me."

He stopped eating. "*Owe* is a big word, child."

"Not as big as *debt*, father."

He studied me for a moment, probably measuring the chances that denying my request would cause him another loss he could not afford. "What is it that I...*owe* you?"

"The lives of those who helped you kill my friends. I'd like to take care of that before your war."

He huffed a chuckle. "Persistence used to be an admirable trait you had as a child."

"When the repercussions were lesser, you mean."

Lowering the fork and knife on the table rather quietly and too calmly for him, he leaned back. "I think you forget—"

"Who were they?" I spoke over him. "Who gave away where to find them? Who told you that you could find them in Eldmoor that day?" I needed the names of who was spying on my husband's every footstep.

"Let her," Melanthe said, cutting through her dinner all poised and unbothered. "We are in no need of those informants, Silas. Let's call it cutting loose ends." She chuckled under a delicate hand. "Your daughter might even learn from this. How important it is to cut loose ends."

My father's brows slowly rose at her words, and they exchanged a not-so-subtle look that all but screamed *'we can make her bait for the Night King'*.

"Fine," he said after some short thinking.

Kilian would know to stay away. He would. He would know not to approach me.

"It is set then," I said, throwing my napkin on the plate and standing. Before I left, I turned to Melanthe whose eyes almost glowed from satisfaction because of whatever she was planning. "Waiting for the right moment is a virtue I've not learned from my father."

She stopped chewing and narrowed her eyes on me when I picked up an apple from the table. The way her body recoiled, almost expecting me to hit her, satisfied me. What a good pet.

"Why pluck a heart that is not yet ripe." I looked over at my father and sang him the same song he had taunted me with, "How terrible it is to have something worth losing."

A child.

A kingdom.

A weapon.

A war.

A future.

"The list is getting long," I said, taking a bite of the sweet fruit and leaving towards the winter gardens—where my mother was still buried.

"He is meeting with the new Unblessed Princes," Moregan said from under the shadows of the winter shrubs. "People say that they are considering doing business with Silas again. Without their king's knowledge."

Of course, that was why he was coming with us. "Doubtful it would pass under his nose."

"You think the Unblessed King will accept it, too?"

"I am not certain. But the princes might be planning a coup. It wouldn't be the first time in Vrammethen history."

"It would be too much ruckus for nothing."

"Or just enough. They might not be joining my father's war, but they would be forfeiting any help they could offer us. Believe me, the losses are greater if the odds end as so." I cleaned my mother's head stone, picking away the moss and the odd vines that had climbed onto the grey marble. "How is Demir?"

"Sick from what I've heard. You were right about the blue gyre."

"Is it working for you?"

"Made me sick at the start, but the symptoms are lessening. I can finally sleep. My mind is not so hazy, and I remember most that has happened during the times I turn into the creature."

"I'll figure out what she's done to you, Skadi. We'll reverse it, or at least take away her control of you."

"I doubt it. I don't know what she's planted in me, but I know it has grown roots deep inside my chest through the years. My people always warned me about dark magic."

"For now, keep taking the blue gyre. Do not stop unless it is causing you harm."

"As you say."

"Skadi."

She hesitated in the evening silence. "Yes?"

"Make sure to free my brother-in-law without being seen. My husband will greatly need your assistance from inside since Elias will probably be sent somewhere far from here now that father does not have something over him. I can already see he doesn't trust Elias as much anymore."

"What about you? Are you going to wait for the Night King?"

"I've only planned it this far."

"Would Silas let you remain heir after? How will we communicate after your return?"

I bent down and traced a finger over my mother's name engraved on the stone. *Wish I didn't leave you here. Wish I'd brought you home again.* "Me and you might not be able to talk for much longer. But my husband will send my bonded, Memphis, to deliver messages to you when he needs word from inside my father's court. Help him take my father down."

I heard her take a step forward. "Snowlin—"

"Goodbye, Skadi."

Melanthe stood before me, holding a portal open. "You have an hour to end it. My magic will pull you back here. Attempt to play any games and you are well aware what will happen to the prince."

"Something you want from my trip? A bracelet, earrings, a spine?" I asked, backing inside the portal. "Self-respect, perhaps?"

Hot wind beat all around the cliff I stood on, facing Theros city. There was a barrier of light over the ivory and aquamarine castle. Melanthe's magic was almost useless before a white witch, but not mine.

I bolted, tearing through it and landing right in the middle of the castle grounds. Not even a second after, horns blared all around the city and guards poured from every nook and corner of the ivory walls.

As if they had been waiting.

So Magnus knew his son was deserving of death.

Yet...he sought to protect him from me.

"What did you give him in exchange for betraying his own father?" I had asked my father.

"A promise to have Solarya as his own after I raise Aurora," father had said.

Magnus's son had betrayed his oath, his family, his position, and an agreement between us for such a weak promise. One my father would definitely not honour. He'd sold his family for fake power. He'd sold mine, too.

A flash of horror shaded Solaryan faces as they aimed their weapons at me, unsure whether to attack or not. The skies began gurgling with a distant rumble, and soon, grey clouds dimmed day and the sun altogether to the point that none of those golden rays could be seen. Before the first arrow broke the air in my direction, hundreds of lightning bolts poured over the city, emitting a cold wave of white electricity that burnt and scorched and blinded. And then, amidst the chaos and noise, I bolted further away inside the open castle. And as I'd predicted, all of it was empty.

An arrow landed an inch from my foot when I took a step forward, the metallic tip that had embedded in the golden floor sizzled, melting deeper through tile and concrete.

"The sun does not give mercy to those who chose the dark. We will hurt you if you do not leave, Your Majesty," a tall man shouted, holding a hand up. Armed to his teeth, the son of the sun and the soldier of seas stood unphased by my presence.

"So you were warned, Caspian." I tilted my head to study the Crown Prince of Solarya. "Did your little brother confess his sins to your noble father?"

His hand lowered and he took a step forward. Brave. But he was brave by blood. "We understand your pain, Snow." Compassionate, too. Those born under the sun were healers, lovers, and forgivers—they were everything I was not even though we'd once gotten along.

Me and him had once been...acquainted. Friends, some might call it. Before he'd lost his older brother to the sea, he'd been like me. The second child, the spare, the one who hid at every ball under tables and observed. And we had observed together. He'd shared his sweets with me along with stories of the vast seas that I had used many nights to battle away nightmares.

"Then you will do the smart thing and move. I would not know mercy even if I saw it. I wouldn't know mercy even if I was capable of feeling it. Consider the fact that I am not levelling your shiny city down to embers as an act of respect." I took a step forward. "Move before I lose that, too."

He shook his head, and every bow was strung tight, ready to set arrows loose on me. "This will be considered an act of war."

"It was war the moment you brother caused death to someone I cared about."

"And he will be punished for it."

"Not the way he deserves to be punished."

"My father is a fair king."

"Believe me, Caspian, what I will do to him will be fair. Deny me my peace, and once I take my father down, it will be your kingdom I come for next. But it will not be just my kingdom and I that will come for you. The woman your brother killed with his betrayal was Queen Moriko's lover, so she will come to my side as well. And there will be no other war. Solarya will vanish as if it never even stood at all."

His hand lowered just a little. "That is a threat you should have not made."

"I do not threaten. My word is law. Which side will you fight beside? Mine, or your traitorous brother who will not hesitate to sell your secrets to my father. It was because of him he got your sceptre piece in the first place." I stepped forward. "Reasoning with you is not something I would have done considering the debt I am owed. But my husband respects your father, and I respect the help he has granted us during these times. I give you grace. What will you give me?"

Every heartbeat around us was loud, almost too loud, except his and mine. His bow lowered, and despite the plea in his ocean eyes, he nodded. "You will kill him no matter what, won't you?"

"He is already dead, Caspian. Now you decide your fate and of those you will soon rule over."

"I do not wish for you to be my foe, Snow. Never have, not even once, not even after finding out about your magic. But mostly, I will not deny you relief for the pain my brother has caused. As someone who has seen every sort of pain enough to recognise it, I can see it in you. My power is to heal, no questions asked." He moved a step to the side, and all of his men lowered their weapons and retreated. "End of this corridor, fourth door to the left."

I slid past him, with a heavier heart in my chest somehow.

"For your friend," he called behind me. "I am sorry."

A breath was stolen out of my chest at that moment, and I swallowed the bitter pain down. "Send word to my husband that in two days we will be heading to Breshall for the last sceptre piece. Let him know that Silas will join us as he plans to meet with the new Vrammetheni Princes in secret while we are there. I suspect he will do so after I retrieve the sceptre first."

"We have not spoken to your husband since you were taken. Father did not permit it after he found out what Otis had done."

"You have my permission to contact him. It is important you do so. We cannot afford for my father to strike another deal with them and lose the support of the unblessed."

He nodded and slowly began retreating away, signalling his soldiers to turn around when I entered the castle.

My whistles were the only sound around the massive halls as I searched for my prey. "Where are they hiding you?" I crooned, skipping along the massive library room. I halted and turned my ear towards the farthest end of the shelves, listening and not taking a single breath until I heard the slow hum of a heartbeat disturbing the flow of electricity in the air. The way it dared beat with such force while hers...hers had stopped. "There, there."

I pushed on the light oak wooden book shelf and the secret door revealed another room. My smile stretched from ear to ear when I saw the little present already wrapped up for me in white and gold. "You must be a fan of hide and seek. It is my favourite game."

He shot to his feet and looked around the empty room as though the lingering spirits around us could be any help for what I was about to do to him.

He backed further away from me. "War will ensue."

"How terrifying. I'm shaking." I took a step forward, and he took one away from me. "First, I will tear your mouth from corner to corner and then I will sew it up with your own intestines since you cannot hold from spilling your guts to just anyone. Hm, how about that?" Unsheathing my dagger, I took another step towards him. "I will do it so prettily. I'm a knitter, you see."

"Do you not want to know why I did it?"

I clicked my tongue. "No. Not really."

The second I bolted on top of the Highwall, my chest expanded with both fear and far longing. The brush of warm air was too thick, too familiar, too reminiscent of what I wanted to forget.

Soldiers gathered around me in no time, and it took them a moment of surprise before they all fell to their knees.

Larg ran towards me and I backed away until he stopped moving.

"My queen," he called hoarsely, reaching a shaking hand to his chest and bowing to me. "You've returned."

"Not for long."

All hope slipped from his face. "How did you—"

There was not much time, and I was too afraid Kilian might come near enough to be caught in whatever trick Melanthe had planned. "I need you to bring someone to me. Quietly."

"Who?"

"And her? What did you promise her?"

"She asked for the Night King's affections, but I could not grant that considering his taste in women. However, I did offer to take you out of his life, and that seemed to please her enough."

My lips curled up. "Nesrin. Bring me Nesrin." I turned to the other soldiers. "Don't let your king come anywhere near me. It is an order."

14

Black Pawn to C5

Kilian

MOREGAN WILL BE OUR help inside. She has agreed to your plan. Everything is set. That was all that was written on the note that Elias had sent us.

We only had a few days to arrange how to get both Snow and Mal out at the same time, and now we actually had help from inside the Isjordian walls as well. The only thing missing was the correct window of events.

The sudden shift of wind was very gentle, almost unnoticeable, but it made everyone sitting around the meeting table go very still. Every head turned towards the massive windows framing Amaris that was slowly being engulfed by a wave of dark grey clouds rolling at a terrifying speed over the city skies. Every hair on my body rose when the air charged with electricity, when the earthy scent of autumn turned soft and flowery.

"Snow." The moment her name was out of my mouth, I faded by the *alaar* and ran the distance over river Nyx towards the Highwall.

And there she was, perched on the roof of the wall, swinging her feet back and forth while she fed the cloud of crows hovering around her pieces of...flesh. An overwhelming shade had blanketed my senses at what I saw. They urged me to move, to have her back in my arms, to hold her, to smell her, to keep her safe. Six months. She'd been gone for six months that had felt like six lifetimes.

Longing had blinded me to the point that I'd missed the blood stains on her face and hands and the stone-cold look she had pointed to the ground while she cut chunks of meat to throw in the air at the death bearers.

I couldn't see her emotion, but I'd learn to read it in her features.

And what I saw terrified me.

She stood, the chains tied to her wrists and neck dangling as she wiped her blood-stained hands on her coat and picked up something from the ground next to her.

Fuck.

She fisted the long brown hair of the severed head, lifting it up before nailing it on a pyre. Nesrin's features were pulled aghast, as if she had met the God of Death himself right before dying. Or perhaps something worse than *Death* himself.

Dozens of my men faded right before me, swords drawn in my direction. "Stay back, my king. It was an order from the queen."

Shadows began crawling around my limbs, a poor attempt to hold me still.

"What makes one wish for death so badly as to lie to me?" I asked, and the darkness slipped out of me, breaking all their shadows apart.

I'd only taken a step forward when hands wrapped around my arm, pulling me back. "It's a trap. They are right. She is right," Eren said even though I could tell from the way he breathed and the dark clouds of despair around him that he wanted to run to her, too. "Elias reported that Silas still has control over her. Think, Kilian. Who is the one other person who can stop my father? Who is the one other person this realm fears more than him? Who is one person who can still ruin his plans? This is a trap. Don't. Let's just see what she will do."

Snow stood there for a while, staring at Nesrin's head before grinning to herself, turning round and disappearing into a portal.

Gone.

Like that.

She was gone.

Again.

I faded Eren and I at the roof of Highwall several moments after she'd left. Soldiers had gathered around Nesrin's head perched on the spear. But they were not looking at her.

When the crowd parted, I realised it was something else that had caught their attention.

She was Silas's spy. The words were written on the grey stone floor in blood—Nesrin's blood.

A portal cracked open behind me, and we all turned to Visha and Oryn slipping from it. "We have news from Solarya," she said. "Snow paid a visit and killed Prince Otis earlier today. Caspian Vayr sends word from her. She's told him that Silas is visiting Vrammethen himself in two days to meet with the princes while they retrieve the last sceptre piece. She doubts an agreement between them is happening without their king's approval or knowledge."

Two days. We finally knew. "Our last window."

"If it even is a window at all," Eren said, and then turned to Visha. "Silas is going with them? Are you certain?"

"Yes."

Eren's brows rose. "My father is leaving Isjord at this time?"

"He must be scared of an alliance against him or desperate for the metal," Oryn argued. "Could bet the new princes are giving him a hard time considering they already have an agreement with you, my king. If they have agreed to meet him, it would mean he has found something else to offer them. Considering no one wishes to best the Night King, it must be something much worse than offering them beasts."

No matter how much we had tried to keep Nia away, she'd found a way to the Highwall. For the past hour, she had not said a single word to anyone, only stared at her sister's severed head still bleeding out on the wooden pike. Something worse than betrayal had filled the colour of her air. Something more painful. It was enough to wilt her hope.

While the rest of us had not been entirely too shocked to have witnessed the murder, we had yet to process the message painted with Nesrin's blood.

She was Silas's spy.

"She's died a traitor's death," Larg sighed, shaking his head. "Stregor's child was a traitor. Word will spread fast," he added. "Let's hope it does because she had her followers, and they might not take what your wife has done very lightly. To think they might be aiding Silas, too, concerns me. Our queen might have wanted this to be known widely."

"I don't think that was my sister's main aim," Eren said, and we all turned to Nia.

"Considering what she's done," Cai spat. "She died an easy death. Did her a favour." He laughed bitterly. "And believe me when I say, her favours are spare. She used this to warn us about Vrammethen and the Adriatian spies working for Silas knowing we might be planning something and details about it would have been leaked, otherwise your councillor would have lived to feel and taste her death."

Thora hummed from the corner of the rooftop where she had sat, petting a crow's feathers. "They are beautiful," she said, still intently observing the bird. "Do you know why they are called soul thieves in the old Eldmoorian folklore?"

Every single soldier had stopped along with us to hear the little sister's words.

She let the bird go and stood. "They take shiny things and hide them. Souls shine more than diamonds however tarnished they are because souls are precious. A pretty tale, isn't it?" she asked, smiling. "Ah, it was Snow who told me that story." Her emerald eyes hardened when they landed on Nesrin's head. "It is a shame that there will be no soul to send out to heaven or hell. The birds picked the shiny thing apart and stole it away along with her flesh. I suppose the bitter end of it all is the fact that a second chance at life will not be granted to a soul who prayed so hard to be given one."

I could swear every man and woman in that terrace flinched.

Thora flashed everyone a girly grin. And it was the most charming and disarming gesture, a power not many could summon. She knew how to use it well to her advantage. To deceive others into thinking of her as weak and incapable and young. A perfect trap. "I might have an idea," she said, reaching Nia's side and leaning her head on her shoulder, fluttering her lashes at her friend.

Nia's gaze softened as she linked an arm around the younger sister's waist and rested her cheek on her head. "That is the most frightening thing you might have ever said."

Part II
Bird's Opening

15

White Knight to E2

Snowlin

I spat blood on the green marble floor of the underground temple that was now cluttered with seared, bloody flesh and chunks of alabaster. Big flakes of the white stone had frayed from the tall sculptures of the unblessed false deities that had taken a hit during our fight with perhaps the ugliest beasts I'd seen. *Harhounds*—that is what Demir had called them. A human creation. A man-made contortion of a wolf and a deer. The unblessed did not use magic. And their human attempts at mimicking it had created something fouler than magic ever could. How odious did the human mind become when power stood between them and the ruination of others.

A herd of *Harhounds* laid in pieces alongside the giant who had guarded the last sceptre piece. It had been fast even though I'd prayed hard we'd struggle and delay them from putting the sceptre together. But the veil had been weak, and the monsters even more so.

Demir stared around rather disappointed for a different reason than mine. He bent down to grab the sceptre piece that had been lodged inside the giant creature's rib cage. "A troll," he sneered, struggling to catch his breath, the wounds on his face healing a little slower than usual. "They had put a fucking troll to guard a piece of her prison."

"You have lived so long amongst us that you have forgotten your kind pays no mind to the divine." Of course that they had not taken caution in its protection. But taking in consideration that craft was the weakest in this land, and that we'd crossed the veil without issue, this was another level of recklessness and sloppiness even for the unblessed.

He glanced at me and then tightened his grip on the sceptre.

Though he didn't say anything else, I knew I'd gotten to his empty green head. I knew how to break someone's spirit. I knew what it took to weaken someone. And as soon as Aurora was raised, he'd become the weakest of them all.

Even though he couldn't see my grin, a growl slipped between his clenched teeth as if he could smell my excitement.

"*Hur,*" I whispered, words barely a breath of air as they left my lips. "*Ma'hazur kahaz.*"

The sceptre piece lit up in his hand and he jerked back, dropping it. It flashed for a few more moments, emitting a chill in the air and causing a shiver in the already weak barrier that held back my magic.

Whatever divine call poured out of it affected him, too, because his skin flashed green and filled with scales while his breathing turned hoarse and heavy. Pure panic seeped into those soulless eyes when he began coughing up blood.

Heavenly magic was bane to dark magic, it helped it surface from every corner it hid, and the blue gyre in his bloodstream was neutralising it.

It was science. As simple as that.

I bent down and picked the silver rod, twirling it between my fingers before offering it to him again. "Be gentle. I want to be the one to put that first bruise on her."

Father looked rather unimpressed after returning from his visit with the Unblessed Princes. He'd been unimpressed with his best soldier, too, when he'd retreated to the ships after he couldn't stop coughing up blood. Poor, poor Demir. He was having a pretty rough day today.

The humidity was thick and left a harsh taste of dust on my tongue as we left the Breshall castle, heading back to the bay where the ships had docked. The stench of craft had variegated in the muddy air, and it was making me nauseous.

Four Crafters were circling me while Melanthe led ahead, and all four were struggling to walk and draw enough magic to keep me chained at the same time.

The wind had gotten colder compared to when we'd arrived, and I was certain it was not because of me or my father. It was nothing spiritual either. Not a warning. Not one from Gods at least. It seemed like the rest of the entourage had also noticed the change as they all slowed their march, attentively surveying our surroundings. It wasn't until howls set off in the distance, making the beasts that were accompanying us turn agitated. And that seemed to have sent the archers mounting their bows while the rest of the soldiers slid their cold white steels out of their sheaths. The slavering green beasts that prowled around us sniffed the air and growled at the faint touch of fog encapsulating the phantom unblessed city that had gone quiet and empty all of a sudden.

The two floor grey houses around us looked like a graveyard, no light, no movement, no sounds, no life at all.

I sucked in a breath, listening to the faint sounds hovering above us, hidden among the fog—too loud to be a flock of birds and too quiet to be thunder.

The way everyone's pulse picked up a steady beat of fear made me giggle a little, and Melanthe turned a scathing look on me. "Quiet."

Her minions circled me, the hold on my magic growing heavier while they grew fainter.

"Like a mouse," I whispered back, watching one of the Crafters starting to sway on her feet.

A shiver drew up my spine when the electricity in the air suddenly packed with a thicket of icy magic—familiar magic.

Fuck.

"Finally, here you are," a soft voice called from the terrace of a two-story building to our right, and every muscle in my body stiffened.

Everyone turned on a similar beat to aim every weapon in my little sister's direction who was hovering at the ledge, swinging her feet back and forth, looking almost bored.

Hells.

What in the hells was she doing here?

What the hells was she thinking?

Fear spiked to my throat while my mind dug out every possible scenario on how this could go very wrong—how she could become my father's plaything, too.

I glanced at the man who stood stupefied beside me, his eyes stripped entirely from any thought while a petrified expression began swelling up in his features until he held a breath.

Thora jumped from the terrace, her landing soft and controlled from the gust of wind circling her. "Papa," she said, dusting her black leather jacket and straightening the rose-coloured bow holding her hair back in a ponytail. "You look well. Unfortunately."

My fists gathered tight, and every part of me prepared to jump between her and the rest. The thought beat relentlessly in my head like a panicked pulse, but no one made a single move, waiting for my father who seemed to have turned into a human statue.

"It cannot be," was all he managed to utter.

"Can be," my sister said, disdain slipping over her mask of calm. "Thanks to your brother and sister."

Everyone looked confused and unsure whether to lower their weapons or jump ahead and attack. The Crafters looked over at Melanthe, waiting for the command that would have them choose between containing me or protecting their king.

Silas glanced at me before turning to my sister. "What are you talking about?"

She tilted her head to the side, an action all too familiar. "Uncle took us that night, hid us in Whitebridge with aunt Eleonor's help, and planned to use us to usurp the throne right under your nose."

My father staggered a step back. "Us?"

My sister smiled all sugar and bane, luring my father right where she wanted to lure him into—distraction. "Eren is alive, too. Healthy. Breathing—" She raised a hand, and flakes of snow danced in the air at her command. "Magical like me and Snow. Now, if the family reunion is quite finished, I need you to hand me my sister."

Father took a moment to process her words, her magic, and her entire presence, turning to look at me as if he had just scored the best strike of luck before offering Thora, "Or you can join me and your sister."

Young she was, yes. Moldable and formidable, too. But she was no longer a child—no longer *his* child.

There was a small beat of silence while my sister blinked at him. "Your humour is unscathed from old age and insanity, papa. How impressive."

"Order your men, Silas," Melanthe seethed, grabbing onto his arm. "This is an attack."

That caught Thora's attention. "Stepmother, how is little sister?" She took a few small, cautious steps forward and gave her a smile. Her emerald eyes flashed with something colder than ice despite the soft expression she wore. "Can't wait to get my hands on the little thing."

Melanthe shot a panicked look at my father before her magic thickened, fortifying the barrier between us and Thora despite the restricted nature of craft in this part of the realm. As if knowing things were about to go absolutely wrong, the witch's attention snapped to me. And she sent me an unspoken threat.

"They sent you to get her?" father asked, doubtful as he was entertained.

Thora straightened her thick fringe with a finger. "I might not be the strongest out of them all, but I surely am a sweet treat to the eye. Alaric keeps saying so. But the man does adore me. Am I a treat, papa?"

That was when I noticed a figure, and then two, hiding between the fog and behind the thin violet barrier shielding my sister. The Skye warriors' silver falcon masks glistened somewhere in the distance behind Thora, silently waiting.

She was not alone.

And if she was here...that meant Kilian had gone to get Mal.

Father narrowed his eyes on her for a moment before signalling his head.

Two beasts leaped in the air, breaking through Melanthe's barrier and landing right before my sister.

It happened almost too quickly. She moved too quickly.

Where two huge bodies once stood remained only floating ashes.

Something glistened in Thora's hold, a simple silver dagger with a small emerald etched to it.

They had done it.

They'd created more *anima accissor* weapons.

Thora took another step forward, wiping the gleaming dagger to her sleeve. "Remember that game you used to play with me?"

"What game?" our father asked, signalling his soldiers to circle her.

The tension turned thick when my sister sang the rhymes that I used to chase her around to, "One, don't run little one. Two, mind your step when you take—" She lifted three fingers up. "A turn at—three."

I took off in a flash before the guards could grasp my intentions, before the chains holding me prisoner tightened and weighed me down.

Something crashed against Melanthe's barrier, tearing a slash through it for me to pass. I felt the tug of magic holding me back, but I forced myself forward despite the blinding pain. And then...out of thin air, a hooded figure faded mid-air, holding a silver sword I knew all too well. The blade bearing my name hit the first phantom chain wrapped around my wrist and then the second one. They twisted the handle, angling the blade to cut through the last tether holding me prisoner to Melanthe. The soul killer slashed through the limbs of dark craft binding me, and hells were about to break loose when I felt the gates of my magic rumble from the force of power surging and pouring to the surface—drowning all of my senses.

I breathed too much air and with too much force. My heart beat too fast and my skin burned too hot. The ground below blanketed in ice, the skies screamed with thunder, and the wind howled with warning when I rose to my feet, breathing control down the seal while violent power coated my sight.

The gust of wind blew back the veil of fog to reveal Macaria and Oryn standing tall at the edge of a building, chanting a string of words that made the blood in my veins hiss and my magic submit to my command.

The skies sung not only from magic speeding out of me but from the collapse of wind against the wings of my soldiers descending the grounds one after the other. Volantians landed all around us along with Tristin, and the Skye soldiers followed suit.

The hooded figure threw my sword at me. And swinging the blade until it glowed with electricity, I turned to my father whose shadows thickened from the blistering light above. My smile was easy. "I've waited for this for so long."

"Kill them all!" he barked, and hundreds of beasts, soldiers, and Crafters poured from the buildings around us—the trap he'd set for whoever he'd expected to come for me.

Soldiers and beasts alike launched towards us. But before the next breath was taken, I bolted right in the midst of them and blasted all what had remained caged inside me for months long. The grounds shook and the screams were too short because lightning crawled all around me, burning skin and melting bone.

Skye warriors rained down on the ground in the hundreds, armed with soul killers.

Melanthe seethed, making her way towards me, her body glowing red. Hundreds of chains coated in thick glowing craft rose from behind her, aiming at me. Only to end up crashing against a thin layer of transparent violet.

The witch raised her pale stare to the roof where Macaria stood, and shouted, "You have always been one to follow and never lead, Macaria. Such talent! Such shame! To die a follower's death when you could have lived a victor's life. This is my last offer to you. Join us as our sisters have and I will grant you the life you were denied."

The old witch echoed back, "I will live, girl. I will live to burn you myself for what you have done."

A growl escaped from Melanthe's tight mouth, and then waves of her magic began knocking back Tristin's soldiers. "I will never burn."

"I can change your mind," I said, advancing towards her. Lighting hit the protective veil around her over and over, power crashing against power. And when it began thinning and waning, a portal opened behind them.

"We will fight. But it won't be today," she said.

Father retreated first, and then she followed, leaving a small army of beasts growling in our direction. They had what they wanted, and father was not willing to put up a fight—not when he was planning a war.

Cowards.

The Skye warriors and Tristin managed to get rid of the last beasts remaining while I tried to gather and rein in control of my powers that had barely seen light in the past six months.

Oryn walked to me, holding an unconscious Macaria in his arms. "My queen, do you need help?"

I shook my head and pointed to the violet witch. "What about her?"

The old man looked down at the woman. "She had to summon a call from the

Otherworld to break Melanthe's and her sister's veils otherwise we would have never been able to get to you. She will be just fine in a couple of days. This one is a strong one."

Small arms wrapped around me tightly all of a sudden, engulfing me with soft heat and notes of honeysuckle perfume—she still smelled like the day she was born. My sister shook in my hold like years ago when they had put her writhing small body in my arms to hold. But this time...she didn't make a sound or breathe at all.

Her skin was cold when I rested my lips on her cheek. My brave sister. "Rora," I called after she would not let me see her. "My little Rora."

She pulled back slowly, her face all hard and grown all of the sudden, no longer the barely adult I'd left behind months ago. "I did well, didn't I?"

"You did so well. So, so well. But you're grounded. So grounded. You're never to do that again," I whispered harshly, holding her tightly to me again. It was not possible to breathe her in as much as I wanted to—to hold her as tightly as I wanted to. "You hear me, never. I can't...I can't lose you, too."

"It is a bit too early to mourn my loss," a hoarse, small voice called from behind me.

And I froze. Too afraid to turn. Too afraid that I might have imagined this day from the start of it. Too afraid that somewhere along the scheming, the grief, the loss, and the small wins I had lost the last bit of sanity I'd clung to.

When a hand rested on my shoulder and pulled me to turn around, I squeezed my eyes shut to shield me from the breaking reality crashing against my fantasy.

I would not allow it.

I would hold onto my mind a little bit longer.

I would not be tempted to lose it because I missed her so fiercely.

I would not—

"Snow," she called again. "Snowlin Skygard, you insane idiot, open your eyes."

A cry left my throat before any words could form to ward off this tempting spirit before it claimed whatever was left of my mind.

She hugged me. And it felt too real. So real.

"I hold no promise but this one I give you," she spoke in my ear words I had once before spoken to her years ago when she and I had been young and afraid. "You will be safe and you will be loved. That's what you told me. But I'm not feeling very loved right now."

It was only then I allowed tears to fall. "How? Please...how?"

"Alastair, it was grandpa," was all she said. She pulled back, taking my wrist in her hands and pulling apart the cuffs still rubbing against my sore skin. And then she did the other. She did them all. Until the only reminder of my time in Isjord was left around my neck. Gently, as if she could even hurt me anymore, she pulled the cuff apart, staring at the red mark it had left there. "Did you show them hell?"

I smiled. "That is a pretty offensive question, Helenia."

16

Black Bishop to D7

Malik

SOMETHING WAS HAPPENING OUTSIDE the prison quarters, but I could not figure out exactly what. Soldiers had been mumbling about the king's trip to Vrammethen for days now, and considering what Snow had told me the last time she'd come down here, the eighth sceptre piece was there. Silas had succeeded. He had collected all of Octa Virga. And in no time, he would be joining it as one.

She still hadn't told me what she'd done in exchange for the healer who had mended my eye. But from the fearful glances of soldiers and murmurs of servants, I assumed it had not been an exchange at all—Silas had been forced to comply with her demands.

The main entrance gates groaned open, letting a bit of corridor light enter my gloomy residence. It was not meal hours and soldiers were usually not brave enough to come down here unless they were forced to check that I had not somehow broken through the five-inch-thick metallic bars. Isjordians really knew how to stroke one's ego.

Someone flashed a torch right between the metallic bars of my home, and my eyeballs almost lit on fire from the sudden brightness.

That someone scoffed. "You look like shit."

That was a new voice. I don't know who was frowning more at whom, but Elias's blonde brows had reached a new low.

"Come to finally pay me a visit?" I asked, sitting up from my royal bed made of hay to greet my unusual visitor. The new position made the figure hiding behind him visible, and I sneered. "What's the bitch doing here?"

Melanthe popped her head over Elias's shoulder, her expression rather flaccid compared to the usual stamped pride and perfumed grace. "My aunt might be a horrible person, but does she really merit that noun?"

I grinned at the sound of her voice. "Let's swap places, Visha, maybe you will know after."

She rolled her eyes and flicked a hand right in front of the metallic bars, unlocking the door. "Let's hurry now. My disguise won't last long."

"How did you manage that?"

The witch itched her cheek. "Paid Melanthe's sister a visit in Venzor before we came here."

"Come on, Silas could be back any moment now," Elias urged, lifting a cloth bag over my head.

I pushed him off. "Is that necessary?"

The bastard grinned and slid it over my head.

Elias and Visha led us through the snow-thick winter gardens and towards the back castle walls that were being rebuilt. No one stopped us. There was no one to stop us at all. "Where are all the soldiers?"

"V gave them orders to clear the area so the transport of our most prized prisoner could go unnoticed from anyone planning to break you free. And there is an attack in the city, so Moregan took most of the guard with her. The others have received word of an ambush on Silas in Vrammethen and are searching and clearing the city parameters before he returns."

"Who has gone to Snow if you are here?"

"Thora and Oryn."

That made me halt on the spot. "The fuck?"

Visha tugged on my chains, urging me to continue. "I see you have not had a chance to exercise much of your vocabulary these days."

"Where is my brother? How did he allow her to go where all the big wolves are? They have the beast and Melanthe, Visha. Fuck, Silas has gone with them, too. This is ridiculous."

"Lower your voice," Elias murmured, looking around the rather empty walls.

She glanced under her lashes at Elias. "The king is here."

I frowned. "What king?" There was a chilling silence between Visha and Elias. "Kilian is here?" No, no, this was what Silas wanted.

The witch nodded as we climbed the spiral stairs leading to the top of the walls and into the blistering, beating wind of the northern kingdom. "He planned it this way on purpose. Silas was going to use Vrammethen to get to Kilian. He'd set dark magic traps everywhere in the area of the unblessed continent for your brother, knowing he would be set on at least saving one of you. Moregan, the general, has taken our side and pointed us exactly where these traps were in Isjord, so we were able to work around them. Vrammethen was another matter, but nothing that would affect Thora since she is an elemental and doesn't rely on dark magic like your brother."

A reply was stuck in my throat when my eyes finally adjusted to the landscape ahead. It was almost frightening how snow had covered all that laid ahead, like it wanted to sink this miserable city under it.

A small, cloaked figure spun around, noticing our presence. The young girl beamed and ran the distance to me, jumping in my arms.

I chuckled. "Missed me, young Pen?"

She wiped a few tears with the back of her glove. "You can say so."

"They got you on the big girl duties now?" Snow would have had a fit by now.

She nodded excitedly. "I've been training loads. Visha and I can break Melanthe's magic now. It's how we got inside the veil. Uhm, it was mostly Visha, but I did help."

"You can tell him later, Penelope. Let's go," Visha ordered, undoing my chains and finally freeing my limbs from the heavy metal. Magic surged through my bones like a hit of the most potent drug. And with that tide, so arose the buried voices of the dead that had not stopped whispering in my ears since I'd woken my unholy blessing. I'd almost enjoyed my time down there. The quiet. The lack of human noise. Almost.

Isjordian soldiers began marching in our direction, and Elias put a hand on my arm to stop me from drawing magic. "V has it under control. They are under her influence. No need to hurt them."

And with death so came emotion. The cloud of shadows surrounding Elias was very confusing. "Are you regretting this? Betraying your kingdom?"

"No," he said, "But I am regretting abandoning them under Silas's rule."

Horns blared all-round the city, louder inside the castle gates as Silas along with his most subservient soldiers marched inside. Their strides were long and angry, all of their movement reflected what they felt. Unbridled anger. Such dark anger. Anger that suddenly morphed and crawled right inside their owners to turn into surprise and almost fear.

Their squadron halted and unsheathed magic and metal in the direction of the castle doors—in the direction of...my brother. Every shadow in the vicinity shivered for a moment before going pin still, solemn and darker—a silent army that stood beside my brother.

What was he doing? Had the idiot gone insane at his delicate age?

Nothing. My brother was nothing and everything, a cloud of packed thunder and a calm sea at the same time as he marched nonchalantly towards Silas.

The Winter King blasted with laughter, signalling his witch. "He has come to the slaughterhouse with his own two feet."

Kil didn't stop, and the closer he got, the more I could see the black shadows leaking from his eyes. What looked like my brother was not my brother.

"I've come to take," Kil said, and everything suddenly burned colder—fiercer than snow, like frost fire. "For every day you have kept my wife prisoner here, I will take something from you, Silas Krigborn."

Silas sneered, suddenly feeling alarmed. "You speak so loud for someone who is right where I've meant to bring you."

Red, glowing chains rose from the snowy ground in Kil's direction, only to go limp right about as they touched his body. Melanthe's magic had not stuck to him.

And I was just as confused as her considering that the whole land we stood on was a shrine for her power.

My brother did not stop. "I am exactly where I am meant to be. You're a man of words, Silas, but I am a man of my word," he said before his body dissolved in the darkest cloud of mist that rose into a vortex and began absolving whatever stood in its reach. It claimed life from everything it touched, even air, leaving only blanched ash and death behind.

Melanthe sent a blast of her magic that crashed against my brother almost as if she had thrown a snowball at him instead. And then she tried again. And failed again. Nothing...nothing would stop my brother from advancing closer and closer to them.

"Melanthe!" Silas bellowed when Kil's magic got closer and closer.

The witch's eyes had gone wide, her magic going right through my brother over and over without hurting or binding him. "I don't understand."

Four more Crafter's portalled close by and my brother's body dissolved in the wind. Leaving them all in a cautious and still silence. Breathing hard and afraid.

"Shall we make haste now?" my brother called from behind us. "I'm eager to see my wife. I rather miss her."

We all spun at the deep command of his voice. He stood leaning against the walls, arms crossed over his chest as if he had been there the whole time.

"How did you do that?" What had attacked Silas and his witch had been only a shadow of his. One that could use magic like him.

He picked some lint from his sleeve. "Let's say that certain things bring certain qualities in me."

"Cockiness?"

The bastard had a crooked grin on his face when he pushed from the wall and opened his arms to greet me like he often had done when we were younger. "Forgive me, brother," he said. "I tried. I tried not to let him take Driada."

"Not your fault that she wanted death more than us, Kil." I clasped his shoulder. "And Snow?"

"She is with Thora."

I nodded, and we all stepped through the portal that Visha and Pen had drawn open. It was only when we had fully stepped through to the other side that blood curdling screams filled the dark, cold air of Tenebrose.

I turned to my brother as the portal began to disappear along with the sounds of pain and death. "What did you do, Kil?"

My brother's eyes were veiled black. "Nothing I regret."

I was going to ask him something. I swear I was. Had my attention not caught on the flash of dark hair held back by those stupid pink bows and big fucking emerald eyes that were far too innocent looking. Thora was breathing hard, and her gaze never left mine as she slowly crossed Visha's chambers and made her way to us.

"Snow?" my brother asked, stopping her.

She smiled at him. "With Alaric and Nia upstairs."

"Well done." He patted her cheek and rushed outside, leaving the two of us alone.

"Your hair has grown back," I said when no one spoke and no one moved.

She touched the end of her hair absently but said nothing.

"Don't I get some sort of greeting for returning alive?"

She extended a hand forward, and my head dropped back from laughter. But I took her hand and shook it. "I was thinking of something more like this," I said, pulling her to me and wrapping my arms around her small frame. "Little bird."

Her hands rested on my back, hesitantly at first. "Malik," she whispered onto my chest, holding me tighter.

When she melted entirely against me, I pressed my face to the top of her head and breathed her in. I inhaled that maddening scent of honey and peach that was so damn sweet—way too sweet. I hated sweetness. I hated every cursed sweet flavour and smell.

"Did he hurt you," she asked quietly, her head still buried in my chest. "Elias said that—"

"No."

She finally lifted her head from where she had hid and raised a hand to the scars on my left eye. The more she stared at me, the more the frown she wore deepened.

"Don't go falling in love with me, little bird."

Pulling away, she sneered at me. "Idiot—"

I put a hand over her mouth to shut her up and locked my arm tightly around her neck until she was wiggling around like a goose in a net.

"Let me go! Malik!"

"Mal," I said in her ear, and she sucked in a sharp breath. "Mal, not Malik. Call me Mal. You know ten ways to end me in one second, so you should probably start calling me that." Twirling her around, I pinched her chin between my fingers. "How about now you tell me how you put your little back side in serious danger."

"My little back side is fine."

"It better be."

Her eyelids faltered and she evaded my gaze, lifting something between us. "Aunt Ada wanted me to give you this. I helped her write it sometime after you and Snow were taken." She swallowed, finally looking up at me again. "I'm sorry."

I brushed my thumb under her eye, wiping away the warm teardrop pooling under her dark lashes. "She was sick, Thora. It would have happened eventually."

"Wouldn't you have wanted to be here for her?"

"It happened for the best that I wasn't."

Even through her dark fringe I could tell her brows were bunching with confusion. "Malik, you can't say that," she whispered, trying to not let her voice tremble.

"There are a few deaths that I never wish to feel, bird," I said, raising my fingers to her brow to push away the short hair covering them. "Hers was one of them." The way my truths slipped away like butter before her made me want to stay as far away from her as possible. "My last memory of her would have remained the most prominent one since death is the most we feel as humans—all emotions at once and yet nothing at all."

Her full, rosy lips parted open. "At...at lake Asterin...with Kilian, you said you felt him die," she breathed, her emerald eyes pacing between mine, looking for denial more than an answer.

I sighed, realising just how much I had told her—how much I'd confided in her. "You should have at least brought me a bottle of liquor as a warm welcome if you were going to pester poor me with questions you already know the answers to."

"Is that what you are going to do? Drink it away?"

"No one says anything when you just *think* your troubles away like it is all supposed to be sunshine and rainbows if you just forget it ever rained."

My ears buzzed at the silence that followed.

She winced a little, stepping back and away from me. Though I could finally breathe without being suffocated in sweetness, the air tasted too stale now in my lungs. "You're right, I am sorry."

No.

No, that was not what I meant to say. It all came out wrong.

What I meant to say was that I envied her. That I was so envious of her, I envied how she could forget because I couldn't. I envied how she was able to paint blue over grey, how she still tried even if her tears ruined the canvas. I envied how she could be afraid of what scared her because I could not. I envied her smiles because I still kept feigning mine and they looked nothing as bright or warm or true as hers even though she lied, too—she lied so much. I envied that she was this small thing that dared to feel so much though she'd never been shown how to, but I was emotion itself and yet I didn't feel a bit. Sometimes not at all.

I grabbed her wrist as she was about to turn and leave, the apology stuck at the tip of my tongue—the one apology I'd promised to never make when I found a cure for my issues. The same apology that no one in all my years had ever tempted me to make. "You could join me. I'll come to your room like before. You know I like your sofa more than my bed."

Slowly, she peeled my fingers away from her skin. I forgot too often how she hated to be touched. And I tried too often to forget just how much I wanted to touch her. "I've been staying in Olympia for some time now," she said, rubbing where I'd held her. "And I will not sit and watch, let alone participate in ruining someone I care for."

17

White Pawn to B3

Snowlin

Oryn had portalled us to Olympia, on top of the tower where I had stood so many times. And my chest filled with pain and relief all at once when I took in the mountains surrounding us, the city bursting with life, the skies drenched in sunlight, and the soft wind that was no longer sharp against my skin, but a soft kiss.

Home, I was home. A bright home.

A hand on my shoulder brought me out of my mourning and right into another sort of grief. Cai towered over me for a moment, studying the whole of me. The brown of his irises had been swallowed by the black of his pupils, almost rendering his bright eyes lifeless. "You should have never made that promise if you were going to break it this many times."

"Cai, I–"

"Don't say you're sorry," he snapped. After a few more silent moments, he let out a long, trembling exhale and stepped back. "We will talk later. Come find me when you have something other than an apology to give."

Eren ran the terrace distance to me, lifting me in his arms and spinning us round while I clung to him hard enough to snap him in half. "I wish we didn't have so many reunions, Lin."

The moment he put me down, I hit his chest with my weak fists. "You never told me. You never told me what he did to you on that godforsaken island. Why wouldn't you tell me, Eren? Why?" My fingers went to the scars on his face. "Why did you lie to me?"

He put a hand on my cheek and shook his head. "Those memories were all erased when I would tuck you and Rora in bed at night. The moment I saw you two...nothing mattered anymore. Nothing hurt. I swear it."

I rested my forehead on his chest, hoping to hide my tears. Last thing I wanted was to cause my people hopelessness. Behind him, my soldiers lined the path down the castle, a hand over their chests as they bowed their heads to me. Alaric stood between them, solemn, not a single wrinkle to betray his stoic expression while he bowed along like the others. "My queen."

The old man reached me, and I rested my head on his chest, wrapping my arms around his waist. In his embrace I always became that little girl who had never been held by a father. In his embrace I always became a loved daughter, an adored daughter—I always became a child. He was why I'd never been jealous of other daughters.

"Kid," he murmured, tightening his hold on me, and I got a taste of safety, of home.

"I am sorry." For Alastair. For Sebastian. For leaving. For everything.

He sighed, rubbing my back. "So am I, kid. So am I."

The comfort of it made my eyes draw shut. Comfort—it felt odd. All this time, my comfort had been something else. Something dark. I'd relied on the shadows beyond the mirror for far too long.

A little thing clung to my leg, and I finally let go of Alaric to pick up Leanna's little monster. She pinched my cheeks with her small fingers and pulled hard. "Lila missed you, auntie. Did you miss Lila?"

"No," I said, and she giggled, hugging my neck and almost suffocating me with her unnatural small child strength.

Another small thing hugged my side, her red head pressed to my chest. Penelope cried silently, holding onto me for dear life. "I know you haven't missed me either," she said, crying louder. "But I have missed you."

"You've grown."

She wailed. Hard. Loud.

I laughed.

And she cried even harder.

Nia had managed to pry the both of them off of me at some point to let me greet my soldiers and court. Amongst the words of welcome, I almost missed the swift change in the wind around me and how much warmer it grew.

My words were cut off when I noticed the figure climbing the steps to the terrace. Like a dream I'd dream too many tortuous nights, he stood there. His brown hair was longer. There were dark shadows covering his face. And even his silver eyes had somewhat turned a deeper shade. His chest rose rapidly despite the calm on his beautiful face.

Slowly, I made my way to him. Slowly...because my whole world was spinning out of its axis, rotating with such speed because every balance that had ever existed in me was broken. He didn't move. I don't think he was even breathing anymore at all. But his eyes followed me, going from the colour of autumn skies to starlight the closer I got to him.

Once I was close enough to touch him, I said, "Hello, handsome."

He slowly raised a shaky hand to graze the ends of my hair, wrapping the strands around his fingers. "Hello, my gorgeous girl."

We moved quicker than light itself. I was in his arms, tucked tightly to his chest, my legs wrapping to lock around his waist while he enveloped me entirely in his embrace, his head buried between my hair.

All this time I'd felt like a part of me had been torn out, pulled from my flesh and left me hollow. It felt like I'd finally become whole again. Two parts of me crashing into place. Everything grew silent around me almost as if someone had snapped their fingers and ordered it. The voices, the sounds, the cries, and laughter. That mocking voice who'd lived in my mind for far too long was gone, too. The emptiness was now filled with only his voice, the sounds of his heart, the pattern of his breaths. And my lungs...my lungs were drowning, inhaling so fast and deep, finally being fed what they'd craved for months—his scent.

"I think you might have missed me," I said.

He laughed. A laugh that turned into breaking sobs. I felt his tears on my skin. I felt his scent of radiant spring brush my face. I felt his warm darkness embrace my longing and my pain. I felt my own senses suddenly come back to life. And I hated it for a moment. Hated that I was suddenly able to feel. Until I remembered that I felt love, too. That I loved him. I hated that it had to be buried with all the rest that I felt. That to love him...I had to hurt, too.

I winced from the dull pain whistling over my bones when his hand rested on the side of my ribs.

And it was all it took for his massive frame to turn stiff, for his breathing to stop, too. As if he was listening and waiting for signs. Or maybe for me to confess.

"A *harhound* knocked me down briefly back in Breshall when I got the sceptre," I said quickly. Perhaps a little too quickly because when he pulled back, the frown that he wore was full of doubt. Another thing I'd missed. I'd missed his worry. His nagging, too.

But I didn't like this. Not at all. The way my inner pain was painted on his face as if he felt what I was feeling—as if he was in as much pain as I was.

"Maybe she needs to see a healer," Nia said, reaching a hand to me. She knew the truth. She would always know. "I'll take her."

My husband shook his head, sticking closely to me. "No—"

"Kilian," Nia said slowly, carefully prying me away from his strong grip. "She won't go anywhere. I'll take her. Deal with the court. You will have to let Olympia know that she is back safely. It is your duty as king. She is safe now," my friend repeated, taking my hand and slowly backing away from him. "I have her. She is safe."

Nia sat before me, crouched on the ground with both her arms around her knees, pointing a guilty look on the floor as the Medi-healer crossed the room to me, carrying her bag of contraptions.

"Thank you for before," I offered quietly, and Nia smiled at me, her hazel eyes drowned with silver tears.

The old healer gasped when I pulled my shirt down, and I quickly put a finger to my lips, knowing that Kilian would break right in if he heard her even breathe a note higher than she normally did.

When Nia spun away from me, refusing to look, something told me I shouldn't have let her in either.

My healer studied the map of wounds and gnarly scars that had healed badly and some that had refused to heal at all. She mouthed a string of curses when I removed my trousers. The same old woman who had not flinched even once before despite how many times I'd seen her in the past thirteen years now looked horrified. "What do you want me to heal?" she asked, looking lost and overwhelmed.

"Everything," I said, peeling my gloves off and showing her my shaking palms. "Starting with them."

She stared at me in disbelief. "Everything? Are you certain?"

"I am." I could not tell which of my scars and wounds were new or old, but he would. I know he would now.

She took a few pieces of colourful crystals from her bag and kneeled before me. "You never have permitted me before."

"I will remember them even if I don't see them." *But he doesn't have to.*

They were only remainders of my hatred, but to him, they would be reminders of my pain.

Watching the raised and mangled flesh disappear under the healer's touch was the strangest pain I'd gone through. It didn't exactly hurt. Or maybe it did.

The room smelled of medicine and sunlight when the healer finished, but I didn't move for some time, inspecting the smooth skin with my fingers until it blurred behind tears. My body was now unmarred by time.

The Olympian skies were drowning under a tangerine-coloured sunset when Nia pulled me up from the bed and helped me onto the bath.

She sat by my side, her head resting on her knees while she quietly told me all that had happened while I was gone.

I ghosted a finger over the scar on her throat. "Does it hurt?"

"A little when I speak. Healers say it's normal since it was caused by dark magic." She lifted a finger to trace the scar on my cheek. "Like yours." Her hazel eyes shone less than they had normally, like a little life had been stolen from them. "You're tired. I should go."

I grabbed her arm, stopping her. "Stay a little longer."

She rested her cheek on the bathtub's edge, looking at me. "Alright. As long as you need me for. I'll stay."

"Lifetimes, Nia. I will need you to stay with me for lifetimes."

"Then I will stay with you for lifetimes." She reached into her jacket pocket and brought something out. "I was going to give this to you before Silas took you to Isjord."

She put something cold in my palm. A gold chain holding an emerald pendant. The same necklace I'd given to the Crafter years ago. My mother's pendant.

"I tried to find it for years, each time you sent me to Eldmoor. But I'd never had any luck. Mal helped me last time. We found the Crafter within an hour. He'd not sold it just like I had thought." She pointed to the back of the pendant, at the swift engraved on the metal. "Myrdur insignia. Rare. More so than the emerald sourced from the Volants. Objects sometimes carry so much power to Crafters. It did to you as well. I know you missed it."

"Never as much as you." I unclasped the necklace and put it around her neck. "Whatever the Crafter would have wanted, I would have given it to him. This is yours. Will forever be yours. I was so scared that day, Nia. I thought he'd filled us with hope for nothing when he just asked about the pendant. Back then, I thought he would ask us for diamonds, gold, and more riches of the same sort. When he pointed to the pendant, I thought we'd been lied to. That we'd searched for so long for the craft metal only to end up disappointed again. It was never about the pendant. I'm so sorry that I let you think it was ever about it, but I didn't want to scare you then."

Two stray tears slid down her cheeks and she reached to wrap her arms around my neck, holding me tightly against her.

I had just dragged myself out of the bath and gotten dressed when he knocked on the door and slowly let himself in. He was out of the black leathers, his dark brown hair was drenched, the long strands falling over his eyes. The more I looked at him, the more suffocating the air grew, the more my heart pulsed madly.

Like before, he stood still and silent, watching me from afar, his chest rising and falling fast.

I sat at the edge of our bed, wondering when had we ever been so cautious of one another. "Why won't you come to me?"

He didn't say anything, but he slowly walked to where I'd sat and kneeled before me. His silver eyes grazed every detail on my face, lingering over my mouth.

"Why won't you touch me?" I whispered, now scared all of a sudden.

Slowly, he raised a hand to my face, and let out a deep sigh when his skin met mine. I could feel the restraint he held, the way it made his touch tremble. Shivers raised down my spine when his fingers grazed my lips. It ignited something I'd thought had been taken from me.

I pushed his long hair back from his eyes. "Why won't you speak to me?"

Never had anyone watched me so gently. "I have so much to say. What should I say first?"

The sound of his voice was the deadliest elixir. Dark and cold and burning like night, and it lit me up like a fire. "Kiss me."

His mouth slowly curved into a smile before he leaned forward, crashing his lips to mine. Our lips locked for a while, resting softly against each other's. And the overwhelming taste of yearning choked me and left me breathless.

I had barely touched him when he pulled back, took my hand and turned my palm up. His thumbs skimmed the skin there for a moment before he traced his fingers up my arms, stopping to run them over where he remembered old scars to have been before. He turned frantic when he inspected my back, my stomach, my legs, and every other limb and found nothing there either.

Hurt and anger flashed on his face. "You didn't want me to see."

Not now. Don't know my truths now. "They had to go anyway."

"Lies."

Let me lie. "I had planned to have them all removed a long time ago."

"Liar," he snapped.

Believe me this once. "It was a hassle for the healer."

"More lies."

"Darling—"

Shadows around us began growing taller and melting off the walls into a puddle of gurgling tar as he demanded, "What did he do to you?" His hands frantically searched my body all over, stopping to graze places where old scars had once been and finding nothing. "Gods, what did he do to you?"

"Nothing I couldn't handle."

The colour of the setting sun outside suddenly was no longer burnt and warm, it darkened and dimmed until it quickly turned to night, enshrouding all of us in darkness. And the violently summoned night covered his grey eyes, too, masking them with obsidian and crawling black veins that spread around them. "Why...why are you lying to me?"

I shivered at the chilling breeze that brushed my neck. "Because."

"Don't," he breathed, almost choking with each inhale.

I didn't say anything, but I did kiss him. And he did kiss me back. My body pressed to his hard one, his fingers tangling in my hair, holding me still while he devoured me. The darkness around us slowly began dispersing to leave hues of a young twilight twinkling over the crystal windows.

He groaned against my mouth, the masculine sound pooling low in my stomach, settling heavily between my legs. His hand slid down my nape and he buried his face on my neck, inhaling my skin, my hair, hungrily. His touch was demanding, so absolute, his restraint finally coming undone. "The conversation was not over."

I reached for the strings of my nightgown and pulled them down, letting the silky fabric slide down around my waist. "Sure. Let's talk." I took his hand and sucked on his thumb, licking at the pad of his finger. "We can start with the weather."

His gaze darkened, onyx spreading over silver. "You're the most stunning creature to exist, yet here I am, only a man," he said, his hand lowering down to my chest, grazing my aching breasts and my trembling stomach. His thumb traced light, torturous circles over my skin until I'd flushed red from frustration and need. "You little trickster."

My mouth parted open to refute that very silly name, but he kissed me, shutting me up. "How empty has the world been," he whispered, licking my lips and wrapping his arms around my body to pull me flush against him. "Without you."

I bit his lip, and he hissed, digging his fingers into my hair and kissing me harder. "Yes, sing verses to me, Adriatian."

His mouth left a trail of wet kisses down my face and neck, stopping only when my moans filled the stark silence. He raised his eyes up at me and smiled, flicking his tongue over my nipple. "I like it better when you do the singing." His hands dropped from my face and down my body, softly brushing against my breasts with his knuckles until gooseflesh puckered over every inch of me. He stopped all too suddenly, his fingers resting over my heart. "Why is it beating so fast?"

"Because I want you to fuck me." I grabbed his hand and cupped it over my breast. "And you're taking your sweet time."

And there it was. That deep, dark laugh of his that soothed all parts of me that I didn't know needed soothing. It was so vibrant yet so rich and dark—I wanted it.

"What's that look for?" he asked, pushing away some hair from my face.

"You're so pretty, Kil."

He grinned wide, doing that silly tongue in cheek thing, and I kicked him with my foot until he dropped back on the floor, chuckling.

"Arrogant prick."

He grabbed my foot and pulled me to the floor too, lifting me up and over his body. "If I recall correctly, you used to like my arrogant prick." His fingers were light on my cheek, handling me so softly. "Has that changed?"

"Well, take it out and let's see."

He would not stop laughing. "The way your romantic words sway me, love of mine." He grabbed me and faded us on top of our bed, my legs straddling his waist.

"Yes, finally," I murmured to myself, sitting up and popping all the buttons on his shirt and then undoing his breeches. The man just stood there, half stunned and half entertained, watching me as I got him naked in record time.

When an unfortunate fist rasped on the door, I saw red. "Go away, we're fucking."

Kilian blasted into gales of laughter, and his brother pushed the door open just a little to say, "I'm glad for you two, but it's dinner time. With the family. Postpone the fucking to a later hour. And keep it down for Gods' sake, your sister is two doors away."

"Who is two doors away?" I heard Thora's voice ask from further down the corridor.

Mal sighed. "I could swear this girl has godly hearing." Then the bickering grew even louder after he shut the door.

Damn it. I rested my forehead on his and tried to calm my raging heart.

Kilian trailed a gentle hand down my spine, holding me close to him. "If this was never real," he murmured over my lips. "If I have somehow made this all up, I want you to know that you are the most devastatingly beautiful thing my mind has ever created."

My eyes drew shut. I'd longed for so long and never had known until him how much I wanted to be wanted. He held me like a flower pressed between his pages, preserved under the warmth of his words. Just how I craved to be held. So delicately. "You must be real," I said, trailing a finger over his beautiful face. "My imagination is pretty lacking to be able to create all this." Starry eyes and all. The only stars I wanted to see day and night. My stars. And mine alone.

He flashed me one of his grins. "That good, huh?"

I nodded and buried my nose in his neck, inhaling the scent I'd tried hard with no success to conjure in my time away from him. My lungs filled with memory and warmth, and like snow, I melted.

His large hand rested on the back of my head, stroking me further into slumber. "I want to feed you before you rest."

I smiled against him, pressing my body closer to his. "I'm well fed."

"Your stomach is telling me otherwise."

That made me frown. "It is not that noisy."

His lips rested softly on my brow. "Don't be mad, my woman. I like it when it growls at me. Missed it even." He lifted me up like I was stuffed with feathers and rolled the nightgown over my head again, his hands skimming every bit of my skin as he did so, making me shiver. His eyes raked over me one last time, the look growing darker before he stood and got a dressing gown to throw over my shoulders. "Come. I want to see you eat."

I resisted the urge to get a pair of gloves and took his hand.

The dining room was busier than usual. Everyone important to me was sitting enjoying their food—food that our cooks usually took the time to prepare during festivities.

Alaric almost gave himself whiplash with how fast his head whipped to me. "Ah, finally. Come on, kid, take a seat. I...I had the cooks make all you like. No funny vegetables and all that."

Nia huffed, shaking her head in disappointment.

"Thank you, old man," I offered, patting his shoulder when I went past.

Mal lifted a hand up in a wave, smirking at me, and I rushed to him, hesitating a little before throwing my arms around his neck. "Sister-in-law," he purred, cradling the back of my head gently, his hand shaking against me.

"Princeling."

He chuckled, and I pulled back to inspect the rough scars around his eye. "I'll have the best of my healers have a look."

"It was made with Adriatian steel, and I am not bothered," he said, patting my cheek. "They made me look even more irresistible."

"Perhaps bring that healer to have a look at his head," my sister said quietly, slurping some soup, and Mal cocked his head to the side to give her a look.

Kilian sat beside me at the head of the table, laying down cutlery, food, and filling me a cup of water. He still held my hand, his thumb tracing circles over my palm.

Alaric cleared his throat. "I would like for this to become a usual...occurrence. Once a week, at least, I'd like for us to all gather for a meal."

Caiden set his fork on the table and narrowed his eyes on the old man. "What have I done to you?"

A loud bang came from underneath the table, and my friend glared at Mal who raised his brows, and said, "Something wrong, my muffin? Did you leave that stick up your arse again?" He cocked his head in my brother's direction. "Did he?"

Eren sputtered water all over the table, coughing, but the rest of us had turned red from holding in laughter.

I could feel a few hard looks on me. And with a sigh, I put the spoon down even though I had barely tasted the food, and looked up at Alaric, Cai, and Eren who had narrowed their eyes on me. "Might I help?"

"Stop planning war, we are eating," Cai said.

"Don't be silly."

Eren lifted a brow. "What were you thinking so hard for?"

"Not war."

Kilian shifted in his seat to look at me, frowning like the rest of the table, and I smiled a bit too innocently. It seemed like I shouldn't have because he frowned even deeper. "You look like Lila when she asks for sweets before bedtime."

I winced. "I look like a beggar?"

"Sneaky."

I shifted my chair closer to his and hooked my legs to wrap around one of his.

He lifted a hand to pinch my chin and pressed a kiss to my mouth. "It won't work," he said, twisting some strands of my hair around his fingers. "The thoughts are practically twisting your hair into curls."

"It is all I have thought the past few months, Kil, I can't seem to help it."

"All?"

"If I thought of you, Mal would have turned into an honourable sacrifice, and I am a dishonourable woman. Couldn't taint my reputation."

He chuckled. "It might be compensated, my light, I've thought of you and of us enough to drive the Goddess of Thought out of her job."

I clutched his shirt. "This is a bad place to talk poetry to me."

"My beautiful girl," he said, running the back of a finger down my cheek. "Tell me you're here. Tell me I'm not sick."

I pulled his face down and kissed him. "I'm here."

Alaric cleared his throat. "I've brought you cake," he said, standing and later returning with a two-layer white cream and lemon cake. "Samira picked it out for you. She said you like this sweet shite."

"I do." I kissed his cheek, and he blinked a bit dazed for a moment, nodding and taking his seat.

Thora cut everyone a slice, and Kil helped her serve it to the whole table.

I'd had two plates already yet he had not even touched his. The entire time, he'd stared at me while I'd been eating, his arm over my backrest and the tips of his fingers hovering and tickling my shoulder.

I broke a piece of cake with my fork and lifted it to his mouth. "It tastes like you. Lemony."

His dark brow hiked up. "Lemony?"

I nodded and he wrapped his pretty lips around the fork.

"Like it?" I asked, scooping some of the cream left on my plate with a finger and licking it. The cream was the best part.

He nodded, grabbing my hand to guide my finger and scoop some cream before sucking and licking it clean. "I missed your taste."

My naked toes curled a little. "I missed your face."

He flashed me a grin. "Want to sit on it later?"

Someone coughed, and Kilian pulled back, lifting a cup of water to disguise his smirk.

"You know we can hear pretty well," Nia said, chewing on some sourdough.

"My Nia, I'd be worried otherwise."

"So," Eren said, stretching back. "Who are you thinking of killing?"

"No one."

He raised a brow. "That person is called *no one*?"

"Funny."

Cai kicked my leg under the table, and I jolted in my seat. "Who?"

The plate before him flew right against his face, smearing cake all over it, and everyone turned to my glaring husband. "If you want her attention, use words such as *'excuse me, Snow,'* or, *'I have something to say, Snow,'*" Kilian nearly spat the words out.

My friend's mouth was pulled in a sneer as he tried to clean his face. "*Well, hello, Snow,*" he enunciated. "Who were you thinking of?"

Kilian lifted a cup of water to his lips. "Much better."

I looked back and forth at everyone. "No one."

Yes, there was someone.

Everyone knew so, but they knew to not poke me more about it.

I had barely given my goodbyes when Kilian threw me over his shoulder, a large hand wrapped around my naked thigh. "Here or Adriata?"

Oooh, choices! "Here."

The second he put me on the bed, I crawled further back, my heart beating out of my chest while I watched him undress. His body had grown bigger, his muscles more defined, his skin even more marked with littering scars. I was going to ask him about that later.

He undid his trousers with a hand and pointed to my underwear with his chin. "Pull them down for me, love. Show me your pretty little cunt."

In moments, there was nothing on me, and I was wet and bare before him.

He crawled to me, hooking his hands under my knees and nuzzling his face between my legs. "Fuck, you're beautiful," he hummed, pressing his mouth between my thighs, kissing my sex.

My back arched off the bed when he licked all of me and sucked on that bundle of nerves that had fire spreading over my spine. Hells. Seven burning hells. "M-maybe we should discuss what's happened first. Catch up on everything."

"Yeah?" he hummed, lapping at the wetness down my centre, and I shuddered when he slipped a finger inside me, then another. My hips rolled against his mouth, and he obeyed all demand, pumping his fingers faster. "Maybe. But fuck, look how wet you are, my love." His arms went under my knees, and he flipped us over until I was on top of his face. "Sit first. I've not had my meal yet."

"How will you breathe?"

"You think I want to breathe when I have your sweet cunt on my face." His palm met my skin hard and he rubbed the sting away, palming and kneading my bottom. "Sit, Snowlin, I'm fucking starving."

My knees buckled on their own and then every other limb of mine turned entirely liquid when his tongue plunged inside of me. The man ravished me, his massive hands wrapped around my hips to keep me there, riding his face.

A tremble raked down my spine when he groaned against me, a hot, coiling pressure pooling between my thighs. "Kil, I can't, Oh, Gods," I cried out, grabbing onto the headboard to hold upright while my body grew weak from the waves of blinding release pulsing in my belly. "Hells, burning sweet hells," I breathed out, giggling and panting for air all at once.

He kept lapping at me leisurely and leaving kisses all over my thighs before he flipped us over again and came to stand right between my legs. His eyes burned a silver flame when they travelled over my body. He palmed his cock, stroking himself over the dark underwear. "What a cruel dream you are, love of mine."

Those words made me swallow hard, and my tongue darted out to lick my lips. "You said you've thought of me," I said, still breathing hard and watching his muscled chest fall and rise rapidly.

His teeth dug into his lower lip when he smiled. "I have."

My eyes dropped to his hips. "How? How have you thought of me? Have you—"

He freed his cock from the underwear. Hard and thick in his hand. "You will find out in a second."

Well, that made me smile. Later—I'd ask him to show me later.

Grabbing the edge of my nightgown, he pulled, and the silky thing parted in two. He cupped my breasts, gently kissing the curves and missing their hardened centres as if to torture me. "Have I told you how much I love your body?" His hands skimmed my stomach while his mouth latched on my neck, his fingers dipping everywhere, grazing places that I had never thought could feel so intense to touch. Finally, he relented to my writhing pleas and wrapped his full lips over a nipple, sucking and teasing it with his tongue until I melted into a puddle of need. "More so how it reacts to me."

He fisted his length, brushing the tip against my wetness and slowly nudging my entrance, stretching me open almost torturously—so slowly that I was about to lose it.

"Gods, you're so big," I cried out, my nails digging into his shoulder.

"And you always take it so well." He groaned in my mouth when his entire length sank inside me in one thrust. His hips were flush against mine and I could feel him in my stomach, my hips rolling against his despite the sting. "Fuck."

"Shit."

"All good down here?" he asked, dropping a small peck on my nose and rolling his hips just a little. "Your body couldn't have forgotten mine so soon. Tell me it hasn't because I remember yours too well. So well."

I felt so full it burned. "It hurts so good," I whispered between hard kisses, my body slowly adjusting to him. "Kilian, ah, yes. It feels so good."

"I want to go slow," he breathed harshly, his cock dragging in and out of me again so torturously slow. "I want to learn you all over again. But I can't be patient. Ask me to be patient. Tell me to be patient."

"No," I whispered over his mouth, sucking on his tongue. "Please."

"Please what?" he taunted.

"Fuck me hard. I need you to fuck me hard, please. You know how I like it."

My jaw went slack, and all sorts of sounds came out of me when his hips started pounding against mine, relentlessly. He devoured my mouth, sucking and licking all moans and whimpers off my tongue. A small shudder rolled over him when I wrapped my legs around his waist and pulled him closer, my breast brushing his chest each time he thrust, relieving just the slightest bit of the ache that had encapsulated me entirely.

The sounds of our bodies grew obscene, louder, heavier, and demanding. I was sure my flesh had bruised from the force of our joining, yet he didn't even slow. Only him, I only ever wanted him to mark my body. However he wanted to.

I'd missed him. I'd missed this. I'd missed feeling wanted, desired, not disgusted by my own skin. Repulsed by my own existence. Each delicate stroke of his hands on my skin, the weight of his body on mine, our joining, his mouth on mine, the same breath we shared, all of it grew so intense all of a sudden.

Kilian leaned back on his haunches, watching where we joined with a little too much satisfaction. "Who is fucking your pretty cunt?"

"My husband," I cried out, reaching to hold onto the headboard behind while his punishing thrusts rocked us.

"That's right." He pulled my leg over his shoulder and bent down again, kissing and pounding against me with all he had. "Your husband."

I came too soon and too violently, the release sending a shudder that racked my entire body, pulses of heat spreading and burning into the most exquisite type of pain I'd ever experienced.

He didn't stop, dragging out what little bit of strength I had left in my spent body. He let out a painful groan, his hips jerking against mine, and I felt his come fill my insides. His mouth was on my neck, my cheek, my eyes, my brow. He smacked big, wet kisses all over me until I was writhing and giggling from the tickles. "I missed you so much, my sweet sin."

I pushed the soft brown waves from his eyes that all of a sudden had turned dark and haunted again. "And I missed you, my darling."

We'd just gotten out of the bath and I was combing my wet hair, sitting on the vanity, when he returned from my dressing chamber, holding a bunch of white shirts in his hand. "This is where all my shirts have gone?"

About that. "They smelled like you. When Penelope found them around, she would wash them and the scent would leave, so I would just get another. I did try rubbing them with the others, but it wouldn't work." Pulling onto my drawer, I got the handkerchief Mal had given me before our wedding. "Driada and Mal gave me a bunch of them, too. They don't smell like you, but they were made by you. Little you, actually."

He took the small square of fabric, running his thumb over the embroidery for a moment. "Since when have you started collecting them?"

I took the handkerchief and folded it back in my Kilian shrine. "The night before our wedding."

"Which wedding?" he asked, sliding a hand to the back of my neck.

"The first."

He kissed me, his hand pulling the towel wrapped around my body and throwing it to the floor. "First you take my heart, my soul, my surname. Become my sun, my stars, my moon, my skies, my everything. But taking my shirts is taking it too far," he said, nudging my nose with his. "Why do you sit in front of it if you will not look at it?"

I glanced at the mirror behind me. "Force of habit, I suppose."

"What is it that you still see in there?"

"Me."

His fingers were soft on my face. "Why would that be so horrible to look at?"

"If you could only see what I see, Kil."

"I see you. I've seen all of you. I want to keep seeing all of you for the rest of our lives."

"I've beguiled you. That night in the snow, my beguiling must have worked."

That made him smile. "With your wicked, murderous wiles, might I add."

"I warned you."

His smile faded a little. "Don't be afraid," he murmured as if he didn't want even the wind to know that I could be afraid. "He did not manage to make you what he wanted to make you."

"He did. You've not seen what I planned to do, what I still want to do, what I've done, the mess I've left in Isjord. How much worse I planned and wanted to do." How much worse I still want to do. My rage might have grown numb, but not my desire for ruin.

"That is his fault. Your only fault is that you're stubborn. But this stubbornness kept you alive, so I don't give a fuck about what that bastard forced you to commit."

"Hells, you cannot be saved."

He chuckled, pushing the stool behind me away and backing me to the vanity desk before spinning me around so my back was to his chest and I was facing the mirror. Though it was mildly dark and my heart was still warm from his words, the shadows were relentless and thick in my reflection.

There was no saving me either.

"Open your eyes," he ordered, the tips of his fingers gently tugging my underwear down and parting my legs with his knee.

Instead of looking straight ahead, I watched the reflection of his hands work over my body, tracing the line of my curves, dipping between my thighs to pet the still sore and sensitive flesh, and then back up to cup my breasts. A moan slipped free when he pinched my nipples and lowered his mouth to suck on my neck. "Don't close them. I want you to watch—watch how fucking beautiful you are. You've got to keep them open, love, to see how exquisite you look when you take me." He kissed my ear. "When you come." His lips were barely touching my skin, teasing and taunting me until my breath hitched from frustration. "Fuck, when you look so needy for me." His fingers slid over my core and he brought one to his mouth and sucked. "Perfect."

My eyes followed his hands at all times, playing with my body, teasing my skin, deceiving and taunting my most sensitive parts which he denied his touch. I didn't say anything—I was entirely too fascinated seeing my body react to him. In a trance, I looked up, staring directly into my eyes.

There was me, but there was him, too. Starlight poured out of his silver eyes that met mine in the reflection, lust dripping like liquid thunder when they lowered down my body that had flushed with want—desperate want. "Hold on to the table, love, and bring your hips to me."

His fingers traced the arch of my back when I bent down a little to grab onto the table edge. His cock nudged my opening, teasing and slowly stretching me open. "Kilian, shit."

"Sore?"

I shook my head, my chest falling and rising fast. "Just...just...you know."

A soft tendril of shadows wrapped around my throat, squeezing lightly. "Look at you." His fingers circled my sensitive core while he fully pushed it. "Look how your pretty little cunt stretches around me," he said, lifting one of my legs on the counter so I could watch where we joined. "Look how beautiful."

My legs began trembling a little when his fingers dug on my hips, holding me tightly while he pounded inside of me frantically.

Wetness dripped between my thighs, soaking his length, making the joining sound of our bodies heavier and louder. He set a brutal pace, my breathless moans drowned by his grunts. All the time, his eyes never left mine, and I watched the pained look on his face with too much pleasure, a shamelessly wicked smile stretching on my face. He was right. It was fascinating. And I was too enthralled by the way his body fit with mine and how perfectly mine fit in his to let my head spin into the abyss again. My mind *was* spinning, but this time because of the burning pressure that built all over me, tipping me between the edge of insanity and pleasure.

He wrapped my hair around his fist, pulling my head back so he could kiss my ear and taunt me with his mouth while my body was still riding my climax, prolonging it till it threatened to collapse. "Watch me fill you up. That's my good girl," he purred when I opened my eyes again. "Watch how hard you make me come."

I did. And it was one of the most insanely attractive things I'd seen. The thigh muscles bulging, the tightening of his abs, the veins on his forearm puckering, the pulse thrumming on his neck, his tight jaw ticking, holding back moans that escaped into breathy groans. He was perfect, more so in the midst of pleasure.

His hips bucked hard against mine and then I felt his warm come spill inside of me. If only to taunt me, he kept thrusting, a hand wrapping around my shoulders to hold my languid, pliable body up.

He kissed my cheek and stepped back a little, breathing hard, his finger catching the come that began seeping out of me. His other hand wrapped around my jaw, probing my mouth open. "In case you've forgotten my taste."

I wrapped my lips around his finger, sucking and licking it clean. "I'd rather drink from the fountain next time," I said, kissing his hand. "But thank you for being so considerate."

He tilted my face up so he could kiss me. "Plenty of time for me to fuck every bit of you."

"Ah, but there is the matter of daylight."

He chuckled, throwing me over his shoulder and heading to the bathroom again.

I laid facing him in the bath, my chin resting on his chest while I looked up to find him smiling at me.

I fingered the little chain tied around his neck. It was new. Besides his wedding band, he had never worn any other jewellery. "You've never worn this before."

He twisted the necklace around and unclasped it, pulling a ring out of the chain. One I had not seen before. One that seemed a little too girly for him. But I was not there to judge. He took my hand and slid it on my ring finger, over the shimmering tattoo of our blessed marriage. "It won't melt this time. I made sure of it."

Awe left me gaping. A yellow diamond stood at the centre of a gold halo, encircled by six smaller white ones, the shape almost resembling a daisy. Dainty, sweet, and so, so pretty. "This is the prettiest thing I've ever seen." I cupped his face in my hands and kissed every corner of it. "Thank you, darling."

He kissed my knuckles and laced our fingers together. "I've always wanted to see you wearing my ring on that finger. You have so much claim over me, woman. I can't look anywhere without wanting to look at you first, smile at anything without smiling at you first. Speak, breathe, eat—all those—I only do them for you. I wanted something to mark my claim over you. The Gods know," he said, touching the tattoo. "Hopefully, a white-haired chicken with a personality as bland as his boiled flesh can now know, too."

I laughed. "Lazarus is harmless."

His jaw tightened. "Don't say his name. Does he need his eyes, you think? I don't want him even looking at you."

"Now, now, Kil." My cheeks hurt from smiling at my gift. "Love the daisy. Is it your favourite?"

"I think it might have been. I found an old design I'd made when I was looking through a box where I keep your things."

"My things? What things? You have a box?"

"Birth certificates, midwife notes, tests your teachers had conducted, and things of the sort. Even some drawings you'd made with some mashed peas because apparently that is how you got rid of them without being seen. It was the only one Eren would give me. It still smells of peas by the way."

My eyes widened. He was insane. "You do not have my birth certificate."

"I do. In fact, I have several copies. Eren once brought me three by mistake."

"You're mad." He looked so calm telling me all this that I had to re-evaluate the mad dynamics in this relationship.

"Obsessed, that is what I've heard. Eren used to call me that once. Now madly in love."

"I have so little of you." I wanted everything of his, too. Every little bit.

He took my hand and put it over his heart. "You have this. I wouldn't say it is my biggest organ, but it is the best one." He slid my hand down his stomach and over his length. "And this. Would not say it the most important one, but holy fuck does it feel like it when it is inside of you."

I didn't know if I loved his mouth on me or talking to me. Every word that came out of it was pure, scalding ecstasy and my body and mind loved the way it burned me. "Are you trying to romance me, husband?"

"Is it working?"

I climbed his lap. "Yes."

18

Black Pawn to C4

Kilian

SHE HADN'T SLEPT ALL night, not even after I'd done everything in my power to tire her. Fucking her to sleep had not worked. Neither smothering her with affection and questions. Or telling her the stories of my scars—this time she'd even listened intently. For a while, she had pretended to be asleep. But knowing her, doing nothing had bored her to bits, so she'd given up pretty quickly to just stare at me for the rest of the night. Blaming it on our reunion, I had let her and basked under the attention.

Despite the lack of rest and the little she had to eat the day before, she looked fiercely concentrated and determined. But there was no fire in her eyes. They were a mirror of pure, cold winter. Unforgiving.

It worried me.

The calmness felt wrong.

She was a storm.

I only wished she rained down on the world, not on herself.

Penelope brushed her hair while I got myself dressed, her golden eyes glued on the arched window overlooking part of the city—the stare empty and distant, different from before. I'd caught her distanced from reality more than five times in less than twenty-four hours. More than one voice in my head told me something was wrong. And I believed them.

When my lips rested on her temple, a smile returned on her face.

She pushed a few strands of hair behind her ear and turned to me, taking my face in her hands. "Ready?"

"No," I said, pinching her nose. "I'm still debating tying you to our bed and keeping you there. It feels too early. I just got you back."

She shook her head. "While I've got time and opportunity to stop my father without a war, I will try. I cannot drag my people to the battlefield without knowing that I did everything I could possibly do to stop him before it came to that."

"Or you can let me deal with it."

"No."

"Could have at least pretended to take it into consideration," I grumbled under my breath, and she laughed, wrapping her arms around my waist and resting her chin on my chest. "Together then."

She nodded. "Together."

"What trouble will you cause today, my missus?"

"I want to go see Jayre."

"Jayre?" Who the damned hells was Jayre?

"The dragon. Pen said you have him."

"So it has a name."

"You knew I'd sent him?"

"The moment I saw him in the skies. Who else would send a dragon my way besides my wife? What is next on your list, love? You've done eudemons, so that is well and gone. It has to be good to beat a dragon."

She reached on her tiptoes and sank her teeth on my neck. "What impeccable old person humour you've got."

For the thousandth time today alone, I brought her to my chest again, burying my face in her hair. "Tell me you love me again."

"I love you, Kil. Just at this particular moment, you're suffocating me, and it is honestly making me reconsider things."

She almost ran towards the stables where the dragon had been sleeping for the past few months.

The clementine-coloured creature rose its head and sniffed the air, pushing to its claws and rushing towards Snow like they were old friends.

Memphis huffed by my side and curled on the grassy floor of the gardens, licking her leg while looking at her bonded and her new pet with annoyance.

I bent down and scratched her head and ears how she liked it. "Can you turn into that?"

The large cat's nose scrunched, and she gave me a pointed look.

"Hm. Thought so."

Snow turned to us, and shouted, "Memphis, come here."

Her bonded quickly ran and hid behind her blue skirts, peeking her head out just a little to look up at the dragon.

"He is from Aita, like you. From long before you were born," Snow explained to her bonded who looked nowhere near convinced until she took a few careful steps forward to sniff the dragon. Then all three suddenly became old friends together.

There was so much enamour in Snow's eyes for both creatures. She had the giddiest smile on while she began animatedly talking to both creatures who could for sure not talk back to her.

Oh, to be a black furred feline and an oversized lizard with wings at this moment.

"It really was her dragon," Larg called, laughing as he crossed the stable distance to us. He sniffled a little and bowed his head to Snow, overtaken with all sorts of emotion. The old man was the most sensitive person I knew. "My queen. It is good to have you back."

"Is it?" Snow teased, patting Jayre's snout one last time and reaching my side again.

"Of course it is. Everything had been bleak with you. Your presence has brought back my king's smile, too. I hope it can bring back his sleep schedule while you're at it."

"You wrinkled busybody," I mumbled between my teeth, and my godfather chuckled under his breath, trying to hide it with a cough.

Like a flash of lightning, Atlas shot through the guards, bushes, and horses in our direction. Tripping, heaving, and coughing while he bowed to Snow a whole one hundred eighty degrees, folding like a neat napkin. "You...you've returned."

My wife opened her arms wide. "Come to mother."

Atlas sighed, his shoulders going slack with relief. "Well, it is good that you're in a teasing mood." He smiled at her, but it looked more like a wince. "That is good. Right, Kil? It has to be good. Did you have a hard time, my queen?"

She slid an arm around my waist, and I pulled her closer to me. "Not as hard as them."

"We heard he made you heir," Larg said. "We thought it odd, but Kilian had an inkling that it was a call made by you."

"It was," she agreed. "I reminded my father of what would happen if the throne remained empty for long. Bringing forgotten fear is what I do best."

My godfather ran a hand over his beard. "What will he do now? He cannot crown a new-born. Not without causing all kinds of ruckus."

"Given how quiet Isjord has been," I said, "I doubt many know that Snow is no longer in Isjord. He will probably make excuses for not bringing her out in public until he is ready to reign war."

The gruff man cleared his throat and flashed her one of his charming smiles. "Contrary to us. We've organised a little get together in Lyra for you."

Snow blinked once. "A beheading perchance?"

Larg laughed hard enough to make all birds fly off into the horizon. "I've missed your jests, my queen."

My wife looked up at me, confused. "Do you burn at the stake? That is such a time-consuming choice. But I respect it."

Everyone was already at the makeshift war room in the Myrdur ruins where both our kingdoms had met these past few months—and it had somehow become a common ground for us. Adriatians had grown comfortable around Olympians, but it couldn't be said the same about the other way round. Olympians were still cautious towards my people. And I couldn't blame anyone. Olympians adored Snow, they would never let go of what was done to and thought of her even if she did.

"Silas's troops are still in Breshall," Tristin said.

"Smells like a trap to me," Mal sighed, propping his feet on the table and covering half of the map.

Caiden pushed them off, almost making him tumble over. "Or Silas could be struggling to portal them past Mahara's channel now that Visha has lifted up her veils again."

My brother clicked his tongue. "My muffin, Silas has plenty of men, Crafters, and beasts to spare, he would not spend so much energy to bring them back to Isjord, not when he has made sure allies. They're either hoping we would go back or are remaining there to make sure we do not. Silas brought Snow when he dealt with the princes. She knows enough to ruin his plans. He expects us to turn the tide again like we did before."

My brother was right. Like most of the times.

"No news from Vidarr?" I asked.

"None," Nia answered. "Not since he'd last seen the Breshall Prince meet with Isjordian Captains in the northern waters where ships are still docked."

"One of my Skye can fly over there," Tristin offered. "No magic they can detect."

"Silas has been hunting us relentlessly, it would not be smart," Caiden said. "He still has contact with the slavers who had the Olympians. They must know a trick or two to trap one of ours considering how many Olympians we've retrieved from them."

"What about me?" Elias asked. "I can go. My magic will blend in with theirs. And they probably think I died when I set the whole eastern camp on fire."

Caiden shook his head. "There is no chance in hells that Silas has bought your death. He must be looking for you, too. Just as persistently. You know Isjord under and over. We can't risk it when you're our most valuable asset against him at the moment."

Elias leaned back and smirked at him. "Yeah?"

Caiden blinked at him and then at all of us. "Did the Isjordian just flirt with me?"

"If you ignore it, he might go away," Visha said, not tearing her eyes from the grimoire on her lap. She was set on figuring out and mastering the dream veil to trap either Vas or Aurora for more than just a few moments.

"Bet you still see me in your dreams, V," Elias smugly said.

"You're the very reason why I thank the dark God every day for giving me a dreamless sleep," she replied boredly.

Elias nodded to himself. "She definitely loves me."

She flicked her eyes up at me, and there was so much violence there that it almost made me laugh. "Do we need him whole? I can just use his brain."

"Too much work, Visha," Oryn said, adjusting his specs. "We've talked about it."

"My death aside," Elias said, clearing his throat. "What are we going to do with the Unblessed Princes? Even if the king still remains on our side like Kilian says, the three isles are a separate entity. They bow to a king, just not to his rule."

"Don't worry," Snow finally said, munching on the cashews Caiden had procured for her. "I'll get them to drop my father in a blink."

"How?" Nia asked.

"You know," my wife said, yawning and stretching in her seat. "I put a knife to their throats. Threaten their progeny and their pets, though I would rather not threaten their pets. Make them bleed a little, burn a little, cry a little, whimper a little, beg a little—"

"Sweet heavens," Eren murmured, rubbing his temples.

Snow shrugged. "If you have a better idea."

"We can offer them help. Shipments. Partnerships. Anything," he replied. "Lin, it is time to make allies not enemies."

Thora raised a shy hand, and I nodded for her to speak. "I like the *bleeding a little, burning a little, crying a little, begging a little* idea. They are already afraid, why not use it?"

My eyes drew shut and I let out a long exhale. Not the two sisters and their capitalising endeavours.

Something touched my lip, and I opened my eyes to find Snow putting a cashew in my mouth. "They are nice and sweet," she said, licking her fingertips. "Want another?"

"Is this an attempt to lower my blood pressure?"

"Why, is it high?"

"Must you ask?"

She smiled, fluttering her lashes at me. "Yes. I love seeing you all frustrated."

"Why are you two with your noses on those damn books?" Caiden asked the two quiet Crafters. "Should you not be dealing with the witches Snow has found in the Deadlands?"

"I'll deal with the witches Snow has found," Snow herself said. "Just waiting for the full moon fog to clear off the Deadlands. Visha says we cannot cross it."

Tristin took a seat, finally. She'd looked more relaxed ever since Snow's return. "What now? There is not much we can do. Are we simply waiting for this thing to play out?"

Snow shook her head. "No, now I will take my father apart little by little."

"How?"

"I've already planted the seeds. Just waiting for them to sprout."

Nia sighed. "Please, no more galleys and oars or seeds and fruit."

"Thought you would have appreciated this one figure of speech." My wife stood, sauntered to her and pinched both her cheeks. "Maybe when they start becoming poisonous little flowers. Just wait."

A little gathering, Larg had said. Little. Small. A few. Those were the words he'd used to describe the crowd of people gathered in his front lawn that was lit with pyres and torches we usually used during celebrations. The open space was decorated with all sorts of glittering shapes that hung all over the house, trees, chairs, and even the blessed bonfire which he was roasting a lamb over and holding a long skewer stacked with dozens of different types of mushrooms.

The loud music did go down just the slightest when Snow and I approached the bunch, but it picked up again when my wife gave everyone a little forced smile.

"Bet they would have preferred that beheading now," she murmured.

"Larg would have never invited anyone who would have wished that."

"Tis true," the big man said, sliding between the two of us and throwing an arm over our shoulders. "My godson would have turned this into *their* beheading for your exclusive entertainment." He patted her head, and Snow blinked a bit taken aback. "I've put some big mushrooms on the bonfire for you. The best I could find. Picked them myself with these hands."

"Could have been worse," Mal said, strutting to us. "He could have picked them with his toes like he picks his ear wax."

Larg sighed. "This boy."

My brother glowered at him. "Where are you hiding the wine?"

"In the grave you are digging for me, you rascal."

"Snow, here!" Penelope shouted from a table positioned in the far distance, under the shade of a willow.

"What's with Thora?" Snow asked Nia who was fanning the younger sister resting her forehead on the table.

The friend winced. "Drank a bit much from Larg's handmade whiskey and I don't have any of my stuff with me."

"Told her it was deadly." My godfather laughed. "She insisted she was deadlier."

That was definitely something the little Skygard would say.

Mal sneaked behind her and blew on her neck, making her jerk upright. "Headache?"

She groaned a little. "The worst."

He extended a hand to her. "Come. Larg has some tea in his kitchen."

Instead of taking his hand, she grabbed onto his sleeve and followed him inside the house.

"Oh, look, it's the children you kidnapped," Caiden said, pulling a chair and taking a seat.

Eren sputtered his drink. "You what?"

Snow took a careful glance at me and then snarled at her friend.

Penelope laughed, missing the tension on the table entirely. "Funny story that one—" The young girl took one look at Snow and then lowered her head over the food. "Never mind. It wasn't that funny really."

Larg returned to the table, lowering a plate overflowing with the earthy vegetable. "I'd start with the pine ones. They are the best in this season. I've sprinkled them with some spiced salt. Handmade by me, of course." He puffed his chest, wiping his hands on the pink apron decorated with pink flowers that he wore. "Jam, liquor, bread, pickled vegetables, cheese. You name it, I make it."

Snow blinked some more at him. "Crafty."

"Simply raised by a tough woman," he said, patting his shoulder. "My ma only had me. So I had to learn some stuff."

She pointed at Alaric who was leisurely chewing on the mushrooms. "He can do a mad moss stitch. You two should have tea together sometimes. Make sweaters and jam for each other."

My godfather belly laughed, patting her head again like she was some cat. "I'm in need of a good sweater, the cold is starting to chill our lands. Now I know who to ask."

Alaric sighed, shaking his head. "Come to me, old friend. I'll fit you one nicely."

Nia snorted. "You still haven't finished my hat."

"Anger keeps getting the best of me," he said roughly and looking almost mad. "I lose it when I miss a loop."

"A family thing," Nia explained to Larg. "We're working on it."

Larg let out a long breath, his eyes filling with tears. "You have a good bunch, Alaric Drava. I hope you know what a lucky bastard you are."

"Yeah," Alaric muttered, lowering his eyes and filling his mouth with more food. "Lucky."

After sniffling and wiping his eyes, Larg patted my shoulder. "I'll pack you some jam, cheese, and liquor to take with you. What about some crackers?"

I nodded. "Thank you, Snow loves them."

"I do?"

"Remember when we were studying Eamon's book?" I asked, stealing a mushroom from her plate. "All Larg's food. Even the apples were from his backyard."

"Oh."

Caiden reached for a mushroom, too, and Snow batted his hand away. "Talking about Eamon," he said, shaking his hand that was almost chopped off. "How is catching V—"

I hit him under the table, and he groaned. "Hells, what was that for?" He looked between his confused friend and I, realising I'd not told her yet. "No business talk on the table, fine."

Oryn blinked a little flustered under Snow's perusal and the poor man's shoulders shrunk. "Is there something, my queen?"

"Snow. And yes, there is." She leaned forward. "I gave blue gyre to Skadi or Moregan, call her what you like, she didn't mind."

"Blue gyre?"

"Dark bane. The name changed about sixty years ago," Nia explained. "Old women and men were hunting it and using it to protect themselves from dark magic during and after the Ater Battles, but ended up severely poisoned after they found out it consumed any other dark emotion as well. Once they became numb from pain, they didn't realise death was nearing."

"I see." He thought about it for a moment. "Any particular reason why she is taking it?"

"She was the first person they turned into a beast. Her symptoms from the dark magic were worse than the rest. Once I tried to see if it affected Vas, she began taking it as well. Her symptoms lessened. She became more coherent, could sleep, even remembered what happened during the time she was transformed. She was struggling to turn at some point and obeying any command from Melanthe."

His eyes slowly widened. "This could be quite the discovery...Snowlin."

"You think we could be able to use this?" I asked.

"Possibly. Dark bane in itself probably won't do much more than just unveil some of the effects of the dark magic. To become potent enough to erase it entirely, it is mixed—"

"With silver," Snow said. "Like Nia told me."

Oryn nodded. "Silver, gold, obsidian, dragon bone powder, diamond powder. However, these are deadly to the human body. It will kill them."

Snow's smile grew. "Will it?"

The table went quiet. Finally realising my wife's line of thoughts.

Larg set down a whole tray filled with ale. "Why is there work talk in my front yard?"

"Would there be a chance we could move our table to the back yard then?" Snow asked, blinking a little confused.

My godfather reminded us all of his belly laugh again, and leaned in my ear, "There is some good old liquor up in my bedroom, on the second drawer on my dresser, between my knickers."

I spat out my drink. "Where?"

"The only place that hellion of a brother you have will not look in. It's good stuff, one hundred and fifty years old. Saved it just for you."

"I'll go fetch it," I said, dropping a kiss to my wife's head and standing. "I'll be back in a moment."

She nodded, too enamoured with her mushrooms to mind me leaving her side.

I stopped at the sounds coming from Larg's kitchen. Hesitating at the foot of the stairwell.

Thora was up on the kitchen counter, my brother between her legs, holding a wet cloth to her forehead. Something he said made her smile. And whatever she replied made him laugh. Their talk grew so animated, loud and young.

Before he'd become aware of my presence, I left.

Larg caught up to me halfway across his yard. "You didn't find it?"

"Keep it here for me."

He understood without me giving the reason why.

The dinner had ended successfully. No injured or bloodied or beheaded, though Snow had not given up hope till the very last minute that there would be some form of execution—had even sighed with disappointment when we'd left with bags of jam instead of guts.

Both her and Mal stood side by side in the middle of the night gardens filled with evening primrose. It was past dusk, and as the waxing crescent moon began glowing against the onyx curtain of night, the yellow flowers around us rose their heads toward the skies and slowly peeled open their petals. The flaxen blanket of evening primrose rippled alive for a mile around us and Driada's grave.

This had always been her favourite spot to be in. Many cold nights I had found her here, adoring the life night gave the flowers—it had often given her life, too. She'd been so alone.

The two did not move from where they stood for a long while. Not until a batch of curious fireflies began swarming the area, colouring the place with brightness and filling Mal with hives. My brother was the friend of death, but a slave to insects. I had done my due diligence years ago, attempting to get him out in nature more often and get him used to it, but he'd usually refused.

He began itching his neck, and Snow's shoulders shook with silent laughter. The two bickered quietly for a short moment before turning and walking the distance to the benches where I'd sat. Snow sat on my left and my brother on my right, both staring at the star draped night.

Snow laid her head on my shoulder, and immediately Mal followed suit. I couldn't help but grin to myself. When Snow linked her hand with mine and Mal did the same, I couldn't hold it anymore, I laughed—harder than I should have.

"Mal," I said. "I do not wish to hurt your feelings, but you're supposed to be past this stage."

"You've got a soft pair of hands, big brother."

"He does, doesn't he?" Snow agreed. "You should touch his hair. Soft like a summer cloud."

My brother did just that and nodded to himself. "It is nice indeed."

I swatted my brother's hand away. "What are the two of you plotting now?"

"You lost her, too," Mal said, leaning forward onto his knees and linking his shaking fingers together.

After a little while, I said, "I did."

My brother's face was tense. "I'm sure she was happy to go."

"Don't hold it against her, Mal, I beg. Set her free of your prejudice on the life she wanted so badly to have. It was her right to want and wish despite what you and I think was wrong."

"Even dead, he took again from me."

Snow reached a hand over my lap to hold Mal's. "Let's not make her death about him because it is not about him. She had what she wanted most. Her family. Her boys. Driada has never regretted her life despite her unfulfilled wish—because she had you two."

He turned to my wife, handing her a mooncake. "Shouldn't you be preaching and teaching me how to crawl into the afterlife and kill the bastard a second time?"

My wife glanced at me, holding back what she truly wanted to say. "Just listen to your brother."

Mal's mouth pulled in a smirk and he shook his head. "You were supposed to be on my side."

She waved a hand. "I've made my sacrifice to you for the regretful choice I've made to be on his side."

My brother laughed. "Cai will say the same. And the fool is not so talkative these days anyway."

That was all it took for Snow's small smile to melt off.

I threw my arm over her neck and pulled her to me. "Regretful?"

"You know a bit of evil tastes nice with my tea." She made a stirring motion with her hand. "Just a sprinkle. You are too good, darling. It might rub off on me."

My brother's mouth was agape while he stared between the two of us. "This is ridiculous."

I smacked a big kiss on her cheek that was swollen with the mooncake she was chewing on. "What is?" I asked him.

"The fact that the two most dangerous people in this realm are sitting in the same stool as I, making eyes at each other when a day ago they were about to obliterate two kingdoms."

"I wouldn't say obliterate," Snow muttered. "The unblessed lands cannot possibly be obliterated more than they already are." She looked up at me. "And my husband doesn't obliterate."

Mal scoffed, and Snow's head snapped to him, her smile slowly falling off when he said, "You didn't see what he did in Isjord before we left."

He knew to leave it at that. My brother stood, ruffled her hair and left.

"Shall we head in?" I asked, holding her closer to shield her from the cold wind that picked up and reminded us that even Adriata experienced the cold seasons.

"A little longer, I like it out here," she said, laying her head back on my shoulder, but instead of the glittery skies, she was looking at me, the gold in her eyes glazing over with sparkles.

"Don't you want to look at the stars?"

"I'm looking." The sun in her eyes became radiant, almost turning the blessed night overhead into divine day. She sighed and adjusted her head. "Darling?"

"Yes, love of mine."

"I have very violent thoughts."

My brows rose. "Towards me?"

Her fingers slipped between the button space in my shirt and rested against my skin. "Not at this moment."

That made me chuckle. "Towards whom or what?"

"You will not like it."

"But you will do it anyway."

"I will," she said quietly.

"Could I try to convince you otherwise?"

She shrugged and shuffled closer to me, almost close enough to crawl under my skin yet it wasn't even damn near close enough. "You could try." Her eyes met mine for an entirely different reason, softening to the colour of honey. "How is your heart?"

"Numb. How is yours?"

"He says he's numb."

The fact that this woman was all mine had me question reality every moment of the day. But she was close to me now, and so when I brushed my hand down her soft cheek, I let myself gloat a little. "The cruellest kindness I've been gifted by the Gods is you. They love to remind me that I am only a man by hurting you." I rested my forehead on hers because I could—I was a lucky bastard like that. Despite their cruelty, Gods had always brought her back in my arms. "My Snow."

"You're not just a man, Kil. I don't know what you are, but when you hold me, it is the safest I've felt all my life."

I shook my head. "I didn't keep you safe."

"You saved me."

"Only because you survived. If you hadn't survived him, there would have been nothing for me to save."

19

White Pawn takes C4

Snowlin

KILIAN'S WORDS FROM THE night before were not letting me think in peace.

I didn't know if I'd survived my father.

I didn't know if I'd even survived my own mind.

Or if I would survive my own power.

My signs of struggle were painted on Visha's ceiling. The more I stared at the burn marks against the grey stone, the more I realised how much worse they had grown over the years. The magic had stopped ageing me two years ago, I'd felt it, but the power itself would never stop maturing, growing, becoming a force that one day I might not be able to contain.

Visha stood above me, her hands touching each side of my temple while red, cinnamon scented magic filled the room. Her brows creased, her soft face twitching because of whatever she was seeing inside my mind. Her breaths had grown fast, too, cold sweat dripping down her cheeks and neck. She suddenly gasped and her eyes peeled open. For the first time, she held my gaze longer than a few seconds, long enough to let me see the horror swimming inside the pool of her green irises.

"Who is it?" I asked. "Who is the girl from the vision?"

She stood and hurried to her cabinet filled with dusty books of all sorts. It took her a while to find what she was looking for, digging through each of them with hurry and panic.

Three books lifted up in the air, circling her. Pages violently fluttered open, stopping when she lifted her hand up. Then her eyes moved fast back and forth between the three.

I slipped from the stony table and stepped close to her, looking up at the dark pages illustrating something resembling nightmares. In the middle of one of the pages stood a veiled creature holding a scythe. Glaring at Visha, I said, "She was a child, Visha, the hells are these?"

"They have many names through realms and heavens," she said, trailing a finger under the writing. "Some call them reapers, seraphs of death, angels. Here, in Numen, we call them Guardians. She is like you. The child of a Death Guardian."

All the books drew shut and dropped to the ground. My Crafter paced back and forth, her many beaded bracelets and necklaces dangling and chiming.

I rolled my eyes. "Either you stop or I cut your feet off, Visha."

She halted mid-step, freezing with one leg still up, and looked for Oryn who stood at the corner of the room, just watching. "It has to be just an illusion."

He shook his head. "No, it was a vision, you know it well," the man said, picking up a piece of chalk and drawing a few lines on the small, stained black board hung on the far wall. "But visions have pathways. Any vision at any point of time is moldable. A slight change of action, a different course of action, a weather change, a mood change. All those will affect the probability of the future replicating that vision. Take Macaria's visions. They are simpler than what the child has shown you. Why? Well, because she only sees a few end fragments of a compilation of pathways." He drew over one particular line over and over. "What you were shown was simply one end to the pathway you have started taking."

Visha put her foot down and hurried to the black board. "How do we know it is not the only one?"

He looked at me. "Do you dream of it—of the vision?"

"Yes. Even when I don't close my eyes. I can sometimes hear the noises when it is quiet."

"Does the original vision change from time to time?"

"Slightly."

"Then it is easy." He dragged the chalk without interruption over the black board, creating swirls and twirls all over. "Unpredictability. Do what Snowlin at that point in time would have never thought of doing. Do the opposite of what was your most intense desire at the point your vision was shown."

I laughed despite the uneasy feeling poisoning my blood. "You both are mad."

The two turned to me, confused.

My grin was wide. "I saw Aurora bleeding and breathless. That is the only end result I want. Why would I want to change it?"

I couldn't grasp the horror and fear in their faces. Wasn't that what we wanted? To defeat Aurora and therefore my father?

Visha touched a hand to my arm, wincing and pulling back like I'd burned her. "You cannot decide on it just like that."

Decide? It looked like it had been decided for me. Like everything else. "Why not?"

Her mouth parted open to speak, but no words came out. She touched me again, her hand tightly warped around my wrist, more to hold herself upright than me. "Sometimes, we accept the fate we think we deserve." She shook her head. "Don't."

"Don't what?"

There was no emotion at all in her face, but the single tear slipping out of her left eye felt like it bore all the emotions this world could possibly bear. "Don't accept it. Whatever you think you deserve, Snow, you're wrong. Look around you. Just a little. Outside of the shadows you see and what those shadows say."

"I am. And every time I look around, I know that what awaits out there if Aurora wins is not the fate my loved ones deserve."

"Snow—"

"If you tell a word about this to anyone," I said, picking up my jacket, "I will slay you both like cattle and let crows feast on you for days."

Not one step I'd taken out of Visha's chambers had registered in my mind until I stood inside the musky, dark dungeon room. "Shut the doors," I said to the guard, backing against a wet, far wall and dropping to the ground.

The metal doors slammed shut, robbing the room out of the very little light it had left until I was in a grey darkness. The sort of darkness that made you hazy. The sort where you could still somewhat distinguish if something stood before you yet not entirely grasp whether it was something real or made up by your mind.

There was this hollowness in me that I had not expected. Death had always been walking along my footsteps. I'd learnt to get along with it. I'd learnt to make it fear me. Why was I feeling so weak now that I would confront it?

Strange. I felt so strange.

Like a part of me was missing.

What was missing?

Sometimes we accept the fate we think we deserve.

Visha was right, in a sense. But I still had not accepted the fate I'd seen. Not entirely. I'd only made peace with it.

I lifted up the dagger I held, watching my reflection. "Shouldn't you be laughing?"

Cai hit me with a hazelnut in my forehead, looking around the open Myrdur ruins as he reached me. "Who were you just talking to?"

No one. Don't know why I even bothered, no one was replying to me anymore. Not even the shadows. They were...gone. The further inside my head I searched, the emptier I found it.

He settled across from me, against a massive rock that had fallen from a statue of our God. My friend looked even angrier from a distance. "He left you alone."

"I'll be your shadow. But be your own light," he'd said this morning, and then he'd let me go through this day alone. "Kilian is not my keeper."

"He should be. It is not smart leaving you alone. The last time he left you even a second alone, you subjected yourself to madness."

"What happened was not his fault. I will not let you say that, even if you think so. I went to—"

"Save Nia. I know."

"I don't think you do. Did you want me to let Silas kill them both?"

"Well, he almost killed her."

I wrapped my hands over my ankles, trying not to gather them into bleeding fists. "Tell me what you wanted me to have done, Cai. If it is my guilt you want, have it, but at least tell me what I am guilty of."

"I don't want your guilt," he said, tapping a finger on top of his knee. "You should have waited. Waited for any of us to come before you began bargaining with them. Do you realise that not once have you been alone since you stepped here thirteen years ago?" He beat a hand to his chest. "I have been beside you. Alaric, Nia, Tristin, the whole damn kingdom has stepped at the same footstep as you for thirteen years, Snow. Now you even have him." He laughed madly. "You actually even let him be there for you. Then you went back again. Why do you act like you're all alone?"

"I don't know."

I didn't know.

He rested his head back on the rock and shut his eyes. "I actually hate this stupid sun." His eyes peeled open again when the light around us dimmed at my command, a grey storm sliding over the blue skies. "Do you not hear them anymore?"

"Hear what?"

"You always wince or cringe when you are down here because of the mist. Do you not hear it anymore?"

"I hear it. It's just that there are louder things in my head now." I shot a look around, over the little life that had sprung around the ruins so unlike before. "Heard Isjord hasn't stepped in Myrdur anymore."

"They haven't." He leaned forward, looking like he wanted to say something but debating whether I should know or not. "Kilian stopped a ship a few weeks back."

"Heard he stopped a few."

"This one had some of our people in it. Trained Olympians being held by slavers. Silas had spent quite a fortune on them."

My eyes drew shut. "Hells."

"What are we doing, Cakes? Are we fighting this thing?"

"No, I was thinking maybe we can talk about it with Aurora and my father first. You think they might reconsider this whole *'destroy the whole realm'* ordeal?"

He hit me with another hazelnut. "What is next? There is a plan, I know there is a plan."

"There is." There always was a plan. This one had to end with me—

Groaning, he stood. "You can't keep hiding."

"I am not hiding."

He shot me a pointed look. "You went to the dungeons this morning."

"Maybe *you* should be my keeper."

"Why did you go down there?"

"To reminisce about the good old days when I could squeeze an answer, any answer, from someone."

"What answers?"

"Why nothing makes sense anymore. Any of it."

He sat back down again. Though I could not see the look of worry, I felt it when the wind turned brisk. "Is it like before?"

"Perhaps. But there are no voices in my head to make me feel like I'm losing it. I'm going insane from the silence. The emptiness."

"He shouldn't have left you alone."

I smiled to myself. "Perhaps not."

My feet were struggling to settle anywhere, anxiously pacing back and forth in our room in Amaris. Waiting. And waiting. It was past midnight and he was not here.

I stopped. My heart beating out of my chest when his presence drew shivers across my skin.

The door cracked open.

Kilian stepped in, covered in blood all over. "Not mine," he said, starting to drop his weapons on the ground and unbuttoning his leathers. "How was your day, my love?"

My jaw nearly snapped from how hard it had set. Had he lost his fucking mind? "How was my day?"

He raised a brow, taking off his jacket until he stood there topless, muscles covered in blood. "Was it not good?"

I followed him into the bathroom, taking the cloth he held under the sink and pulling him to face me. "What happened?" I asked, cleaning his face first and then his body, making sure to be careful around the bruising and the scratches.

He watched me so intently, gaze latching onto every little detail on my face. "Why was your day not good?"

"Kil, what the hells happened?"

Then those silver eyes turned so gentle, so soft. "Did something happen?"

I sighed. "Kil."

He lifted a blood-stained hand to my face, ghosting it over my jaw. "Something is wrong."

"Yes. Look at you."

"No. Something else."

I pulled his hand down and cleaned it, pulling his wedding band off to rinse it under the sink. "Get in the bath."

His reflection remained behind me for a long while, but he obeyed my words and slowly got in the bath. "You don't want to tell me."

"I don't know what to tell you."

He leaned his head back and just looked at me. Distracted and lost in his perusal, I had not noticed how dark the room had grown, or how cold it had become, or that the yellow candlelight had turned grey.

"Whose blood is it?" I asked, washing his hair.

"Didn't have time to ask for their names."

"Is this why you let me spend the day alone, so you could go around doing this?"

"No." He raised a hand and pinched my chin. "Missed me?"

"Yes. Hated this stupid idea. Why would I need to be out there on my own when I can simply be with you?"

"Thought you might have wanted or needed the time."

"Never again."

His mouth slowly pulled in the most sinful smile. "The second drawer on my desk. Check it."

Still confused, I stood and reached for the pile of papers in his second drawer. Notes of all sorts about a...dream veil. Kilian had come across my notes on Eamon's Book of Dreams and finally made some more sense to my discovery.

He slipped behind me, still soaked, a towel around his waist. "Smart girl."

Heavens. He'd figured out so much. "You really think we can replicate the dream veil to trap them again?"

He headed for the dressing chambers, and I followed shortly after, flipping through pages and pages of detailed craft. "At some degree. We tracked Vas for a while and Moriko managed to locate him one day down southwest of the Hanaian border. Visha had him trapped for a good solid ten seconds, and it would have taken two more for me to have held him entirely chained under it. But he got out. Barely."

I gaped, realisation hitting me, remembering how weak Vas had looked, wheezing and holding his chest at times. "Is this why he looked injured?"

"That's good to hear."

The papers dropped from my hands. "You were hunting Vas today?"

He dug through his clothes. "Wouldn't call it hunting if I knew where he was."

"Kilian, that is dangerous."

He looked at me over his shoulder, throwing a shirt on. "Is it now?"

"You fought him again today?"

"No. He just stood there and screamed till his witch portalled him out of there."

"The blood—"

"The Aura he had with him. Adriatians. Felt...poetic to do it manually. Sort of had forgotten how bloody people are though."

Glaring at him, I returned to lay down on our bed, picking up some of the calculations Visha had made for the dream veils that she was practising to trap Vas with. Something cold and scaly and familiar and raw touched my shoulder, and I flinched, crawling and stumbling away from the bed until my back met the far wall. My breath misted, old shivers rising over my skin, frost sliding over marble and spreading through the room. Black specks blurred my vision, and when I looked down at my arms, there were bite marks all over again.

I choked, struggling to breathe, feeling something slither against my throat.

Kilian was already on his knees in front of me. "Where...what...what hurts? Love, what's wrong?"

"Don't...don't touch me."

He stilled. Not breathing. Not moving. "There are easier ways to tell me to go die."

Hot tears slipped down my cheeks and I reached for him. "I'm sorry. All...over. They're all over."

He took me on his lap, tracing my skin with his fingers, searching and searching. It took him less time than me to realise that there was nothing there, but he didn't stop, as if to comfort me. He blew on my skin and brushed his hand all over, slowly washing away the veil of memory. "It's alright. They're gone. See?" he asked, slowly kissing my arms. "Gone."

For a brief moment, I tore my eyes from his and looked down.

Gone.

They were gone.

Leaving only a haunted feeling behind.

Memphis wriggled and yowled, hiding in the corner of our bedroom, her cries piercing my heart. It had been her, just her. "I'm sorry."

Kilian looked between her and I. "Come here, Memphis," he called, reaching a hand to her while he held me with the other.

My animal looked unsure, but she slowly prowled to us, her eyes downcast and guilty.

He took my hand and put it on her head, letting me feel my bonded's warm fur. "It's just Memphis, my heart."

She came closer, resting her head on my shoulder, and I hugged her tightly to me. "I'm sorry, M."

I'm sorry, too, her voice echoed back inside my head. She nudged my arms with her snout, and Kilian's hand gently grabbed my own, prying it from where I was scratching against my skin there. He left to return with a warm wet cloth, cleaning the blood. "What is it that you thought touched you?"

I opened my mouth to speak and then shut it when Memphis let out a long trill of broken notes.

Immediately, his eyes lifted to mine again. They searched and searched for answers that he always got correctly. He didn't say it out loud, but he'd figured it all out.

Someone knocked on our door.

Kilian looked like he didn't even hear it. Nor the second or the third knock. His eyes were entirely on me, burning though every layer of truth and past every lie I was planning on telling him.

"Come in," I said when he wouldn't answer.

Mal leaned against my door, dishevelled head to toe, his eyes drowsy with sleep while they bore into me. "What happened? Why are you bleeding?"

"N-nothing."

He raised a brow. "Nothing? It doesn't look like nothing. Why is my brother on the verge of losing his mind?"

I looked over at Kilian, those silver eyes of his were now lost behind a curtain of black, void of life, sucking in every bit of light from the room. "Darling?"

Mal straightened and cautiously pushed into the room. "Kil?" He took a few more careful steps forward. "Brother."

The air chilled from a different sort of frost.

"Get out," Mal ordered me, slowly reaching closer. "Go, Snow, now."

I shook my head. "I'm not leaving him. What is happening?"

"Snow," Mal barked, and Kilian's head snapped in his direction. "Oh, hells. I was being nice, come on now, big brother," he said, raising both hands up. "You know I'm nice to her."

"Mal, what is happening?"

The younger brother kneeled between us, putting a hand on Kilian. Black spidery veins crawled over his face and he groaned almost in pain, his breathing growing laboured.

Kilian caught his wrist and pushed him off. "You're making this a habit," my husband said, returning back to normal.

Mal dropped to the floor, panting and cringing. "You ungrateful shit."

Kilian stretched his neck. "And don't ever shout at my wife."

Mal scoffed, glancing at the little half-moon scratches on my arm and freezing entirely. His gaze remained fixed there, the dark pupils pulsing almost.

A lighter knock rang about the quiet room. "Can I come in now?" Thora asked, peeking over the door. "Oh, I can." She rushed to us, kneeling beside Mal and whispering in his ear, "What is that we're doing?"

"Nothing," I said, giving her a smile and lifting my knees to my chest to cover up my arms.

Her forehead creased. "Malik said he felt something and told me to stay back until it wasn't dangerous. Did something happen?"

"Nothing."

"Say that word one more time," Mal gritted out, his jaw ticking.

"Speak to her like that one more time," Kilian bit back, and the two brothers shared a dark look.

"Why? You're going to lose your shit again? You could have hurt her."

My husband flinched.

I put a hand on his, trying to pull him towards me. "You can never hurt me."

Mal scoffed, shaking his head. "Like hell he can."

Thora reached for him, wrapping her hand around his wrist. "Let's go now, Malik, they are doing fine. Please," she pleaded again when he wouldn't move, and the younger brother's eyes rose to her.

He stood along with her, slowly and discreetly sliding his hand down to hers until their fingers were laced together. "If you're struggling to control your magic, Kil, maybe you might need to take one page from our daddy dearest's practice books."

Hurt like no other crossed Kilian's face, but he nodded. "I will."

The moment they left, I rushed and hugged him to my chest. "What did he mean?"

"Not much, my heart. Shall we go to bed?"

I swallowed hard. "If I tell you what I think touched me, would you tell me what he meant?"

His eyes raised to me again, more hurt flashing through the vivid grey. "Do you want to tell me?"

"I want to know what he meant."

"You don't have to tell me by force, only when you are ready. I'll tell you what he meant though it doesn't matter much." He picked me up and laid me on the bed before following after and tucking me to his chest. "Silence. Darkness. Quiet. My magic feeds on those. Thrives when I've mastered those. Remember what I told you before how I trained it? How my father used to train me?"

I pushed back from him, hurt filling my throat. "He didn't...he didn't mean—"

"Those methods helped, Snow, whether they were wrong or not."

I rose to my knees. "You won't do that. Promise me, Kil. Promise me you will never do that again."

His hand came to cup my face. "Alright, my heart. I promise you. Come here and let me hold you now."

20

Black Bishop to A4

Kilian

SET ON NOT DELAYING action, she'd spent the whole day down at the training courts, tiring her much thinned body along with Caiden who had been anything but a gentle teacher with her. No matter the threatening looks I had sent his way, he had not faltered from battering her up as if she was a ragdoll.

He was angry at her—so goddamn angry.

But he was hurt, too, and because of that, I grit my teeth, dug my feet in the rubble, and resisted the desire to rip out his heart with my bare hands.

Something from the night before had caused the sudden change in her. Reminding me much of the time back in Isjord. Reminding me that I was useless and helpless to her. She wouldn't tell me anything, and I had a vivid imagination that was weakly holding me back from marching inside Tenebrose again. To kill.

"That's enough," I barked when Caiden landed another hard punch on her stomach.

He shot me an unamused look over his shoulder. "Will you be there to coach Silas or any of his pets to hit her gently?"

"You are not training her, you are hurting her."

"She needs to get familiar with pain."

This fucker was trying to mess with me, not her. I shot up from my seat and stalked to him. "You know damn well—"

"Boys," Snow said, panting from where she'd laid on the ground. "I swear, if you start measuring whose cock is bigger, I'm going to bolt myself right in front of a hungry bear and just lay there until it has licked up all my cartilages. Might even thank it."

When I reached to help her up, Caiden batted my hand away. "She can get up by herself."

And that was it. I punched him.

Snow shot up and came between us, her hands resting on my chest. "Darling, it is fine."

"See," Caiden said, wiping blood from his mouth. "She can get up."

I sneered. "I really want to see you get up after I'm gone with you."

Snow's fingers were gentle on me, she pulled my face down to hers and kissed me. "What is it?"

"He was being too rough and you know it."

"He is always like that."

"No, no he is not."

"Kil. He is," she said, pointing under her elbow, the finger shaking. "I had a big gash here, remember? I was about seventeen and he gave me a playful shove while I was standing next to an alcove. I tumbled for a good solid minute down the cliff because of that."

"Then by right I ought to punch him again."

She bit her smile down. "Alright, horses down, big boy."

"Snow," I said, cradling her face in my hands. "Whatever it is that you are doing, stop it."

She was silent again. So silent.

If she wanted me to say it for her, I would. "It won't fix what he thinks you broke, Snow. Not his trust in you. Not the promise you gave him. It will not take away the fact that he almost lost you. Whatever you let him do to you. Whatever punishment you want from him or Alaric. You are not deserving of any of that. Tell me that you know it."

She swallowed and tore her eyes away from mine.

"Deny it," I said. Lying would be better than nothing. Better than this silence.

Her lips parted, but nothing came out. Silent again. When had she ever been this silent? Not when I was her enemy. Not when she had hated me. Not after she'd told me she loved me. Never.

"Leave," I said to Caiden. "There is something I need to talk about with my wife."

Snow did not turn to look at her friend who lazily descended the training courts and left. She didn't look at me either.

I rested my lips against her temple. "Why are you keeping me from here? Do you...do you not trust me anymore?"

Her head whipped back and her eyes shot wide. "Kil, no."

"My queen," Visha called, and Snow's attention went to her. "Might I see you for a moment?"

"She'll come to you in a second, Visha. After she tells me at least one truth."

Snow got to her tiptoes and pressed a kiss on my lips. "I trust you. I do not trust myself."

She slipped from my hands just like that, rushing to drag Visha away.

I didn't think twice, I faded to where Caiden was, following after him while he manoeuvred through the city and took a seat inside a tavern.

"I'll tell you what you want to know," he answered before I even asked. "Sit. I can't have this conversation while I'm starving."

"You'd go against her word?"

"Not if she had asked me to keep it a secret. But she hasn't."

"So, you'll just tell me to spite her?"

He sneered, breaking some bread sticks in half, probably wishing it was my neck instead. "I'll tell you because you're the only person who can seem to get through her head."

I took a seat. "Speak then."

"She thinks she has forgotten."

"Forgotten what?"

"Pain. She says it doesn't bother her and that she doesn't notice much of it anymore. She fears that she might be hurt, but wouldn't notice if she really is hurt or just imagining it. It is all in her head, Kilian. I know it. I think she just wants to be treated normal again. Treated as a normal human being."

I took a moment to process what he was trying to say. "By beating her up?"

He shrugged. "If I went gently on her, it would never work. She wouldn't have bought it." His eyes rolled up to me. "You don't know her how I do. You haven't seen her like I have, Your Majesty. She needs this."

I leaned forward and stole one of his bread sticks. "I'm still going to break those arms one day for what you did today."

He glanced between me and the breadstick I stole. "You'll help her?"

"Without touching a single hair on her pretty head. You said she wants to feel normal. Pain was her normal. I don't want her to think that is all that will be normal to her. That pain is the only constant thing in her life. She has stopped hurting in one way and is still trying to compensate by hurting in another way. Both aren't the solution, Caiden. You want her to feel normal? Start creating another normal for her. From the beginning. Without pain being the foundation holding it up. I know you two share difficult history and it might be hard for you to move past it, but I ask, if not for the sake of you, do it for the sake of her."

He leaned back on his seat and sighed. "You're unbearable."

I took a bite from the breadstick. "That's the nicest thing you've ever told me."

"I really don't wish to see you right now."

"Not really a choice," I said, taking another breadstick and dipping it in his stew. "I'm your king." I pointed the breadstick at him. "Touch my woman like you did today and I'll introduce you to a new concept of death."

I watched her from afar as she made her way through Taren. Following her every step around her kingdom through shadows. I knew she'd felt me because from time to time, she smiled to herself and glanced at her own shadows.

Her presence was soft around her people, quieter this time round. And even they'd noticed.

Olympians knew how to feed her strength though. One house she went by fed her butter scones. Then there was a navy scarf wrapped around her when she came out of another one with two elderly women. A family by the edge of the city gave her a brand new string of marble beads which she counted all the way to where Nia and

Thora were waiting for her. The three went by so many shops that I had to shake myself awake at times. When they settled by a small bakery to have some assortments of biscuits and tea, my love glanced at the setting orange sunset in the distance and waved.

I faded behind her, and leaned to whisper in her ear, "Wrong way."

"Stalker."

"You loved it," I said, taking a bite from the biscuit she had in her hand and settling in a chair between the three women. "How was your day, ladies?"

Nia rolled her eyes up at me. "Bet you can give us better details about it."

Thora gaped between us three. "You were following us? Why did no one tell me?"

"I was hoping he'd grow tired from the shopping and eventually leave," Nia added.

"A good attempt," I said, leaning back on my chair and throwing an arm around my quiet wife's shoulders.

She turned to me and put a biscuit in my mouth. "Is Cai alive? A few had seen you dine together."

"Still deciding on it." I took a sip from her tea. "What did Visha want earlier on?"

"The full moon fog is starting to clear from the Deadlands and I can soon go and hunt some very naughty witches." She blinked innocently. "Why? You want another moment to escape and go after Vas?"

"It was your idea," Nia said, shrugging.

Snow shot her a look. "Let me remind you that your lover helped in this."

Nia's eyes jumped between us. "Mor listens to him. That is not my fault."

Another body dropped to the chair next to Thora. My brother groaned from a headache it seemed and squinted at all of us. "What are we eating?"

Thora got up. "I'll get you something savoury, these are all sweet."

"Where were you?" I asked.

"Highwall. We checked for that blind spot Moregan said spies were exchanging information with Silas." He stretched in his seat, sprawling wide. "Never realised how big that stupid wall is."

Nia raised a brow at him. "And there is a tavern there, too?"

My brother gave her a wolfish grin. "I carry all the necessary assortments for entertainment, Helenia," he said, his eyes following the younger Skygard as she walked out of the bakery, returning to us.

"Cheese scones," Thora said to him and sat down.

He tugged at her rose coloured bow and stuffed it in his pocket. "Thank you, little bird."

Thora sneered, annoyed, but did nothing to claim her hair tie back.

Snow had gone quiet again, not looking at anyone. Her attention returned only when I wrapped a hand over her thigh. Her head rose to me and she leaned to kiss me. "Hey."

"Hey," I murmured back at her, tucking some of her dark hair back.

It was the fourth night in a row that she was sleeping in my arms after six long months. She was restless as the other three previous ones. Pretending to fall asleep. Pretending she wasn't afraid to dream. And I was tired of pretending that I didn't know, but I didn't want to scare her away—I didn't want to scare her back into her shell like that night. The way she was answering me less and less, the ways she spoke softer...all of it terrified me. It terrified me because I knew her thoughts were not as gentle as she was being. And Snow never thought softly or gently or so little.

Very slowly and carefully, she turned around to face me. Even though my eyes were closed, I could feel her studying me. Holding back that smile was the hardest thing I had done these past few days.

"You're not sleeping," she whispered. It wasn't a question, nor a statement. She was unsure.

Still, I didn't stir or let on that I wasn't indeed asleep. Cautiously, she pushed up to her elbows and started leaving small pecks all over my face, down my neck, and all over my ear.

I groaned so loudly that she flinched and let out a little surprised squeal when I wrapped my arms around her tightly. How undeserving I often felt to hear the sounds she made from happiness. "What troubles you, love of mine?" I asked, cupping the back of her head and pulling her lips to mine. In my hold she was silken, gentle, roses and soft stars. By my side she was nothing but a titan of power, no sky stood above her, it was simply being held for her.

She gasped when I deepened the kiss, moaning softly around my tongue. Her mouth would be raw by the time I was sated with her taste. She kept kissing me as she leaned to my ear, and whispered seductively, "I want a glass of milk."

There was one moment of pure silence before I howled with laughter like a mad man. "Milk?"

She nodded even though her brows were pulled in a scorning scowl at my reaction to the odd request. "It helps me sleep. Alaric used to bring me milk every night when I was little. He had read it somewhere that it helps you sleep."

"You can't sleep?"

"You know it, so stop acting like you don't."

Weaving my fingers through her hair, I pulled her closer so I could see those gilded irises better. "How do you feel?"

She opened her mouth and then shut it, reluctantly thinking for a moment before answering me, "Like I need to run."

Fucking finally. The words *fine* and *alright* were about to drive me insane knowing she was none of that.

"Then let's run," I said, wrapping an arm around her waist and standing. I sat her on my lap as I reached to put her boots on, and then threw one of my jackets over her naked shoulders.

She blinked, watching me roll the sleeves up. "What do you mean by *let's run?*"

"Exactly that." I kissed her cheek and faded us to the middle of Soren Forest.

Wind howled eerily around us and loud enough to warn of the change in seasons. Winter was almost here.

I put her down and pushed her hair back. "What you feel won't change so easily, Snow, no matter what good things happen after the bad. Healing is simply not that simple. Falling back to habits does not always have to be destructive. If running helps, then run. But don't run alone." I let go of her and slowly stepped back. The way she traced my movement with her eyes had my body react with such force that I was struggling to take those steps away. "You can run, but I will be right behind."

She swallowed and shifted on her feet. "Will you chase me?"

I shook my head. "I already have you. It cannot be a chase. But I will play with you."

Her mouth pulled up in a subtle smirk. "Games have rules. What rules do we have?"

"Don't let me catch you," I started, taking another step back and swivelling a look over her naked legs that I was going to have wrapped around my waist by the end of this night. "That is the only rule."

"And if you do?"

"Better run fast, my love."

She shivered and her mouth parted, her tongue sweeping over her rosy lips to wet them. "Alright."

There was not a moment of hesitation before she backed away and sprinted into the forest. I waited a little for her steps to falter and blend with the sounds of night, and then chased in her direction. The air was brisk and sharp, filled with the taste of pine and winter, but it carried her maddening scent of lily. Folk of all sorts began fluttering close by, and the shadows surrounding me blurred and blended together, distracting me enough to lose grasp where Snow was for a moment.

Hells, she was fucking fast.

But I knew the shape of her shadows better than I knew the shape of the moon. And she needn't be hung in any skies for her to be bright. For her to glow.

Moonlight had cast a halo over her form, her black hair glistening as wind weaved its hands around it while she ran. The little white satin nightgown she wore had ridden up along with the jacket, and I had the most explicitly delicious view of her silken thighs that puckered with muscles each time her feet met the ground.

Her giggles were contagious, echoing like a dreamy lullaby in the dark forest. She glanced back from time to time, throwing me a massive grin over her shoulder.

She didn't slow. She only ran faster. The burn, the breathlessness, all made her run faster. When her giggles faded and she wouldn't look back at me anymore, I knew she needed to be in my arms.

I deviated around her and crossed the forest almost diagonally in her direction, and once I was close enough, I wrapped my arm around her waist and lifted her up. She screamed and giggled when I threw her over my shoulder, smacking the soft flesh of her arse and biting her thigh. "Should have run faster, my love."

"Maybe I didn't want to," she said breathlessly, wiggling like mad in my hold.

I lowered her down, wrapping her legs around my waist. "What should I do to you first, hm?" I kissed her soft mouth until she was melting around my tongue. Her hips moved against mine, and my already painful erection was straining hard against my trousers.

She pulled back for a breath, her golden gaze was glossy and glistening with lust. "Please don't hurt me, mighty Night King," she whispered, feigning the dramatic plea, and my cock loved that. "Should I yell for help? Am I in big, big trouble?"

I chuckled and bit her shoulder, groaning when she moaned in my ear. "I'm going fuck you until you will be too sore to walk let alone run."

"Oh, no," she mockingly gasped.

A cloud of black shadows rose up and around our periphery, shielding us from the world.

"What secret are you about to tell me in the dark?" she murmured, rolling her hips against mine.

I braced her back against a tree and unbuttoned my trousers. "How about I show you?"

"Can't see."

"No need to see this one," I said, pulling the thin material of her underwear to the side and pushing myself inside her. She was already wet, her cunt soaking my cock and letting me easily slip in and out of her.

"My sweet sin," I murmured over her throat, chasing kisses to her ear. "Did the chase excite you?"

Her back arched under my touch when she took all of me, adjusting so, so well to my size, her soft, full, and perfect tits pressing against my chest, letting me feel all of her. "Yes," she breathed, a long string of whimpers following.

Her fingers dug on my shoulders, in my hair, my neck, desperately grabbing and holding me to her while I fucked her. She didn't know how perfect she looked even in the dark, how much she glowed against it, how envious of her it was when she smiled drunkenly, not realising anyone could see it.

I ran my hands all over her, pushing the jacket off of her shoulders and feeling her cool skin over my own, cupping my hands all over her curves, feeling what belonged to me. From the way her body responded to my touch, leaning in and shivering, I knew my claim on her. Her mind—I wanted to know my claim there, too. "Say you're mine."

She bit on my lip, hard, sucking on a droplet of blood seeping out the broken skin. "I'm yours. Fuck, Kil, I am yours." Her fingers ran down my chest, lightly scratching skin and making my abs and my breath tighten. "But you are mine, too."

When she smiled against my mouth, so victorious of the way she broke any control I had, any sanity I held, there was no restraint in the way I claimed her after.

Her body bucked and she cried out, the divine sounds bouncing back around the darkness to torment me, to tempt me. Throwing me right at the edge of delirium.

"I love you," I said over her mouth, still ravishing her notes of ecstasy, the way her tight cunt pulsed around me, and how her body puckered with gooseflesh and stained redness when I drew out her release.

Her fingers grabbed at my hair, gently pulling to kiss me how she wanted to—so hungrily. "And I love you, Kil."

Fuck, I wanted to remain buried in her.

She swayed in my arms when I put her down, her lips parted, panting for air. "That was," she breathed out, giggling. "That was good, so good."

I buttoned up my trousers. "Thank you."

"Most welcome."

"From now on," I said, kissing the tip of her nose and adjusting her night gown to cover all her pretty tits now covered in my marks. "Always run with me. Walk with me. Go places with me. Decide with me. Act on all the madness you can think of, but do it with me by your side."

She had finally caught her breath but decided to hold it at my last words. "How long will you hold that against me?"

"I've not decided on a date just yet. Perhaps a calendar year, perhaps two."

She bit her lip and peered up at me under her thick lashes so innocently she could make the dead faint right back to their graves a second time. "Forgive me?"

"Forgiven," I said, and her face broke into the most radiant smile she had given me since her return. "So forgiven," I repeated, kissing her mouth. "Do you feel better?"

She stretched like a cat. "Oh, I feel fantastic."

"Snowlin Castemont."

"Yes. Much. I think I just needed to realise that I could run. That nothing was holding me back."

The sigh I breathed out lessened some weight from my chest. I bent down and hoisted her up on my shoulder. "Let's go so I can perform some husbandly duties."

She wiggled her feet. "In the bath. Let's fuck in the bath."

"I was thinking of feeding you, my missus," I said, smacking her bottom. And before she could say something that I knew she was going to say, I added, "Food. Feed you food."

She sighed, her body sagging in my hold. "I've become predictable. My end is near."

"Believe me, I don't think you will ever become predictable. You will always find a way to startle me to a young death."

She pinched my backside. Definitely still unpredictable. "They are so perfect from this angle," she said in awe, fondling my buttocks. "No wonder Cai turned to your side so quickly after being an adamant hater of yours. I want to bite them."

I might have laughed a bit too loud because all the curious folk who had carefully left their homes to spy on our conversation retreated back at the speed of light. "An adamant hater of mine, you say?"

"Oh, Gods, we used to have such heated conversations about you and your stupidly handsome face."

"Hm. Was that before you fell in love with my stupidly handsome face or after?"

She cleared her throat and hesitated a bit before mumbling, "Blood is rushing down my head from the way you are holding me, so I might be a bit...befuddled about it."

I grinned to myself and pulled her down, wrapping her bare legs around my waist as I carried us further inside the forest. "Better?"

"Might have been both," she said quickly, resting her cheek on my shoulder. "Before and after. You were such a prick."

I bit her soft cheek, her neck, her shoulder just to see her writhe and giggle again. "Good thing I was such a prick. Look what it got me."

The noise of people and horses grew closer, and so did the edge of Fernfoss village.

The tavern closest to the forest was already full. People ate, drank, laughed, and danced, as if they were clueless to the war ahead. But they all knew. They all knew well. Most of those sitting around us were soldiers. Adriatian. Olympian. Hanaian. Even a few odd Red Coven Crafters.

I pulled her to a table hidden behind a wooden pillar that concealed us from the rest of the room. Surely, an Isjordian soldier or two must be roaming around the area and reporting back to their king. Snow and I would be recognised in an instant. And how long would it take him to dispatch his minions and turn this village into a graveyard?

The young server's eyes doubled when he noticed Snow, and his body almost instantly folded into a bow had she not kicked his shin. He yelped, clutching his leg, and Snow sneered at him. "Where is your father?"

The boy blinked at both of us, and leaned in to whisper, "Gone over to Whitebridge for some supplies. It's been only me and ma for a week now."

Snow frowned. "Whitebridge?"

He nodded. "Eldmoor and Hanai cut trade with the continent because...because of...the Winter King. We have been cooking with barely any salt. Most of our dishes are boiled now because we have no oil either."

She looked over at me, coming to some realisation.

"Send word for your father to return," I said. "I'll deal with the spice issue."

His eyes darted from Snow's hand to mine, and they went wide a second time. He almost bowed again. "How, my king?"

"Leave it to me. Spread word to those you trust to not travel out of the old Olympian borders for any reason from now until it is past winter season. It is dangerous."

The moment he was out of earshot, Snow asked, "It was you, wasn't it? The one who cut my father's trades?"

I nodded. "How come this side of Olympia is so distanced from the rest? I was hoping your people had spread the word down here, otherwise I would have done so myself and not let them starve." Guilt was now digging a hole in my stomach.

"Whoever remains here chooses to remain in ignorance about what lies beyond the *zgahna*. Just in case my father were to torture the truth out of them. Even with the little help we give them, it has to be made in absolute secrecy and sometimes without their knowledge."

"But why remain here? Why not join the rest of Olympia?"

"All Olympians who have decided to remain here are from Myrdur. Survivors who either managed to hide or escape. Most returned a few years after the Night of *Draugr*. *Breitg goh dysin agh tah fana us berzgha. Born to die in the land that birthed you.* A swift always returns to die in its nest. All of them refuse to abandon the land again despite the risks. One day, I hope to build the city and return to live here. Cai and I found the old architectural notes and sketches of the city in the Taren library when we were younger. We were going to build it back exactly how it was." Her eyes drifted over her people. "One day."

I pinched her chin and turned her face to me. "I'll build you your city. Exactly how you want it."

Her eyes gleamed. "You will?"

"You have my word."

"Kil, you don't—"

"You have my word," I repeated. "If you want the stars, I will get you the stars. If you want the moon, I will get you the moon. Every wish that you have, everything you desire, I'll bring it to your feet. You only have to tell me, nothing else."

She took my hands, leaving a kiss on top of both. "You have to tell me, too. I'll give you all *you* want."

"You've already given me all I want."

The inn keeper had given us a room on the top floor after we'd debated for a minute or so how safe it would be for us to remain here. The decision came quickly after Snow had started petting my thigh and kissing my neck. Watching her try to stifle her moans and failing had made me come harder than before. The looks we were going to get after we'd leave this room was something to be dealt with at another time because she'd gone to sleep. Dreamlessly.

Her body laid naked, sprawled on top of me, softly snoring. Until I suddenly felt her breath seize for a moment, and then two. She jolted awake, eyes wide and panting for air.

"Hey," I whispered, bringing her to me again. "It's okay."

She swallowed and shook her head. "It is not. There is something—" She didn't finish her sentence. "It wasn't a dream." Quickly, she got to her feet and rushed towards the window. Her right hand shook, and she blew on it as if it burned while her eyes were narrowed on the direction of the village.

"Love, what is it?" I asked, walking up to her.

Then I felt it.

Like the smell of incense burning.

Magic.

Black magic.

Tasting like death.

I grabbed her hand and lifted it up. A black tattoo sprung from the middle of her right palm, spreading and blooming into the shape of a spider lily. "What have you done, Snow?"

"A deal."

"With whom?"

"The Prince of Ustrina. I promised him a life he cannot take and now I can feel Vas's presence."

Gods help me. "Love—"

"Please don't be mad."

My eyes drew shut. "Snowlin."

"Please, Kil." She hurriedly began searching the room for her clothes. "Why is he looking to enter my lands?" she asked herself more than me, dressing haphazardly.

"Someone must have seen us."

Once we were somewhat dressed, I faded the two of us to the edge of the village, right where the white of winter separated against the warm soil of old Olympia.

There were no beasts. There was just one beast. Far inside the coniferous forest, just slightly over the old Olympian border. A pair of glowing green eyes stared at us from the distance—a protected distance of dark magic stinking of mint and rot.

"Well, well," Snow shouted, her voice booming around the stretch of silence. "Why is the little mouse hiding? Afraid?" She stepped forward, her feet sinking into the snow, and with every move she made, my shadows followed, creating a shield of protection around her. "What are you so afraid of, Vas? Why are you always so afraid?" She took a few more steps ahead as if to lure him towards her. "Doesn't it suffocate you, to live in fear? It must be terrifying."

The glow of green eyes grew closer to her. "Sometimes," he drawled, voice hoarse and breathy. "It is good to be afraid, Snowlin."

Night melted onto the ground, the moon above hiding entirely at my order. But the blanket of shadows crashed against a veil. As I'd thought, he was well shielded from my magic, and had expected it even. He'd learnt much from our last encounters. Considering he'd barely healed in places, he'd learnt well.

Her smile was wicked. "Nonsense. Why should I be afraid when you can be afraid for me, too?"

He stood tall, no longer hiding behind the forest shade. "Arrogance is the death of many. It shall be the death of you."

"How funny is that coming out of you," Snow said, stepping further forward, almost taunting him to step just outside Melanthe's protection. "Look where you stand."

A howl called in the distance, and we both tensed.

It was a forewarning.

He stepped forward, but not outside the invisible craft halo that was protecting him. "In plain sight, where better to hide, is it not? You would not say where your people hide, so I will have to just slaughter them all. Olympians or not. This will all be on you. Every death tonight will be on you."

Fuck.

A trap.

Snow's movements were feline, predatory. "I like this. Watching you so afraid of my people. Picturing you gathered in the middle of the night, discussing and worrying about...a *few* Olympians gets me all giggly."

Almost lured, he dared step forward and then retreated as if he had caught himself. "What about the fact that I knew you were exactly here tonight, does that excite you? I knew where to hunt you. In fact, it was no hunt at all."

An unnatural shift in the village behind us caught my attention. Bodies moved hurriedly, my shadows following them along. They hopped from one house to the other. Humans, not beasts.

"Like old times," Vas growled, his fangs gleaming when screams and flames broke through the night.

Snow shed my jacket, throwing it to the side, her fists glowing with thunder whilst mine summoned every thick shadow cast by the moon.

"They're in the village," I said to her in Darsan, and her whole body tensed. "Go. I have him."

The ground beneath our feet began vibrating, the forest behind him suddenly disturbing, creatures fleeing from all sides. All sorts of terrifying sounds pealed through the night silence.

Snow hesitated. One step ready to take off towards the village and the other bracing for what was coming towards us. "I'm not leaving you."

"I've got this. Your people need you. Save as many as you can. Go, my love."

Reluctantly, she nodded, her steps still heavy when she backed away and bolted towards the village.

The smell of rot seeped into the crisp night air. Then they were there, pushing and crawling all over each other, some launching in the air and others running directly for me. Including Vas.

The man stopped when Caiden portalled right between us, both his hands raised forward, pulling them apart as did Vas's body, without even touching him at all. The Olympian general twisted two daggers in his hands and stalked to Vas's remains, tearing through beasts one after the other, my shadows forming a protection space around him while I held back the massive herd aiming for the village.

Visha portalled next, then Eren, Alaric, the Skye, Larg, and Triad followed by more soldiers and Aura.

What Silas and his band of idiots didn't know was that we all had eyes on every corner of this realm.

"Evacuate the village," Alaric shouted to the Skye.

"Too late for that," Vas growled, rising from the ground again, his flesh mending.

Just not quick enough because Caiden was already pulling him apart. Over and over. Each time his body mended, it broke apart within seconds.

"How long do you think you can keep doing that!" he bellowed, trying to reach Caiden, only to be caught in a web of my darkness, not realising he'd stepped out of protection, his flesh sizzling from the touch of death he was cursed to never know.

"Melanthe!" he shouted, and then vanished away like the wind.

If I had a gold dar for every time he'd done that when he faced me, I'd be a much richer king. However, just as I was studying him, he was studying us, learning our boundaries, learning how to mess with our heads.

Perhaps that is what tonight's ambush had all been about.

Instigating fear. Torment.

Night had turned into day from the fire lit behind us, it had enveloped the village for miles around, almost catching on the forest behind it. The beasts had been many—many more that we'd expected Silas to spare for an ambush.

Heavy rain poured on us, and the master of the storm came and went inside the village houses, trying to evacuate as many as he could from the fire. Eren's hands were full, sometimes holding people, and at other times commanding ice and rain to douse the fires.

Except, there was no dousing the fire that was lit with dark magic. Blackfire kept burning endlessly.

Darkness poured from me, slithering down the village floors and spreading over the fires enveloping the buildings until there was no more trace of it.

Blackfire barely doused from water and frost like it doused from my magic, evaporating entirely from my touch, no toxic smoke following after to poison the air.

An Adriatian had planned this. I was sure of it. They'd known to use just that.

Survivors had crowded the entry to the Myrdur ruins. Healers worked fast between the hundreds and thousands of villagers who had sustained burns and many more wounds from the blasting ice summoned by the Isjordian soldiers who'd hid amongst them. The people were quiet, their eyes all glued on one person alone.

Snow sat at the edge of the ruins with a little girl on her lap, soot covering both of their faces. Something had been robbed out of her today. Maybe even before and I'd just noticed. The empty stares—this was why she'd hid them from me. To not let me know that her father still held prisoner some part of her down in those dungeons. Torturing her still. Endlessly.

"I can't find her parents," she said to me in Darsan, her voice hopeless. "The house where they were sleeping was on fire when I went in, she had tried to douse the flames with wind and everything else around her had burned even worse. I should have looked."

Her chest began rising fast, and I took the girl from her arms, lulling her to sleep with a slip of magic. "You did all you could," I said, kneeling before her. "These people live because of you."

She shook her head. "The first thing that came to mind when I saw the flames was to run, just like I was told that night. I've never saved a single thing in my life, Kil. This is what happens when I try to save something." Her face hardened, the icy gold fire returning to them again. "But...one thought separates me from getting up and showing the whole of Isjord what it feels to truly burn. That is my power. To destroy." She looked over her shoulder at her people. "Will they look at me the same if I do just that? Or will I become just another thing they fear?"

"Is that what you want to do?"

Her voice was small. "Yes. Do *you* fear me?"

"No, but I fear what it would do to you." *It would kill her.* I ran my fingers over her face. Realisation crushing me and making my heart ache like never before. "You don't, do you? You don't fear what would happen to you."

"I want to burn, Kil. No matter if I burn with it. But if I burn, I might burn you. What stands between my father and the fate he deserves is you." She wiped the lone tear escaping her eye, her hand shaking. "It will pass. It will surely pass."

"Your Majesty," a healer called for her. "Would you mind helping us with some burn wounds?"

Snow looked at me first and then nodded, taking the girl from my arms and following shortly after the healer through the ruins to where more people had taken shelter. The feigned smiles she offered to those around her tore at my heart, ripping it little by little, but it comforted her people.

Caiden stood in the middle of the burnt remains of the village, staring at two Isjordian soldiers kneeling before him. "They'd been living amongst us for years. I knew these two idiots," he said, kicking his foot on their faces. "They had identified all the Olympians here, slowly gotten to know everyone. My people had welcomed them into their homes. Fed, clothed, and housed them."

One of the men laughed under his breath. "They should have all just died back then."

Caiden lowered before him, and the man choked from the lack of air. "Oh? What else, tell me."

The man's skin turned purple, his hands clawing and digging at his throat and chest. Every little vein in his eyes popped, turning the white sclera red.

"What was that?" the Olympian general asked, cupping a hand to his ear. "Ah, perfect. Silent. Like all of your sort should be." He tilted his head back, watching them all slowly choke. "Are they afraid of me, Kilian?"

"Very."

He clicked his tongue at them, his magic retreating, and the men heaved, finally breathing. "Don't be. It gets our Crafter's magic all dizzy, and she might cut up your brains wrong."

Both men looked behind us at where Visha was standing, already waiting for them. They almost, almost begged not to be taken when Visha portalled away with them.

Tristin landed close to us. "Memphis had a note attached to her. Moregan's warning came a bit late. I think they were expecting to find a resistance of sorts down here, not just odd families trying to get by. Many soldiers and beasts left very soon after the attack."

Caiden wiped a hand over his mouth. "Yeah, their miscalculations cost us a lot, Tris. How long have these people been around us? How much do they know?"

"Mal's Eldritch Command will be here shortly," I assured. "They will go through everyone and make sure no others have slipped by."

"Lies," Mal said, strutting to us with all his men. "I'm already here."

Caiden's eyes darted all over the Eldritch soldiers spreading through the village and towards the Myrdur ruins. "Just don't scare anyone. Most have lost everything they had, even family."

My brother put a hand to his chest. "With this face? Muffin, you injure me."

"Silas has been looking for Olympians for ages, this was not unexpected," Eren said, dragging another Isjordian for Visha to take next.

The man sputtered, gasping for air and crawling away from everyone, his eyes wide and mad with fear as they focused on Eren. "Don't hurt me. I beg. I know nothing!"

"Be quiet now," Eren ordered, looking around. "Where is Snow?"

"Being a queen for once, not just the crazy lady," Nia said, heading to Caiden to wrap his burnt arm with some gauze. "Don't move, you idiot, I can smell the grey salt in the air. Verglasers are growing smarter. They know how to utilise their magic to the fullest. Ice and grey salt will melt your flesh to the bone, and won't let any magic heal it either."

"Moregan might have showed them," Eren said, blowing a heavy breath. "I've seen Isliners using the same technique."

Nia looked up at me. "Why are you so quiet?"

Because half of me is torn and pretending she is not. "No one returns to their homes in Fernfoss. It is time Olympians join their kind across the mist whether they made an oath to the land or not. The rest of the people remaining will be welcomed in Adriata. Nia, ask Moriko if she would be willing to let any in Hanai."

"We leave Fernfoss?"

"No, we will come back to Fernfoss. We will raise our war banners in this land, all of them. Silas's war started here, and it will end here."

Some screaming ensued, a telling sign that my brother was at work. Not minutes later, he returned with more men to join our circle. "What a cute attempt, eh? Hiding between the rest with burn marks and smoke on their faces yet not one hair out of place," he said, shaking his head at them. "All I could salvage, I am afraid. Your wife's anger got the best of her. Yet again."

"Just wanted to see if I could melt their mouth shut," she said, walking to us. "How would I know his whole brain would explode?"

"A simple guess, maybe?" my brother said, leaning against a porch rail. "I know that look."

Everyone looked over at Snow after his words.

She awkwardly took my side, fisting the back of my shirt to hold onto me for dear life. "What look?"

"Vengeance," Tristin said. "You're going to get it."

My wife pressed her face to my arm to hide her wicked smile.

21

White Pawn to C3

MACARIA STARED AT ME over her teacup. All of the Red Coven witches did so while we sat in their dining room, eating almond biscuits and making no conversation whatsoever.

Except Mal. He'd flirted with half of the women while the other half had already given into his charm without him even batting an eyelid at them.

Visha sat quietly beside me, her tea growing cold in her lap while she stared at the empty velvet emerald armchair that stood at the centre of the sitting formation. Considering that none, including Macaria, had not sat there, I imagined it belonged to her mother.

"Did Penelope not wish to come with you?" Macaria asked, clearing her throat.

"I do not bring children along with me in these types of ventures."

"To a tea gathering?"

"To a murder scene."

The violet witch choked on a sip and coughed her lungs out for a moment. "M-murder?"

"I believe Visha has told you that Melanthe intends to take over Red Coven."

Macaria nodded. "She did, and we have made sure it will remain an impossible task for her. Grand Maiden or not, our coven has never fallen."

"Yet. Not fallen *yet*." I lowered my cup. "I have a simple solution for a problem that is possibly costing you time, energy, supplies, and patience."

She raked her eyes over my attire and all of my weapons. "You can't just find and accuse every Crafter of being her accomplice."

"Not every Crafter. And might I remind you that there is a debt remaining uncollected from your people. Consider this as making you aware that my debts are always collected." I stood to study the portraits on her walls, and said, "I need to trace a Crafter."

"Which?"

"Salma was her name." I looked around the room for the heart that suddenly beat quicker than the rest, and unsheathed a dagger. The scent of magic around their hiding place inside the Deadlands had not been Melanthe's, so my next best guess was her second in command. "I'm hoping that at least one of you must be blood related to her. It's only a drop that I want."

"The one in the corner," Visha said quietly, sipping her tea.

With the help of the blood trace, Visha had portalled us not far from where Melanthe's coven was hidden in the undead forest, concealed under its barren crown and heavy scent of rotting.

Mal let out a low whistle, surveying the dead grounds. "I promised a few ladies I'd bring back souvenirs, sis-in-law. Where on the crescent heaven have you brought us?"

I shot Visha a look over my shoulder. "Verdict?"

"You may kill them all," she said plainly, stepping back and raising her glowing hands towards the veil over the coven.

"You'll get your souvenirs," I said to Mal, putting my gloves on and unsheathing my daggers, skipping along to a tune Lysander had once taught me, said to have been sung once upon a time during the death of a Crafter. I had much respect for their traditions, you see.

"No limbs. And for Gods' sake, no eyeballs or tongues," Mal said. "Nothing soft."

Not bothering with knocking, I pushed the handle, finding it open just as I had predicted. There was a herd of sounds coming from all over the sage scented house and one particular gasp from a stunned Crafter standing right before me.

Before she could scream, I sent a dagger flying right between her eyes, and caught her body as it was about to drop to the ground and attract unwanted attention.

There were five other Crafters bleeding on the old oak floors when I reached the makeshift war room where Melanthe and Salma with her little minions had been making their plans to move against Macaria and take over Red Coven—and eventually all of Eldmoor.

None noticed my presence, not until I slammed the door behind me and loudly dragged a chair to sit beside them.

All of them shot up like the ground below had lit on fire, red magic gleaming from their hands. So much power in one small room.

Shadows began elongating and melting off the walls, slithering like phantom serpents on the ground and crawling over their bodies, drying them off magic at Malik's silent command and wrapping around their throats.

"Sit," I said, lifting my dagger to the neck of the young Crafter sitting on my right. "All of you."

"Melanthe will know you are here," one said calmly, how only witches knew to keep calm. None were afraid of death. Death was their bitter blessing. But this batch should be scared of their deaths—perhaps not entirely scared, but wary of it. They all knew they had signed a faulty contract with Melanthe, even if they didn't wish to accept it.

"I'm betting on it." I propped my feet on the table. "Though hopes are faint considering Visha Delcour is outside and Melanthe could lay an egg before all of your heads hatch from your bodies."

The witches exchanged wide looks amongst one another. "Visha...she is well?" Salma asked.

"Healthy and red," I said. "Like the day she came to me."

Guinevere shot up. "You cannot mean—"

"You heard me right. She came to me with her own two feet, safe and sound, and has been by my side for years I've now lost count of. Despite whatever lie Melanthe has told you."

"What do you want?" the oldest of them asked. "We have nothing that will help you in any form."

I tilted my head to the side, really trying to see their point from every angle. "One of you little airheads caused me to lose my kin, almost made me lose a sister, set me back months of work I had done in Isjord, and even helped Melanthe keep me chained when you all knew better. And that is not even the worst. I cannot lose Eldmoor to my father. So, I will make sure to drain that air out of all of you and fill your head with some knowledge before I soak your lungs with blood."

The same young-looking crone said, "Killing us will do nothing for you."

"Wrong. Target practice with some willing participants. There is yet a book to be written on how to skin a witch. I'm hopeful about a writing journey. Now, priorities first, where is Urinthia?"

Dead silence stretched until I made the girl on my right bleed a little. "We do not know," one said.

I dug and dragged my dagger over the young Crafter's throat, parting her head from her body in one cut. "I really do not like lies unless they are coming out of my mouth," I said, standing and pacing the room. "Which head is next?" My feet stopped right before Guinevere. Clutching her long red hair, I pulled her head back and pressed my blade to her throat. "This one perhaps?"

"We don—"

Blood splattered on the table and on all of their faces, and they all screamed murder.

Mmm. That's it. "Eeny, meeny, miny, moe," I counted, pointing the end of my blade to another.

The girl began quivering when I approached her despite the empty look on her face. "In Isjord. She is in Isjord."

I pressed the sharp edge harder to her neck. "You've got to be more precise, dear."

She shook her head. "Physically she is in Isjord. To locate exactly where, you might have to find her astral form first. You...you cannot conceal Urinthia's magic as she is tied to Eldmoor one way or the other like all of us. It would be easy to feel the surge of dark craft if she had started mending the sceptre, but—" Her eyes drifted to her sisters and filled with more fear.

"But?"

"None of us have felt her. There are certain ways to conceal your magic. Like the Elder Crafters hid the sceptre pieces. If King Silas has begun the ritual of waking the Guardian, even a simple Crafter would have felt it and known it. He must be doing it...out...not in this realm."

"Like a pocket realm?"

"Possibly. But those are impossible to open without the blood of an Elder Crafter. Even Melanthe would not be able to open one. No one of us can do so without permission from Gods. Celesteel took that right from us after the Ater battles."

"But Urinthia can?"

"I've seen it."

Seen it? I leaned in. "And where would your Grand Maiden open these pocket realms? What God would still allow her?"

She blinked rapidly, her mouth opening and closing as she tried to think.

"Golgotha," another said. "In Golgotha's realm. She has been the Demon King's lover for centuries. The only entity that would allow her to open a pocket realm between Numen and theirs would be him. Perhaps even step in it. His dark realm might be but ash and no air, but it is still a realm and a viable space to craft an in-between pocket."

Well, well. "Interesting." Letting go of the girl, I walked over to Salma. The woman was glaring murder at her subordinates who had disobeyed her treacherous self. Her body recoiled a little when I sat right beside her. "Someone bring a pen and paper out. It's homework time."

Reluctantly, a few looked around and laid paper and ink on the table. Tapping the end of my blood-stained dagger on the edge of the white sheet, I said, "Every name of every Crafter on Melanthe's side better be written down. Along with their location and preferably an encouraging message for me at the end. It looks like I have the work cut out for me now that fear of your God has left your systems."

"We have no fear of our God. Death is our reward," Salma mumbled between her clenched teeth. "Lest you all forget."

Resting my feet on the table, I leaned back. "Let me remind you of the words written in your own holy book, dear. *There might be sin and there might be flaws to condemn you not for as wardens of this realm, Caligo, and the in-between. But choosing to commit sin without regard of Numen or bearing ill on your motherland, will bring you flames before mercy when you step in the land of the Death God.* Cannot remember the chapter, but that exact line is in your holy book. Is it not?"

Her mouth curled into a snarl. "It is not as simple as you make it."

"But it is. Witch betrays her Maiden. Witch plots against her Maiden. Witch aids a man who wants to make a God blessed land his own hell, contest your God. Witch is bad. Witch is really bad. Witch burns. Witch gets no say. See?"

Someone sniffled across the table, and I clicked my tongue. "Don't get tears on my paper, dear, the ink will smudge."

When everyone handed over a list with names, maps, and all sorts of details they had used in their usurping ventures, I stood and stretched my legs, ready to leave.

Salma didn't even raise her eyes to look at me when I gripped her jaw hard, prying her mouth open and pressing my bloodied blade to her tongue. "Tell me, does betrayal taste bitter?"

She swallowed hard, tart tears sliding down her pale cheeks. "You will never win."

That made me laugh hard. "I've already won. Over you. And that is the only win you will ever remember."

I dragged my sword back, and blood sprayed on my face and leathers.

It was almost noon by the time I had come out of the dim coven. I stretched my arms up, trying to crack a kink on my neck when a yawn overtook me. "Well," I said, yawning again. "That was relatively pleasant."

Mal cringed at my sight. "Define pleasant."

I threw him the map and the lists I'd collected which were marked with points where all of Melanthe's supporters remained hidden. "The souvenirs."

He looked at the map and the names, and his brow raised. "I'd better take that limb now if it isn't late."

I kicked my elbow back in his stomach, and he threw an arm around my shoulders. "I'll come with my men to search for them all."

"Thank you, Mal."

My witch stared at the blood-orange distance when the sun faded beneath the dead forest trees. "Melanthe was like an aunt to me, a mother almost. I shared a room with Salma," she said quietly, "along with most of my secrets, my concerns, my grief. Hera was one of my wetnurses. Guinevere's mother brought me a lamb for my sixth birthday."

"How domestic."

She turned to me, blinking slowly. "Should I not be feeling something?"

"What a waste of energy it would be."

"It is my fault, isn't it? Why they all turned on my mother. Why Silas has come so far in destroying this realm. For what happened to you and the others. For what happened to Nia."

"The blessed moon," Mal cursed under his breath and turned to face the sunset, suddenly interesting to him now.

It was not like Visha to think like this. But she did take someone's life to give it to another and that must have some form of tax on someone's soul. Despite what my witch showed the world, I knew that somewhat of a gentle soul laid beneath the granite exterior. Very, very, very, very deeply beneath. "Greed is the coin of the treacherous, witchling. It is no one's fault how they deal their hands but their own. They believed Melanthe's child would grant them the power they craved. Greed for more greed. That is no follower. That is a leech. Waste your tears on dying puppies and starved kittens."

"Do *you* blame me?" she asked bluntly.

"I blame someone. But that someone is not you." If there was someone deserving of blame, it would be me. I should have gutted my father when I had my chance. My vengeance should have come second to the safety of those I care about.

Mal turned at my words and just stared at me. He did that for some time. The look growing haunted, tortured, and filled with the same monsters I saw in the mirror.

Someone else had once looked at me like that.

Not with pity.

With pain. That's what he'd told me that look was—pain.

I wanted to ask why he kept looking at me the way he did since we'd returned from Isjord, but I knew he hated being asked.

"Can we go now?" Visha asked. "The Deadlands are dangerous after sunset."

Mal caught my arm when we faded back to Olympia, waiting until Visha returned to her chambers before saying, "Do you think no one has noticed how you touch your wrists and your neck? Or when your hands shake each time you lift them up because there is no longer weight to them—no more chains."

Then, like the world had peeled off to reveal an older reality, I felt phantom chains wrap around my limbs again. "I don't know, but I'm glad they are not saying anything about it."

The brown in his eyes flashed black entirely. "Do you know that the guards would speak, and I could hear your screams down there." His hand around my arm tightened, and so did every breath I took after. "How do I forget them? How did you forget them, tell me, please? I hear them all day, all around me. Nothing I do is working. How have they not taken the fight out of you the same way they've taken it out of me?"

My stomach sank, nausea climbing up to my mouth. "I'm sorry."

He let me go, his chest shaking with laughter—heart breaking laughter. "You never begged. Not once. But I begged for you. I begged them for you every day. I begged them to stop."

Tears blurred the spinning world. "I'm sorry."

He rubbed a hand over his eyes, his skin had turned so pale "You don't remember, but they brought me to watch a few times."

Oh Gods. I couldn't breathe. Oh gods. "Mal—"

"They threw about a hundred snakes in there with you. And I watched and watched. For forty-three days I watched them torture you. Forty-three days!"

I shut my eyes tightly. "Please."

He laughed again, but a strangled cry slipped through this time, making his voice tremble. "Now you beg?"

"I'm sorry."

His fingers nervously picked at the skin on his thumb until it bled. "How can you care about someone who doesn't care about themselves? Thora said that to me once and I don't think I understood what she meant until...until we were there. You knew how to get out of there. You're smart like that. You're the smartest person I know. It did not take you forty-three days to think of a way!" he bellowed, his voice quivering. "Why did you, Snow, hm? Why did you let them do that to you?"

"I'm sorry, I did not know. Mal, I didn't know you were there."

He struggled to breathe, backing away towards the edge of the terrace, trying to grasp something to hold onto. "I need...I need—"

Then he left.

What had I done?

What had I done?

I collapsed to the ground, digging my nails on the cold marble, trying not to close my fists again. The reflection on the white floor only stared back this time. The eyes looking back were my own. And it terrified me more.

"Say something," I whispered, hitting it. "Say something!"

You deserved it, all of it, they hissed, and then went entirely silent.

Everything went entirely silent again.

The reflection settled.

My tear drops twisting its shape.

I had caught the Adriatian Court meeting right at the very end. Kilian had gathered his councillors since dawn, and even though most were bone tired, none refused to leave without welcoming me back. Cautiousness had slipped somewhere along the lines and now I was just doubtful whether they forced the pleasantries out of fear of me or my husband.

Triad and Larg still hovered over Kilian who had sprawled wide in his chair, rubbing a hand over his stubbly jaw.

"Can I have him now?" I asked, and the two large men spun to bow at me. I needed him so much. I needed him to hold me. Just to feel his skin against mine. To quieten the world. To quieten my mind.

My husband's expression started to fall the more he looked at me. The way he felt what I felt scared me so much—it terrified me senseless.

"We were just about to leave," Larg said, offering me a wide, toothy grin and a grizzly old man laughter.

"Sure we were," Triad murmured to himself, shaking his head at the general.

"She needs to hear this, too," Kilian said to the two and stretched his arm out, offering me to take his hand. He pulled me to sit on his lap, and I finally breathed without restriction. He leaned in my ear. "What is wrong?"

"Nothing, darling. What do I need to know?"

He was not convinced. Not at all. And only worried worse, his brows creasing full of doubt.

Triad cleared his throat. "We have doubts that there is someone else in our court or near our court reporting to Silas. The Fernfoss incident was a given, but there might have been another soon. The Skye luckily caught another messenger before they had gone too far into Kirkwall. Your soldiers risked much, but potentially saved us from Silas figuring out how we have been holding Mahara's channel safe."

"Not surprised considering that my father let me kill Nesrin. He wouldn't have sacrificed his only spy so easily. Anyone you doubt?"

"None, Your Majesty," Larg said. "All are younglings I've raised and trained myself."

Triad huffed. "Tenderness and fondness will one day be your death, you old fool."

To ease the hurt in Larg's face, I asked, "Was Nesrin close with anyone? Your men perhaps have a lover or family who gets the information without any of them knowing that they are feeding it to a spy."

"Could be possible," Triad agreed.

"Have your most trusted spread around different false information, something that my father would profit from knowing," I added. "Whichever gets to Isjord the fastest, that is our spy. Moregan will send back word in a breath."

Both men nodded and left.

Kilian's nose grazed my skin, and he left a trail of pecks up to my cheek. "You bathed. Without me."

"It was not the type of bath water we could have shared."

He surveyed the red patches of skin I had scrubbed raw and rested his lips on top, leaving barely there kisses. "Got any answers?"

"Plenty. Macaria and Mal will be handling the witches who are working for Melanthe, and I think I might have found a way to get to Urinthia."

"Hm. I can smell danger." His finger slid down my jaw. "Perhaps it is just the lily soap."

"I need to ponder on it first." There was too much to think about. First, would it even be possible to get to Golgotha? Second, would my husband lose his mind at my request to see the God of Demons? Most importantly, would this affect the end I'd seen?

He smiled. "Alright, my love, you ponder on it. But are you going to tell me what's wrong?"

"Nothing is," I said, holding onto him tightly. Nothing was ever wrong when I was in his arms. "Did Nesrin have any siblings?" Besides Nia. Though I was sure no one was even aware she was her sister.

"No. Stregor was a proud man. When his legitimate first born turned out powerless, he was embarrassed. Some shunned him. Others doubted his sincerity, nobility, and belief, so he made sure his wife could not get pregnant again. He chose to not have any more children than be cast out. Why do you ask?"

"I'm sure whoever is spying for my father is close to her. Friend, family. Someone who might be angry at me for what I did."

He was silent for a moment.

He had thought of someone.

"Will you not tell me?" I asked.

"Will you try killing him without proving it to be true first?"

Oooh, it was a *him*. "Can I lie?"

He threw his head back and laughed. "Yes, lie to me, woman. It's better for my blood pressure."

"Such an old man."

He sighed, a languid smile pulling at his lips when he laid his head back on the chair rest. "I am not that old." His knuckles gently touched my chin. "My soul was only born that day when you told me you loved me back. But it might die from whatever is tormenting my heart."

"I'll kill it, Kil."

"Not a doubt, my heart."

22

Black Kingside Castling

Snowlin

CHEWING ON SOME MOONCAKES, I sat on a white terrace overlooking the busy main street of Amaris, watching Grey, a Captain at Highwall, linger by a bunch of children playing ball.

Though I'd promised not to kill him if I wasn't fully sure he was our spy, there was no *'don't hurt him'* clause on the terms and conditions I'd agreed with Kilian when he gave me this name.

Atlas handed me another mooncake. And apparently the boy was allergic to sugar because he pinched my sweets as if they were to suddenly explode. "Do we have to sit here?"

"If I am too close, I will strangle the words out of him, and I sort of gave my word that I wouldn't."

The young priest nodded. "I see, I see."

"Do you know him well?"

Atlas gathered his large robes tightly to him and scooted closer to the terrace edge. "Y-yes. His family comes to my temple during celebrations. Both mother and father are religious. His little sister is married to a Lyran priest even."

A religious fanatic was the best guess in my bingo card and Atlas had just stamped the spot for me. "He and Nesrin, were they close?"

"I believe so. His peers often tease him because he's been chasing her around since they were children while she never showed any interest in him."

Because she wanted my husband. I looked at him. "You know quite a bit."

"People gossip around me all the time. It's...it's almost as if I am invisible. Maybe they ignored me enough, and I truly became invisible."

I patted his head. "You're not. I can see you well, Atlas. There is a big bee on your shoulder by the way," I said, turning to look at my target, watching him be approached by a child in his early teens and hand him a bag with bread and...a piece of folded paper under it.

That was my mark. Pushing to the corner, I jumped on the street and slowly approached him. "Grey, right?"

The entire street had halted and was attentively looking at me when the captain spun like he'd been called by Henah herself, staggering back like he was in her presence, too. "You...I mean...my queen."

I raised a brow. "Since pleasantries are out of the way, I needed some help."

"Help?"

"I need to get to the main library and these streets are dizzying me."

Still obviously stunned, he blinked for a moment. "Of course...of course. Follow me," he said, looking over his shoulder from time to time, and I shot him a sweet smile. The man's eyes grew wide, and he quickly whipped his head forward, clutching the bag of bread and carefully slipping the piece of paper inside it not so discreetly.

"Apologies," I said so very gently, catching up to him so we stood side by side. "Did I interrupt something? You've bought bread. Were you heading home?"

He tightened his hold on the cloth bag. "Uh, yes. Yes, my queen."

"Isn't your family in Lyra?"

His step slowed, but his heartbeat only grew faster. "They've come to Amaris."

"Hm."

"Do you often come to the city?"

"Yes." I turned my palm to him. "Mind if I have a slice? The smell is driving me hungry."

His whole face fell, and he barked an uncomfortable laugh, hesitantly reaching inside the bag. "Sure."

"Actually, let me buy you a new one. That one grew cold because of me," I said, snatching the bag from him.

He jumped forward to retrieve it, and I wrapped a hand around his throat, ice slipping in the air and coating his lungs and throat until he collapsed to his knees, breathless. Clicking my tongue, I said, "How rude."

"Grey, my man, you're looking a bit ashen," Mal said, striding towards us, and I threw him the bread bag.

He'd avoided me for days. Only resurfaced when I'd told him I was going to corner Grey who he had a grudge against.

While Grey choked for air, I unfolded the paper and read the first few lines written in Darsan. "Me and you are going to have a little chat," I said, pulling him to his feet and dragging him to follow me into the library.

Thora was already there, waiting and ready. The moment I had him sat on a chair, I let go of his throat, letting him breathe. "Fucking bitch!" he howled.

"You kiss the mother I'm going to kill with that mouth?"

He shook violently from anger, turning red. "Heavens will take my justice. They will take all of our justice, you filthy whore!"

Mal chuckled around a mouthful of bread and then kicked his foot right on Grey's chest, knocking him to the ground breathless. "She sat you politely on the chair," he said, crouching to the ground and smacking Grey's head with a slice of bread. "I rather think you'd be more comfortable on the floor. Get used to the cold ground before she buries you shallow in it and lets birds pick you out of it little by little."

The Highwall Captain snarled, baring his teeth, almost feral. "From you I'd expected it. But from your brother, never. To fall for her trickeries and seduction that will lead your souls to hell. To hell!" he bellowed.

I crouched next to Mal and flipped the paper open, turning it to him. "Talking about hell. Using children to send back and forth to the border, really?" Flicking the paper to his face, I pulled out a dagger. "How long have you been attempting to kill your king?"

He pressed his lips tightly together, staring me dead in the eyes, refusing to answer.

"Actually, scratch that," I said, fisting his hair and pulling him up. "Let's go see your family."

Mal put a hand over my arm. "I've got a better thought." A grin spread over his face. "But he seems like a screamer. Are your ears going to be okay, my queen? I don't want my brother coming after my dick."

I rolled my eyes. "He isn't that scary."

"To you," my brother-in-law said, grabbing Grey's neck, his brown eyes disappearing under a curtain of black. Spidery veins spread over his face, and the captain bellowed, the entire library shaking from his screams and incoherent mumbles that sounded like the most desperate pleas I'd ever heard. "Hm? Did you hear something, sis." Mal patted his cheek. "Got words for me, cupcake, or should I keep going?"

"His heart is about to stop, Mal."

"I know when it's enough. I've stopped enough hearts in my lifetime."

Just then, Grey's mouth began foaming, his eyes rolling back, and he blacked out, his body going stock-still.

"Wake him, little bird," Mal said to my sister, taking a seat and leaning back while she put a hand to Grey's chest, pumping air into his lungs, causing him to jolt awake.

The man had turned violet from pain, veins almost bursting through skin, and he no longer had a voice to use for screaming, so he gaped like a dying fish, moaning his pain silently.

"That was sorrow," Mal said, chewing on bread, and my head snapped to him. "Anguish is next." He gripped Grey's jaw, forcing the captain to look at him. "You know what I am capable of, Grey. Do not try to find out. There has yet to be a man brave enough."

Grey sniffled, his mouth trembling. "The...p-prophecy...lives," he mumbled. "People...are...afraid. I am...afraid."

Mal leaned forward. "That was not what she asked."

Grey's eyes slowly turned to me. So much disgust and hatred filling them. "I've been trying to kill that fucker for a while, but no one could get close enough. He has not stayed in Adriata for months, and now that she is back, he is never alone."

That made me giggle a little. "You think you could best Kilian that easily?"

"Everyone has weaknesses."

"And what is my husband's, if I might ask?"

"Family." His mouth stretched into a grin. "You know what poisons an Obscur's heart? Pain. Like father, like son. Silas took you, and I made sure to pass to him what your father did to you—he had written it in such impeccable detail, my heart almost broke for you, my queen. Nesrin took Driada. Tainted her fragile mind and soul little by little with despair to the point even Kilian could not ward off death." He turned to Mal. "I would have taken you. With poison, my prince." He laughed maniacally, tears and snot dripping down his quivering mouth. "It has been so easy to slip it in your drink when you're only half conscious and aware most of the time. Even if I failed, you would have poisoned yourself eventually, one drink at a time. And that is how you kill the Night King."

Venom seeped into my blood at his words. There was no time to feel anger or anything at all. The urge to hurt shook me entirely.

"You killed Driada?" my sister asked, tears streaming down her face.

"Too easily," he sneered, swivelling a look over her. "I've had my eye on you. The little mistress."

Thora bent down to him. "You don't know who I am?"

Grey's brows creased. "A whore?"

I grabbed Mal who rushed to launch at the man, eyes dark and shadows even darker. "Let her."

She put a gentle hand on Grey's cheek, barely touching, and frost spread fast over his skin—faster than he could grasp that his air was leaving his lungs at the same time. "My mother gave me the name belonging to the Warden of Storms. It is a very rare name. Certainly, you must know it. Thora. Isa. Krigborn."

I'd never seen a man's face drop so fast. Grey looked between the two of us, shaking. "W-what?"

"And that is how you kill a pathetic man like you," she said, and his mouth parted wide open, trying to breathe but failing. She killed him so slow, enough to see every possible reaction cross his face. Fear so intense and pure.

Quiet fell once Grey's body stopped writhing, surrendering to death.

None of us spoke.

None of us looked at the other.

Mal headed to leave first, slipping from my hold. But before I could run for him, my sister did, tugging at his sleeve and pulling him between a row of shelves somewhere in the far corner of the library. From the little space between books, I could see her tip toeing close to him, his face in her hands and so close to her own. Like that day in lake Asterin, her voice was soft and comforting and strong when she spoke.

There was little in me that could soothe someone like that.

There was something else I did excellently.

Whatever remained of Grey was not heavy to drag outside on the streets, but every muscle and bone in my body felt heavier. By the time I reached the city square, I was breathless. From all corners, I could see those shadows hunting me again like they'd hunted me long ago. Every eye that landed on me suddenly turned black, their faces grew teeth and claws, and venom dripped from their mouths.

A guard approached me. Carefully lowering his weapons to the ground before standing in front of me. "My queen. Is there something wrong?"

"Bring me his family and everyone who goes to the same temple as him. Bring me everyone he has spoken to this week. I want to show your people what happens when you try to kill your king—when you hurt those your king loves. Call for everyone over sixteen to gather and watch. Everyone better be here, or I'll drag them out to the pyre with him."

The guard looked at Grey, his face turning to steel. "At your order."

Rage had coated my sight entirely, but somewhere between madness and awareness,

I saw Atlas part through the crowd. Watching.

"Go, Atlas."

He gave me a sad smile. "I'd like to stay. Be here...for you, my queen."

The room was empty. It could have been full, too, but I wouldn't have seen anything. I could barely see enough to wash the blood off my hands. Should I count? Should I not count? The question had been hammering in my head all the way to our room. I'd finally lost the count. Should I have started it again? Would it matter? It didn't, did it? No one would bloody tell me anymore. Not the silent shadows. Not their voice.

Not even *you.*

His spring scented warmth slipped behind me, and my eyes drew shut. I didn't know my hands had been shaking until he held them under the water stream, gently washing them.

"Where is Mal?" I rasped.

"He is with Thora in her room."

"You saw?" I had felt him there, watching somewhere in the distance.

"I did." He kissed my temple, and leaned to whisper in my ear, "That is the most romantic thing anyone has ever done for me."

I couldn't help my smile after seeing his in the mirror. "You should have stopped me."

"I don't care how many times you stain these hands with blood," he said, his thumbs stroking my palms. "As long as it is not yours."

"He wanted to kill you."

"If it could be that easy."

"He had found a way."

He put a white envelope sealed with my father's crest on the basin table. "It really is *not* that easy."

My heart was too loud to allow any thoughts to taunt me at all. "Did you read it?"

"I was tempted. Several times. But there is this thing, my love," he said, continuing to wash my fingers. "When emotion is intense, it tends to bleed into the things near you. Whatever words he put in there, he intended to hurt me with them. The malice still lingers around the paper edges. Also, I still have faith that you will one day tell me yourself. If only to liberate you from the burden of remembering alone." He turned the tap off, taking a towel to pat my hands dry. "The letter is yours. Do with it as you wish."

"Thank you."

He sighed, pulling me to his chest to hold me tightly. "What am I going to do with you, hm?" he murmured, kissing the top of my head.

Kilian held me on his lap as he went through document after document, checking and double checking on everything before the tip of his pen touched the paper to sign off his permission. He was so serious, gilded, harsh. The lines on his face were so straight and sharp when he was focused. He was different at times. In court. Before danger. Around me. Around my family. Around his own. So many shades of this man.

I had found my favourite new thing to do. And he didn't seem to mind at all.

The melancholic rain pattering against the glass windows of our room and Memphis's soft purrs were already lulling me to sleep which I was trying hard to refuse because I wanted to spend all the time I had left staring at him.

As if he could read my mind, his mouth pulled into a smile. "Sleep, my heart. You will wear my face off."

"No."

He chuckled, lines breaking to form soft curves.

A phantom shadow hand crawled from behind him to turn the page while he held me. It was fascinating how his magic was an extension of him while mine used me as its conduit.

I lifted my hand to the shadows and let a little skitter of electricity twirl around my fingers. His darkness did not budge, but my magic did abate, softly fading at the touch. When I'd returned from Whitebridge after saving Thora and Eren, he'd done the same, his magic had helped tame mine. I don't know how, but it had worked. Same as it was working now.

"Perfect," I whispered to myself, playing with his shadows.

He wrapped a hand around my wrist and pulled my arm down to my side. "The more you feed it, the more it will ask for. Once magic becomes dull, it will seek life. It is how it compensates to keep itself powerful." He kissed each of my fingertips and then my lips. "Death is unpredictable."

"But you are it. You would not hurt me. You have never hurt me."

His forehead rested on mine as he said, "No. I would never hurt you."

"Then contain me. Instead of teaching me to face it, use it to contain me while I draw more of it. Enough to fight another...like me. Enough to fight Aurora if need comes."

"What if I fail, what if it is not enough?"

"We will stay within bounds—within our limits."

He studied me intently, measuring the odds and the possibilities that this would and could actually work. "Within our limits." He sighed and pinched my cheek. "I'll think about it."

Memphis's snout nudged my leg, and I patted my lap for her to rest her head there. "What do you think, M?"

Her mouth opened in a massive yawn in response, and so did mine. After shaking her head, she pushed the balcony doors open and shifted into a raven, cawing and launching into the storm.

"She is restless," I said, craning my neck back to see her disappearing from view entirely. My creature had spent less and less time with me than any time before. Surveying skies, land, and seas. She'd become a soldier more than a companion.

"So is her bonded." He stood with me in his arms despite my protests and threw me over his shoulder as he walked to the bed. I was too tired to protest being handled like a potato sack—a very pretty potato sack if I might say so.

He lowered me on the bed and caged me in under him, kissing me in all the tickling spots. "Sleep."

"You're not being very convincing."

"Hm," he hummed, licking a trail over my throat, and a trickle of warmth slipped down my stomach. "I know you are tired, stop fighting it."

And then it slipped lower and lower until the thin nightgown I wore became unbearably uncomfortable against my skin. "Touch me."

"Sleep."

"Fine." My hand slid over my stomach and over my centre where tension was about to snap me in half. "Watch and learn."

His smile was so sinfully cruel and sweet and maddening all at once when his eyes slid between us, watching me touch myself under my underwear. "Take them off, let me see what's mine," he ordered, leaning in my ear, still not touching me where I needed him to touch me.

But I did as told.

It was nowhere near enough compared to his touch, and I wanted to rub myself on him, feel him against me, but I was aching and tired, so I obeyed, sliding my fingers between my legs, over my swollen nerves and the slick wetness. Trying to chase something that only he knew how to chase.

He hummed in my ear, kissing and nibbling on my earlobe. "Are you wet, my love? Are you wet for me?"

A bit down on my lip, holding back a moan. "Yes."

He pulled one of my nightgown straps down, cupping my breast and lowering his mouth to suck on a nipple. "Good. Put a finger inside your needy cunt."

"I need you."

"And you will have me. Do as I say."

He chuckled when I huffed but did as told, sliding a finger and stifling a whimper at the fullness that was not nearly enough.

"Stop planning on how to get back at me."

"Stop giving me reason and just fuck me," I whined, desperately.

"Do. As. I. Say." He bit on my nipple, making me hiss and arch my back for more. "Put another one in. Good girl," he whispered, trailing kisses down my stomach and watching my fingers disappear inside of me with darkening eyes. "Such a good girl." He rose to his haunches and unbuttoned his britches, stopping when I stopped pumping my fingers. "Keep going. Make yourself come for me."

His gaze grew heavy as he watched me writhe and moan, slowly taking off his clothes and freeing his hard cock. The sight of his naked body tipped me to the edge, and I felt myself get wetter and my spine string tight while a hazy release crashed through me, leaving my body languid, surrendered on the bed.

He grabbed my wrist and sucked my fingers clean. And the feel of his tongue sent shivers down my spine, making my stomach knot with want again. "Open for me, love."

Even though I was bone tired, I quickly parted my legs for him.

He bit on his smile, his eyes perusing the whole of me. "Wider," he said. "Let me see you."

I spread my legs further, and he left small pecks over my thighs and all over my spent body, his beard tickling everywhere. "Beautiful." He settled between my legs and guided them to link over his back. "Still not sleepy?"

I quickly shook my head, jittery, and lowered my hands to explore his body, trailing my fingers down his stomach muscles, between each dent and swell and then over his back. He let me explore him how I wanted to, his breath hitching with each stroke of my hand. How was he so...perfect?

He pushed inside of me just a little, and I gasped.

"I love that sound," he murmured, dragging my lips between his teeth, pumping his hips unhurriedly against mine, burying himself deeper each time. "I love every inch of you. And I love how you take every inch of me." He pulled one of my legs over his shoulder and thrust a little harder, a little deeper. "I love when you come around my cock," he crooned the words, not even letting me breathe out a whimper as his tongue was in my mouth, sucking and licking the air and words out of me.

"Such a good girl," he murmured. "Are you my good girl?"

Not a day in my life had I been good, but for him...yes, sure, fine, whatever.

He grabbed my jaw and kissed me. "Answer me."

"We both know that is not true," I moaned, my eyes drawing shut from the wave of pleasure that took me under.

"You are good for *me*. So good. So obedient." His hand wrapped round my neck, squeezing just a little, his thumb brushing my pulse. "Listen to that. The only reason I can breathe. Listen how it obeys me."

He slammed his cock inside of me—hard—with need and desperation all at once. Just as desperately, I sought more and more of him. My hands were all over him, my mouth never left his. My body strung so tight I shook. Release crashing until I was rolled blind under it.

I was still shaking when he pulled out of me, his head thrown back, his hand quickly working his length.

Hooking my leg around his waist, I said, "No, look at me when you come."

He opened his eyes and stared at me under his dark lashes, a half grin taking over his slack jaw. A guttural groan tore through his throat and he came on my belly and all over my chest. He stood there, still stroking his cock, breathing hard and looking so utterly satisfied with himself. "That's one hell of a look on you, my love. You look like a painting." Leaning forward, he took a sensitive nipple in his mouth and pulled back with a pop. "Perfect. I knew they'd look perfect with my come all over them."

I rolled my eyes, and he laughed hard, bringing those tiny jitters back in my stomach that was still tingling with remnants of pleasure.

Turning on my side, I watched him go into the bathroom to fetch a wet cloth. Watching his hard body move did unexplainable things to me. He was all mine. All mine.

He raised a smug brow, returning to clean me up. "Why are you grinning, my little vixen?"

I rested my foot on his stomach, trailing it up his body, and he shuddered, grabbing my ankle and leaving a kiss there. "I want to eat you alive," I told him. "Devour you entirely."

He hummed to himself while he cleaned me up and got my nightgown back on me again. "And when did this side effect present itself? Shall I call a healer?"

"Ha ha."

He grabbed my jaw, squishing my cheeks, and he dropped about a dozen pecks on my puckered mouth. "Have I told you how much I fucking love this sassy mouth, hm?"

"You can always tell me again," I mumbled, and he laughed a little, letting go of my face and kissing both of my cheeks.

"I love your sassy mouth."

"Kilian."

He blew the candles off. "Yes, my heart?"

"Kil."

He tucked the both of us under the blanket and pulled me to his chest. "Hm?"

The yawn almost tore my jaw in half. "Good night." *Don't let me sleep. I really don't want to sleep. I want to look at you till my eyes bleed. In my dreams you're bloodied and screaming for me. The world in my dreams is ruined. I just want to look at you before what I see in my sleep becomes reality. Before you learn to hate me for leaving you alone.*

He hesitated, and the piercing silence that followed made me nervous—it was as if he could read the thoughts crossing my mind. "Goodnight, my Snow."

It had been a mistake. Sleeping had been a mistake.

I woke up covered in sweat. Alone. Not remembering exactly what had chased me in my sleep. The only thing I remembered was Mal watching in the distance. The heaviness on my chest had lessened, only because my heart had shattered over and over seeing my friend's tormented face. Maybe I had seen him there and I just didn't want to remember. Maybe I'd forgotten on purpose.

I patted the bed for him.

Where...where was he?

Was I still dreaming?

Panic almost struck me again.

"Come here," he called, and I looked up to find him sitting in the armchair in the corner of our room, watching me, the silver moon throwing a waterfall of light on him and him alone. He looked angry, the muscles on his face about to snap in half. His whole body was tense and so was his magic because shadows quivered all around the room uncontrollably, like a forest under thunder.

"Why did you leave me?" I asked, trying my best not to collapse on the way to him.

"If I stayed," he said, pulling me to his lap, arms and shadows holding me tightly. "I would have done something you would have hated. Taken all of it away. Every single nightmare. You would have resented me, and I would not have cared at all."

I pointed to his drink. "Can I have a little?"

He tipped the glass to my lips and let me have the smallest sip. "Tasty?"

I shuddered. "Revolting."

He laughed, downing the rest of the drink. "Perhaps," he said, kissing me, letting me taste the flavour on his lips and tongue. "This is better?"

"Delectable," I hummed, sucking on his lips, licking the flavour away.

He showered every inch of my face with pecks. "What do you see when you close your pretty eyes?"

"I think you know, Kil." He knew. He'd filled in between the lines. The only thing missing were the details which I was still unsure I wanted him to know.

His chest rose faster. "Let me help you."

"You can't banish them away this time, darling, the monsters are human. They don't even hide in the dark anymore. They're not even scared of me, no matter how much stronger and worse I am." I ran my hand over his heart, not knowing how to calm it any other way. "But they are afraid of you. So do not leave me."

"Why are they afraid of me?"

"Because you are powerful, and you can do very bad things to them."

He weaved a strong hand through my hair. "You are powerful, too."

"They still force me to wear chains, Kil. But you can't see them."

His face fell and steeled like iron all at once. "Tell me how to break them."

"It must be me. It has to be me."

"Then let me help you."

I looked up at him, realising that I'd found the pure absence of madness again, the same comfort I'd found in Isjord by my mother's grave. It was him. Why everything had quietened down again. It had always been him. The reason my nightmares had disappeared entirely. "Alright. Help me."

"Shall we try to sleep again? I won't leave you, ever."

When my mind screamed, begged, and pleaded to say no, I said, "Yes."

Then I let them scream and beg and plead far in the distance. Watched them crawl far back inside the pits of my mind where they'd been raised from. Until they were entirely gone. And gone was the weight on my chest, my wrists, and my neck. Gone. My mind was anew when I laid my cheek on his chest, when I breathed in the scent of lemon blossoms from his skin.

23

White Knight to D2

Snowlin

KILIAN WAS STILL GIVING Thora and Visha orders even though he'd been repeating them like a song for the past hour. The two were struggling to keep awake at this point.

He sighed and turned to face me, scowling while he closed our distance. "You're looking too happy while leading me to a heart attack, love of mine."

"You trust me so little," I said, shedding every piece of metal from my body. Steel acted like a conduit sometimes, helping me channel magic in a more controlled manner, but considering that I was about to test my limits, I did not need any conduits or control.

He helped me unstrap belts and whatnot, making sure his hands lingered over my body. "Trust is not my issue."

I cupped his jaw and buried my face in his neck, inhaling his taunting scent for a moment. "I know."

"The day you walked out of here," he said, a finger pointing to his heart, "was the last day of not fearing. Can't say I don't miss feeling untouchable."

"You are untouchable, Night King."

His knuckles touched my chin lightly. "How can you say that when my heart walks around with the mind of a rock and no sense of danger."

"You will protect me."

"I failed more than once."

"You never failed."

"Snow—"

"Darling, I have the mind of a rock and no sense of danger. It is no one's fault but my own. Please," I said, pulling him to me, "let me wear my own consequences and regrets."

His lips lingered over my own for a while until Visha cleared her throat. "If you two are quite done."

Thora giggled. "Hells hath no fury like a woman who gags at the sight of love."

My witch did not do anything more than just blink at us to signal that she was already bored to bits and wanted to get out of here.

I let go of Kilian, stepping back, and so did he. He'd chosen to train us in Amaris since the land was already used to absorbing massive lumps of magic. Though the Fogling had not resurfaced since Cori's death, we were still weary of drawing heavy magic within Olympian grounds, fearing that it would attract them back.

Overwhelming air gathered around me when I felt the gates of my magic slide slightly open, and power that I'd so rarely let myself feel filled the air around me. Clouds gurgled and warned us of the unnatural thunder gathering above our heads. Like metal drawn to a magnet, it circled me. I was the eye of the storm.

"That is as far as I can get it open before it becomes a problem for me to close down," Visha informed us.

Electricity powered through me and gathered around all my limbs. Black tattoos curled and twirled over my skin as I tried to rein control of it and channel it to my command. It obeyed somehow, clinging to me just slightly even though it hammered around me uncontrollably. Were Kilian's exercises working?

His eyes veiled black and darkness slithered under him and over the grassy floor, turning the air and ground into cold, grey ash. When phantom tendrils of darkness touched the electricity around me, sliding against it and eventually enveloping all of it and me under it, I felt a flutter of absolute control. The deeper Kilian's shadows slipped inside of the lightning barrier, intertwining and bracing against it, the lighter the weight of my magic felt, and the more control I reined over it.

It was like a switch. The shield of lightning around me shrunk and enlarged at my command. A switch rather than a dam that endlessly poured and needed heavy gates to be pushed and pulled each time I wanted to command it.

A stuttering laughter left me when I kept playing around, letting my magic dance across my body, pulling and pushing it back inside the bounds it came from entirely too easily.

"Love?" Kilian asked, almost panicked, and it made me smile a little.

"Yes, my darling?"

His sigh was loud enough to hear over the magnetic sound of our magic colliding. Our magic fit like a glove.

It was the most fascinating thing I'd ever seen.

From the look on Visha's face, she thought the same.

The strain I usually felt when I used magic had slipped off, it felt like I could flex my joints after never being able to before. It easily floated when I wanted it to float, turn how I wanted to turn. It obeyed with ease.

"More," I said to Visha.

"No," my husband said sharply. "The more darkness absorbs, the more it seeks. If you feed it too much, it will aim to take it all. My heart, I beg, enough for today. We'll progress gradually."

The desperation in his voice made my black heart break and bleed a little. I'd promised to stay within bounds. "You're right."

"I will pull back," he said when I maintained the pull of lighting, and the arms of darkness began retracting away from around me. When all of his magic was safely tucked within him again, Visha summoned the seal to close entirely.

A breath whooshed out of me, and I collapsed to the ground, dizzy while my ears rang with a thundering noise that threatened to burst my brain open.

So, this was a little taste of what I was keeping prisoner.

Warm arms wrapped around me, and I sagged onto him, counting my inhales as I breathed in his scent to calm me down.

"Did it hurt?" he asked.

"Not like I thought it would. Feels more like a bad hangover."

There was a stunned moment of silence when I saw what we had caused to happen around us. Ash hovered in the wind above the land that had once been a vibrant green. It was now covered with black, burning embers and fully sprouted white flowers growing amidst. An eerie sight—a graveyard.

Life amongst death.

"What in the hells?" Thora murmured, studying the death around us and the flowers blooming from between it.

Kilian bent down, glancing at the flowers and then me. He rested a palm flat against the soil and shut his eyes for a few seconds.

I got up. "What is it?"

His eyes peeled open. "The land died when my magic touched it. The soil would never grow anything, every life under it would have died, too." He plucked a flower and stood. "Galanthus." He extended it to Visha. "Have a look for me. See how they managed to sprout in dead soil."

"It's just a flower," I said, blinking between them.

"It works," my Crafter said blankly, pocketing the flower in one of her pouches. "If you can contain her, then you can contain Aurora. At least until we can manage to pry the sceptre off Silas's hands. We can work on a dream veil dome. Infuse my magic with yours to contain Aurora and Snow, too."

Thora looked over her shoulder to us, still crouched down to the ground and making a bouquet with the white flowers. "What about killing her?"

The words chilled the air.

Then the visions I'd seen in Seraphim flashed all over.

Dead. I'd see her dead.

Visha opened her palms, a red sceptre forming in the air, two spheres of light floating out of it. "The sceptre acts as a guard, she shares part of her life with it. If she dies under someone's control, she will be brought back, continuously. The only way to stop her is to command her back inside the sceptre." The witch swallowed. "Then freed again by Snow's command in order to be killed." The sceptre illusion vanished, and she looked at me. "Have you asked him, my queen?"

Damn you, Visha.

My husband raised a brow. "Ask me what?"

"Kil," I started carefully, "I want to meet Golgotha."

He glanced at Visha and then at me. "And why would you, love of mine, want to meet the God of Demons? For tea or?"

Funny man my man was. "To find Urinthia."

He narrowed his eyes briefly on Visha again, and my witch winced a little. "And how can he help us find her?"

"He can locate the pocket realm she has opened to hide and assemble the Octa Virga in."

Kilian measured my words for a moment and then heaved out a sigh. "I'll see to it."

"Will you really?"

"If we weren't trying to prevent a war from breaking, I would have allowed it over my dead body."

It was my time to flinch, and he reached a hand to me, pulling me in his arms and kissing my brow. "You know what I mean."

I buried my face in his chest and inhaled him. All it mattered now was that he was here. If I thought about it any longer, the old memories would drown me. "Yeah."

One day I would ask again.

One day I would ask him to tell me all.

Kilian had gone to sleep soon after I'd started petting his hair, his face pressed to his favourite spot between my breasts. He'd spent all day assembling camp in Fernfoss after our little training and had returned to Amaris bone tired. There was no waking him, he was completely gone. Carefully, I slipped away towards the door, quietly tiptoeing outside without waking him at all.

Nia was with Thora in her room like we'd planned. My little sister threw a cover on Mal who had fallen asleep on her sofa, and then joined us in her bed.

"Kilian is going to be so mad," Nia said, bringing some goodies out of her bag. "He was so mad when you asked him about Golgotha. Imagine when he knows about this."

Well, the Isline Queen was no God at least.

"Nonsense. He loves me," I said, chewing on the worst snacks I'd ever had. This was why Cai was my snack person, not Nia. What sane person snacked on dried grapes?

"You really think the Islines might really want to help us?" Thora quietly asked.

Nia shook her head. "The answer to that is definitely a *no*, Rora. I think Snow is thinking of something else."

True, I was.

Thora stuffed her mouth with dried grapes and then gagged, spitting them on a piece of paper. "Like?"

"Throw our father off," I said. "Cause some trouble in Isjord. His numbers are terrifying the more I think about it. He's slowly encircling us all even before raising Aurora. Which means one of the two. He either fears Aurora will fail him. Or is prepared for us to put up a real fight with her. He knows you and Eren live, if he was worried about me finding a way to control it, he is now triple worried. Father has this *thing* despite his skill of war."

My sister leaned forward, all curious. "What thing?"

"He doubts himself."

"How do you know?"

"It took him so little thought to decide to make me an heir. I know that man inside out. He is weak. Like a turtle."

"Oh God," Nia mumbled, enjoying her dried grapes. "Here we go again."

My sister blinked. "Like a...turtle?"

"Strong armour. Boneless flesh underneath. He's got his beast, his witch, an old Ice Queen, and soon a whole Guardian. Take the turtle apart. Strip the veils and the sun shields. Take away his four horsemen. What remains underneath is only a man with some decent powers. Besides, his fourth horseman already rides for me."

"I'll speak to Mor about the Islines, see what she thinks. They've been neighbours for millennia, she might give us a clear perspective on this," Nia said, nodding. "It will be dangerous, Snow. They are not nice people from all that I've heard, and they will probably use this opportunity against your bloodline. We cannot deal with two enemies."

My little sister nodded. "I agree with Nia. But with you, too. This could work. Isjord thrives on meticulousness, a set of straight rules, and protocol. Imagine throwing them into chaos."

"Exactly."

The two went quiet all of a sudden. Both looked behind me, over at the doors, so I turned as well. Kilian was standing there only in his underwear, his hair all over the place, his cheeks stained pink, and he was staring at me with the sleepiest eyes that made me feel all guilty for some reason. "You weren't there." Even his voice was all sleepy.

"I totally get it now," Nia chuckled under her breath, and Thora joined, both giggling like hens.

"I'll come back to bed in a moment, darling."

He blinked fast. "How long of a moment?"

I got on my feet. "Is there something wrong?"

"Yes."

Hells, had he heard us? I was not ready to tell him about it yet. "What?"

"You're mine at night."

A flush crept all the way down my face, neck, and chest, and his eyes dropped there. "I suppose it will be a short moment," he said, lifting his amused eyes back to mine and walking away.

"Don't say a word," I warned the two behind me who were already preparing to embarrass me more.

They pressed their mouths tightly shut, but the moment I sat down, Nia repeated in an almost perfect Kilian voice, "*You're mine at night.*"

I winced.

Then Thora did the same. Trying her best at doing a Kilian's impersonation.

I grabbed a pillow and struck them both. "So. Not. Funny."

Mal groaned, shifting to his side, and Thora sneered, glaring death at him and hitting him with dried grapes. "I want to choke the hells out of him."

"What did you say to him in the library that day?"

She swallowed, looking down at her hands. "Things. Silly things. He likes hearing silly things. The sillier they are, the more he likes them, the more he will listen to me. Apparently, many of the things I say are silly because he likes most of what I say."

"Just...that?" I asked.

She shrugged. "Cai tells you to breathe, I tell him silly things."

Nia looked at me before asking her, "Why does he sleep here?"

"I asked him to stay with me when I came to stay over here in Adriata. He just never stopped." My sister chewed on her bottom lip, and then whispered to us, "Mal is sort of...good at these war things. Are we telling him?"

"A little too fucking late," he said, startling all of us out of our skin. He rolled on his back again and sighed. "Crescent heavens, why are you all screaming?"

I put a hand to my chest, shaking from laughter. And soon, Nia and Thora were laughing as well. We laughed until tears were streaming down our cheeks and our bellies hurt. Suddenly, it felt like the whole dim room had sprung to life.

When Mal laughed with us, I realised then that the room had really taken life, the shadows had loured, and the candles were glowing brighter. Even the colour on the walls appeared vivid somehow.

"Want to gossip with us?" Thora asked, patting the spot next to her. "We have snacks."

Mal got up and stretched, taking a set next to her and raising a brow at the dried grapes. "I was deceived."

"What do you think?" Nia asked, offering him some carrot slices instead.

His mouth curled up a bit at the sight of the vegetable, but he took one. "It is good thinking. There are some things we need to consider. How will Silas react to it. Do we want him to kill these people? I can't think of another way for him to be able to stop the rioting. Isjord takes no useless prisoners, remember?"

"You're right," I said, sighing, and all of them looked surprised at my answer. "What, I don't want innocents dead?"

They all stuffed their mouths with the dried fruit, looking at one another.

Mal was the one to ask since the other two didn't, "Since when?"

"Since the fact that Isjordians love to be oppressed. They will sing to my father's brutality. I've seen it before. This might win completely against us."

"Ah," Nia said.

"Ah," Thora followed, nodding.

Mal nudged my shoulder. "Why are we not telling Kil?"

"I'm scared for his health. He keeps saying blood pressure this, blood pressure that. Starting to think he is not joking."

My brother-in-law found it funny, extremely funny. Hilarious even. He howled. To the point that the wolves in the distance howled back. "The bastard will live. Just tell him."

"When my plan is perfect and I'm sure he won't find an argument that will make me doubt all of it." I dusted my hands and stood. "I'll leave you to it. Let me know tomorrow if you think of anything else."

"Mhm," Nia chuckled, and Thora followed.

Just before I took off, I spun and threw my arms around Mal, clinging to his neck so I could whisper, "Don't hate me."

After a moment, he put his hands around me. "I don't hate you," he whispered back. "Never have. You can go to him now or he will avenge his stolen time."

Damn it. "You heard?"

He threw a bunch of dried grapes on his mouth, wincing at the taste. "No?"

Kilian was waiting in his armchair in the far corner of the room, drinking, eyes travelling all over me when I made my way to him.

"You scared me before," I said, throwing him a glare.

"Yeah, I was scared, too. You promised me a cuddle. Preferably with your tits in my face. You left mid-cuddle. Imagine my horror when they were just...gone."

"Kilian Henrik Castemont," I hissed, taking a pillow from our bed and throwing it at him. "You absolute fool."

"And the full name returns," he chuckled, catching the pillow. "Am I in trouble?"

"Yes." No, he was not.

"I'd like to know why."

"Well, you barged in naked."

"I had my underwear on. I did not barge, I knocked. And I woke up with you missing from my side."

"Then you said I'm yours at night." Which I was. Don't know where I was trying to go with this.

"That you are." He cocked his head back. "Why did you have to slip away from me like that? What wicked things were you planning on doing?"

"Nothing."

"The things you do to me when you lie," he said, adjusting in his seat.

Heavenly thigh Gods. "Even so," I said, a little bit louder than normally, and his brows hiked up. "I can do wicked things. I can keep things from you. Lie to you." I wanted to do neither of those things, ever.

"Of course."

Oh. "Yes, of course. I don't have to take permission for anything." But I wanted him to approve of what I was doing.

"No, you don't."

Oh. "No, I don't." I stopped pacing back and forth when I caught him smiling from the corner of my eye. "Something funny?"

"I love it when you are cruel to me."

"We are arguing, Kilian." I pointed between us. "This is us arguing right now."

He cleared his throat and forced the smile away. "Alright. I'm sorry. As you were saying."

"Try and look like you're enjoying this a little less."

"I'll try, but not all of me agrees," he said, pouring another glass of his horrible tasting liquor.

I grabbed another pillow and smacked him with it. "Maybe I can convince the stubborn parts."

He grabbed my wrist and pulled me to him. "You violent little thing. Maybe," he purred, stroking pieces of hair out of my face, "I should have started with some news first."

I shuddered. "What news?"

"But you've hurt my feelings," he said, pulling back, leaving me all cold and empty. "Fool."

He bit his lip. "Ah, my poor heart."

I straddled his lap, and he groaned at the back of his throat. "Tell me."

"Say please."

"Please," I grit out between clenched teeth.

He grinned, downing the rest of his drink. "I've found a way to sail us through the Sea of the Dark."

"You have?"

"Yes. Triad has already gone to overlook the ship being fortified with Adriatian steel. Already tested, it won't melt from the contact with the acid waters further in, but no more than about five of us can go because of the weight it has added. I spoke to Cai earlier today. We will need him to steer the ship with wind since there is none inside the eudemon space, and he agreed."

"He did?"

"Mhm. So did Mal. He'll lead us towards life."

Oh. "Why did you wait to tell me?"

"I didn't want it to keep you awake all night from excitement, but now that I think about it, it might have actually helped you sleep."

"Yeah."

"Are you still mad at me?" he asked, his nose nudging mine. "Are we still arguing? Or can I have my cuddle now?"

"Say please."

"Pretty please," he murmured, kissing my mouth repeatedly. "Please, hm? Haven't I been good?"

I kissed him back, trying hard not to smile. "Mhm."

24

Black Bishop to C2

Snowlin

THERE WAS NO OTHER way to cross the Sea of the Dark to the underwater city of Hellas besides by ship—though a ship wasn't a way either because no one had actually managed to reach the other point without paying the price.

No matter how much Kilian had insisted he went alone, I'd refused. If we were to pay a price like the rest, we'd pay it together. And besides, I might be the only one who Golgotha might be willing to speak to. He was known to be a prideful God.

Mal jumped from the ship deck and dusted his hands together, glaring at my sister who was shifting from one foot to the other while she stared ahead at the gurgling, dark storm gathered above the bizarre waters.

"Her fascination with odd things sometimes scares me," I said.

Kilian pointed an accusing look at me. "Does it now?"

"Unbelievable," Mal murmured.

Kilian lifted his gaze up from the map to him, already knowing what he was going to say. "There is no wind in this sea to stir us, brother, and you know it. Thora is needed to guide the ship."

"It could have been anyone else."

"They all backed away when she volunteered," my husband said with some humour, glancing at my little sister. "She's got a way with words."

"Sure," Cai said, shaking his head as he came to join us by the ship. "Words. Men are bloody fools. Fools for girls with pretty eyes, dark hair, and the most ominous sense of humour to exist."

My sister looked between all the men, seeming a bit confused at the fuss, before she got dragged to the ship deck by Cai who showed her around and explained which sail they needed to push for the ship to stir in the direction we wanted it to go.

Nia stepped before us, handing me a little sachet of foul-smelling herbs. "Blood bark," she explained, giving the rest of the entourage one, too. "Macaria sourced me some of the plant and I mixed it with white rue to hide your scents from eudemons, like what we used for our Nimbus when they flew over this area to lure them inside Adriata. The creatures might think they hate your taste until they smell your magic."

"Hope you packed a bigger one for my muffin," Mal said, throwing my friend a teasing glance. "His attitude fucking stinks. One of them tentacled things might want to snog it out of him."

Cai bumped hard against Mal's shoulder as he reached to get the satchel from Nia. He patted her cheek. "Be safe. Alright?"

Nia nodded at him. "I will."

On the way back to the ship, he bumped hard against Mal's shoulder again. "Fucker."

"Never got a piece of this," Mal spat back. "Is that why you are acting so silly, my muffin?"

"You're not my type, arsehole."

"I'm everybody's type," Mal shouted back, and then turned to throw me a wink.

Kilian pinched the bridge of his nose and sighed. "We're all going to be some eudemon's lunch today, aren't we?"

"It will be a fine dining experience for them. The selection is impeccable," Nia said over her shoulder, waving us goodbye.

Kilian linked his fingers to mine and pulled me on deck. "No one looks down at the waters or up at the mist. No one stares directly in a eudemon's eyes or whatever else you see when we leave land. Clear?"

"But those are just tales they tell to scare children," Thora said. "They don't really hypnotise you to follow them and then drown you before eating your corpse." She blinked up at Mal. "Do they?"

"Of course it's tales," the princeling said, and my sister let out a whoosh of relief. "They don't drown you first." He leaned in and gently bit her cheek. "It takes away the spice."

She nodded to herself as she rubbed her cheek. "Understandable."

Cai chuckled and threw an arm over her neck. "We won't let anything eat you, Rora. We'll throw him first. Once they get to his fatty brains, they won't think about eating us at all."

I had almost finished my almond snack and the entertainment was getting too good before even hitting waters.

Kilian did not think so though, and my grin slipped into an apologetic smile.

I put an almond in his mouth. "I wonder if I taste nice. I mean, I'm not exactly human, they might like me."

His eyes drew tightly shut while he chewed on the almond. "Woman."

Mal patted his shoulder. "Calm down, brother."

My husband blinked at Mal and then at me, almost offended. "Did he just tell me to calm down?"

I lifted another almond to his mouth. "Almond?"

"Yes, and matter of fact," he said, folding the map and pointing away from the ship. "Go fetch some more."

I rolled my eyes. "Prick."

For the first time today, he actually smiled. "Are we about to have another argument? You know I love those."

"Enough with the long fucking stares. We get it," Mal said, sliding between us and pushing us apart. "Let's get this ship going. I'm getting nauseous without hitting water yet."

We'd sailed for about an hour, and according to Kilian, that was an hour too long for Golgotha to be so quiet.

The grey fog encircled the ship in the shape of a dome, repelled by my husband's presence.

"How long has it been since someone has gotten this far into these waters and returned to tell the tale?" Cai asked, shifting his hands back and forth, drawing and guiding wind to stir us further in the depths of the eudemon waters.

"Centuries," Mal said, tilting his head and narrowing his eyes into the fog ahead of us. "And they didn't exactly tell any tale as much as they screamed and cried and retched. These creatures were once of heavens, still are. In the book of our Goddess, it is said that they terrorised realms restlessly. They were never meant to hide and remain peaceful. It was what made them so powerful amongst the divine panes."

Cai leaned on the border, staring ahead. "Never understood how a realm like Dissiri fell."

Kilian leaned back on a sail, crossing his arms. "It is said through scriptures that the three Demon Gods were planning on claiming the throne of all Gods back when all three first Gods, the *Goddess of Nothing*, the *God of Most*, and the *God of Some*, coexisted in union and not as rulers of their own part of the realm expanse. And their horror did reign all over for a little while, dark skies with no sun and moon. No dead were allowed to leave for heaven or hell. To the Demon Gods, their existence was both heaven and hell. Souls and the living walked along. Golgotha did not agree to his brothers' decisions. Reigning chaos would never bring more chaos, only hope for peace and light. And all Demon Gods fed on chaos, horror, misery. If no one prayed for it, there would be no more Demon Gods at all. At this point, Fader, once the *God of Some*, had become an entity, built his own space and crowned Ithicea the reigning heaven over some part of the realm expanse. Golgotha sought his help after being denied by his own mother, Nihilia, and the God of Most. The demon realms all eventually fell as he'd predicted from lack of prayer and faith. The other two brothers were taken prisoner by the *Goddess of Nothing* for the damage they had caused over many realms and billions of lives across them. Fader tried to keep Dissiri alive since Golgotha had been a helping hand in taking his brothers down, but none of his realms would relent to praying for chaos. The last offer he had for Golgotha, who was now a fallen God, was to live here, in a realm where human desire was darker than most. It was enough to keep him and his creatures alive, but not enough to bring life back into his realm."

Mal faked a snore, and Kilian shot him a dark look.

The younger brother chuckled. "My explanation was intended to be much shorter.

Demon King had no prayer. Demon king fell. The end. But his explanation will do it."

"Never mind him," I murmured to my husband. "I love it when you speak history to me."

"I saw you doze off a little."

Only because he had told me about this last night in bed. I would have never missed listening to his stories. "Just resting my eyelids, darling."

Mal suddenly rushed to the quarter deck, narrowing his eyes on the black waters that were so heavy and thick in density it almost resembled tar. "Bother," he warned, and Kilian's darkness dripped around us, clouds of black formed skeletal shapes with glowing eyes, hissing at the very air around us.

The ship swayed, and Kilian wrapped an arm around my waist to steady me.

Everyone went quiet.

There was not a sound of nature around us.

The sea was silent. And so was the air. So silent that I could hear all five of our heartbeats. And then...another much louder sixth one ticking like a clock. Growing closer and closer.

I spun around before the massive serpent-like eudaemon broke the water and shrilled in the air, raising chills on my skin.

Its body froze at my command and then the sharp brush of cutting wind blew the body into small pieces.

Cai stood behind me. "What were you waiting for?" he sneered. "A bloody invitation?"

"Wanted to see if it could really hypnotise me."

Ignoring me, he turned to survey the murky waters that had begun gurgling beneath us with more movement.

"Uhm," my sister said, pointing below us. "Why is it spinning?"

We all leaned over deck to watch as the water around our ships began spinning into a vortex and lowering us inside it—slowly engulfing the whole ship.

"Air pocket!" Cai shouted, and both he and Thora formed a barrier of wind around us when the water rose almost to the deck.

"He is inviting us in," Kil said too calmly while his shapes of night doubled and then tripled around us.

It was too dark to see anything, but when the ship shook, I knew we had touched the bottom of the sea.

Dozens, hundreds, and thousands of heartbeats circled us, growing more and more somewhere between the layer of water that was being held away by wind.

"What do you see?" I asked Kilian when his hand tightened around my wrist.

I felt his body slide before mine as if to shield me. "Nothing I want you to see."

"Mal?" I called.

"I've got them," he echoed.

Electricity lit my fingertips, bringing light all around us.

My eyes doubled at what stood not even a couple of feet before us. "Hells." All sorts of creatures floated in the dark waters we were submerged under. Horns, talons, and teeth, pimpled flesh and veiny skins, mangled bodies with either too many limbs or barely any. Eyes too dark and some too pale were focused on us—on me—unmoving behind the shield of air though I was sure it would be no struggle for them to break through it. Yet they weren't. The creatures finally moved, parting in the middle to make space for something else swimming in our direction. The body looked human from afar, up until it got close enough for me to see its features—or the lack of them. No eyes, mouth, or nose. Wrinkled skin covered its face and the rest of its body. It got close to the shield of air and rested a three fingered hand on it before pointing one at me.

The water around us suddenly dispelled, creating a vortex that revealed the sandy floor of the sea and a massive rocky city standing right before us, surrounded by mile tall walls of black water. At its centre stood a giant fortress the size of a mountain, metallic gates bound the entrance of it shut.

"Hellas," Mal murmured, his eyes wide ahead. "Thought this one was a bloody legend. There really is a city down here."

The thing pointed its finger to me again and backed away, bowing its head.

"They want you to go alone," Mal said. "Golgotha might be a fallen God, but his pride still remains. He won't grant an audience with us, only you. Someone equal to him."

Kilian was not going to let me go. And considering I had to leave him behind, I was not going to let him go either. To my surprise, his fingers slowly unwrapped from mine and he pulled me before him. He kissed my brow and cupped my face. "Make no bargains. Fall for no temptation he might offer."

"You're letting me do this?"

A little smile grazed his lips. "I would have kneeled before you the second you would have batted those lashes at me."

"I wouldn't have gone."

"And you would have ended up resenting yourself for not doing it."

My mouth parted open. "Oh."

He kissed me. "Mhm. *Oh.*" His finger went under my chin to lift my gaze to his. "I can't live knowing that."

"I love you," I said, backing away. "Say it back."

"When you return to me. Be careful."

Dagger in hand, I followed after the four-legged thing with the skin covered in tar and pustules filled with something that stank. The city was oddly full of life, creatures roamed around, unbothered by my presence.

The metallic gates of the castle-like fortress creaked open before we'd even neared, making the hinges shake and groan as if they were struggling to open. The dark and wide corridor walls were crawling with barnacles and seaweed, dripping water all over us and echoing a sound that was about to pop my eardrums out from frustration. But what struck me was the fact that it was lit with an ashy looking fire, almost like the black flames that lit around Kilian sometimes—they oozed a sense of doom and terror.

The creature thing stopped when we arrived at an open chamber, and luckily, I did, too before crashing into it.

More luminescent grey flamed torches lined the empty, massive cave with a tall bone dais in its centre that looked almost like a theatre podium.

I'd marvel at it, but the dripping water sounds that echoed around were driving me absolutely insane.

"A word would have been nice," a gritty, dark voice called from behind me, and I spun to face the tall, half-naked man that was standing not even two feet away from me. His long, black hair was streaked with white and fell down to his unclothed chest. He was young but not so young at the same time—old in a sense that I was sure only some could feel. And surprisingly handsome. "Don't humans do that anymore?" he asked, walking to his dais made of odd bones and rock, looking more God than human despite the deceiving skin he wore. "Send word and then I supposedly welcome you into my home." He leaned back in his seat, narrowing his black eyes on me. "It's not polite to kill my servants."

"It's not like they can talk, and you're sort of missing a letter box."

He flashed me a crooked grin. "We've lived amongst you for many lifetimes and not once have you been curious to learn our way of communicating."

"Should be grateful for our disrespect," I said. "We tend to deface and vandalise what we deem curious in nature. Even worse, your creatures would have been mocked. Used. Played with. Pointed at. Made a caricature of evil only to disguise true monsters. What looks like a monster is not nearly as close to being one up there."

"You would know, wouldn't you?" he asked, studying the whole of me. "I've not sensed this much chaos in such a small body in some time."

"You flatter me, God of Demons. To be acknowledged by you is a privilege."

He grunted, tilting his head to observe the whole of me. "Is there something you seek from this visit?"

"Answers."

"Good," he sighed, stretching in his seat. "I've got no food you'd like if you had come to wine and dine with me."

Gods and dry humour went hand in hand. "Urinthia has been taken by my father."

He perked up a little in his seat. "Has she now?"

"But you knew that, didn't you?"

His smirk was crooked. "My women don't simply go missing."

"How brilliant," I said, stepping closer. "Then lead me to her. I'd like a word." *Before I unburden her shoulders from the weight of her head.*

He raised both hands. "I am a prisoner in these waters. A man with no land in a no man's land. I gave her permission to enter my old realm whenever she pleases. I, on the other hand, am denied return. The land permits me not after I could not feed it what it needed to stay alive—power."

"Then permit me to enter your lands and I'll search for her myself."

There was a moment of silence before he said, "You speak so bravely for someone who does not know what lies beyond. If you can survive it or not."

"I'll survive."

"You seem sure."

"My husband will tear you apart if you don't ensure that I do."

His brow twitched. "Your husband." The God of Demons stood and descended the stairs of his human throne. "Presents no threat to me."

"Then why do you look threatened?" If one could recognise fear and caution, it would be me.

There was barely a foot between us when he raised a hand to the side and cracked open a crooked portal that framed an ashen land with no skies, no light, no wind, and no life. Ruins upon ruins piled for tall miles towards the empty space that should have been lined with the blue colours of Nubil and lit by Henah or Cyra.

Nothing. If nothingness looked like something, it would look like what I was seeing. An emptiness so desolate that it stirred a sense of doom inside my chest.

And that was just a small taste of what Numen would turn if Aurora was to be raised.

"I am not threatened," he almost growled. "Because I am sure the need for his retribution will not come, Guardian of Lightning." The way his dark eyes flashed tied a knot in my stomach. "You may enter."

My pulse was pounding in my ears when I took a step forward and then another until I stood right in front of the door to another realm. Not an in-between. A whole other realm.

I reached a hand forward, letting my fingers graze the reality beyond the portal. Then, holding a breath, I jumped in it.

My lungs seized like they often did in panic. Dizziness washed over me from the sudden weight to my bones and the pressure that wanted me to fold flat to the ground.

I shook my head, warding off the flashing spots of black from my vision, and then I calmed my breaths until I was sure I would not grow faint from inhaling what too little air remained in the burnt atmosphere of Dissiri.

Silence stretched wide over the grey graveyard made of crumpled rock soiling the ground and floating about in the air. Whatever faint brightness illuminated the realm was not natural—only a murky glow without source.

I stood in the middle of the absence of nothing. No life. No death. Until a faint familiar sensation trickled electricity down my neck. I spun around, trying to grasp where the call of the sceptre was coming from.

"Go'ya," a ghostly whisper brushed close, and I jerked forward, heart pounding against my rib cage that was starting to hurt. The words resounded far in the distance. Until they disappeared. Unfamiliar yet familiar. A language I'd not heard but could understand.

Something warm and light as wind touched my face, and I stumbled back a few feet when it murmured in my ear, "Bah." Run.

"What?"

"Go'ya." Guardian, the same whisper repeated in the distance again, and I followed after it—until the mumbles began growing into more unfamiliar words. Unfamiliar words I could somehow understand. Leave. Run. Go.

The deeper into the ruins I entered, the fainter I grew, struggling to keep my eyes open. My whole body felt weak—as if every ounce of my energy was being drained off, sucked right out of me.

A flash of red in the distance made me force my eyelids open again. The Grand Maiden had kneeled in the middle of a massive craft halo and before the silver sceptre pieces laid on the ground.

"Urinthia." I tried to call but I wasn't sure if even murmurs were leaving my lips. At my will, magic left its bounds and crawled over me, feeding more than electrici- ty—feeding me strength. "Urinthia!"

The witch's head snapped to me, sage eyes wide when they landed on me. She stood, and the glow of the craft halo beneath her dimmed, chains bearing Melanthe's scent dangling from her limbs. "Snowlin." She shook her head and drummed a hand over the thin crimson veil surrounding her. "No, no, no. You have to get back, child. Now!"

Pure rage held me to my feet. I pulled my dagger out again and walked towards her. "Not until I have your heart in my hand."

"You should not be here!" she bellowed just as something crashed in the distance. "You will die."

"Lies," I mumbled, shaking my head again to ward off the spells of dizziness. "But you're good at telling lies, aren't you?"

"If I could spare my child a fate written with the purpose to ruin her, I would have told every lie it took."

"Selfish bitch."

"I am a mother!" she cried out. "Snowlin, this cannot be stopped. It is not meant to."

"It can!"

Another crash echoed behind me, the ground beneath my feet shaking and a chilling cold wind brushed my cheek, making me halt on the spot. Why was I feeling wind in a dead realm not graced by the blessing of Nubil?

Her words were cut off when she looked behind me at the stones floating in the air beginning to drop down to the ground. "Go!" she bellowed. "It is too late for me to do anything. It is. But not for you. You will stop her. You can stop her."

My throat filled with bitter words that nearly made me choke, and my damned tears threatened to spill. "At what cost?"

Her face fell and she staggered a step back. "You know of the cost?"

"Like hell I do!" I screamed, lifting one foot after the other almost as if they weighed like rocks.

She shook off a confused look. "Your seal is opening."

I looked down at my hands curling with countless black veins and then at her. "You know about my seal?"

"I helped Lysander create them." Tears skittered down her eyes. "Now go. Dissiri is feeding from you—not only from your magic, but from your presence, too. It will do so until its core is brought to life, it won't care whether it takes yours entirely."

"If I can end this here, I don't ca—"

"Don't fucking finish that sentence," Kilian's voice bellowed in the empty distance. Another portal door had cracked open close to us, and he stood behind it, breathing hard and angry—Gods, he was so angry. Golgotha stood on his knees with Kilian's hand wrapped around his throat. "Come," my husband said gently and reached a hand in the distance he could not cross.

Few more steps, just a few more and I could reach Urinthia, rip her heart out and Aurora would never see the light of my days.

A wave of dizziness washed over me again and then a sharp pain on my back knocked me breathless. The seal. The bloody seal was opening.

"Come!" Kilian ordered, loud enough that I finally felt a flash of his power even realms apart. Death was cold, so cold. *Not like him*, I thought just until I turned to see the look on his face. Black mist poured out of his eyes, the tips of his fingers had turned black and his nails had sharpened to black claws. "Come here," he repeated, and his magic slithered inside the portal, hovering and burning the air and grounds of Dissiri, coating them a colour of onyx. His magic encircled me, not letting the fallen realm feed from me, enough for me to gather some energy and stand.

Step after regretful step, I walked to him, grasping his extended hand.

He let go of Golgotha and pulled me into his arms, tightly holding me when my strength gave away and threatened to topple me to the ground. His hands were colder than ice when they rested on my skin, but the moment he sighed with relief, everything warmed up.

I turned to the portal again, staring ahead into the ruins of Dissiri as it began shrinking and closing. Somewhere in the long distance was Urinthia, assembling the ultimate weapon of destruction for my father to use. The opportunity to end this all stood before me, and I'd lost it. Again.

The God of Demons rubbed a hand over his throat, more annoyed at my hesitance than at Kilian who'd almost squeezed his eternity out of him. He glanced at my husband and then me, and said, "You let a man make decisions for you?"

My heart was still too loud and my limbs were too weak for me to gouge his eyes out. "You wanted to feed my magic to your realm. I don't need judgement from you."

"There is plenty to spare. You would have not died, do not be pathetic," he said simply, and a phantom shadow wrapped around his throat again.

Kilian bent down at him, raising a dark brow. "So, if I reach to tear half of your soul out of your body right now, you would not die either?"

"I'm powerless, boy, she is power itself. Tell me you do not feel it. How can anyone not possibly feel it. Last I felt something like her power was when Cyra bid me goodbye. Your wife could fuel another sun—create another realm. Do you realise the power that she holds? Are you so selfish to want it only for yourself?"

"I am. She's fucking mine. I gave no permission for you to touch what is mine. Do you know what that means?" Kilian backed away and let go of him. "One day I'm going to claim retribution for what you caused today. Wait for me."

Golgotha's jaw tightened. "And I will wait for you, Godling."

Kilian suddenly halted and turned to narrow his eyes one last time at Golgotha.

The fallen God walked back to his dais, a chain of words falling from his lips—strange words, the same language I'd heard in Dissiri. "You will not be able to control her."

Kilian tightened his grip on my hand, and everything darkened in the empty cave, lanterns dying off when darkness whispered against the walls to crawl around the Demon God. "Do not listen," he said to me.

Golgotha sniffed as he laid back on his seat, his dark eyes falling to the black tattoos still crawling over my skin. "Not in the poor condition you're in. You're only half of what she is now. You're not her equal."

I glanced at him over my shoulder. "You believe I trust you?"

"And yourself? Do you not trust yourself? Your own body is telling you that."

Kilian didn't speak or look at me as we made our way back to the ship.

"You understood what he said?" I asked, trying to keep up with his heavy steps.

"Yes."

"What language was it?"

"I don't know."

Thora jumped in my arms right the second we left Golgotha's home. Her dark lashes were wet. "Kilian thought—" She sniffled. "The tattoo band on his finger...it faded and disappeared."

I glanced at Kilian's hand still wrapped around mine, the mark of our union was still bruised grey in places, not entirely the strong obsidian colour it usually was.

He wouldn't look at me at all when we climbed back on the ship. And he didn't talk to me either on the way back. Or even blinked at all. But at least he didn't let go of my hand and did not push me away when I tentatively rested my head on his chest.

Mal was not as forgiving as him though. The looks he gave me were scalding. Maybe he wanted to take back what he'd told me the night before. He looked like he did hate me.

Visha was at the shore waiting for our return.

My witch looked hopeful. The first time she remotely looked close to feeling any sort of emotion.

"I tried," I said to her. "Now you can let this go. Let me have those nightmares in peace."

Her head lowered. "I will not stop."

If Kilian had not pinned a dubious look on me, I would have ripped desire out of her entirely. "You will have to. I order it," was all I said.

She stopped me again. "When I was led to you, when I walked for weeks through lands that should not have existed to come to you, I carried a heavy promise. To serve you until I can't. And until I can't, I will still serve you." She spun and then disappeared out of sight.

Narrowly. I'd missed finding Urinthia so narrowly that I was about to pluck my hair out one by one with tweezers.

Kilian opened the doors and strutted in, still flipping through countless documents, hardly even realising I was laying down on the bed. Or so I thought. When his eyes landed on me, they widened just a fraction—with happiness.

Cursed be my pride.

I had spent the night after returning from the Sea of the Dark in Thora's bed, watching her sleep and snore softly. Then the night after I'd gone to Nia's, letting her tell me about all sorts of flowers she'd harvested from Aru that she was planning on making medicine with until she had fallen asleep with her head on my lap.

Tonight, both had refused to let me sleep in their beds. Apparently, they needed something called privacy, and I'd avoided talking to him for much too long.

Guilt was such an odd sensation. Gnawing. Hollow. I'd barely realised I was feeling it from the hopelessness I'd encapsulated myself in. Which was an oddly filling sensation, I'd figured.

"You're angry," he said, shedding his clothes, and I tried my hardest to keep my eyes trained on the book before me. Though, my nerves had strung so tight that no letter was making sense. What language was this?

He sighed, reached to grab my book, and spun it round in the right direction. Oh.

He sat on the edge of the bed next to me, his hand petting my thigh back and forth, and my toes curled under the blanket. "Love. My love. Won't you speak to me?" he asked, leaning to kiss my cheek, and I almost burst a vein from struggling to not kiss him back. "Hm? Please? Punish me some other way." His mouth dipped lower, and his hand slid between my thighs. "I missed you so much," he said, kissing his way back to my lips. "So, so much."

Me too. "I want to read my book."

He slowly pulled back and nodded. "Alright, my love. I'll leave you to it."

My heart ached and I really didn't want to be stubborn about this, but this put fear back in my blood. I had...hope. So much of it. And I'd lost it.

It was my fault for hoping again in the first place.

He returned after his bath, water rivulets still clinging to his skin as he dried his hair with a towel. He caught me looking, and when he smiled at me, I wanted to give up right then.

"What is it about?" he asked, laying on his side of the bed, and I blinked at him. He pointed a finger on the page. "The book."

"Nothing that would be interesting to you," I said, flipping a page. Truly. It wasn't interesting for me either. Where had I found this absolute nonsense about gut health?

It felt like I'd stabbed at my own heart when his brows creased. "I see."

We were silent for what felt like hours. I'd stolen glances at him from time to time, but his gaze had never left a tiny spot on my glittery ceiling filled with countless stones that turned a luminescent silver when they were hit by the round moonlight.

Too tired to continue this day, I shut my book, blew off the bunch of candles on my nightstand, and laid down, forcing my blood shot eyes shut.

His voice was smoother than night, "Can I at least hold you?"

Yes. Yes. Yes. I rolled around and let him wrap his arm around me. Heaven—I was in heaven. Lemon scented heaven.

His fingers were gentle on my back. "Thank you. Will you tell me goodnight as well?"

"Good night."

"What about a kiss?"

I pressed my lips to his for a moment and then ducked my head back to my hiding spot in his chest.

Silence rang for a short while. "Please forgive me," he murmured between my hair. "I was selfish, I know. But I swear it to you, my heart, I've rarely ever been selfish before you were in my life. Can't I be selfish with you? Hm?"

When his voice shook, the heartache returned so fiercely it was making me dizzy. I had forced Cai and Nia to accept my eventual death, schooled them to let me face it as I wished. But him...he would never...he'd never accept it, would he? How had I just realised that?

I trailed a hand down his back and sneaked it under his shirt, feeling his warm skin on my cold one. He sighed at my touch, and I shuffled closer to him, slipping a leg between his and adjusting my face on his chest. I felt the still angry scars on his chest brush my cheek and remembered the moment I had wanted to be selfish for him, too. I would have wasted that wish in Rokko's realm a million other times to have him back. I would have wasted any wish in this realm to have him with me.

"I'm scared, Kil. So scared. Like never before."

There it all was. Out in the open. Spoken and real now.

I didn't fear dying. I feared failing them.

He suddenly pulled back and kissed me, ravenously—inhaling my every breath until his own filled my lungs. "I am so scared, too, Snow. Terrified. But I'm more scared of losing you. If I had found you dead, nothing would have mattered in this world enough for me to stay in it. I won't lose you again for the sake of anything. You hear me? For the sake of absolutely anything. Fuck the world."

My mouth dropped open. "Kilian Castemont."

"You heard me," he said, pulling me close to him again and burying his head on the crook of my neck. "Hold me, woman, and hold me tight. Nearly had a heart attack at my young age that day."

I dragged my nails through his scalp, letting his incredibly silky hair slide between my fingers. "Poor baby."

A squeak left my mouth when he bit my neck. "Evil woman."

"But you love me," I whispered, giggling a little.

He left a dozen pecks on my shoulder. "So much it terrifies me. If you hadn't taken my hand—"

"I will always take your hand."

"You hesitated."

"If there is a world where you are safe in it, I would have given everything. Even my life." *I will, still.*

"Don't break my heart, Snow."

"I already warned you, darling. Long ago."

25

White Pawn to F3

Kilian

SNOW HOPPED FROM ONE book aisle to the other with Atlas and Oryn following every step she took. And she finally stopped to peruse the long lines of the chained books that had not been opened in perhaps the last ten centuries or so.

"Kil!" Snow called from somewhere deep in the library, and I pushed off the wall I'd leaned against to go to her.

"Yes, love?"

She pointed a finger to the top shelf where a thick volume of an Esmeray diary was chained. "Get me that one."

"What's in it for me?" I asked, taking the book and holding it up and over her head.

"Depends, what do you want?"

I puckered my lips and lowered my face down to her.

Chuckling, she puckered her lips, too, and we both shared a little awkward peck. "Ah, so easily pleased."

"What have you found, my hellcat?"

She traced a few lines under the simple book title. "Blood and something, something...Guardian."

"Blood of an Ithicea Guardian." I took her hand and traced my finger over her palm, forming the letter. "That stands for first heaven, or what we call Ithicea. You learn fast." Old Darsan was not easy.

"Had to," she said mindlessly, already flipping through the pages of *Hereditas*. She smoothed a palm over the blank pages. "You said these were written with the blood of a fallen Guardian. Which fallen Guardian? As far as I know, no Guardian of the prime heavens has fallen. It is said they could fall, but there has never been a mention of anyone fallen from what I've read. I don't believe Aurora is a fallen Guardian either. And most of these were written long before she became the Octa Virga."

"With the blood of Oneira, a Guardian of Dreams, who still served the *Goddess of Nothing*. She'd sent dreams to a man sentenced with a life of nightmares. Not out of pity, love or care, but out of jealousy of her sister, Efelia, a Guardian of Nightmares who'd lived among praise because of the terror she'd caused to those she visited. Back when terror was praised. Doing so, she'd broken the foundation of what she was created on and therefore fallen from the heavens and sent to live out her days as a simple woman who was a slave of nights full of nightmares. Esmeray had met her in her travels to the lower realms that were not overlooked by Gods—some say she had searched for her purposefully, to write these books, and that the Guardian had willingly gifted her last days to her."

She chewed on her bottom lip to the point it was bleeding. "We have no portals or gates to other realms in Numen. Only to the heavens of our Gods."

"There once were many. When the three reigning deities, Gods of *Nothing, Some,* and *Most,* lived peacefully together and undivided. But that was pretty long ago, my heart."

She swallowed and lifted her eyes to me, and her voice was low when she said, "Kil, I saw something in Seraphim."

Though it was hardly possible that any gates had remained in our time, it couldn't be entirely impossible. And since Snow was perhaps the only one who could open them from our realm, she would not be just her father's target. "You saw *nothing* in Seraphim. You hear me?"

She nodded and took my hand, pulling me to a seat where Thora was already sitting with Nia before a large dictionary that was one page flip away from falling apart.

"Please remind me to buy Atlas something nice for himself," Nia said, quickly scribbling notes on a thick notebook that was also a drop of ink away from turning entirely black. "Don't know where he dug this from or from what cold skeleton's hands he pried it off, but I know he deserves something nice."

Snow smirked at her friend. "You look like you're one page away from moaning."

A pen hit my wife right in the head from an unimpressed Nia. "It's gold. This is gold," she insisted, pointing a finger to the book. "This language, these letters have not been seen since the time when Gods walked back to their heavens."

Snow hooked a thumb in my direction, puffing her shoulders proudly. "He speaks it. Reads it. Knows it."

"Mal, too," Thora mumbled while intently trying to trace whatever words were on another Esmeray diary into a piece of paper for Nia to translate.

"Where is the idiot?" Nia asked. "He could be here cutting us time."

Thora looked absolutely unbothered as she calmly said, "Having his ego stroked amongst many other things."

Snow snorted and then blasted into a cough, almost choking on a breath of air when Mal strutted in, frowning exactly at her sister. He looked worn out, just not in the type of way Thora had described. And Snow had though the same apparently because she turned to her sister, and said, "I thought you meant—"

The younger sister lifted her head up, blinking slowly and so innocently. "Training. Men get very touchy when they fight. It's like they can't keep their hands off of one another."

Mal took a seat beside her, forcing her to scoot further away despite there being more space literally all around the table. "Little bird, your hands are all over me when I train you as well."

Thora suddenly shot up, looking at the entrance of the library where Neo stood, waving a shy hand over at her. She pushed the chair back, ignoring Mal's severely inappropriate remark. "Excuse me for a moment."

My brother grabbed onto her wrist, but then quickly let go as if he had caught himself. Thora, too, hesitated a moment after, before shaking her head and rushing to Neo.

Snow's eyes jumped between her sister and my brother, and then her sister and Neo. Despite the quiet library, the two were talking in hushed tones and that was causing my wife some sort of distress because her knee bumped against the table over and over until I put a hand on her thigh.

"Love."

"Hush. That's a boy. She is talking to a boy."

"No," my brother said, yawning, "she is talking to a dead man."

"Thora likes him and you can see he likes her back," Nia added, not paying attention to us. "Leave them be."

Snow's brows hiked up and she turned to me. "He likes her back? You knew about this?"

"Yes."

"Knew what?" Thora asked, returning to her seat. "Did you find something?"

Nia sighed. "Nothing but a slew of boring details about the origin of their creation. And none so far are about Guardians forged by Adan or any of their weaknesses or flaws." She looked up at Snow and then me. "There are some paragraphs about her—a Caelum born."

"Am not," Snow crooned, continuing to cross reference letters with one another.

"There was only one family," Nia continued, and Snow's pen stopped moving. "The Aerin. Born from Nubil's brother, the God of Thunder, Goltar. And a lower Goddess called Theena. Goltar's first child followed Nubil to Caelum and later swore his loyalty to him, serving as the heaven's second in command."

"Nia," Snow warned.

"Nubil never reinstated the spot after Zephyr surrendered his title. It still belongs to an Aerin blood. It belongs to you. It will belong to your children. Or Thora's. Or Eren's. To whoever Elding who will claim it."

Snow lowered her pen on the table and rolled her eyes up to her friend. "I'm a Skygard. Queen of Olympia. And that is enough."

"Ours, too," Mal said, leaning back.

She clicked her fingers and pointed at him. "Yeah, Adriata, too."

"If matter comes to war," Nia started, "would you consider asking them for help?"

My wife blinked once. "Who?"

"The God you're supposed to serve."

"I serve one God, my Nia. And that is my desire."

"Fine, but what can it do to help us fight off a Guardian?"

"We're working on it," my wife said quietly, tracing more notes down. "If I have to bow before any deity, it will have to be my own power."

Her friend's voice was broken when she said, "Snow, it could kill you."

"And godly interference hasn't been trying enough already?"

"You think you can take on a fight with her?" Mal asked, tapping a nervous finger on the table.

"Yes. Then all we need to do is kill my father to free the Octa Virga from his command. From there I can handle the rest."

Kill her—that is what she'd meant. "You keep forgetting that Snow is not alone," I said. "We will be right beside her."

Snow put a hand on my thigh. "If we have to."

"There is us as well," Thora added, giving her sister a smile.

My wife sighed. "That doesn't console me much, Rora."

Mal fingered the bow tying her hair back and then pulled it loose, letting the silky rose ribbon slide off and onto his grasp before stuffing it in his pocket. "No soldier of mine has ever worn a pink bow to a fight."

She reached for the ribbon. "I am no soldier of yours, Malik."

My brother grunted. "You are being trained by me. That makes you my soldier. Mine."

She huffed. "Trained? Sitting and breathing with my eyes closed all day does not count as training."

"It counts for most of our training," I explained. "If you wish to learn how he creates tugs of magic and attaches them to the dead he summons, meditation will be the hardest part of your training. Connecting the physical to the spiritual is beyond difficult. You have to visualise the invisible threads, imagine where they are and attach them to your mana to bring them to life."

"That is something she can do?" Nia asked, finally abandoning her study.

"Considering what she is, with some effort—easily."

Nia's eyes were slightly wider than normal. "So, if she were to summon, let's say, an army of ice soldiers—"

"Depending on the tug she has on her magic, a solid battalion."

"Only a battalion?"

"Easy, Nia," Mal said. "At best a battalion."

"I saw you raise more than a battalion in the battle at Highwall."

His finger tapped quicker against the table. "If I wanted, I would have raised more."

"But?"

"But it consumes parts of us," I added. "Darkness consumes as it grows. Death, too. Shadows, too. For us to grow our magic, we have to bargain for something else. Like elementals rely on their mana, we rely on the strengths of—"

"Our soul," she finished for me.

"Not exactly," Mal explained. "Kil and I have mastered control over it. For it to consume us entirely would take a while. But, yes, it does consume parts of it. Any part. If you are unlucky, it could consume your empathy and therefore your entire ability to understand emotion let alone control it. But for an elemental, they would have to fragment their own magic into tiny threads to extend out of them which will leave less mana in their bodies to do normal things like breathe. An easy case with Thora since she has an unlimited source of it. And so far into our training, we've yet to find what tax she will pay for it." He lifted a piece of paper with the Esmeray inscriptions on it. "What exactly are we looking for?"

"Vas," Snow said quickly. "Details on Aurora and her one flaw, anything I can use against them."

My brother cocked his head back. "How about lightning? Quicker and more efficient than this bullshit."

She shook her head. "Vas cannot be killed, that is his curse. What I can do is kill my father, command her back to the sceptre, and trap Vas. To do all that, I have to know their weaknesses."

"Trap?"

"She means inside his mind," Visha spoke from the table next to ours, still busy reading her grimoire. "That would be me. And Kilian."

My brother's attention returned to me. "How would my brother do that?"

She stood and put down a piece of paper with heavy craft written in Borsich. "I will tattoo that on him—a dream veil. Along with his summon of dark magic, he will be able to create a physical dome which will serve to control Snow and contain Aurora. I doubt we can subject their minds to another dream veil, not unless it is cast by an Elder Crafter, but we can trap them inside one physically, by tricking their mind into thinking they cannot leave it. Once Aurora is convinced that she cannot possibly get out of it, Kilian will drain her magic, and Snow will make sure to keep her busy enough not to worry why her mind is playing with her."

"Sounds dangerous," Mal said, snatching the paper and going through it. "How do you know it will work?"

"Because I've tested it," I said. "I can contain Snow, and Vas fell into one of my traps some time ago."

"Huh," he hummed, but my brother did not seem convinced. However, he did remain amongst us and even helped translate a few bits.

Nia looked outside the massive library door, at the setting sun lowering under the Moor Sea. "Alaric is going to kill us."

Thora shot up. "Hells. Dinner."

The library soon emptied until only my brother and the two Crafters were left.

Before we exited along, I stepped before Mal, and he dropped his head back, sighing, knowing what I was about to say. "We've not had this talk." He had to be made strictly aware he was not to toy with Thora.

"No need for this, brother, I have no intentions of the sort."

"Then let her be. Don't get between her and Neo." Somehow, I was convinced he would do just that. He felt possessive over her.

It was then his dark eyes met mine. "You do not understand."

"Make me understand."

"I will not have her in my arms crying over some man."

"Why would she come cry in your arms?"

"That is between me and her."

"Have you been drinking again?"

He halted again. "Do you want me to apologise or stop? Make your intentions clear, daddy Kilian."

"I want to know why. To understand. To at least understand. Just something. Give me one thing. I beg. Is it my fault? At least tell me it is my fault even if you do not know whose fault it really is. Blame me, Mal, just blame me." I cupped his head and rested my brow on his. "Blame me, little brother. Not yourself. Nothing has ever been your fault. You understand?"

For the slightest moment, I was tricked into thinking I had him back. But he sucked in a deep breath and pulled away. My little brother was slipping through my fingers, and I'd just let it happen. How had I let that happen? He was mine to look after. "Don't make me hate you, Kil. You're the last thing I want to hate. Let it go and let me be."

I drew my eyes shut, not bearing to watch him leave towards where he went to punish himself every evening.

"Kilian," Visha called, and I forced my eyes open, my brother now gone. "Can I have a moment?"

"Is there something wrong?"

She shook her head, raising a palm to open a portal beside us. "There is something I want you to see."

She'd taken us to the edge of a cliff in Olympia overlooking a vale occupied with cattle and sheep. The sun had yet to set entirely in this part of the realm, and it was enough time to enjoy the afternoon beauty of the Olympian heights.

I raised a brow. "Sightseeing? Did Larg put you up to this?"

"We are in Amur, where you and Snow fought the Fogling before Cori died. She led them from down there, through this cliff, and up the mountain behind us so they would be far enough from the city.."

"And?"

"Look behind us."

A soft colour of white had blanketed the sharp rock in front of me. Galanthus had sprouted all over, covering the entirety of the mountain that was not hidden by clouds.

"I visited a few places—places where Snow has used magic before—but this was the only place where you used magic along with hers. An Amur local confirmed that the rock below was already dead, nothing would ever grow on it, grass, shrubs, anything. Yet, despite the land and your magic, these sprouted."

"What are you trying to say?"

"The land is not just accepting Snow's magic." She extended a hand forward, and a gust of red mist enshrouded the surface of the flowers. When they didn't budge from the touch of death, she pulled back. "It is using it, too. When an Adriatian Aura becomes a Malefic, or when we bury a Crafter, the land will absorb their magic to feed itself, not to nourish from it." Her breathing grew a bit faster. "It is like...like—"

"The land is healing."

"Yes," she agreed. "It is healing. Snow will not like this, will she? Maybe we should not tell her."

"She doesn't have to like it, Visha, but no one will keep a single other secret from her, understood?"

She nodded. "You're right."

I faded to Fernfoss where Caiden was settling with the soldiers. He and Eren had sat close to the fire in the middle of the camp, eating together away from the crowds. And pretending that no one with two working eyes could tell the two had probably seen each other's d—

Hells, where was I going with this?

The dickhead threw his head back and groaned when he saw me approach. "What can I do for you, Your Majesty?"

"It would be too hard to ask you to stop existing since my wife still somehow likes you. But if you can find a way to do it without hurting her, I'd really appreciate it."

"I'd laugh if your presence wasn't the vilest encounter I've had all day."

"Look at us agreeing. Surely soon we might get along."

"You must be desperate to seek me."

"I'd go down on my knees, too, if only they didn't scream for me to turn the other way every time I see you."

Eren chuckled under his breath. Despite his secret lover's glares and narrowed stares, he didn't stop. "Sit, please, Kilian. The night was growing boring."

Caiden stretched back into the tree stump and sneered at him. "Was it?"

Eren nodded. "If you tell me that you like my eyes, I'd like to also know why. Otherwise, I'm bored."

The dickhead so poetically said, "You have beautiful eyes. They are green. Like the trees. I like trees. Don't want to fuck trees though, much rather I do you. How about that?"

"How about that," Eren repeated, laughing to himself.

For crescent's sake. "They are not *green*," I said, settling beside Eren. "A moss colour more like it, and he's got some dark specks on his left one, making it almost hazel looking. Especially at night-time. I wouldn't say they resemble trees. Perhaps a shamrock meadow. They're pretty nice in the morning covered in dew. Children love running through those."

"What do you want, you bastard?" Caiden asked when Eren lifted a brow at him, and it was my turn to laugh.

"Manners, please. And yes, I do want something from you. It has to do with my brother."

Caiden stopped chewing and lowered his food down, his entire mood shifting. "What about him?"

"I'm worried."

"So am I, but what is that you want me to do behind his back?"

"Not behind his back. You can tell him that I came to you if you wish. I want him to know that I am trying even if he hates me trying. I cannot give up on him, Caiden."

"Leave it to me. It is not my first ride with that...sort of behaviour," he said. "You trust me, don't you?"

"With all the lives of the ones I love most."

"What colour are my eyes?" he asked, smirking.

"This little moment between us could have lasted a bit longer."

"Could've. If you knew the colour of my eyes."

"Brown. Like stomach sickness."

"Royal prick," he muttered under his breath when I stood to leave.

"Dickhead."

26

Black Bishop to C5

Snowlin

MY SKYE COMMANDER HAD finally given me the nod that I'd shed all my rust away. Physically, I felt the sturdiest I'd felt in a long while. Mentally—

Perhaps it was because of sleep. This time I could sleep, I just didn't want to.

Tristin sighed, dropping down on the bench I'd sat on, and her wing almost scooped an eyeball of mine out. "You've not done that before. Should I be concerned?" She turned her head to me. "You rarely fight to kill. You always dance around those you fight, turn them into prey rather than an opponent, taunt and lure them, trick and direct them into slicing the dagger that they once used against you over their own throats."

Leaning back, I squinted at the sun. "The game is no longer fun." And I was entirely too hollow to feel anything from it.

"I see."

She passed a cigarette to me, and I touched the tip with my finger, letting the clove tobacco burn on the heat of electricity. "You need to quit, Tristin."

The stony woman nodded. "I will. My hands are fidgety lately. Lea says it happens because they've been soaking in blood for so long—and this waiting taunts me more than any fight. Shocking as it is, this is the least bad thing I can do with them at this point."

"I can't find what to do with mine. Perhaps I need to start an incredibly toxic habit like you."

She was quiet for a moment before she said, "This is not your fault, Snow. I hope you know that."

Except that it was.

I'd barely inhaled a couple puffs when the cigarette was snatched out of my hand. Kilian stood behind me, a hand in his pocket while the other brought my cigarette to his lips. He exhaled a cloud of smoke and then flicked the rest of it to the ground. After briefly touching his lips to mine, he said, "That shit is bad for you."

It had been one long day since he'd gone down to Moriko to observe the situation east of Hanai where we were expecting my father's troops to attack the Autumn Kingdom. Though Elias had burned down the camp, there was another one built just close to it. Hanaians were loyal to the bone, and my father had absolutely no spying eye inside Moriko's court. His spies were already attempting to sneak in, trying to gather intel on what side she would be locating her forces.

Kilian's thumb brushed my chin lightly. "What is it?"

"I thought you went to take care of the Isjordians entering Hanai?"

"I did."

"You did?" Looking like that?

"Not much care was involved, my love. They rather...dissolved without a trace?"

"Oh." I shifted in my seat, the sweet ache between my thighs growing uncomfortable when he sat beside me, draped an arm over my lap, and curled a big hand around my ankle, drawing circles over my skin with his thumb.

In his dark navy suit lined with specks of silver and glistening dark sapphire buttons, he looked so royal.

He raised a brow when my eyes dropped below his hips, where the tight trousers strained against his muscles and—

"It's still where you last saw it, my heart," he murmured in my ear. Slowly, as if on purpose, he stood and unbuttoned the jacket, setting it over the training court fence. He hooked a finger at me, walking backwards and folding his sleeves. "Bring your pretty face here."

Hopping from my seat, I stretched my arms up and fired electricity all over my body as if I hadn't just charged the whole skies of Numen with thunder not even a few minutes before.

"I've gotten better at mimicking the dream veil, Snow. Your mind might start to play up, too. Keep focus," he said.

My mind.

The one thing I still was trying to master.

The wind died off entirely when the strands of darkness pouring out of him touched the space of air. Little by little, it crawled to me, spreading around, doubling, and tripling while it lifted to engulf me under it.

My own magic formed a shield around me, keeping it under control and away from reaching me. I jerked when a cold hand wrapped at the back of my neck. But there was no cold hand on my neck no matter how many times I searched. My skin was still warm at the touch. The same cold hand then wrapped around my ankle, wrists, and throat, feeling like chains because of how frosted it was against my skin.

Lightning blasted around me, panicked and uncontrollably.

A black blade cut right through the thick black mist in my direction, and I managed to lean back, narrowly avoiding being cut by it. My heart pounded hard against my chest while I spun around to grasp a presence in the darkness.

Mal's laughter echoed around me though I couldn't see or feel him.

"If concentrating on keeping your magic steady takes away this much of your attention," Kilian's voice slipped through the darkness as if he was speaking in my ear, "then what is the point of doing this if you are going to lose control of it still. Concentrate."

Everything grew louder when I tried to focus on my surroundings, and so did my magic, suddenly pouring out more than I was allowing it to. It was loud. So loud. Every noise in the distance, below, and above was heightened, echoing, reverberating, extending to confuse me. My magic grew its own mind the more mine slipped out of focus.

Kilian's voice whispered in my ear again, "It's part of you, stop treating it like its own creature."

But it was its own creature.

A prisoned creature who'd just gotten a taste of freedom.

"Snow," he warned, feeling the seal on my back start to slip open more than usual.

Shaking my head, I shut my eyes and just listened to the movement, letting the wind guide me until someone knocked me from behind, causing me to greet the gravel with my face.

"Mal, I am going to cut your fucking hands," came Kilian's sleek voice from around the blinding darkness.

The younger brother chuckled somewhere in the distance while I hoisted myself up. Too much noise. Too much of everything. The wind. The birds. My own thoughts. Especially them. Why—why was I letting myself be haunted again?

Darkness vanished, revealing the white snow flowers blooming over the ground, and the panic I had hid in it.

My husband looked between Mal and I, and whatever he could not read in me, he read on his brother because hurt flashed on his cold face.

Kilian picked me up and threw me over his shoulder. "Change of plans."

"What?"

He faded us in the middle of the Amaris castle gardens and lowered me down on a bench before disappearing to return with a bunch of garden tools in his hands. "I know you don't mind getting those hands dirty, so come here," he said, pointing his chin to where he was.

I picked up a glove. "You want me to...garden?"

"Mhm."

The moment I saw a worm writhe in the fresh soil, I gagged. "Darling, I can't possibly."

He chuckled, lowering me beside him in front of a little square patch already half planted with some daffodils. "They don't bite," he said, picking the disgusting creature in his palm and moving it further away from us. "And they're good guys. They help the soil breathe."

"Doesn't make them less disgusting."

He nudged my shoulder. "Come on, woman, they are adorable."

I gaped, offended. "You've called me adorable before. Do we fall in the same category?"

The look of shock in his face told me much. "No?"

"You're lucky I'm not wearing a dress," I mumbled, putting on the bloody garden gloves a bit too angrily. "What now?"

He took a small pot planted with a daffodil and turned it upside down, shaking it until the flower came out along with the slab of soil. "They've been growing in the greenhouse for a little while, and we can now plant them in the soil. Atlas has already spread fertiliser on it, so we just make room," he explained, digging a little hole in the soil with his hand and placing the plant in it. "That's it. Now we do it a few hundred times."

I laughed.

But I shouldn't have. Because there I was, digging up hole number thirty-six for a cute yellow daffodil when I could be digging up some enemy graves instead, trimming ears and tongues, not leaves and long roots.

I glanced at him, still elbow deep in soil, trying to dig up the roots of a thick rose bush. Dear heavenly Gods. His shirt had matted to his back, sculpting every muscle so perfectly. The fancy trousers had pulled even more tightly against his thick thighs and his perfect back. I wanted to lick the thick sweat on his brow and perhaps even further down.

Though his back was to me, he shook his head. "Stop drooling. More planting. They better be symmetrical or you're going to have to dig them up again."

My smile faded. "Why do you like this stupid garden so much?"

"It helps me calm down," he said quietly. "And it keeps Kaliantha's presence around still. My mother built them. These gardens were hers. I never really knew her, and I'm certain whatever memory of hers that I have is made up by me. But recognizing the flowers she liked most, keeping safe the creatures that do remember her, and preserving whatever tradition she'd allowed to be held in these gardens, all of it makes me feel like I do know her, too."

I let out a heavy sigh, and he turned to me with such urgency, taking my gloved hands in his, searching for something. "Did you cut yourself somewhere?"

"Yes, my black heart just bled a little. You've never told me," I said, turning to lash out my anger on the soil before me, striking it down with my trowel. "I've ruined them every time I've bolted here."

He pried the trowel from my hand and helped me dig up a hole for the next daffodil. "They can always be fixed, my love, that is the beauty of it. You wanted to hurt me, and I wanted to let you. My own hurt never matched yours, not even slightly. I could nourish my mother's memory whenever I wanted. You didn't have the same chance."

"I need you to start putting *you* first, Kil."

He grinned, returning to dig up the rose bush. "Oh, I did. Many times. That is how I got myself the finest woman in the realm even after she tried to kill me several times, kidnaped my niblings, threatened my mother, my brother, my kingdom and all its people. So on and so forth."

I took a pebble and hit him with it. When did he become so funny?

He rubbed his shoulder. "Ah, shit, that hurt, my love."

It did? I quickly rushed to him. "Darling, I'm sorry."

He tapped my nose with a rose. "When did you become so gullible?"

"Yeah, when?" I muttered to myself, returning to my post and hurrying through my duties. "I've been softened like manure. My enemies can smell the gullibility miles away."

By daffodil number sixty-two, I was about to chew off my own clavicles to let my arms dangle freely and fall off my damn body. "Kill me and be done with it," I whispered to a worm wiggling through my newly planted patch.

Kilian came from behind me and put something over my eyes. A piece of cloth of some sort. His warm breath fanned over my neck and then tickled my ear. "Time to do this without looking."

My body leaned against his hard one. "I can tell you something else I can do without looking. On my knees." I raised my hands up. "Without even touching you at all."

His mouth ghosted over my neck, brushing so gently against my skin. "You're definitely going to be watching me fuck your mouth. Be good for me now and do what I say."

"And? What do I get?"

"Whatever you want. My woman always gets what she wants."

"Fine," I said, patting the ground to find my tools and the pots. How hard could it be?

It was hard.

I'd not done so much mathematics since the age of thirteen.

I had not concentrated like this even when I plucked my eyebrows or carefully scooped eyeballs out to make sure no one bled too much or too soon.

One last time, I reached for a pot only to not find any. Did I do them all?

His fingers grazed my cheek briefly before sliding behind me to undo the cloth. "Well done, my heart. Was it hard?"

I looked over my shoulder, at the little patch I'd been working on, and my mouth parted a little in awe. My gardening skills were not exemplary and the daffodils were more or less tilting in odd positions, but I had planted them almost symmetrical to one another. Same spacing. Same lines.

This was why he wanted me to garden?

Kilian took a watering can and sprinkled the patches all over. "There are bees, birds, noise from the courts, many people have passed by and about, there are too many scents, loud wind, your own thoughts amongst all that. Can you tell me if you noticed anything? Heard anything else?"

"No. I didn't."

"Exactly. Shut the world off. Use your senses in one direction. I know you can, I've seen you do it thousands of times before. It doesn't matter what lurks in my darkness. Or the one inside you. What it whispers to you. You've not forgotten to shut the world, you're just readjusting the ways you use." He turned to me. "You've stopped using pain as a switch."

I dropped my gaze at my gloved hands. "Couldn't you've just told me?"

"No." He threw his gloves away. "That's so damn pretty."

I huffed at the flowers swaying gently and weakly at the touch of wind, their necks crooked from the weight of their own bodies. "Daffodils are the ugliest flower to exist." And so weak.

"I meant you. All roughed up, dirty, sweaty. Angrily staring at me." He swivelled a look all over me. "Exquisite."

I threw off my own gloves and went down on my knees before him, trailing my hands up and down his thighs to feel those muscles I'd eyed all day.

He hissed, cursing under his breath when I cupped his cock, stroking him over the thin material of the trousers. "Not on your knees," he said, grabbing my hand when I went to unbutton them.

Slowly, I undid the buttons, looking up at him. "I love the view though," I said, leaving kisses on his strong thighs and pulling his thick length out of his underwear. "So panoramic."

His fingers slipped through my hair, tugging so I would look up at him again. "You should see mine."

I sucked the tip just to watch his face purse with pleasure—almost with pain, too. The further I took him in mouth, the more his chest raised, a small, tortured whimper leaving his lips when his length hit the back of my throat.

"Fuck, that's it," he groaned, pushing hair out of my face while I wrapped my hand around the base of his cock and swallow as much of him as I could, gagging and moaning around this thick, long length.

Heat pooled between my legs, the thin underwear I wore uncomfortably plastered against my wetness. The torture was intoxicating—one different from what I was used to. I figured I liked torturing the man I loved. And he liked it back because he didn't take control this time. I slipped him off my mouth, stroking him in my hand while I ran my tongue all over, sucking licking, tasting—exploring him how I wanted. How he often did with me.

When I looked up, I found him already looking down at me, his mouth parting with a moan when I sucked more of him, so many dirty sounds blended with nature, growing louder, needier. His hips started moving along with me, and tears pricked my eyes from the intensity.

"Snow," he groaned my name, his hips jerking forward, and I felt him spill on my tongue, his hand tightening on my hair to hold me there, buried in my mouth.

I coughed when he pulled out, trying to swallow every bit of him.

He kissed the top of my head and got me to my feet, wiping the drool from my lips and the tears from my eyes and cheeks. "The only tears I want in your face are these."

I swiped my tongue over my lips, tasting him there still. "Thank you for being such a patient teacher."

"Anything for my best student." He grabbed my chin and kissed me—all over. "Always the overachiever."

"Prick."

His hand slipped over my throat. "I ought to bend you over my lap and teach you a lesson." He dragged my lip between his teeth, a shiver making my legs almost give away. "But I need you to be able to sit for our next lesson. I really have to know where all this attitude is coming from."

Nothing had left me remotely as sore as gardening combined with last night's activities, but despite the great difficulty, I'd managed to get myself up for the meeting. Vidarr had sent news that the last of my father's troops had sailed out of Comnhall entirely last night and that he was most certain that Isjord had left with a deal as he'd seen shipments being dropped off secretly and hauled inside Breshall castle. Some shipments would have not been cause for concern considering that Isjord had imported coal and horses from the unblessed for centuries in exchange for jewels and gold, but I knew there were no jewels or gold in those containers. After letting them sniff power, they had probably demanded more from my father.

Now, why wasn't I across the continent, holding a boot over an Unblessed Prince's neck and squeezing an answer out of their lungs, but sitting here and mulling it over with our courts?

One answer.

Kilian and the '*We could lose a potential ally and your father could gain a stronger, angrier one fuelled with motive. You saw how they reacted when you staged the ship accidents. They believe he is reigning war, not destruction, and they will believe just that till flames melt their bodies. They do not know their fate, they won't believe their fate, they have no fate. Their fate has always been dependent on us.*' whole speech.

After he'd made me come a few times, those words had sounded remotely close to prose by a philosopher. Now that I thought about it, they only made me angry.

When my gaze slid across the room to look over at Leanna speaking, I caught him looking at me, and heat crawled up my face at the sight of his slightly bruised lip. Maybe I should have not bit him that hard.

What? I mouthed.

His silver stare dropped to my mouth and then slowly back up at me. *Nothing. Just looking*, he replied.

Why was he sitting so far from me?

He raised a brow and asked, *What?*

I love you.

He slowly grinned all pleased and proud with himself, and my eyes rolled back. Before I could add a 'fuck you' to my confession, he stood and asked Tristin if he could have her seat.

The commander shot me an amused look before standing and offering her king the seat that she should have freed long ago.

"Hello, gorgeous," he said, sliding a hand over my thigh.

"Hello, handsome," I whispered back and grabbed onto his arm.

He leaned down and kissed my cheek. "I love you, too."

"It is a matter if they will be swayed," Cai said loud enough to pull my attention back to the meeting. "We all are aware they know no loyalty, not even to their own kind."

"The king made us a promise," Larg said. "He is still shipping us metal. This had to have been done without his permission."

"Metal? We are nearing an unavoidable war, there is something more precious than metal the unblessed princes can offer to it. Forgers, a fleet, bodies for his armies," Cai added. "Gods know what Silas might have offered them this time. Even if it is just the princes without the help of their king, it would not be the first time in history to tell of a fallen unblessed ruler usurped by his own kin. And hasn't Drystan ruled Comnhall for a decade now? No Unblessed King has managed to keep a head on their shoulders for that long sitting on their wooden throne."

Kilian was quiet. He'd told me that the Comnhall King would not betray his word and I could tell that he still thought so. He knew Drystan better than us, spent enough time to analyse the man like only he knew how. If Kilian thought the king would not be swayed, then I believed him.

"I will have a word with them," I said, and then before they could sigh or huff or puff, I added, "A nice word."

"They do not care for what you are," Alaric said. "You cannot sway them with promises of power or gold." He pointed a finger at me. "And no killing. We cannot weave our way out of this by killing anyone."

"I've got something else for them. A blessing of sorts. What they have always wanted."

Everyone went dead quiet except Alaric who seemed rather alarmed. "What blessing, kid?"

"A curse disguised as a blessing," Visha revealed. "The blood of someone who can never die. Snow returned inside the *zgahna* and retrieved the limbs she had cut off from Vas when he came to cross the mist. I've studied the limb and managed to salvage some of what he possessed. Snow had also made some helpful observations in Isjord which confirmed some of my suspicions."

Kilian tightened his hand on my thigh but didn't speak. Probably aware there was more to it, and he wanted me to dish it out before reprimanding me.

Eren rubbed a hand over his eyes. "This is turning into something more than war, Lin. If we do this, what makes you any different from Silas?"

"I'm younger. Better looking." I leaned forward. "Sometimes fishing is just a hobby, not necessarily about catching fish. Hook, line, and sinker."

"Not the metaphors again," Nia sighed under her breath, and I shot her a look.

"You want to trick the unblessed folk?" Eren asked what everyone was thinking.

"Trick? No, I don't trick, brother. I do, however, deceive."

Visha put a small vial filled with red liquid on the table and then another empty one next to it. "*Nohas*." *Reveal*, Visha chanted in Borsich, and the liquid stirred inside the glass, bubbling and steaming, turning into a black, ink-like consistency. "*Teih*." *Hide*, she ordered, and the once black liquid turned clear while the empty vial filled with smoke.

"A mask," Kilian said quietly.

"Like a mirkroot. A temporary burst of magic that will eventually fade," Visha explained, pocketing the vials and pointing a finger at me. "It was her idea. I didn't know it would be possible until Oryn helped."

I sneered at her. Why was she so scared of Kilian?

The old man's head snapped up from the book he was reading, and he turned beet red with guilt. "I...I only gave an idea or two. The queen made all the important calculations."

Incredible. I was speechless. Had two of my most trusted people just thrown me in front of carriage wheels?

"You are telling us that you've basically manufactured a new drug that could potentially make someone unkillable?" Kilian asked, his jaw set tight. "Even an unblessed?"

Visha might have blinked a little too fast when she cleared her throat, and said, "As I previously explained, it was all her idea."

I gave my husband a bright, saccharine smile. "Well spank me for being brilliant."

He liked the joke, but not so much the plan. "We will see about that."

"Being brilliant or the spanking?"

He shook his head and stood to follow with Visha and Oryn, probably to confirm that the new drug was not faulty.

Cai, Thora, and Nia had little to say about what I was doing, they looked as if they had anticipated something of the sort, but Eren just looked...disappointed.

As the room began clearing, an unexpected visitor made their way inside. Moriko bowed her head. "I'm glad you're back, Snowlin."

"Your enthusiasm takes me back every time, Mor." Resting back on my seat, I put a hand over my heart. "I'm touched."

Her mouth twitched as she slipped forward and sat across from me. "You were missed."

"I'm certain."

"By many."

I flashed her a smile. "By all who count."

"There is a matter I'd like to discuss with you."

"Any of the obvious will have to wait. My husband is waiting to berate me for going behind his back." *Again.*

"Not an obvious matter," she said, leaning forward. "Obvious to me, but maybe not obvious to many. Though I do think it might be obvious to you as well."

"Quit yattering. You're making me nauseous."

"Well," she said, clearing her throat. "I'd like your blessings."

"You flatter me."

"To wed Nia."

When I remained wordless, she continued, "I would have married her one day. Today, tomorrow, a hundred years from now, it doesn't matter, but we might not have a today or a tomorrow let alone a hundred more years. I know what you mean to her and what she means to you, so this is why I came to ask."

"You will not hurt her."

"A promise I can give."

"If you do, Mor dearest, hells hath no fury."

"Understood."

"Do you love her?"

"More than I thought I was able to. Much more."

"One can always try harder."

She nodded. "Indeed."

Since love was out of the way. "This might be dangerous to Nia. You are both Aura."

"I assure that no harm will come to her. My people live in the land blessed by the Goddess of Life who fell in love with death. They know that if love must be measured by any means, it is not measured by who we love, but by how."

I shivered. She reminded me so much of Kilian that it was creeping me out. "You will ask for a blessing from the Gods?"

"I do not see why we would be denied."

Neither could I, so I nodded.

As if she had been waiting, Nia slipped inside the room just as Moriko was about to leave.

"My *ahana*." The cold queen rested her forehead on my friend's and kissed her cheek before leaving me alone with her.

Nia nervously hopped from one foot to the other on the spot she stood. "You said yes?"

"Should I have said no?"

She smiled at me and ran the distance to suffocate me in a hug. "Thank you."

"Is it like in your books?" I asked, holding her tightly to me.

"So much better."

Good.

"Oh! She must have said yes," Thora said, skipping inside the room and jumping to sit on the table.

Heavens. "Why do you look like wolves have had a bite of you?"

Nia sighed, shaking her head at her. "She's worse than you. Bruised half of the Skye warriors after she learned how to fly."

My sister grinned shyly, trying to fix her messy fringe. "Proud?"

"Very," I said, kissing her cheek. "I saw you've returned to Adriata entirely. Your room was empty here. Is there something wrong?"

She shook her head. "No. Mal and I meditate in the evenings to help me learn how to string my magic like he does. Afterwards he either falls asleep on my sofa or is too drunk to bring me back, so I stay there. And since you've returned, I don't want to bother you and Kilian."

"As long as there is nothing wrong, you can stay wherever you wish."

She gave us all a bright smile and clapped her hands. "Shouldn't we celebrate Nia's engagement? Oh, we must! Please, let's celebrate," my sister said, linking her arms with Nia and I.

Kilian was hunched over his desk when I returned to Amaris. And from the way he narrowed his eyes on me when I slipped on his lap, he was not impressed with what I had hidden from him.

"We were going to discuss my brilliance," I said, pushing his hair from his brow and leaving a kiss on his frown. And then about a hundred others on the rest of his face.

He sighed, resting his forehead on mine. "Why didn't you tell me?"

"Too much on my mind."

"What were you planning to do with it before you thought of giving it to corrupt the unblessed?"

"Nothing, really." Truly.

He pulled me closer on his lap. "Nothing, huh?"

I took his hand and put it over my heart—perhaps a bit more to the left. "I swear it."

His eyes dropped between us for a moment and then returned to mine. "You are one dangerous woman, Snowlin Castemont," he said, wrapping the same hand around my throat, his thumb skimming my pulse. "Play with fire. But don't play with darkness."

"So, am I brilliant?"

His grip tightened, and I held a breath. "Wicked. That's what you are," he said, leaving soft pecks over my jaw. "You're lucky Visha and Oryn have morals and would blindly follow you into a ditch all while pushing you into one, too, if necessary. If it had been anyone else, Snow, this would have gone terribly wrong. Beyond terribly, my heart."

"I know, Kil."

His lips finally met mine, sucking what little air I had in my lungs. "And that is the only reason why I am alright with it. Now, unless you have something else to tell me, I need you to get some sleep. I beg, my love, catch just a little rest for me, hm? Sleep in my lap if you want, anywhere."

And so I did.

For him, I tried to endure what came with sleep.

The endless visions that had finally settled back to the original one.

For every time I tried to fight it, to change its course, it showed me someone else dead.

Sometimes him as well.

Mostly him.

Always him.

Death knew how to taunt me.

I'd awoken much rested and with a whole bunch of people standing in our bedroom. I knew why he'd asked me to rest. Apparently, self-discovery really was a journey. Mine was more like a loop around the realm, except it never stopped.

No matter how many times Visha had explained to me the twisted logic between me and healing...the land, I could not grasp whether my witch was losing it or if she'd lost it some time ago and I never noticed.

Oryn set a flower before me, forcing me to look at it. "Have you not noticed at all?"

Greenery did not impress me much. "No. Should I have?"

"Maybe."

"I've been using my magic for years, Oryn, even when I was not supposed to. So why now?"

He pointed a finger to my chest. "The icy hearth there in your chest must be warming."

I looked down. "I assure you it is not."

"They have sprouted everywhere you and Kilian have trained," Nia said. "But they have sprouted somewhere else, too."

My enemies' graves? That would be so poetic.

"In Isjord," Elias added. "All over. Mostly around places you've been. The castle, training grounds, even in the Isline village where you were taken by the Solaryans. The exact place."

I yawned, glaring at Kilian who had brought this trick upon me. "And?"

Oryn stepped a little forward. What a brave man he was. "Could mean that Isjord is...dying, Your Majesty, as the flowers have only sprouted on dead soil elsewhere. It could mean that the soil under Isjord is dying, or has already died."

"My, my, are the odds spinning in my favour?"

The old Crafter cleared his throat and cupped the air with his hands, letting his mauve shadows form a tree. "The whole of Numen is sort of like a...plant. One stem rots, the whole thing will rot with it. If it has already started, it won't be long until the rest follows." Like his words, the mauve began growing black at the roots until it engulfed the whole tree.

"Well, we are trying to fix it, aren't we? Silas will die shortly and promptly." I clapped my hands. "Oooh, we could sacrifice him to the land."

"Sacrifices are legends," Atlas chimed in, raising a hand. "Your...Your Majesty."

"Silas might have watered the rot, but it is not only because of him that it has spread," Oryn continued. "It is not how it works."

"He means to say that faith is weak," Elias explained.

I tilted my head to my Crafter. "Who got your tongue, Visha?"

She remained hidden under the shadow of the library. "Something doesn't feel right about any of it. Until I am sure none of this is prompted, by either Gods or humans, I say we do and think nothing of it."

"What is it that we can do to begin with?" Thora asked, chewing on her fingernail.

"Evacuate Isjordians?" Eren threw out there, silencing all beside me. He narrowed his eyes when I laughed. "Offer them sanctuary, Lin. You cannot tell me that you think all of Isjord wants what our father wants? He is forcing innocents, children, and paying the poor to fight in this war."

"You'd be surprised how many are willing." I pointed my chin at Elias. "Tell them. He's seen both sides of that frozen world. If the land is rotting, it definitely has been doing so with their help."

"Both of you are right," Elias said. "But I stand with V, we wait it out till we have something more to go about this."

"And then?" Eren asked again. "What then?"

"I'm not going to potentially invite father's spies and crooks anywhere where our people reside, Eren. Not to spare Isjord from dying."

He stood. "Think about it, Lin. Just think about it first."

"Visha, you stay," I said when everyone turned to leave.

The witch waited for everyone to leave and shut the door.

"What's wrong with you?"

She lifted her dull green eyes up at me, looking exhausted all of a sudden. "The land rots. And suddenly...there is someone who can feed it."

"You are thinking too much into this."

"Am I?" Visha asked. "All we've done is not think enough. We throw a rock into a lake and find out it's an ocean." She took a deep breath, straightening her shoulders. "I'm coming to you not only because I think something is wrong. I can feel something wrong, Snowlin. Ever since...since...lately, I've felt more."

"Of what?"

"Everything." She looked at me then, the look spoke more than words—words that

Kilian could never know. *Since I saw your visions.*

I paced back and forth in my room after she left. Thinking of this whole thing from its start. From the time my exile ended until now. Visha was right. First the *zgahna*, then I find out of my blood, and now...now I'm apparently feeding the land? The Gods were playing. The fools only knew how to throw dice. And every time they tossed, a whole new side showed.

A shadow in Kilian's garden made me halt.

My brother stood there, alone in the middle of the night, hunched over, staring at his own feet. I'd never noticed how alone he always looked. How alone he always was.

"I might be biased because he was my friend first before my brother-in-law," Kilian said, laying down in our bed, flipping through one of my annotated books. "But he was right. In his sense, he was right. Though you were right in yours as well."

"I'll be back in a moment." Grabbing Kilian's jacket, I rushed towards where my brother stood, watching the shy creatures of the garden finally circle the flowers.

Eren opened an arm for me to snuggle closely to him. "Everyone is trying to understand what you are feeling. But I am afraid if you are feeling at all."

Nothing had changed. He still worried about the world, but who worried about him? "What about you? Are *you* feeling at all?"

He looked at me with the same soft smile as before. "I think so, but not giving emotions a face almost convinces you that you have no emotion at all, doesn't it? It is how they are. To be worn. If they are not worn, they end up being eaten by moths at the depths of a closet and you are left but with scraps of them, torn, no longer wearable, faded. One might try to salvage them, but would they be the same? Would they feel the same?" He sighed. "I doubt them sometimes, the scraps I was left with after being made to hide them for so long. I doubt whether I feel things as I should. Whether I react as I should, or if I am not reacting at all to something I should react to. Whether I am truly feeling what I feel or just projecting what my mind is saying I should feel. So, I hesitate. I let go. I forget. I don't take much to heart. But I am grateful to feel even those little scraps."

He kissed my brow, pulling me closer to him. "Father's torn through yours entirely, hasn't he?"

I leaned onto him entirely, wiping a hand over my eyes. "I don't know. Father took something from me this time. I don't know what, but...he took something." I turned to him. "The same thing he has taken from you. So you must know what it is."

His expression was gentle and so was his sad smile. "I'll think about it. If I find out, I'll let you know. You will tell me as well, right?"

"Right." I sucked in a sharp breath. "What you said before, I will think about it."

"Because you want to weaken our father's support, is it not?"

"Well, my motives might not be decent, but it does work in Isjordians' favour, doesn't it?"

"It does."

"I don't think I can change, Eren. It will also be unfair to expect you to change for me because you are the person with the purest heart that I know. But I got my brother back and I don't want to lose him again, so maybe we can fall to some agreement?"

He held me even tighter, resting his cheek on my head while he swayed the two of us back and forth, how he used to lull me back then. "Whatever you do, I might be the other voice, but I will always be on your side, no matter what."

Part III
King's Gambit

27

White Pawn to A4

Kilian

It was no longer about metal. No longer about trades and new alliances made out of pettiness and whose coin weighed the most. Stepping in unblessed soil today meant that negotiations of war had begun and the worst was upon us. And we had yet to prepare for the worst.

Snow wore the Adriatian crown today, dressed in the Adriatian garments, too—navy silks and gold threads. Her obsidian hair spilled loosely down her back, shimmering despite the faint gloomy sun gracing Vrammetheni shores. She looked nothing but godly, nothing human, nothing touchable. And if you were caught by her gaze, locked into the abyss of gold, one would go down to their knees and heed to her order without a single word being spoken.

She glanced at me from the corner of her eye and gave me a taste of her power. "What's with the ogling?"

"It is my right."

Her cheeks stained a rosy pink. "Do a little less of it. The king will think I might have put some sort of spell on you."

"He'd be right. Free me, woman, I'm going insane," I said, wrapping an arm around her waist and pulling her to my chest, kissing her neck until she was kicking and writhing.

"If you two are quite done," her brother said, side eyeing me as he passed us to enter the castle. "Let's meet this king and be done with it."

"Drystan is a rather patient man," I said, letting go of my wife. "He will understand."

She huffed. "Charming another's pants off?"

"He kept them on at all times."

"He better have."

We had left the docking site accompanied by a horde of Olympian and Adriatian guards, but it was her people that had caused the unblessed soldiers to all gape and stare at our entirely unnecessary entourage. They murmured some sort of prayer to their saints and human deities as they studied their wings. Just as Snow had said before we'd left: they're for shock value.

Eren took position by the doors and stopped his sister. "They have fickle egos. Be polite."

"Most men do, brother, I've learned to work around them," she said, flicking her eyelashes all innocence at him. "Then crush it ever so slowly until I can see every crack of it."

King Drystan was a lanky, fragile man who by human years was past looking as young as he did. Though the unblessed were denied any blessings, nothing had stopped them from profiting from magic despite its costly nature. Costly, because the Dark Crafter who had stood beside him at each of my visits was rather powerful considering that Vrammethen was not only far from the gates where the Celesteel-blessed drew their power, but it was also a land where false prayers and belief were a conduit of godly anger. Each craft here had a ninety nine percent chance of being cast wrong.

The king grunted when he stood from his bronze dais, leaning on his cane and walking to us. "Welcome," he greeted in a perfectly polished common tongue. As always, the royal families of the unblessed used education to their benefit. For what they lacked in power, they attempted to compensate in knowledge.

His eyes landed behind Snow, at her soldiers, and fascination gleamed on his rather lifeless eyes. "Incredible." He cleared his throat and pointed at the settees. "Please, sit. It must have been quite the journey because of the darkening weather."

"Quite the contrary," Snow said, sitting beside me. "It was rather pleasant."

"How odd."

"Not odd at all. My people control the skies, the wind, the weather."

Drystan looked again rather fascinated. "I've heard. I've heard. Fascinating that your kind survived. Now that is what I'd count as a blessing," he said, blasting in boisterous laughter.

"A jest of ours," I explained to my frowning wife. "He couldn't quite grasp my powers. Or consider them entirely useful."

"Besides in times of war," Drystan said, opening a glass jar to take some sort of candy out of it.

"Besides in times of war," I agreed.

Snow took one of the candies he offered. My wife was less interested in eating it than studying the soft jelly dipped in powdered sugar.

That made the Unblessed King chuckle. "Imported," he explained, taking a seat and rubbing his aching knee. "Like most of our foods. Our lands are rather—"

"Barren," Snow continued for him. "It must cost you a fortune."

Drystan seemed rather pleased to quench Snow's curiosity. "We've found ways to compensate for gold and riches. Fishing, manpower, artisanal skills, metal, fine horses."

Snow nodded. "Commendable."

"A necessity," he corrected. "To survive in a land that wanted us to disappear."

My wife fought whatever intrusive thought was trying to escape her tightly pressed mouth. It made me smile a little, and the Unblessed King noticed.

"Your wife is quite the beauty. But being her father's child, I can't not think that she's not used that trait to her advantage," he said, surveying her with some scrutiny now.

"Believe me," she said, chewing on the sweet, "if you were beautiful, too, you'd want to use it to your advantage."

He laughed. "I've never been called ugly more graciously."

"If this conversation continues any more in this direction, you will find that I was less gracious than I was direct."

His brows rose and he glanced between my wife and I. "You've come for business, I apologise. Though I cannot understand what business exactly since your husband and I have already set connections, and I've given my word to solely trade with him alone. Especially since your father is now looking to open war on the realm."

"It is not your loyalty I deem faulty," Snow said, and Drystan narrowed his eyes on her. "But your chosen."

"You mean the princes?" He laughed. "I can assure you, my kin no longer serves your father."

"Your kin already is serving my father."

"Impossible," he said, signalling his Dark Crafter to take his side.

"Quite the opposite," my wife said. "Father was in Breshall not long ago, with the purpose to meet your kin. Who, by the way, had politely agreed to hold an audience."

Drystan's shadows twirled with an array of disbelief and curdled with fear. "And you are certain of this?"

Snow leaned back on the seat and crossed her legs. "I've got no desire to turn a precious ally useless. And useless you would be if an unfortunate civil war was to overtake your lands right about when my father is to declare ruin on all the realm. You human kings are weak. It would not take a day to take you down, perhaps even less considering they have my father's aid."

He turned to me. "Is it true?"

I nodded. "Unfortunately."

He rubbed a shaky hand to his jaw and signalled his Dark Crafter who didn't delay to portal away. "Your father is quite set on causing ruckus in my kingdom."

Snow's mouth twitched a little and she forced a saccharine smile on. "Don't take it personally."

Not even a few minutes later, a knock sounded on the doors behind us, and three men strode in, their expressionless faces suddenly turning a shade of cautious when they took notice of us. Their shadows, however, were rather thick with fear. Fear was so ever present in the unblessed lands that it was starting to stink, too.

"What is the meaning of this, uncle?" the shortest one said, stepping forward. The Prince of Norodoh looked annoyed. "We have cities to run and no time to waste chewing candy on the mainland with your drunken court."

Snow stood and faced them, her smile turning cruel. "Apologies, did we interrupt your meetings on how to usurp your king, you useless pests?" They blanched the colour of paper at her harsh words. "What did my rotten father offer you for your rotten souls, huh? Whores? Gold? Power that he cannot give you?"

He stepped forward. "How dare—"

Darkness spilled from me, coating the room and air with thick obsidian fog that hissed when it touched the air. Death was so present in Vrammethen that it wasn't at all difficult to summon it. "Sit," I said simply and rather politely, but the men quickly rushed their shaking limbs towards the empty settee across from us. All which made me feel bad since I was not in the business of making men with groomed moustaches feel afraid and threatened.

Snow's lashes had drooped, and she did not even bother glaring at the three princes. "It is idiots like you that give soliciting a bad name."

"I beg your pardon?" one of them barked, his eyes nearly bulging out from the offence. The nepotistic hierarchy of this kingdom made for some spoiled rulers. Wars caused by a fragile ego were not a new concept in this part of the realm.

"It is not for me to pardon," my wife said more gracefully than usual. "Though the Goddess of Deceit might appreciate a few prayers in these very dark times."

"Your Gods are cruel," one huffed.

Snow swivelled a look over them. "I can see that."

The youngest one, the Darmain Prince, shot their king a look. "Are they here to break the deal?"

"Break?" I asked, leaning back and throwing an arm around my wife's shoulders. "No, but it was also not to my knowledge that I gave *you* permission to break it by accepting another from Silas Krigborn."

"You must know well," the Breshall prince said, sneering. "The highest bidder wins by bringing the biggest bid. We promised metal, not our loyalty. We are free to bargain whatever trade we wish and with whoever we wish as long as we provide you that metal."

That made me chuckle. "Biggest bidder? I offered you no bid. What I did offer on the other hand is not a single other option besides trading with me." I pointed my head to their king who'd heard the terms and repercussions of denying me. "Ask your king."

Snow's mouth curled into a sly smile, and she murmured only for me to hear, "So you threatened him?"

"The chance presented itself, my heart." Drystan had asked what his other choices were besides trading with me, and I'd laid out the fact that the whole of Comnhall would have not seen light until they'd withered under the shade of night and died if he would have denied his first and only choice.

The three princes turned to their kin. "Uncle?"

Drystan's look was cold. "The monarchy will die when my blood dies. This throne will remain under my family name until my very last breath, or remain no more. No other name will sit where mine has sat. If I must force my hand on you, then I will. If he must force his hand on you, then I will let that happen as well."

"Fine by us," the Norodoh Prince said. "We will take our chances."

Snow groaned, already bored. "If this had been another time, I would have melted your flesh like wax. However, we do not have the time nor the patience to play chase the mouse with either three of you buffoons or with any other three buffoons." She pulled the vials from a small silk sachet and put them on the table before us.

"What is this trick?" the Breshall Prince asked, and Drystan leaned forward on his throne to observe the blood vial.

"Longevity. Eternity. Immortality. There are many words for it."

One of them laughed while the other two just stared incredulously at my wife. "You expect us to be fooled so simply?"

"Quite honestly, I've seen you be fooled by less." She pushed the vial a couple inches towards them. "But try it."

The Norodoh prince lifted a painted brow. "It could be poison."

My wife cackled, and they all went pin straight when lighting hit just outside the window and slithered inside to twirl around the princes. "Why would I need to poison you? I like seeing blood, bone, guts, and much like that."

One of them shakily reached for the vial and reluctantly drank all of it, gagging for a moment at the taste.

Snow took out a dagger from her side and threw it on the table. "Someone kill him. I'd rather not stain my dress."

"W-what?" They all shot at their feet. "You can't possibly—"

I faded behind the Breshall Prince and slashed the dagger over his throat. He dropped to the ground, gurgling and choking on his own blood, but only for a moment as the wound on his neck began sowing together until he finally sucked a full breath again.

"What in the crown jewels," Drystan murmured in astonishment when his nephew got up from the floor, soiled in his blood, more alive than he had been before I'd killed him. "Impossible. This is impossible."

"Would you like for me to kill him again?" I asked, straightening my jacket.

The prince stumbled back, waving a hand. "Once was enough."

"Thought so," I said, sitting beside Snow again.

"Have I come from the dead?" he asked, still in shock.

"No," Snow answered. "The potion kicks in before you die and slowly mends what has been damaged."

"This is impossible," Drystan repeated, looking at his Dark Crafter whose eyes had shot wide at what she'd seen.

Finally, the witch met our eyes briefly, terror skittering through the vivid blue of her irises before she nodded at Drystan. "Times...have changed, my king."

"Indeed," Snow said, smiling at her, a silent threat behind it. Someone as skilled as this witch would understand that there was a bargain made between death and life when the potion was consumed—one at the expense of more than just the soul. Would we live long enough to witness it?

The Dark Crafter heeded to the threat because she said nothing else.

"You would sell this to us?" one of the princes asked.

Snow sneered. "Yes."

His hand shook, lifting the empty vial up to inspect what little was left in it. A moment of absolute madness, almost cathartic, flashed through his cloud of emotion before faltering to intense desire. "For what price? What price could buy this...miracle?"

Snow must have felt something because she reached to link her fingers with mine. "Loyalty."

All four of the unblessed rulers looked at each other. "That is a broad expense."

"Of every kind there is. From now until Isjord is no longer in my father's hands."

"Are you asking us to join your war?"

"You would've been made to join Silas's," I said. "For little to nothing in exchange for more than your lives. Believe me, that death would have been short of nothing but agony. Here and beyond. Whether our Gods are cruel or not."

Snow leaned forward. "A dose a month for a hundred of you."

"For how long?" Drystan asked, rubbing a shaky hand to his knee.

Her fingers tightened over mine. "Until my witch can figure out how to make it permanent. She happens to work quicker and grows inspired by those who hold their promises. Not a ship sails to my father. Not one weapon. A single piece of wood or coal or horse. Nothing. If I see your ships cross the Mahara channel, they better be at my order, or they will sink by my order."

"And if we disagree?" one of the princes asked.

This was indeed tiring. "If I must kill an entire kingdom in order to prevent my enemy from receiving their help, then I will simply do so. Between lunch and dinner is plenty of time actually. Might even be able to squeeze some quality time with my family there, too."

The Breshall Prince almost jumped from his seat. "Is that a threat of war?"

"No. It is a pesky chore I really do not want to do. But if I don't do it, my wife here will do it, and I am not the type of husband who lets his wife concern herself with chores. Unless the said chore takes care of itself."

Drystan rubbed a hand over his jaw. "It will be discussed."

"It will be decided. Right now," I said, kissing Snow's temple, letting her sweet scent soothe my nerves that were being tested like a battle horse today.

"It is a deal," Drystan said after the princes gave him some shaky, confirming nods. "You have the metal and our loyalty in exchange for the potion."

"There is one other thing," Snow said. "I'm interested in finding someone's bloodline here in your lands. You might have heard of him, they called him the son of seas. Vas, son of Zoltan, born on Norodoh."

"You mean Vas Hutlenn?" Drystan laughed. "He is but a legend, I'm afraid. Sailors sing of him to encourage themselves in the harsh seas. He was said to have slayed monsters, and you know there are no monsters in our seas."

"Why does he interest you?" the Breshall Prince asked.

"I came across the name in something I was reading, and I wish to quell my curiosity on the matter since I'm already in your lands and the odds are very little for my return," she easily lied, and they so easily bought it, their egos overfed on my wife's interest.

We left the Vrammetheni castle with a deal and no wounded or bleeding, though my wife's eyes had pleaded with me several times during the visit.

A smile slipped over my lips when I heard a slight rumble coming from her stomach. "Hungry, my love?"

"A little." She glanced at me through the corner of her eye. "That was very king-like."

"I *am* a king, my woman."

Drystan's Dark Crafter, Erna, led us further into the sparse village of Norodoh, where Vas was said to have been born. She cast us a careful glance over her shoulder from time to time, but remained quiet otherwise.

"He must pay you well," Snow said, trying to buy her intentions. "I hope he treats you well, too."

The Crafter slowed her step a little and nodded at Snow. "He does."

"The marks on your skin say otherwise," Snow gritted out, her jaw tight when Erna pulled her sleeves down to cover the scars.

"They are old, very old."

"Didn't ask when, but why."

"They're not from him, Your Majesty. They were done by one of my own kind." She pulled her hood back a little, revealing thick streaks of white over the blood red hair. "You know Vas, don't you?"

"What makes you say that?" I asked.

She came to a stop and faced us. "Because I know who Vas Hutlenn was and that it was his blood you made those vials with."

"My," Snow crooned. "Drystan might be the luckiest godless man to live in this realm to find a Crafter who possesses such forbidden knowledge."

"I served a man long before I came to serve him. An Elder Crafter, the same one who hid the sceptre piece here in Vrammethen."

Snow took her in from head to toe. "You're old."

"Old as one can be. No longer a mother, daughter, or a sister."

"Eldmoor would have welcomed you back. They can make you their sister."

"I cannot return to Eldmoor without being hunted by death." She pulled her sleeve back to reveal the same mark Kilian had on his back, her hands shaking. "The Elder Crafter I served was also my husband. He beat me to death and then...then he brought me back because he was not done with hurting me. He was not as skilled as most despite his titles, only a pitiful Potioner who kept stealing recipes from his neophytes and talented younglings he came across," she said, her voice growing smaller. "He didn't know how to hide the Octa Virga scent like the others, so he tied me here, for me to hide it. My magic has faltered through the ages from it, but I felt it return again when you got the sceptre piece."

Snow's face was filled with such red rage. "You can leave this place. The sceptre is in my father's hands, there is nothing to guard anymore."

"I don't want to. Drystan...he treats me well. I think I know why you wanted to come here, and I can help you get what you need to kill Vas. Consider it my contribution to the war that is coming."

Snow went rigid at the word but nodded.

28

Black Knight to F6

Snowlin

WAR WAS THE SHORTEST word with the most difficult meaning. The *why* and *how* made it even more bizarre to understand. Before, the answers were at the tip of my tongue. For revenge. For my anger. For my justice. For the destruction of all that wanted to destroy me. I'd gone from planning to ruin, to planning to protect.

Except...protecting was not something I was good at.

Kilian straightened my jacket, buttoning it all the way up to my neck, and then he pulled my hair to rest on one side so he could tie the white cloth bearing the insignia of my kingdom over the other side. "There, my queen," he said, leaving a kiss on my knuckles, and then fading the two of us on top of the castle bridge leading towards Taren.

"We can do this together," I said.

"You're not only their queen, Snow, all those people have seen you grow up, fed you at least once in their homes. Their children serve in your armies not from duty, but because they adore you."

"You don't know that."

"I've spent every moment I could those six months in this city. I know. They need to hear it from you alone. Not a document plastered on their walls, not a guard announcing it, not the two of us standing by one another like rulers. By you, the girl they knew, the woman they watched you become. The protector who they trust." He kissed me and then backed away. "I will always be somewhere close to you, watching you. Always."

As I walked into the city, rehearsing my words and those he'd told me, I realised that I'd always been consumed by vengeance, but my people never have been even though they suffered the most. I lost my mother, but they lost their lands, families, their entire life, their hopes, futures, and dreams. Not once had they felt anything more than just enmity and caution. Not even exactly hatred.

The city of Taren was alive and loud, my people rushed around, children laughed as they crawled between stools and over tables, some of the elderly shook their heads at the young ones and others simply laughed. So much life despite all that my father had taken.

"Auntie Snow," Lila bellowed, ignoring the game she was playing with her friends and dashing like a bull towards me.

I caught and swung her around before resting her on my hip. "How many times do I have to tell you to not call me auntie Snow."

"But you are my auntie."

I pulled her finger from her nose. "Don't have to announce it to the whole world, kid. Makes me sound old."

"Makes me seem important," she murmured, resting her head on my shoulder. "The other kids don't ignore me when they know you are my aunt."

"Who is ignoring you?"

She giggled. "Don't turn scary."

I sneered down at her, pulling her finger out of her nose again. "I'm always scary."

"Not to me."

Gods, I was losing my touch. "Fear me, kid."

"Okay." She blinked up at me, hopeful and waiting for approval. "I can scream if you want. Like the people in the valley."

Sigh. This was pointless. "Screaming children do nothing for my ego. Only hurts my precious ears."

"Where is uncle?" she asked. "I like uncle. He always visits me and brings me pretty flowers."

"He does?"

She nodded quickly. "He even took me to the flower land and I played with flower people. Oh, auntie, he even got me a flower dress!" the little demon screeched.

"Flower la—" Oh. The gardens in Amaris.

"Babysitting duties?" Cai asked, strutting all dark and tall towards me. He took Lila from my arms and threw her up in the air a couple times, making her squeal like a piglet.

"You too?"

He sighed. "I was kicked out of the training courts by Tristin."

"My, shall I take a guess as to why? Bullying another newbie?"

He gave me an unimpressed look before tugging on my cheek hard enough to hurt and then flicking my forehead. "How will you drop this on our people?"

"There is no gentle way to go about this," I murmured, rubbing where he'd flicked me.

"As if you would ever have a gentle way to go about things."

I gave him a shove. "Should have asked Nia to come with me, not you."

"Come on, Cakes," he teased back. "I can be inspiring. Supportive. All qualities you looked for when you befriended me."

I rolled my eyes. "We bonded over sugar and hate."

"Ah," he said, grinning, "similar taste. Forgot about that one."

My people crowded the maze-like city square moments after we'd arrived, and I climbed on top of the centre fountain. Lila still sat on Cai's lap, blissfully unaware of how turbulent her future was at present—how she might not have a future at all.

How it was all my fault for it.

Emotion welled my throat when thousands of hopeful eyes looked up at me, expectant of the worst. My people knew to always expect the worst. Yet there was such bliss in there, too, admiration that injected courage in my weak, black heart.

But there was no voice coming out of my mouth no matter how many times I opened it to speak.

An older gentleman slowly reached where Cai and I stood and put a string of white beads on my hand, closing my fingers around them. "With courage, my queen."

"And if I lack it?"

"I've never known you to lack courage. Why start now?"

I nodded and held onto the beads tightly until I felt the skin under the smooth stones mark red from force.

Silence rippled over the crowd, and I stepped forward. "I thought and hoped to never gather you here for what I am about to tell you. I had hoped we'd left wars and battles behind. So I had thought. And I had thought wrong."

Expectant silence pushed me to continue. "There is war ahead of us, one that was already started long ago. But this time we are not alone. There will be night again, but night will be by our side. There will be frost, but frost will be by our side, too. Most of you have already fought against my father once and I cannot ask you to fight against him again. Our young are too young and our old are too old. Our chances against what my father prepares might leave us with no chance at all. But until my last breath, I swear to keep him from this land and keep you safe. And with my last breath, I vow to never let my father threaten it again. I come today to break my oath and ask you the favour I swore to never ask. To fight my father again."

Lila shot up from Cai's arms and ran towards the crowd, right in Tristin's arms. "There was no fight, my queen," she said, hoisting her daughter up. "No battle or war. The Night of *Draugr* was slaughter. For our people, for those we lost that day in Myrdur, this will be their justice. We've waited a long time. We've hid for far too long." The Skye Commander bowed her head, and her soldiers followed suit. One by one, the rest of the crowd followed. When silence rippled, the wind quietened with them.

Bile rose to my throat, realising I'd just asked my people to give their life for this...and they had just accepted. I had hoped...hoped they would ask me to destroy all, to use what I was and do what I wanted to do. Instead—

Cai's comforting hand landed on my shoulder and then air entered my lungs at the calming speed he dictated. "Breathe."

"Olympia could hide," I whispered to him, heavy tears clinging to my lashes.

My friend shook his head. "We've hidden for far too long."

"They don't have to fight this."

"You said this was a war started long ago. And it has. Now we get the chance to end it."

"I can end it."

"Not without it ending you."

I turned to him, silently pleading. No words were spoken, but he'd learnt to read all the words I never spoke.

The vein on his brow ticked and he took a step closer, anger rippling through his face at what he'd realised. "Whatever that look means, it better be some sort of joke, Snowlin."

A small hand tugged on my jacket, and I looked down at Lila, reaching to hold her up as she was asking. Her little finger trailed a long line on my forehead. "Don't be sad, auntie."

"What do you know, kid> The hells do you know?"

Lila put a hand over my mouth. "That's a bad word."

"We all might be going there soon, so strap your flowery boots on."

Cai snatched her from my arms. "Alright. I think auntie Snow just needs to fucking calm down for a moment."

"That's another bad word, uncle," Lila murmured, glancing at Tristin who was glaring daggers at us.

Cai noticed the Skye Commander and almost threw her child back at me. "Have to go, Cakes. They are expecting me back."

"Coward," I snarled when he quickly portalled away.

Tristin took her little girl back and glowered at me. "You have that look on your face."

"What look?"

"The same look that has me doing three stacks worth of reports."

I flicked my hand back. "You know I never read those."

She sighed, rubbing her eyes. "Who are you after now?"

"Nobody. She is already here," I nearly sang, tying my hands behind my back and skipping into the city. "Hope she wants to play with me. I really want to play."

"I want to play with you, auntie!" Lila screamed, and her mother winced.

"Not with this toy, kid. She bites."

"Ah, the fresh scent of desperation," I said, crossing through the Valley of Death. The tune of my whistle travelled down and between the wide ravine corridors, letting the sound grow louder and rumble across the mountains, echoing.

I stopped and turned, crouching down to her. "You look pale, Malena. How are you enjoying Olympia so far?"

She shivered despite her cold blessing. Her face had sunken below the frost covering her skin and malnourishment, and even her beady, large black eyes had shrivelled. Crawling away from me, she hid her face between her knees and her long white hair.

"Do not be afraid. What is the worst I can do to you, dear? Kill you?" I laughed—loud enough for the echo to return almost like the sound of thunder.

"Do it," she whispered, shaking. "Kill me."

I tilted my head to the side, considering. "Beg." Had she even given my people a chance to do so that night? Had she let children, men, women, and elderly beg when she'd slayed them that night?

Her mouth trembled. "Please...please kill me."

How anticlimactic. "How about I make a deal with you," I said, picking up her chain and tugging until she was standing right beneath my feet. "A redemption of sorts. You've got a load of redeeming to do in my hell first before you go to any other."

All faint wrinkles of hope creasing her forehead disappeared and she curled into herself again. It annoyed me beyond belief. "Why do you protect him when he did nothing to protect you? He threw you out of your position, his court, his side, and your home when you no longer served him any purpose."

"Serving him was my purpose. That purpose expired. It is nothing I hold against him."

What an idiot. What an idiotic way to live. "Don't make me feel sorry for you, Malena. I am not very nice to those I pity and I want to be nice to you," I said, brushing her hair away from her face.

Her eyes were empty, looking up at me. "What do you want from me that you have to speak to me to get?"

"But I like hearing your voice," I said, sitting cross-legged before her. "Especially when it is so fearful and shivering. And I am feeling somewhat kind lately. You look like someone who might need some of my kindness."

She shook her head. "You've wasted your time."

"I really don't think so." I laid back on my hands and pointed my chin to a man a couple feet away from us. "You see him? I was thirteen when I chained him here and he was in his late human teen years when that happened. Does he look a day over nineteen when he should be in his thirties? You will not grow a day old, Malena, not an hour older than you were when I chained you here. Might want to consider it for a moment." I stood and twirled my finger in the air. "I can go for a walk and come back if you want that moment. You might not appreciate my contemporary art pieces, but the view is mesmerising from up top. Pale, bleak, and so hopeless. And exquisite composition."

Her voice was faint, "Wait."

"What was that?"

"In exchange for my death, what do you want?"

"Everything. From my father's weaknesses to his biggest strengths. If there was someone he shared those with, it would be you. And do you want to know how I am aware of that?"

She looked confused.

"Right before I sent my soldiers to take you, your precious king had sent his mercenaries to kill you. Why would anyone want to kill an old crone like yourself except if it wasn't utmost unnecessary."

She shook her head, denial crossing her dark eyes. "Cannot be."

"Do I need a pen and paper?" I asked, sitting before her again.

Nia and Thora were waiting for me at the entrance of the valley, both had refused to join me in questioning the old Lady of Grasmere.

"Who wants some scones?" I asked, throwing my arms around both their shoulders. "You will want to celebrate when you hear what I've just learnt."

Nia brought a bag of baby carrots from her pocket and stuffed one in my mouth. "What did you torture out of her this time?"

"I didn't torture anyone."

"You offered to kill her?"

"Yes."

She raised a smug brow at me. "You did it?"

"Of course not. No one that hurts my people just simply dies." I put a finger to my lips and threw her a wink. "I lied."

Something screeched above us and everyone's attention turned to the skies, watching Jayre circle around the heights of our mountains before settling on top of a castle tower. The massive thing had pinned its stare on me across the distance while it rested. It didn't take long for Memphis to return, too, cowing as she shifted from an eagle to a massive cat.

My bonded nudged my leg and I bent down to pat her head. "Well done, M."

"Where did you send them?"

"To confirm what I was just told. A sea snake is still a snake. Sometimes even more venomous. Why would I believe anything she said? Right, M?"

My animal rolled her eyes, leaving me stunned and gapping. "Excuse me?"

"It was the metaphors," Nia said, steering Thora down the street.

"Most definitely," my sister agreed.

I sat back in the seamstress's settee, already blind by the white fabrics scattered just about everywhere while Thora curiously hopped from one to the other, inspecting the bejewelled cloths between her fingers. "So pretty," she murmured to herself, her round eyes widening and glistening.

"Should I buy you some?"

She spun to me. "Why would I need it?"

"For when your day comes."

She shook her head. "I will never get married."

I surveyed my wedding ring, running a finger over the daisy. "Twas what I said."

Her smile was soft like our mother's and it hid so much, just like hers had. Why did she hide from me, too? "You deserve it. All of it."

"So do you," I said, brushing some strands of hair from her face, and she flinched. My hand curled into a fist, shaking as I tried not to dig my nails into my palm. What had I done? "I'm sorry."

She pushed her hair back and smiled at me again. "Nothing to be sorry about. I didn't...didn't mean to do that."

"Do I scare you?"

Her eyes went wide. "No! No, Snow, you don't scare me." She quickly took my hand and held it between hers. "See, I'm not scared. Nothing scares me, really."

"Beside badgers."

A little sneer pulled on her lip and she glared at me. Our resemblance was uncanny, and it made me smile. "Bully."

I pulled her to me and wrapped my arms tightly around her. "Should have been there to do it years ago. A bit of sibling bullying gives one character."

Her hands curled on my jacket. "Eren did a pretty decent job."

"Eren, a bully?"

She sighed. "A little mean one. He wouldn't let me talk to boys until I was sixteen."

"Who says you can talk to them now?" I kissed her cheek and pulled back to cup her face. "You are so little."

"Am not."

"To me, you will always be little."

Her emerald eyes glossed over. "Thank you for finding us."

I rested my forehead against hers. Holding my little sister like this felt unreal—a dream. "Thank you for staying alive."

Nia pushed her head out between the two thick, brown curtains of the changing room. "I am certainly not going to be wearing this or anything of the kind."

She'd dreamt of wearing these huge gowns. Used to parade around my room with quilts tied to her waist and a bunch of herbs in her hand at least one night a week. "Show us."

"Absolutely not."

She absolutely was. I stood, and she scrambled back into the changing room, clutching the curtains to cover her body. "Helenia," I hissed, pulling them back. "Let me see."

The seamstress cocked both fists on her hips and sighed. "It is not done, hen. It will look much different once I fit it to your measurements."

Nia breathed heavy, still covered by the brown curtains. "I look like a cake topper."

The old woman clicked her tongue and pried the curtains from her hands, trying to pull them back. "A bride is the decoration at her wedding."

Nia huffed. "Moriko can wear the gown."

Both Thora and I snorted at the same time. "You're lucky she comes without armour," I said, crossing my arms. "Does she ever even take it off?"

"Oh, she must," Thora said, a sly smirk rising on her lips. "I'm sure of it. Now let's see what the queen will take off of you on your wedding night." My sister ducked and crawled under the curtains to the other side of the changing room and gasped. "Nia!"

The words were muffled, but I heard Nia ask, "You like it?"

"I've never seen anything more perfect."

I laid back on the sofa, just listening to their dimed voices and giggles. The world felt so light and airy. And all of a sudden, I was in that meadow in the middle of nowhere, basking under a spring sunset, surrounded by flowers and hay.

I must have laid my head back because sleep was thrust upon me.

For the first time in a while, I didn't dream.

What I saw was not a dream.

Not emptiness either.

Only a far desire that had only halfway come to life.

I woke to a gentle touch on my cheek and the brush of sunset tangerine rays warming my brow.

"Slept well?" Kilian asked.

"What time is it?"

"Dinner time."

"Where did Nia and Thora go?"

"Moriko came and took them to Aru for the night. She needed them to make a few arrangements for the wedding venue. Nia didn't want to wake you, so she called me."

The seamstress returned from the storage room and bowed to Kilian. "My king."

"Thank you for looking after her."

The woman shook her head at me. "Everyone knows she falls asleep in the most ungodly places. We are used to it. These streets you walked have raised that little grump you call a wife."

Kilian dragged me out of there before I could show the old hag what a grump I was.

We perused the market for a little, but my stomach had protested for food, and he'd pulled me to a faraway stall where they were selling some of my favourite salty dishes. The man who had known me for a decade and had fed me most of my dinners throughout my teenage years pulled two stools back and made us take a seat right in front of where he was cooking.

"Evan makes the best meatless pies," I said, taking a fork and biting on a tinsel while the man stirred the vegetable fillings over the hob.

"I know."

The tinsel slipped from my teeth. "You know?"

"Heard you visited him the most, so I've come to have my dinners here for a while now." Apparently, I must have been looking at him funny because he smiled. "What?"

"Nothing."

Evan set two plates before us with some massive portions of pie and sauces. "He was more curious about the stories than the food."

I stopped chewing. "What stories?"

Evan gave me a sly look. "Exactly. What stories? There were too many to tell."

Glaring up at Evan, I said, "I can ruin you."

The man did not even flinch. "You will starve."

Fair.

"So," Kilian started, resting an arm over the back of my chair. "What did you get out of Malena?"

"They told you?"

"Who?"

"Nia and Thora."

"No," the man said, smirking at me. "Your soldiers did. They are good gossip. They know you well. Your habits, too."

I lowered the fork before taking a bite out of my food. "Are you preparing for an exam or what?"

"I'd like to know about my woman. It's not fair that random men know you better than me." His fingers skimmed the back of my neck. "So, are you going to tell me or would it be better for my health to live in the dark?"

My cheeks were about to explode with how much food I'd stuffed in my mouth, so he waited, looking very entertained considering the grin he had on his face. "No, I will tell you," I said after swallowing the big bite.

He stopped the other helping of pie I had loaded up on my fork. Carefully prying the utensil from my strong fingers, he separated a bite size chunk and lifted it to my mouth. "I love watching you eat, woman. Love seeing you get your appetite back."

"Why lie to her?" Cai asked, sliding on the stool next to mine and stealing my plate of food, immediately gobbling up the pie in one bite. "She's the ugliest when she eats."

"That is why she is married to me, not to you, Caiden," Kilian said, pushing his plate in front of me and lifting a spoonful of the warm stew to my lips.

Ignoring him, my friend helped himself with seconds without even asking Evan. "So, what did the sea bitch tell you?"

"Father has mercenaries all over Solarya. Two of Magnus's court members are on his side and plan on locking the city when the fleet he's dispatching soon arrives on their shores. His plan has apparently always been to take care of Solarya first—quietly."

"Like Olympia. At night. City gates locked from the inside, making it impossible for troops to go in or out." Cai sighed, leaning back. "Silas is a one-party trick sort of man. What else?"

"Adriata was next. Day time. Ambushed south by his supposed unblessed alliance and held up north by Eldmoor. Also trapped. Then Hanai. Trapped, too. This time on all sides. Apparently, he already had ships stationed in the Sayuri before Jayre burned the ones in Heyes. Doubt Moriko can abandon the west borders to guard the east, too."

"Could be what Silas wants," Kilian said. "Weaken the west's defence by separating her guard."

Cai shook his head. "All this without even considering Aurora and Demir. He knew an alliance would form. He is trying to separate us from facing him head on."

"He had not counted for me or Olympia. From what Malena said, Kil was his biggest bump in the plan and he'd hoped I would have taken care of it when he set up the marriage arrangement. Aryan kidnapping and killing me was apparently *plan B* all along. My father had wanted to keep using me until I didn't follow his script."

"He has not made a single move. If Silas is quiet, it means he will strike soon." Cai rubbed a hand over his blood red eyes that had not taken a rest for sleep in weeks. "Should have tried to convince Nia and Moriko not to hold the ceremony."

"It will give people a sense of normalcy," Kilian said. "It can be very damaging to morale if all you see is loss. Ignoring the problem for a day is not ignoring the entire problem. They deserve to celebrate."

My friend huffed. "Don't you feel like you're being schooled like a child every time he speaks?"

"Then grow up," my husband said, leaning back to glare at Cai.

"Fuck you."

Kilian lifted his left hand up, flashing him the silver ring he wore on top of our band of blessing. "Very much taken. But I appreciate the sentiment."

I lifted a forkful of pie to his mouth, and he ate it. And before I could give a bite to Cai, he grabbed my wrist and directed the fork back to his mouth again. "This isn't a *kiss and make up* situation, love. He's pissing me off."

Cai threw an arm over my shoulders, and Kilian pushed it off, resting his instead.

"For the love of all that is holy," my friend snarled. "I do not want your woman."

"My woman does not want you either," Kilian snarled back. "Still processing why she even likes you in the first place."

Dear Gods. "Boys—"

"Listen up," Kilian said, chewing rather angrily. "She's talking to you, little one."

Then something I did not expect happened. Cai threw his head back and laughed. And then laughed some more. Hard. Much harder than he'd ever laughed with me. There were almost tears in his eyes as he heaved, holding his stomach. The fool then stood with no explanation, kissed my forehead and then Kilian's, snatched another pie and left, whistling away into the city. "Put it on their bill, Evan!"

Kilian's mouth was slightly agape, watching my friend disappear among the evening crowd. "He has lost it."

"Good thing I didn't tell him that father might already have a fleet ready to send to Whitebridge. Memphis and Jayre already spotted them."

He shut his eyes tightly. "Love."

"Hm. Something tells me I should have told him."

"Eat. I'll talk to him later."

"Don't yell at him. He's sad, Kil, and I'm worried."

He rested his forehead on mine and kissed the tip of my nose. "I won't. Want something sweet now? We can stop by Samira's."

"Yeah, I want to take something sweet to someone else as well."

My throat would not allow me to draw a single breath when I saw Memphis already there, curled up in the meadow of overgrown anemones, guarding the three stone graves.

I reached to rub her brow how she liked it. "You liked Cori a lot, didn't you?"

My bonded did not make much noise, her nose sniffing the piece of cake I lowered where my young tribe leader's belongings were buried. Olympian folklore had the prettiest tales in my opinion. They said spirits would return to the realms they had once lived if you buried their belongings in the soil of their motherland.

"Do you think she has returned?"

Kilian looked at the sunset overhead. "Why do you think Memphis comes up here?"

I looked up at him. "If—" *I die.*

His eyes grew dark. "Like hells you're finishing that damn sentence. Get up."

"Up, yes. Make sure it is somewhere I can clearly see all seven skies."

"Snowlin!"

"Memphis loves heights. No shitty flowers sprout so far up either. No white headstone. Something colourful, but not yellow. I would come down as lightning, so every time that height would be hit by thunder, you would know it is me coming down."

He was so angry at me.

"Promise me?" I asked.

"No."

"Promise me, please? No one else holds my promises because I have never held theirs like I've held yours. Promise me this. I want to return to this wretched realm and visit."

"I can't."

"Kil, please."

"I can't because I will be up there with you."

I stood and hit him.

He grabbed me as I turned to leave, wrapping an arm around my waist and lifting me up so he could speak in my ear. "So, every time I've told you my heart burns and bleeds and rips without you in my arms, without your scent all over me, without feeling your warmth on me, all those times I've told you I love you, you've never believed me once? Is that it?"

What was I going to do? I had not thought of this. In the midst of my plans, preparing for the inevitable end, I had not counted this. Why was he thinking with his heart?

"Answer me, Snowlin! Did you think I fucking lied when I told you that I would not stay in a world where you are not?"

"You have to."

"I have to do nothing."

"For me. You would stay for me. If something happened to me, you would stay and look after what I leave behind."

"Now you're just looking to make me angry." He pressed his head to mine, and I felt his quick breaths on the back of my neck. "Tell me that's it. Tell me you're just wanting to make me mad."

"Yes." I lied.

And he accepted that lie.

29

White Bishop to A3

Kilian

EREN PUT A HAND on my shoulder. "It is enough for tonight, let's head back."

Cai shook his head. "There are troops ready to sail to Whitebridge as early as tomorrow morning. If we head down to help Magnus, we might be able to delay Silas making a move out of Dardanes." The general breathed hard, resting both hands on the table to study the map spread on top. "This is telling us something."

"Or this could easily be another trap. All these early moves could easily be traps," Mal said, observing the map. "We know the sceptre is not ready yet. This is something else. Either distraction or traps. Either for Snow and Kil or even Magnus and Moriko."

"My guess is for Kilian," Tristin said. "He doesn't know how to get Snow's reaction, especially now that Fernfoss is gone. Otis Vayr has reported of your constant relationship with Magnus, so Silas must think you two have an agreement of sorts. The trap is for you. Snow would probably say that. Who, by the way, will reprimand each and every one of us for even gathering tonight."

"No, no," Cai said, narrowing his eyes on the distance between Whitebridge and Isjord. "We are missing something."

"He could be right," Elias said. "Why send ships from Grasmere when he could have easily sent them from Brogmere. Closer. With a couple of Verglasers aboard to break the icy waters they would have docked on the island within the day."

"Did Moregan say who or what were they loading in them?"

"No, only that they had received direct order from Silas to prepare the southern fleet for sail."

"All of it?"

Elias nodded. "All."

"He is leading us astray," I said. "Tempt us to move most of our fleet away from our waters in his direction."

"Adriata," Cai said. "He wants to attack Adriata first."

"No, he wants to trap us all in Adriata. If his troops have us surrounded south and north, then he wants to fight all of Numen separately."

"And dirty," Eren added, his eyes wide. "He will go for civilians to keep us occupied and remove resistance."

"So we let Solarya be attacked?" Cai asked.

"We will speak with Magnus," I said. "I think it is time we force contact whether his pride is hurt or not."

Giggles of all sorts were pouring out of her room, and the closer I reached to it, the louder they got. I could recognise hers amongst the others. They were so light and vibrant at the same time, and the way they brushed past my ears made my whole skin erupt in shivers.

Before my fist even rested on the wood to knock, the doors were flung open by a tipsy Nia. The scene behind her was...unseen for lack of a better word. Visha lay sprawled on the floor, passed out, her face covered with red hair while she snored like a horse. Thora rested her head on the witch's stomach, glaring at the ceiling and mumbling to herself. And my Snow—

"You need to take her. Immediately," Nia said.

My brow arched and I glanced over her shoulder at my wife sitting cross legged on the floor before a line of liquor bottles, the one who oddly seemed less affected by their whole celebration. I was still so angry at her for what she'd said the day before. "Hm."

"Hm?" Nia asked loudly, her eyes doubling. "She is a lunatic. Take her."

Right then, my wife's head flung in my direction, her porcelain skin had tinted red, and her gilded eyes had dropped. The more she looked at me, the more she perked up. "Oh, wow. And who might you be?" she asked, leaning back and almost sprawling over the floor, attempting to give me her best shot at a sultry pose.

Gods, I was supposed to be so angry at her. "You know very well who I am, love of mine."

She blinked. I blinked.

And then her mouth tipped up. "Kilian." My name was honey and fire at the same time when it poured out of her lips, "*My* Kilian."

Wasn't the death of me extraordinarily beautiful on this particular evening? I walked to her, bent down and hooked my arms under her shoulders and knees, hoisting her up. And she let loose a string of giggles that might as well have been composed by the finest orchestra to ever play the land of the living.

"You raging alcoholic," I said, shaking my head.

She gave me a shy smile. "Am I still heavenly beautiful?"

"This is why you should never drink. How can you even doubt that?"

She threw a look over her shoulders at the ladies attentively glaring at us over their liquor glasses. "See, being evil and heartless is not all that disadvantageous." She flapped her feet all excited, and shouted, "To bed!" She kissed my neck, and murmured in my ear, "So you can do bad things to me. And I can do very bad things to you." Her hand slipped between the button space of my shirt and her fingers were tickling my stomach. "Very, very bad things."

"Good try," I murmured back, and kissed her cheek repeatedly only so I could hear her giggle again. "Not when you are this drunk."

She rolled her eyes up at me and just glared as if I would submit entirely before her—perhaps I would someday. I was only a man. And she was everything this man had.

I turned to the others. "Don't stay drinking too late."

"Yes, father," Nia murmured under her breath, and they all laughed.

Sigh.

Mal walked in our direction just as I was about to turn to our corridor. "Is she still there?"

Thora. "Yes."

He patted my shoulder and slipped by to enter their room. Not even a second later, screams travelled down the silent corridor, and then some bickering followed.

Then a ton more bickering. And a ton more screams.

Snow wrapped her arms around my neck and rested her head on my shoulder, humming to herself while I walked us back to our bedroom. When the melody grew grim and the first touch of tears touched my skin, l halted my step.

I could not move as my heart slowly tore to pieces.

She sobbed silently, her head buried in the crook of my neck.

I lowered the both of us to the floor though we stood in the middle of the corridor, and gathered her in my lap, brushing back strands of black silken hair shielding her face from me. "Snow?"

Her body shivered, her skin had gone colder than the touch of snow, and slowly, candles put out in the corridor while the air coated with a film of hoar frost.

Panic wrapped around my throat. "Love of mine, if you must break my heart, break it with reason. Tell me, I beg of you to tell me."

"I don't know," she whispered. "I really don't know, Kil."

"Let me take it away. Please," I begged. The pain, the anguish, the memory. All of it. Whatever she was still keeping from me, I didn't want to know it anymore, only to destroy it.

She shook her head and her fingers clasped my shirt tighter. "How would that hurt any less?"

Gently, I pulled her face up and rested my forehead on hers. Tears streaked her pink cheeks and glazed her sun-coloured eyes, turning them into a soft honey shade. I ran my fingers over her face, down her nose, over her lips, and around her eyes. With every stroke of my touch over her skin, her breathing evened out and her sobs bounced to chest aching hiccups.

She nudged my nose with hers and pressed her lips to my chin for a long moment before pulling back. "It drives me insane, you know."

The littlest of smiles then graced her lips, and I breathed out some relief. "You're never even taking a whiff of anything alcoholic again. Grape juice even."

She sniffled and then began to sob again for an entirely different reason. "But I love grapes. I can't live without grapes. Grapes are all I have. I can kill for grapes."

I shouldn't have laughed, not really, because she cried louder, her face scrunched up with such sadness for her grapes. "Keep the grapes. All of the grapes."

She was going to be so embarrassed about this later. I couldn't wait.

When I had Snow inside the covers and made sure that the candles in the room were no longer burning, I slid beside her and gathered her body to mine, pressing her back to my chest.

Just holding her brought some peace and calm back into me. Too many nights I'd spent holding just her memory. Nights that I would never allow to happen again.

Though, it seemed that her drunken endeavours had yet to end. She began squirming. Giggling and squirming, pressing closer and closer to me and shimmying her back right over—

"Love," I groaned, gripping her hips and spinning her to face me. She took that as an invite of some sort and climbed on top of me. I pushed her wild hair away from her eyes. "Suppose you're not sleepy."

"Not one bit," the little temptress purred, biting her lip and looking at me like she was about to feast on my bones.

I caught her hands before they went to my one happy bone. "Don't make me put you on the naughty corner."

"Why?"

"Not when you're like this. If you're not sleepy, I can carry you around on my back like that lad Simon. And that is the only ride you're getting out of me tonight."

She sighed and leaned down to kiss my neck so torturously slow, her tongue trailing over my pulse before she dug her teeth on my flesh. Fuck. "Give me just a kiss then," she said, cupping my face and licking my bottom lip.

"Sleep, you vixen."

Her face scrunched up. "Kilian, if you do not kiss me right now I will die."

The severity in her voice had me in tears from laughter. "What am I going to do with you, hm?" I kissed her lips. "I don't even know what to do with myself anymore. So overwhelming. What do I do, Snow? What does one do to not go mad from happiness?"

"You're happy?" she asked carefully, as if she didn't already know that she'd been the one to show me happiness.

"Deliriously happy."

"So am I," she admitted in a whisper. "How long until we aren't anymore?"

"I'd give up forever for one moment of delirious happiness. And remember," I said, stroking her cheek. "Your husband is a fearsome man. If anyone ever again threatens to ruin your happiness, I will do some very bad things that rhyme with hill and bill."

"Have I corrupted you to the dark side, my darling?" she whispered, leaving wet kisses on my neck that had my blood shooting south.

"I am a simple man. Easily persuaded."

She smiled over my skin and then licked a trail to my ear. "I remember it differently.

I remember it taking quite a bit to persuade you." Her hot breath fanned my skin, and I had to physically peel her from me before I lost the last strand of sanity I held together with some glue made of the same material as her.

She growled, kicking her arms and legs in the air for a moment before surrendering and collecting all the blanket to her side of the bed. "*Klaghne.*" *Idiot*, she murmured in Calgnan, and then recited a long line of curses that would have made the hot sun blush.

"Come here. Be angry in my arms, woman. You vowed to me. Twice."

She collected the blanket again, sulkily laid her head on my chest and let me gather her in my hold.

I kissed her head. "That's my good girl."

When her little snores started filling the room, I decided to close my own eyes for some sleep.

My hold felt empty, my body colder, and panic made me jolt awake. Only to find Snow sat at the end of the bed, looking at me, her chin resting on her knees that had gathered to her chest.

She couldn't sleep again. How many nights had it been now? She had to be exhausted.

"You're awake," she said softly, looking like every cruel dream of mine under the faint lights of sunrise. "Finally."

"Why, were you waiting for me to awaken?"

She lifted her head and stretched her legs to the side. "Yes."

"Yes?"

She nodded and sat up on her knees before pulling her thin nightgown up and over her head till she was naked before me. She crawled to me and straddled my hips, sitting right over my aching cock. "Can't believe you made me beg for it."

"You didn't beg," I said, and it was the wrong thing to say because she ground her hips against mine for a very torturous, brief moment and then lifted herself up, leaving me aching and searching for her touch.

"Did you want me to beg?" she murmured in my ear, her hand travelling lower down my stomach, but not low enough. Her fingers skimmed over the band on my trousers, and every nerve end on my body collapsed at the sensation. "Is that it?"

"Fuck no."

She dragged her hips over mine again, making me pay for what I'd done. Reminding me I was so painfully hard. "Then why is it so difficult to ride my husband's cock?"

I'd beg if I didn't know she liked begging me more. "A please would do."

"Pretty please," she hissed over my mouth, sliding her hand over my length.

Hells.

I grabbed her jaw and pulled her mouth to me. "Pretty please what?"

"Pretty please fuck me," she moaned, breathless, her small hand stroking me root to tip. "Fuck me like only you know how to fuck me. Make me come apart and then let me feel you come apart."

Burning seven hells, if she didn't stop, I would come just like this. "You want me to fill you up?"

Her hand moved faster. "Yes. Yes, please."

I grabbed her and spun her on her back, under me, fucking naked and panting with need. Her black hair pooled around her like the darkest, most alluring night, framing her face stained with the prettiest blush. Every soft curve of hers stood out against the navy silk sheets.

She knew my brain well. Her hands travelled over her stomach and cupped her full tits while she writhed with need, kneading her soft flesh and rubbing her hard nipples. She watched me with hooded eyes, teeth sinking into her fleshy lip while I pressed soft kisses to her sex.

Her body jerked when I wrapped my lips and sucked where I knew would have her writhing and calling all the Gods. Her hand shot through my hair to hold me there. And sinking two fingers inside her wet cunt, I watched her come apart, tasted her sweetness on my tongue, and then savoured those little moans and screams when pleasure threw her over the edge.

"On your stomach, my sweet wife," I ordered, pulling out of her and licking her wetness off my fingers.

She took orders ardently, flipping over and giving me a chance to leave my red print on her skin. I pulled her hips up until she was on her hands and knees, her pink cunt glistening with want, stretching around me as I sank myself to the hilt inside her.

Her body jerked in my hold, and she half hissed and half moaned a curse when I thrust in her again.

"Fuck, Kil," she breathed, her back arching as I slammed myself inside her warm cunt, those two dimples above her round back making an appearance. She took each of my thrusts, bouncing against me, meeting my pace. Insatiable like I was. Only for me.

My hand left her soft, full breast and lowered over her stomach, down between her legs, and I felt her get wetter when I circled her sensitive flesh. "How do you want me?" I asked, kissing her neck. "Tell me how you want me, love."

She was panting and breathless, but managed to give me a stuttering response, "You know how I want you."

That's my girl. "Both hands on the headboard," I ordered, cupping both her breasts and palming them raw, twisting her pretty pink nipples till she moaned again, her thighs shaking when I readjusted my hips against hers how she liked it.

I slid my hands over her body, over the shrine I prayed on every day, grabbing her soft hips tightly in my palms and slamming my entire length hard inside her, feeling her cunt pulse and tighten around me. She felt so good, not only around my cock, but in my hold, how she moulded against my chest, how soft she was under my touch, how she sounded while she took me.

There was only one woman I'd ever let myself go with, and that woman was currently whispering my name in so many shades of pleasure, her cunt weeping around my cock, her tits filling my palms so perfectly.

The bedframe creaked as I picked up my pace, and so did her little whimpers and breathy moans. "Kil, I'm coming," my wife cried out, her limbs weakening and quivering when I didn't stop until she was all spent.

When she started writhing, her body turning soft and pliable, I wrapped my hand around her jaw and pulled her face to me. "I want you to come again for me, love. I'm not done with you."

The drowsiness in her face was a stunning look on her. "I can't."

"You can." She could. My girl loved to come several times on my cock.

Phantom hands of darkness substituted mine, draping all around her limbs, over her throat and between her legs, wrapping and licking her skin with heat.

Her swollen pink mouth parted wide open with a moan when they slid over her wet cunt, massaging every other sensitive spot while I kept fucking her.

I wrapped her long, soft hair around my fist twice and pulled her head to me, marking her throat, whispering how good she was for me, how well she was taking me, until her eyes rolled back and she cried out again.

That sound...that was my undoing.

She was my undoing.

Fuck. I groaned against her neck as blinding ecstasy crashed through me and I came inside of her.

She collapsed face down on the bed, her small shoulders lifting up rapidly while she tried to catch a breath.

I laid down, picking her up and putting her against my chest on top of me, waiting until both our heartbeats began calming against each other.

She looked up at me when I hummed to myself. "Why are you smiling for?"

I have a taste of heaven every time I hold you. Then I'm reminded that it is heaven I'm holding when you speak or when you smile or when you simply just lay there for me to watch. "I just fucked my wife. Who is mine. I get to do that for the rest of my life."

"After all this," she said, her eyes fluttering shut when I trailed my hand over her spine, feeling her shiver at the touch. "After all this, after I put my father so far down this soil that he can taste the Otherworld, after that joyful event, let's...let's...I mean—" She swallowed. "Stop taking the potion."

My hand stopped moving. "You want—"

"I want," she quickly agreed, lifting her eyes to me again.

Children. A family. Our own family.

"Come on," I said, sitting up with her still against me. "Get up, there is a war to plan, soldiers to count, borders to check. A king to kill."

She blinked and then howled with laughter. Trailing her hands over my torso, she pushed me down again and kissed me breathless. "Are you still set on none, six or seven of them?" she chuckled.

"I'm set on however many you want. As long as they are with you, as long as I have you, as long as I am raising them with you." I twirled a piece of dark hair around my fingers. "We can name them Storm, Hail, Rain, Thunder, Sunshine, and such, so I can have all the weather in tiny black-haired children who will one day frighten me to an early death. Like their mother."

Her smile was bright, so bright, yet there was a terrifying forlornness behind them. "Okay."

"Okay?"

She nodded.

I smoothed my thumb over her soft lips. "You are being very agreeable about this."

"We might not be here soon. I might as well let you name all of our imaginary children atrocious names."

"My missus, since when have you started giving up before a fight?"

"I'm not giving up, darling."

"Then stop calling our precious future children imaginary."

She grinned at me. "The names are still atrocious though."

"Let me down gently for once in your life, woman. I thought it to be quite the idea."

"What if they are like me?"

"I'd be heavily entertained for the rest of my life."

"Bad, Kil."

"You're not bad."

She raised a brow and poked a finger on my chest, right over my heart. "Love does make you a fool."

"You are not bad, Snow. The world has wanted to take everything from you and you only fought back to get what you were owed. Never more. Never what your father wants. Never at the urge of greed."

"I'm told anger is just as bad."

I shut my eyes tightly. "I don't know what you're talking about, love. Age has robbed my sight. And I can't really hear so well either."

She laughed. Hard. Her entire body shaking from amusement. If there was one thing I loved, it was making her laugh because I knew she only laughed like that for me.

A heavy knock cut through my mood like an axe, and my very sleepy brother cracked the door just slightly open. "Brother, it is not even six in the bloody morning."

"I'm sure it is still night-time somewhere out there," Snow replied, and then turned to whisper to me, "We weren't that loud, were we?"

"That is before you asked me to come inside of you or after?"

She sneered at me. "Pri—"

Mal knocked again, louder this time. "For the love of all dark heavens, change the bed hinges, dust was flying off my walls. You'd think the mighty king of fucking Adriata would have better quality woodwork," I heard him mumble whilst he retreated back to his room.

"What about Sleet?" I asked.

She lifted her eyes to mine, blinking confused. "Sleet?"

"You're absolutely right, they are bad names."

She shot up, bewildered. "You'd name our child *Sleet*?"

30

Black Bishop to E3

Snowlin

THE SWEET, APPLE AND orange scented afternoon air of Aru was filled with soft touches of floating blossoms. It was like two seasons had merged together in one and were dancing around, blowing gusts of soft northern wind against the Hanaian palace.

People had gathered in the cherry blossom forest just outside the walls to celebrate. Chairs were scattered in neat lines on both sides of a rosy petal altar floor pointing to an arbour made of pastel-coloured flowers. And the stunning arch was situated under the soft shadow of an older blossom. It was an exact description of the dreams Nia would tell me when we were young girls and dared to imagine what ifs. Moriko had brought them to life for her. Moriko had brought her biggest desire to life, too—to find love.

The murmurs of joy and celebration were soft and yet all so loud with happiness. Perhaps that's what it was. Perhaps it wasn't the flowery blossoms at all that made everything so dreamlike—just happiness.

Is that what I smelled from him? Happiness?

Though he was in the furthest corner of the celebrations and away from me, his eyes immediately found mine the second I looked at him. A layer of stone rigour shed from his features when he offered me a smile. It was a command my body obeyed without question—it demanded that I return it.

I love you, he mouthed.

And I love you, darling, I mouthed back, and a stupidly massive grin overtook his features.

Cai stepped before me and I sneered, looking over his shoulder at where my husband was not a second ago. Where did he run off so fast?

"What?" I hissed.

"She wants to see you. Only you."

Worry filled me like a sinking ship, and whatever amusement I wore, it all shed away as I rushed to take off. Jayre and Memphis circled the skies of Hanai, vigilant, and soldiers circled all parameters, armed to their teeth and with a straight order of kill. But even they could have missed something.

My friend rested a hand on my shoulder, stopping me. "It is nothing like that, Cakes. Take a breath." It wasn't until I'd calmed down that he let go of me, portalling us right in front of our friend's room in her new home.

Nia opened the door before I even got a chance to knock, and she practically dragged me inside.

For a second, for a very long second, I stood there frozen still and astounded. "Nia," I murmured, my eyes hovering over the white tulle ball gown spreading far and wide around her, decorated with all sorts of embroidery and specs of light rose coloured petals, pearls, and glimmer. Her curls were up and pinned back while a golden crown of leaves and flowers rested just above her brow. And my mother's pendant around her neck. "They do exist," I said with some awe.

She blinked a little. "Who?"

"Faeries. Those creatures in old story books that Alaric swears up and down the seven skies that have never existed in Numen."

She smiled, and I truly believed it then that they did exist. She sighed and nervously paced back and forth. "Tell me, do I look stupid?"

"What?"

"I look stupid," she said, nervously picking at the tips of her gloves before lifting them to her neck, to the slight remnants of the scar and then down her arms covered with white gloves, hiding even more of them. "And exposed. So exposed. Why did I pick this one? Why did you let me pick this one?"

I shook my head, still in awe at my friend. "No, you look perfect. Simply perfect. The most stunning thing I've ever seen, Nia."

Her breaths came and went fast. "I told her it would be too much. All of this is too much. I can barely deal with you. I can't...I can't marry a queen, Snow."

"She loves you like she has never loved anyone. And she wants the realm to know it," Kilian said, stepping inside the room, and I spun round to him and then quickly back to Nia.

"I called him, too," she said, chewing on her lip. "I need a logical answer to balance your biased ones." I glared at her, and she chuckled. "And clearly, I was right."

Kilian neared her and rested a hand on her shoulder. "She loves you and you know it. Not only have you seen it like I have, but you've felt it as well. No, this is not happening too soon, I decided to marry my wife when I was barely fourteen and she had no idea about the said marriage. No, it won't matter to Snow or the rest of your family that you will be away from her as long as your happiness is on the line. Yes, Alastair left Drava to you and one day you will pass it on to your children or whoever you chose as right for the position. Drava will always be your homeland no matter where you are. You will be queen consort and you will be the best this kingdom has ever had. Anything else?"

She shook her head, breathing out a long exhale. "I think that was mostly it."

My husband patted her cheek. "You look beautiful, Helenia. As always. Moriko is one lucky woman, as are you."

My friend smiled at him and then at me. "He always says the right thing, doesn't he?"

I rolled my eyes. "It is terribly annoying."

He extended a hand for me to take and left a kiss on my knuckles. "It charmed you, didn't it?"

I huffed. "Just barely."

Everyone sat silently in their chairs, simply enjoying the way the willow branches overhead swayed softly at the lull of sunset autumn air. A soft bell chimed in the distance, and we all spun in our seats to see the most radiant woman I knew walking down the carpet of pink petals with Alaric and Cai on each of her arms.

The strings of a violin slowly gave the air a melody, too. The notes curled around and accompanied my friend's steps towards the one she loved. Moriko's chest rose rapidly, and her cold face was betrayed by the silver rimming her eyes. The old queen bowed her head at Alaric and Cai, and extended a hand to Nia, pulling her closer. Too close apparently because the stern Hanaian priest cleared his throat in warning.

The two kneeled before one another, still holding onto each other as the priest lowered a metallic basin filled with water between them. When their eyes met across the small distance, something changed in the wind. It was then I saw all doubt and worry entirely melt off my friend's face.

Kilian squeezed my hand when they began reciting vows to one another. The lines made of promises repeated by both and celebrated by the whole crowd.

No one breathed, waiting for the last call of the priest made to seek Gods' blessing. There had been only one other marriage of two Aura that had been accepted by them and blessed—ours. And I still had faint doubts that it had been because of my threats. Faint doubts that abated when the smoke of the burning flowers that the priest held began curling in the air, wrapping around my friend and her wife before breaking apart in the wind and disappearing.

A stuttering breath and laugh left me at once when clapping thundered around us and Moriko leaned in to kiss Nia, their hands and fingers now bearing a golden vine tattoo, the mark of their blessed union.

"Were you making threats in your head?" Cai asked quietly. "You had a weird face on just a second ago."

I frowned. "No."

"She was," Kilian said, still clapping and looking ahead with a small smile playing on his lips.

"Mhm," Mal agreed, nodding.

I don't do threats. I would have simply burnt them all.

"There," Cai murmured. "The face came back."

Kilian nodded in agreement. "She just did it again."

"Yeap," Mal echoed.

Eren laughed just then, and the three men spun to look at him like it was the first time he'd done so.

I sat at the head table alone, watching Nia being spun around by Mal and Cai in the middle of the ballroom. Thora had her head resting on Alaric's chest, her eyes closed as they swayed slowly to the music. Eren, Kilian, and Mor were all standing, a drink in their hands, their manners serious and stony as they most probably strung along a conversation of the most boring kind only them three knew how to sting. Even Oryn was dancing—with a shy Macaria blinking down, refusing to look up at him. Visha and her equally crimson-haired protege had cornered Elias who laughed and made their frowns go lower and lower.

I enjoyed this. I enjoyed seeing the world move.

Though I craved vengeance like summer soil sought rain, there was something else I desired more than to expand my collection of souls with their heads on pikes lining my castle walls like solstice decoration. I wanted to protect—I wanted to protect this more than I wanted retribution.

As I lifted the cup of water to my lips, I muttered a whisper so the Gods would not miss it. *Till my last breath.*

"Who are you thinking of killing, kid?" Alaric asked, sighing as he stretched on the chair next to mine like his bones were one hundred years older than they had been before I'd gone to Isjord.

"Why is it creaking?"

He lifted up an amused brow. "What is creaking?"

"Your skeleton, Alaric."

He chuckled. "I'm old."

I lowered my cup and sat up straight in my chair. He, too, noticed the change in me because all amusement vanished from our air. More so when I said, "No."

Immediately, he looked away, his gaze guilty and tired. "I don't need your permission, hen."

To die. That is what he was not brave enough to say. He was going to let himself age like Alastair. "Remember to repeat that when I have you chained down my dungeons and force you to grow five hundred more bloody years old."

"I want to grow old, kid."

I didn't look at him as I said, "And I am not losing my father. The only parent I have ever had."

"You are not losing me, Snow. Death takes us all."

"Not without my permission."

He sighed, rubbing his eyes. "I am no longer needed."

I finally spun to him. "Says who?"

His eyes were lined with tears. "Kid."

"Says who?" I hissed, my voice shaking from anger, desperation, and heartache. "You have been with me through misery and hurt and anger. Stay. Stay while I try to find happiness, too. While the rest of them find happiness and give it back to you.

It is an order from your queen and a selfish plea from your daughter. Stay, please," I begged, shaking my head. "Sam will have you for the rest of eternity. And you know my whole ordeal with hells. Besides, you sweat a river in Olympian summers, and I'm scared you might have a stroke near hellfire if they do grant you a visit."

He cracked a sad smile. "You might have just convinced me."

"That would be a first."

He patted my cheek. "There are a lot of firsts I am seeing lately."

"Put up a little fight. I feel like you're just lying to me."

"I'm old, kid. Deceiving my child is the last thing on my agenda."

"What's first?"

He pointed his chin at the food tables. "Them honey scones. Want some?"

"Would love some."

Something nudged my knee under the table, and Memphis poked her little snout from behind the linen cover and rested her head on my lap.

"Scones, M?" I offered.

My bonded sniffed and then licked the bun. So me, her, and Alaric munched on sweet scones for most of the evening, observing the world I wanted to protect, watching it spin around and fill with laughter.

That was until a pair of very handsome hands had pried me to the dance floor and were now holding onto me while their owner swayed us at the soft fading melody of the orchestra. Only here, in this embrace, was I the one being protected from it all—no longer the protector. How did he do it?

"I want to put you in a big white dress and marry you again," he murmured in my ear, shifting his hand on my back lower.

"Wasn't doing it twice not enough?"

"No," he said simply, and lifted his gaze somewhere over my shoulder. "They are perfect together."

I twisted my head a little to the side to see the newlyweds sitting near each other, smiling and exchanging conversation. "They better be."

"Their shadows complement each other. Like brackets. Or colouring within lines—Mor is the lines, and she is her colour. What she feels matches hers entirely too perfectly."

I squinted though I was very sure I would not be growing another blessing. "It better."

He chuckled and spun me round once and then twice. "Are you going to threaten her all the way through this lifetime?"

"Yes. I'm persistent."

His nose gently nudged mine. "An admirable quality of yours, my heart."

Mal tapped on his shoulder. "Let me have a spin, brother. Quit hoarding her."

The moment Kilian handed me to him, the younger brother spun me around until I got dizzy. I would have said something...if only it hadn't made him smile.

"You look dashing today," I said, patting his chest and smoothing the black fabric of his suit.

"I know you're regretting marrying my brother instead of me," he said, spinning me one more time. "But I did get a friend out of it."

"You're more than a friend to me, Mal."

His smirk was ridiculously smug. "Ah, the sweet days when you were threatening my life morning, noon, and night."

"Why should I keep at it when you're the worst that can happen to you?"

"Ouch."

"It did burn a little when I was told the same by you." I looked up at him. "We've never spoken of Isjord again after that day. Of what happened there and what you saw."

That empty look fell over his face again. "I figured you would never tell me why you did what you did."

Except that I would tell him. For him...if it helped him...I would.

"When I was little," I started, already feeling my throat choke up, preparing to tell the story I'd never told and sworn to never tell. "There were one of two ways I used to forget it all. Pain was such an easy fix. It started small, so small that I didn't even realise I was doing it. But soon...it simply wasn't enough. I sought a second way. More pain, at the hand of someone who wanted my pain the same as I did. And the more they dished out, the more I wanted. Yet again, it grew not to be enough. I realised that all that time I'd craved something else entirely, not pain, but I couldn't have it. Not when I loved Rora and Eren so much that even the thought of death made me sick."

We'd stopped moving, but the world around me spun so fast. He had to know—for him, I'd say it. So, I focused on the second button of his shirt, and continued, "In Isjord, it wasn't so much about forgetting. It was more of a punishment. I believed I deserved the pain, and then the pain helped me forget. I wanted it. I wanted the pain. I wanted the punishment because I still couldn't have death."

Silence.

He didn't move or speak or breathe. Even his heart went silent.

He wiped my cheeks with the back of his hand. "Does Kil know?"

All the sound then returned at once. "He guessed. Most of it actually, but I've never told him the whole thing."

"Why did you tell me?"

"Maybe you can see what it can do to those around you even if you don't care what it does to you." I looked over at Thora, still afraid to look at him. "I think you know, Mal, why she...why she hates heights." A sob tore through my chest. "It's because of me, isn't it?"

He didn't answer me. Didn't need to. But he did wrap his arms around me and let me bury my face in his chest to hide me from the world yet again. His heart was so loud, and it drowned all the noises in my head along with those in the room.

"I'm sorry," he murmured, his hands shaking.

"Not your fault, Mal."

He let out a shuddering exhale. "Not yours either."

"Snow, it's raining" Thora called, and Mal quickly wiped the rest of my tears away. She dragged a slightly tipsy Nia behind, heading for me quickly despite the heavy dress she wore. "We should dance under it. Like when we were children." After kicking the bottom of her dress forward, she took my hand in her free one and dragged me with them outside and right under the soft start of a storm.

My little sister giggled at the skies before cupping her hands over her mouth, and shouting, "More!"

Obeying her request silently as always, Eren made it rain even harder for her. I looked over her shoulder to see my brother leaning against the doorway, smiling at us. Had she realised that it had always been him? That her small piece of heaven was Eren?

She pulled us further into the cherry blossom gardens and spun us around with her while rain completely drenched our hair and clothes, turning my pretty pink dress, a soggy maroon.

"You're going to catch a fucking cold, little bird," Mal shouted.

My sister was still grinning at the skies. "I don't catch colds. Never have."

That made me slow my step a little and stare at her. No, she never had. She'd never been cold either.

She and Nia giggled, furiously spinning, the ground beneath their feet turning muddy and staining their dresses. They looked so happy.

Everyone behind me looked happy.

Even the world looked happy for the first time in a long, long while.

It would remain happy.

I was going to make sure it did.

A hand wrapped over my own, pulling me back under the building hood.

"My little, wet hellcat," Kilian murmured, dabbing a small towel to my face. "In an adorable pink wet dress."

"Like a worm," I said through rattling teeth.

He smirked, shedding his jacket and throwing it over my shoulders, guiding my hands through the massive sleeves. "The prettiest worm."

"I thought I was a stunning, murderous vase? A steel, stunning, murderous vase. A broken, steel, stunning, murderous vase, but mended somehow. A beautifully mended, once broken, stunning, murderous steel vase."

There were no more smirks or smiles, he laughed so hard that his whole body shook. "You forgot witty. I remember I said witty as well."

"Damn it. I thought I was a stunning, murderous, witty vas—"

He kissed me, his lips warming my skin, his touch warming my soul. "Who would have thought, huh?"

"I'm still so angry you got to trick me the way you did." I hit his chest. "Guard? You, a guard? How did I fall for it?"

He grabbed the lapels of his jacket, pulling me to him. "I was so greedy for you. I still am so greedy for you."

I shivered. And it was because of him, not the cold.

Laughter pulled my attention again. Penelope had joined the other two, pulling a non-cooperative Visha behind. The witchling was stiff as a board from the rain soaking her entirely. She'd finally left her robes and dressed in the same rosy colour as the rest of us. And regretting it considering the way she'd hugged herself.

Elias stepped out in the rain and threw his jacket over her shoulders, prying her from the other bunch and sitting the bored woman on a corner to warm her up. Something he said had her eyes gleaming red with magic. The Venzor heir only lifted his hands up and retreated a couple steps, laughing.

"My bet is that he'll lose a hand by the end of the night," Cai said to Mal.

Mal snorted. "I bet he'll lose more than his hand."

Elias shot them both a look. "I've survived fine."

"Survived being the keyword," Eren added, and Visha gave him a little smile.

"Why would I take his hand or anything of the sort?" Visha asked disinterestedly.

Elias smirked back at us. "See?"

Her deadly, red gleaming eyes rolled up to his. "I'd take out his soul."

The man's face fell fast, and the rest of us laughed.

And we laughed.

And laughed.

Kilian wrapped his massive body behind me, tucking me to him while we spent the rest of the night and dawn and sunrise under the rain, laughing even more.

31

White Knight to F1

Snowlin

THERE WAS STILL A hue of happiness in the atmosphere even days after Nia's wedding. It was bothering me.

"Love," Kilian called from where he had leaned against the headboard, flipping through the scribbles I'd copied from Esmeray diaries, still searching for answers to questions I didn't even know we had. I'd gone to the woman's grave and attempted to dig her up several times before Kilian had mildly convinced me she wouldn't die a second time. "Are you trying to kill me, woman?"

My feet were burning from how much I had paced back and forth. I flicked a hand at him. "You know I'm over it now, darling."

He threw his head back and laughed hard enough to get my attention. "Come here, my old nemesis, and give me a kiss. My back is killing me."

"Old man."

"Brat." He patted the space next to him, and I sat right where he wanted me. "My obedient brat."

"Where is my kiss?"

He smiled, lowering his mouth to mine and kissing me. "Care to tell me why you are trying to outrun lady time?"

"It's quiet."

He took a moment to process my words and whatever was written on my face. After abandoning the notes on the other side of the bed, he gathered me in his arms and just held me. "Do you want to run?"

"No, but maybe we could go for a walk. Can't have your back give out on you so soon, not when I've got so many activities planned where you need your back."

"Is that so?"

"That is indeed so," I agreed.

"Alright, my missus, let's go for a walk."

"Actually. Let's do something else. Something you like."

"Something I like?"

I nodded. "There must be something."

His smile was so soft that I could almost melt to the floor. "There is."

I had to bite my lip from smiling. "Something else."

He thought about it for a moment. "There might be a place I want to show you."

Amaris was loud at midnight. Most people walking the city streets were either heading to work or preparing to start work.

"How does it work?" I asked. "Night and day?" There was still so much I didn't know about his people—his kingdom. Mine as well, I guess.

"Some sleep during the day, some at night. Most Aura cannot fall asleep during the time of our Goddess. There is a rush of adrenaline and power when the skies turn dark, as shadows grow taller and thicker, too. So they sleep during the day."

"But you sleep both times."

"Depends. There is not a particular time I feel the surge of my magic, I simply feel it all the time," he explained, handing a street baker a few coins in exchange for a fluffy pastry of sorts. "Day and night. But I do sleep better at night sometimes. Light bothers me. Though I've been told by many scholars that it has nothing to do with being an Obscur. Not a general trait we possess."

Cause you were made to hate it, darling.

I might have moaned when the flavour of the treat melted on my tongue, because he chuckled. "That good, huh?"

"Keep talking," I mumbled between chewing big bites of my snack. "Tell me more. I want to know all of it."

He pointed to a building on top of the hill, at what looked like a temple. "I was born there. My mother was Sidran, and her father was a priest. They were quite set that I was to be born under the southern star, right below Henah's second heaven, like Sidran tradition required."

"Why not under the moon? I hear it is good luck for your people."

"There was no moon when I was born. Only darkness. No Obscur is ever born under moonlight. There was no southern star either, no stars at all, but the temple sits exactly where it should be."

We stopped again, this time for him to buy me some fluffy colourful candy wrapped around a stick.

My eyes rolled back at the taste. "Go on," I said, putting some of the cottony stuff in his mouth. Perhaps this was my new favourite thing. Feeling normal was...enjoyable. Even if it was for just a fleeting moment. Because when he looked at me, nothing about it made me feel normal. No power, no magic had ever made me feel as exquisite as that.

"Do you know why the heavenly creatures have remained in Amaris?" he asked, pointing to where a few flower folk were hurrying to close the petals of their homes for the night.

Driada had mentioned something about them once. Him being the reason why they were not afraid to remain among humans. "You? In all fairness, I would have stayed, too, if I was a little flower spirit. To fawn over you. Would have worked like a dog to spread my happy dust on everything if you were my king and I was a little woodland creature."

He threw his head back and laughed, the whole city turning to look at us. More at him. Eyes wide. Not wider than me though. He was so pretty when he laughed.

He threw an arm over my shoulder. "I *am* your king. And you'd be an exquisite woodland creature, but I like my queen as she is. Only spreading happy dust on me," he said, throwing me a wink and stealing some of my fluffy candy.

"So, why do they stay if they're not here to fawn over you?"

"They go where they feel the land needs them most."

"Your people are the closest with their faith. Your lands also seem to be doing fine."

"Debatable. Faith is a two-edged sword. You cut using it, it will cut you back. These people have suffered most because they love to use faith. But it is not because of them the creatures stay, it is because of me and those who were like me. Obscurs can no longer be buried or set free at sea. Their power lingers after death. If not for these creatures, the land below would have slowly and eventually died from housing an Obscur, so they remain here to nurture it."

"I still think it's because of what I said."

His smile kept growing bigger, his eyes nearly glowing like moonlight. "Yeah? Any more fun facts for tonight? Or can I take you to see that secret place of mine?"

I inhaled the remaining candy and nodded. "Curiosity sated for now."

"Hold tight," he said, fading again, this time at the edge of a tall cliff that overlooked the Moor Sea gleaming under the round and full moonlight. The breeze was ever so gentle, almost as gentle as his hand on my waist. "Are you nauseous? I thought the smell of fish wasn't so bad down this coast. No one comes to fish here."

"No, just...it's beautiful." The silver cast of the moon had draped such exquisite shadows over his face as well as the sea.

"It's even better down there," he said, lacing our hands together and pulling me down the stone stairs that led to the open sandy beach enclosed between tall cliffs. The space felt like a secret. A pocket where you stored hidden gems. The sapphire waters. The white sand. The stars above. Those down here below that looked at me the same as some looked at the skies.

He took off my coat and bent down to unlace my boots, and then his until we were both barefooted and wearing barely anything. "The water is not cold," he said, walking backward and pulling me towards the shore where waves brushed the sand softly.

Our feet met water. And the deeper we got, the warmer it felt. He pulled me to him when my feet no longer reached the ground, and I wrapped my arms around his neck.

His lips were warm against mine. "Wait for it," he murmured, and then almost at his command, the water below us began glowing a fluorescent blue. His fingers skimmed my cheek. "Now you know."

I did not know why my chest felt so heavy, why my words were choked out when I spun around to look at the marvel illuminating the clear waters around us and the sand below. My fingers grazed the water, watching the blue hue shift and glow more when the small waves rolled over the calm surface.

So there were wonders as such.

Resting my forehead on his, I said, "I want to know them all. As much as you can show me. All your favourite places."

"Everywhere that you are, those are all my favourite places. This is simply a place. It became special the moment you stepped on it."

This hurt. It shouldn't hurt.

I wanted to live out every fantasy of ours. Every single one. Leave our mark everywhere. I wanted to picture our life ten, twenty, one hundred years from now. But there was so little time, and there was so much to live through. Things I've not told him, things I want to do with him, things I wanted to share with him. Things I wanted to give him. Just like that little fantasy that night. I would have let him name our children every ridiculous name he wanted. But they were the sacrifice I had to make to ensure many others had a future. Lila deserved a future. Nia and Mor deserved to know how their love would grow old. Thora and Eren had been prisoners for most of their lives, and they were just finally learning life again. Mal—Mal had to live and dare to know how beautiful the other side was. And Kil. My darling. He'd make sure all that happened, that they would be safe and happy. I was sure he would eventually be happy, too.

His thumbs brushed my cheeks. "Why do you cry, my love? Why must you break my heart again?"

"Because," I whispered, my voice shivering, "I regret the time I could have learned so much more of you."

He kissed both my eyes. "There is time for everything. I'll show you every little thing I know until you are sick of it."

"I can't be sick of anything you say or do."

"I'll remember this when we argue next time."

"I wasn't even angry last time. And it wasn't an argument, really."

His dark brows pulled together. "What? It wasn't? But it looked so real?"

I splashed water on his face. "Fool." Something slimy touched my ankle and I jolted. "Kil. Something touched me."

"Probably a small fish."

I gagged and shivered, jumping in his arms. "Take me out. Take me out. Take me out."

He lifted me up and somehow managed to have me sitting on his shoulders, his head between my legs, all while he laughed himself to tears. "Better now?" he asked, kissing the inner part of my thigh and smoothing his hands over my legs.

At least I could see my feet now. "Yeah, thank you."

"How does the world look up there?"

"Shinny."

He tilted his head back to look at me. "Maybe I should carry you like this all the time."

Even backwards, his smile was so pretty, his face was so pretty, his eyes—oh, his eyes. For some reason, he looked away into the distance, smiling to himself almost shyly.

"What?" I asked, wrapping my hand under his jaw and lifting his face up to me again.

The fool grinned at me, the dimple on his chin deepening. "I like how you look at me." He spun me off his shoulders so easily to wrap my legs around his waist and pull me flush against his body, my chest pressed to his. The wet silk of my nightgown suddenly became unbearably painful against my hardened nipples as he trailed a hand down my back, and I gasped when his mouth latched on my neck, kissing a path to my ear.

Something splashed besides us, soaking my hair with salt water.

Another splash followed, drenching me entirely.

Then, screams and snickers ensued.

Kilian groaned. "Malik."

My brother-in-law swam to us with my little sister following. "Please tell me you're not swimming naked?"

"Maybe we should have been," Kil grumbled.

"This is so nice," Thora sighed, swimming on her back, staring at the skies above.

Kilian glared at his brother. "You better have a good goddamn reason for following us here."

"I do," Mal said. "Silas was seen leaving towards Whitebridge with Melanthe. Apparently, your aunt has taken over in his name, claiming the capital as an Isjordian front. Thought you might want to know that." He jumped from the water, raising his hands up. "Throw her."

"Throw who—"

Then, I was up in the air, crashing against water. Mal picked me up and then threw me to Kilian who couldn't stop laughing.

He wrapped an arm around my waist and wiped the water off my face while I kicked and writhed in his hold. "I'm going to kill you."

"Thought you were over that," he said in my ear, making me shiver entirely. "You look adorable all wet, my little hellcat."

"No, no, Malik!" my sister screamed before being thrown up in the air.

When she burst out of the water surface, it was revenge time. Her eyes burned while she launched towards Mal. Or it could have been the salt because mine were burning as well.

I clung to Kilian and shouted at Mal who was still trying to swim away from my sister, "Did Skadi say why he's gone himself?"

"Didn't say, but my guess is to scare Magnus," he shouted back. "He must be thinking we've already gathered an alliance with him. Wants to corner him like a mouse until he's forced inside his city walls and abandons any plan he might have made with us."

"Mal," I called again.

He finally stopped moving and let my sister climb his back, putting his neck on a chokehold. "Yes?"

I glanced at Kilian who had narrowed his eyes on me. "Never mind."

The moment I woke up, I'd already made the decision. Father was in Whitebridge along with his witch, doing Gods knew what. Probably getting Prince Arun to join his assembly of merry men and lizards. Demir was bed ridden, having people poke at his arse for human sickness since apparently all of Melanthe's trials had failed to detect what was wrong with him magically.

"Don't," Kilian warned as if he could read my mind before I even made to step away from the bed.

"Hear me out first."

His eyes were still shut, laying sprawled naked beside me like he was about to be painted by the finest painters in the realm. "No."

"Yes."

"Snow," he groaned into the pillow.

I stood and headed towards the dressing room with him following shortly after. He wrapped a sheet around his middle, already ruining my morning. "Darling, it is an immaculate idea. What a waste of thoughts it would be."

He put a hand on the hanger I'd pulled out, holding my grey leathers hostage. "We'll mourn the loss together. I'll even send a little prayer to the heavens for it."

"Kil."

"Don't *Kil* me."

I bit on my lip to hold back a smile as I trailed my fingers over his torso. "You can come with."

His eyes dropped down to where I was touching him, and his jaw ticked. "How considerate." He grabbed my hand before it ended under the sheet, and he clicked his tongue at my poor attempt at distracting him. "Cute, really cute."

"Visha thought it to be brilliant."

"I'll deal with her later."

"Darling," I said, stopping to face him. "I will not sit and wait for war. If I can stop him, slow him, kill him, I will try. And no better way to do so than through his own people."

He grabbed my face so I could look at him. "Isjordians are people of war. They thrive in it and for it. It was Krig's silent blessing. To keep them greedy, powerful. It is not worth risking yourself for this. They will not be convinced whatever you have to say to them."

So I'd thought as well, but one short conversation with Eren had opened my eyes to something else. I knew our father far better than him, and he knew Isjordians far better than me. "And you forget that more than half of Isjord is not even Isjordian. You forget that most of my father's people are brought there from war caused by him. Because of markets he's ruined from his unfair trades. A wall he raised, monsters he raised, prices he raised, fear he raised. Most are there to make a living for families they have elsewhere. Some are bound by coin and poverty. Some are bound by force and war. Some have no choice. But give them one and they will take it. And then the other half, darling, are people who've never been to war. Never seen war. Never even heard of it outside of school books and prayers they hold once a year at solstice. They are people. Simple people. Harsh, distrusting, loyal to a fault, greedy? Perhaps. But they are harsh because of the land they live in, distrusting because they are being lied to by the very man they believe most in, loyal because they are made blind, greedy because they are fed so much avarice that they are made to feel starvation for it. They will listen. That is all I ask of them. To listen. Nothing else."

That and so much more that Eren had shown and taught me.

Slowly, his mouth pulled into a smile, and he lightly pinched my cheek. "You're right, love. Very much so."

I was? "Thank you."

"You're most welcome, my blushing wife."

"Don't look at me like that."

"Like what?"

"Like you're proud."

"I am."

"Don't be. I intend nothing nice. That is all what Eren told me, not conclusions made by me. I could care less to come to any conclusions about those people," I said in one breath, making myself cough.

"You remembered and cared enough to rely on his conclusions. And you put trust in your brother. He must have been happy just telling you all that and seeing you listen."

"You're making me sound and look nice."

"I'd like to think my wife is nice."

"Don't act like you don't know who you married."

He pulled me to him and kissed me. At last. "My sweet sin, I've drunk too much of you to consider sinning anything but good."

"What have I done to you?"

"You're dragging me to hell, so I might as well try to fit the environment." He pulled my face up and left a little kiss on my nose. "Mal will come with you. No *buts*."

"About that. He and I have already agreed a while ago."

He nodded, backing away from me. "I see. I see."

"Don't look hurt."

"Am not."

It was my turn to chase him around. "Kil, I am so used to not telling anyone about what I do, it doesn't really hit me until I've already set it to motion. I didn't mean to keep it from you."

He stopped getting dressed and cradled my face in his palms. "Love, you've told me. Now, two days, ten weeks ago, anytime, matters not. What matters is that you've told me. I really do not mind."

"Why do you look disappointed then?"

"I am supposed to be your partner in crime. Thought I would have been your first choice about this. Guess I am the spare second."

"Fool."

"What a way to comfort me."

"Poor baby."

He pointed between us, backing away. "This is an argument. We are arguing right now, Snowlin."

The second he gave me his back, I ran and tackled him, climbing him like a tree.

"Oh," he said, still walking around like I wasn't clinging to his back for dear life. "It is fine when you want to argue, but not when I want to argue."

"Yes."

"Yes?"

I smacked a dozen kisses on his neck until he moaned. "I meant no. What was the question again?"

He turned his head just a little, his cheek brushing against my lips. "Are we going to get dressed or should I show you the appropriate way to ride me?"

"What is option C?"

"We can continue arguing."

"Option B. Most certainly option B."

"Fantastic choice," he said, smacking my thighs.

I stood right at the edge of Highwall with Visha, Mal, and Oryn by my side.

"What are the chances that father thinks I would do this at this moment?"

Mal leaned against a wall. "Not entirely low."

"But low."

I looked over at Visha who had kept an unblinking gaze on the veil surrounding the city of Kirkwall below. Her aunt was at the strongest a Dark Crafter could be. She was a daughter, a sister, a mother. She'd completed the cycle of her blessing. While Visha was destined to become the Grand Maiden, the child of the most powerful Dark Crafter to exist and the most knowledgeable of her sort, she was still hovering around the edges of her magic which she had sworn to leave untouched when she'd surrendered her fate—when she gave up on her written path in exchange for the one she was trying to write for herself.

"You fear her."

A portal cracked open before us, framing the city of Venzor, and she turned to face me, her expression harder than usual. "It would be smart to fear her."

"Fear me more."

Her head snapped back and green eyes glowed red while she mumbled a string of words that caused Melanthe's veil to falter around the edges of the sea city. "Mal's magic will draw the beasts, but you don't have too much time."

Lightning hit overhead, and in the snap of a second, I stood on top of the tallest tower in Venzor, overlooking the second biggest city in the kingdom. While Mal hovered just on the street below.

It didn't take a blink of a moment for gasps and shouts to pull a crowd of people beneath me, Mal disappearing between them. And then the faintest shiver tingled my neck—the stink of dark craft and godly magic made my eyes water.

I unsheathed my new daggers that glowed a bright, glittering white, channelling magic onto the steel.

A howl and then some sort of a mangled growl blared like a warning siren in the air before the large body of a green beast jumped right in front of my face. I'd escaped its claws by a fraction of a second before another one crowded me from behind, aiming for me again.

I bolted just right behind it and threw my dagger in its skull. And the thing turned to dust and vanished in the northern wind in seconds.

People ran all around me when beasts poured in the hundreds from the tall buildings surrounding the city, not caring about the people being stomped, shoved, and crushed against one another. Not caring to avoid hurting them while aiming to hurt me. Just what I wanted them to do. Show Isjordians my father's true intentions.

I bolted again before claws could reach me. Only to be caught by another pair just as I landed on top of a building. The beast's strength made me stagger forward and almost greet the ground with my face. I bolted again. Fighting hundreds of beasts was not my aim. But the moment I landed, another pair of claws were aiming for my throat.

Hells.

They were hungrier than ever before.

Bolting again, I landed right on a ship deck that had docked on the Venzorian port. It took them longer to find me, but yet not long enough.

Again and again, I bolted from spot to spot until I'd gathered the attention of every soldier, beast, and Crafter. And had every bow, sword, and spear directed at me.

Wind began beating harsher against me, and then amongst the ruckus of the fight, a low growl slipped into the cold Isjordian air. Then fire burned tall and wide, over dozens, hundreds of ships that had docked on my father's port. Jayre disappeared between skies faster than he'd appeared.

Amidst that disarray, the beasts had stopped, sniffing the air and running away opposite from me. Somewhere Mal was luring them to.

A portal opened mid-air, and I jumped in it, standing right at the centre square of Tenebrose, leaving chaos sort itself in Venzor. In a breath, the seal concealing my magic snapped in place—entirely. I closed down every bit of magic I possessed, the scent of my power disappearing from the air entirely like I'd done so many times over the years to hide what I was.

One Isjordian, a dozen, and then eventually a crowd formed in the city square. Whispers of surprise ghosted around me. Awe, horror, fascination, and...hope was written in their faces before they all bowed.

They began to bow, but I spoke over their respect, "I am not your heir, no need to bow."

They all lifted their heads again, this time confusion dawning upon their reaction. "Never have been. Never will be. My blood might be Krigborn, but my place and palace are among the skies. The cold hurts me, it bothers me, it haunts me in my worst nightmares. It will soon haunt you all too if my father continues standing upon his throne. If this land keeps feeding him respect, loyalty, and your youngling to his armies that will soon march to war with the realm. You must know of the war. *This* war might be the last for many. For all perhaps. Your king has summoned a divine weapon, the Octa Virga, the same weapon King of Seraphim summoned to climb heavens and ended up ruining his land."

A wave of gasps made me stop for a breath before continuing, "He used me to collect the sceptre that binds a Guardian of Ithicea. He used many of your children, brothers, sisters, fathers, and mothers, too, sacrificing them to get to this weapon. The weapon he will use to turn the realm to ash in order for him to reign over it—as your new God," I said, stepping forward. "I know that you do not desire this. I know many of you desire peace. The bravest thing I have done in my life was hope. Hope that I would be free from my father, from his greed, from his control. I wish that you are all brave enough to hope, too. To hope for peace. For a future that might not come if my father does this." Reaching onto my pocket, I grabbed the little flower that had not died for weeks after it had bloomed, and handed it to a girl. For the first time, I hoped that the flower grown because of me would not turn into a curse. "He held me in chains you have not seen for far too long. He has been holding all of you in chains you cannot see for far too long. He's held winter as his prisoner, too. With the false pretence of being his servant. But winter is no one's servant. It is no one's enemy. Why have you all let it become yours? Do not join him in destroying this realm. Do not let him ruin the home of many. If you do, I will not forgive. Whoever marches with my father in his war will burn under my storm and be buried under my wrath. There will be no mercy to give once I see who spares no mercy to the realm!"

They all looked overhead, gasping at the sight of Jayre leaping through clouds and at the thunder gathering overhead at my command.

"Whoever I see at that battle will find hell. My hell! And that I swear an oath that you will all burn. Walk south, walk east or west, and we will welcome you should you choose to leave my father's side."

I backed into the portal Visha had opened behind me, watching the people of Isjord disappear from ahead.

Two beasts stood chained in the middle of Visha's quarters that suddenly looked entirely too small. "Well, well, well. Look at you making friends, Visha."

My witch stared at me rather amused. "Look at you giving speeches."

"It was good, wasn't it?"

"Better have been," Cai said, stepping inside the crowded room. "You risked a lot for that little stunt." He nudged a beast with his foot. "Nothing could convince me to turn into this. How the hells do they still have a brain after drinking Vas's blood soiled with all that Caligo shit?"

"They don't," Visha said, pulling open one of her cookbooks. "The Caligo substance poisons the head. They would be...feral, like the beasts from the Ater battles. Except, those wanted to invoke chaos without direction and these can cause chaos by order. Brainless but thinking."

"How?"

Visha shut her grimoire. "They've planted something inside of them that controls their minds while they are in that state."

I studied the creatures my father had made, tilting my head to get a better look at the mark on their neck, right where their small incisions were. "Interesting."

"What is?" my friend asked, crossing his arms.

"A *khamir*," Visha said, grinding some sort of herb. "The mark of a spirit still living in its vessel after death. Some stubborn souls tend to do this after passing."

Penelope shot up from her seat, startling me. "P-p-possession? Spirit possessions aren't real. You said they aren't real, aunt. No spirit can cross the mantle of the Mid-world."

"It is not possession. A *khamir* mark is usually harmless. A way to let us know that a soul needs help to be guided beyond. No spirit has the ability to use their human form after death. This would also mean that Melanthe had to kill them first before turning them into beasts, and that makes absolutely no sense at all because they can turn back into their human form. Have lives, speak, walk, eat, and remember." She walked to them, slashing a dagger to her forearm and letting her blood drip to the floor. "One would also think that puppeting a dead soul is an easier, much easier thing to do than controlling someone alive. If she was the God of Death himself. But at best, she is a light joke that he's been told at dinner. Souls in their spirit form are one of the most difficult to control. They bear strong grudges, regret, love, longing happiness, intense desire. Easier to persuade one's mind than one's soul."

Pen winced at her mentor's bloody mess. "Alaric is going to be mad."

Cai pushed off the wall that he'd leaned against to reach closer to the beasts. "Moregan has told us that her body has no command when she heeds Melanthe's call. Is it their mind? Perhaps she really is controlling their minds."

"No. A powerful enough Crafter can control only two or three at a time. There are a million of these beasts. She has definitely found a way to use souls, I just have to figure out whose or what part. Perhaps...something else entirely." The blood began moving over the marble, circling the beasts at the command of Visha's chant. She blew on the powder she'd ground on the mortar, letting it spread in the air, and the creatures began convulsing, shaking, and foaming from their mouth and nostrils, slowly turning back to their human form.

"Are they dead?" Pen asked, leaving her bench and crouching before the circle.

"They are," I said. "But breathing somehow."

"P-possession?" Penelope asked, looking up at Visha.

"No, their spirits have already departed. Whatever rot Melanthe has planted in them to control them in their beast form has killed their bodies, too."

I frowned. "Moregan told me she was struggling to remember, wake, sleep, and eat before taking the blue gyre. Was it this? Something corrupting her from the inside?"

"Possibly. The dark bane has kept the rot at bay. Slowed it."

Penelope chewed on her finger, looking between Visha and I. "Aunt, but how is Melanthe controlling them?"

"It isn't Melanthe controlling them," Visha said, her fingers curling in the air to turn it a hue of red. Time changed around us, it remained almost unmoving—almost as if we were in a new one entirely. The in between as they called it, or the Mid-world, stretched parallel to us, visible under Visha's magic. Between the crimson smoke around us, two black strings hovered afloat, tied around the men's necks that extended towards the windows and for long miles ahead, disappearing in the distance. "Another spiritual Aura is."

Cai's eyes were wide. "Adriatians?"

Visha slid a finger over the strings. "With some help from a Crafter. I've never known any Adriatian Aura besides Kilian and Malik to have any affinity with death and beyond it. To manipulate souls outside their bodies or tie strings to control them after death."

As if they had been summoned at the mention of their names, the two brothers stood leaning on each side of the door, their hard focus on the black strings. Both of their looks grave.

Visha's palm opened and the red mask between the two worlds disappeared. "My first assumption is simple. They were fed the potion with Vas's blood so they could turn into the immortal creature. Then planted with a beacon of sorts that would make it possible to control them in their animal form. This beacon feeds on mana. Once it consumes all the mana, it kills the host. And to keep the bodies from rotting, they do not turn back into their human form." Visha blinked once, utterly emotionless as she said, "That is about five rules of living and dying broken. Melanthe is doomed."

"So this is the work of an Adriatian?" I asked.

Kil remained still. "Yes. Empaths."

"What about what Elias said, the whistle?" Penelope asked. "An Empath would not need to whistle, they would simply just—" She frantically moved her hands around. "Do that."

Mal looked at Kil, sighed, and said, "There was an old trick once used by Lyran grandmothers to dispel spirits from a child's room when they used to have continuous nightmares or dreams. Some used rocks, sticks, chants, or songs, but also whistles. The call stops them from lingering close by. It makes sense." He pointed his chin to the men. "When they turn, their souls essentially go into a sedentary state in the Mid-world, still tied to their bodies. The whistle could be a summoning call for whatever Melanthe has put in them, and then once she has their attention, an Empath ties emotional strings to them to control their desire, anger. Lure them to a particular target. Feed hate into a particular direction."

"Then it is easy," Cai said, and everyone looked at him. "We've got plenty of Empaths who can do what Silas's Empaths are doing."

"The strings are unique, my muffin," Mal explained. "You can make it so that their spirits are warded off or come to attention or attack, but only to a specific order designed by the one who has attached those strings. Our best chance is finding these Empaths and killing them."

"He could have hundreds."

Kil shook his head. "A dozen at best. We keep a strict record for the safety of our people. Every parent is required to hand their child's name once the blessing surfaces. The punishment for failing to do so is worse than death. Mal, have the priests draw up the names of every Empath in Adriata and then pay them all a visit. See who and how many are missing."

"I'll come with you," Cai said. "This is creeping me out."

The princeling smirked and smacked my friend's behind. "If you wanted some alone time with me, you could have just asked, sweet bun."

My friend backed away. "On a second thought—"

Mal grabbed the front of his jacket and pulled him out of the room.

I shook my head. "It just doesn't make sense. How could she have thought of all of this? And what beacon?" Crouching down beside Pen, I reached a finger to the *khamir* mark only to be stopped by Kilian's hand wrapped around my wrist.

"Melanthe could have easily predicted that we'd do something like this. Might have even wanted us to do this." He kissed my fingertips. "The *khamir* mark is more than just a mark. It is a powerful seal. Until we find out what it could be sealing, let's keep our hands to ourselves."

"Would I have lost a finger?"

"No, you could have lost your soul."

"Can't be worse than losing a finger." Unimpressed by my statement, he bit my hand, and I jumped upright. "Ah."

Leaning forward, he murmured only for me to hear, "I'd like to see all five of your fingers wrapped around my cock, so try and keep them all for me, my love." As if he'd not left me gawking, he looked over my shoulder at Visha who was blankly staring at the two bodies, blissfully unaware. "Oryn could look at this better, he knows both sides of magic. Call him."

She snapped to attention and nodded. "I will."

"Penelope," he called, and the little carrot stood so fast she got dizzy. "Could you run to Adriata and get Atlas, too."

"Why Atlas?"

"He is an Empath."

"He is?" the both of us asked at once.

"A non-practising one, he gave up the rights when he wore the robes, but he has one of the best understandings of the magic. Mal has been training him since he was a small kid to keep it under control."

"What if we can't find the Empaths?"

"Then we will have to kill my cousin. The proper Crafter way," Visha said nonchalantly, messing around with a few vials and returning beside us with a bowl of water and a small bottle of an oily sort of substance. "Simple as that. This all is tied, bound, and connected to her magic. The potion, the strings. If there is no grand master, there are no puppets."

"You'd think it would be as easy as that?" Nia asked, strutting along with Eren. They both kneeled before the beasts as we had. "She will probably be hiding during the battle. Puppeting the war she orchestrated from afar."

Visha calmly replied, "Until I solidify my conclusions, my best proposal remains as that."

I shrugged. "Mine, too."

"I bet," Nia muttered under her breath, taking a seat.

Visha wet her hands in the water and then spilled some of the orange tinted oil on her fingertips, rubbing them together before she brushed them on top of the *khamir* mark. The black lines melted into each other under her touch, spinning until they formed a circle the size of a fist. Her red brows creased. "There is a presence of a soul. This doesn't make sense."

What didn't?

"Careful now," Kilian warned, tendrils of darkness and shadows climbing up the walls.

Visha's fingers glowed red as she plunged them inside the tattoo space, through the man's skin, and pulled out holding something in her hand. A small, black larva that stunk so bad it made me gag. My Crafter's eyes were wide. "We were wrong. So wrong."

I put a hand over my nose and mouth. "The hells is that?"

Visha turned to Nia. "Get my grimoire."

Nia got to her feet and sprinted to return with the massive book. The pages parted in half and began flicking through rapidly until they stopped on an almost blank page towards the end. A dark illustration of the small creature was drawn on the old, stained beige paper. Along with a short paragraph written in Borsich beside it.

Visha's horrified eyes filled with tears. "What...what has she done?"

Kilian straightened, his body tense. "Kill it."

My witch shook her head, and I was beyond confused when tears poured out of her eyes. "So much pain."

Kilian stepped forward. "I know, Visha, but you have to kill it or I will. We both know which is best."

I clutched his arm. "Kil, what is it?"

"A seedling. The soul of a stillborn. No memory, no experience of life, no emotion. An unformed soul. Innocent. Extremely easy to control. Easy to feed emotion and tie strings around."

Nia collapsed to the ground, eyes wide. "This is madness. She was planting these inside people?"

Kilian held me close, rubbing a hand over his eyes. "Souls are difficult to keep under submission. Not these souls. These are obedient, pliable. Empty."

Penelope rushed in along with Oryn and Atlas, but the latter remained at the doorstep when he saw the scene set before his eyes.

The older Crafter took the small creature from Visha's hands and laid it on the floor, a violet craft halo illuminating under it before it vanished into dust. He turned to me. "You said the blue gyre worked on Skadi?"

"Yes, she said she was getting better."

"We'll tell her to double the dose. The flower might be neutralising the effect, but it won't kill the seedling without ingesting silver which would probably kill *her* eventually." The old Crafter brought a shaky hand to his head and then looked up at Nia. "You think you could concoct something for me? I'll draw up everything about the seedling. Crafters are of no use against it. Death and more death do not go hand in hand. We need something that can poison the seedling and then kill it without killing the carrier."

Nia nodded, pulling a vial from Visha's table and collecting some blood from the Isjordians. "I can try. We might need to keep the other to test if I can manage to create something."

"No," Oryn said. "These two are gone. Dead shells. The seedling had the entire control. We need to test someone who is still in their human form."

"What about Skadi?" I asked. "But I couldn't feel her heartbeat either. None of theirs. Are they all dead?"

Oryn grabbed a scalpel close by, dragging it right across one of the dead Isjordian's chest. The heart under the rib cage was entirely surrounded by black roots. "The seedling feeds from the heart. If Skadi is still conscious, that probably means the heart is not infested with roots. Once the seedling dies along with its roots, the heart will return to pump for the body again. I'm afraid not many will be as lucky. The woman is a prime Verglaser, ancient as time and just as powerful. I suspect that made her the perfect first candidate. It would also make her our perfect first try at solving this."

Penelope dropped to the floor. "We'll never be able to save them."

Save. "I didn't know we were trying to save anyone. This is good news to us. Let's hope they will eventually fall off and die like rotten fruit."

"Is it?" she asked. "My mother said she knows some of the boys and girls who got turned. They used to go to school with me. I don't want them to die, Snow."

"It's war, little carrot. You should see how many boys and girls like them I'm going to have to force to get up and fight soon."

32

Black Bishop to A7

Caiden

NIA HAD NOT COME out of her old quarters for days, not even to eat or drink or shower. Little did she know, stinking and starving did not really do much in terms of saving the world. Tired of thinking of the *eventually*, I barged into her chambers, breaking the lock.

She jolted upright in her chair, a hand over her heart. "Who let you in?"

"*I* let me in, sweet Nia." Throwing an arm around her shoulders, I gave her a little hug she liked for whatever reason. "Brought you a snack."

Her eyes widened at the carrots, so animatedly that I regretted not bringing her the whole fresh crate I'd bought at the market. Immediately, she dropped whatever grassy plant she was grinding on the mortar. "With a spicy yoghurt dip?"

"With a spicy yoghurt dip," I said, pulling a small jar from my pocket.

She hugged me again. I let her. She could have whatever she liked.

Once she settled on a stool to eat, I went through her notes. Neat and clear as always. Concise. Lined with pretty pen colours. Many visual aids were drawn beside the heavy writing. I was in the presence of a genius. "Any discovery?"

Her head lowered. "This is supposed to be the work of a Potioner, but minus the dark magic. I am no Potioner, not even a Magi-healer, Cai, I have no idea what I am doing."

"Doesn't look like it to me."

She sighed. "Oryn said Macaria was going to send a Potioner to help me figure out some stuff, but she can't get close to where I am working. This is no use. I'm wasting time for nothing."

"Nonsense," Snow said, skipping inside the room, touching every little potted plant in sight like she was some flower spirit. "Ohh, carrots. Yum." She swallowed, her mouth pulling into a small cringe, not even hiding her revulsion to anything and everything orange. "I brought you some cheese and honey pastry from Samira's." She smugly showed me her tongue when our starved friend jumped up and down from happiness.

Nia squirmed in her seat, peeling the paper bag open and taking a massive bite on Samira's specialty. "The future's looking brighter now. Scratch all that hogwash I said before."

"Changing the world one hungry friend at a time," I said, pinching Snow's fatty cheek.

"Hands off," her husband growled, suddenly overcrowding my space. He lowered a concoction of a grass-like assortment before Nia and then pried Snow to his side. "Hazelnut and balsamic vinegar salad. Your favourite."

"It is not," I said. Who the fuck had a favourite salad?

"It is," Nia whispered for only me to hear and then ducked her head.

"Don't let hunger get the best of you," I whispered back.

"I am a weak woman, I'm sorry."

During the whole ordeal, Snow had found herself right in front of some cacti, poking her finger on them. "She's on the loose again," I said to her husband.

He glanced at her and then at me. "So?"

"In about a minute—"

"Ah," Snow yelped, sucking on her finger.

I nodded. "A small miscalculation."

"By fifty-nine seconds. Not small at all," Nia mumbled, her mouth fully stuffed with food.

I sneered. "Eat your *salad*, Nia."

"Why is this thing breathing?" Snow asked, still by the cacti, reminding me well why she did indeed need her *keeper*.

Thankfully, he'd already taken her side, a little closer than necessary. Letting me see well how happy he made her. How easily he'd made that happen.

"An aqua cactus," Nia replied. "Sort of breathes like a human when it is out of water. I used to make mud foam for your stomach with it."

Kilian uncapped a water bottle and handed it to Nia. The bastard was a bit too nice for my liking. "Have you managed anything yet?"

"Not enough to test it."

He patted her shoulder. "You're doing great, Nia, do not push yourself harder than you can bear. We still have the *anima accissor* if nothing can be done any other way. This is not a burden you need to bear alone. Do you understand?"

I sneered. The sweet tongued bastard.

Nia looked at Snow who had stopped before a vase filled with snow drops—the new nightmare that was chasing her lately. "This could save many lives, Kilian. Not all volunteered for this war. So many were forced. Snow knows it. She just has a hard time understanding that some people deserve saving."

"To hells with saving."

"Cai," Nia pleaded.

"We're fighting for survival. Survival, Nia. Saving comes later. If we even survive this thing. And the odds are not looking much in our favour. Like Kilian said, we have the *anima accissor*. The potion or medicine you are making is not our priority, only a backup in case we fail to come up with any other way to stop Melanthe. Stop thinking of this as a way to cure the sickness, more of a way to kill it. Perhaps it will come faster to you."

She chewed on her lip, her eyes falling to the ground. "Because I learned to do this to kill?"

"No, because it is easier to kill than to heal. The world has come up with more ways to kill than heal. It has to be a tell."

"He is right," Kilian said.

I huffed. "What a joy."

His eyes darkened. "Will be the day that you stop exis—"

Snow wrapped her arms around him, and he stopped talking, glaring at me instead.

It was becoming more difficult by the day to be ungrateful to him. He was who I was most grateful to. He didn't help only Snow, he helped Nia, he helped my people, he helped Alaric through his grief when I didn't know how. Shame he was such a piece of work.

"Why are you smiling like that for?" Nia asked, nudging my foot. "You look a bit mad. Stop it."

I grabbed Snow's hand and dragged her outside. Thankfully, Kilian knew not to follow. Her quick, tiny steps chased rapidly after me, hurrying to catch my pace.

Once we stood at the roof of the castle, I let her go. "Why did I catch Visha lurking around Myrdur ruins last night?" I asked.

"Contrary to popular belief, I don't keep her on a leash at night."

"She can hear our peoples' call, doesn't she? It's how and why she came to Taren in the first place."

She pointed a finger to her head. "I'm sure she hears many things."

"The mist, Snow."

"And?"

So, she knew. "Why is she out there having full blown conversations with condensation?" I caught her finger before she pointed it to her head again. We both knew the only crazy one among us was her, not Visha. "Spit it out."

"Cannot. It's a secret."

"Oh?"

Miss Madness closed her eyes and nodded. "Mhm."

"In relation to what or who?"

"Me. Remember that galanthus crap?"

"Yeah. How does this correlate?"

"Apparently, the mist sends out the same sort of magical signals as the flowers. Visha thinks that is how my ancestors have managed to turn themselves into it, why it acts as protection for our kingdom and why it has never been absorbed by the earth below. I might not be the only one who has or had this...ability. It is more like a Skygard...trait."

"Why does this matter to begin with?"

The moment she gave me that sneaky, wicked smile I knew she would not tell me. "That's the secret."

"Does Kilian know?"

Her smile faded. "Not all of it."

That was not good.

I flicked her forehead and put a hand over her mouth before she made a sound that would have my legs cut. "The second I see anything dubious, I will tell him. Screw our friendship or whatever."

She frowned, rubbing her forehead and then nodding. "Fine."

I'd just gotten out of the bath when the fool broke into my room like it was his and dropped on my bed. At least he didn't fade and sneak on me like last time. Could be because I almost gutted him by mistake. Probably not. He had enjoyed it.

He whistled, raking his eyes over my naked chest marked in places with fresh scratches. "Look at that. Who did those?" His grin was wicked. "Never mind, I know."

Apparently, the whole world knew of *us*. The only ones who had no idea what we were doing were me and...*him*. Even though I slept in his bed most nights, I still could not figure out if there was an *us*. The night I had kissed him and he'd kissed me back we'd been too far down each other's pants to talk. Then far too drunk in euphoria to be able to talk. Then too far down one another's anger to bother with talking. Then too needy to let ourselves talk. If we talked, he'd ruin me, and not in the way he or I would like.

"What are you doing here?"

"You honestly have been bruising my feelings all over, sweet bun."

"No, I meant, why are you here with me not—"

He groaned. "Don't say her name. It pisses me off."

Then there was him. And *her*. If they stopped talking like they did, they might realise they could do much more to one another than talk. Except. They both liked talking.

I got my leathers on. The only time they were off my body was during the bath and sometimes at night, but only when I had his hot body pressed to mine. Sometimes, he even liked it when I kept them on. "What did she do now?"

"She keeps mimicking what I do. I take a step, she takes a step. It started all funny as shit. But then, I have a drink, she has a drink. I have a bottle, she has a bottle. Can't even be angry at myself because she'll randomly start sulking in front of a mirror. You see where I am going with this?"

Yes, because that is what she and I agreed on. "Not really."

"I can't do anything I am dying to do."

"Why not?" I raised my brow at him. "Scared she'll waste her life away like you?"

He stood all of a sudden, coming right in front of me. "You know something about it, don't you?"

After tying my boots securely, I stood, coming chest to chest with him. "And?"

"You would tell me, would you not? If she was doing this on purpose, not to just annoy me."

"Don't pull those puppy eyes with me, Mal. I wouldn't tell you even if I knew."

"If they were green, would it have worked?"

"Fuck you. And they are not green. More of a moss-like colour." I froze, a holster falling off my hand. The damned hells did that come from? Kilian, that bastard.

"Oh, more of a moss-like colour." He snorted, shaking with laughter. "And don't ever fucking lie to me."

"Or what? You'll stop being a thorn in my foot?"

"I'm trying—"

"To protect her? Fuck that, she is better than any man I have trained. She can protect herself."

"So, it's fine when she is reckless, but not fine when Snow is reckless."

And that was something he knew not to say. "Snow is not reckless, Mal. Thora will confront danger, Snow tries to outbid it. You realise the difference between reckless and suicidal, right? Thora is young. We've all been young and reckless. She'll grow out of it."

He cupped my face with a hand and rested his forehead on mine, breathing hard and so angry, his fingers digging in my jaw. "If something happens to her because of this, I'm going to bury you so far down this earth that you'll burn both here and in hell at the same time."

"If you're not going to kiss," Eren said, leaning against my bedroom door. "Can I borrow you for a second?"

Mal pushed back from me, still warning me with his eyes as he retreated away towards the exit. "Never noticed your eyes," he said to Eren, patting his shoulder. "A nice mossy colour, aren't they?"

Eren dug his teeth on his lip to keep from grinning, and it pissed me off even more because those stupid dimples took my attention away from his mouth.

"Don't ask," I said, drying my hair with a towel and searching the shelves for a hair tie.

He slipped behind me, his hand digging in my hair and pulling my head back so he could bury his face on my neck. "You smell good."

Burning skies. "Is this what you wanted that second for?"

"No." He pressed his hard body closer to mine, and I leaned onto him. "Can I not change my mind?"

"If you'd come earlier like I asked you."

"Couldn't leave Mahara's channel sooner. Father's ships are persistent to the point of stupidity."

I turned, grabbed his face and kissed him, backing him to the wall. "I told you to let the Volants deal with it," I said, nipping at the corner of his mouth where a scar ran over. It drove me insane.

"Takes four dozen men to do what I can do alone, Cai. It is not fair."

Scratch that. *He* drove me insane. "It is not fair that you sleep only two hours a day. Are you trying to prove something, huh?"

"You've counted?"

He groaned in my mouth when I pushed my hips against his. "You guard for twenty, I fuck you for two, and you sleep for two. Shittiest bargain with death I've seen."

No, it was me who had bargained with death. What had death and I tussled about so it could now haunt me with one of his smiles alone?

His hands lowered to undo my belt, and a knock banged on my door, forcing me to pull back. "Shit. Who is it?"

"Mother spring," Alaric answered. "Get your arse to the camp, kid. Something else is waiting for you."

Something else.

"What I wanted to talk about," Eren said, straightening himself and doing my belt up. "We hunted down the slave traders who were selling Olympians assassins."

They didn't blink. They didn't even look like they were breathing. The whole two dozen Olympians didn't even look remotely human anymore.

"Conditioned," Snow said. "They inhale and exhale so little to burn less energy, less magic. They haven't said a word or even sat down. Nor ate or drank. For days." Her head slowly turned to the slave tradesmen chained by a stump, her eyes gleaming. She started laughing, her shoulders shaking with more than amusement. "I'm going to have so much fun."

They flinched. But not because of the thunder howling like mad above us. Whatever they saw on Snow's face had the men start scrambling back and gathering next to one another like hens in a coop.

I glanced at Kilian who was standing in the far distance, watching her and her alone. He'd relaxed against a tree, arms crossed and attentive on her still, making no move to stop her while she walked to the men. If he wasn't beside her, his shadows were. If there were no shadows around, night was. If there was no night, he'd found a way to make death his slave only with the purpose to look over her.

Until him, I'd not realised my mistake with her. I'd tried to raise walls around her. While he had raised those same walls around the world instead.

"If you won't speak, I'll just make you sing," she said sweetly. "Then we can all dance. Perhaps the men whose tongues you've cut will dance with us. Isn't it so? You speak and they obey?"

They all scrambled back when her fingers lit with electricity. She put a hand on a man's leg, melting it to the knee. And it wasn't just his screams that started off my migraine. All the men screamed like they were all part of a symphony of sorts.

"Shut it!" I shouted, their lungs seizing at my command. "Better."

Still, none of the Olympian soldiers budged, blinked, or breathed any heavier. Nothing.

"How lucky you are to have two same limbs," she said, melting off his other leg up until the knee. "Oooh, look how many limbs you all have together. Who's next? Eeny, meeny—"

A man leaned forward. "My neck," he said in Borsich.

Eldmoorians? They were Eldmoorians?

"Nice offer, but that would kill you," Snow replied.

The man shook his head fast. "No, no, my neck. A necklace."

I reached for the gold necklace hidden under his shirt, breaking the chain and turning the gold pendant around for any sort of inscription. A whole list of...names was carved on the back.

"It is craft," he said. "We use craft. They obey at the call of their name. A name only we know."

"How many have you sold to Silas Krigborn?" I asked, pocketing the necklace.

"A dozen, but I heard they were lost at sea."

"What else?"

"Much. We've been doing business for decades. He sent us after Olympian Aura. Wanted them trained well before they would be handed back to him."

Few knew that Silas Krigborn was a spineless coward, but it pleased me to know he feared us in any capacity.

"What else have you sold to him? I need a detailed list."

"C-criminals. We've broken many out of all eight kingdoms for years, I cannot remember every single one of them. Banned elixirs. Blood of Dyurin blessed. Dragon bone, the heart of a sphinx, hundreds of Aura. And, uh...uh, what were those called? We had to dig all over for years."

"Seedlings?" Snow asked, frowning, her whole body vibrating from the force she was using to keep still.

"Yes, yes, seedlings. A tedious process."

She glanced at me over her shoulder. "A tedious process, he says."

"We need you to dig for us again," I told them.

He blinked fast, starting to shake. "What for?"

Your own graves.

33

White Pawn to A5

Kilian

DESPITE OUR BUSY SCHEDULES and what we'd come to learn about the *khamir* beasts, Alaric had ordered us to at least join one meal a day to have together. Moriko had graced us with her presence today and she was currently sharing a silent stare down with my wife.

"Any news from Magnus?" Caiden asked, slicing his meal rather quickly. Anyone could tell that him being here instead of down at Highwall or Myrdur was stressing him out.

"No war talk on my dinner table," Alaric grumbled.

"Not yet," Nia answered, and her father sighed.

"I wonder why," Moriko murmured under her breath, and Snow slammed her cutlery down on the table.

"What was that?" my wife asked, blinking sweetly at the Autumn Queen.

"No bickering on my dinner table," Alaric repeated for the fifth time today, slamming his own cutlery on the table, and everyone lowered their heads on their meals and continued to eat quietly.

"Maybe we should approach them again," Eren said carefully, looking at his sister.

Caiden scoffed. "So she can kill another one of his sons?"

"Otis deserved what he got," Mal said, flashing my wife a charming grin. "Did you really hang him upside down?"

"Like the moon," Snow replied rather excitedly, and my brother chuckled.

"Maybe Snow can actually tell him the truth about it all," Nia suggested.

Caiden shook his head. "That might actually scare him off. It will be worse when he actually realises in whose hands the power lies."

"I am a humble matron of my power," my wife said, cutting her vegetables rather graciously and unhurriedly. "Nothing to be afraid of." Surprise almost overtook me until I saw that the vegetables in question were a piece of broccoli, beans, and baby carrots that she most certainly was not going to eat.

Everyone dropped their cutlery and raised their eyes up at Snow, all except Alaric who was silently chuckling while he enjoyed his meal.

"Humble?" Moriko asked. "I heard you once claimed that you are a God amongst men."

Once? I was sure it had happened more than once.

"That wasn't a claim," Snow replied, almost gagging on a single piece of bean.

"Humbleness was at discussion," Moriko pushed.

"Humbleness, not truthfulness. Why should we lie so unnecessarily?" She turned to me. "Right, darling?"

I rested a hand against her cool cheek and wiped her lip with my thumb. "Yes, my heart. We mustn't."

She smiled and kissed my palm before turning a *I told you so* look on Moriko who scoffed.

"No, Snow," Nia said, hesitating. "About Olympia. Let's tell Magnus about us. All of it. Let them know how big this fight is, how much we ourselves are sacrificing before asking him to sacrifice."

Everyone stopped eating and looked over at Snow.

Eren spoke first, "I agree."

"I do, too," Caiden said, and that was enough to make Snow's attention return from wherever her thoughts had taken her.

"You agree?" she asked.

Her friend nodded. "As you said to our people, we aren't the nation from the Night of the *Draugr*, we've never been, but we let it define us because we were afraid someone would be able to reduce us to that again. But that is not true. That night...that night will never repeat. You and I will never let it repeat, just like we've made sure this far."

And it was all it took for Snow to nod in agreement, and say, "Then we don't hide anymore."

"Right, my king?" Caiden asked, raising a brow at me and attempting to contain a victorious smirk.

"Since you've been polite for once," I said, "I do agree with you."

"Feels nice," he said, chewing like a smug idiot. "To be agreed with for once."

Penelope burst through the dining room, wearing a massive grin and few streaks of smoke on her freckled cheeks. "I got it!" she said, waving a piece of what looked like fur on her hand.

"Rabies?" Thora asked, scrunching her nose. "That's nothing to be excited about, Penny."

Penelope's excitement died down and she stood there, panting and with hair that looked like she'd been struck by lightning. "No, I got my first charm. I mean, I made it. With magic. It protects the person you made the charm for. This was a tricky one. It is for Snow," she said with a small voice, hiding the trinket behind her back, embarrassed all of a sudden. "So it can protect you in battle now that we are definitely going to war."

Snow raised her eyes to the young girl and extended a hand forward. "Let's see."

Penelope hesitated and then slowly walked to her, leaving a small corner of fur strung on a piece of tie on Snow's palm. "Maybe it won't work."

Snow studied the thing for a moment and then tied it to her waist belt. "I'll let you know, little carrot."

The girl beamed. "Alright."

"Thank you," Snow offered, securing the small token to her belt. "No one has ever made me something like this. Not for my protection, at least."

"Macaria said you might need it," the young Crafter revealed, and everyone went silent once again. "She taught me herself how to make it."

I leaned back. "What did she say?"

Penelope went beet red when she glanced at Snow's sneer. "Uhm...uh...not sure, but she mentioned something about Isjord and Islines."

Snow stopped chewing and carefully glanced at me. "I don't know what she is talking about."

"There you are, Penelope," Visha said, gliding inside the room and reaching Snow to hand her a folded piece of paper. "News from Moregan."

My wife quickly read the note and rolled her eyes up to her witch. "What does Elias say?"

"Fernfoss has welcomed around a thousand Isjordians this morning alone. He personally checked on them one by one after the Eldritch command was done. Not many have been as lucky though."

"What do you mean?" I asked.

"Silas sank three ships of Isjordians leaving for Solaryan last night and turned the rest of those that tried to flee."

"Turned?" I asked.

Visha's mouth quivered a little. "Into *khamir* beasts. Moregan said they forced the potion down their throats. And there were not just odd thousands. But tens of thousands were seen trying to flee winter lands from all corners. Silas is using this to his advantage."

"Father is losing it," Eren murmured, grabbing the paper to read for himself. "How...how is his court allowing this?"

"Silas is past the point where he needs a court," Alaric grumbled, throwing his cutlery on the table and standing. "You kids will need to start preparing, need to start gathering allies. It has been delayed more than it should have. The war is here."

Snow looked around and then blinked up at her guardian. "Tis not."

"Kid, this is not my first time. We are losing time."

Snow shook her head as she slowly cut through her food. "The wars you speak of were not of survival. When you have a chance to escape, many choose not to fight, but this has no chance of escaping. Everyone will fight. And until all my ducks are in a row and fucking quacking, there is no war. Just a simple threat," my wife said, dabbing a handkerchief to the corner of her lips. "Sit down and finish your meal."

Moriko drank a whole goblet of water in one go and blew a heavy breath, turning to her wife. "My *ahana*, rationalise with her, I am exhausted."

Snow sneered. "If I was as old as you, I'd be exhausted, too."

Nia chuckled, and her lover shot her a betrayed look. "You think I'm old?"

"I think you are beautiful," Nia said, staring up at her. "But your joints do creak."

"They do indeed," Moriko agreed curtly. "So do me a favour and walk me out to the terrace."

Nia tilted her head to the side. "Exercise will do you good."

Like this was all my fault, Moriko pinned her accusatory look on me. Why did she always think it was my fault "I bid you all goodbye."

"And we bid you goodbye, too," my wife mocked in a curt voice, making everyone on the table besides Alaric chuckle under their breath.

Nia shook her head and turned to me. "Can this hostility be categorised as a war risk since they are both queens?"

Moriko stood, finally giving up on her silent fight with my wife. "Perhaps you will accompany me, Kilian."

I stood as well, kissing Snow's head. "Actually, yes. I'd like to go over a few details about the east wall."

My wife gaped at me, looking betrayed. "If you must."

Moriko's expression was cold and bored when she asked, "Is this the secret to a happy marriage? Begrudging behaviour?"

Snow slowly rolled her eyes at Moriko. "Yes, that and his huge c—"

I put a hand over her mouth. "Love of mine, secrets are meant to be kept."

"Why would I deprive them of finding happiness in their marriage also," the vixen said, smiling innocently.

I halted not even a foot inside our bedroom, my eyes swivelling over my wife clad in the littlest red nightgown I'd ever seen, reaching barely over her back side. She'd bent over my table, scribbling something down on a piece of paper. Absolutely ignoring me.

"Hello, love."

She turned and braced her hip on the desk, flicking a bunch of black hair behind her shoulder. "Any trouble in Hanai?"

"Not particularly," I said, shedding my jacket and raking my eyes over her again. It looked like trouble was waiting for me at home.

She melted at my touch, closing her eyes and sighing when I slipped my hand behind her neck and kissed her cheek. She smelled like heavens. But beneath the innocent scent of vanilla and lily perfume she wore, I could smell the ulterior motive. "Do you want to be fucked or is this a way to fuck me over?"

She smiled a little and bit her lip, rolling her alluring eyes up at me. "Both?"

I was fucking doomed.

I sank my teeth on her cheek and tugged lightly. "Mistress of my heart, you play too much. What is it that you want from me? Tell it."

"Nothing. I just need you to not worry."

"Asking about the impossible."

"To trust me?"

"Now you're just being mean."

"But you trust me?"

"More than my own self."

"And if I tell you that I want to go speak with the Isline queen, would you trust me then?"

"What next? Want to go diving in some volcano?"

She sneered like an adorable feral cat. "Aren't you funny, ey?"

"Why are you wanting to meet the old queen? Are you hoping to get them to help against your father?"

"Not exactly. They certainly might not be convinced to join the battle, but I am hoping to convince them to help me discourage more Isjordians to leave my father's side. An Isjordian is a child of winter before they are my father's people. If they believe that winter is stirring them away from their king's lead, then they will be led away."

"This might cause more trouble than you think. The Isliners have not meddled with Isjordians since the time of Old Isea. Are you certain about this?"

"New times are coming, Kil. King Edric used to say that only ice could break ice, but look at two Verglasers fighting. The balance rarely tips in favour of any. One will win over the other from wit, not magic. Ice cannot battle ice with a victor. Ice can battle ice with a cheater. Everyone knows how Tenebrose won his crown, and they praised him for it. If I am going to cheat my father on his own game, why not bring someone who is at his level?"

Smart girl. "You believe they will take the time to hear your reasoning?"

"I'm a Krigborn. By right, I can contest the Isline throne. They will want to hear what I say before I try to do so. Besides, I have an inkling they will be thrilled to know that I, the Isjordian heir, am conspiring against the king they loathe."

"Alright, we will go."

She patted my chest. "You will stay here. I will go."

"Absolutely not."

"Darling, someone needs to be here. Besides me, only you can handle Aurora. Me and you should never even be in one place at this point. Also, Mal and Thora are coming with me."

That made me frown. Twice now I'd been the second choice. "They already know?"

"Yes. We sort of discussed it all together a long while ago."

I fingered a thin red strap of her nightgown. "So you knew this would work."

She shrugged. "I had back up if it didn't."

"Back up?"

She pulled the edge of her nightgown up to reveal red lacy underwear. "Bought them just the other day."

"How long have you been planning this attack for?"

"A while," she revealed, starting to unbutton my shirt. "Moregan proposed it to me back in Isjord actually."

"You trust her this much?"

"I did and do. With my life and Malik's. She was going to get him out if you hadn't. She helped me plan Fren's...situation."

"Murder."

She tilted her head back and forth. "There wasn't much murdering happening. I really didn't put much effort in it. Even her own bones were not putting much effort to hold her up at all. She came apart so easily I had to wait for them for so long and ran out of daydreaming scenarios to the point my ears were ringing from silence."

"That ought to go in the dictionary. Not murder if not much effort is put into it."
The hellcat snarled. "Are you mocking me?"

"Wouldn't dare." I said, sliding the nightgown off her body. "You don't have to do this. I would have listened to you regardless. Whatever insane plans you have, as long as I know them, they will always be fine with me."

She frowned. "This was my favourite part of the whole plan. Pretend you've fallen for my seduction so I can gloat victoriously."

That made me chuckle. "I'm obsessed with you, woman. With everything that you do." I ran my nose down her neck. "With how you smell. With how you feel in my hands. With how you come apart when I fuck you."

"Make sweet love to me, you mean."

"Yes," I said, tasting the sweetness of her skin on my tongue. "Make sweet love to you. You might gloat victoriously knowing that I am absolutely ruined by one thought of you."

"This is suicide. When I said find an ally, I didn't mean this," Alaric grumbled, staring down at the partial map of Islines that we had. Like me, the man had not been thrilled about Snow's idea. "These people are vicious, they will dig their teeth into this. The concept of help will go over their heads."

Eren tensed a little. "This is their war, too. They need to be given an opportunity to fight it just the same as us."

"He is right, Ric," Nia agreed, lifting a hand to her throat. "They will understand that Silas will not spare them either."

Visha and Oryn entered the meeting, the two exchanged a look before she spoke, "There might be a...way to keep Canes and the *khamir* beasts from reaching Snow before she crosses the Isline border." She turned to look at me. "You, my king."

Snow's head whipped to her. "What are you talking about, witchling?"

"It would be nearly impossible for you to be ten seconds in Isjordian soil without Melanthe finding you. Not even ten seconds. We were lucky last time, and they have now learned what luck we used, they are prepared," Visha clarified. "However, if there was something else as much as a target as you, keeping them occupied, you could slip through the old temple tunnels quick enough for them not to detect your presence."

Mal took his feet off the table and yawned, leaning back on his seat. "Silas might be preparing for one of you to do just that. If you think about it," he said, looking around. "It seems to be the only way. Both of them have some sort of blood track on. And it just happens that when they are preoccupied with one of you, the other doesn't seem to be of importance. Doesn't that make you think a bit about it?"

"Father has done it on purpose," Snow murmured to herself.

Oryn cleared his throat and looked over at Moriko. "What about the Hanaian side?"

Mal shook his head. "We won't be able to fade within the Isline lands—elder magic surrounds the whole mountain range."

"Yes. But I am not talking about magic," Oryn explained.

"It could take weeks to climb it," Alaric said. "Without even considering the chances that whatever lives up there will even let anyone climb it at all."

"There is another way," the old Crafter revealed, drawing a line on the map through Hanai mountains to the Isline villages. "My congregation used to take the mountain route to the temples on the other sides of the mountains. We've visited Islines many times by foot."

"He is correct, there is a way," the Autumn Queen said, walking to Nia's side. "Just not a very nice one. There are tunnels running through the old mountains that take you to the Isline temples in Isjord. We sealed them all after the Terian War against Silas's father when they snuck through the night and slaughtered villages while they were sleeping."

"Once inside the temple, Melanthe would be no issue, right?" Cai asked and then turned to Visha. "How long could you keep Melanthe from being alerted of her presence if she keeps her magic tightly sealed?"

"A minute at best," Visha said after thinking about it for a bit. "The blood trace they have on is not only connected to their magic."

"A minute could be enough," Oryn agreed. "The tunnels inside the temples take you right over to the other side. I'll make the map for you."

"Can't someone just fade her to the other side?" Pen asked.

"The old magic around the mountains won't allow it. And besides," my brother said, "that minute might be cut short if I use my magic. Considering the beasts are appearing out of thin air whenever they can feel us use it, I doubt we would even have a couple of seconds."

I pulled Snow to sit on my lap, and murmured in her ear, "Eren has travelled through Islines. How about asking him to join you?"

"No. Whatever is out there is still haunting him, I know it. When he speaks of that place, it feels the same way as when I speak about that night at the solstice."

"You still don't want me to come?" I asked one last time. I had said yes, but my mind had begged to say no.

She nudged her nose with mine. "Nope."

Nope?

Not even no?

Nope?

34

Black Rook to D3

Snowlin

WE STOOD FACING A cave sealed by a boulder. Even all the way across from Isjord, I could feel the chill of winter down my neck. Unnatural winter. The season beyond was no blessing, no divine touch—it was all human and manmade, desecrated and stripped from all its meaning.

"If I say you grab my hand," Mal said to us as he tightened my sister's holsters. "You grab my hand, understand?"

Both Thora and I nodded, pulling our hoods up.

Eren turned to us three. I'd given the order for him to stay back. No matter what he knew about the Islines, I would not force him to face that place again. "Whatever you see out there, it will be something you've never seen or fought or felt before. The magic of these people is intense, so intense that they have created a sense of bonding with the environment. Like a morph bonds to a human. Do not try to kill anything that doesn't try to kill you first. Even if you see a beast, go past it, pretend it does not exist, even if it looks threatening, do not kill. It is very tempting to be afraid beyond there. They've preserved everything to remain the same as it was the first day Krig touched the land—fanatically. And no lightning," he said to me, and then turned to Mal and Thora. "No shadows or wind. Only ice. Casting magic out there is dangerous, especially for you, Mal. Their spiritual is not the same as ours out there. I've seen...I've seen grown men and women gouge their own eyes out only so they wouldn't see what the land beyond wanted them to see."

Thora's eyes were wide. "What the hells has happened to you out there, Eren?"

"Nothing I can properly describe. Do as I say, and you will find the north easily. Follow the wind, it will take you there. Never walk against it, only where it sends you."

Mal threw an arm over my shoulders and Thora's. "Scared, ladies? Why so?" The smug fool smirked. "Big bad Mal is here to protect you."

Eren ruffled his hair and the younger Castemont remained stunned on the spot. "Big bad Mal also used to pick on his boogers with a crane."

Mal shut his eyes, his head dropping back. "Fuck me."

"I'll have to pass on that," Eren muttered, fixing Thora's hood.

The corridors were wet and dark, thin stalactites hanging from the ceiling, dripping all over the muddy floor.

I shot a thin line of lightning ahead, the magic travelling all the way to its end to find it empty. Instead, something else just as fearful caught our eye.

From the sturdy walls, frozen figures protruded out the rock, petrified from the saltiness and the cold atmosphere of the cave.

"They must have never realised," Mal said, waving the torch around to illuminate each and every one of them while we passed through. "Probably came here to hide from the cold only to be deceived by it. There is still fear lingering around them, but they didn't die from fear or with fear."

Thora grabbed onto his sleeve, her hold tight while she closed the distance between them until her arm was brushing his. She wasn't scared. Not for herself at least considering the way she carefully glanced at Mal.

Cold wind blasted around us as we exited the tunnel, howling and sharp. Where once stood a proud Isjordian village, remained only a graveyard sunken six feet under snow. The only thing still visible was the temple, protected by dark craft.

The veil was still there. And the memories it had induced once were still fresh in my mind, too. Luckily, we deviated around it, into a stray selection of hidden tunnels under Krig's statue. Oryn's map had cut our search to just a couple of minutes, and before we knew it, only a wooden gate creaking from the billowing wind separated us from the other part of old Isea.

Mal pushed the door open, the old, rusty lock easily giving away. The howling wind of the true north blasted right into our faces and plastered about a layer of frost on my poor skin that would need some long recovery from it.

The moment I gained footing on the dense snow beyond the door, I lost my focus between the mile long white canvas that appeared to have no end and no start.

Thora followed shortly besides us, not at all bothered by the cold, the wind, or the thick snow. By nothing actually. She let a thin layer of wind wrap around and shield us from the harsh environment.

Mal swung to her. "No magic, bird."

"You want to die? Besides, it's barely anything and we aren't using it against anyone."

Mal threw me a side glare. "Did *she* have to come?"

My sister huffed and then reduced the wind bubble to wrap only around me and her, leaving Mal in the blistering wind. That reminded me why I'd asked her to come.

"Fine!" he howled, clenching his jaw tight from the cold. "Fine."

"If I wasn't so nice, Malik," she said, extending it again to cover him, too, "you would have been a pretty nice ice sculpture."

With Thora clearing our path from the foot tall snow and Mal directing us towards where he could feel life, we headed inside the heart of Islines—what remained from old Isea.

I was the moral support companion. And for the first time, maybe a silent companion because I had done and said nothing as I stood between the bickering two. They had not stopped. Jabs after jabs, insulting every inch of each other's looks down to Thora's apparently crooked small toe. Which my sister seemed to be particularly sensitive about because she almost knocked him unconscious with a slap. Mal had laughed and that seemed to set her off even worse. Now they had fallen silent, shooting one another a taunting look from time to time as if to see who will crack first.

Like Eren had said, Islines were full of odd life. The creatures were some of the ugliest, but they had remained quiet, in a rogue path ahead and unbothered by anything around them. A herd of some feathery looking sheep with no eyes had even accompanied us for a part of our trip. Not even acknowledging us, yet also being aware of our presence. Even the frost covered trees breathed with life, twisting in our direction when we went past them. Watching and observing like everything else around.

Something caught on my foot, and I stumbled forward, almost face planting the white ground had Mal not caught me. I felt liquid soak the insides of my leathers and then a fresh sting on my flesh. There was a slash across my boots that had lessened the impact of whatever had almost cut my leg off. "Fuck, that hurts." Why was everything hurting more these days? Was it age? Was twenty-five the end of it all?

Mal bent down and surveyed my leg, tearing parts of his undershirt to wrap around my calf. "Dispel the snow, little bird. Something is hiding under it," he said calmly, surveying our surroundings while putting the last knot on the makeshift bandage. "You alright?"

"Just a little cut."

He looked up at me. "Yeah, he'll still kill me."

Thora did as told without hesitation, lifting tons of snow in the air and dispelling it to create a mile radius of barren rock around us. "Nothing."

"I would have felt a presence, Mal," I said, attempting to set my foot down. "It must have been a rock or—"

He put a finger to his mouth, slowly standing. His sword was in his hand and slashing forward before I could blink twice. Where once stood nothing but air, a shape materialised, turning visible and dropping to the ground. The remains were not human. Not quite a monster either. A mangled, thin shape made of several arms and legs with a ghastly head in the middle.

"Seven hells, that is one ugly creature."

Mal shot me a stunned look. "It has feelings. Feelings you can hurt."

I rolled my eyes. "Apologise for killing it and then I'll apologise for hurting its feelings."

Thora jerked forward as if she'd been kicked, and landed on the ground, groaning and clutching her side.

Mal faded right beside her, helping her up and wrapping an arm around her waist, carrying her as he came to help me. "Up, my queen," he teased. "Or Kilian will have my precious dick served to street dogs."

I pushed myself up, lifting my sword towards...well, nothing. "I can't feel any presence. No heartbeat. Nothing is disturbing the wind. Or the electricity."

"It's because they are not a presence. More like a manifestation. My father might have mentioned something like this some time ago. A lingering presence that feeds on magic similar to the Fogling, except that these have never even breathed air or possessed a soul. They just simply exist out of nothing. Like most of the creatures we've passed today. Empty, just holding onto some odd sense of life."

I spun around, searching for anything. "How can you see them?"

"Because they are alive. They emit life. Some sort of life my magic seems to like." His stupid smirk was back. "This suits my taste well."

"No magic, Mal," I warned.

He cocked his head to the side, black spidery veins crawling around his eyes. "Just a smidge."

"Can I cut your legs just a smidge, too?"

He cracked his neck, shadows pulling away. "Fair."

Thora unsheathed her daggers, tentatively swinging them around in the air. "Do you think they are what Eren has seen?"

"Don't know," I said, letting ice slip over the ground around us. "But we can find out now."

"Here goes my dick," Mal sighed.

"It will be one short story to tell," Thora mumbled.

He tugged her harder against him and bent down to murmur something in her ear that had her writhing and screaming. His head suddenly snapped up and he covered her mouth with a large hand. "Shhhh, little bird."

Still holding Thora, he faded beside me and slashed his sword a hair away from my left shoulder.

Another creature fell slain to the ground. Black blood and bile getting on my leathers. Ugh. "This was my favourite pair."

"Fuck," he hissed, spinning round.

"What?"

"Don't panic, but about a hundred of them are closing in on us."

"On the ground?" I asked.

He nudged the thing laying slain on the ground, kicking its three fingered foot. "They seem to have legs, so yes, on the ground."

Thora looked at me, already reading my intentions. "You think we can be fast enough?"

"My poor pride might never recover." I clasped my sister's hand and we both lifted the other forward. At the flash of a second...countless, tall, sharp shards of ice rose around us, piercing everything above the ground until we were locked in the middle of a field created by them. Bodies and black blood became visible, the latter dripping and sliding between cracks of ice until it soaked our boots.

When the ice melted away at our command, a graveyard of mangled bodies encircled us, and somewhere in the distance, a faint trickle of a pulse caught my attention. Eventually, the count of heartbeats began doubling and tripling. Steady heartbeats—human heartbeats—resting hidden right below the mantle of their cold blessing.

The men poked their heads out of the snow piles they had buried themselves in, finally giving away their disguise. They were dressed rather lightly compared to us. There was only a thin layer of brown leather and pelt between them and the blistering cold.

Standing at their full height, they pointed the end of their bone spears toward us, muttering all sorts of curses and prayers in old Ysolt to their unheeding God.

Shivering, really.

How had they managed to have the odd creatures protect them?

In fact, how did they manage to have such control over every creature existing in their land?

Murmurs grew like the buzzing of bees when they slowly approached us, studying me and the colour of my eyes.

"What are you?" an older man rasped in the old language, narrowing his icy gaze on me.

"My name is Snowlin Edlynne Krigborn, first of my name, blood and kin of Edric, he who wore the first crown. Queen of Olympia and the seven skies." I'm sure I'd missed something.

"And Queen of Adriata," Mal said, clearing his throat.

"And Queen of Adriata," I repeated.

"We know who you are," a gravelly voice called, and the Isline men parted for the gruff giant with excellently plated braids to go through. Even buried under those thick, pale blonde brows that needed a desperate trim, his yellow eyes met mine. "Kin knows kin and the winds have spoken of you. He asked what you are, not who."

I didn't tell him that we were kin as much as penguins were kin to chickens, but I did raise a brow at him. "What I am is also who I am."

"I'm afraid word play is not our thing."

"Don't be afraid. And since we are past introductions," I said, clasping my hands behind me. "Where is your queen, I need to see her."

"We have no queen."

"How progressive of you to abolish the monarchy. Foolish, however, considering it might now be free to take."

He surveyed me top to bottom, the strange eyes we shared lingered over my scar and then my eyes. "Are you here to take?"

"Gods, no. Krig would absolutely shit himself from laughter if I did though."

Few gasped, and the man narrowed his eyes on me. "Then what have you come to do where you are not welcomed?"

I put a hand to my chest. "Where is the kindness?"

"You are the child of a traitorous king."

"Ah, another man after my pride. I need a word with your queen."

"I told you, we have no queen."

Huh. Had Skadi's sister died? "King then. Priest, shepherd, bard, whoever you follow."

"He is listening."

My brows rose. Did Skadi know? "Your Majesty," I said, flashing him a smile. "I've come to bargain."

He spat on the ground. "Bargains are evil's doing. We do not bargain."

"You will find dealing with this evil rather merciful."

"We are in no need of mercy."

"It is because of mercy that you exist. How easy it would have been for my ancestors to have killed you instead of banishing you here. The very foundations you stand and sit and slide on are made of pity and mercy. But my father is less graceful with his mercy than his predecessor. And once he assembles what Tenebrose failed to, you will be the first he will come after."

He was quiet for a moment. "Assemble?"

"The Octa Virga."

Few more glances and gasps were exchanged. What an impressionable crowd. Knowledgeable, too, it seemed.

"Why should I believe this is not a trick from your father to have us lower our guard?" a tall woman standing beside him said, stepping forward. Another prime Verglaser by the colour of her eyes. Perhaps another Krigborn?

"Lower your guard? Dear, you have no guard at all. My father has been roaming your mountains for months searching for the sceptre piece hidden in your temples and you've not once caught him. I came here without a hitch, a minute's walk from Isjord to here. Did you know that?" I stepped forward. "If I wanted your lands, I would have taken them with a toothpick and a dream."

The man and girl shared a look. "What are you asking?"

"Not asking, I'm offering you a choice. Die here, expecting. Or die in the battle that is about to ensue."

"It is not much of an offer," the king huffed.

"It is not much of a choice."

The woman sneered. "Your father has no business with us. I'm sure he will be satisfied with whatever he steals from the rest of you false believers."

I shook my head. "Not when you have something he desires."

"And what is that?"

"Your death. As long as you live, you have something he wants."

Looks were exchanged—concerned looks—but the man still said, "We will take our chances."

Thora stepped by my side. "Our father has already started killing you. The war might not be your place to die and he might not be interested in having your lands, but he is killing you, nonetheless, without you even realising. Has winter left since it last came?" she asked, her old Ysolt strong—much stronger than mine. "When have you last seen skies, sun, fruit, and herbs? Winter was a blessing and a cleanse, not the suffocation it has become. If *I* feel it, I'm sure you do, too." She lowered and sank a hand in the snow. "This is no blessing. This is not our God's blessing. Not his curse either. This is a grave. And you're being buried. Abandoned. Godless though you still waste prayers to someone who has already abandoned you."

"Strong words from such a small thing," the Isline King sneered, his smile cruel. "To make wild claims in the name of our sacred is deserving of death in this land. Have you come to die on my lands, child?"

My sister stood, her hard gaze landing on him. "Wild is the assumption that you can kill me before you are buried alive in your pitiful blessing."

He stepped forward, his sword in his hand and aimed at my sister who slipped from my grip and walked right to the edge of it.

She grabbed the steel and directed it right to her throat. When blood began soaking and staining her grey leathers, Mal's chest rattled with a low growl, shadows raising around us.

"Wait," I said, grabbing him. "He will be ash before he even thinks of hurting her. Let's wait a moment."

The barbarian king's eyes travelled between the three of us and then at the thunder above before they dropped back to my sister's. "What is it to you if we die out here or with you?"

"Fear," Thora said. "Father fears you. You ride besides us, and we have the pleasure of seeing him seethe with fear. Your numbers will not raise us or cost us, but it might be what will cost the King of Isjord courage and what might give his people tenancy to their own decisions. If he sees you ride with us, he will fear. If people see you ride with us, they will think twice about riding with him."

Mal smirked, and murmured under his breath. "Little bird is a little wolf."

"Fear," the king repeated, looking over at me. "For fear."

"For fear," I agreed. "And your magic. Only ice can break ice." *Only a fraud can deceive another fraud.*

He slowly pulled the blade away and stepped back. "Who rides against him?"

"My kingdom, Olympia. My husband's kingdom, Adriata. And Hanai, too. I expect more to join."

The look he had on did not warm up, but the harshness lessened. "What an impressive foe your father has created."

"Numbers are solely numbers. And my father has more."

"I meant you. A creature like you."

Mal slid before me, his eyes dark and his voice darker. "Call my queen a *creature* again, I dare."

The king surveyed the darkening shadows and raised a hand. "An honest mistake. I will remember it in the future."

The woman who had stood next to him looked livid, grabbing onto his arm, and pleading, "Papa, you can't possibly—"

"Only ice can break ice," he echoed back, repeating the words King Edric had said to his two sons, Isline and Tenebrose, right before they had decided that they would solve their dispute for the throne with violence. From the look he gave me, I was thankful to have paid attention in that particular history class and that he still believed King Edric was not an absolute cunt of a man. "If there is a threat to my people and the land we were bestowed to protect, we ought to take it to heart."

"Do we have a bargain?" I asked when Thora retreated to my side.

The king nodded. "Have your bargain, Krigborn child."

I grit my teeth and held back the tongue that wanted to say 'Skygard'. I handed him the plaque Visha had prepared for me. "It is a means of communication." When he took the grey stone, studying it with some horror, I added, "It will heat and glow when I send a call for you. Speak my name to it when you wish to communicate with me."

"Dark magic, papa," the woman snarled. "We do not mess with dark magic."

I cocked my head to the side. "Just magic, princess. It can't be any darker than plain magic in the hands of the wrong Aura." Before we turned to leave, I asked, "What happened to Skadi's sister?"

The king froze. "Skadi? How do you know my aunt?"

Well, well. "Do you know where your aunt is?" I asked, avoiding his question that could possibly turn them against me—depending on what Skadi had done to deserve her banishment.

"Dead."

That drew a giggle out of me. "Says who?"

"My mother."

"And why would your mother lie to you?"

He frowned. "My aunt was killed by your father when she was banished."

"Why was she banished for?"

"What game is this?"

I rolled my eyes. "The answer cannot be so complicated."

"It is not. Our rules, however, might not seem...as easy to understand by outsiders."

Heavens. "Well, humour me."

"She wanted a child."

"Heinous."

He grunted. "By means not accepted by Gods."

"Oh. Is coitus forbidden in these lands? Do men just hand women a tablespoon of their...*seed* when they wish to reproduce?"

He looked over at my entourage. "Is she trying to be humorous?"

"Afraid not," Mal said, holding back a laugh.

The king turned to me, and calmly explained, "By means of dark magic. A Crafter is what you call them."

I blinked. "Why, were your own men not willing?"

He looked over at Mal again and sighed when he remained positively serious. "My aunt was a warrior, a huntress. She went on week-long hunts and fed villages with it for months. During that time, she also sustained injuries, suffered malnourishment, and slept in rough conditions. One's body can only do so much despite the gift of magic. When she settled and got crowned as queen after my grandfather, village healers told her of her situation. She could not bear a child. From then, she became inconsolable, seeking all treatment there was until she stumbled by one possessing dark magic who promised to find aid for her condition."

"That's it? She sought help so she could be a mother and you banished her for it?"

The woman next to him bared her teeth at me, almost growling like a wild thing. "We do not need judgement from an outsider."

"A punch more like it," Thora muttered, pulling me back. "We will speak soon. Farewell."

My two noisy entourage had not spoken a word after we'd left the Islines. But once Thora settled in one of Visha's chairs and sighed, holding a piece of cloth over her neck wound, Mal exploded, "You irresponsible girl."

My sister blinked at him. I blinked at him.

"Do you have any idea how dangerous that was?" he spat loudly, pointing a finger at her. "What were you trying to do, have your pretty head end up on a pike and roasted along their pines to have for their next lunch? He would have not thought about it twice, Thora, I saw his intentions. He would have gutted you if he had not been scared shitless of your sister. What when she is not there, huh, will you test your luck again? Will you grab a man's sword and put it to your neck again?" He stopped for a breath and then narrowed his eyes on her. "You didn't listen to anything I said, did you?"

My sister offered him a little smile. "Got a bit distracted after you called my head pretty."

His head dropped back. "You're five feet too small to act like this."

"Five feet four," she corrected. "And a little half. But I'm still growing into it."

He turned to me. "When the Gods gave me patience, they were not prepared for this. How are you fine with what she did?"

"I'm not. Just waiting for you to finish."

Thora shot to her feet. "Snow, please, you know I did nothing wrong."

"It was dangerous."

Visha slipped inside her quarters and sighed, pinching Thora's sleeve and pulling her towards another room where a healer was waiting.

Once she was gone, I asked Mal, "You think she is pretty?"

He cocked his head to the side. "Unsettlingly so." His big hand wrapped around my jaw to squeeze my cheeks together while he shook my head until my brain started to rattle against my skull. "But you're prettier."

"Liar," I spat.

His wolfish grin grew wicked, and he backed away to leave without denying it.

The room was silent when I entered, and Kilian was not in his usual spot on the table besides the window where he did his work. Papers were neatly folded on top of each other, and he'd placed the seal back in its place, meaning he was mine for the evening. Shedding my leathers and quickly slipping through my night gown, I stepped onto the bathroom where I could smell his scent of lemon flowers.

He'd laid in the tub with his eyes closed and head propped back, his strong arms grasping the sides.

Some gazed at stars. Some gazed at sunsets. Yet I'd not found either as fascinating as I found him.

As usual, he remained still, waiting for me to make that first move, but his mouth twitched just slightly as if he was withholding a smile.

I pulled a stool and sat behind him, pouring some soap on my palm and lathering his hair with it. It was then his face broke into a stupid grin. He groaned softly when I massaged his head and rinsed his hair that had grown long enough to put it in small ponytails. "What did I do to deserve this?"

I curled my fingers in his hair and pulled his head back to kiss him. Warmth curled in my stomach when his tongue slipped in my mouth and he pulled me closer. "For resisting the urge to come after me." Nia had told me the man had been half mad before he'd retreated back to our room. She had kept a close watch on him till he'd finished all his work, doubting that he might truly come after us.

"Am I to be rewarded any more?"

"Maybe," I said, standing and returning with a razor.

He raised a brow at me when I began lathering his face with soap. "I thought you liked my beard."

"I do. But I still have burns on my thighs from it. Sacrifices have to be made."

He slipped a hand right between my legs and softly brushed his knuckles an inch or so from my core where my skin had turned red the last time his face had been there. "How did it go?"

The touch made me suck a short breath, but his voice demanded my attention. "Business talk, huh? What have you done to my Kilian?"

He chuckled, his fingers gently skimming the rest of my thigh. "Speak to me. Anything."

"It went well. I think."

"Hm."

"Hm? What do you mean by *hm*?"

His silver eyes peeled open. "Did you threaten them?"

"No?" I couldn't particularly recall. Had I? Even so, did it matter?

"No?"

"No. And why would it matter?" I washed the soap from his face and kissed him all over. Particularly the little dimple on his chin that had been hidden all this time. "There, my pretty man."

He stood up straight and hooked an arm around my waist, hoisting me up effortlessly into the bath. Clothed. And the water was freezing.

"Kil!"

He silenced me with his mouth. "Love of mine," he murmured, smiling against my lips. "Don't mess like that with my poor heart. It is still pretty sore with worry."

I bit his chin lightly and kissed him again. "Oh, to be loved by a poet." My fingers sank in his thick hair, pulling him closer to me. "Oh, to be loved at all."

He tugged on my nightgown, ripping it apart in half before turning the rest of my undergarments into bare scraps. He pulled back just a little, looking worried. "You're freezing."

"The water is cold."

He frowned. "It is not."

"Kil, the water is freezing."

He frowned for a moment and then stood, lifting me up on his arms and taking us both out of the water. I sighed when he wrapped a massive towel around us, still shaking a little. He kissed my temple and set me on the basin counter. "Forgive me, I didn't realise."

"Warm me up then if you are so sorry."

He patted the towel over my wet hair, trying to dry me the best he could.

The absolute idiot.

Snatching and throwing away the towel he held, I wrapped my legs around his middle. "I was thinking of something along these lines, perhaps?"

He plastered his naked body flush against mine, letting me feel every bit of him on me. "Have I told you I love the way you think?"

I rocked against his hard cock. "Actions speak more than words it seems."

His mouth was hot against mine. So were his hands.

"Still cold?" he asked.

"No, it's just you," I said, rubbing the goose flesh on my thighs.

His mouth curled in a smirk and he kneeled before me, lowering his face between my legs to kiss the sensitive inner part of my thighs. "Open up for me. Feet on the counter."

There was no teasing or taunting, his mouth latched on my sex, sucking hard on that tightening of nerves until it felt like I was about to snap in half. "I love the taste of you," he cooed, flicking his tongue over my opening, licking at the wetness already gathering there. His hands came up to my body, palming my breasts and kneading them raw, twisting and playing with my hardened nipples while he fucked me with his tongue.

My hand shot forward, clutching and pushing at his head while I rolled my hips against his mouth. "Fuck, Kil."

"That's it, ride my face." He thrust a finger inside of me, and I cried out as release crashed against me, drowning me in haziness. He didn't finish, not until I'd stopped shaking. He lapped at me until he'd licked me clean.

When he fully stood, he hissed as he stroked himself like he was in pain. "That got me rock hard. What will you do about it?"

"Seems like a *you* problem," I said, reaching to wrap my arms around his neck, already knowing I was going to have to beg for it after what I'd said. But I loved begging him, being at his mercy, obeying what he said, being good for him. Loved all of it.

He lifted me up, arms wrapped tightly around my waist while he took us to our bed. "Warm yet?"

I kissed him, tasting myself on his tongue. "Getting there."

He lowered us down. "Yeah?"

"Yeah," I said, wrapping my legs around his waist and pulling him against me. There were not enough words in any language I knew to explain how just holding him against me like this felt. There were not enough hours in a day or days in a week to get enough of the high it sent through me to be held like this. Not enough lifetimes to douse the need. "Say you're mine."

"I'm yours," he breathed, his touch fanning over my arms, down my waist, and legs. His hands traced the silhouette of my body while he kissed me relentlessly, endlessly. Melting and moulding me into the most pliable shape.

I squirmed and writhed like a new flame trying to feed on his air. Only to find out that he's gasoline and that I was an uncontrollable fire instead. "Please, enough torturing me. Please. Please."

His massive hand wrapped around my jaw and bit on my lip. "Where are these manners when you go dashing inside burning flames, hm?"

I moaned when he gave me what I begged for. "I save them for special occasions."

His other hand dug hard into the flesh of my thigh, holding my hips steady as his thrusts picked up a pace. "You evil woman."

"Tell me," I breathed between kisses, my nails dragging against his biceps that had caged my head. "How does the dark side feel, my darling?"

His shadows slithered over my arms, pulling them up and over my head, pinning them still. "You first. Tell me in detail how it feels filling you up." The same shadows crawled back down my body, curling over my legs and parting them even more for him. He sat back in his haunches, looking down between us where his thick cock disappeared inside of me. "Fuck, love, your cunt feels so good." I'd rarely seen such a boyish grin on his face. He licked a finger, lowering it on my centre where nerves were burning like fireworks, circling the sensitive spot until my thighs started quivering and begging for that release it was chasing.

He pulled out of me and spun me around to my stomach, his shadows slithering under my belly to push my hips up for him. "Mmm," he hummed, brushing a rough palm down my spine and over my bottom. "My little hellcat."

I hissed when his palm met my skin once and then twice, and the burn ached so good that it was hard to cover the sounds even with my face pressed against the sheets.

Kilian's hand wrapped around the length of my hair a couple times and he pulled my head back just as he slammed back inside of me. "You deny me that sound again and both me and you say goodnight right now."

"I can't," I panted, my arms shaking. "Kil, I'm going to come."

"Tell me to fuck you harder. I know you can take it," he breathed in my ear. "Tell me this cunt is mine and that I can fuck it harder."

I wanted to scream yes, but my body was shaking to the point I was afraid I was going to black out. So I frantically nodded instead. "Yours."

There was nothing soft about the way he handled me. It was carnal, bruising, sinful. Yours and mine became so vague the more he fucked me. Yours and mine became such empty words from the way he so savagely claimed my body and I claimed his. Yours and mine were so simple compared to the way my body reacted to his sounds of wanton pleasure. So, so simple they became when he spilled inside of me. Grew entirely amorphous when my own release tore through me, breaking and breaking until I felt like the thinnest glass crashing against the thickest rock.

His breathing was loud.

Mine was louder.

"How pretty you come," he purred in my ears, slapping my sex and then rubbing the sting away, dragging a long and tired moan out of me along another rippling wave of pleasure.

I hissed when he pulled out of me. My arms could not bear the weight of my body anymore and I collapsed face down on the mattress. His mouth latched on my spine that still tingled with licks of electricity. He trailed gentle kisses all over my body, and then pulled my hair back to kiss my cheek. "You're going to go to sleep with my come running out of you?"

My eyes were so heavy. "Deal with your own mess," I mumbled, still hot, sweating and out of breath.

The mattress dipped when he stood and then returned from the bathroom. A gentle whack on my bottom made me jerk, my hips arching back just a little. "Warm now?" he asked, cleaning me up and then digging his teeth on my backside.

Apparently, I looked funny when I glared.

A string of laughter poured out of him and echoed all around our bedroom. He laughed cleaning up, dressing up, laying down, pulling me for a cuddle. It was suffocatingly hot, but I pressed my cheek to his strong arm that was wrapped around my head tightly enough to suffocate me.

Fine, it was a bit tighter than just that. "Why do you have me in a headlock?"

He jolted, his hold on me loosening. "Shit, did I hurt you?"

I cracked an eye open. "Kil, I'm fine, darling. Not going anywhere either."

"Before you end my life for not telling you earlier," he said, reaching the nightstand and handing me a letter. "Solarya sent word to us."

I shot up, quickly unfolding the paper to read the three short lines.

My shields have lowered for you. Magnus Llyr Vayr, King of Solarya.

I huffed, feeling slightly stunned. "What is this? A love letter? *My shields have lowered for you,*" I mocked, rolling my eyes at the melodramatic delivery of words.

"Let us hope he loves me enough to send love letters, my love," the fool said, pulling me to him again. "Maybe I can seduce him to help us."

I gaped at him, and he threw his head back, laughing some more.

"Not funny."

"It was a little," he murmured, tucking his head in my hair like a cat. "Love me now."

"Or what? Magnus will steal your heart?"

His whole body shook from chuckles again. "I love it when you're jealous."

I did not.

35

White Pawn to C5

Kilian

MAGNUS LOOKED TIRED AMONGST the many shades of emotion that crossed his surroundings when I made my way across his large throne room. Cora was nowhere to be seen, but Caspian had joined him today. His heir spent most of his life at sea, so if he had returned to land, they all knew what awaited ahead.

Magnus cocked his head back, studying me and the two guards behind me. "Might I suggest that if you've come bearing bad news to at least wear a smile. You've withered our sun, Night King."

"I believe that is because of your humour, Magnus."

The man threw his head back and laughed, hard. "You come alone. I would have not harmed your wife."

You would have not been able to. "I could not guarantee she would have not wanted to harm you." *And she probably thinks you have plenty of sons to spare.*

"Yet you asked to see me."

"There are more important matters at hand than my own grudges."

"Your wife does not think so."

"My wife was hurt. My wife had no grudges. She came for what she was owed."

"She killed my son. My. Son," the king repeated, and old, bitter pain seeped from his chest.

The pain of losing a child was one I often wished to never see, but as a king, he would have lost much more from the carelessness of his son. "It was unfortunate that what she was owed was a life. Whether it was yours, your son's, or her own, she would have taken it nonetheless and without doubt."

He sighed and glanced over at Caspian who stood tall and proud despite the disdain colouring his air—disdain for his brother. The heir was talked about all over the three seas. Bone and flesh of a soldier. Blood and magic of a healer. Given the way his emotions were so cleanly separated from one another, almost as if cut by a knife, he felt a different pain from his father. Betrayal. "You asked me to let him in my palace,"

Magnus said to his son. "You tell me if it is worth my grief to listen to what he has to say."

"Speak, Kilian," Caspian said. "There will be time for us to mourn our loss after we can no longer fear Silas Krigborn."

I nodded and reached for my baldric, wrapping a white cloth bearing the Olympian crest over the whitestone blade attached to a silver hilt carved by the finest artisan in Taren, and extending it forward to them.

"You need not concern yourself with gifts," Magnus grunted, raising a brow at my offering.

"It is a truth. Call it a gift or a curse after you see and hear it."

Caspian slipped down the dais steps and took the dagger from my hands before returning by his father's side.

Magnus's eyes went from narrowed in curiosity to wide with almost...horror when he touched the transparent blade and then the vines around the hilt that twirled over an eagle's head. His hand stilled over the letters engraved around the hilt. The letters forming his name. "What is the meaning of this?"

"That blade you hold was forged not long ago."

His brows pulled together. "Impossible. Whitestone was only mined in Olympia. Whatever had been left in Myrdur has already been unearthed by many. And that is without saying that any old smith who had the knowledge to forge one could not have survived the Night of the *Draugr*."

"It was not forged in Myrdur. But beyond."

He looked confused. "No one can move past the mist, no one can get to the mountains. Even if there were Olympians roaming beyond, I doubt...I doubt—"

"Millions. Tens of cities. A court. A queen. An entire kingdom concealed behind the mist that my wife's ancestors drew to protect their lands along with the many truths. Olympia never fell. There is no old or new Olympia. Myrdur fell. Only a tribe out of the thirteen to exist."

Caspian reached for the cloth bearing the Olympian crest, studying the eagle and the feel of the white cloth. "Snowlin," he murmured, and looked up at me. "She is their queen. The last Elding."

I nodded. "Crowned at sixteen by the twelve tribe leaders of the kingdom."

Magnus's shadows still poured with disbelief. "Who knows?"

"Moriko, the Grand Maiden and her second, and now you."

"Silas?"

"No. Not entirely."

"What truths?" Caspian asked. "You said there were other truths concealed."

And so I told them. All of it. From the beginning to this very end. The story of Olympia's survival, Silas's intentions, my wife's origin and her power.

Their horror was almost offensive.

Silence was heavy. It grew heavier when I saw the threat surrounding Magnus. "Aren't you afraid?"

"For her? Every day of my life. Of her? Never. Perhaps when her friend steals the last bite of her food. It's her favourite part of the meal."

Magnus shook his head. "She is not human."

"Then why does she feel so fragile in my hands? Why does she hurt and cry? Why does she bleed? How can I make it so that she is not?" *So she stops hurting every day. So she stops hurting so profoundly.*

"My sister's blood did not change from the time you spoke to her, met her, dined with her, saw her," Eren said, removing his hood and stepping forward. "If you did not fear her then, why fear her now? Is *knowing* all so frightening that your perception of her as a person has changed though she still is who she was back then?"

Caspian's eyes widened and he quickly descended the stairs again. "Eren Krigborn?"

"The very same. And made of the same blood that runs through my sister, the one you title as inhuman."

Magnus glanced from me to him. "You've been alive all this time?"

He nodded. "We come for a matter that needs more urgent dealing than my existence," he started. "Silas still has ears in your court. More than ears. Two of your members are conspiring to lead his soldiers inside Theros."

"How have you come about this?" Magnus asked, looking over to his son for support. "I cannot point fingers at my people without knowing well this is the truth."

"Malena, the old Lady of Grasmere, was the one to tell us. And no need to point fingers. We have both names," I said.

Caspian was still in somewhat of an awe, staring at Eren, ignoring what was being said entirely. "Does your father know?"

"Yes."

"So the prophecy lives," he said, and turned to me. "Is it still?"

"Yes."

The doors behind us groaned open. "It does not matter," Cora said, walking across the massive chamber to us, wiping blood from her fingers with the corner of her white dress. She stopped before Eren and ghosted a hand over his face. "Son. It is great to know you live. And I am glad your sister has returned safely back to you."

"Thank you, aunt Cora."

Magnus sighed, raking a look over her. "You went to *observe.*"

"So I did," she said, and raised her hands up. "But the Goddess gifted me these and I know how to use them extremely well."

The Sun King extended a hand to her in the distance. "Come to my side, Cora. I might start thinking you're a mirage soon. The deserts have seen you more than I have these days."

"Ever so amorous, my sweet husband," she said, throwing us a smile over her shoulder before going to Magnus's side. "Like the day you won my heart."

He cleared his throat when she settled on his lap. "They come to warn us."

"And we shall thank them."

"Is there a reason why you are bloodied?" I asked.

She looked down at herself. "A resistance has started in Whitebridge. It seems that the land does not wish to belong to us again—or live under our sun. Many injured have fled over these past few weeks and have overfilled our hospitals."

So we were too late. It had not been a trick. Silas really wanted to divide us all before battle. "And prince Arun?"

"Killed," Cora said. "A few weeks ago by his wife and presumably by her brother's order."

Hells. "My condolences for your loss," I offered. The two had lost two children within such a short time yet they carried their pain too graciously for the hurt they'd gone through.

Her eyes fell to the ground. "We should have known better, but my son did love her. And we thought she loved him back. Maybe she did. Just not more than her duty to her brother. Also, it happens that she had quite a bit of a following on her side." The Sun Queen's strong gaze faltered for a moment, and she turned to the fading sun setting on the balcony, almost seeking the comfort of it. Just then, I saw a flash of her real emotion. Bruised violet and fresh—grief was a harsh colour on her. "Enough of them to cause trouble, hence the blood. Whitebridge might not be entirely Cyra blessed, but the people are still Solaryan in all sense. Silas knows he will not turn the people against us and that his next best choice is to eradicate them. He wants to cleanse the land. He started with ours."

Eren said, "He's been planning this for a long while. He wishes to discourage you from facing what is to come, to lock you inside your walls, afraid."

"And what is to come?" she asked.

"The inevitable," I said. "He has the sceptre and Urinthia is mending it together. The Guardian will rise any day now."

The Sun King shut his eyes and heaved a heavy sigh. "It would come, the day would come."

"We come to ask you to join us."

His eyes snapped open, heat blistering the space between us. "And leave my kingdom?"

"Perhaps you will want to listen to what we have to offer before you consider Silas's option and wait to be slaughtered in your motherland. To listen to us and others that will join us in this war by making the same sacrifices as you. Meet with all of us in three days' time in Olympia."

Snow was already in her absolutely and barely anything of a nightgown, lying on her back in the middle of our bed, reading a bunch of letters. When I got closer to her, I realised she was reading my letters.

I don't think I had ever blushed in my life, but the ripple of dither in my stomach reminded me much of the same sensation I had often seen in others. Just the loose memory of what I'd written back when I'd been a boy made me cringe.

It didn't seem to have the same effect on her though. She was fully grinning despite the silver shine to her golden irises. "You were adorable. I think I fell in love again," she said, holding the letters tightly to her chest.

Collapsing beside her, I picked the letters from her hand and put them aside. A churning of jealousy soured my mood and I suddenly wanted all of her attention—I was greedy for all of her attention. "Don't love him. He was an idiot."

She climbed over me, straddling my lap. "My idiot. And since are you no longer an idiot?"

I smacked her plump arse and pulled her down to me. "You have a way to my heart, woman. Certainly with violence."

She cleared her throat, resting her chin on my chest. "Your Winter Princess, huh?"

"You were," I said, running a finger down the bridge of her nose. "My Night Queen."

She bit on the tip of my finger. "I am not sure what I am at this point. Might as well be that, too."

"Have you thought about returning to Valda Acme?"

Her features sharpened. "Heavens will not get the pleasure of my company ever again. Not unless they have it in them to repent. On their knees. Possibly bleeding in some form. Suffering without blood is rather pale." She wiggled her fingers almost to signal marvel. "I'd love to see some heavenly blood."

"Are you not curious? Of who you are?"

"No, Kil. All I already am is enough and sometimes too much. It might have been different before, but not now—not anymore."

"Before?"

"When the solution to my nightmares was to destroy all that had caused them."

"And now?"

"I don't want it any less, Kil. I am just tired—tired of getting so close to it only to lose something else. If I knew what I was able to do, I would have not hesitated to use it. Now, the less I know the better. And...my nightmares are not so terrifying anymore. The darkness does not hold so many monsters now." She sighed, trailing her fingers down my face. "Magnus will join us, won't he?"

"He will."

"Of course. I only killed a son. He has like seven others."

"Six. Arun is dead."

"Hells. Who got to him before me?"

I shook my head. "Silly girl."

She giggled, sticking her hands under my shirt. This dream of mine looked so happy. "Should have seduced him. Gotten it over and done with."

There was a sharp knock on our door, and Snow shot straight up, elbowing me right in the stomach.

Thora strutted in with my brother following right behind.

"Keep your promiscuous hands off of me," the young one said, slipping from my brother's grip.

What had he done now?

The red fury around my brother made me arch a brow up. Could he not hide it or did he not want to hide it? "I caught her at Highwall."

"Caught?" Thora choked out, stunned. "Caught? What am I, some sort of prisoner? I can stand guard."

My brother howled with cruel laughter and then sneered at her. "Little bird, I cannot keep chasing you around."

"No one is asking you to. And I am not for you to keep in a cage."

"Keeping you safe is not keeping you in a cage!" my brother bellowed.

Snow tilted her head back to me, frowning and confused. "Does this seem familiar to you somehow?"

I wrapped an arm around her and pulled her to me. "Look again."

Her mouth parted a little, studying my brother and her sister. "Ah."

"Nia was there with me!" Thora screamed back in his face.

"Nia is capable."

Hurt crossed her young face. "I am, too. And you don't know what I am made of either, Malik! I trained with Snow! I was my father's soldier as she was! I was his killer!" She took a deep stuttering breath, attempting to calm herself down and locking herself in her own invisible cage instead. The change was so sudden, from one face to the other. More than a mask. A separate reality that she could switch between.

Snow tensed for a moment in my arms, knowing the look well. She stood up entirely, reaching her sister's side and cautiously sliding a hand through Thora's. "Hey."

The little sister turned to hug her, but pulled away as if she had caught herself doing something she wasn't supposed to do.

My wife's brows dipped lower, and she hugged Thora to her despite her hesitation. "Talk to me, Rora."

"I don't want you to protect me anymore."

"You can't ask me that."

"I am not your responsibility anymore."

"You are my sister," Snow said harshly, hugging her tighter. "It is what sisters do."

I turned my attention to my brother who was still exhaling fumes of anger, demanding an explanation that came before the question. "She had joined the ground guard in Isjord. Kirkwall."

Hells.

"Rora!" Snow bellowed.

The younger sister turned to me. "Tell them it is not this bad."

"You are powerful, Thora, but all three of you most probably have a blood track on you." I glared at Mal. "Perhaps if he had taken the time to explain to you why that was so very wrong."

"He told me," she said, lowering her eyes. "Fine. I was in the wrong." Thora kissed Snow's cheek and turned a withering glare on my brother while the two walked outside. "I hate you," she hissed under her breath.

Mal put a hand to his chest. "And here I am, thinking that you loved me."

Once Thora stomped away, Snow stood from the bed again and caught up with my brother, shutting the doors so I wouldn't hear.

They were there for quite a while.

She spoke more than him from the faint whispers I heard.

When she returned to my side, she looked tired and upset, her pretty dark brows all tense. She curled up against my chest, burying her face there. "He saw."

"Saw what?"

"All they did to me in Isjord. I didn't realise why they had not tortured him until he told me they'd made him watch me."

My blood grew cold. The night grew colder. "He told you that?"

"He did. That was why he was so angry at me." She swallowed, and whispered so faintly I almost didn't hear her, I stayed."

"Stayed?"

Her fingers curled over my heart. "In there—in the dungeons. For days. Even though I knew how to get out."

"Look at me."

She didn't. Her hand slipped from my heart.

"Look at me, Snow."

Her eyes finally lifted to mine, empty again, her hands tight around my arms as if to not close into fists. "Don't ask me."

"You don't want to tell?"

"I don't want it to hurt you."

"Hurt me." I rested my forehead against hers, and begged, "Hurt me, please."

So she told me. Everything. Numbly recalling the details. Her voice foreign to my ears, cold and distant.

By the end, it did hurt. So, so much. More than I had thought it would. More than I thought I could hurt. But seeing the relief on her face, I'd ask her to tell me again. I'd ask her to tell it to me a thousand times until she was relieved from the memory entirely.

And I'd finally found what Silas had stolen from her.

Hope—he'd stolen her hope.

36

Black Rook to D8

Eren

IT WAS THE CINNAMON-SCENTED autumn wind that always brought me out of nightmares these days—it was always the wind. It dried my sweat and quietly calmed my terrified breaths, wrapping around me like a pair of comforting arms. The man sleeping next to me did not stir when I pushed myself up to rest against the headboard, trying to grasp hold of my reality and distance myself from what plagued my nights and my many thoughts. At night, I was still a soldier. In my dreams, the wind beating against my skin was harsh. And the scene that I saw there was an old one.

I ran a hand over the burned skin all over my arms, spreading frost over it until the pain settled again. The scars carved by blackfire were gnarly, sickening. Made by flames that burned like any other, but that was part of the deceit, as different from the rest...it burned a forever burn. It was made of dark magic—some of the darkest kind. Adriatians had tried to make sure nothing would come out alive that night when they had attacked. They had been prepared.

The doors to my room burst open and Lin strutted in, with heavy steps and breathing fast, followed by her husband who sighed and leaned against the door. My little sister paced back and forth at the foot of my bed for a moment before acknowledging me and her friend laying next to me, both of us...naked.

Cai opened an eye and groaned, going back to sleep as if this was just another time Snow had done this.

I clutched the sheets up to my chest and made sure my little sister remained unconcerned and not haunted by the visions of me naked. "Lin, what's wrong?"

She sneered at Kilian. "Aggravating man."

"Aggravating woman," he threw back at her.

"Are they divorcing?" Cai groaned, still half asleep. "That was bloody fast."

I sighed. "One of you talk, please."

Snow crossed her arms. "We are waiting for Memphis to return from Isjord with news from Skadi. She took Nia's potion last night."

"And? Where is the issue?"

"She wants to go to Isjord and see herself," Kilian said. "Doesn't trust it entirely until she can see it herself."

Cai laughed first, and then I followed. But it was not the right thing to do considering the shift in Lin's face.

My sister looked furious. "My bonded has not returned."

Kilian finally reached a hand to her. "She will return, my heart. Memphis will never be caught by them."

Snow took his hand. "But—"

"No *buts*, my missus."

I looked between the two sickly-in-love fools. "Why did you come to argue in my room?"

My sister threw me a scathing glare. "You two are the only ones left in the whole castle, would you believe. Can't go down the dungeons for advice, can I? They only ask not to be killed, which is the worst advice ever. Why on this earth would they want to even remain alive for?"

Cai's head popped up, startling her. "What did you say?"

Kilian dragged Snow outside. "We will let you get ready. We will be on the terrace waiting for news from Skadi and whoever is joining the meeting in the Dravan Isle later today."

I nodded. "I'll be up there in a moment."

Cai's eyes were still half shut with sleep as he got himself dressed. Tired as always, he stood and left a small kiss on my neck. "See you tonight?"

"Is there something between you and daylight that I need to know of?"

He huffed, trying to button his trousers. There was so much in his mind. There had to be. He was only ever so quiet when his mind was loud.

Just when he was about to pull away, I grabbed onto his shirt and pulled him to me, wrapping my arms around his body and just...held him. One, then two, and three. He didn't move. But I'm sure he wanted to, I could feel the way his muscles went rigid against mine. "What is it, Cai? You know you can talk to me," I whispered, not daring to raise my voice any louder and push him away with words—words he never gave me.

Perhaps he hadn't heard me.

It would have been better if he hadn't.

Because he so cruelly said, "If I wanted someone to talk to, I'd go visit my father's grave. At least he won't give me life changing advice that won't be so life changing for me."

Maybe I forced my smile a bit too much because he looked away, searching the whole room only so he wouldn't look at me. "Am I that bad to talk to?"

I'd always been told to not speak, to not say what I wanted to say or express what frustration I had. To not even think. By my father. My mother, too, had asked me to be quiet as talking would often only bring me trouble. Alaric and Lysander as well had asked that of me because they feared I would say the wrong thing and expose us. Somewhere between those lines, I must have forgotten how to say anything at all.

Maybe I should still do so. Maybe I really was bad to talk to.

It was alright, though. I didn't have to talk back. He could talk to me.

But he didn't even want to do that.

He rubbed his eyes, tired again—always so tired. "Eren—"

"You can go, Cai. Don't feel like you have to stay because you don't," I said, picking up some fresh clothes and heading towards my bathroom.

His arms wrapped around my middle, forcing me to stop. My eyes drew shut when his lips trailed kisses on my shoulder. But the soft sensation soon disappeared behind some foreign feeling that made my whole body shake, sickness filling my empty stomach.

Always needed, never wanted. That was my fate.

He went still, too, moving away from me. "Hey, what happened?"

"If I wanted to talk to someone, I'd find someone who does want to listen." I turned, giving him a smile and a light kiss that stirred my insides in a way no kiss should. "Go, I will see you tonight."

And he did.

He did leave.

As always.

And I could finally heave out all that I held back. If I could only retch what I felt, not only how I felt. If it could only empty my heart. And my head, too.

A soft knock rasped on the bathroom door and Nia poked her head in. After one look at me, she rushed to my side, digging through a pouch. "Take this," she said, lifting a small vial of a greenish liquid that smelled like rosemary to my lips. She helped me sit on the ground for a moment. "Cai didn't say it was your stomach."

"Cai?"

"He came and got me from my quarters, said you were feeling unwell. A headache. But he got that wrong." She gathered her knees to her chest, her voice was small when she said, "Doesn't seem like a stomach-ache either though."

"No?"

"Seems like a Skygard sibling sort of sickness. Silas induced type of sickness," she said, wiping a cloth over my forehead and down my temples.

That made me smile. "What is my cure, young Nia?"

"I've yet to make one," she said regretfully. "Tried for almost ten years and my specimen was never very cooperative. My treatments made her fussy."

I chuckled. "Sounds just like my little sister." I patted her cheek. "She must have given you loads of trouble."

"No trouble. But...but I worried a lot—Cai did, too. And he's become the same again. Same as he was back when she was in the thick of her rage. Distant. Only waking, eating, sleeping. I'm not sure if he even realises that the world has not stopped. That he is not the only one in it. That it is just him who has stopped. Stopped trying, too." She looked up at me. "You like him."

"I've never been known for my taste in men."

She snorted. "Neither have I."

That made me laugh, but coming down from that high was a little painful.

"I know how you feel," she said quietly. "I've felt like that once."

"Do I wear my heart on my sleeve?"

"No, not really, but I've learned to not rely on seeing shadows to know how one feels. Snow has no shadows at all. And Cai's are always so confusing."

"And yours?"

"Mine...mine have always been passing. I've felt all one can feel, but nothing really stuck with me long enough."

"Besides love."

"Besides that," she said, smiling shyly. "I think I am just too grateful to have what I have to acknowledge what I once did not have. Forgetting was easy for me. Snow, Cai, Alaric, this whole kingdom made it easy."

"Are you suggesting I try to forget?"

"You aren't like Snow, trying to grasp lingering pains to use as a weapon. On the contrary, you use it as a poison, as if existing is wrong and your past sufferings made it right again. It would be difficult to forget. Like with poison, you'd go into withdrawal. But...rewriting what you think of yourself, of your existence...that could be easier. It was easier for me. Your poison could easily be medicine with a little change in what part of your past you use. Roots, stems, leaves, don't use them. Use the flower. What came out of them. A loving, caring, bright, and righteous human being." The silence following her words was perplexing. "Am I wrong?" she asked a while later.

"No. No, Nia, you aren't."

She scooted a bit closer and leaned in to whisper, "He is waiting at your door for me. Will probably want to know what was wrong."

"He is?"

A nod. "What do I tell him?" she asked, gently resting a gloved hand on my arms, where the thickest burns were.

"My stomach. Tell him it was my stomach."

"Eren, maybe—"

"We do not talk, Nia," I said, standing and helping her up as well. "I don't think he even knows my middle name."

Kilian stood in the far corner of the terrace, leaning against a wall, all dark and brooding as he'd always been since he was younger. He watched my sister speak to her men, his eyes only on her even though Lazarus had gotten a little bit too close to his wife.

His brows dipped a little when he saw me, a reaction so minute it would have been unnoticeable on everyone else. His Majesty was too stern for his own good.

"Have I upset you, old friend?" I asked, clasping his shoulder, but the man was unphased by my nonchalance.

"Should it upset me?"

"No."

"Then why is it?"

"You put much unnecessary thought in what you see." I pointed my chin to Lazarus. "Don't you mind that he still circles her like a vulture?"

"Who cares who looks at her," he said, pushing his hands in his pockets. "When she looks at me like that."

I glanced over at my sister to find her looking at Kilian.

My arrogant friend puffed his shoulders a bit, dusting some invisible lint from his perfectly cut and ironed jacket. "I'm not scared of pigeons, Eren."

"You've gotten worse. A severe case of madness."

"Yet here I am, married to the woman I love. Your prick of a lover can't even guess your eye colour correctly."

Sigh. "He is not my lover."

"Hm. If I recall this morning correctly, both your di—"

"Fine," I gritted out, and he raised an amused brow. "We are...*lovers*."

Memphis cawed as she lowered from the skies, shifting into a large cat and rushing to my sister who almost squeezed her life out of her, hugging her bonded to her chest.

Snow unwrapped the letter attached to her collar and quickly read it, her shoulders raising and falling fast. Her face had paled beyond her normal colour.

It had not worked then.

Nia's potion had not worked.

"It has worked," Snow said, a stuttering laughter leaving her. "It worked. Skadi vomited the seedling last night."

"It worked?"

I turned to Cai's voice coming behind us. His face lit up with a grin when Snow flew in his arms, kicking her feet and writhing in excitement.

"I thought you didn't want to save anyone," I said.

She gave me an unimpressed look. "No matter how you look at this, it is a win against my father. Besides, I didn't wish to lose Skadi. She is more valuable than all of you think. Silas's personal guard is her. And she will be beside him during the battle. She might be able to give us an opening to him."

I bought none of that, but nodded nonetheless.

Contrary to the rest of the people on the terrace, I knew she'd cried every time a tree was cut in Isjord because squirrels were left homeless. She'd fought hard for their property rights. When she'd drafted a proposal to our father about and it had not worked to get his attention, she'd gone and stabbed the work men, nailed a warning on the city news post, and officially made the whole of Tenebrose think she was a witch sent directly from the frozen hells.

"What now?" I asked.

"We sneak as many of these inside Isjord," Kilian answered. "The rest we use afterwards. Whoever will remain."

Atlas rushed to the terrace, tripping over his robes and tumbling a couple of times. "V-Vrammetheni ships and Solaryan ships were seen entering Mahara's channel. Sailing towards the Dravan Isle," he said quickly. "Tristin sent me to notify you immediately."

I backed away, blowing a sharp whistle for Jayre who immediately launched from a mountain cliff in our direction. "I will go make sure that they arrive safely to our shores and keep away whatever might have followed them."

Cai grabbed my arm when I went past him. "Tristin and her Skye are there."

"I heard."

He sighed, his hand moving from my arm to my waist, and he closed the distance between us. "Nia said you're still unwell."

Jayre landed on the roof, lowering his head so I could climb his back.

"That is my problem, Cai."

His hold on me loosened and he nodded, backing off while I climbed Jayre and launched to disappear inside clouds—the only place I could think and talk and feel without being afraid I was doing them wrong.

37

White King to F2

Kilian

Snow got dressed rather languidly, alone this time. The black dress she wore had several chains dangling over her shoulders, arms, and chest, almost resembling an armour. For some reason, she even put her gorgeous, long hair up, pinning it at the back and letting silver earrings dangle down her ears. Her eyes were on the mirror, but from time to time, they looked over at mine, almost seeking reassurance. The crown she wore was Olympian, but it might as well have been Adriatian. The silver spikes were decorated all over with obsidian and dark diamonds that almost seemed to inhale every sunray in the room.

Sliding behind her, I picked up the reddest lipstick I could find and turned her to me, pinching her chin to stain her lips until they looked like the most perfect sin.

She smacked her lips together. "Pretty?"

"Very."

"Don't let me strangle Magnus."

"You wouldn't do that to the sweet man who writes me love letters and lowers entire city shields to welcome me into his home."

She hit me, kept slapping my arms until I caught her hands and spun her around, bringing her back against my chest. "I love you," I murmured in her ear.

She looked at our reflection in the mirror, and smiled. "More than your lover?"

"You're my lover. My missus. My mistress. My friend. You're everything."

I faded us at the high cliffs of Drava, watching Solaryan and Vrammetheni ships reach the shores. The meeting between kingdoms would be held out in the open sky as everyone had agreed. The mist had cleared off from the patch of land at Snow's command to allow them a safe approach.

Below us, a circle of chairs made of greystone gathered around to form a large circle with the Olympian crest engraved in its centre. Once, Gods had sat on those chairs, now they lay empty for us to fill.

Moriko and Nia stepped out of a portal. The two stood hand in hand, and sat right by each other, next to where Drystan was already waiting along with his Crafter.

Macaria arrived next, followed by two of her sisters.

And last was Magnus, Cora, and Caspian.

Tension was thick in the air, but Snow was calmer than I had anticipated. Though, the look on her face did make me slightly cautious. She looked battle ready—cruel smile, gleaming eyes, and steady heartbeat.

"So it came to this after all," Cora said, breaking the heavy silence accompanied by the crashing waves and the accusing stares.

"Unfortunately," Moriko answered, holding Nia's hand, her knuckles turning white because of how hard she clung to her wife. "This was unavoidable, it seems."

My wife's fingers curled, stopping right before they became a tight fist. I could see the words she wanted to say in the way she looked ahead.

I could have stopped him.

I was so close to stopping him.

This could have been stopped by me.

Except that she was wrong.

But she liked being wrong.

"Do I have permission to presume you have called us here to join you in battle?" Magnus asked.

"If I wanted your moral support, Your Majesty, I would have sent you a postcard," Snow said, slanting a look at him.

Nia cleared her throat. "Our chances would be greater if we stopped Silas and Aurora before they spread across the continent."

"What you are asking," Magnus said, "is for me to abandon my city at the mercy of none and volunteer my troops to join yours. We already have lost Whitebridge. And Silas's troops are now no more than half a day from my cities."

"Die in Dardanes soil or die in Solaryan soil," Snow said. "Choices are not lush, but fortunate for you, you still have the option."

Magnus tapped a shaky finger on his chair. "He will send Aurora where he finds it easier to send her. The army is just a start," he added.

He'd heard the plan from me, but he needed to hear it from her now, so I kept silent.

"His armies are a distraction," Snow assured. "A means to separate us from joining against him. The forces he's sent to Whitebridge and the Sayuri are nothing compared to those counted in the mainland camps. His plan is to keep you occupied for a few mere moments, perhaps even let you win, only to have you lower your guards for what will come next. And Aurora will be dealt with. She is not to be feared."

He sat up straight, looking at all of us before he turned to my wife, asking, "Dealt with? How does one deal with a Guardian?"

All eyes were on Snow when she said, "The same how they've dealt with her before. Using another Guardian." My wife's hands were shaking. She would forever be made a weapon of the realm if she were to admit her fate. "I will fight her like all my ancestors have."

"As well as I," I added. "We've created shields and magic and weapons against her and Silas's other monsters."

Cora spoke first, "But the sceptre is in Silas's hands. Do we even know how to control her?"

The Violet Witch pointed at Snow. "Her kind was given the duty to control Aurora when need would rise," Macaria spoke. "She can control her. I doubt Silas will be able to hold onto the power for long despite the machinery he's made. Once she's free from the bounds, Snowlin will be able to command her back to the sceptre."

A lie. Snow wanted her dead.

"And the Grand Maiden knew of all this?" Magnus asked.

"All Grand Maiden knew," Macaria confirmed. "The knowledge is passed to the new generation without fail."

He sneered. "So Eldmoor was aware of what Silas was planning all along when he wed a Skygard Princess? This could have been prevented at the roots? Is that what you are saying?"

"Not entirely, no," Macaria added. "When Silas married Serene Skygard, Valas and Urinthia had a meeting with him and his court, as the ones who guarded the balance that Silas was threatening to ruin. The reasonings she'd seen had been greedious, driven by a hunger for power. An alliance with King Jonah would have granted him a new position in the realm." She glanced briefly at my wife before saying, "But his intentions were also driven by love."

Snow's head snapped to her. "You did not just dare speak lies to cover your own faults."

Macaria swallowed with fear, but did not falter despite the electric threat ricocheting around the glens behind us, now relentlessly being hit by lightning. "That is the truth, Snowlin," she said to her, and turned to Magnus again. "It was tradition that a Delcour would join the Skygard as their hand—a spiritual guide. Urinthia and Valas never trusted Melanthe enough to send her to the Skygards after their last Delcour Crafter died, for her to be their guide through the powers even they themselves could not understand. So Valas, as the Grand Maiden at the time, sent my son under the guise of banishing him, led him to Alaric Drava, and hid the truth from everyone else after I'd told her of my visions that would soon turn into a message of Gods." Her hands shook when she revealed, "Under Nubil skies and on Krig's lands, stood three Eldingchildren."

"The prophecy," Nia said, her eyes wide. "You saw the prophecy before it was written?"

The air grew colder, and Snow breathed out frost. She'd been lied to again. "You knew all of it, all of what was to come yet you led my father inside Olympia?"

Macaria shivered. "Not on purpose. Not to destroy it. But to make sure you three would exist. He needed a Skygard, the plan was to use your cousin. But no God dictated it that way. Cranes and visions and writings on the stone predicted so much worse chaos to come. It had to be you. It was necessary that you three would exist. The balance of the realm was at stake. What would follow would be worse than simple destruction. It would be annihilation. A sickness that would have spread further than our realm—a sickness that has already started in many others." Her dark eyes glowed violet. "A dark new age has started. It has corrupted our land."

Snow's hands curled tightly and the skies above screamed her anger so loud that my hearing buzzed for a while after. She took a shaky inhale, her golden eyes crawling with red veins and unshed tears. "The balance of realms?" Her shoulders shook from the rough laughter that left her throat so heavy and pained. "The balance of the realms," she repeated, more to herself than anyone else. "My kingdom fell. My people were slain. My kin vanished, got used, abused, and tortured. For the balance of the realms?"

Macaria lowered her head with guilt. "Everyone gathered here needed to know the true burden of what is to come. The true burden that the realm has borne in order to keep alive. It is important to know."

Drystan cleared his throat. "I've heard all I needed to hear. We've built enough of a relationship between us to say for certain that Vrammethen will be by your side in this war."

"The unblessed will fight?" Macaria asked doubtfully.

The human king drummed his trembling fingers on the stone chair. "Indeed."

There was doubt in Macaria's eyes that jumped between his silent Crafter and us. "Eldmoor, too. Urinthia would have wanted it so. We might not have armies and artillery, but we have magic—powerful magic. From now and until he is defeated, Red Coven and our Crafters will be at your service."

I nodded at both.

"We have stood together before we even knew what we were standing together for," Moriko said. "Hanai will fight beside you, even if I have to leave my own city to the mercy of none."

Everyone waited for Magnus to speak, but the man had pinned his attention on my wife who silently writhed in pain beside me, her expression stolid and unforgiving despite the thick tears lining her eyes, refusing to shed. "You believe we can win this way?" he asked her.

She finally looked up, two stray tears falling down her face. There was steel in those eyes, anger, fury, and violence. Her mouth trembled more from rage and a desire to claim blood than fear. No, there was no fear in there. Not at all. "Yes," she breathed, and the thunder above struck earth and water.

"You already have a plan," Caspian said to Snow, his wide eyes growing wider as he stared at my wife. "You always had a plan."

"I do."

Magnus stood. "Then we ride with you." He bowed his head to me. "Both of you. Our troops will sail for Dardanes by tonight at the latest."

Just like that, it was set.

All six kingdoms would fight against Silas as one.

Snow's shoulders rose and fell rapidly. She stared ahead at the violent seas swinging from the angry command she gave the skies. Her whole body relaxed when I slipped behind her, wrapping my arms around her waist and resting my forehead on her shoulder.

One could only bear so much.

To hear your existence was manufactured only for suffering crossed any threshold. Yet she still stood tall before it all.

"Tell me," I breathed, begged.

She sucked in a sharp breath. "Every step I take, I learn something new about myself that I didn't wish to know. Take it all away, Kil, all I am supposed to be and all that they've made me, and then what is left of me? What am I if I am anything at all?" She turned in my arms to face me. "Purpose is all I hear. That it is my purpose. I am where I'm supposed to be, who I'm supposed to be. So I wasn't meant for anything else at all besides possessing this blood only to carry it further, controlling the sceptre, keeping peace, being divine?" She was breathing hard—choking with each inhale. "Myrdur was ruined. My family perished. My mother is dead. Two kingdoms almost thrown into war. And all for what? So I could suffer at my father's hands and ultimately die there, too?"

She stilled at the last words she spoke as if she hadn't meant for them to be spoken aloud, and so did I, the air chilling again.

"Snow, my heart. Who do you think will pry you off my hands so easily?" I drew her close to me. "Death? But I am it. Nothing can claim you. Not when I've claimed you first. Nothing will dare."

Her eyes drew shut and heavy tears slipped down her cheeks. "Hide me, Kil. I want to hide."

I unbuttoned my jacket and pulled her close to me before buttoning it back again. We stood there a while, a long while. She did not cry. She did not speak. Her silence was heavy and painful.

"Defy it," I said. "Defy this purpose. If you do not have the strength, then let me defy it for you."

She lifted her head again. A strange look in her eyes. Almost surrendered. But it shifted quickly. A realisation of sorts took over. And just when I was about to ask, she looked over my shoulder at the presence that had joined us.

I turned to Thora as well. She was standing there, waiting. Quiet. So quiet. She must have heard what her sister had said because there was no need to read shadows to know of her devastation.

"Yes, Thora," I said, and Snow pulled back a little to look at her, too.

"There is someone you still have not asked to join us."

Part IV
The Four
Knights Game

38

Black Knight to D7

Thora

MALIK DID NOT SPEAK one word to me while he helped me put my leathers on. The Adriatian contraptions were still heavier and more complicated to put on than the Olympian ones, but if I went to Olympia, Alaric was going to chain me to the dungeons and not let me do this.

Malik's hands slid down my thigh to secure the dagger holders, and I tried my best to even out my breaths. Failing when he went down to his knees to tie my boots on.

"Scared now?" he asked.

I kicked his shin. "Don't read me."

He finally raised his eyes up at me, holding my foot down so I wouldn't kick him again. "Read you? Bird, your heartbeat is going to drive me insane any moment now."

Not because I was afraid. It was because of something far worse. "You didn't have to come. You didn't even need to do this. If it is so annoying to you, just leave."

He tugged on my bow, pulling the ribbon until it fell from my hair. "I'd rather you not die and take my secrets beyond the grave where I cannot keep you silent. And you would have strangled yourself with these contraptions like last time. And lastly, luckily for you, I enjoy being annoyed." He pulled me to him. "Hold tight, bird, this will be a bumpy journey."

He had not lied. Fading between whatever forces or magic surrounded the Sea of the Dark was indeed bumpy despite the access we'd been given by the king himself. We'd waited for nightfall so his magic would be at its strongest, and it was still not enough. The moment we touched the city of Hellas, I heaved out all that I'd eaten during the day.

Golgotha let us through his stony, wet city with no issue. His creatures paying no mind at all when we passed through to his...cave? Castle that looked like a cave?

He sat on a dais made of bones, studying me from my hair and down to my toes. "You looked a bit different last time. Little angrier. Taller? Didn't you have a scar on your face?"

"I am her sister."

"Ah," he said, drumming his fingers on the chair. His eyes thinned, the irises elongating, resembling the eyes of a serpent. "You're a fascinating creature as well." His nose twitched, sniffing the air, and he turned to swivel a look over Malik. "Two fascinating creatures."

My friend looked annoyed. Unimpressed, too. "Your smell does scream fascinating to me, so if you're expecting a compliment back, move on."

Some more finger drumming later, Golgotha said, "How might I entertain you tonight?"

I blinked. "Tonight?"

"Well, you've chosen a bad time to visit. Near night. My creatures heed no call at the time of Henah. If they wish to attack you, I cannot stop them. This humble home of mine is the only safe space. We are one of a sort, you see, Henah and I," he explained. "Born out of the same womb. The eudemons get...confused. Tonight, you will be my guests since I'd rather not anger your brother or your sister," he said, turning to me. He clicked his fingers, and a large table loaded with all sorts of foods appeared in the middle of the cave out of thin air. "We will dine while you tell me about your journey."

Malik grabbed my arm, pulling me behind him. "Absolutely the fuck not."

"Impolite, but you have a point. The crab is...acquired taste," Golgotha said, descending his throne and taking a seat at the head of the table. "Sit. We'll discuss whatever you've come here to discuss."

Mal held a hand on my back the entire time, even after we'd sat, his fingers wrapping round my waist a little tighter each time Golgotha would look at me.

The fallen God took some big gulps of his blood-red wine. "You want me to join your war, is that it?"

"Not exactly," Malik gritted out. "You can't harm the human kind, it would be a useless attempt to have you out there with us despite your well-known skills in battle. And your creatures can barely survive a few hours on dry land."

"What use do you have for me then?"

"Melanthe Delcour, you know of her?"

"Urinthia's niece. Of course. Quite the troublemaker that one."

"She's gathered quite the power by consuming some blood of Aurora's lover."

Golgotha's pupils thinned again. "The immortal man."

"More than a man now. He's consumed Caligo blood and can turn into a dark beast. I know the Dark Crafters' magic will suffer with you around. And if the odds favour us, the beasts could, too. They will sense you as the biggest danger instead of us. Riveting and prodigious dark power tasting so akin to death it could mock it, and all of that crap unholy books say about you. You'd disable the Winter King's shields, stultify his strong line of craft defences without lifting a finger."

"So you want to use me as a target."

"Why would you be a target? The Winter King will have his hands plenty busy with us," Mal said, leaning back on his chair and throwing him a wink.

Golgotha chewed on some odd, dried squid leg, narrowing his eyes on Malik. "Well thought."

"I never think unwell thoughts."

Idiot.

The Demon King chuckled. "Arrogance was a good friend of mine. He would like you."

"I'm a likeable man," Malik said, leaning forward again, his hand moving a bit lower on my waist. "Will you join us then?"

"What do I win from all this bother?"

Malik's jaw twitched. "You'll get to see sunlight, breathe fresh air, touch some grass, and watch people slaughter one another. All four joys of life."

Golgotha's smile was serpentine. "The last should have been the first. I would have spared you your voice."

"I'm quite enamoured by myself, I like hearing my own voice."

I gaped at him, and he threw me a shameless wink. "Close your mouth, sweetheart, something from this shithole might fly in."

Golgotha's eudemon servant pointed a finger across the hall to a bedroom door and then at me. When it pointed again to another room for Malik, my friend grabbed my hand and pulled me to the first bedroom. "Like hells you are sleeping alone in this place."

"I wasn't going to," I said. "Was going to ask if you would stay with me. Perhaps you'd be scared enough of these pimply guys to cuddle tonight."

"Menace," he mumbled, smiling a little as he shut the door behind us.

The room was massive and oddly modern. Black wood furniture and paintings of all sorts decorated the windowless square space lit by grey candlelight. "Is it an illusion?"

"No. He is powerful like that. Can turn chaos into reality."

"Like the man who could spin wool into gold. From the tales."

He threw an amused look over his shoulder at me. "Like him."

"What now?"

"We sleep and pray this night ends faster than it started. The stink of this place is making me nauseous."

"We shouldn't have dressed for battle," I complained, tugging at a belt around my waist. "That man is smart. Scared when he needs to be scared."

He pulled me to him, undoing all the buckles holding up my leathers. His hands touched me where no other hands but mine had touched. Eliciting things no other man had elicited from me. "Don't do that. He wants us to underestimate him and lower our guard."

I lifted my hands forward, undoing his leathers as he was undoing mine.

He looked down at my fingers. "What are you doing, little bird?"

"Helping."

"I don't need help."

"Neither did I, but what are friends for?"

Thankfully, he didn't mention that friends did indeed not help each other undress.

After all the heavy stuff was off, he grabbed a thick blanket from the bed and laid it on the floor.

"The bed is big," I said.

"The floor is big, too. Any other observations you'd like to make?"

"Why are you being so mean to me?" I asked, crawling on the bed and jumping inside the warm covers that smelled of lavender.

"Go to sleep."

I knew though, he didn't need to tell me. He was angry I'd given Snow an ultimatum about coming here. It was my idea. Besides, Kilian would never let her return here without killing Golgotha first. Which would defeat the purpose.

I sighed, rolling back and forth in bed, struggling to find a comfortable spot. "Malik, for hells' sake, come up here." He'd never slept on the same bed as me no matter how many nights he'd spent in my room. But he'd never slept on the ground either, and there was no sofa around.

"Sleep, Thora, or I'll swaddle you with those sheets until you can't move."

I gathered my blanket and laid it on the ground, next to him, chucking a pillow at him, too.

"Thora, get up from the fucking floor."

"No."

"Hellion." He blew out a heavy exhale and hoisted me up, throwing me on the bed and then laying beside me. "Better?"

I spat some hair from my mouth. "Yes."

Yet, an hour had passed and I couldn't get my eyes to shut at all. Carefully, I turned to look at him. "Malik?" I whispered.

Nothing. Not even a little twitch. His breath was even, his whole body relaxed.

I shuffled closer just a little to his side and he still didn't move. "Malik?"

No answer again. Was he really asleep?

I'd gotten so close that his face was only a few inches away. "Malik?"

"What?"

I jerked a little. "I'm cold."

"That is such a shitty lie."

It was. "Alright, I'm scared." Not the slightest actually. This was quite thrilling. I'd always dreamt of going on quests and dark adventures, and this was the closest to one. Quite frankly, I was enjoying myself.

"The lies are getting worse."

"Lonely?"

"Getting colder and colder, Thora."

I swallowed. "Uhm, what if there is a monster under the bed?"

He peeled his eyes open and they gleamed black. "Why would it be under? It's sitting right beside you."

At that moment, one might have been scared. He did scare me, just not like he'd intended to. "You're not funny."

He wrapped an arm around my shoulders and pulled me to him. But it was not the first time he'd lent me that part of his. "I'm not a cuddler, little bird, so keep your hands to yourself."

"Alright," I said, resting my cheek on his shoulder. But my hands were twitching so badly from being told to be still. "Malik?"

He squeezed his eyes tightly, sighing. "Fuck. You can put your hands on me."

Phew. So I did. Except...now I could feel his hard body beneath my palm, the heat emitting out of him, his slow breaths. He smelled so good, too.

"Malik?"

His body began shaking, and I flinched, whipping my head back to look at him. Only to find him laughing himself to tears. "Yes, what now?"

"Can I lower my hand a little? It feels uncomfortable up here."

He grabbed my hand and lowered it to his stomach. "Good?"

No. No. Not at all. "Yeah, better."

It was too hot. Suffocatingly hot. Like I was wearing a massive wool scarf in the middle of July heat.

I forced an eye open, looking around the dark room, expecting to see sunlight from how rested I felt. There was no sunlight. But there were arms wrapped around my middle, a body plastered closely to mine from behind, and a face buried in the crook of my neck, breathing steadily. Instead of feeling creeping panic chill my skin as usual when I felt someone so close to me, my spine arched a little from the hot shiver travelling down my body, sinking a weight down my stomach.

His scent was all over me. In my hair, on my pillow, in the air. Rosewood, chamomile, and something else—orris. He smelled like morning rain on a field of flowers.

He shifted a little, his lips grazing my neck, and I pressed my eyes shut.

The moment my breath hitched, his inhales stopped entirely. He opened a large palm, trailing it up my stomach and resting it over my chest. "Breathe, little bird," he said, voice darker and coarser, heavy with sleep, and an ache suddenly pulsed between my legs when his hand lowered again, grazing a sliver of skin exposed on my stomach.

My heart was pounding so embarrassingly loud.

"Don't move," he said when I squirmed.

I froze. "Why?"

His fingers trailed barely there circles on my skin, dipping just slightly under the band of my trousers. His nose brushed my skin, and I shivered. "Just don't." One fragment of a moment longer, he remained there pressed against me, his hand slightly sliding further and further down, touching places that no one had touched before.

I flinched when he suddenly got up and sat upright.

I was panting. Struggling to breathe. My mind alone had just run about a dozen laps. If he'd moved his hand just a little lower, whatever friendship we had, it would have ended. "When do I move?"

He didn't answer immediately. "You can move now."

"Did you let a spider crawl down my back?" I asked, shaking my arms, trying to scare off the spider that could have potentially entered my clothing. It was something he would do.

"Maybe I should have. Get dressed," he said, collecting his stuff from the armchair.

"Where are you going?"

"To pray this bath has ice cold water."

Golgotha looked between the two of us. "Slept well?"

"No. You?" I asked, and he laughed.

"I don't sleep, girl."

"That explains the dark circles," I said, playing with a fork, trying to avoid looking at Malik.

"I thought about what you told me last night," Golgotha said, cutting through his breakfast. "About Urinthia's niece and the seedlings she has used to take control of the beasts she has created."

"And?" Malik asked.

"Presuming you are looking to kill her, that could possibly mean the death of those she has turned."

"All?" I asked, almost jumping from my seat. "But that's in the millions."

"Thora," Mal said, almost gravely. "He wishes to use that."

I blinked fast. "Use what?"

"The chaos that will ensue, the disruption of the balance of souls leaving for Caligo will overwhelm the Mid-world and the Otherworld. Each time you kill a beast, two souls will leave," Golgotha said. "It is tragic, very much so, but tragedy feeds me." He let out a sigh, abandoning his cutlery. "You can of course refuse. I will still join you regardless as I'd like to see Urinthia on the other side of my bed again. But that would be it."

Malik stood. "When will you join us?"

"As early as tomorrow. My presence could be discouraging to any courageous witch on the Winter King's side who might want to play before the war."

My friend nodded, taking my hand and pulling me towards the exit without another word.

"Snow would have said yes to what he asked," I said, trying to catch up with his steps.

"She would have not."

"I don't think so."

"Snow will fight more than just Aurora. She is already fighting herself. Adding a fallen God looking to feed his realm life by using the misery of her people is not something she would do. Choice or no choice in the matter."

He was right. Again.

Once we stood right outside the cave entrance, he turned to me. He pinched my chin and pulled my face up so I could look at him. "Why the awkwardness?"

"No awkwardness."

His eyes narrowed at me. "Stinks like a lie."

"Lies really stink to an Empath?"

"Don't play with me, Thora." He closed a step near me, our chests meeting each time he took a hard breath. "You know what else an Empath can smell?"

"No? Like literally?"

"No, not literally, but I bet it would smell just as sickly sweet as it looked. Pretend last night or this morning didn't happen or exist because I will."

"If I knew we could do this, that we could forget so easily, I would have done worse like I wanted to. I would have put my hands where I wanted to. I would have not left you aching this morning either. I would have let you have me however you wanted to have me. I would have stopped saving my firsts."

"Thora," he gritted out, his eyes drawing tightly shut. "Fuck."

"All is forgotten," I said, giving him a smile he would never buy. "All of it." I nudged his shoulder, trying to lighten the mood. "You are too easy to tease, Malik."

39

White Knight to E3

Snowlin

SO IT HAD STARTED. Our last ally had been made considering the smug look on Mal's and Thora's face when they crossed through the Fernfoss camps.

"Thought you'd send an army after us for not returning sooner," Mal said, throwing an arm over my shoulders.

"She did," Visha murmured from somewhere behind me, still not lifting her eyes up from the grimoire she was reading. "Golgotha sent word to shore that you were going to stay the night in Hellas. The king and her camped by the shores of Sitara all night just in case he'd lied."

"Matters not," I said, ignoring the snitch. "He agreed, I gather?"

"He did. Even wants to join us tomorrow and remain here to try and deter Silas's Crafters from playing any dirty tricks on us before the war."

"You believe that?"

"Not one bit, but I will be keeping an eye on him."

I glanced at him and my sister. At their frozen stances. At the distance between them. Narrowing my eyes at their side glances. "What's wrong with you two?"

He gave my sister a massive shove and stretched his neck. "She's been annoying me these days."

Thora got up from the ground, dusting her leathers, unbothered. "Thought you liked being annoyed."

"Moderately, little bird, moderately," he said, retreating and disappearing.

I raised a questioning brow at her, and she flashed me a sweet grin like she'd done when she was younger and didn't want to be told off. "We are getting ready now, aren't we?" she asked, linking an arm around mine while we walked back to the main tent.

Hammers, footsteps, and orders thundered louder than the skies above. There were many flags raised around the camp in Fernfoss that was now but a ghost of a village. Solaryan, Hanaian, Eldmoorian, and Vrammetheni insignia had joined Olympia's and Adriata's side. The colour of our armours and leathers were so starkly different, but we'd gathered to fight as one.

"Any day now, Rora. Any day."

Caspian parted with his soldiers and crossed the distance to us. "My father is leading the last group of civilians out of Theros." He searched above for the sun hidden between fog and clouds. "Are you certain Silas will aim for our city first?"

"Positive."

"Then why are we abandoning the city for them to take so easily?"

"Take? What are they taking? What's there to rob in an empty house? What do four empty walls turn to when the door is shut?"

He looked at Thora and then back at me.

"A trap, Caspian."

My little sister formed a circle with her hands, and whispered, "*The Snow Slaughterhouse*. That's what we've decided to call it."

He blew a long sigh, still doubting my plan. "Any more news from your friend in his court?"

"Ally, not friend." I handed him the last letter she had given Memphis. "His troops have left the northern and eastern camps and are preparing to march south and southeast. From there I presume they will head towards the west of Hanai and then Adriata."

He ran a hand over his jaw. "It is too soon. How do they plan on tearing the Adriatian walls down—" His words were cut in half when he read the last few sentences.

The sceptre has been put together. Urinthia has been seen by the guards down in the dungeons.

He folded the paper and sighed. "She will do it for him. So that is the plan then? You're commanding her back to the sceptre?"

Thora tensed beside me, her grip on my arm tightening.

"Not exactly," I said. "I have other plans for her."

He followed us inside the main tent where the whole lot was waiting, circling the massive map laying on the round table. I'd planned much in my short lifetime. Schemed. Plotted. But never war of this scale. My plans of war were more of a one-man sort of strategy.

Magnus, Alaric, and Moriko stood side by side. The three had once fought and planned war side by side, too. They were our advantage. But none had planned against my father. This was why Eren and I were the back up. We knew him best.

"The beasts," Elias said, leaning against the table and pointing all around the Hanaian border. "Stationed there mostly. From what other captains gathered, they are mainly being held on the main ground camps. Too difficult to move them on ships, most got sick the further they left from land."

"The gates of Celesteel," Macaria said from the corner she had sat. "The essence is still the strongest in Dardanes. Easier for the magic to draw fuel."

"Can confirm," Magnus agreed. "We haven't sighted many in Whitebridge and most have stayed within the island's waters."

"Isn't that perfect," I said.

"How?"

My fingers lit up with lightning. "Have you seen how easily human flesh melts? It is the mainland that bothers me. Moregan said that Silas has turned into beasts all those who had escaped Isjord after my visit. We might have to supply most of our *anima accissor* to the soldiers here."

Alaric let out a long breath. "Fighting 'em will be bloody, kid. We've fought beasts before. Once our artillery has been used, what then? Do we just wait for the people we've sent out there to be killed one after the other?"

"My potion worked," Nia said. "We could prepare big batches of it."

Oryn shook his head. "Much work and not enough time to make this the first and only solution. A remedy for thereafter, yes but during...I doubt we will be given grace in battle let alone time."

Kilian rested a hand on Nia's shoulder. "We'll prepare some to have as a reserve, just in case."

"Our best option still remains killing Melanthe," Cai sighed. "Her shields, her creatures, everything would disappear."

"We can get inside the Tenebrose castle," Tristin said, pointing at Elias. "He can find her."

"Doubt she will be at the castle," Macaria replied. "Crane bones do not see her in Isjord no matter how many times I toss them. I do not think she would remain there either. A Delcour is always stronger in her soil."

"A goose chase," Moriko said, shaking her head. "Your land is a deep hole, the further in you get, the more it confuses you. We'll never be able to find her."

"What about the Empaths?" Nia asked. "They have to be connected to one another and close to the battlefield to properly control the beasts so they don't slay one another or their own soldiers. We find the Empaths and they will lead us to her."

"It could work," Visha finally said, though she was not paying attention to anything other than her thick grimoire. Determined to find a cure for what I didn't wish to cure. The future.

Nia stepped forward, her chest rose and fell fast. "I'll find the Empaths. I'll find where she hides and kill her."

Kilian's eyes immediately landed on me from across the room. He knew I wanted to scream the word no. But there was another reason why Nia wanted to do this, and for the sake of that, I did not. Maybe I wished someone else would scream it for me. But her wife remained unforgivingly phlegmatic.

"You can't just simply kill her," Visha spoke again. "Even though the strings controlling the beasts will snap, her magic will linger. Beasts will not aim just for us, but anyone they see, uncontrollably. Whoever can still shift into their human form will not be able to do so anymore, not without her command. Melanthe has to be stripped of it entirely. Every trace of her magic needs to return where it belonged when she first died."

"How?" Cai asked.

"Daughter. Sister. Mother. Three of Delcour blood will need to perform a craft called. *D'mora*."

My, my. The little witch had finally picked up a thing or two from our...friendship? Only a few knew what that craft was.

The Violet Witch shot up, her violet eyes wide on Visha. Well, she knew. "Child, you cannot—"

Visha did not blink once. "Save your pity for the dead, Macaria. They will need it if she isn't stripped of the very essence she feeds on."

"You said three. Where do we find three of you?" Cai asked.

My witch glanced over her shoulder at where Penelope had shyly sat down. "There will be three of us. Aradia, Melanthe's sister, has agreed to join us."

Nia nodded. "It is set. I find her. You three kill her."

Moriko opened her mouth to speak and shut it just as fast, her jaw tightening as did her fists. The surface of stone on her face broke to reveal some even tougher stone.

"Next would be Silas," Mal said, dropping on a chair beside Macaria and throwing her a wink, making the woman flinch from surprise. "You and Kilian will be plenty busy with Aurora. Who will hunt him down?"

"That would be me," Eren said, and Cai almost sprung up like a coil from his seat.

"No, Silas is mine," Alaric grumbled. "An old debt. An even older regret."

"I want to kill him," Thora's voice was sweet, but loud and strong, and it got all the attention.

The room went entirely quiet.

The worst was...none were surprised by what she'd said, they were only afraid of what I would say next.

I stepped forward. "Rora—"

"He is mine, Snow," she bit out, her lips quivering, the whole of her shaking.

No one breathed louder than a fly.

"It will not be easy," I said. I'd seen her magic, what she could do, but I could not send her towards our father.

"Can't be harder than trying to kill a Guardian, is it now? Do you see me objecting despite always wanting to?"

Another sort of quiet fell over the tent.

Oryn and Visha both raised their heads, looking at one another for a long moment before returning their attention back to what they were reading. Not uttering a word of the truth only they knew. The truth of my end.

I couldn't...couldn't look at Kilian to see the fear and doubt there. It terrified and drove me away from the future I wanted. It would make me doubt, I knew it—I'd already doubted it every moment I saw, heard, touched, kissed, and smelled him. So, I didn't look at him at all.

"The girl says Silas is hers to kill," Magnus spoke. "And so she will kill him. I've seen her out there with the soldiers, with the Eldritch commander, with my own. She says she will kill him, then she will."

My little sister offered him a smile and nodded. "It is set. Silas is mine. Anyone against?" She looked around the room, but no one stepped forward. Not even our guardian. Alaric looked proud. Afraid, but proud.

He rubbed a scarred hand over his face and sighed. "And the old Krigborns?"

"They will remain in Hanai, closer to the main cities," Kilian said.

Elias nodded, pointing to the map. "They will be at a bigger disadvantage if they fight on dry land. Winter will favour both, it will not be a fight anymore no matter who is wittier. Then this war will go on forever. Our biggest hope is that Isjordian troops might surrender when Snow fights Aurora. It is important that they surrender," he said, looking at everyone around the room. "And they will surrender. My people are tired, weak, poisoned." He turned to me, standing fully. "There are children in his lines. They will surrender."

Every head swivelled in my direction, and I raised a brow. "If you are certain, then there is no doubt."

"You will seize the attack once that happens, right?" he asked.

"Sure."

It was funny how easily everyone believed that little four-letter word in desperate times.

Only one who had very little faith in four letter words doubted what I'd said, and he had for sure narrowed his eyes on me.

The meeting ended not too long after. Everyone suddenly had an allocated square in my game, it was no longer the queen against all. The worst I'd thought would happen was now happening. They'd be there, all of them, fighting.

When everyone left, I pulled Thora to the side. "Plea—"

She didn't even let me finish that one word. "You've always protected me from monsters. Hid me. Slayed them for me. This once, let me protect you. Let me hide you. Let me slay them for you. *I* will kill our father. He will die by my hands."

"I'd take a dagger or two. He has a thick neck and your hands are too little to wrap all the way around it."

She laughed, and so did I. "Thank you."

I cupped her face. "You must live. Don't make your death my burden to bear."

"I have faith you will kill Aurora like you say you will. Have some faith in me, too," she said, backing away and leaving me with him.

The moment we were alone, his hands were wrapped around me, his face buried in the crook of my neck. "Why did you hide those eyes of yours from me the whole time?"

"Because I worry about other things entirely different from this war when I look at you."

"What other things?"

"You."

"Why would you worry about me, my heart? Don't you know who I am?"

"Yes, but your heart has a reckless mind."

"I know. I will try to keep her safe, not make her a prisoner. She can have her reckless mind as long as she shares it with me. Don't hide your eyes from me."

Macaria cleared her throat and the both of us turned to the tent entrance where the Violet Witch stood awkwardly. "You said...kill Aurora. Your sister said you will try to kill Aurora."

"You're attentive. My congratulations."

She blinked a bit stunned, her dark eyes faltering and then widening. "Kill a Guardian?"

"Macaria, if I had the patience for this type of conversation, I would have become a kindergarten teacher instead."

Her chest fell and rose quickly, her black eyes flashed violet for a moment before she nodded and retreated away. Leaving an eerie air behind.

"Boo," Kilian whispered in my ear, and I jumped a little.

I elbowed his stomach when he started laughing. "Laugh all you want, but she creeps me out."

The waiting game was driving me absolutely insane. Still alive, still impatient. Though I was sure I was going to be an impatient corpse, too.

Kilian circled me, magic howling from both our sides. It was becoming less and less of a fight taming our power using the other's. He had managed to create an environment of sorts, a dome that drew life away from those underneath it, protecting those outside of it. Visha had given him a gate to her magic, tattooed all over his right hand. He could create a mock of a dream veil, an environment where his dark magic worked against the mind—and he'd mastered it only in weeks. Kilian was magnificent in all he did, but magic was not even second nature to him. He was it, in all sense.

"Feeling faint?" he asked, looking worried.

"A little. You should have really put a shirt on."

He bit his lip, trying not to smile. "Push some more out."

"You sure?"

He nodded. "I'll tell you when to stop."

"What if I can't?"

"You can. You're pretty obedient to my demands. I have little doubt," he said, still walking around me.

I pushed more like he asked, and the bubble of lightning surrounding me thickened and grew a bit bigger. One breath, one command from me to set it free, it would open a hole in the entire continent. Yet, no matter how much more power I fed to it, the more I pushed the gates of my magic, the control remained—the tattoos on my hands greyed and pulled back.

Drawing and controlling my magic was more or less painful for me. But inside here, there was no pain at all, it simply slipped in and out of my seal like a breath did—as if it was something that came naturally. The control was absolute and it gave me back precision.

At the start, we'd only been able to keep going for a few hours, now we were almost past using it through a whole day. The longer the better. We didn't know how long the battle would last.

He patted a towel to my brow, wiping the sweat off. "What is worrying you, my missus?"

"It will not be only I under the dome, Kil, she will be there as well. What if you can't—"

"If you had a little bit of faith in everyone around you, my love, you would not feel so alone in this war." His hands travelled up and down my arms. "You are not alone, I hope you remember this."

"It doesn't comfort me. If I have to keep looking over my shoulder for the rest of you, I might not be able to keep fighting."

"I'll make sure to keep you inside darkness for as long as I can, so you don't have to look over your shoulder."

"So unfunny," I sneered, slapping his chest.

"Alright, my hellcat," he said, touching his knuckles to my chin. "I'll come get you in a moment. Stay here while I talk to Visha for a moment. Her craft is starting to itch."

Golgotha had leaned back against a tree stump, watching us all throughout the training session. Particularly Kilian and I. It was always us he watched from the day he'd stepped in Fernfoss. Both of us had yet to reach our limits, but we'd tapped so much of our power to contain one another that Visha and Penelope both had to be present in order to make sure we didn't harm anything or anyone around us. However, the fallen God looked unimpressed.

"You look like you wish to bless me with some wisdom," I said, collecting my jacket.

"You are trying too hard."

"We all should sometimes."

"But you don't have to try so hard. And you know it." He sauntered to me. "You don't strike me as someone who...limits herself."

"So many words that you use to come to one simple conclusion."

"You're a monster," the God of Demons said. "*Be* a monster."

"You also slabber like a dog," Mal said, strutting to us and throwing an arm around my shoulders. "Yet, no one tells you to bark. How about we stick to moaning about the injustice of Gods and the inferiority complex it has given you to reside among us dirty humans, rather than giving the advice you were not asked to give?"

"You also know that I am right," Golgotha said, pointing a finger at him. "Wouldn't this senseless war never have a start if she just did what she truly wants to do?" He turned to me. "I might be humbled, but I did not turn into a fool. You've thought about it—about destroying the obstacle before the obstacle destroys you. Why not do it? Why not free your power and rain down hell on all of Isjord? Turn it all to crumbs."

By becoming the prophecy, he forgot to add. "You'd like that, wouldn't you?" I asked. "A world drowned in despair, suddenly destroyed by a monster, chaos for skies and ruins for a sun. And who would people begin praying again to? You, of course." I clicked my tongue. "Why are you throwing checker stones when I clearly set up a chess game? Must you be so hungry when hunger was what drove you realmless?"

He was very little offended by my words. "How long do you think you can starve for?"

"Long enough."

He cocked his head back, studying me. Those terrifying eyes of his thinned in their middle, almost resembling those of a serpent. "How calm you are. Facing what no other man has faced."

"I am no man."

"But you can still die like one." He nodded when I remained quiet, backing away, those eyes glowing as they bore into me. "I see now. Everything is becoming so much clearer. When did the reaper visit you?"

Shit.

Mal's hand tightened around my shoulder and shadows suddenly grew with life. "I'll say this one more time. No one wants to hear your crap."

Golgotha raised both hands and grinned. "Only stating what I see."

"What was he talking about?" Mal asked once the two of us were left alone.

"Thought you didn't care for his crap."

"Yeah, but I care about you, and something is telling me that maybe I should have let him shit all of it out." He crossed his arms, pinning a cold look on me. "I can call him back. Maybe Kilian will want to hear some of it, too. He's dealt with a lot of shit, he'll know if this one will stink or not."

"Mal, it is nothing."

"It is one thing to not want to tell me, and quite the other to lie to me." He tilted his head to the side. "Is this how we are going to be now?"

"Are you trying to manipulate me?"

"Yes."

I sighed. Mal and I shared the same wounds. He would understand. He would know the importance of what I was keeping hidden from everyone. And he would help me with Kilian. "I saw something."

40

Black Knight takes C5

Malik

I SAW SOMETHING. AND for the sake of all, I think you will keep this to yourself.

"What's wrong?" Thora asked, lowering her hands and the threads of magic stemming from her disappeared—the little ice creatures attached to them vanished, too. She sat on the floor across from me, leaning against my library, but even that far I could see the immediate worry, the sheer panic.

"Come here."

Her lashes fluttered fast and she thought about it for a moment before going on all fours and hurrying to my side. Driving me insane little by little, only the way she knew how to.

"Is it supposed to be a secret?" she whispered, looking around my room as if it wasn't the safest space in the whole of Numen.

I tugged on her bow and set her hair loose. Peaches—her hair smelled like peaches. Never had I felt more drunk than that night in Hellas, when my face had been pressed against her locks. "This ridiculous thing was bothering me." Before she could take it from me, I wrapped it around my wrist and tied it securely. "You're never quick enough, little bird."

"Fine." She curled her arms around her knees, resting her chin on top of them. "I've got like a thousand of them."

"I'll burn them all."

Her round eyes looked up at me so innocently. "Do you not want to tell me?"

"I want to tell you everything. This one...it is not my secret to tell. I still badly want to tell you though." I lifted my hand to her hair and curled a strand around my finger, watching her chest begin to rise and fall fast. "Look at me."

And she did. She did look at me.

"It's just me, Rora."

Her voice was small when she said, "I know. But it was just him, too. Just my uncle."

I grabbed her face and turned it to me again. "Don't cry," I said, my breaths burning.

"Because I swear to Gods, I will hunt down his soul beyond just to rip it out again."

"I'm not crying."

"Good. You look ugly as fuck when you cry."

She sniffled and then sighed. "So this is what hate feels like."

I laughed, enjoying the blank look of anger on her soft face. "You don't hate me, little bird."

"I really want to."

I stood. "Come, I'll make you hate me in a blink when I kick your arse again."

"Aren't we going to keep trying to multiply my threads to control more frost animals?"

"We might be running out of time, and you already know all the science behind it."

"Need my ribbon back, please," she said, lifting her palm to me. "Can't kick your arse back with my hair flying all over the place."

I turned her around, pulling all her hair back and loosely braiding it, taking my time to run my fingers through the soft, sweetly scented locks that she only allowed me to touch. I took the tie holding my own hair up and securely tied the ends. "There."

"I've always wanted to braid hair with my best friend," she said, petting the long braid. "I just imagined we'd be in our pyjamas, gossiping about boys, telling scary stories, and eating chocolate."

My hand lifted to push the thick fringe covering her brow to the side. "Haven't we done most of those?"

She straightened it back. "You never put on pyjamas."

"You know I like to sleep naked."

"Your scary stories are traumatising."

"No, they are just true."

"You hate chocolate."

"I can still eat it."

"And we've never gossiped about boys."

"We did."

"No, you calling Neo every enfeebling name in the dictionary does not count as gossiping."

I pinched her nose and faded us to the Fernfoss camps. Except that our usual spot was taken by Kilian and a bunch of Hanaian and Olympian soldiers being taught how to avoid getting trapped by an Adriatian Aura's magic.

Thora ran to Snow who had sat on a little bench, just staring at my brother from a distance. "Shouldn't you be in Solarya helping them set up?"

"Shhh," my sister-in-law said, tilting her head, her eyes never leaving Kilian. "I'll go in a minute."

I crouched beside her and wiped the drool off her mouth. "I really don't understand the obsession."

"I want to have that man's babies, Mal. Unless you come to understand the urge, shhhh." As if she could hear my thoughts screaming, she turned a little to me, her eyes pleading. "It will be alright."

"You don't believe in that shitty word, you heathen."

She smiled and shot to her feet when the training court cleared. And my topless brother remained there waiting for her. We were in public, but the way he watched her did not belong in public. Leave it to your big sibling to embarrass the shit out of you.

Thora crouched down. "I love watching them do this."

I did, too.

I'd never seen life dance with death the way it did when she unleashed thunder and he unleashed darkness. Neither fighting the other. Neither consuming the other. Simply taming—embracing and comforting till the two found a ground where neither was spiralling out of control.

Thora's emerald eyes widened and glowed from the reflection of her sister's magic, the skin of her arms pimpling with goosebumps from the mess of warm, controlled chaos it created against Kilian's. "Do you think it is because they share one soul?"

"What is?"

She looked up at me. "That neither allows the other to kill them. That neither lets itself kill the other."

"The two are great masters of their magic. It has nothing to do with that."

Her nose scrunched with disappointment at my answer. "Would it be so disdainful to think this romantic?"

"Yes."

She snorted. "Please don't break into hives."

"Too late. Look what you've done. You got to rub me up in ointment now, little bird." I crouched down next to her and tugged on her braid until she turned to face me. "But you would probably think that romantic as well, so now poor old me has to do it himself."

Her smile was so damn sweet. Rose berries were sweet too, but fucking poisonous. "Seeing you haven't been to your whores in weeks, poor old you might be excellent at doing things himself."

This little shit. No one could make me laugh like her.

She was right though. And it was not for lack of trying. Even the thought repulsed me these days. What happens when you sober up, I guess. You can't realise if the vomit rising up your throat is your feelings or just bile.

I hooked a finger on her necklace and pulled her up to her feet. "If only you were as good at rendering me defenceless as you can render me speechless," I said, dragging her to another court.

She sucked a sharp breath when I wrapped the necklace around my finger until the chain was tightly pressing against her neck, digging into her smooth skin where my mouth had been not even days ago.

"Try pushing me off without touching me or using magic directly on me," I said.

My eyes never left hers, but from the corner of my vision, I could see ice taking shape and then two creatures prowling towards me.

Ice crashed against shadows before they even got close enough to stand near the shade of my shadow. "Ah, isn't that cute, bird?"

She refused to look away or give up. More wolves of ice took shape, doubling, tripling, not even hesitating to launch towards me this time.

I clicked my tongue when they didn't even last a full five seconds. "Now that is just stinking adorable."

"Stop taunting me."

"Taunting you?" I stepped closer to her. "Thora, you've never heard the noise of battle. The chaos. The absolute insanity that crosses you when you can hear or see nothing. If you cannot shut your mind off from your surroundings, the tethers will fade or won't be as strong. You're an elemental, one too many tries and your fuel ends, then the seal opens. What happens when that seal opens?"

"Bad things."

"Very bad things, sweetheart."

She swallowed, her eyes dropping to my hand that was now pressed to her throat. "Malik, p—"

"Don't beg me, Thora. Push me off."

"I can't."

"You can."

"I don't want to hurt you."

"You actually just did. By insinuating that you can even get to me."

More creatures of ice rose around us. Angry little bird was quite the character.

She didn't hold back, and neither did I.

The wolves evaded my shadows more efficiently, but still crashed against my magic. This time, however, she was relentless. Each time she tried, each wolf that rose, it lasted longer than the previous. Avoiding being met by my shadows, jumping, and sliding between them, until...the tip of an icy paw flashed in front of my face for a fraction of a second before it crushed against shadows.

"Very good."

"It was not," she said, breathing just a little bit heavier from the use of magic.

I let go of her and stepped back. "It was. No one gets that close to me."

"Then you must have let me."

"Just a little. But that was some good effort."

"I'd accept that," Kilian said, finally throwing a shirt on. "My Eldritch Commander is very frugal with his compliments."

"Nonsense," Snow said, wrapping her arms around my brother's sweaty chest. "He gives me compliments all the time."

I pried her hands off my brother and kissed her knuckles. "Only for you, sister-in-law."

Kilian grabbed her hands from mine and put them back on his chest, fading away to probably do what only Gods and the whole Amaris Castle knew.

Cai crossed the camp, dumping a bunch of weapons in the pile behind us. "You should be keeping an eye on Golgotha or training your men, not romancing your brother's wife."

"Golgotha is taking a little rest by the hearth because the daylight was stressing him out, and my soldiers don't need to learn how to kill. I've only ever taught them how not to. Since we are going to war, killing is what we want, isn't it, honey buns?"

"Do you need help?" Thora asked, folding back her sleeves and following him.

I grabbed her shirt, pulling her back to my side. "He's got it. Don't—" *Leave me.*

Shit. I was losing my shit.

This was not good.

Not good at all.

"Actually, go help," I said, backing away, but she grabbed me this time, her fingers clinging to my jacket.

"I don't want to leave you."

Hells.

Sweet hells.

Cai broke us apart, pushing through between us. "Helping or not helping?"

"Not helping," I said at the same time she said, "Helping."

Her brows fell. "Malik, please."

Drowsiness began fogging my vision and I swayed on my feet. "Later, bird."

I'd faded right where my mind had pounded me for weeks to go, finally falling to the temptation of wanting to feel numb again.

Though...it seemed like someone else had the same idea as I.

Snow leaned against the tavern door, arms crossed, a blank look on her face. "Have a walk with me." She pointed her chin down the street. "Lead the way or I'll get the both of us lost."

"Thought my brother and you were keeping each other busy. That was quick."

She took my side while we made our way towards the Amaris balcony, the cliffs overlooking the Moor Sea stretching wide and blending as one with the sky. "He is waiting by the brothel," she said. "I decided to wait here. I guess I made the right bet."

"How did you know where I would be?"

"I had Nia follow you before Silas took us. I know all the places you go to when you feel the way you do."

"You're wearing the necklace I gave you."

She lifted her left hand to it. "Matches my ring nicely."

"What are you doing, Snow?"

"I don't know. I'm not Kilian. Words are usually not the best way for me to express my thoughts. I'm more of an 'action' kind of girl. Burying, burning, drowning, those sorts of things. And Kilian advised me against it. Said you'd be very much willing. Which concerns me even more somehow."

"Snow—"

She jumped upright, pointing at a bunch of children vandalising the street with colourful chalk. "Oy, kids, can I have—"

They all turned to Snow, taking her presence head to toe before they screamed their lungs out and ran off.

"That is one way to do it," Snow mumbled to herself, kneeling to pick up some chalks, and even handing me a few. "I've always wanted to do this."

"Chalk the streets?"

"Yeah." She looked so amazed at the opportunity, her eyes gleaming as she searched for space to draw on.

I took a front row seat on a city bench, watching her atrocious skills at work. Mushy figures, stick figures, loads of stars and moons. Once she was done, she stood up, hands on her hips and fully satisfied with her work. "Perfect."

"That's absolutely horrendous."

She hit me precisely in the middle of my forehead with a chalk. "It's Dolunay," she said, pointing to the clip on her head—the one I'd gotten her. "I never got to see it this year. You promised to take me. I think it would look a bit like this, would it not? Loads of stars, people walking the streets searching for sweets, and things of the sort."

Something heavy settled on top of my chest, like a weight pinning my lungs down. When had I let myself get so attached to another that would leave me as well?

I grabbed the chalks from her hand, pushing her to sit down and watch. I had not drawn anything in ages, didn't know if I even could still, but I tried. Tried my best at recalling a Dolunay where I'd not been drunk enough to forget. I wanted her to see whatever she wanted to see. The whole world if she asked.

It was almost past sunset when I finished. The lack of daylight had not dimmed the bright colours of the chalk at all, only given them more life. When I moved back, there was horror crawling over me. Some relief there, too.

"Wow," Snow murmured, her mouth agape while she looked at what I'd drawn. "Much better than what I'd envisioned. Thank you, Mal." She hopped from one drawing to the other, crouching down so she could see the details, trailing a finger over them as she made more sounds of awe.

"Tell Kilian." *Please, please, please, please, please—*

Her head snapped to me. "You know I can't."

My chest, the pain, I couldn't bear to carry it on my own. I needed my brother...I needed him to fix this for me again. "To hells, Snow, to hells with it all."

Her chin quivered, her eyes glazing with thick tears that would not stop pouring. "Absolutely not. Never."

"Grey was right. Even if we win, he will not...he cannot live without you, Snow. I know...I know that is the truth."

"He will have you. Our family. All of it. He will have to. Force him if you must. You gave me your word, Mal, please."

My head was pounding. Tugging and pulling at my hair did not grant me any relief at all. The fucking thoughts were so loud, crowding other each other. Every emotion in the distance grew so close. Of a child screaming, a man coughing from sickness, a happy mother singing her baby to sleep. It was all too much.

"I need you, Mal."

Like that, everything disappeared. "Fight it. I'll fight it with you. You want me to beg again? I'll beg again for you."

Her face fell, more stray tears chasing down her face. I couldn't even stop those. "Every night when I dream of it, I see a small detail change. Details so minute you would think there was no change at all. The screams sometimes call my name, sometimes they call yours or Thora's. Sometimes I'm burning and sometimes you or Thora or Cai or Nia or Eren or...he is burning instead of me. You know when that change happens? After every time I go to bed convincing myself that I will wake up the next day and erase it." A heart wracking sob made her shake. "They are taunting me, Mal."

I caught her tears again. Her pain was hidden from me yet I could feel it so intensely from that one desperate way she said my name. "Alright. Alright, Snow."

"Promise me you will not let your brother do anything that I don't want him to do."

"I promise."

41

White Knight to D4

Nia

IT WAS GROWING COLDER in Aru, and Hanaians had been in the fields trying to nourish their crops with heat all day, yet their queen's main intentions at the moment were to just be angry at me. Straight after I'd returned from Drava, she'd abandoned every other duty and had called for me to join her at her private training grounds.

I swung at her again after ducking and evading every attack she'd brought my way. And as always, she caught me, and this time she wrapped a hand around my jaw and backed me to the court wall. She breathed hard and so angry. "*Ahana*, I don't want to hurt you, but if it had been someone else—"

"No one can get this close to my heart, Mor. You wanted me to sweat out an apology. And the least I can do is let you make me sweat since I will not be making that apology. You forget who I am. What I am. It was just that one time I got hurt, Mor, just that once. Why won't you have a little more faith in me?"

She rested her forehead against mine and let out a long sigh. "You know what plagues my thoughts?"

"If only. Perhaps we would have little of these disagreements."

"Every time you fade somewhere, there is this...feeling that you might not return to me."

"Truth is that I might not one day. But it should not be a reason to fear living."

Her fingers were gentle on my face. "This is not living, *ahana*."

"For now, it is."

She shut her eyes. "I should have married a docile woman."

"Oh?" I asked, grasping her shirt and pulling her closer. "I thought you liked me wilful. What docile woman would know what to do with you?"

She braced her hands on the wall behind me and pressed her body over mine, her mouth lowering to my neck. "But you're docile for me," she said, returning to kiss me, her knee parting mine to slide between my legs.

A guard stepped towards us, forcing her to pull away from me. "We have guests."

I sighed, dropping my head back. We had barely gotten a moment alone since the wedding. "Maybe we shouldn't be so welcoming, Mor."

The guard laughed a little. "It is the Isline King, Your Majesty, so maybe we indeed shouldn't be."

King Sigurd Krigborn had studied each paint stroke on the meeting room walls. Everything seemed oddly fascinating to the man who had stripped almost naked from the 'unbearable' heat as he had called it. His chest and arms were covered in an almost faded pattern of tattoos made with bluish ink.

"*Ôol*," he said, sitting down on the chair opposite Mor's even though his eyes were on me and my curiosity. "The tattoos. They are a map of the Isline mountains we have travelled. It is an Isliner's greatest honour to be covered as I am. To have seen them all."

"I know."

He titled his head back to study me. "Why would my culture interest you?"

"Much interests me. I wouldn't flatter yourself." The enemy of my enemy was my enemy, too, and I had to know them just as well.

"Your lands are strangely...pleasant," he said to Mor, an attempt to soften the hostility in the air. "Much too warm, but pleasant."

"Thank you."

He studied my cold wife for a moment. "The Skygard Queen has asked that we remain here until the war, but if we are not welcomed—"

"You will be welcome in my lands as long as peace is the only aim."

He tapped a finger on the table. "But you think that is not our aim?"

"I've got a few years on my back, Sigurd, and if I am taught one thing from age, it is that a Krigborn never has just one aim. And definitely never desires peace."

"Then why ask us to join you if there is so little trust?"

Moriko rested her head back on the chair and sighed. "Because we do not need trust to ensure that your aim remains true. Right, Snowlin?"

My friend stood at the door, leaning against it. Pure humour was written on her face. "Most certainly. But must we be so hostile to our guests?"

"*My* guests," Mor threw back.

Snow rolled her eyes. "Yeah, yeah." She pushed off the door to sit beside Sigurd. "I hope your trip has been pleasant."

He grunted. "As pleasant as you would expect for someone who has never left our borders. The cold of the north guides us, and if it hadn't been for your guide, we would have been lost in these lands." Sigurd turned to Mor and I. "Lands I have no desire to step on let alone wish to claim."

"Well, since we got that out of the way," Snow said, stretching back. "Who is hungry? I'm famished."

"You look quite happy," Mor commented.

Snow slid a piece of paper to us. "A note from Moregan."

I looked at Sigurd, not one reaction written on his face. So Snow had not told him his aunt was our insider.

Isjordians are retreating again. There have been revolts in the cities when they got news of the Islines joining Queen Moriko. Silas is struggling to squash them this time. No more potions, say the whispers, the herbs have been faulty and killed a few hundreds before Melanthe realised. Not enough people are willing to dig up graves for innocents either. Soldiers are losing spirits. Even more so when we spread word that those who turn into beasts die when they turn.

"More Isjordians have joined our camps?" Mor asked.

Snow nodded. "I still think it's because of my warm hospitality. Once you figure out what that is, you should try it."

The way Snow irritated Mor should not make me laugh, but it always did.

The Isliners had camped close to the Koy City borders, hidden under the protection of the forest nearby. Unlike their cold blessing, they had blended rather well between Hanaians, the odd Adriatians, and the Olympians circling the borders. The only cautionary looks came from one person alone.

I handed Sigurd a bowl of warm, herby stew. "You've been watching them all day. Why are Olympians so fascinating to you?"

"Have *you* been watching me all day?"

"It is my duty. Or was," I said, sitting beside him.

"Thought your duty was to be married to the grumpy woman."

"Gods let me pick my struggles as the day goes."

He laughed, and the sound was so strange even to him because his shadows were murky with sad amusement almost.

"Why are Olympians something that makes you feel cautious?" *And fearful.*

He glanced at me. "You're one of them, aren't you?"

"Adriatian, by blood. So, what is the answer to your perplexity?"

He ate a few spoonfuls from the stew, chewing hurriedly. "There was once this...boy I met in our lands. He had black hair like the Sky Queen and was blessed by the Sky God like her—a little too much, if you ask me. I've never felt the sort of horror in my life like when I saw him that day." Sigurd shook his head, his blue eyes drowning in some memory. "Sky and earth became one, and I felt the clouds filled with thunder touch my fingertips. Hail rained down in the shape of blades, but sharper and deadlier. And the wind cut through your skin like glass. But that was not even the worst. Have you seen a man being drained of their entire air?" He stuffed his mouth with more stew even though he looked like he wanted to be sick. "And even though he'd slayed a whole village and injured me to the point of death, he cried and apologised, holding his shaking hands over my bleeding wounds...trying to save me. He stayed and nursed me to recovery in the middle of nowhere, begging for forgiveness till the day he left to march back where the damned hells he'd come from. That might be the only day in my dreary life that I've been afraid." He pointed his spoon over at the Olympians who were proudly wearing our crest across their chests. "These might be men, but he seemed like a man too."

I breathed fast when I asked, "When...when was this?"

Sigurd stopped chewing, thinking about it for a moment. "My daughter was about eight back then, so around fourteen years ago."

Fourteen years ago. *He had dark hair like the Sky Queen.* Hells.

"I saw how you fought at the courts," he said, pulling my attention again. "Dirty."

"Using my intelligence, knowledge, and my opponent's lack of them, is not playing dirty. It's called being smart."

He huffed a short laugh. "You remind me of my daughter, Iskyla, she is much the same in a sense, but she likes to call it *playing dirty*. She takes big pride in her tricks."

Ah, the one Thora had called *'a massive bitch'*? "Do you take pride in your tricks?"

"I have no desire for trickery. Lived too many lives to care for much."

"You're a king. Desire and greed are a pillar in your foundations. Not to mention your blessing being war. Why would anyone reign war on anything if not for greed?"

He lowered his bowl down, staring right ahead at both of my people. "Where I am from, that word does not bear much meaning. I'm just a man others follow when the wind is too harsh to guide them. Our blessing is indeed war. And we are at war every day, girl. Me, you, them. With ourselves, our anger, our happiness, our own thoughts. We've become great masters of those. Our souls are at peace because we won those wars—the greatest wars. It is why we found peace even after being banished by our own kind in a rough corner of this marvellous realm. I cannot say that all have won those wars. Some make their blessing their curse. There is good, there is bad, there are lost, and there are those who don't want to be found, as there always will be." He flashed me a crooked grin. "Did I pass your test? Have I lied?"

So, he knew of my intentions. "No. You haven't lied," I said, drinking my stew. Old knowledge always beat the new. What he said was too fascinating to my ears to ignore.

He shook his head. "Smart woman indeed."

Eren had sat alone by the large fire set up between camps in Fernfoss, his attention was on Cai who stood a few feet away, speaking to Snow.

He gave a big brotherly smile when I sat next to him. "You look exhausted," he said, kneading my shoulders, and a little whoosh of relief left my lungs.

"Eren?"

"Yes?"

"Snow, she used to tell me stories you had told her—Isline stories. Big monsters and stuff of the sort," I carefully said. "What...monsters did you really see up there?"

The crackling of the fire grew a little louder, or maybe it didn't, it could have been because of the silence that ricocheted between us.

"I only ever saw one monster, Nia, and I am sure it would not enrich your knowledge of the place much."

"Why?"

His hand slipped away from me. "Because the monster was me. Father sent me there once to hunt one. Except that I only found strange animals trying to protect themselves." He laughed a little. "Sure, they were ugly, but they were peaceful." He tilted his head to me, looking a little too much like Snow when he said, "But you should've seen me. Whatever was in that air, it wanted to draw the worst out of me. Except that it did. No mirror could have told me better what monster I was than the eyes of the people I killed."

My heart hurt for him. "You're not a monster, Eren."

He shook his head. "I'd sworn, Nia. To die before drawing a breath of magic that would harm innocents. What I did that day in those mountains made me deserving of death."

"You lied to Snow and Thora about what you saw there."

"My little sisters are hot headed, and were even worse back then. They were so curious of the Islines, they saw how their father loathed that place and wanted it even more." He toasted his drink to mine. "Good thing they were little scaredy cats back then and are still now."

I snorted. "Them, scaredy cats?"

"Thora would cry at the sight of a snail, so I used to tell her that the beasts in the mountains left a big trail of slime and muck. Snow had a thing about livers. She hated how much they bled, so I told her that they ate livers."

"Yeah, Snow still hates livers."

"And Thora still cries at the sight of snails."

I hadn't laughed this much in a while, but it looked like neither had he. Eren was like calm waters, I always found myself drawn to his side every time I felt storms overhead.

"So you can laugh," Cai said, dropping down next to Eren, looking smug and ready to say something he shouldn't by the look he had on his face. "But why do you do it so rarely?"

Ugh. I'd witnessed him flirting too many times to consider this his best shot. Especially considering how Eren reacted.

The eldest Skygard took a sip from his drink. "You've never been remotely funny."

"Thought you liked it better when my mouth was busy with other things than telling jokes."

My nose burned from the ale I'd inhaled.

"The more I think about it," Eren replied, leaning back. "The less you say, the better we get along, so I suppose I do like your mouth occupied with other things."

Oh, no.

When Cai's eyes dropped to Eren's mouth, I stood up and left. Perusing the camp until I found another loner doing lone people stuff. Visha had curled into a ball and was drawing something on the ground with a crane.

"Don't creep up on people, Helenia," she said boredly. "You were released from your duties as a spy."

Observing and watching was ingrained in me, it was no longer about a duty. "Who are you hiding from?" I asked, kneeling beside her. "A six foot two blond captain, perhaps?"

She stopped drawing with the crane and turned to me. "Must you taunt me?"

"Must you not tell me though you let your shadows freely encircle you in my presence? Isn't it for me to see?"

"I trust you, that is why I allow you to see. It doesn't necessarily mean I want to acknowledge anything. But yes, if I see him, I might sacrifice myself to the seven hells and let them burn me ever so slowly just so I can escape the torture of hearing him speak."

"Hearing him flirt with you," I corrected.

She blinked once. "I felt a bit sick just now."

I pressed my lips together, holding back a laugh, and pointed to the runes she'd drawn down on the soil. "What are those for?"

"We will have guests."

"Guests?"

She nodded. "I needed to read intentions before I could let them through our waters."

Just then, heavy footsteps thumped from the camp entrance. Tristin and her soldiers were escorting two women. One was tall, with auburn hair, golden brown skin, and the other was not much shorter, her golden hair was cut to her shoulders, and the robes she wore covered every inch of skin. There were clear intentions of peace and reluctance circling them, and an old air about their magic seeped through the wind—a magic I could not entirely grasp.

Snow came out of the main camp, looking a bit surprised at the auburn-haired woman. "Nilsa?"

The woman bowed her head. "Guardian."

"Snow, just Snow," my friend said, pointing inside the tent for them to enter.

"Who are they?" I asked.

Visha stood and threw the stick away. "King Kegans's daughter. The one who freed Aurora five hundred years ago. They called her Nilsa Veranesi. The woman behind is Alyone Morfir, a high priestess in Heyes temple."

"The hells are they doing here?"

"I brought them here."

My eyes were wide on the witch. "What?"

Visha and I followed shortly, standing on a corner while Snow narrowed her eyes on the woman and her companion.

"What you said to me back then," Nilsa started. "You were right."

"Of course," Snow admitted, crossing her legs and giving her an innocent smile. "Could have written me a letter though, but this is a nice ego boost, so thank you."

"I come with help."

Snow raised a brow, glancing at Alyone. "Help?"

The two nodded. "We have managed to take over your father's camps in Heyes. His last ships retreated towards the Sayuri in an attempt to flee our attack. As far as we've searched Seraphim, no Isjordian remains."

Snow arched a brow. "*Our* attack?"

"Me and my people managed to chase them out."

"So they listened," my friend sighed, pleased with what she was hearing.

"They did. I am grateful for your anger, and so are my people." She unstrapped a dagger and put it on the table in front of Snow. "We are not many. And few of us still are fearful of our own blessing. But we will help and we will fight however we can. If your offer still stands, of course." She looked over her shoulder at us and then at Kilian. "Though you do already have a strong side."

"We'd be thankful," Snow said, and I knew the words tasted bitter. She was protecting the realm she'd sworn to take apart not even that long ago. All because of the people in this room and for her people behind the mountains. Though she had not told me or showed it, I knew the decision was haunting her.

"It is us who are thankful," Nilsa said, bowing again. "That you are willing to fight for us all."

Snow's eyes found mine. Maybe we did hear each other's thoughts like she used to say long ago. "That is me," she replied, standing and taking Nilsa's dagger, trailing a finger over the sharp edge. "The ever loved...hero."

Kilian pushed from where he'd sat. "I'm her husband, Kilian Castemont."

"The Adriatian King," Nilsa said, bowing her head at him. "I'd recognise the scent of your magic anywhere."

He glanced back at Snow and then pointed to the exit. "I'll show you around the camp and get your people settled in." He hugged my friend to his chest for a moment and then left.

And Visha followed shortly behind like a creepy red-haired shadow.

Snow and I were alone. For the first time in weeks. Or months.

My friend stepped before me. Her war face on. "You want to ditch Mor?"

I laughed. "No?"

"Oh. What's wrong then?"

"You know I can feel you still sometimes."

"Well, that's awful. I'm sorry."

I pulled the big idiot and hugged her. "You don't have to pretend to be alright with all of this. With the heavy weight you've been bestowed."

She sighed and rested her cheek on my shoulder. "No one bestowed me anything, Nia. It is to protect you, all of our family, and Olympia."

"You waited for so long to get what you wanted."

"I have all I want. More, even."

"Then why does something feel so wrong? I cannot explain it, Snow, but every time I sense you, it feels like my heart is about to rip in half."

She tensed against me and promptly pulled back.

I held my breath, feeling that same spark of foreign anguish in my chest.

There was something wrong.

I knew it.

Two hands landed on our shoulders, spinning us around. Alaric looked mad. He had that type face he put on when he was about to scold us. "You both missed dinner. Again."

Snow rolled her eyes. "Silas is about to roast us in white fire, I'm sure all the domesticity can be pushed to a later date."

I hooked my thumb in Snow's direction. "What she said."

The gruff man grunted. "I'd like to see my kids more often. Whether we're about to be roasted or not."

Snow turned to me. "Does he need glasses? Or is it a memory thing? When was he last seen by a physician?"

The fact that she was not joking made me shake with laughter.

She gave me a shove. "You were responsible for looking after his health. Cai after his wealth. And my duty was to keep him sane."

"You three separated duties?" Alaric asked, stunned. "You're *my* children, not the opposite."

"You're old," Snow plainly said.

"I know I'm old, kid."

She pointed at him. "See, he is sane. So it is definitely an eye thing."

He sighed and pointed at the two of us. "The world could be falling out of the skies and you still need to attend the next dinner."

Snow frowned. "Maybe it is not an eye thing. How could the world be falling out of the skies?"

Alaric retreated away, shaking his head and mumbling to himself all sorts of prayers.

I grabbed her hand before she was about to leave, too. "Are you going to run away from answering me again?"

"No. But if I tell you to trust me, will you?"

I let her go. "Always."

Maybe this time I shouldn't have done either. Trust or let her go.

Because she'd lied.

The tent curtains pulled open, and I flinched a little. "The hells, Cai."

He frowned at me, rushing to put a hand on my brow and another on my pulse. "You look unwell? Shall I call for a healer? What is it, Nia? Where does it hurt, is it your scar again?"

"Cai, I am fine. You on the other hand—"

"It is not me," he said quickly. "It's Eren. I think his stomach is bothering him again. Do you think you can check on him again? He just left for Taren."

We both knew it was not his stomach. "Why do you care, you don't even know his middle name." With that, I pushed past him and left.

"Jonah," he called after me, and I stopped. "His middle name is Jonah. I have no idea why that matters, but please, do this one favour to me." Lifting a salted caramel candy between us, he waited, the wrapper shaking just like his hand. "Please."

I took the candy. "You know I hate sweets."

He smacked a big kiss on my cheek. "Can't really carry carrots with me at all times, little rabbit."

42

Black Bishop to B3

Snowlin

THE MUSIC WAS LOUDER than usual in Alaric's favourite old tavern in Fernfoss that had opened after weeks just to house this one last night. The space was packed, and most bodies were sweating and laughing away. These were perhaps their last days dancing to the sound of strings and drums. They would be marching to them soon.

Nia and Moriko were there first. The Autumn Queen had spent more and more time in Olympia, learning Nia's culture, interacting with it and letting her spend more time in her city despite her new court duties in Hanai as Queen Consort.

Surprisingly, Mal and Thora arrived both at different times while Cai and Eren came together. My husband was last to arrive, and I quickly patted the space beside me for him to sit.

The table had gone through at least five rounds of ale, but I'd only occasionally sipped Kilian's in an attempt to be conscious enough to remember this night with all of us together before we'd leave to our allocated camps tomorrow.

Kilian's ears were almost steaming. He glared at his brother and his chosen companion. Mal had brought the woman he often visited in one of his preferred brothels.

Cecilia, was it not? Like that sheep disease. Was it a sheep disease?

I nudged Kil's shoulder to stop him from being such a prickly bastard, and his jaw tightened. "This was time to spend with family."

"He clearly sees her a lot and probably considers her family." I frowned at him. "Don't tell me that you don't approve of her because of what she does?"

"I don't approve of her because she sees no issue in feeding all my brother's addictions. The drunker, the more tired, the more vulnerable he is, the more pleased she is." He ran a finger down my cheek in an attempt to smooth my confusion. "They met when he was just sixteen, Snow, and you might have guessed correctly if you thought she must have been older than him. The woman is also an Empath. Make the connections on why she chose my brother who was half her age to be the one who keeps her the richest whore in Adriata."

"Want me to kill her?" I whispered.

He chuckled, throwing an arm over my shoulders and tucking me to his side. "You think I am below murdering her?"

"A little?"

"It wouldn't be the first, my love, and perhaps not the last that I would and have killed for him. If only...if only I could kill what haunts him inside that thick, fat head of his."

Himself. You would have to kill him.

He downed his drink. "Maybe I'll just kill her first. Give myself an early birthday present. I never do nice stuff for myself anymore."

I snorted, burying my face in his arm, and he showered me with a bunch of kisses.

"Hello, Selia," my sister greeted, joining our table.

I sipped the foam from my ale. Nope. She was not named after the sheep disease.

The woman's eyes turned animated with excitement. "Princess, I haven't seen you in some time." Selia's eyes dropped to the dress Thora wore, envy glowing in the blue of her irises. "You look...different."

"It is Snow's," my sister said, chewing on some apple slices. Her hair was curlier, the dress fit her tightly around her body that had gained weight and muscle over time—she did look different. Mature. Grown.

Mal frowned at both of them. "You know each other?"

Thora nodded. "She came to the castle a couple of months after my father took you. Concerned her best lay was not visiting her anymore."

"Almost had a fright," Selia said, laughing a little louder than the percussion. "Thought you got hitched or something, Gods forbid." She ran her hand over his chest, and bile rose to my throat along with the urge to pick her orange red nails one after the other with a butter knife. "Never letting that happen for as long as I breathe."

I sipped some more ale foam, mumbling to myself, "That is an easy fix."

My sister snorted, coughing around a sip of ale. "He is safe," she said, wiping her mouth. "He isn't able to keep a woman around him unless he gives her coin for favours. You are his perfect find, Selia. No need for a fright."

Selia let out what looked like an uncomfortable laugh before she stood, and announced, "I will go dance if anyone wishes to join me. You bunch are no fun whilst sat down. Anyone?"

Mal had narrowed his eyes on my sister over his ale cup, not even bothering to join the woman he'd brought himself.

Why the hells had he even brought her?

My sister stopped chewing and looked up at him. "What?"

He scooted across the bench to her, throwing an arm over her chair. "Bird," he purred, his eyes lowering to her mouth.

"Fox," my sister murmured with her lips still on the glass pint, but he'd heard it—we all had.

"Foxes eat little birds," Mal said, sprawling wide on the bench and resting his head back on my sister's shoulder. He was grinning up at her and his breathing grew heavy when she turned to look down at him.

I stopped sipping the ale foam from Kilian's cup, watching them and my husband with the corner of my eye.

My sister sighed. "Malik."

"Pretty bird," he purred, pinching her chin, and the dark parts of his ember eyes thickened until his gaze was a piercing black.

"You're not a fox," she said, pinching his cheeks together until his lips puckered like a duck's. "You're a drunk skunk."

Except that he wasn't.

He didn't say anything, just held her gaze, his breathing growing faster and faster. The hand he had on her face slipped over her jaw like melting ice, and he tucked a bunch of hair behind her ear.

Even I held my breath with them.

I threw a careful glance to Kilian who had probably realised my thoughts before they had even formed in my head.

"No," he said, dropping a peck to the tip of my nose. "To his own Gods damned luck."

"Would it be so bad?"

"Your sister's first heartbreak won't be from him."

Thora almost jumped from her seat when Cai dropped on her other side, forcing the two to finally separate and straighten on their seats.

"Did you not bring Neo?" he asked.

Mal's hand tightened around the water glass he had before him.

My sister shrugged, scrunching her nose. "Don't want him anymore."

Eren's head snapped to her. "Rora."

"But he is so vain, brother. Nice, polite, sweet, but vain."

"I see you've been taking Snow's lessons," Cai said, and Leanna laughed a little louder than normal from the table conjoined to ours, and the little demon on her lap laughed along for no reason at all.

I sneered. "What's so funny?"

"Oh, nothing," the woman said, handing her daughter some fruit.

"Ma used to think you would die a spinstress queen," Lila screeched.

Leanna put a hand over her daughter's mouth a little too late, her eyes wide. "I did not say that."

"You did, mama," Lila said, nodding and chewing at the same time.

She glared at her daughter. "Fine, I did, but I was proven wrong. Happy?"

I sneered. "Will be, when I weave myself a knitting bobbin with your yellow hair for a nice winter hat."

"Please do not threaten my hair," the tribe leader said, touching her hair. "I've started to develop a complex after you choked that poor witch in Fernfoss with her own hair."

"The complex will go away, Leanna, when I pluck it all out."

"Auntie," Lila started, rolling her deceitful eyes up at me. "Lila wants to play in the snow like uncle Cai. He gave me a ball of snow yesterday, but it disappeared. Must have lost it in the room when I went to play with Pelin."

"Aren't you your mother's child," I said, kissing her cheek, and Leanna shot me a look. "I'll take you to play with snow."

"After the battle." She put her hand up, counting along as she said, "Lila has school tomorrow and the day after and the day after and the day after."

I heaved a heavy sigh. "You've got to learn the days of the week, kid."

She sighed, too, devastated. "They're so hard, auntie. But will you take me?"

Mal stood from his seat and headed to leave, bumping hard against everybody he came across.

Seeing him like that returned an emptiness in my heart that only grew more shallow. "Yes. I'll take you, Lila."

"I'm frightened for your child's life," Moriko calmly said, lifting the ale cup to her mouth all while shooting me a smug look. "Death by snowball."

Before I could launch the most perfect verbal attack on the woman, Kilian wrapped an arm around my waist and faded us outside the tavern.

He cupped my face while I angrily panted. "Before you violently obliterate me, listen first."

"You have ten seconds," I said, looking around. "Where have you brought us?" It looked like the Taren River under caves where we held our monthly rituals.

He took my hand, guiding me towards the path I'd snuck through when I was younger a million times. There was an Olympian priest waiting at the little peninsula created in the middle of the cave lake, formed by the river flowing under the rock and down to Moor Sea.

"Remember when I said I wanted to put you in a big white dress and marry you again?"

I looked down at my pretty grey silk dress and blinked a little confused. "Yes?"

"I thought of something better," he said, pulling me towards where the Olympian priest had sat cross legged in the middle of the rocky space floating around water.

The old man bowed to us. "My king and queen."

"Apologies for calling you so late," Kilian offered.

"No matter the time, I will always be in the service of love."

Kilian and I kneeled before one another again. "To honour both of our traditions," he said, and I grinned up at him until his cheeks flushed like they always did.

"Your hand," the priest asked, and I extended my palm to him like I'd seen others do at their own ceremonies. He drew the symbol for the soul in Calgnan with white paint in the middle of my palm. Then on Kilian's before joining our hands together.

It was different for us—for my kind. The prayers usually were sung to the skies, not told like by most. Nubil adored songs of love. It was said he spied from realm to realm every time they were sung by his blessed. Tradition said that the mountains would echo it around for all to hear, heaven, water, and earth alike. The song vibrated on the water, on the stone, and air around. It was beautiful, enchanting. A dream. Now mine as well.

We marked the stone with our names in white ink.

We marked the air with sage.

We marked the water with our touch.

All three would know if they already didn't, that him and I were one and would always be.

The priest stood after the last prayer. "Your vow ceremonies are private between you and your faith," he said, bowing his head to us and leaving.

"You need to take your shirt off," I said, taking my own clothes off.

He had a stupid smirk on his face when he saw what I was wearing under my dress.

The red slip he'd gifted me some time ago.

I soaked my finger in paint and drew all over his chest, dipping a little under his trousers, and he raised a brow at me. "What vow might that be now?"

"Might I always be gloriously fucked by my husband."

He threw his head back, his laughter thundering all around the cave. Once he was done, he picked me up and sat me on his lap. After staining his fingers with paint, he drew something on my face and kissed my lips. "Might she always smile at me like she smiles at no one."

"No need for a prayer, Kil," I said, grinding my hips against his.

I put a hand over his mouth when he moaned, feeling his smile against my palm. "This is a sacred place, remember?"

His hands dug on my naked thighs, forcing me to shift over his bulge again. "I am going to do some unholy things to you if you keep rubbing your cunt on me like that."

Ignoring the thrill lighting between my legs, I reached for the white paint again and traced a few more marks on his chest, down his stomach, and waist. I took my time just to feel him shake under my touch, to feel his warm breath rush over my skin. Watching his resolve break little by little.

"Evil woman," he gritted out, a whimper escaping him when I rolled my hips again over his hardening length.

I shifted closer to him, my breasts pressed to his naked chest. Looking over his shoulder, I drew some more vows down his back. All the time he looked at me, his lips leaving feathery kisses on my arm and shoulder. He murmured so many praises, sung taunting promises, and sneaked barely there touches down my thighs, his finger grazing the thin lace of the underwear I wore to torture me back. When I shifted up on my knees to reach the space on his lower back, his mouth latched on the soft flesh of my breast, and my moan travelled down the cave.

"Shhh, my sweet sin," he purred, licking and sucking, staining my skin with purple bruises.

"This is cheating," I hissed low when he pushed back the silk straps of my nightgown to free one of my breasts.

"You put them in my face," he said, his tongue slipping out to flick my nipple before he bit on it and tugged until my knees buckled. In one tear, the nightgown was off my body. He grabbed my hips, dragging me over him and rocking me over his length until I could feel flames lick down my stomach.

"Don't make me come like this. I want you."

"Turn around," he ordered, and I spun in his lap so my back was against his chest. His fingers dipped in paint again, and I shivered when they traced words on my spine. He hummed, his fingers travelling low down my back. "I love these two little dimples."

Biting on my lip to keep quiet, I squirmed on his lap, shamelessly riding on my pleasure.

His hands cupped my hips, angling me forward and taking apart my underwear. His knuckles brushed my wet core while he undid the belt buckle and buttons of his trousers. "You're going to ride me like a good girl," he said, the thick head of his cock pushing against my entrance until he was all inside me, my eyes rolling back when it hit all the right places. "All the way down, love."

I hissed when my hips rested flush against his, taking all of him.

"All good?"

"So good," I breathed, riding him.

His mouth trailed a line of kisses to my neck while his hands cupped my breasts, kneading them in his rough palms. "Go slow," he moaned in my ear. "I want to remember, I want to remember how you feel tonight till the last of my days."

I leaned my head back on his shoulder and kissed him, sinking down on his cock slower. "I don't think I could ever forget any of my moments with you," I said, my chest raising fast from the buildup of heat in my veins. "They've not been inked like these vows, they've been branded. I remember every single touch of yours. Every single time you've touched me. Every single time you've told me you've loved me, even...even when I've not said it back. The one regret I will have for all of my lives." I crushed my mouth to his again when he made to speak. Whatever he wanted to say, it would have broken my heart, I knew it.

His hand slid down my stomach, the touch so gentle it felt like the lick of spring wind. While the other hand tangled in my hair, holding my head still while he kissed me back.

Heat coiled at the pit of my stomach, teasing and taunting me the more erratic the joining of our bodies grew. His fingers circled my centre while I rode him, slapping my sex every time I went faster than he wanted me to. Little did he know, it only spurted me worse, drove me insane, the heated flesh growing hotter while his thickness bruised me from inside. It hit me too suddenly, the wave of release rolling too unexpectedly, and he put a hand over my mouth to drown my tense moans.

I didn't stop, no matter the breathlessness or the tiredness that threatened to collapse my very bones. I didn't stop until I felt him thicken and jerk inside of me, until he buried his face on my neck to suppress his own moans.

My body slumped against his. Tired to even move even the slightest.

I looked down at my body still connected to his, over at the red marks he'd left everywhere, grinning to myself. "Do you think they will like the change of rules? This instead of white ink?"

He smacked a few big, wet kisses on my cheek. "We make our own rules, as always. We've always made our own rules."

For a fraction of a second, I held my breath. And a clock slowly ticked at the back of my mind.

It was like the whole game had reset at hearing those words.

The coin had already been tossed by fate and the foe behind the white lines was another.

One move had already been made and the Fischer clock on the side counted not days or hours—it counted months.

Waiting for me to make my own move.

Fate had sat across, counting my every move on every game since I'd started playing with it.

All of my moves had changed from time to time and it had shown me each endgame. All end games. Only one detail had always remained the same in each of them.

Aurora. Dead.

The one strategy I'd never changed.

"Love?" Kilian called, bringing me out of the depths of flashing thoughts dating from the start of it all.

Shit There was so much I had missed. So much I had overlooked.

I smiled at Kilian. "You're so smart, my darling."

His brows rose and he chuckled, that little dimple distracting me again. "Am I now?" He carefully held onto me while reaching the edge of the patch of land we stood on, touching the water surface. "It is a bit cold. Do you mind it?"

"It is supposed to be cold," I said, flicking a few drops on his face.

He cupped a bit of water on his hand and began washing the white paint from my skin, little by little, unhurriedly and so gently. Then it was my turn and I wasn't so gentle as him. Wherever I wanted to touch, I touched. More inappropriate places than where I'd painted, so my turn took twice as long.

"There," I whispered. "They've gone to the heavens, all of our vows." How could I have ever...ever thought of not fighting back whatever force, divine or not, for him? Just for him and him alone. This...he was what I deserved.

I deserved this.

Him.

The future I wanted.

His stupid smile grew ridiculous. "They have. Long ago. When I was fifteen and the girl with silk black hair made me swear I would wait on her."

"Thank you for staying a brunette for me," I said, tussling his wavy wet locks. "I really don't like blonds."

The whole cave echoed my squeals when he threw me over his shoulder.

The sound of the crackling wood and the chitters of night were lulling. Even the heavy noises of the camp around us suddenly sounded majestic. It didn't help that I was tucked in Kilian's embrace, braced by his body heat, as I stared up at the clear night skies and the thin crescent moon, feeling bone tired and so, so adored.

Not once had he stopped murmuring gentle words in my ear the whole time he'd held me there, swaying us.

And sleep came softly. But the dreams did not.

Dreams I'd dreamt of before. More vivid and detailed than before.

Vast white emptiness surrounded me.

The little white-haired girl in the forest beyond the portal was staring back at me again. Black eyes widening. The whisper of death calling again. All flashed so quickly before I was thrust inside the same vision I'd seen back in Seraphim. Chaos. Flame and ashes stained with blood. Burned bodies covered by snow littered around me. Desperate calls carrying my name screamed in the distance, they were voices I knew so well.

Everything was the same.

Except.

This time I saw who pushed the blade through my chest, almost felt it, even. In the middle of it all, I stood there, bleeding and surrounded by white fire, feathers scattered everywhere, burning and charring, spreading with the northern cold wind. The Guardian did not lay dead. Nor defeated.

A pale hand wrapped around the hilt, belonging to the woman with pearlescent white flaming hair and the darkest, deepest eyes I'd ever stared into. Aurora tilted her head to the side, her massive white wings folding back. "*You can see me.*"

I jerked awake, words and air robbed out of me, heaving from pain and the burning sensation dressing my skin.

I didn't need to see to know who had just pressed his forehead to mine, slowly rocking us back and forth and murmuring repeatedly, "Come back to me."

Her words were still whispering in my ear, blocking the call of comfort my husband's voice was chanting.

But he didn't stop. Not even for a breath. Calling until I heard nothing else but him.

"She's awake, Kil. Aurora is awake." My fingers trembled when I tried to lift them up to see if I had truly bled. And I had, but from much smaller wounds only deep enough to remind me of pain. "I'm sorry. So sorry. I didn't mean—"

He held my hands, bringing them to his chest that was beating furiously. "It's alright. You're alright. You're alright," he repeated more to himself than me.

Over Kilian's shoulder, Golgotha had narrowed his eyes on me from the distance of the forest. Confused, he stepped closer and closer, frowning and coming to a halt when I grinned.

I breathed in the man holding me. "Call Visha for me, darling, please."

And so he did.

The moment Kilian and Visha had left, Golgotha took a seat on the fire next to me while I tried to drink the herby tea Nia had made for my headache.

"Born a villain," he said, carving a piece of wood with a knife. "Will die a hero. The history books will love you."

"Look around," I said. "What hero would take all those they love to battle? A hero would have died alone. I'm no hero. No martyr."

"You will be a hero."

"I'll make sure to *graze* a couple of soldiers on my way out. Make sure that bright light is not shone on my character as well as my deeds."

He laughed harshly and then narrowed his eyes at the dark distance ahead. "You summoned her on purpose, didn't you, in your vision?"

"Did I?" I asked, sipping my tea a bit loudly.

"And then you let the witch enter your head after the vision."

I took another loud sip from my tea. "Hm." Didn't need the remainder, my head was still pounding from Visha's craft.

He kept carving the small wooden piece in his hand. "To collect her essence, I presume. I've got no other answer why you would subject yourself to the pain."

I slowly nodded, trying to finish my tea.

"You found her weakness, her flaw, didn't you?"

Leaning back, I sighed. "I did. Found mine as well. And *Death's*. Fate's, too. I have found out a lot."

His knife stopped carving and he finally looked at me. "You think you can escape what you were shown by a *Reaper of Death*?"

"Escaping would require running and hiding. Do you see me running or hiding?"

He went silent, his eyes thinning. When he opened his mouth to speak, I asked, "Tell me, Master of Chaos, what would happen upon the death of a Guardian like Aurora?"

Macaria had told me all about it after we'd returned from the caves, but a second opinion was always good.

His serpent eyes thinned. "Pure chaos," he replied. "The balance of magic would tip the realm into destruction. The way mine lacked it, yours will be overwhelmed with it. Drowned and then deformed." His eyes spun like a dark abyss, flashing with quick images. "Burning cold ice would come first, then the sun would rain down fire. The skies would collapse. Earth would sink." Finally, his eyes went back to normal and he relaxed back on the tree stump. "And more like it. She's made of flames, forged from the purity of white fire. There is a reason why such chaos is locked into someone—to make it controllable. If the vessel holding it dies, it will set loose."

If I'd learned one thing from all this, it was that nothing happened to me without cause. The child I'd seen through the portal was no coincidence. Neither were the visions she'd shown me. Why the damned hells it had taken me so long to figure it out was a question for the books.

A warning.

All was a warning of what would happen if I killed Aurora as I'd always planned to do.

Guardians had an essence, according to what Nia had read. Some were made to ruin and others made to heal. Like Meira, Nubil's old lover. The land had accepted her gift to heal after she'd died. Nia had read that the Guardian had been born out of a child's laughter, another form of pure chaos. Just a chaos that was not destructive like Aurora's.

"And mine? What would happen if I died?"

"You know, don't you?"

I looked over at the *zgahna*, over where my ancestors' power lay and remained after years and decades. "I do."

It would protect.

43

White King to E2

Kilian

WHATEVER HANGOVER LINGERED OVER our people from the night before had disappeared by dawn. Every face I passed through our camps was hardened with deep concentration. They'd all seen Snow's panic last night. It had for some reason steeled them harder, especially her people. There was no forgiveness in their eyes. No doubt either.

Tristin landed right in front of me before I got to enter the tent where my wife had chosen to spend solitude. She breathed hard. "Silas's creatures have just left the cities and are marching towards ours and Moriko's borders."

"And the Guardian?"

"Nowhere to be seen, my king. Crafters are saying they cannot feel her presence anywhere near us."

"Because she is not," Visha said, walking out of a tent along with Penelope. "It means Silas has not given her a command yet, her state is still dormant. He could be scared to let her free from the sceptre for longer than necessary, like Kegan."

"Where is Snow?" Tristin asked. "The men should see her before they march towards Isjord."

"Brooding," Cai said, buttoning up his grey leathers. "She gets to slay Silas's dreams. She's taking this extremely well. Any news from Mal and Elias?"

"They are inside Tenebrose along with Golgotha," Visha explained.

He laughed. "Bet Golgotha's scent is driving the witches mad."

Penelope coughed a little. "I can attest to that. The magic print around him feels foul. I'm glad he is gone."

Snow was alone in the main tent, standing before the map, her eyes on one object—the lone king figurine standing in the castle. "So, he will not fight."

"Skadi had heard healers say that Silas lost half of his vision when he held the sceptre for the first time after it joined. However powerful his armour is, there will be tax when using magic he is not supposed to use. It will work in our favour. The target will no longer be moving. Elias knows that place inside out and Moregan will wait for her on the other side. His defences will be down when Thora goes to him." The moment Memphis brought the news to camp, Elias had joined Mal and Golgotha in Tenebrose. Details had changed quickly and we'd had to make new adjustments.

Her fingers drummed on the table. "Everything is ready now. Everyone is where everyone is supposed to be. I guess the real game starts now."

"And are you?"

She turned to me, leaning against the table. "Darling, you might say I was born with a taste for blood."

"This is more than a hunt, my little huntress."

"Indeed," she said, running her hands up and down my chest. "It's my best hunt. No more lists, no more counting. If I take her down, no one will ever make it on any list of mine. What would you think about putting her head on our bedroom wall? I was thinking of displaying her wings in our living room."

"Confidence is really running high, huh?"

"Do you know who my husband is? He can do very, very bad things to people at a click of his fingers."

Bells rang in the far distance, and she shut her eyes tightly, trying to calm her breaths. She took my right hand, her shaky fingers tracing the golden tattoo of our blessing. "Don't let me hurt you, promise me."

I pressed my lips against hers. "You can never hurt me."

Nilsa, Caspian, Larg, Triad, Cai, and Tristin were already gathering around the battalions they were commanding. The six along with me would direct the troops in Isjord. Mal and Thora would soon join from inside Isjord, and Eren—

I looked up at the skies already rousing with heavy winds.

He'd join us soon like the rest.

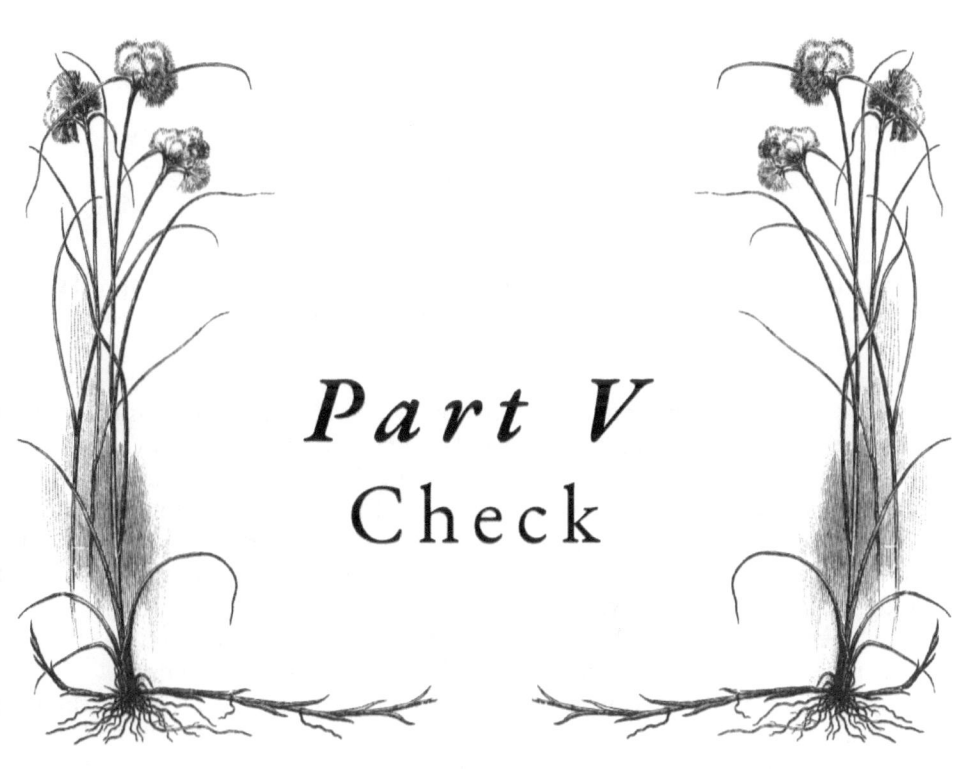

Part V
Check

44

Black Rook takes C3

Snowlin

I HAD FELT HER before the sirens had gone off in the distance of our camp. I'd seen her before I'd even felt her presence stain the air.

I would face her today, but so would my people.

Armed, their grey leathers dyed black to blend amongst the Adriatian soldiers flawlessly, their faces emotionless and streaked with white marks of blessings from their loved ones, they had marched early today towards Isjord, unshaken.

"I hope one day you will forgive me," I said to my generals who lined up for orders to lead their troops ahead. "For bringing you here. For not being able to stop this."

Tristin stepped forward. "It is an honour we get to fight it with you by our side and leading us, my queen. Your father took our hope when he took your mother, but he brought it back to us unknowingly when he gave us you."

Cai bowed his head and all of his men followed. "We will rise!" he shouted.

"Between clouds and skies!" his soldiers echoed, disappearing into portals.

My friend stepped before me, clasping my shoulder. "Don't die. I want to rebuild that bakery in Myrdur and take you to smell the apple in the sunset." He lifted a hand between us, holding a little salted caramel candy up to me. "Bury me right under there if I die."

My eyes drew shut and I clasped his hand, bringing it to my chest. "I've never thanked you for the cake." For saving me when I did not want to be saved.

He smiled. "Could be your last chance to say those dreaded words."

"I love you, Cai."

He pulled me to his chest and held me tightly. It was brief, but I knew he hated himself for letting emotion overtake his rage. "I love you, too, Cakes."

Then I watched fathers, mothers, daughters, and sons give each other a final good-bye. I watched them struggle to tear themselves from their loved ones. I watched lovers retreat back with small children in their arms, bidding perhaps a forever goodbye to whoever they were sending off. I watched the elderly put on a brave face over their regret and apology as they wished good luck and prayers of return to their children, nieces, and nephews.

Kilian reached my side and pressed his forehead to mine. And we stood there for a while. What did one say at this moment? That I loved him? Would it compensate for the many more times we would have said it if we survived today—for the lifetime we promised one another? "In this life and all the next."

"In this life," he breathed, reaching for the bowl of white paint and dipping the tip of his finger in it. He drew a line across my forehead and another down my chin—the marks of my tribe. The mark of Myrdur. "First in this life."

"Kilian—"

"I'm going to have you in this life until we are sick of it. Until we are sick of all the laughter and happiness. I'm going to have you in this life first. I am done losing you. I will fight until I can't fight anymore, but I will fight."

I dipped my fingers in the paint and drew the mark of my people on him. "I will, too."

"Good." He kissed me. And it wasn't a kiss of goodbye. It was lingering with a promise for later. For another. For many others. Unfinished. Incomplete. He unbuttoned the front of his leathers and guided my palm over the paint before resting it on his chest, letting me mark him and feel his heart beat so roughly under my touch. "I will see you out there."

"Be careful."

He let go of me and very slowly forced himself to step back. "You forget who I am," he said, puffing his shoulders and flicking some invisible dust from his black leathers.

"Show-off."

"You love it."

"I love *you*."

His steps halted and we stood there silently still in the distance. If he came and if he held me again, I would break. So I stepped back, too, putting distance between us. "Say it."

"I'll say it after this ends."

With one last smile, he turned around and disappeared between other bodies.

After. He'd say it after.

A line of tears traced a hot path down my face.

"After," I echoed long after he'd gone.

There would be an after.

There would be...an after.

It would.

And I will get to live every single fantasy of mine.

I would not fail today.

Memphis nudged my leg and I bent down to her, showering her with pets, kisses, and hugs that I had probably denied her often. "Fly to Olympia."

Her large yellow eyes shivered and she let out a low yowl that made me regret every moment in this life that I had spent with her and not held her tighter.

"Go," I said, hugging her to me one last time. "Keep watch over Olympia for me."

She rested her forehead against mine. *Forever your eyes in the skies.*

"Forever," I repeated back, letting her go.

My bonded shifted into an eagle, screeching a high-pitched sound that caused the wind to halt as if in command before she launched towards the blue skies, disappearing into their depths.

"Are you certain about this?" Visha nervously called, and I spun to her.

"No." I was not sure about anything that would happen today. I was not even sure what I'd realised the night before was even true or if it was just a way my mind had found to cope with it all—with my death. "But I was hoping you would be since this was mostly your idea."

She shivered, her pale eyelids fluttering fast. "You will not tell Kilian this was my idea, will you?"

"Keep me alive first."

She shakily nodded. "Do not be tempted to kill Aurora. You know her weakness, you are her weakness, but do not be tempted to kill her whatever she does or whoever she hurts. She has to be commanded back to the sceptre. Keep holding her back until we've got the sceptre."

"And if I can't? If I lose control?"

Oryn appeared behind her along with Macaria and Penelope. "If the king fails to bind you with his magic, we will try to contain you for as long as we can," the man said, almost regretfully. "Then we will direct your magic to another realm that accepts it without stealing away your control over it. A realm that needs it."

I was also not sure how they would do that either no matter how many times Visha had explained to me.

Penelope had blanched and she shook entirely. "I don't want to do this. It is not what we talked about in the meeting, Snow, please." She cried. "I don't want to do this. If your seal opens entirely—"

Macaria put a hand on her shoulder. "We will try, won't we, my sweet child? For the sake of many."

Pen's tear-filled gaze lifted up to mine. "Let's tell him, Snow. Kilian needs to know what you told us all. What might happen." The young one's eyes pleaded with me one last time. But soon she gave up altogether, giving her grandmother a nod despite the tears. "Alright then."

The four Crafters linked their hands in a circle around me. Ancient letters flew out of their tongues, and slithery tentacles of glistening red raced between their linked fingers to hover in my air.

A vacuum suddenly opened above me, feeding onto their magic, and then...I felt the seal open halfway through, much more than it had ever opened before.

The power came like the clash of two storms and a barrelling thunder.

Pain struck me hard, immediate and relentless, pounding against my bones and branding my skin. The seal on my back peeled open like a wound. And my magic crawled out of it like burning salt.

I felt...I felt—

So much.

I could taste the air, touch it, sense every living thing around it—heartbeats, voices, the buzz of wings, the faraway roll of waves—everything. The muffled noise of the *zgahna* had finally stopped, and the words were now clear, no longer a buzz. A shiver went down my spine at the voices I heard. The voices it had collected all of those years.

Laughter, screams, the cooing of a child, orders, prayer. All...all it had witnessed over the centuries it had protected us.

All four Crafters turned towards the rumbling Volants behind them. Watching the ancient fog roll down the mountains in a terrifying wave, engulfing everything under it. The ruins, forest, and village, heading towards where the battle ahead awaited.

I bolted to the top of the Theros walls, watching the Isjordian army enter the Sun City entirely, finding it empty, unprotected. Their confusion was evident. So much so that no one looked victorious as much as they looked afraid.

Cora appeared beside me, battle ready. "You can give them a choice. They still can have the choice to abandon this war, Snowlin."

"They had a choice. They've chosen to die."

And when all city gates rolled down all at once, the ground below shook from the force and so did the sunny skies from the immediate storm rolling over the blinding sun.

Then...thunder rained. Furiously. Blinding. Burning. Heavy. Unexpectedly. For miles along, the scenery glowed brighter and hotter than the sun itself. There was no time for screams or pleas or running away, they all melted under the heavy weight of their armour and greed.

The beige stone walls of the massive city were stained with soot and blood. The air was choking with the electric taste, but it stank of burning flesh and smoke.

Solaryan soldiers rolled out from their hiding spot, archers lining the whole city wall perimeter.

Every *khamir* beast that slowly revived from my attack, did not escape the soul killers pouring down like hail on them. There was no battle to ensue when Solaryan soldiers descended below. Only slaughter. No bodies to bury. Ash had already settled.

I turned to Cora who had overlooked the small battalion here. "And Magnus?" My voice was not my own, and the Sun Queen hesitated as did I, her eyes wide.

"What remains of the Isjordian fleet will not last long. My husband is one with the seas, he will not need help. Go, we will all meet in Isjord."

Nodding, I floated overhead until the city below grew smaller and smaller, and then I bolted again much further away. I had an oath to keep and my hands were itching to burn and unburden myself from the promise I'd given to those who'd dared fight against me.

The moment I reappeared over Hanaian waters, the small distance between the Sayuri and Aru where Isjordians were sailing to attack the Autumn Kingdom, the wind halted and so did the ships being stirred by it. Soldiers put a hand over their brows, squinting up at me, grasping it a little too late what I was about to do.

Skies raged once again.

And the Borough waters boiled from the temperature, tall waves crashing and sizzling against each other, thick steam lifting towards the skies where Volantians hid and waited for the survivors to reappear.

I did not wait this time to see the beasts evaporate from soul killers, I bolted again.

45

White Bishop to B2

Malik

AMERIE CRADLED A SLEEPING Serene in her arms, carefully looking through her curtains outside where Tenebrose city guards were patrolling the streets

Elias paced back and forth enough to annoy the shit out of me. "We should be out there."

"You're the only one who knows how to get inside the castle walls without being seen. Follow the plan and Snow won't skin you. But most importantly," I said, pulling him away from the window, "my brother won't rip your blonde soul out."

The Demon God who had occupied Amerie's sofa grunted. "I do agree with the yellow-headed human. We shouldn't be hiding."

"Unless his excellency can whip out some magical powers to get inside that castle where Silas has sat his bony arse to enjoy the show, then he should shut up."

He narrowed his dark eyes on me. "You're rude, boy. You know I am not allowed to fight your kind and my purpose was to mask your magic. Haven't I done enough? Not one witch has sniffed you out while you offended every deity of death alive when you raised the whole city graveyard on its feet." He swivelled a look over me. "Godling of Death."

The moment the war horns blared through the city of Tenebrose to signal the advance of their troops, Elias tensed.

"That's my signal," I said, backing away from them. "Find Silas and help Thora when she comes."

Elias's jaw was set tight, his hand tightening around the hilt of his sword. "*If* she comes."

"She will come. Do not die recklessly. Wait for her. My army of the dead will break through the city soon. Do not let any Isjordians get out of their homes. My dead cannot tell the difference when it comes to killing. They will attack whoever they see in these streets." I pointed to Golgotha who was picking out the raisins from Amerie's biscuits. "Don't do anything a squid wouldn't do."

And then I faded right in front of the Isjordian troops, heavily marching towards our own. I kneeled and sank my fingers into the snow until I was able to feel the soil beneath along with the pulse of death. There was no struggle to find signs of it because bones of all sorts rose from under the cold blanket of winter.

Dozens.

Hundreds.

Thousands.

Tens of thousands of skeletons broke the surface. All around me for miles along.

And more approached from behind them in distance, descending the hill of Tenebrose cemetery to trap the army from all sides.

Human. Aura. Animal. I was the master of all death.

They stood when I stood, their steps matching mine, obeying to my command.

Cold wind blew a cast of frost back, and then monsters of another sort prowled along the dead army. Wolves made of frost, taller than I, bigger than a boulder. And there were hundreds of them. Thora appeared through a portal right beside me. Her creatures matching their master's steps who took my side, her bow strung tight, aimed ahead at the figures that were sharpening and getting closer to us.

Her lips trembled a little and I knew it wasn't from the cold.

"Aim true, Thora."

She sucked in a sharp breath and held it, her bow tightening when black tattoos began appearing over her hands. Her arrow pierced through the misty surface hiding Isjordian troops, and the whole blanket of frost pulled back entirely, peeling from the gust of powerful wind that blew at her silent command to reveal lines and lines of navy clad soldiers and beasts stretching for miles, marching in our direction.

The *anima accissor* tipped arrow had etched on the body of a *khamir* beast, its limbs already melting into dust.

Lightning flashed across the skies, blue blinding light casting strong shadows below—stronger than the darkness did—and they elongated, twisted, grew claws and teeth, wrapping around soldiers.

The touch of first blood grazed the white snow and it felt like time stilled.

I didn't know who launched towards who first, but within the next second of the wind revealing everything, deafening chaos ensued. The dead twisted around the living, pulling and tugging them apart. Beasts crashed against frost wolves laced with blue gyre and silver, sending splintering ice and black blood raining down on the battle ground. Thunder grew loud, but not loud enough to drown the noise below.

Grabbing onto Thora, I faded the two of us back to our front lines blocking the Isjordian path.

"Elias?" my brother asked, stepping forward and rolling his shoulders.

"He is in."

"And the dead?"

"Attacking. More are rising and descending Tenebrose as we speak."

The empty field of snow ahead began filling. Isjordian troops finally made their way out of Sable Abyss Forest that had concealed their vast numbers. Millions marched towards us. More monsters than humans.

"Good," my brother said. "Step back, the both of you."

The taste of death filling the space packed with frost made my stomach twist.

Darkness deeper than tar, thicker than tar, hungrier than a starved serpent, dripped from my brother, and the bounds he'd put to control it broke free for the very first time. His fingers began turning black, phantom claws growing, his eyes hidden beyond the veil of darkness. A blanket of death crawled ahead, prowling like a hunting beast, an icy black fire burning wherever it touched, turning the snowy ground a solid grey ice that was colder than anything. We all watched my brother's magic rise like tidal waves for long miles and engulf thousands of soldiers and beasts under.

There were no screams, no pleas, no fight at all as many disappeared into it. Nothing echoed for a minute. Just pure silence. No corpses collapsed, no weapons dropped. They all simply vanished. Consumed by death. My brother's magic had eaten almost halfway through the enemy lines.

Kilian stopped before I could tell him to. Already seeing his colourful shadows turn entirely black.

Isjordians still continued pouring endlessly despite the damage Kilian had done. Soldiers crashed against soldiers. I fed on Isjordian fear and our soldiers' bravery, my strings thickening, doubling, and elongating to summon more dead, fortifying our numbers.

Smoke and steam blurred all sight, blocking most of our surroundings, and I tore through dozens of beasts, my sword already soaked and dented, to reach somewhat close to her.

Thora stood between a circle of wolves, firing rounds of arrows on the *khamir* beasts. No one was able to get close to her, all were shredded the second they would step near her radius. And now I could finally focus on finding the Empaths that were controlling the beasts.

But each one I found slit their own throat the second they saw me.

"Fuck," I hissed.

I pushed through the bodies again, fading, cutting, inflicting pain on every Isjordian force I came across, searching for more Empaths. The further in I dove, the louder the noises grew, the more bitter death tasted. All my senses were heightened. Chaos and death feeding them like a drug.

Then...sudden burning heat melted the cold wind into steam. Specks of white fire burned under Kilian's gusts of darkness until they began breaking through.

Something bright shone overhead, almost as strongly as the sun.

The Guardian stood overhead watching all of us like prey. White wings and hair dipped in pearlescent fire, her skin gleaming with specks of glitter. She spoke no words or lifted no limb when a wash of fire rained down on us.

The skies turned to night in a blink and the fire evaporated against Kilian's darkness. Adriatian Aura took the lead, profiting from night, and beasts and soldiers stilled and were slayed without a fight.

Aurora's presence had dimmed, but not diminished.

And the next wave of her attack was even more severe.

Yet my brother withstood and took the impact of it.

Over and over.

46

Black Rook takes E3

Caiden

MORE. THERE WERE MORE of them that we had counted, and now their main weapon hovered over our heads, sputtering fire that burned the air itself. The moment a sliver of it touched skin, the whole body burned into ash. But none...not even she had taken as many lives as the creature I was walking towards had.

The immortal general turned his head to me, bearing sharp teeth and claws, prowling in my direction and launching in the air. Only to crash against my air shield, his whole body shook when I seized the air in his lungs. You see, I was quicker than most. It was why Alaric had recruited me to train long ago, and since then, I'd only gotten better.

I chuckled. "Go on. Breathe. It is not so hard."

"I remember you," he wheezed, raising one shaky limb at a time. "I remember your scent. Not from the village. Before. Even earlier on. You look just like him, too. Like your father."

I must have faltered, because he suddenly got back on his feet, almost grazing my stomach with his claws.

The wind turned sharp at my order, slashing thin strips of wounds all over his scaled flesh, black blood spurting everywhere.

"Skilled just like him, I see," he groaned when my daggers flew towards him and embedded deep in his forearms.

This man knew my own father better than me. He'd gotten to see him, to remember his face, and I hadn't. This man had been the one to deprive me of the only thing I'd ever desired. This man had robbed me of everything.

"He was hard to kill." He launched in the air again, breaking through the barrier of air I'd lifted, causing me to stumble back to avoid another hit. "But with a little effort," he growled, a slabbery sneer curling over his fangs, "I got there."

My fist shot forward, hard wind knocking him back, and then he was struggling to breathe again. "He died protecting our people," I said, reaching and slashing my sword through his chest to nail him to the ground. "And I will die killing you."

"I cannot be killed."

His clawed hand wrapped around the magic forged steel and a blood curdling growl of pain escaped him when the metal hissed and steamed against his skin.

"Blue gyre," I whispered, nailing another dagger on his hand to pin him down. "All over your bloodstream and all over my metal. You weak, pathetic, son of a bitch."

He laughed when a wave of screams tore the air, the sound so rough and dark and wicked. Kilian's shield had broken in places from Aurora's attack and the white fire had consumed most that it had rained over. "You're useless. Just like him, just like your father," he taunted. "What are you going to—"

His words were cut in half. The greyed ceiling above cried and shook the grounds below, thunderous rain poured on us, and a thick, stentorian lightning suddenly shot from the skies, knocking Aurora to the ground.

I laughed in the beast's face, feeling my friend's power fill the atmosphere so intensely. "Knock, knock, motherfucker."

The thing began breathing faster, his eyes darting around relentlessly trying to find where Aurora had disappeared.

I nailed another dagger on his hand, and another. Many others. Making sure to prepare him nicely for who was to serve his cold and painful slow death.

A whistle rang close by, and every beast's head snapped in my direction, growling and then running towards me at his order.

I nailed another dagger on his other arm and stood, unsheathing my sword. "Shit."

Something crashed on the ground next to me, a boom echoing right after. It was like two slabs of land had hit each other, sending an icy wind nearly piercing everything in sight. Eren's face was covered in black markings. Wind and ice manipulating and twisting at his command, blowing and slicing the beasts and soldiers into a thousand pieces. Red and black blood sprayed all over...all over for miles.

And he wasn't done.

No. Not even close to being done.

The part of the battlefield we stood on cleared, emptied. Only death remained. "Cai!" he shouted, backing towards our troops. "Look back."

Vas broke free just when Eren was about to turn his attention to him. But instead of crashing against wind or ice, he stilled on the spot, eyes wide and starting to glow red.

She was right on time.

He dropped to the ground, revealing Visha standing behind him. Her fingers twirled with red shadows, slithering like serpents around her body and over the icy ground until they engulfed Vas entirely. "Hello, Vas."

Both of their figures disappeared soon after. And so did Eren.

I was alone in a pit of beasts, fighting off as many as I could, searching and sorting through dead bodies to find him. "Eren!"

47

White King takes E3

Visha

NOTHINGNESS SURROUNDED US. AN empty white pane stretching for miles ahead. Both above and below.

Vas was in his human form, staring back at me. "Your aunt underestimates you," he said, his voice muffled in the wide expanse.

"No. She has appropriately estimated me. You, on the other hand, underestimate how afraid a man can be. Of simple things." It was not difficult to draw the memory. Not from his thoughts. From the lingering spirits of people he once had loved that still hovered around our worlds.

The unblessed had this curse, you see. To linger. To fester. To hate. Erna, Drystan's Crafter, had a gift to call and heed. So, she had called on all those spirits and lingering souls who had known him. Drained them out of every bit of memory they had of him and given them to me. It had taken me three storage units worth of vials and a whole month to go through them all.

"So," he said, spinning round. "You're going to keep me here all the way through the battle? Locked up inside my own mind."

"No. Only until I break you."

"I can't be broken."

"But your soul can."

His amusement faltered into bitter disgust. "You cannot break my soul, *witch*."

"I've never seen Snow so perplexed trying to figure out something. However, as usual, she was right. Fader kept your body undying, eternal, void from sickness and disease, fortified it in a way no one could touch. But death is not death if both body and soul have not been taken. And life is not life if both body and soul are not alive. Though many have attempted to defy Celesteel, the order of life and death cannot be defied even by the greatest God there is. It is as simple as that."

Snow had doubted it long ago, but only confirmed it when she'd struck the deal with the Prince of Ustrina. Vas had no soul. She'd played her luck that day and won more than just a bargain.

Melanthe had used the seedling to control the other beasts, but he was the only one who had absolute control over his body.

Because there was no soul in it to be corrupted by the magic of the Caligo beast blood.

He clapped languidly, the sound echoing. "What a fantastic discovery. I. Am. Unbeatable. That much I thought you knew."

"I found it. I found your soul."

His hands dropped to the side, his face twisting with anger and wild disbelief. "What?"

"In order for a life to be unclaimable, both soul and body must be parted from one another. Usually impossible. A body cannot survive without a soul, but Fader fixed that. Part of you is in the Mid-world. Part of you walked Numen. That is how Fader could defy rules older than him, placed by deities greater than him. Now, I can defy him." At the click of my fingers, a cold shadow appeared beside me, and it seemed to impress my guest because his eyes grew wide. "It was swimming in the Sea of the Dark, so alone and lost like no soul in this God blessed realm should ever be. You have Snow to thank for this reunion. For your...salvation. Welcome inside my mind, Vas," I said, and the surroundings twirled into colourful patterns to slowly form a memory—a painful one. I could not plant it back in his mind, but I could plant it in mine. Like a dream veil almost. "Let's break yours."

48

Black Knight to E6

Kilian

SILAS'S MEN AND MONSTERS crashed heavily against our front.

Like silk, darkness slipped from my fingertips, a cloud of onyx smoke enveloping the enemy lines.

At the click of my fingers, the cloud disappeared, leaving behind floating ash that blew in the northern wind, disappearing without leaving any trace of a soul or its flesh.

I felt a splinter somewhere deep and far inside my mind with how many deaths my darkness had consumed so far. Just a splinter.

I'd bear a thousand more by the end.

Power leaked in the air, filling the cold winter wind with unnatural heat which was almost synthetic in feel against my own. The snow below began melting away, the wind halted altogether, and the skies cleared when Aurora rose again from under my control. Isjordian troops halted and took shield from what was hovering above them, bracing for her attack that did not spare them any grace either.

The white-haired woman loomed above us, studying the ground below—expectant. She lifted a pale white hand towards us and white sparks began appearing out of nowhere, lighting the air itself in white flames.

No wind, ice, or shadow resisted its spread no matter how many Aura called upon their blessing to shield from the burn.

Not until it crashed against darkness, soon then dissipating and disappearing, letting wind blow again, the cold air returning to pimple our skin.

She tried again.

And again, it was met with darkness.

Howls rang in the air and the Isjordian forces continued to launch towards us, but this time they were aiming for me.

I faded away, avoiding impact, disappearing and reappearing between fighting bodies, claiming as many lives as I could while I took the impact of Aurora's attacks.

Her pale eyes landed on me and she suddenly dropped to the ground, the force causing those around her to melt and the ground to liquify into mud. She slowly stalked in my direction, tilting her head and studying my magic as it wrapped around her in a large dome to shield those around us, causing her to falter in her steps.

The air hissed the words even before she opened her mouth to speak, "What are you?"

I panted heavily. "Night." And at my command, the skies darkened again, the sun hid, and the full moon glazed the white winter earth. Aurora stood out in the dark, the pearlescent flames dripping from her skin and hair had lit her like a torch, creating a slew of extended shadows just underneath her and nowhere else.

She glanced down at her many shadows that had gone pin still and began elongating and extending far in the distance until they turned into thin strings attached to the Umbra hiding in the darkness far from here who'd been waiting for this moment.

And while she was bound in place, I let cold death and darkness pour out of me, crawling and surrounding her until she was engulfed by them. Overwhelmed with life, death only grew larger. But so did her flames. The ground beneath began melting, the snow turning into water, and the air sizzling like burnt ashes.

An echo of screams followed suit, skin and bone melting from the unbearable heat she was emitting. And soon, the shadows under her burned, too. Setting her free again.

Fuck.

Macaria's Crafters between the lines of battle lit up in the glow of their magic, red and violet phantom chains rising from the muddy earth, shooting and wrapping towards Aurora's limbs. Once she was trapped, her mana seeped through the leaching metal that bound her.

Fed from the harrowing death littering my surroundings, darkness crawled like a hungry beast, rising from every little drop of blood, scream, clatter of metal, and caused by the purest forms of emotion—anger, greed, rage.

Those that stepped in my direction all melted into the air, turning and vanishing to dust, feeding the beast made of darkness even more till it rose tall enough and big enough to encircle the Guardian. She fought against it, but this time she struggled, faltered, white flames disappearing from her body, her skin greying.

She took a deep breath, her body forming a ball of fire as she rose to the skies again before blasting flames all over us. Hurting many below. Isjordians, too.

Then...the skies grew blue again. But not at my order.

And something chilled the air. Not winter. It wasn't something human or divine in perception at all.

Pellets of rain touched my skin as a warning before a downpour blurred the field of vision, soaking all those below. A cloud carrying a heavy storm moved quickly above us, painting the day with grey and filling the wind with a touch of electricity.

Aurora's white flames hissed at the touch of rain, dowsing a little, and she raised her head towards the skies, searching for something.

When the heavy clouds above began gurling beyond disturbed, I knew something was wrong...before even tasting the sweetness of her magic colouring the air.

Aurora's attention left me to search the skies again that had decided to paint a piece of unadulterated chaos.

All the hair on my body rose, and a metallic taste filled my mouth when the wind vibrated and a bolt of blinding lightning struck Aurora—the impact so severe that her body flew back for miles, disappearing between the thick forest, inside a deep crater that stretched the size of a small city.

Quiet fell all around us. The sound of metal clanging faded into faint hisses until it stopped altogether. Everyone waited to see the White Flame Guardian rise into the skies again, her mangled limbs that had contorted, broken, and blistered slowly cracked back into place, her ashen skin mending together to hide all scratches and wounds.

Her face slowly broke, going from stoic calm to twisting with rage. Her pale eyes had shot wide, searching the ground for what had struck her.

Our surroundings were packed with intense and overwhelming magic when dust, smoke, and steam cleared. It was like time had slowed and a sense of doom settled in.

A sense darker than death.

Something like destruction.

Heavy...the gravity had grown heavier too.

A hand thrust out from the snowy ground, luminescent veins drawn over the skin I'd touched so many times. Slowly, Snow rose from the white earth, almost reborn. Her dark hair floated around from electricity, her breathing hard, her golden eyes gone, hidden behind a white glow. She looked up at Aurora, her body floating in the air to stand before the Guardian.

There was no longer a barrier around Snow's magic, concealing and containing it like it had always been. Instead, the ancient power hovered around her in a twirl of terrifying magnificence, composing a tumultuous symphony with roaring thunder.

Aurora hesitated, studying Snow as Snow was studying her. Two of a kind. But all so different. Terribly different. A soldier facing a huntress.

Even though I could not see her face, I knew what was painted on my wife's features. Rage. Fury. Bloodthirst. "You hurt him," she spoke, and the words hissed along with the wind, repeating like a whisper all around us, over and over.

You hurt him. You hurt him. You hurt him. You hurt him. You hurt him. You hurt him. You hurt him. You hurt him.

And when she drew a breath, the wind drew a breath, too. "You shouldn't have done that."

"I will hurt many," Aurora's voice blared like a muffled horn. "It is easier if I started with just one first." She tilted her head to the side, looking over Snow's shoulder to me. "He would have done fine. But you are in my way."

"Time must have gone slowly locked in that sceptre," Snow crooned, and thunder cracked over the greying skies, pouring over Isjordian soldiers. Screams blended so naturally with nature almost as if they belonged in it. It wasn't until Snow drew out her sword that Aurora blinked. Not until the blade lit and heated with electricity did the old Guardian frown and draw out her own weapon—a simple staff with flaming edges. My wife chuckled. "I'd warn you to back away, but where would the fun be in that?"

"There is no backing away. Not anymore. This realm will be the ashes that I raise from with freedom. That sceptre will no longer be my prison."

"I'd disagree and add that my father's accommodations are much worse." Snow took her in head to toe, and the flames on the Guardian's wings shivered. "Take it from me, I've been in your...sandals."

"I am not his prisoner."

"Even more unfortunate for you to die belonging to no one—not even a master."

"And who is your master, might I ask?"

"You're looking at her."

Snow bolted, landing right before Aurora who caught the hit of her blade with the staff which cracked and broke in two from the strength and electricity. Snow swung again, and Aurora launched up, avoiding her blow. It took my wife not even a fraction of a second to bolt before her again and send the Guardian plummeting to the ground a second time. Except that this time, Aurora's large wings pulled back once, gliding against the strong wind, and helped her launch back up in the skies again. Barely halfway up in the air to Snow, lightning rained down on her body, restless bolts thicker than pillars, nailing her hard to the ground that hollowed and cracked into a large steaming hole the size of a volcano crater.

"Skygard," the Guardian hissed, struggling this time to drag herself up. "But you're not like the others, are you?" Aurora rose again, white flames burning around her, blasting to heat the air and burn the ground, along with all of us on it.

Thora and Eren were just as quick as I, and thin hoar frost froze the air, meeting and touching the white fire in the middle and dowsing it while my darkness surrounded and protected my wife, carefully latching onto her to keep her magic contained.

For the first time since she'd appeared, I saw Snow's shoulders raise with steady inhales. She had to be in pain from setting the seal free. Pain that I could not see.

Aurora's head tilted again to study us on the ground. "More Skygards."

Snow's smile was ungodly, her eyes were golden flames through the pale glow over them, radiating even in the far distance. "Whatever can kill a Guardian, we have it."

"Kill?" Aurora asked, almost amused.

"I never fight to spare." Snow looked over her shoulder at me and nodded.

And a dark dome of shadows rose up from the ground, engulfing the two in it. The magic was not perfect, but it was enough, mimicking the dream veil in Nephthys. It would protect her, and weaken Aurora, trapping her mind. Hopefully, enough to have her guards lowered and returned to the sceptre.

The White Flame Guardian looked at the shadows dimming her surroundings, but it was too late for her to fly out of the dome as pure darkness fuelled by the purest thunder crashed against her quicker than she could, her mind already locking.

And so it began.

White fire and lightning.

But not just lightning.

Cold lightning. Almost frozen.

Snow breathed out frost around us, and Aurora shivered, looking around utterly afraid.

"I know what your weakness is," Snow started, ice encapsulating even the shadow dome walls. "Do you know mine?"

49

White Rook to A3

Visha

It was strange. The struggle he put up was strange.

I'd twisted his memories, his mind, his perception of time and sense altogether. Yet he fought with such persistence. Snow was wrong. Anger was not the biggest driving force. Jealousy was. He had wanted what he'd been denied to the point of destruction. So much so that he'd convinced himself that what he felt for Aurora was love. The insane obsession he'd developed for her when Esmeray had introduced them was sickening, but I'd soon found out that her obsession for him had been worse.

It took time, patience, and an insane amount of magic to pull apart a soul from its living host. But to mend it together? Even more—more that I wasn't sure I even had. But like Snow, my own limits were being tested.

While I occupied his mind with haunting memories, letting his mind replay them until it bled dry, his soul was mending to his body one stitch at a time, each one threaded by my hand. Every single emotion. Every single feeling he'd had through life. Every single memory. There was so much. He'd lived for far too long. Felt things far too intensely. Even more so after he'd met Aurora.

He broke faster when it was her memories I planted back inside his empty mind. It was him lowering Melanthe's defences from the inside, opening the gates little by little for me to enter deeper, wanting more of her...more of that feeling he'd given her—elation of the highest form.

Every moment they'd spent together was an epiphany of sorts. She had been a drug to him. And the side effects had festered violently, just like the rush of the hit.

The air was stale from dark magic, unmoving, yet a chilling breeze blew past my neck, and I stiffened.

Something felt wrong.

It was only for a fraction of a moment that my consciousness slipped between the walls of my mind and reality to feel Snow's power spiral when Vas's green form let out a deep growl. "You should have kept all eyes on me, little witch."

His hand slipped through my protection veil before it rose entirely to shield me, claws not even an inch away from slicing my throat when something crashed against him.

My hand reached to my neck and I breathed out a sigh when no blood stained my palm. Blessed death.

A huge dire wolf made entirely of frost pinned Vas down, dragging its fangs through his throat.

Snow coated my eyelashes that were soaked with tears. "I had him. I...I had him." There was so little left to mend back. Only a little longer.

"Leave him," Thora shouted, pulling me back and dragging me away. "Snow needs you. Something is wrong. Why can I feel her, Visha? Her power keeps commanding me. It is driving me insane, I can't even focus to draw enough magic."

"We've freed the seal. Now it is about to open entirely. Sooner than I had expected."

Thora's mouth parted open with horror. "No, no, no, Visha. No!"

"Leave," Nilsa said, her fists burning as she walked in our direction. "The both of you, leave him and go help her. I've got an old debt to pay back."

The ice wolf was crushed to bits and Vas rose to his feet again, breathing fast and angry. "Down memory lane, aren't we, miss Veranesi?"

Nilsa's eyes burned, too. "Don't you look awful, old friend."

Thora let an arrow loose, hitting something behind me. "Help. Snow!" she bellowed, breathing hard, struggling to figure out which beast to aim at.

Raising a protection veil around me, I sat on the ground, drawing a binding halo with my blood around me and sinking my hands inside the snow to feel the ground below.

"This has to work," I murmured, my hands shaking. "It has to work."

"Penelope," I called, my own voice echoing down the chambers of my mind. *"It is time we call to Numengarth, to the soil and the air, the skies and the sun above, Snow's seal is opening. Heed to this call when you find my mother."*

But first, before I shut all the gates feeding Snow's magic to Ustrina, before I closed every single stream of her magic intercepting the in-between to enter Caligo, before I broke the connection entirely, I made the call to another gate—a call that I'd never made before.

To a realm that was no heaven.

To our realm.

My magic pierced the earth, seeking a new gate.

"Please, help her and she will help you," I chanted over and over in my mother tongue.

And then the waiting game began.

For a call that would perhaps never be accepted.

"Save her and she will save you," I whispered to the soil, the air, and the skies.

50

Black Knight takes D4

Nia

THE GROUND BENEATH OUR feet trembled from the force of the march of Isjordian troops towards us. The strong wind had misted from snow and disturbance, cloaking the view ahead and tricking our sight. Hanaian border walls were not tall—not tall enough to withstand the force of what was coming, but the small advantage had refrained us from waiting for Silas's army down below in his lands.

"I can fade closer to see how far they are," I said. The beasts had no heartbeat, no emotion, I could not feel anything even if they were to stand right in front of me.

Alaric answered before Moriko could, "Absolutely not."

"We can see nothing. They might be right below our walls for all it matters."

"And for all it matters," he said, "we will fight 'em still, near or far. Below or above. Battle is about patience, hen. Blood will be spilled one way or another."

"Your father is right," Sigurd said, leaning against the walls and squinting at the far distance. "They might want to lure us out there, that is why they are being so quiet. Their king knows our forces have joined yours. This is a trap. We'll wait."

Mor tensed for a moment, placing her hand on the wall border. "Maybe don't get too comfortable." Faster than I could notice, she pulled out her slender sword and jumped down the wall. The mist pulled around her and she emerged below shortly with black blood on her blade, a *khamir* body already disappearing into ashes. "Shields up!" she ordered, and the sound of the shields being raised ricocheted all throughout the length of the wall until it faded in the long distance.

"Archers!" her general called, and the whole wall was lined with soldiers aiming their bows ahead.

It was only then I caught heavy shadows approaching us, piercing the thick fog and barrelling ahead with all they had.

I held my breath, panic raking my bones when Mor did not return back to the wall terrace.

When thousands of arrows slid through the silent air, chaos broke loose.

I lost sight of her in less than a second.

A strong wind blew the misty disguise away to reveal thousands of beasts and soldiers crawling up the border walls and filling the field ahead. I appeared between them, engulfed between shadows, fading rapidly from corner to corner, searching and feeling the air for the Empaths that were controlling them. The sounds of battle were dizzying, the vibrations of metal meeting metal almost nauseating.

Luckily, the Glares were melting the cold earth below and warming the air, causing Isjordian attacks to weaken.

Isliners barrelled through bodies, recklessly almost, slaughtering away viciously.

"Come on," I muttered, black blood staining my face as I swung the soul killers through thick flesh and scales all while trying to grasp the location of the Empaths. "Come on. Show yourself. Come on."

The moment the skies suddenly changed to night, my vision turned bright—brighter than during the day—and every shadow in the periphery grew colours, thick colours.

It was so easy to tell apart an Empath. The colours they wore, the heavy emotions that carried along with their own, the foreign specks lingering in them.

I faded right before the man, but he was quick to know of my intentions as he grabbed my hand and smirked. "Do you enjoy pain?"

When nothing happened, when the infliction he intended to pass to me only floated free in the wind, I said, "Do you?" Twisting my hand and gripping his, I squeezed until I felt the bone crumble and then sliced my dagger through his throat.

A set of claws grazed my shoulder before I could fade again, the touch of dark magic seeping in my blood hurt more than the wound, but I shook away the pain—I'd tasted worse pain.

Earth and rock crashed against ice and monsters, creating a dirty fog that was blurring my field of vision. No matter how many times I faded, I could not see who I needed to see, and the whole entire wall of Hanai was now overwhelmed with beasts crawling to get inside the city.

A strong hand wrapped around my arm and hoisted me up from the ground. "On your feet, girl," the Isline King shouted, pushing me behind him and bearing the weight of the attack before slicing the beast open. "Go! Find who you want to find. You're smart, you will get to the bottom of it."

"Plan B," I murmured to myself, backing away. "Plan. Fucking. B."

My vision was filled with black specs and the wound on my shoulder pulsed with more than pain. So, I reached into my pocket and pulled a small vial of mirkroot, chugging it. Shrugging the dizziness off, I waited for the dangerous potion I'd been concocting for months to work. My chest weighed the size of six rocks with the next breath I took. And everything started to veil with bright colours that pulsated and glowed, my heartbeat louder than drums with each emotion my shadows dug their claws into. When my senses had reached their most intense peak, I searched and searched, fading and breaking through bodies until...until I spotted another Empath hidden in the distance.

The man nocked an arrow and aimed at me, the sharp tip flying directly through my raised palm, breaking only the leather of my gloves and trapped between the metal bars on my hands. The fight was not even a fight. The man was bleeding and wheezing under my grip when I took out the sachet of red clary that had taken me months to collect. *Das a'fasea*. *Death of a witch*, that is what they called it. The small flower grew only on a Celesteel blessed land where the blood of a Crafter had been spilled.

There was pain. And there was this.

I pried the barely conscious Empath's mouth open and spilled the crushed powder of dried red clary on his tongue.

His eyes immediately flew open and he took a long, deep breath before he screamed like death himself was crawling out of his veins.

"Melanthe," I said, barely swallowing and rubbing a hand over the scar on my throat that was throbbing with sharp pain. "Where is she?"

He only screamed, his face turning red, and veins popping beneath the skin that was turning ashen and blue. "P-please," he murmured. "Please."

"Where is she!" I screamed, and blood filled my mouth. "Tell me where she is and I spare you the pain."

When he pressed his lips tightly shut, shaking his head, I spilled some more powder on my glove and rubbed it over his skin until black boils and puss began leaking out of the crack that the burn of the flower left behind.

My voice shook when I said, "Please. Please. I beg...I beg you. There are children behind that wall. Parents. Sisters and brothers. Please, do not make me hurt you when the whole world is hurting. Please. Let's end this. Help me end this. Please." Given up, I wiped tears away with the back on my hand and took out my dagger, ready to spare him the torture of the poison, but he put trembling hand on mine, stopping me.

"Lagoon...the Crimson Lagoon of souls," he choked out. "Near the old gates...of...Caligo. I'm sorry, I'm sorry...for all of it."

Sobs shook me entirely, but I managed to nod at him. "Thank you. Thank you so much." He drew his eyes shut before I plunged my dagger in his heart.

Backing away from the snow stained red, I faded to Red Coven, finding Penelope waiting right by the door along with Aradia.

The two hurried down the steps and almost crashed against me. "Where to?" Pen asked.

"Crimson Lagoon of Souls."

From her belt, she pulled the dagger Sam had gifted Snow and clutched it tightly in her hand before she opened a portal. "Let's go."

I threw a look behind her. "Where is Visha?"

"Visha has to remain in Isjord."

I grabbed and pulled her back. "Why?"

Her lips trembled. "Snow has opened the seal."

I staggered a step back, the pain from my shoulder growing intensely and spreading everywhere. "She...she's done what?"

"Nia, please," she pleaded, holding onto my arm. "We have no time. We have to help her."

"W—what about killing Melanthe?"

"Melanthe has Urinthia. Urinthia will be there. She will help us. Visha said so. Macaria said so."

The lagoon water was transparent, but thick and stained a rosy colour, almost mir-
roring the skies and fog around us as it poured from three tall waterfalls. Crows cawed
a continuous song and made the wind eerier, not making it any easier for us to swim
the distance to the caves hidden under the heavy stream of the centre waterfall.

My stomach pulsed with vomit from the stink of magic encircling the round cave
the size of a castle.

At its centre marked with a blood drawn craft halo, stood Melanthe, a grimoire
floating before her while she chanted an eerie song.

Her eyes rolled open and a wicked smile stretched across her face when she studied
me and the two companions following me along. "You are dying," she said sweetly.

Sweat coated my temples and it was becoming harder and harder to breathe, but
death was still crossing the waters of Keres to me. There was enough time. Plenty of
time to end this until he'd come for me. "I am not afraid," I said, walking around the
craft halo she was hiding in and sliding right past to where Urinthia was chained in the
far corner. The veil around her was thick and crafted meticulously to never be broken
through with means of whatever magic that was not Melanthe's.

I took off my glove and rested the tip of my finger against it, feeling the heat of magic
all over my spine before thrusting my hand entirely inside it and grabbing the Grand
Maiden. *Craft metal. Special, apparently,* Snow had said when she had brought me to
the Crafter who had mended my hands that day. *Very magical.*

Melanthe staggered back, eyes wide and wild, the floating grimoire before her falling
to the ground with a thud. Her jaw was set tight and her smile turned into a snarl when
I broke the chains binding Urinthia and pulled her out of the veil.

Melanthe's following attack was useless. I faded back to where Penelope was standing, narrowly missing the hit.

She laughed, the sound so terrifying when it rolled and reverberated all around the
hollow cave. "This war was long over. No matter what you do next."

I grabbed the Grand Maiden and turned her to me. "Dishonour your daughter
again and I will rip your heart out like she asked me to," I said to her, tugging on the
last chain around her wrists. "Banish her. Cast *d'mora.*"

Death in a human body, as they called it.

A cruel craft.

One so powerful it took three Delcour to cast. Three prime Crafters.

Her eyes widened and she quickly glanced at the two young Crafters behind me
before nodding.

Keres might have been rowing too fast down the River of Sorrows because my feet
gave in and I collapsed to the ground, barely managing to hold myself up to watch
Penelope, Urinthia, and Aradia gather around Melanthe.

"Do you two know the words?" Urinthia asked carefully.

Both young girls nodded and the Grand Maiden nodded along.

Melanthe let out a scathing cackle. "What on this God blessed land do you think
you are doing?"

"Mother," Urinthia chanted, spreading her arms wide, and chains rose from under her feet to surround Melanthe's veil.

"Sister," Aradia continued, and more chains covered Melanthe under. *Forgive me,* she mouthed to her sister buried under them.

At last, Melanthe realised the craft they were summoning, her mouth trembling, tears gathering in her eyes. "What sort of nonsense—"

"Daughter," Penelope echoed, and Melanthe's eyes went wide when more chains slid over the veil.

"No, no," she murmured more to herself than anyone else, still engulfed in her delusions of power and greed. "Three Delcour. You need three Delcour" You cannot take my magic, aunt. You cannot take my magic! Please, aunt, please!"

"By God they were given," Urinthia called loudly, and a strong, unnatural wind blew inside the cave. "By God they will be taken. I call!" she chanted.

"I call," Penelope and Aradia repeated.

The craft was twisted. The common tongue lacked many words spoken in Borsich to explain the *d'mora* cast.

Melanthe's eyes rolled back, her bones bending and twisting until she dropped to the ground, convulsing while crimson-coloured shadows leaked from her mouth, floating and disappearing until there was only a shell of an old human left behind.

Her hair had turned white, her skin pale, and her pale eyes half mad and half terrified. She raised them to me when I kneeled before her now fragile body and pulled a dagger out from my baldric. "I cannot lose," she wheezed out. "I cannot lose. My child. What of my child, please? My daughter, please, she will need me."

"She will receive the punishment you've set her up for. We all have lost one way or another. Because of you," I said, gripping her hair and reaching close so I could see the thin lines of her irises. "Look at me. Snow will want to know in detail how light faded from these eyes, so keep them on me."

It was taught to me that a kill needed to be quick, painless. But as I dragged my dagger over her throat, a part of me understood why Snow liked giving a slow death.

Urinthia turned to Penelope, cupping her face. "Lysander's daughter?"

She nodded, clasping her hands. "Please, Visha needs you."

The Grand Maiden's brows creased. "My child needs me?"

The dagger dropped from my hand, clattering to the ground, my own body surrendering to the poison of black magic seeping inside my veins. "To help...her. Help...Snow."

51

White King to F4

Thora

NILSA'S BODY LAY TORN beside me. She had not survived long against Vas who had now disappeared to Gods knew where, limping, burned, and injured. Finally struggling to heal. Her fire had turned the once snowy ground into a miry slush. Blood and melted skin had soaked through it and even given it an argil tint. Whatever bile tried to raise up my throat from the smell and the feel of it beneath my soles went down really quickly when the *khamir* beasts overwhelmed us again. Pouring—endlessly, relentlessly, killing with a single graze.

From the distance, I saw Jayre crash on land, beasts already crawling and feasting on his body. I couldn't even allow myself to close my eyes for a moment to mourn either of them.

A horde of beasts suddenly stopped as if on command and all turned to face me, growling and slowly prowling in my direction before launching into the air to attack.

And I ran towards them with all I had, my ice creatures following closely behind as I forced my feet to move quicker than they had ever moved. But before I could slice my dagger through their limbs, they all went still. Eyes and mouths aghast, collapsing to the ground.

Gooseflesh rose over my skin when the rest of them crumpled to the ground one after the other, leaving the battlefield bare from beasts. The slithery, scaly skin they wore peeled back to reveal human bodies. Some dead. And others almost there.

Nia.

Nia had done it.

"Oh Gods." My hands shook, my breath shook, too.

Nia had done it!

"Your turn," Visha's voice boomed in my head, and a portal opened just a foot away from me.

My turn.

It was my turn.

Sucking in a steady breath, I clutched my weapon tightly and ran inside of it.

She had portalled me inside Tenebrose castle, right in the middle of the quiet winter gardens. Everything was the same as I remembered it. And all that terrified me. Nightmares and reality stood still and solid for a moment, close enough for me to touch.

Shaking the memory away, I ran towards where I felt a hum of familiar magic—towards the same sensation Snow had described feeling. Like a call, it summoned me to it. Like calls to like.

Someone appeared before me, but they drew their weapon back soon after. The woman blinked stunned. "You made it."

"Skadi?" I asked, and then I had no answer for what possessed me to launch forward and hug her.

She stood frozen. "P-princess?"

"It is nice to see you."

"Uh, nice to see you as well. Are you here for—"

"My father."

Pulling back, she pointed to the red rose gardens. "All the Crafters protecting him are dead, but I do not know where he keeps his Magi-healers that are feeding him life. They are linked to him."

"Then I will have to kill him until all his lives are run through."

She nodded. "Elias and I will keep every soldier away. He is all yours."

"Thank you," I offered, slipping between walls that hid servant pathways and tunnels, hoping that the ember salt was enough to mask my magic from the guards. Many twists and turns later, I felt the same hum sing to me, as if luring me in its direction.

Then I saw him. Sat in a steel dais in the middle of the red rose gardens that overlooked the war beyond the ruined walls of Tenebrose. His armour glistened despite the murk and smoke covering the daylight, it glistened with something else, something unnatural.

Alone.

At last.

Excitement and something else bubbled inside of me. Something fierce. Something like hate.

The snow beneath my feet hardened and turned to ice as I walked towards him. I drew my bow and nocked an arrow, pulling tight on the string, aiming at my father's head. I waited for the wind to heed to my command and change direction before I released the *anima accissor* tipped arrow.

The sun barrier around him broke for the arrow to go through and hit my father's head. The head piece he wore braced the impact of the kill, but the strength of the hit made him jerk forward and almost topple from his seat.

He whipped around, bewildered, raising a hand to his armoured head. Father looked back and forth, searching the surroundings for support. Only to find himself entirely alone with me.

"Child," he sneered, looking overhead at the canopy of ice slowly enshrouding us inside of it at my command. "What do you think you are doing?"

I strapped back my bow and pulled both daggers from their holster, slowly walking to my father who found the situation beyond entertaining and had blasted in a boisterous laughter. But it was an amusement that did not go on for long because serpent-like shards of ice crawled from the walls around us in his direction.

He managed to evade most but not all, his heavy armour slightly denting where my magic had touched him.

And then I ran in his direction, sliding and slashing one dagger through the sun barrier, cutting straight over the leather band holding his left calf plate. The piece of metal dangled loose but did not come off. "One. A thousand more times to go," I said, rising to my feet again and twisting the daggers back into my hold.

He raised a hand and the ice beneath him rose and morphed into the shape of two large, twisted serpents. "The biggest shame of all," he said, stepping back and letting the two frost creations launch their attack on me, "to kill such magnificent creatures as you and your siblings. You would have been exceptional in my hands."

"We were in your hands," I shouted, sliding down between the serpents, rising two sharp stalactites of ice piercing through them. Twisting in place and blowing the splinters of broken ice in his direction with only one thought while sending a dagger flying in his direction, too.

He lifted a hand, and the ice splinters stopped mid-air between us. The force of the wind and the hit of the blade against his armour made him stumble a few steps back though. The more he looked at me, the more he realised that there was no match. Slowly, he raised his other hand and the fragments crumbled and twisted to form dozens of frost serpents that shot up and aimed for me.

They broke again against my shield of wind, the shards twisting into slick pin needles. At the flick of my fingers, they were raining down on my father. Except...this time, he was not able to stop them all in time. "Do you like my tricks, papa?" I waved both hands at him. "I can do them with no hands at all. Just a thought."

He'd stumbled back at the impact of the attack, and a stream of blood trickled under the left arm plate. Stunned, he breathed heavily, staring at me like no father should stare at their child. He cracked his neck and gathered his hands into fists, throwing one in the air forward—and a column of ice knocked me from behind, slamming me to the ground. Dozens of them rose up, and each time father swung his fist, they aimed at me. Relentlessly they crashed against the shield of wind, but an odd one managed to knock my body to the ground, bruising my flesh. He still had the blood of a prime, I suppose. But so did I.

I stood and spat blood on the ground, taking the same stance my father had taken. Then...I mimicked each and every one of his moves. Over and over and over. Each of his attacks were blocked by mine and each of mine blocked by his. This was no longer a fight, but a wicked dance of whose body would surrender to exhaustion first. I'd not even moved a muscle and he was panting.

"Give it up!" he shouted. "And I spare your life."

"Give it up! I shouted back, unsheathing my daggers again. "And I take yours. Gently."

He attacked again, and my moves mimicked his, except that when I blocked his blow, I released my daggers in the air and blasted a gust of air, launching them towards my father who was half blind behind the pillar of ice, letting wind guide them directly to his flesh.

I heard a groan and then the sound of metal crashing against ice.

Father kneeled on the ground, one of my blades had pierced through his breast plates and the other through those over his thigh. Blood gushed from his stomach and leg over the shining silver steel, dripping and tainting the ice and snow below a dark crimson.

"You should have trained, papa, like we did. Might have learned a trick or two instead of hiding like a coward." I pulled my bow while father growled with fury and agony, and mounted an arrow.

The arrow hit him right between a sliver of flesh exposed on his knee and leg steel plate. And the other hit him on his hand, nailing him on the ground.

Father spat blood, pulled the arrow from his hand, and stood fully again. The air chilled and the temperature dropped to the point my bones began quaking. The ground vibrated as pillars of ice rose up and began pushing up on the shield roof, attempting to break it. "I hope you have the energy to keep this up for one hundred times."

So a hundred times it was.

I mounted another arrow. "Ninety-nine," I said, letting go of the string. The arrow slid forward, gliding between the gusts of wind directing it at my command. It slipped between the curving hands of the ice that my father had summoned, and hit him right between his eyes.

All of his magic scent died off. Ice dissipated into thin flakes of snow and the air no longer carried the metallic scent of his blessing.

I held my breath, watching blood gush down his face, his yellow eyes fluttering shut.

He pulled the arrow out of his skull and dropped to the ground with a heavy thud. Lifeless.

Ninety-nine.

"Ninety-nine," I whispered to myself, forcing my feet to move forward. "Ninety-nine. Don't forget. Ninety-nine." My shaking hands pulled frantically on the *anima accissor* dagger still etched on his stomach and slashed the leather belts holding his breast plate in place.

I gasped when his hand wrapped tightly around my wrist and his eyes fluttered open. "I cannot be killed," he hissed so maliciously, eyes glowing a vile shade of rage. "I cannot be killed!"

"Let's meet in hell, papa." I raised a dagger, and before he could utter a single word of plea or bargain or hate or whatever other venom, I struck down on his chest, piercing his heart.

He gagged on blood and his eyes shot wide almost astound at what I had done.

Ninety-eight.

The flare of unconsciousness and the saltiness of death lasted only for a split second because he turned conscious again. "Child!" he roared, ready to push me off.

So I struck again. And again. And again. Every time he came back to life.

Ninety.

Blood pooled beneath my feet, and bile rose to my throat when it began sinking into my clothes and plastering against my skin.

"Seventy-four," I counted, clasping the hilt with both hands, forcing the shaking to stop as I drove it through his heart again and again.

"Thirty-five!" I screamed. "Fifteen. Nine."

Tears blurred everything. Only red was visible as I counted down to one. I didn't know how many times I pierced my father's heart after that, didn't know how loud I was screaming, didn't know how hard I was sobbing, didn't know how little I was breathing, how fast the world was spinning.

"All I wanted," I heaved. "All I wanted was to play in the snow like others. To hunt wild berries with ma. I wanted the first blood I saw to be mine, not belonging to the first person I killed," I screamed between cries. "I wanted a sister, not a protector. I wanted a brother, not a mentor. You took from me. You only ever took from me!"

A pair of hands I could recognise with my eyes shut pulled me away from my father's mangled dead body.

My voice had grown beyond hoarse, but my chest wanted to let it all out. "I never wanted anything! I never got to want anything!"

"Hey," Malik called, searching my eyes. "Come on, little bird. Come on, Rora."

Fixed on the puzzling pattern of his irises, I lifted the dagger up, my hand still shaking. "I killed him." Why did that make me so mad? Why did it make me so angry? "I killed him, Malik."

He rested his forehead against mine, and it was like the world suddenly breathed another air. My chest lightened and my cries turned to silent gasps of air. His fingers brushed my cheek, wiping away my father's blood. "You did well, Rora. You did so well."

"The sceptre," I said, my senses finally returning. I stood and reached his dais, pulling the Octa Virga out of the holder. "Why is it still glowing?"

Malik reached close to it, tendrils of shadows slithering in the air towards it, hissing and shaking when they touched the sceptre. "Pull back the ice dome."

The shield around us blasted and melted into soft pellets of snow that blew with the fast northern wind, revealing what I did not wish to see. In the distance, Kilian's dome was still up. And inside, Snow was still fighting Aurora.

"Enough," I commanded, gripping the sceptre tightly. "I command you to retreat!"

But nothing happened. No matter what words I used. No matter what languages I used.

It did not budge at all no matter how much I shook it.

Gods. Oh Gods.

I looked up at him. "Malik," his name came out as a desperate call. "What is happening?"

The defeated look on his face made my stomach sink. "She has taken control. The sceptre is useless."

I shook my head. "Snow cannot kill her. No one can. This will not stop."

"We will stop it, little bird. I'll find Visha. This is not the last you will see of me," he promised, ready to fade.

"What if it was the last you saw of me?" I asked, pulling him back. We didn't have time to wait. But we might have no time at all after this.

There was a brief moment of hesitation.

His eyes begged and pleaded for me to take the words back, for me to dismiss what I had said, to take back the question.

I stepped closer. "Mal, please."

He cupped my face so gently for a man who did not know the word gentle, the rough pads of his thumbs softly brushing my cheek. "Don't beg me," he breathed, his inhales almost tortured. "Don't beg me. I can't bear it." It might have been but a sliver of a moment, but it felt like the longest moment I had lived in when he held me there. Eyes locked. Our breathing synced. His skin on mine. His touch was not burning but igniting. "If I am to die with guilt, let it be for this sin," he said, pulling me to him so every inch of my body was moulded to his hard one.

His lips were soft against mine. He kissed me unhurriedly, gently, and carefully—so carefully.

It would haunt me. It would always haunt me, dead or alive. Hells or heavens, it would haunt me.

"So sweet," he murmured over my lips. "Always so damn sweet."

Let it haunt me.

I wrapped my arms around his neck and kissed him back like I wanted him to kiss me. And he did. Finally unsaddling whatever restraint he always held with me.

He felt like rain.

He was rain to me.

"That will take a lot of repenting, little bird," he said, softly biting my lower lip. "For far too long."

"We might not have that long."

He left a few last, lingering pecks on my mouth before pulling back. "We will. You will get to kiss many others. You will get your happy ending and you will find someone who wants you like you want to be wanted. You will get it all, I will make sure that you do."

Except that rain was passing. And I hated sunshine. "I...I want—"

You.

You.

I want you.

He rested his forehead against mine. "What you want is not what you deserve, little bird. You deserve so much more than what you want. One day you will find who you deserve."

For a moment, I thought about telling him that I didn't care. That I could die happy just wanting him even if I couldn't have him. But only for a moment. If we lived, I didn't want him to leave me.

And he would—he would leave me.

Tears burned my eyes, and it took everything in me not to cry. "Promise?"

He touched my lips still tasting of him. "It is a promise." Slowly, he backed away, holding the sceptre. "Stay here. No matter what, do not come down there, alright?"

"What? Why?"

He looked over my shoulder, at where Moregan was now standing. "Make sure she does not go anywhere," he said to her. "Keep her safe."

No. No. I shook my head. "Why? They need us. I cannot stay here."

"Do you trust me?"

"Yes. You're the only one that I trust."

His steps almost faltered. "Then you will stay here."

One moment he was there, and the next...he was gone.

52

Black Bishop to C5

Snowlin

LIGHTNING, FROST, AND FLAMES roared around us. Everything had lit awake and the ground burned in shades of pearl, no longer icy, no longer cold.

Kilian stood just a few steps behind me, shadows and darkness pouring out of him like tidal waves, drowning Aurora's fire and weakening her mind that was struggling to stay focused on the fight before her.

The white flames hissed and crackled when they came in contact with his magic and mine. She lay there, finally trapped between the dome and his outpouring power, attempting to escape the lightning and frost chasing her every movement.

I bolted just beside Aurora and gripped her arm tightly, letting ice spread over her skin to freeze her limbs before I threw her back to the ground, her lithe body rolling in the cold, icy mud.

I tilted my head back, clicking my tongue. "Ice. Such a strange yet ironic weakness to have for a Fire Guardian."

She tried to stand, her wings heavy and muddied. "I have no weakness."

"Perhaps it is not ice. Perhaps your weakness is arrogance."

Bolting again, this time exactly before her, I wrapped a hand over her throat and willed all gates of power to crack open, frost pouring out of me, killing her fire and freezing her body. Gales of winter rolled from my fingertips, ice so cold that the wind blowing around our bodies began solidifying into spider-like webs of frost.

"Have you found mine yet?" I asked, and even the ice around us shivered.

Her legs weakened and she went down kneeling before me, choking and fighting, her body almost...almost encapsulated by ice, her fire gone, the pungent scent of her flowery magic disappearing.

"Anger," I hissed in her face. "My weakness is anger. Rage. You feed my weakness so well. Threaten me again, threaten all that I love again. Go on, do it."

Her mouth opened and closed, struggling to breathe. "St—"

I put a finger to my lips. "Shhhh."

My hands shook from the force of pouring frost.

Almost...I was almost there. I'd almost had her. Had Vas's body not slammed against mine and sent me crashing to the ground.

Sound of ringing filled my head. It took my bones a moment to adjust to the force of the hit while my magic barely needed a second to heal whatever muscle had torn from the impact.

Before Vas's green form launched towards me again, I bolted right beside him and stabbed a dagger on his back. Then I bolted again and again and again, faster than what his enhanced senses could catch on, puncturing him all over till he was dizzy and leaking probably more blood than he had.

I'd never been faster. Stronger. Lighter. It was like my body had become one with air. And my human loved the Godly power it poured out so much that it had sent me into a high. Such a blinding high. "I see you have met the other half of you. The true half of you." Soul and flesh finally made one again. Well, V.

He raged, growling and attempting to catch me.

From the corner of my eye, I saw Aurora thaw and stand again, breathing like fury and shouting her lover's name like a beast. "Do not touch him!"

Darkness immediately roared in the air, hungry like a starved beast, and twirled around her faster than a hurricane. Kilian faded before her and more darkness and death seeped under his fingertips, battling the fire and dousing it. Aurora struggled, the flames dissipating just as quickly as she summoned them. Her struggle was enough for Vas to forget just who he was facing and long enough for him to expose his heart to me.

I rammed my sword through his chest, and he let out a pained roar heard by every corner of heavens and hells. The beast swayed on his feet and dropped to the ground, failing to pull out the blade before I nailed a dagger right in his skull, between his slithery green eyes that froze, staring into mine. Visha had done it. She'd made a man whole again. She'd made him weak.

"Mourn her," I whispered, and the wind whispered with me, "and be done with it."

Vas's eyes filled with silver tears, fluttering and struggling to remain open to see me walk up to his old lover engulfed and struggling to fight off death. He wouldn't die. Not yet. Not until he was mended all together. Not until I'd walk him to hell myself.

My limbs were melting to liquid, turning entirely a glistening white. There was little time left. So little.

"*Visha,*" the heavy voice at the back of my mind called desperately. "*Am I dying today?*"

"*I'm sorry,*" her voice echoed back. "*I'm sorry.*"

It wouldn't work.

The land would not accept my magic.

Shaking, I walked inside and beside death, warm and embracing as always. My darkness was always so warm. My magic faltered inside of it like it always had, but not enough, barely enough this time.

This was it.

There was no changing fate.

Not entirely.

Aurora's breathing picked up when she noticed me through Kilian's shadows, her magic almost useless inside the veil of my husband's cold gift that had grown.

I reached forward and wrapped a hand around her throat, squeezing hard, ice forming beneath my palm and spreading all over her skin again. "Where were we?"

She laughed madly. A mad amusement I knew well. "You cannot kill what I am."

"We have the sceptre," Visha yelled inside my head. *"We can command her back."*

"That was in the past. Change of plans. I'm sending you home. Now bend," I said, and the dark shadows fluttered with the harsh command. Aurora choked, struggling and attempting to summon more of the white fire smothered between ice and death. "Bend!" I shouted, and the ground beneath my feet shook, cracked and hollowed into a massive crater. "I said. Bend!"

Aurora's half frozen body shook, and her knees gave away, but she still burned hot under my touch. Her choked laughter drew shivers over my bones and rage overtook me when she said, "By law of Gods, I never bend to the lesser."

I sucked in a sharp breath.

Lesser.

I was not beneath her.

But what I chose to be was. Somehow, between the layers of madness and violence and rage of the monster I was...hid but merely a human woman. *Ybris* by name. Aura by birth. But there was just this one thing I had yet accepted to be. Because the cost was not something I could afford.

I glanced at my sword still etched in Vas's body and the dagger I held in my hand. *Soul killers.* The sword etched in my chest from the visions, it was a soul killer.

A sob slipped between my shaky chuckles.

Everything was clear now.

What had to be done was clear now.

Aurora would not bend to a half human. To someone half divine. To an incomplete half. To two incomplete halves.

The game had changed and was nearing its end.

And it had the same ending despite what moves I'd changed.

"Snow, no, not yet," Visha's voice screamed at the back of my mind. *"Do not kill her."*

"I won't. Make sure to send her back to where she came from after I command her back to the sceptre. Send Eren to Valda Acme with it. Tell them all goodbye for me. And that I am sorry. Tell Mal to do as I have said, to hold Kilian back."

"What? Snow, wait."

"The seal has to open now. I can't hold her for long."

"Snow, wait, I can hear—"

I shut her voice down.

Another sob escaped my lips and my eyes drew shut when a brush of his spring air caressed my cheek.

The seal had to be opened. I had to be all that I was. Human. Monster. Ybris. Aura. Guardian. I had to be all that. And to be all that, the barrier holding my magic back had to break.

But once the seal opened, there was only one way to keep them safe from me.

Soul killer.

I no longer held back. For all of them I would no longer hold back. My lips moved to silently form the words that I'd promised Lysander and Visha with my life to never say.

"*Osca argata.*" *Open entirely,* I ordered.

And so it did.

Every inch of my skin turned a glowing white. Bones, blood, and whatever soul I had left turned into pure lightning. I felt the power hum against my bones and sing to my blood, a melody of drenching power—a melody of destruction.

Power slipped through my fingers and it surged out of me uncontrollably. And just before all sense of control began to disappear, my lips formed the words, "*Hur ma'hazur kahaz.*" *Kneel to the power.*

Aurora's eyes were wide. "No—"

"Yes."

Ice blasted all around us, and Kilian's shadows and darkness blew into the wind that howled uncontrollably, dissipating and screaming almost in agony, crawling back into their master. The dome peeled back, lowering to reveal the battlefield around us.

Aurora's head hung low, a hand over her chest, her power flailing and her form freezing into a sculpture of ice which then vanished like fog.

Hur ma'hazur kahaz, the voices in the wind echoed.

When all signature and scent of her magic disappeared as if it had never even been summoned, I breathed out a shaky exhale of relief and fell to the ground, struggling to contain what spilled from my fingers.

Power.

So much of it.

Too much of it.

The seal had broken entirely. The seal I had since the day I'd been born.

I had become what the realm had always feared. What the prophecy had sung since before my birth.

I had become it.

And I would end it.

The hand to push a blade through my heart had been mine.

So...I had not stopped it. The fate I thought I no longer deserved.

"Snow?" his voice called, and my eyes drew shut, failing to hold back the tears that spilled down my cheeks. The fate I wanted, needed and begged for, called my name with such desperation that I dared doubt one last time.

So little time. Always so little time for me and him.

A slow curtain fell over my eyes, beginning to overtake my sight. My voice died entirely at the call of his name, "Kil."

53

White Rook to A1

Kilian

SILENCE FOLLOWED LIKE THE collapse of dominoes, then it turned so loud it began echoing along the battlefield. No one moved. Not a soul, Isjordian or Adriatian. Aurora had disappeared back into the sceptre, and Demir had the soul killer nailed in his chest, laying defeated on the ground.

But it wasn't him or their disappearing weapon that everyone was looking at.

They were looking at her.

And the skies.

They felt the wind shift, horrifying power filling the space.

Prayers of fear left Adriatian lips.

Praises of awe hummed from the Solaryans and Hanaians.

Worry was etched on Olympian faces—worry for their queen.

And sounds of surrender clapped when Isjordians dropped all their weapons and went down to a knee, all facing her.

But they didn't see what I saw. They didn't see my wife fail to lock back her magic. They all saw her fist hit the ground over and over, willing and shouting for her power to lock back inside her seal, but didn't understand the sentencing Snow had issued to herself.

Not yet, but they soon did.

When skies rolled with liquid thunder and heavy, thick rain, hail and lightning poured over us, hitting the battlefield aimlessly—uncontrollably—over those that had already surrendered. Killing and injuring everyone, including our people and allies.

Her shoulders rose fast, the ground beneath her feet turning into cool, cold molten lava that was starting to slowly spread all over.

"Love," I breathed, nearing her.

She didn't answer. Her attention turned towards the Isjordian forces.

"Snow."

Her hand began lifting up in their direction, a ball of white power glowing at her fingertips.

"Snowlin!" I called one last time, running fast towards her.

Her head snapped in my direction, and her eyes peeled from power for a moment, revealing golden defeat despite her victory. Realisation had coated them with tears.

The seal had opened. She could not control it.

Darkness enshrouded us again, but she stood there, inside the blackest pit of my most haunting fears, glowing like the southern star. Her eyes drew shut when my magic grazed her, stripping off the glow of thunder to reveal her skin again. To reveal my love haunted by so much.

The way she looked at me...she didn't need to spell it for me to hear her goodbye. She was wrapped in divine power, but for the first time, she had never looked so human and fragile to me. She cried, tears glowing against her skin.

"We did it," I said, reaching to hold her, but she slipped from my hands like she had promised to never do. Backing away, afraid of what she could do to me.

It was the first time I felt the burn of her magic. And so did my darkness, it began crackling, dowsing, and faltering. I was not enough to contain her. And I couldn't...I couldn't do it for much longer.

She lifted her dagger up from the ground and held it in her hand for a moment. Only to let me know of her next move. Her lips parted open to speak but couldn't, so she mouthed the words to me. *All the next lives.*

No.

She clutched the dagger with both hands and aimed the tip of its blade to her heart.

No.

My bones barely held the weight I forced on them when I pushed towards her. "I'll do it. Wait, wait! I will do it! Please, let me do it."

Her hand lowered a little and she slowly nodded, her chest shaking with cries.

My love.

My sweet love.

I collapsed before her, shaking entirely. My heart slowing, my breathing slowing. Not one part of me wanted to live without her.

"I'll do it," I muttered to myself as if it could convince me I could do what I was about to do. "I'll do it." Her figure blurred behind tears and her face dropped when sobs ripped out of my throat. I willed more magic out of me—the most I had ever allowed to pour out. No more a stain of death—now death itself.

No matter how much she burned, I'd burn with her, so one last time, I kissed her. I held her. I held my burning stars and sun. One last time. "I love you. I love you so much. I'm sorry, I should have said it before. I should have said it more."

Tears slid down her face. "I love you, Kil."

The air around her burned colder than ice. I reached to rest a hand over her chest. "I can't," I whispered, magic gilding from around me and wrapped around her, absorbing hers...killing hers. "I can't do it."

She put a hand over mine, stopping me from pulling back. "Please. I want it to be you."

I ached like I'd never ached before.

My soul and heart ached so fiercely I wished for an unkind death. I wished for any kind of death. Harrowing death. Anything to escape this cruel pain.

Whatever was beyond this life, hell or heaven, I'd never let her part without me.

Pulling a dagger from my holster, I aimed it to my chest, slowly forcing it through my flesh.

She gasped, trying to pull back. "No, please," she cried, more tears pouring out of her golden eyes that held my sun, the only sun I've ever known. The only sun I would ever know. The only sun I would bask under. I held her hand tightly, and for every part of her I killed, I dug the blade deeper into my heart. "Please, no! Please, Kil. Please!"

They tore me—her cries tore at me viciously.

But they slowly died with her.

Weakness falling over her limbs.

"We would have definitely named at least one black haired baby Rain," I murmured over her lips, holding her close to me. "You would have let me. Rain is a pretty name. Would have suited a girl or a boy."

She gave me a shaky smile and nodded. The glow over her skin dowsing and slowly fading, and so did the taste of electric power in the air. Her eyes were struggling to remain open, but she murmured, "Rain."

"There was this one place," I continued, death howling around us still. "I wanted to take you there. We...we could have seen the sunrise on top of it."

She blinked slowly along her dying breath, the gold of her irises vibrant, so vibrant. There was not much strength left in me either, but I used it all to keep my eyes open for as long as I could, to just look at her.

"Snow?"

She didn't answer.

Her chest was not moving.

Her heart was silent.

Skies were silent.

So silent.

I swayed the two of us, holding onto her for as long as I could. My whole body was numb. Ready to surrender. Holding on just to hold her a bit longer. I cried with her in my arms. Bled with her in my arms. "My love. My heart. My Snow."

The faded blue brightness of the day peaked through the shield of darkness that abated, and a body landed near mine, a hand pulling against my shoulder. My brother pulled the dagger out of my chest, holding his hands over the wound. "No," he roared, shaking and crying. "I promised her. I gave her my word. Do not do this to me, Kil. Do not do this to me!"

Oryn came next, his mouth moved fast, but I couldn't hear anything and couldn't feel anything beside the wetness of blood dripping down my stomach and my lover's warmth fading away.

Visha kneeled beside Snow and so did Penelope and Urinthia. There was no fight left in me when they pried Snow's lifeless body from my arms.

A flash of blinding red was the last thing I saw before I felt myself take one last short breath.

54

Check

Eren

"Eren!" someone shouted in the distance, and I jolted awake. Not exactly awake. I was locked tightly between a pile of bodies, crushed between the weight of them, not even able to shuffle any of my limbs for space.

The sounds had stopped.

Eerie quiet had fallen through the battlefield.

And I couldn't feel Aurora's presence in the air anymore. But I also couldn't feel my sister's. Not even a whisper. Nothing. Nothing at all.

"Eren!" the voice called again, this time panicked. "Gods, please, Eren, answer me!"

Body after body was piled on top of me and I struggled to push them off. Even air was hard to get past my lips and to my lungs. And every part of me fought off the sliver of will and magic that was pounding for me to stay awake. So I did. Not only stay awake.

I opened a small gate of magic, letting it usher through my veins and fuel my lungs with air, my body with strength. Magic I so little had explored out of fear. Magic that had scared little Snow so much so that she'd stayed away from me for days. Magic I'd sworn to never show her again. Yet I had. To protect her. Only to fail again.

"Eren!" The voice had come closer—he'd come closer.

Slowly, I reached my hand through the layer of the dead until I could grasp nothing but wind and smoke with my fingers. Once I'd freed my hand, the rest of me followed easily.

Bile filled my mouth once the pressure was off my body, and I heaved a wet cough, the sting of blood crawling up my throat. When the fog cleared out of my sight and my eyes focused on the field of bodies laying for miles, I searched for him. "Cai," I called. "I'm here."

"Eren?"

I still couldn't see him, but his voice grew closer. Was I imagining it all?

I had not.

He rushed to me, sliding to a stop until his hands were on me, on my face, on my body. There were tears on his face, streaking lines down his smoke covered cheeks. More fell silently while he searched my body for wounds. "Gods," he breathed, almost stunned. "Good Gods." He pressed me to his body, tightly—his body that shook from exhaustion and...cries.

"Hey," I said, holding him like he was holding me. "It's fine. I'm fine."

He fell back to the ground, his fingers tugging onto his long hair while rocking back and forth, refusing to look at me.

I kneeled before him and cupped his face. "Cai, what is it? Did something happen to Snow or Rora? Cai, please."

"No." He shook his head, his eyelids tightly pressed shut, refusing to look at me. "I can't do this. I can't do this."

"Cai–"

"I can't do this, Eren. I just can't."

"Do what?"

He wiped his eyes with the back of his hand and stood, backing away from me. "I can't do this."

And all I did was watch him slip away from me, disappearing in the distance of the quiet battlefield. All I did was...nothing.

I'd come out alive, just not entirely.

Somewhere in this battlefield, I'd lost my heart.

I had lost despite what we had won.

Tristin landed before me, bloodied but not injured. "We need help. Are you alright to help?"

"Is...is Aurora gone?"

She nodded.

"And my sister?"

Nothing betrayed her features, or her heartbeat when she said, "I do not know."

I took the hand she held out and stood. The world turned entirely grim the moment I saw what remained from before. Bodies upon bodies. Snow piling on top of them, staining at the touch of blood from the dead that had yet to entirely turn cold—already buried underneath it.

"Hells."

The *zgahna* peeled from the Isjordian air and earth, rolling, and retreating down south, back to where it had rested for centuries protecting Olympia. It revealed the most gruesome scenery I would ever come to see in any existence.

Tristin portalled us further inside the remains of my father's war where bodies were beyond unrecognisable, laying on top of each other.

Less alive than we'd expected were pulled out from the ruin. The touch of the *khamir* beasts had been unforgiving. Healers and Crafters moved fast amongst bodies, healing and injecting Nia's potion on those who had survived the dark magic that Melanthe had used to turn them into beasts.

My eyes drew shut when I noticed Jayre's remains laying between the forest and Snow's bonded trying to awaken him. Memphis's yowls were strained, she nudged her head on the dragon's wings, attempting to move him despite the crater of a wound in his stomach.

"Memphis," I called, and the animal limped to me, letting me touch her for the first time. "It is alright. He is home again, M. He is home now."

Thora rushed past the battlefield, searching and searching, until she saw me in the distance. She flew in my arms, hugging me tightly. "I killed him."

Relief washed over me. "You might have saved us all."

She shook her head fast. "It didn't stop Aurora. Snow...she had to stop her."

My blood grew cold, colder than ice. "Where is she?"

"No one can find her. No one will tell me where she is either. Or Kilian." She sniffled a little. "They are okay, right?"

"Yeah, yeah, Rora, they are fine."

She looked over my shoulder, tensing. "King Sigurd."

The Isline ruler walked to us, bloodied and wounded in places. His eyes did not meet mine, not even once. "You've won your war. This is where me and my people retreat."

"Wait," I called. "You might not remember me—"

"I remember you, Son of Skies, though I do not wish to." He pointed to the scar over my lip. "You've got that reminder on your skin still. I hoped you would have taken the message."

"For your help today, thank you," I offered though I knew he did not want my gratitude.

The man huffed, shaking his head and picking up his weapons. "Let us never see one another again."

"Let us not."

Thora grabbed onto my arm. "You know him?"

I nodded, ready to free the truth. "Father sent me on a mission a week before the solstice. The order was to imprison a beast that he had his eyes on. A rare one. That beast guarded his village. That man killed three dozen Isjordians with a snow pick alone, and almost killed me, too. I used a few means I regret to prevent him from doing so. Did more damage than just protect myself. I nearly wiped the whole village out and ended up killing the beast, too."

She took my hand in hers. "It is alright, Eren."

"It was not."

"It is to me."

Footsteps approach us. "Kids."

We both spun to Alaric who clutched a blood-stained white cloth embroidered with the Olympian falcon. Gold threats ran through its edges, similar to mine. Penelope had only embroidered three of them for us as a gift. My hand went to my shoulder where my own was still attached. "Rora, where is yours...where...where—"

Alaric's face lowered, his shoulders shaking. "It is Snow's."

Part VI
Checkmate

55

White King to G4

Snowlin

MY BACK WAS AGAINST something cold and hard. Everything ached and I was sure I could not even move my tongue that had settled so uncomfortably against the roof of my dry mouth.

A sound reverberated around me.

My sound. A groan when I tried to shift from where I'd laid.

As I was trying to crack an eye open, a gentle hand rested on my forehead.

"The temperature has gone down," a much too motherly voice announced. "Well done, my daughter. You've outdone every Maiden and Crafter before you."

"I'll hang the trophy over my grave for you, mother," another commented.

"Snow?" a small voice whispered near my ear. "Visha! She's awake!"

Gods. I cracked my eyes open and glared at the little carrot who had nearly screamed inside my ear.

The little red head grinned. "And she is feeling exceptionally well." She pointed at me, jumping up and down excitedly. "Look, she is angry already."

What?

Why was I dreaming this?

I stared at the ceiling I'd stared at for almost fourteen years and waited for the dream to fade me some place else. Some place with him.

But the dream did not fade. And hard arms lifted me up from where I laid, cradling me. A bearded face was pressed to my own, his tears wetting my cheeks. "Oh, kid, my kid."

Hells were warm apparently, not hot, and they were cruel. This was cruel. So, so cruel.

I swallowed. "Alaric?"

"Shhh. All is well. All is well. I am here."

Hot tears slipped from my aching eyes. "You are?"

His whole body trembled against mine, shaking with violent sobs. "I am."

My sister and Nia, too, hovered over me, hugging each other before launching towards me, crying on my shoulders and holding me tightly. So tightly. Too tightly because I coughed.

What–

What was happening?

I lifted a hand up and weaved my fingers through Nia's too-real-looking curls. And my hand jerked back as if I'd pressed it against scorching embers instead. "Tell me something only Nia Drava would know about me," I asked, maybe a little breathless.

My friend wiped her tears, and said, "You stole Alaric's tobacco pipe one night and stuffed it with grass because you bet with Cai that he *would never even tell the bloody difference.*'You blamed it on that errand boy who kept selling him tobacco. It worked because he quit for about three months."

Alaric shot up to his feet. "That was her? It was grass? You let me smoke grass?"

It was like all life had returned to my body, and I sat up, looking around.

If I was still alive—

Ignoring all pleas and shouts and whatever they were all saying, I stood and ran down my castle corridors, hurriedly opening door after door, panic crawling up my throat as did relentless fear, until—

A sob raked through my chest. So painfully that I had to clutch it with a hand to lessen the ache.

He laid on our bed, propped against the headboard, speaking to his glaring brother. Bandage was wrapped all around his chest and there were several healing craft halos painted black on his skin. He looked tired—but alive.

Don't be a dream.

Please, Gods, do not be a dream.

His attention snapped to me and he immediately tried to stand.

I rushed to his side, but I didn't touch him. What if he disappeared? "Darling?" I breathed, my voice hoarse and defeated.

But his voice was strong, cold, and powerful as always. "My heart." He reached a hand to my face, his thumb catching stray tears.

"Is this a dream?"

"I'd feel very flattered to be in it," Mal said, and it sounded all too real.

"Not a dream," Kilian agreed, cupping my face with both hands, and I finally made a step closer to him, yet still too afraid to touch him.

"Not a dream," I repeated, and ghosted my fingers over his jaw, brushing my knuckle lightly against the little scar I'd given him there. "Not a dream."

"Not a dream," he said, and kissed me.

I was drowning again.

In a sea of happiness.

But drowning nonetheless. His lips rested against mine, his tongue sought mine, his sounds forming a thrill on my stomach. Somewhere between kisses, I had pressed my body against his and my fingers grazed the gauze covering the wound he'd intended to hurt me with.

I pulled back a little, and whispered harshly, "I will never, ever, Kilian Henrik Castemont, forgive you for it. I will never forgive you."

"You're my heartache," he said, resting his forehead against mine and sighing.

"What is one pain for another but unfair?"

"Unforgivable."

"I'd do it again."

"So nobody is happy *I* am alive?" Mal asked, leaning against the wall, grinning at us.

"Cai and Eren?"

He grunted. "They were also not very happy I was alive either."

I laughed, grabbing his shirt and pulling the idiot into a hug.

"You were some other level of heavenly that day, my queen," he murmured, pressing his face to my shoulder, and my shirt dampened against my skin. "You should have told me you would fight it."

"I wasn't going to, Mal. Visha did."

"I've always liked her."

The both of us shook with laughter, and he pulled back, straightening. "Thora was right. About the whole soul thing. Kil cannot kill you and you cannot kill him." He rested a finger on my chest. "His darkness did not manage to kill you, not entirely, it never touched your heart. And whatever little life you had left in you, kept him alive as well. You will tell him now. All of it. No excuse."

I glanced at him, at my darling looking at me with tears in his eyes. "I will."

I had not said a word when Medi-healers and Crafters had come to visit us. Plastered to his side, an arm around his waist, I'd witnessed it all and wordlessly hated Kilian who seemed to enjoy the glares and the huffs. The bastard had even dared to smile. Albeit he'd tried to hide it, but how could the sun hide even on a cloudy day.

When Visha and Oryn came inside and ordered everyone else out, I shifted and stood a little, still not letting go of Kilian.

I wanted answers for so many questions.

The two bowed and reached our side. Visha looked beyond exhausted. She'd even tied her hair up and folded back her sleeves a couple of times over her elbows.

"How?" I asked. *How am I here? How is he here? How is my magic still present? Why is there no seal on my back? Has the land accepted my magic?*

She took out a white flower from her sachet. "It was the galanthus all along," she began. "We Crafters draw magic from portals while simultaneously pouring magic into it, feeding it back to the realm that gifted us our blessing—an act of gratefulness, but also one of survival. We are simply carriers of death, and if we do not guide it away, it would consume us too, like your magic did. In a way, you are doing the same, but you are not Eldmoorian, so the magic becomes tricky. And the God of Death is the last one you wish to trick. In exchange for some freedom, you gave away the entire control of it."

"Instead of pouring it into Caligo," Oryn continued, seeing as Visha's words were muddled from exhaustion. "Your magic will pour into this realm, it will pour into

Numengarth, it will feed its lands. A blessing you are giving like your ancestors have and like your God did millennia ago."

"How is that possible?"

"A grounding. That's what we've called it. We don't know what the magic will do to the land, but the land has accepted it. Perhaps after surviving so long on forgotten belief, it needed it. To heal, to recover. It saved it from dying. You can now tap into the fullest extent of your magic, and when control begins slipping, you will be able to share the magic with the land, draw from it, grow from it, live amongst it, and much more. A gate. No longer a seal to keep it shut. If it weren't for the blood of three Delcour, it would have been unachievable, my queen. Penelope, Visha, and her mother made it happen, they called a summon upon the land—a summon that was accepted because the land was dying. We are hoping that your children, your siblings, and their children will be able to do so, too. We...we've found it," he said, tearing up a little. "We can help other creatures such as us to live without pain or prejudice. Or fear. There might be dozens of realms out there who would welcome magic like ours did with yours. We only have to reach out and search." He gave us all a lachrymose smile. "This...I worked all my life for this. I knew we were no curse. I've always known it."

"Thank you, Oryn," Kilian offered, holding me tightly. "We will always be in your debt."

The Crafter shook his head quickly. "They were only simple calculations on my behalf. As I said, this was the work of the Delcour witches."

Visha blinked sheepishly. "Accept it, Oryn. I would have never figured this out on my own." She scratched her bare arms that were still marred with specks of blood and faint wounds. "He convinced my mother this would work."

"And Aurora?"

My Crafter suppressed a yawn, her nostrils flaring. "The sceptre is in our possession and so is the beast. Both under my veils."

I nodded. "What about Isjord?"

Visha looked at Kilian who said, "Thora has taken permanent lead until you decide as their new queen what you wish to do. The lands are distraught, Snow. Many lives were lost. They will need you."

"They will certainly need someone, but it won't be me," I said.

Kilian kissed my temple. "Isjord is not a burden to bear, love. And certainly not your brother's."

"Not Eren's, Kil." I turned to them again. "Will he be alright? The dagger he used was a soul killer."

The two nodded, and I breathed out a sigh of relief.

"Visha," I called before she left. "Thank you. For all of it. For not giving up. For trying."

"You gave me back my life, I am happy I could help you do the same, my queen," she said, bowing.

Hidden behind the slightly open door, I could see Penelope's red hair. "Come inside, little carrot."

She jumped, startled, her hair jumping with her, too. Shyly, still wiping her eyes, she came inside and joined her mentor's side. "It worked," she said, tugging on with something small in her hand. "You had worn it under your leathers. My protection spell worked."

"It did. You saved me, Penelope."

She finally looked up, sobbing uncontrollably, and for some reason so did I.

Once the chest rattling wave of cries passed, I asked, "Will you forgive me for forcing you to do what you did?"

She nodded. "I will."

"Hand me back my trinket," I said, holding a hand up.

The piece of wolf fur was coarse now and stained with blood, mine or his, I didn't know. Maybe this had been what saved me. Maybe not. No one would know. Not even the little girl beyond the portal who'd shown me my fate.

Cerina.

People hugged and kissed and cried all around me. The blanket of peace had finally warmed their expressions that were still marred with the weight and losses of war. There had been too many to bury. More than I'd ever thought there would have been. Even two days later, we were still not even close to being done. My arms were sore and heavy were my shoulders, but I'd gone past the day without relenting to my own grief. There were too many to console. Too many 'I am sorry' to give. And an abandoned kingdom sitting under ruin, all of its eyes on me, full of hope yet again.

Winter in Isjord had somewhat softened even though we were dead in the middle of it. Perhaps it was the white flame that warmed the season, perhaps it was something else. Perhaps it was the white flowers children were plucking and leaving over graves that had lined the periphery.

"Should you be up and about?" Cai asked, throwing an arm over my shoulders.

"I feel...I feel—" What did I even feel? "I've never felt better. So lightless. Never so powerful. Before I had to summon my magic, now it just rests at the tip of my fingers. The wind stops at my call. Skies thunder without command at all, only with a simple thought." I kneeled and rested my palm on the snow, feeling the magnetic pull on my skin from the layer of magic beneath. "The land has suffered, too, my magic and presence could heal it now that it feeds from me."

"What now? Isjord is yours how you always wanted. So what now?"

My skin still felt cold. The snow felt foreign. The only thing that would remain warm in the midst of every winter from now on would be my thoughts—unburdened by my father's existence. "I'm not the only Krigborn."

He swallowed, his eyes searching the snowy expanse to land on my brother. "Eren does not want this. You know it."

I sighed and nudged his side. "You need to sleep. And most importantly, a bath, Cai. You need a good fucking bath."

He tugged me closer and covered my face with his armpit while I writhed and kicked until he let me breathe fresh air again. He burst out laughing when I gagged a little. "Your flowery king has softened your taste. Remember when we climbed our mountains without bathing for days? You stank worse than me."

"Never again will I be doing that."

"Come on, that was fun. The most fun I've ever had, actually," he said, his laughter fading to an almost sad smile when his eyes landed on my brother again. "Don't let him go. Not him, Cai. Not this time. Not again."

"Better than to be let go." He nudged my shoulder with his. "Go home. That bastard of a husband you have will lose his mind, and a mad king is not on my deck of cards for the foreseeable future."

My attention shifted over my people again. Over our allies helping along. "Not yet."

The Seraphim people looked lost, but were trying their best to aid despite their own losses. They all stopped what they were doing when I approached.

I sat between them, pulling some bandage from my bag and wrapping it around a young girl's arm. "I heard you've asked to bury Nilsa here."

"If it is permitted," a girl no older than me said—Alyone, the priestess who had fought beside Nilsa. "We would like it to be so. Our fallen must be honoured in the land they died whilst protecting. If it was the seas, we would have let them drift on its waves. If it was the skies, we would have set ashes astray in the wind. But it is on snow she died, and under it she must be buried."

"We would be honoured," I said. "And always indebted. What will you do now?"

A cast of obscurity fell over her face. "Return home. Mend as much as we can."

"My people are not travellers, but they would spare a hand to help you build your home again, to build back your kingdom. However we can."

She shook her head. "We have no king, no queen, no kingdom to build back."

"Then crown one." Reaching a hand to her, I said, "Hand me your sword." Though doubtful, she did as asked, and I let the metal heat up with electricity until it was soft enough to mould and twist into the shape of a mangled crown. "Here. Now you only need someone willing enough to put their life away for the sake of many. And that is enough. I see how your people look at you. How they follow you. But most importantly, I see how you look at them. How you lead them. And if there is no throne to sit on, build it."

She took the makeshift crown, clutching it tightly in her hands for a moment before looking over at her people and nodding when they nodded in approval at her. "We thank you. Your kind will always be welcomed in our lands."

"As will be in ours," Magnus said, and I spun to him. The man wore his pride on his shoulders today, not on his head like a crown. It was a heavy mantle because his steps towards me were heavy. "I doubted many things. But would you believe I never once doubted you would be able to come out alive at the end of this?"

"I did."

"I know. I saw it in your eyes. I've always seen it in your eyes. I hope to see it no more. This realm needs you to live. Your family needs you to live."

"Will your people recover?"

"Our cities will mend. The realm will mend. We have that opportunity now because of you."

"You do not need to fear me so much, Magnus."

He grinned. "Respect is indeed something to be frightened of. I remember the first time your husband and I met, I wanted to despise the man. I want to despise you as well. What a shame. You're easy to despise, but so much easier to respect." Retreating away, he pointed a finger at me. "Stay away from the rest of my sons."

Rather than mad I'd abandoned him for the entire day, Kilian was asleep. Nia was by his side, quietly changing the wet cloths soaked in medicine that were spread all over his body to help him heal.

"He's never slept so soundlessly before," I said, climbing the bed to him and kissing his cheek, pressing my nose to his skin to inhale the scent of spring. His features looked so soft, so sweet and relaxed. So unusual. "He must be extremely tired."

"I had to slip something in his drink."

I snorted. "Nia."

"I've never seen someone so tense as him. It was the only way to get him to settle." She shrugged, grinning when my husband did not stir despite our giggles. "How does it look out there?"

"The skies are blue and the sun is shining. It will be better."

We both sighed on que and more giggling ensued. "Let's be happy, alright?" she whispered, holding her tears back.

"Alright. Let's be happy. But go now, or Moriko will stir up an avalanche in my mountains if you do not see her in the next hour or so. She was grunting and glaring so hard when I showed up out there without you, I thought weeds would sprout out of me." I kissed my husband's cheek again and again. "I have him now."

She stood and stretched her legs. "I will pass by Thora before I return home tonight, see if she is suiting well with her new duties." Before leaving, she stopped by the door, just looking at us, her hazel eyes glistening in the distance.

"What is it?"

"Nothing," she said, shaking her head. "I like this. The quiet."

"So do I."

Kilian groaned, his face scrunching up a little as he began stirring awake. His hands patted the space next to him until he found my hand. "Snow?"

"Yes, darling?"

He sighed, relaxing again. It took him a moment to open his eyes. "Why are you so far from me?"

"I don't want to hurt you," I said, snuggling to him a bit closer.

"Nia put something on my medicine, didn't she?"

"No?"

"Hm. Closer," he ordered, and I plastered myself to him, resting my cheek on his shoulder.

He looked at me and I looked at him. For a while. A long, long while. The quiet of the evening was filled with the soft patter of rain, clicking against the marble floor of the open balcony, slowly growing louder and stronger, the air chilling with the most tender wind and the sweetest smell. This felt...this...I felt it. Whatever it was, I was feeling it so intensely my whole body hummed.

He brushed his thumb on my cheek. "Why are you blushing?"

I pushed a few locks aways from his eyes. "I'm so in love with you, Kilian Castemont. But once you are out of that bandage, I will strangle you."

He chuckled, reaching to kiss my brow, my eyes, and the tip of my nose. "And I am so in love with you, Snowlin Castemont. So much so that I will let you strangle me when I am out of this bandage."

I pressed my nose against his cheek and just inhaled his gentle scent of spring. "Kilian?"

"Yes, my heart."

"Heal quickly. I want to devour your bones."

He chuckled. "No kissing my pain away? It could speed up the process."

"If only, darling."

"It does. Flesh is flesh, it mends. But no one can patch up what hurts inside of me besides you."

I lifted my eyes up at him. "Something hurts inside of you?"

"It does. Maybe it always will. Every time I close my eyes, I see you dying in my arms."

Like that, I almost suffocated the man with a shower of kisses. I stopped for a breath, and he smiled up at me, my own face mimicked his happiness. "Heal quickly," I said over his lips. "So I can give you black haired babies for you to worry about."

"You know what," he started, throwing off all the cloths filled with medicine that were all over his body. "The pain was never that bad. Felt more like a pinch anyway."

I bit his shoulder until he groaned from true pain and I then picked up all the medicine cloths to neatly lay them back on his wounded skin. "Fool."

He kissed me so hungrily that I had to hold back from climbing his still broken body. "Do not tempt me."

"Heal first."

He cupped a hand over my cheek. "Then you must also heal first."

"I'm not wounded, darling, I told you that the magic healed me."

His hand dropped down to rest on my chest. "Here." Then it lifted on top of my head. "And here."

"Kil—"

"Then...then we have black haired babies who will worry us both to death."

I pressed my face to the crook of his neck and just held him, trying not to be too happy that I could simply do that again. "Alright."

He sighed. "How is the world?"

My ceiling glistened, reflecting the light rain and thunder outside. "Alive. It is alive."

My father was gone.

He was finally gone.

A laugh burst out of me.

And another.

Many others.

As did tears.

So many tears.

Yet no cries.

Only tears.

Kilian pressed his brow to mine, his eyes tightly shut while he held me in the midst of the many realisations. In the midst of relief.

Relief was strange. Like a lock. It had held so much behind.

I could...I could do, think, hope, wish, expect, want, need, crave, desire anything. Anything without fearing it might be the last thing I did, thought, hoped, wished, wanted, needed, craved, desired.

There was a future.

Many nights—so many nights I could hold him like this.

Without fearing.

56

Checkmate

Snowlin

ALARIC AND HIS DINNER plans had not been stopped even by war. The old man had lost so much weight and sleep these past few weeks that none of us had even made a sound when he'd ordered us to sit and quietly eat.

"I am retiring," he said, and the room went even more quiet. "Going to live in Drava, in my old man's house. The city noise is doing my head in."

The hells he was.

"With all due respect, it might be a bit difficult," Kilian said, lowering his cutlery. "There is this project I need your help with."

He stopped chewing and looked around at us. "What project, son?"

"Myrdur," my husband said. "Let's rebuild it. Cai, Nia, Snow, and I have already decided on it. Once this coming summer passes, we will begin. One stone at a time if we must."

My guardian's eyes widened, filling with tears. The pain etched there was heart-breaking. The old man sniffled and nodded, violently cutting through his steak like he was about to eat the plate, too. "Maybe I won't retire then. You might need my help with where everything goes and all that."

My husband looked over at Cai who was hiding a grin behind his water cup and shaking his head. "Most definitely."

Penelope cleared her throat. "Atlas and I are courting," she said, all serious. "Since we are throwing...things out there."

Kilian almost choked on a sip of water. "Courting?"

Nia giggled a little, reaching for little Pen's hand. "Oh, Pen, I am so happy for you two."

The little carrot blushed. "Thank you, Nia."

"Courting?" Kilian murmured in my ear. "What is that supposed to mean?"

I lifted a brow at him. "Kil, darling."

He nodded, returning to his food, though I was fully sure he still did not know exactly what Pen had meant by courting.

"Well, since it's confession time," Mal said, leaning back on his seat. "I'm heading down to Seraphim. Alyone asked for my help."

My eyes went directly to someone, and it wasn't him.

Thora stopped chewing, her gaze downcast. I'd not seen the two even exchange more than a few words these past few weeks.

"For how long?" I asked.

"For as long as they need me. A week, a month, a year, ten years. Kilian freed me from my duties as Eldritch Commander. Neo is taking over for the time being."

"Temporarily," Kilian grumbled under his breath.

Thora did not look so surprised anymore.

"You knew?" I asked her.

"Neo told me a few nights ago," she replied meekly, cutting through her food.

Mal sneered. "I see he is already going around spreading important information."

"He only told me. He said he had told the news to only those important to him." She chewed on the food languidly, quietly adding, "Just how I deserve to be to someone."

Nia cleared her throat and shot us all a smile. "Mor and I have adopted a dog."

Her wife huffed a little and murmured to herself. "I have to share her affections with a dog now as well. What have I done to be punished as such?"

Nia threw her a glare, and the old queen nodded, adding, "He is...as they say...a-adorable."

Visha quietly put a small wooden bird and a piece of paper on the table next to my plate. "Golgotha left these for you before retreating to Hellas."

I took the little sculpture, running my thumb over the immaculate details.

Four wings.

A lightning mark trailing down its head and its long tail.

Four claws.

A thunderbird.

Like the prophecy, you were just as exquisite. You are perhaps the only rebirth I will ever witness in my eternal life. Let us not see each other again, Guardian. You remind me why I thrive on chaos, the excellence of it. I wish to desire no more. My creatures are happy and alive. I've learned those few days I remained between you that perhaps that is all that matters.

The wind was sweet despite the weather shifting further into winter. It was the sweetest on the roofs of Taren castle overlooking my peaceful city sitting and taking a breath after all they had been through. It was the best way to celebrate survival. We had not won much and we'd lost too much. Over the three weeks after the war, we had realised that perhaps we'd not won at all. There had been no winners. Only those that had lost a little less than the other side.

"What will you do if they reject what you have to say?" Alaric asked from where he stood beside me, observing the face of the city that was glistening under the sun.

"When has slighting me become a smart choice?"

"They are Gods, kid. They might not even deign you an audience."

"Alaric," I said, turning to him. "I am the fucking audience."

Grabbing the sceptre, I jumped from the roof and bolted to Valda Acme. The climb was gentler this time and I realised why many took this path so often in their lifetimes. To be only with my thoughts calmed me a little before I reached the top, but it for sure parched my tongue. And the moment I reached the roof of the mountain, anger surged through me again for not bringing food and beverage for my little walk.

"Mighty Guardian of the Gates," I called, looking around. She should have been here already considering their godly ears must be itching from all the badmouthing that had taken place at the council gathering this morning.

Calandra showed up almost immediately after my call. Mighty and divine as she'd been the first time we'd met. Her eyes widened, staring between the sceptre and me. "What is the meaning of this?"

"Call your God," I said, stabbing the sceptre on the ground and taking a seat on the anemone covered floor. "Actually, call all of them."

She huffed a short laugh that was not filled with any amusement. And when I didn't laugh back, her reaction turned agitated. "They—"

"They will come at my call. If they are not concerned by it, then I might take a walk inside your realm and make it a concern," I said. "Hurry now. I'm rather hungry. If I wait too long, I might be hungry for blood."

Reluctantly, she backed away into the silver pillars and disappeared into thin air.

I waited.

And waited.

Perhaps seconds or perhaps hours, I didn't know because I was truly, really, and absolutely famished. Hunger often made time go too slow or too fast.

When she returned, someone else stood by her side. Someone I'd seen before. At lake Asterin, right after I'd almost lost Kilian. With long white hair and a pleasant face, the God smiled at me brightly. He'd been the one to bring Kilian back to me.

"I've never been demanded before," he said smoothly, his voice was silk and clouds, and it made me sit up straight as if it had been a command. There was a connection between us, the sort only kin were connected to one another. A distant sense of incaution. And there were only a few I felt that about.

"How precious," I said, leaning back on my hands, and his brows hiked up a little, noticing my unladylike posture. My back was killing me from that climb. "Where is the rest of you?"

Just when I asked, they all poured out of the gates. One more stunning than the other. I recognised them all. All eight prime Gods of Ithicea stood before me an exact reproduction of my imagination. Mighty—that was the perfect word for what they looked like.

The woman with dark, straight, silky long hair raised a thin brow at me and then at Nubil. "She's truly a fascinating creature."

Nubil nodded proudly. "I thank you."

"No one is to thank but my insane father," I said, interrupting their ridiculous conversation. I pointed the sceptre at each of them. "Which, by the way, is all your fault."

Nubil lowered his chin to hide his grin, and said, "Warned you that she's little rough around the edges."

"Our fault?" one asked, offended.

I'd recognise that ego everywhere. "Ah, you must be Krig. I thought you had a moustache." I clicked my fingers. "No, that was Henah. The woman who weaved an intelligible prophecy and raised a whole nation to come kill me. But wait, it gets better. Apparently, I am their only hope, too."

She still stood stoic and unapologetic. "It is a testament to human nature, and it is my gift to weave the future."

"Or your poor skills, lady," I sneered. My reaction slipped off when I noticed one of them playing with a small blue bird in their hand, not even paying mind to me.

The God of Animals noticed me staring and offered me a smile. "Jayre is well. Among his beloved. Dragons are lonely creatures, and they are happiest in their nests. He is happy."

I nodded. "He better be." Then I found Cyra amongst them, a proud looking woman, a warrior among pampered deities.

She too answered before I could ask, "He is well. But every sunrise he waits for you."

The blur of tears was so sudden, the world sinking around me. I wiped my cheeks with the back of my hand and stood, throwing the sceptre to their feet. "She goes back. Aurora does not belong here."

They all stared in disbelief.

"She was a gift," Henah said, looking down at the sceptre. "A gift cannot be returned."

"She was a curse. Fader bestowed a curse on us."

"Do not let hurt misguide your words," a woman with rosy coloured hair said, stepping forward. From the way she clung to the man who scarily resembled his son, it had to be Plantae.

"Think," I said. "Your rules do not allow for divine weapons to be bestowed to us human realms, but Aurora was handed as a weapon. Fader can break many rules, and he already broke so many when he banished her and gave immortality to a faithless mortal—the rules he set himself. But breaking rules has repercussions. So says every gospel, every whisper, and book, and song. Look at me. I am the repercussion of breaking rules. Not one. Not even two. So many were broken to create me, and look at the chain of consequences it followed. Look at the consequences Fader's curse caused. Fallen kingdoms, greedy kings. Turned man against man. But it turned man against God, too. What will it be next? Will it be our end next? That was what Fader wanted to see, wasn't it? How we would come to survive it. If we are worth surviving it or not. A cleanse of sorts. Sorting out realms that would not be hit by the *disease* that has hit the rest of the realm expanse—faithlessness." I looked up at the skies, opening my arms wide. "Isn't that it, you piece of shit?"

Cyra snorted, and Krig shot her a look.

Pointing at them again, I said, "But it is what you all little prickly pests spend your free time on—toying with those who bow at your feet."

Krig glared at me. "You're brave—"

"I am simply tired," I sneered at the Winter God. "You do not wish to see me exhausted, believe me."

"You misunderstand us," Plantae said. "Severely. We cannot meddle so easily with human life. Sometimes, the only way we can help will cause hurt."

"Then don't help."

"The land will die," she said. "As it was."

"Why do you care? Are you all so hungry for our prayers?"

"Last night," Henah said. "A little child prayed that she could see the stars more often. And the moon. She prayed she could see the sun, too. And the skies. She loves snow, though. And fire, too. She plays around fire. There are little souls that no matter how many times any of us wants to no longer shine light over you, they will always bring us back. But her little prayers do not overshadow malice. To protect those little souls, we must do whatever we can do. You should be proud, Snowlin, to protect so many little wishes that were made last night."

Guilt was also a long trip around. Except, it wrapped like a cord on one's throat. "What a way to justify incompetence. Throwing me right in there with guilt, like it was all my fault to begin with. Like all I went through was justifiable for the sake of many."

Her look grew dark. "You do not understand."

"Much, it seems. But *you* understand nothing at all."

"We still cannot take it back," Krig said, crossing his arms and looking away from me into the distance of my kingdom.

"This realm already has a Guardian. It is in no need of her."

"You are not a Guardian of Realms, Eldingchild," Krig purred. "Your seat is in Caelum, the heaven you serve. Therefore, you cannot dictate or order anything pertaining to this soil."

"Then I must abandon this seat I apparently serve in Caelum."

A few gasped.

"Nonsense," Nubil said, flashing me a smile and waving his hand. "You can share the spot."

Plantae's eyes were round and oh-so wide. "She can?"

The white-haired man sweetly said, "Well, I do not wish for her to scorch my lands, do I now? You all heard what she said that day."

They did?

Nubil reached a hand to me. "I will take the Guardian," he said, kissing my knuckles, the touch so light and inhuman. When his eyes raised up at me, a blue flash crossed them, almost like a fallen star. "Fader owes me a favour. And I so impatiently have been waiting to ask this one from him."

"Do they all owe you favours?"

"Some. Others have already paid their dues. You must owe me one at some point." His smile was sleek. "I'd love to be owed a favour by you, Snowlin."

Kilian was going to have a heart attack. "Fine. I need a favour."

His brows hiked up. "Do tell."

"Make it so my children or those belonging to my siblings do not suffer as I did with their magic. Mine will share this cursed blood of mine as well as an Obscur's."

He flashed me his teeth. "Done. And I'd like to cash in my favour."

"Go on."

"Seat by my side when I need you."

Hells. "How often will that be?"

"Time will tell. But I do not have any intentions to keep you long from your loved ones."

"Then so be it."

His eyes flashed. "So be it then, Guardian."

"Why did you abandon this realm?" I asked as they retreated back into the portal, and they all halted, turning to face me again. "You left and never returned, only to still feed from this land's prayers."

It was Adan who answered, "Faith dissipated. It became more so something they relied on than something of comfort. When it no longer satisfied their needs, they wrote us into books and twisted our words to fit their narrative. Obscuring most of what we stood for, most of what we offered. The people of Numen needed a reason and a reminder to pray again. Not only to us, but to themselves. From time to time, we send them a reminder. They have a reason again now. You made them believe again."

Unbelievable. "Fuck. You."

The tall, pale man with red eyes and the darkest hair burst into a boisterous laughter. "You will fit right in with my family. You and your husband must dine with us sometime," Celesteel offered.

"I'd rather choke on sweaty boot soles worn by a troll."

"A rather...odd way to die," the Death God said, blinking a bit confused. "But there are always new ways to surprise me."

"Honey," Plantae whispered to him. "She was being sarcastic."

"Oh, we like that, too—in hells," he said proudly, waving a hand while they retreated back to the gates. "You do not consume meat, do you? I shall ask for all the vegetables your heart desires. Actually, I'll ask *Desire* myself when I come across her. No need to do anything at all, Snowlin."

For a little while, I remained there, gaping at the empty gates.

Stunned.

Nubil remained there, too, for a moment. Almost proudly looking at me.

"Thank you," I gritted out a little too quietly. *For bringing him to me.*

"I should be the one to thank you," he said. "The seat by my side is filled again. I shall no longer remain bored."

"For saving him."

"Kilian saved himself. I only asked for the gates to this world to open back again for him. Even Celesteel did not need much convincing. Your husband swam the River of Sorrows back to you. Fought spirits and divine to return to you. No man has ever done so. But he is no man, is he?"

"And for the visions, too. For warning me. For not letting me commit the mistake I was going to commit."

He smirked. "You knew it was me who opened the portal and sent you the little Reaper?"

"And you knew I would kill Aurora. You wanted me to see what would happen if I did kill her."

"Your anger is strong. We all had doubts. Fader did, too."

"You grew the galanthus."

"Spring should show itself when it comes."

"And the gates to Numen? For letting the realm accept my magic?"

He shook his head. "I only let the signs show. I knew they would find a way to save you."

"You helped. They said you cannot help."

"Did I?" he asked, retreating back. "Did I help? Have your check mate, Snowlin. You won this game all by yourself."

Once again, I walked the Deadlands. The skies were still red, the ground still barren, the air still warm. Fascinating that after all that had happened it felt just like any other day, as if I'd imagined it all.

I crossed the monolith, tugging on the chains that bound a man more than a beast. Vas, no longer Demir. Visha had managed to draw all the essence of Caligo he'd consumed to turn into the green lizard and left the shell of the immortal man behind. Most had not been as lucky as him. Others had been so infected by the seedling planted in them that they had passed long before their souls had departed, leaving behind only a rotten body.

"How unfortunate. No feather blanket or leather boots for me," I sighed, manoeuvring the thick forest made of branches that concealed the scorched lands. "I'm beyond disappointed."

He didn't speak. But it could be because of the sock I'd stuffed in his mouth. Or not. I'd never had a sock stuffed in my mouth so I would not know.

The flaky woman was still there, still reciting her gibberish when I stepped through the thick gelatine-like shield and into the small land of hell in Numengarth that no one knew existed.

Vas fell to his knees, struggling to breathe from the heat, and I tugged hard for him to stand. Finally, I even pulled the sock out of his mouth in need of some conversation to pass this lonely time. "Up. Up. Don't make me drag you there."

"Where are you taking me?"

"To fulfil a bargain."

He grabbed onto my jacket. "You cannot take my life."

I pried his hands off of me. "I never intended to take it. Much rather see you burn for eternity. Deathless. Painfully. Everyone has heard hellfire is not so kind to selfishness. It despises the greedy. And won't you burn so lovely."

The way Vas's irises trembled and sank drew such happiness on my face. Now that his soul was fully stitched back to his body, he looked much more of what he truly was—just a man.

He was already there. The Prince of Ustrina leaned back against one of the walls, his eyes closed, and a small smirk splayed on his rather handsome face. "I'm impressed," he said, keenly observing me, my price, and something behind me. "Your lover worries too much."

"Not enough, would you believe," my husband said, stepping right beside me and shooting a *'we will talk about this later'* look down at me. "She comes to bargain with hells, and I come as a reminder of what happens when you do such dangerous acts."

Shit. What was he doing here? I looked around. How had he gotten down here? Men weren't allowed to enter this part of Deadlands.

"Lies are such impractical but gentle cover ups," Ezekiel said, raking a look over Kilian. "Is that what they keep telling you still? That a Henah blessed Aura made a deal with a Guardian of Caligo and ended up cursed? My aunt would have ripped my father a new one if he would have allowed such a bargain."

"What do you mean?" I asked when Kilian remained silent, only scowling distrustfully at the prince.

"Your husband's ancestors do not come from Numen. There is no Aura such as an Obscur. That is just a name his people gave themselves when they came here."

The hells was he on about?

Kilian's jaw was set tight. "My people?"

"The people of Astra. A realm not far from here, belonging to the Goddess of Nothing, my grandmother. You can see and feel death, see and feel emotion, crave silence whilst desiring chaos. Feed from light and darkness, life and death. You are all, everything, and nothing, too. Where you are from, what you are is called a *Godling*. A child born from the soil where the blood of the three first Gods was spilled. As you might have guessed, that makes you a rarity." He pointed a finger at the two of us. "That would make you two quite the couple. Extraordinary, actually. The very essence of a God and the purest creation of another two Gods."

"He is lying, right?" I asked, glancing at my husband whose hand tightened around mine.

He didn't say anything, only narrowed his eyes on the Prince of Hells who took the silence as an invitation to continue, "Your ancestors wrote themselves into history with permission of Henah. People of Astra were and still are travellers of worlds, their realm is an epicentre of species from many other worlds. Though...I am still unsure why Godling blood settled in this particularly unimpressive realm when they had so much to choose from. So much to rule over—not just humans, but over divine creatures, too." Satisfied by our confusion, he extended a hand forward. "Consider this knowledge a gift. It gives me utmost pleasure to be related to such creatures as you and your husband. The future is finally looking somewhat exciting. Will you hand me the price of our bargain now? Unless there is something else. Quelling human curiosity is indeed turning into a new hobby of mine."

"Not nineteen," I said.

Ezekiel's brows rose. "Not nineteen?"

"Lilith will be at least twenty-one years of age when you marry her."

His smirk stretched into a grin. "I'm a patient man, and she can be one hundred when I take her as my bride for all I care, but no bargain will keep me from taking her and marrying her. She's my fate. As I am hers." He fashioned a bow and then disappeared from sight along with Vas.

"It changes nothing," Kilian said, still holding tightly onto my hand while we ducked under branches to leave the undead forest.

"It changes some little things," I said, throwing his arm over my neck and pressing my body to his. "You're from a whole other realm, Kil. And you're a...Godling, not Aura. Whatever that means."

He kissed my brow and then my lips. "It won't matter to anyone, they do not need to know."

"What about Mal? He deserves to know. To not feel cursed by the Gods."

"Has knowing what you are helped you?"

"Mal and I sometimes are one of the same yet completely the opposite. What did not bring me relief might bring him comfort."

He sighed, kissing me again and again. "You're right. So very right. I will tell him."

Urinthia and Macaria were waiting for us on the other side. The two powerful witches had all sorts of regret painted across their faces.

"Lilith will remain here with you till the day of her twenty-first," I said. "You will raise her as you wish."

Urinthia's callous expression broke into surprise. "Twenty first?"

"Call it a bargain with hells."

The Grand Maiden's mouth parted, but words did not come out, so Macaria spoke for her, "We thank you, Your Majesty."

"Nothing to thank me for, witch. My half-sister is still destined to an undying death besides a Lord of Death himself. She did not get to choose her future. But for twenty-one years, she will make her own choices and live how she wishes, as normal as it can be for her to grow. Groom her to be a fighter not just a Maiden for a day. What awaits her in those realms is something I only wish to those who have slighted me."

"Will you not stand by her?" Urinthia finally asked. "By your kin? Do you not wish to see her?"

"She is not my kin. And unless she is to tell me anything useful, no, I do not wish to see her. Let's keep it that way. Do not come to me if she is in trouble or hurting. Do not come to me when she speaks for the first time or takes the first step. She and I are tied for all the worst reasons. Reasons which I can untie, but that will mean her death and then yours. And I did make Visha a promise. Because of her, you both live."

57

0-1

Kilian

SNOW HAD A COLD determined look on her face, and for some reason, it worried me. If she made Eren King of Isjord, her brother would be ultimately sentenced to the punishment he'd always wanted to be rid of. Though he would not hold it against her, I was worried what it would do to my friend.

Thora was already there, chatting with Skadi, Elias, and a few who seemed to be court members. The little sister's shoulders seemed heavier, her features more grown. She had killed Silas. And only Gods knew how she had managed that.

Even the air itself went quiet when Snow approached. They all bowed their heads while court members and soldiers went to their knees. "My queen," they chanted in unison.

"Rise," my wife said sharply, and led everyone inside the meeting room, sitting opposite the monarch's seat and leaving it empty.

There were too many questions hovering in the air. And Snow had the answer for every single one of them.

She slanted a look on everyone. "Do you know why I have gathered you today?"

A throat cleared from her side, an older gentleman. "To sit on your throne, Your Majesty. The people of Isjord are discouraged, helpless, and beaten from it all, they look at you for hope of a better, newer, troubleless Isjord."

"They think and hope wrong," my wife said, and a few mouths dropped agape. "I've got no desire to rule Isjord. My blood is more Skygard than it is Krigborn, it has always been and proven even more so after I learned of my blood inheritance."

"No Krigborn has abdicated the throne, my queen," one said, looking at others for support. "The land will not survive. We will not survive."

"I'm not abdicating, Lord, simply passing my crown to another Krigborn, to someone who actually has it in them to care for this land. Someone who will never put greed before their people."

Eren raised his chin when everyone's attention went to him, standing ready for his sister's announcement that would never come.

"Thora Isa Krigborn," Snow said, and every head around the table snapped in the little sister's direction. "My crown is yours. The throne is yours. The kingdom is yours."

If a pin dropped to the ground, it would have sounded like an earthquake from how silent it became.

"W–what?" the little sister asked, staring between Eren and Snow. "Me? Why me?"

"You killed Silas, weakened and freed the Octa Virga, and therefore aided me and my husband in taking Aurora down. Saving us all." She leaned back in her seat and tilted her head back to look at the court members. "Isn't it so?"

Awe and admiration floated around Isjordians when they looked at their new queen, but so did fear. Thora was young, too young to sit on a throne worn out by aged men with fine greed and desire for war.

"It was my duty," Thora said hoarsely. "It should not grant me a crown, Snow."

Snow's exterior cracked just a little seeing the emotion on her sister's face. "And you carried it well. I've got faith you will carry this duty I'm giving you just as well. No one is born for the seat of a ruler. They are all made. Elias and Skadi will stand by your side at all times, to guide you as they know the land and your people. And Oryn wishes to remain here with you as your Crafter and become part of your court."

"There is much work," I said, wrapping my hand around Snow's, "but we will all be here to help."

"And Eren?" Thora asked.

Snow's eyes were downcast. "He and I settled an agreement."

"What agreement, love?" I asked, looking between the two siblings who had not exchanged a single word since the start of the meeting.

"He will remain by Lilith's side in Eldmoor until she leaves for Ustrina."

Thora's mouth dropped. "Snow, you can't—"

"I asked, Rora," Eren said, surprising us both. "It was my request that I do so."

Betrayal filled Thora's eyes and she looked sick all of a sudden. "Why...why would you ask that?"

"She has no one."

Snow tensed by my side, but she did not say anything—but it was not necessary to speak the words of disappointment that were written all over her face.

"And I, who do I have?" Thora asked. She took a calm breath and let the mask of feigned calm fall over her eyes. "If you've decided so, then I will not question your choices." She leaned back. "Only let their repercussions follow."

Eren's face fell. "Rora—"

"If you wish to be out of my life, then be gone. How convenient you already have another sister to substitute me with. I will not even be missed."

Before her brother could utter a single word or explanation, she stood and exited the room.

Snow stood, too, and Eren clasped her arm. "Snow, you—"

"I hope the trip to Eldmoor goes smoothly. Let me know if you need assistance with packing," she said, pulling away and exiting after her sister.

"Tell me you understand," he said, his eyes pleading.

I rested a hand on his shoulder. "I do. But I hope you do, too, old friend. Your intentions are not entirely unselfish. You're not doing it entirely for Lilith."

"Have I told you how much I hate when you do this?"

"Hate it all you want, you coward. You will visit, won't you?"

"They might not want to see me."

"My wife's heart has burned and yearned just to know you still breathe for relentless years. Thora loves you more than herself. The only one who doesn't wish to see you, is you, Eren. Once you're done hiding and being afraid, they will be happy to be by your side again. Raise the girl. She's only a guiltless child with an unfortunate fate, but I want you to be there when I raise mine. I want you to be there for those two women who still need you and will always need you. I want you to let them be there for you as well. Learning to unlearn pain and suffering is a process, so take the time you need. Just do not take the exit entirely."

Snow and I sat out on the balcony, eating dinner quietly for the first time. And hopefully ever after. But I didn't like this quiet, not when I'd almost lost her. If she didn't keep speaking to me at all times, I would think this was a terribly long and detailed dream.

The fork she held stopped halfway to her mouth and her eyes rose to mine. "What?"

"Why are you so far from me?"

She stood and dragged her chair to my side. "Better?"

I pushed her chair back again and lifted her up and onto my lap, pressing her against my chest. "This is better."

"What now?" she whispered, glancing back at me.

"Whatever we wish for," I said. "What does my heart wish for?"

"I have what I wish for. And he is so pretty."

"Is he now?"

Her fingers skimmed my jaw, stopping over the little scar for a moment. "You would not believe it if I described to you how pretty he is."

"I'm glad you find me so pleasant."

"And you should see his huge c—"

I kissed her, shutting her up, her mouth curling into a smile against mine.

"You two need to start frequenting Olympia more," Mal shouted from beneath our balcony.

Snow hurried over the balcony edge, looking down at where Mal was sitting on a garden bench, eating...biscuits. "Come up."

"I need to be close to somewhere I can hurl."

"Come up, Malik Castemont," she sneered.

He grinned and then faded beside my wife, throwing an arm around her shoulders. "You two should be working on making me an uncle."

She hit him. "This uncle is leaving for maybe a week, a month, a year or ten," she mocked, and he laughed, squeezing her cheeks with a hand and shaking her head viciously.

"Do you think I don't know what you did?" he whispered to her.

Did? What had she done?

Snow smiled so, so innocently, and it almost made the both of us forget, but her eyes gleamed and her innocent smile turned into a cruel smirk. "She should have known what happens when you mess with children."

My brother looked up at me. "You told her?"

Hm. So that is why she'd wished me an early happy birthday the other night. She'd killed Selia then. "Didn't think it mattered much. You told me so yourself when I caught you the first time. *Don't give a shit what anyone says, or what you say.* That's it, those were the words."

"You old fuck—"

Snow hit him. "I'll kill them all, Mal. I'll even kill you, if I must."

My brother grinned at her. "And we're back to threatening me morning, noon, and night. Might I persuade you to spare me a while longer?"

"How?"

He brought a little bag out of his jacket pocket. "A snack."

"Mooncakes."

Oh to be a boiled and burnt sugary little treat.

"When do you leave?" I asked him.

He grabbed Snow's hand and took a bite from her dessert. "Two days from now."

I expected rage, fury, blood. But Snow did not react to the stolen bite. She did react to him leaving though. "Stay."

He shook his head. "I need this. If I don't go somewhere far from her—" He caught himself, leaving that sentence hanging for a few seconds. "I need the space."

"Come visit. At Dolunay," my wife said.

He threw an arm around her neck and kissed her head. "I will. At Dolunay. Every one of them."

Epilogue: Endgame

Kilian (five years later)

IT WAS ODDLY SILENT, and it was a silence I no longer liked after years of loving chaos—of adoring and worshipping chaos. I missed it. It was also silent enough for me to hear the steady small breaths of the small human plastered to my chest while I finished signing approval for the new deliveries to the unblessed isles. My son slept softly against me, his dark hair was plastered to his sweaty forehead and his pale cheeks had turned a soft hue of pink. He had so much of his mother's features, yet everyone insisted he resembled me most. But how could they say that when he snored identically to her.

He would be three soon. We had waited. We'd waited and healed first. Though not entirely, the small one had joined us in that process, too.

The skies gurgled outside and lightning struck ahead, but Sam didn't stir. He was already used to it as he often preferred to sleep in his grandfather's bed in Olympia amongst thunder and rain, surrounded by the noise and grandness of it. For the first few months of his life, the sounds of the skies had been the only thing to calm him down, to soothe his cries and many restless nights.

Slowly, I threw a jacket over his small body, and I stood, heading in the direction of lightning I had not seen in nearly a week.

She walked along Atlas who was rambling a list of things that he had prepared during her week-long stay in Isjord to aid Thora, now Queen of Isjord.

When she took notice of us, she smiled wide and rushed her steps as did I.

"Darling," she whispered, kissing me. She pulled back the jacket covering our son to reveal his face and kissed his cheek. "My little darling."

I pulled her to me and kissed her again. Apparently too much because Atlas slowly backed away and fled the scene. "How are my girls?"

Her head dropped back and she groaned. "Famished. If I see another bowl of pine soup in my periphery I will scream."

Still chuckling, I went down on one knee and kissed her round stomach. "What shall I feed my little princess and her mother, hm?"

She licked her lips and thought about it for a moment. From the way she scrunched her nose as if she could already feel the sourness of her favourite fruit in her mouth, I already knew.

"No more munching on lemons," I said.

"Can't help it."

"It hurts your stomach, my heart."

"An orange then."

"Oranges, too, if you do not eat something else before."

"Kil—"

"One slice," I said, finally relenting. With Sam, she had consumed so much salted mushrooms I thought some were going to grow out of her. Larg's hands had been raw from collecting them all over Adriata by the end of the ninth month. With our girl, all she craved was sourness. Moriko had not handpicked anything, but she surely would soon grow tired of sending us fresh lemon crates every week.

Sam had finally woken and sat on Snow's lap, letting her feed him little pieces of buttered bread whilst he coloured on a sheet of paper.

"Son, do you want to sit with me? Your mother must be tired."

He shook his head and blinked up at her. "Ma, are you tired?"

She showered his face with kisses. "Just a little, but not for you."

Caiden marched in, unbothered and finally for once bathed before dinner. He patted Snow's head, picked my son up like a leather ball and sat on a chair. "You didn't come to see me at training today, soldier."

"I had a nap," my son said, yawning. "Papa said I could have one, uncle."

"You can have many of them," Caiden agreed, chewing on some pie. "Got to put a few feet on you if you want to be part of my command."

"How do you allow him to say things like that?" Nia asked, strutting in and picking up Sam from Caiden's lap and putting him on her own.

My son wrapped his small arms around her and rested his head on her shoulder, all shy as he blinked up at her. "Auntie Lenia."

"Sweet baby." Nia cut up some grapes in half and handed them to him before asking Snow, "So, how are things in Isjord?"

Snow only huffed in response, glaring and sneering at a spot on the table like it bore all faults.

"Mor and Rora are being too secretive for my liking," Nia somewhat agreed with her. "If the Islines are giving her trouble, why won't she just ask for your aid?"

"Because she is stubborn."

"Because she wants to give her people a choice. Something they never had before," I said, sliding my hand over Snow's. "If the Islines want to create another Tenebrose and Isline situation, then so be it. Thora is capable."

My wife huffed. "But so is their new queen. They are calling Thora half a Krigborn. Iskyla this, Iskyla that. This blood talk is driving me mad. As if it matters. Isjord is thriving, her people should be happy. Why aren't they happy? Why are they never happy being ruled by someone who cares about them? Why do they care about blood so much they are willing to have another wicked ruler on the throne?"

"It won't come to that," Alaric said, walking in and taking Sam from Nia. "And quit bothering my grandson's ears with nonsense. Eat."

Sam blinked up at him. "What is nonsense, grandpapa?"

"All adult talk, kid."

My son nodded and turned to me. "You speak nonsense all day, papa?"

"If you ask your mother, she will say I've only ever spoken nonsense."

Sam quickly chewed his grapes till he was out of breath before telling his mother, "I also think papa speaks a lot of nonsense. He speaks it to the papers, too, mama, all day!"

"He does," my wife agreed.

"Will anyone else grace us with their presence?" Alaric asked, trying to count who was missing.

"Eren is not coming until the week after," Nia explained. "Visha has gone all mad Crafter on her new apprentices. Penelope is off frolicking with Atlas who had prepared a picnic for her. Mal won't return from Seraphim until spring. Thora won't breathe outside of Isjord until she is rid of the Isline Queen. And my own wife is inspecting the autumn crops for the upcoming festival. Who have I missed?"

Snow raised a brow at her. "You know your duties as my spy ended five years ago, Queen Consort of Hanai."

Nia threw a grape at Snow, and Snow threw a whole bunch back at her. This then ensued a whole food war which my son jollily began participating in by throwing pickings of cheese at his grandfather's beard and hair.

Caiden sighed, asking me, "Your turn to stop it this time."

"No. It's yours. I was the one who got between Snow and Visha last week, remember?"

His eyes drew shut. "Fuck."

I threw a grape at him, hitting the idiot on his head. "That is a bad word to use around my child."

Sam was fighting off sleep and trying to attentively listen to the same story I'd told him a hundred times already. The story people had composed songs and poems about—the Battle of Two Guardians. Squished between his mother and I in our bed, he glanced from me to her in approval of my story telling. After all, she was one of the Guardians. Snow nodded slowly in approval, brushing his hair back from his brow, almost giving up to sleep herself.

He yawned, his mismatched eyes disappearing behind heavy lids. One of them was mine and one was his mother's. Silver and gold.

"Shall I take you to your room, my prince?"

He nodded and turned to kiss his mother's forehead. A habit he'd picked up from me some time ago now. "Night, ma."

"Night, my little darling. Sleep well."

I extended a hand to him, and we walked to the end of the corridor, to the bedroom Mal had painted the colours of the night sky. A first birthday present from his uncle who was Gods knew where by now after I had temporarily freed him of his duties almost five years ago.

Memphis raised her head from the corner of his room, watching my son while I tucked him in. He sighed like all the world was weighing on his shoulders, and it made me laugh a little. He did carry my entire world on his shoulders. The day he was born, the weight of my world had doubled. He held some. His mother held some. Soon, my little daughter would hold some.

Sam blinked up at me. "Will the monsters ever come for ma again?"

I shook my head. "No. She has me and you now. We will never let them back, will we?" *And we've already chased so many of them away.*

"Wait until I become a big Aura like you, papa. We can fight them together."

I kissed both of his little hands before tucking them under his blanket. "Alright, my prince."

She was still sitting up in bed when I returned, one hand holding a book and the other on her stomach, rubbing slow circles. All day—I waited all day to see this. Her in my bed, wearing my ring, carrying my child, wearing my shirt. The sense of belonging I'd always missed...I'd finally found it.

"What are we reading today?" I asked, grabbing the rosehip oil she used and kneeling beside her in bed.

She glared at me. "Last time I told you that, you put me in this situation."

I recalled it differently. "Good thing I didn't ask you that two hours ago when I fucked you on the bath, on the table, and on the sofa. Several times."

Her sneer was feral. "Weren't you about to be useful?"

"Yes, my queen. Pardon my insolence." I pulled the shirt up, and she flapped her feet when I poured the oil on her stomach and began rubbing it in her skin.

She sighed, her head dropping back.

I kissed her belly. "Is my daughter giving you a hard time?"

"Her aunt is. Your daughter is well behaved."

"Thora will get around it. She is well capable, my love. You trusted her five years ago, why not trust her still?"

"She is too stubborn, Kil."

"Hm. Reminds me of a particular someone."

"Not like me."

"Very much like you, my little grump." I grinned when I felt a little kick under my palm. "We've woken her."

"She just likes your voice," Snow said, disappointed. "She never does that with me."

After pulling her shirt down, I shifted to lay beside her. It was too uncomfortable for her to lay facing me, so for now, she curled herself into my chest instead of hugging me like she loved to. "Snow, my Snow," I murmured, burying my face on the crook of her shoulder. "Don't disappear when I wake up, alright?"

She lowered my hand to rest it against the swell of her stomach, and I waited in the silence to hear my daughter's small heartbeat along with her strong one. "I'll be right here. We will be right here."

Just before I drifted to sleep, a shy knock rang and the door cracked open a little, letting a sliver of light slip inside and reveal the face of my sleepy son followed by Memphis.

I lifted myself up. "Sam?"

Our son shyly walked to our bed. "Can I sleep here tonight?" He rubbed his tired eyes and yawned. "Ma will be safer if we are both here."

Snow looked between us, her chin trembling a little, silver gleaming on her lids. "Yes, come here."

I made space between his mother and I, and patted the bed for him. He ducked under the covers and hugged Snow's middle, falling asleep in a blink.

I patted my other side for Memphis to join us, and the bed immediately dipped to accommodate her heavy form. Bright yellow eyes blinked softly over us, protectively, refusing to draw shut until ours did. "Go to sleep, Memphis," I murmured, patting her head, and the morph obeyed.

For a small moment, I stood there watching them too, watching my little family. Safely under my sight. Safely in my hold. Safely.

Snow lifted a hand to my face. "What is it?"

I kissed her palm and laid close to them, tucking my son and wife to my chest. This was the closest my heart had been inside my ribs in years. "Nothing." *And everything.* "Goodnight, love of mine."

"Good night, Kil."

September mornings had always been some of the most alluring. Sunsets even more so.

Snow stood at the edge of Soren Forest, looking over the Seer Sea while Alaric kept Sam entertained with a small leather ball. Dawn was still thick and refusing to reveal sunrise despite the late hour, and I could see Snow nervously twisting her fingers on her side. She caught herself several times from closing her fists, flexing her hands open and closing her eyes, taking several slow and steady breaths.

I stepped behind her and pulled Sam's sunstone necklace over her neck, clasping it on her. Gently, I pulled her hair over it and fixed the stone to lay straight on her.

She turned to me, her eyes filled with silver, glassy grief. "I don't want to say goodbye."

"It isn't goodbye, my heart. Never goodbye. You know he deserves his rest."

"Yes," she nodded. "Yes, he does."

"Ma!" Sam yelled from Alaric's arms, pointing at the eastern skies as the sun made its shy appearance. "Look!"

We turned to see the skies painted vivid with morning colours, and Snow's necklace began glowing a pearly bright gleam, glistening like a beacon around us and vibrating a wave of warmth over us all.

First stray tears dropped from Snow's eyes when she forced them shut and lowered her head.

I cupped her face and lifted it up to me. "Open them, love."

Her gilded irises gleamed bright too, looking down at the sun necklace still pulsating light. Then she looked over at the sunrise. And our son. And her tearful father proudly standing tall before his fallen loved one.

We stood there, admiring the blessing and sacrifice Samuel had left behind, mourning his presence and wishing for him until the sun was brightly round and the sunstone had settled to the pale, opaque white colour.

"Goodbye, Sam," she whispered.

"Goodbye, grandpa Sam," our son shouted with all he could, waving at the skies still.

The end.
Yet...is there ever such a thing as an end?

Acknowledgements

There was a whole list of people I wanted to thank this time round, but I have decided to save it for the next book in the series. I want to acknowledge one person this time, one person that I often forget to acknowledge. Wendy from three years ago, thank you for staying in this world even if you really didn't want to. I wish I could tell you how much easier and better it gets, but I know you wouldn't believe me. I know your own shadows in the mirror would have not let you listen to anyone. But thank you. I am so grateful that you stayed and that we wrote this story.

About the author

Wendy Heiss is a indie author debuting with a new adult fantasy trilogy, Winter Gods & Serpents, the first book in The Auran Chronicles. She has graduated with a Forensics Science degree in the United Kingdom, but literature has been one of her passions since she could manage to read and write. Despite being severely tempted to ride the Agatha Christie route to crime novels, she chose to follow the Tolkien path to fantasy. She forwent fingerprint powder for ball pen ink inevitably forgoing her parents hope for a good life and becoming what they always feared...a figuratively starving artist, which is why she won't quit her day time job any time soon.

Any whom and how, she likes cats, coffee, particularly that cr*p from instant sachets. Loves, loves when spring doesn't try to give her at least one asthma attack every year and threaten her life. 'Claims' to despise mafia romance from the pits of her gall bladder but will probably end up writing one herself to try and outwrite the greatest line in history: Are you alright, babygirl?

Also, fried sweet potatoes, she can definitely eat some of those without claiming to be allergic to yet another vegetable. On that last note before straying too far from a simple bio, please read her books.

Dictionary

Aura: Humans veiled with God like magic and abilities.

Din-Aura: Humans that were blessed by Gods, but powerless.

Dark Crafter: Human blessed with magic, but different from Auras. They draw mana to power their magic from the realm of Caligo, or otherwise known as Otherworld (hells and heavens of the God of Death)

Grand Maiden: Ruler of Eldmoor, head Dark Crafter

Ybris: Hybrid Aura, a child of two different Aura.

Eudemon: Creatures of Golgotha, God of Demons. They reside in the Sea of the Dark after their realm, Dissiri, fell.

Mid-world: A spirit pane, between life and death. Crowded by trapped, revengeful, or fearful souls.

Astrum liber: Holy book of Adriata, followed by believers and followers of Goddess Henah.

Caelus liber: Holy book of all Gods. Made up of godly laws, rules, and principles.

Eirlys book: Holy book of Isjord, followed by believers and followers of God Krig.

Hodr: Heaven of God Krig.

Cynth: Heaven of Henah, the moon.

Caligo: Heaven of Celesteel, the Otherworld.

Hemera: Heaven of goddess Cyra, the sun.

Mankai: Heaven of goddess Plantae.

Empyrea: Heaven of Adan.

Caelum: Heaven of Nubil

Neith: Heaven of Dyurin

Kemeri: Language of Hanai

Darsan: Language of Adriata

Dahaara: Steel tongued

Borsich: Language of Eldmoor

Calgnan: Language of Olympia

Zgahna: Calgnan word for magic mist.

Alaar: Darsan word for magic mist

Tahuma: Language of Solarya

Old Ysolt: Language of Isjord, but no longer spoken in the mainland, Isjord. Only used by Isline Krigborn's.

Karndu: Language of Seraphim

Laoghrikrease: Language of the unblessed, spoken main land Vrammethen and

Islands of Comnhall

Anima Accisor: Soul Killer

Soul Gates: Entrance to the Otherworld

Canes: Magical creature used to sniff and detect magic

Ithicea: Heaven of God Fader, father of all Gods

Fogling: Bat like creature born from the soul remnants of those who died in Myrdur during the Draugr Night attack

Breshall: Unblessed Island

Norodoh: Unblessed Island

The Darmain: Unblessed Island

Valda Acme: The highest point in the Volant Mountains, the place where the gates to Caelum Heaven are (the climb to this point is an old Olympian tradition to pay respect to the God)

Khamir: mark of a spirit still living in tis dead vessel

D'mora: a spell cast by three witches of Delcour/prime blood to banish the magic of a witch/crafter. Also called: death in a human body

Ôol: traditional Isline tattoos, usually received by an elderly after you travel the harsh territory of the kingdom. They mark the hierarchy and status amongst the tribe.

Also by

The Auran Chronicles
Winter Gods & Serpents
Spring Guardians & Songbirds
Season Warriors & Wolves
Autumn Queens & Shadows
Summer Heirs & Fire (Early 2025)
Daughters of Chaos
City of Alabaster (Autumn 2024)
Blue Fairytales
At the end there was you
The last war we ever fought
Where the light no longer follows